The Wild Prince's Favorite

By Jenny Fox

Published by IngramSpark.
Made in United Kingdom
2025 First Edition

First published in 2025.

Copyright © 2024 by Jenny Fox
Cover & Back Cover credit: GermanDesigns
ISBN-13: 978-1-7395289-4-2

Author Jenny Fox
Find me on Facebook & Instagram.

Contents

*This one is for everyone
who's ever needed a second chance.*

*At love, at life, at anything.
You deserve every attempt it takes.
Don't let the fear of failure hold you back.
Everyone who succeeded?
They were the ones who didn't give up.*

Chapter 1

The Northern Mountains.

For those who could only see them from afar, they were white, cold giants of stone and ice sitting at the far end of the continent like monolithic sentinels. Some claimed there were exactly one hundred mountains. Some claimed there was but one mountain that had gradually split into dozens to form a long, twisted chain around itself. Those natural monuments were mysterious to most, and even more to those who dared to approach. Like a god's twisted labyrinth, the deeper one got into them, the more they turned into a death trap. There was not one single, clear pathway into them. The first mountains were smaller, smoother, like gentle mermaids calling the fearless to trap them in the depths of their older sisters. Once one passed the first trials of those stone giants, the task only grew harder. The paths were no longer paths, but ragged trails and climbing challenges, often to find one cornered in some deep cave, or at the edge of a bottomless and surely fatal precipice. They were unpredictable, and the snow was like their mischievous friend, making the task even harder and the land impossible to conquer. With each snowfall, the game was reinvented; the once-safe roads were back to being hazardous and lethal again. If one didn't get killed falling off a cliff or from being trapped in the biting ice and snow, they would surely get lost in the dead ends and resign themselves to the cruel sentence of starvation.

Only those who were born and blessed by the mountains could navigate their tortuous paths and befriend those giants of stone to try to find and learn almost all of their secrets. To the Northern people, the clans inhabiting those mountains, climbing around and going from one end of those dangerous ice queens to another was child's play. They never feared the heights, the dark caves, nor the bite of the cold; all of those things were part of their world like the ground under their feet. Those mountains were their whole world; a small, cruel world. Even to those who knew how to tame the rock giants, the elements weren't kind. They could climb as much as they wanted, but food was terribly scarce, and finding a bush of berries that had outlived the biting cold was a blessing; being able to keep the livestock alive was another. Not many species could live in this cold, and the survival of a single sheep could mean one week with a full stomach... or an empty one.

Amongst those people, a young woman was perhaps a bit more blessed than the others, in invisible ways. Her piercing black eyes were the best at spotting the tiniest little gem of color through the thick veils of white snow. She could track the smallest sparkle of a red berry hidden underneath a layer of frost, leading to a full bush of precious food. She could climb better than most; like a snow cat, her fingers as secure as claws against the rock, her feet swift and light. She could see well in the darkness of any cave, and find her way through the most complex maze of tunnels. She was truly a child of the mountains, born and raised not to live but to survive her hostile homeland.

Ironically, her heart was often turned far away from there.

When her feet took her to some cliff at the edge of her sky-grazing home, her eyes would always turn toward the vast, vast land beneath them. Her world was far too high and north for her to see what was going on at the other end of the continent, but her mind would find ways to imagine. She could weave full stories out of the threads of rumors she had heard from others. She imagined a land where the sun kissed its inhabitants' skin all the time, and where the darkness of night wasn't enough to chase away the warmth. Where they had food everywhere, full bushes of colorful berries blooming all around, huge flocks of livestock, and even fish flooding their rivers... She envied those people, although it was a fine line between envy and resentment. Whenever she would turn her eyes toward the foot of her mountain, the anger inevitably rose.

"Alezya!"

The voice of her father echoed from afar, and a chill went down her spine despite her thick coat. She was late. She grabbed her basket full of berries, harnessed it to her back, and started running. No one could really run on the mountains. Not without the risk to trip and open their head on some stalagmite, or break their neck on a sheet of ice. One had to learn to run slowly, to jump from one place to another, and ensure there was stable ground under their feet while keeping their head up and eyes open so as not to trip or slide to their death. Alezya was good at this. She climbed faster than most thanks to her well-trained body, her knowledge of the mountains, and the confidence she had in finding her way home.

Her home was on one of the largest mountains, where her clan had asserted their dominance and established themselves before anyone else generations ago, taking ownership of that prime location. She liked that mountain the most but hated that it was theirs alone. She loved all of the mountains equally and wished the clans could see it that way too. Sadly, the Northern clans were even more divided than the tips of those mountains, and not likely to ever unite as one again...

Alezya hurried as fast as she could to climb and run back, risking her own safety a couple of times in the process. Her father's anger was scarier than the darkness of an abyss trying to bite her from below. Her heart beating fast and the blood rushing to her cheeks, she tried to breathe as much as she could as the air up there wasn't as nourishing to her lungs. Her clan was hidden high in the mountains, but they were sovereign over a lot of the mountain's land below them. Closer to the base, one could see their little flocks of tahrs busy eating all the grass they could find, while the shepherds watched out for the snow cats trying to eat them. Alezya was one of the few not to hate the snow cats for stealing their food; those feline stomachs were probably just as hard to fill as theirs, and their prey just happened to be the same...

She finally reached the entrance of the first tunnel and made her way into the maze, briefly greeting the few people of her clan she walked past. Most of them didn't return the greeting, or worse, avoided her eyes as if they hadn't seen her; their cold attitudes were like little daggers to her heart. Still, Alezya kept going, biting her lip and swallowing the bitterness. Those people all used to treat her well, but now, she was a pariah...

Finally, she reached the larger cave where she was met with her father's furious glare. He was an imposing man that had a constant dark expression on his long, square face, and thick bear fur draped over his shoulders.

"Where have you been?!"

"I was picking fruits," she calmly answered, showing her full basket.

The few eyes around them couldn't help but glance at all the food she had gathered, but her father did not care a single bit. Instead, he stormed up to her, grabbed the basket, and threw it to the ground, glaring while he towered over her. Alezya lowered her head, knowing what was coming.

"Do not give me that attitude!" he shouted. "You think you can act like this?! You don't get to stay here and roam freely after how you dishonored our family! Are you going to keep acting like this? You're an eyesore! You should be sorry!"

She didn't answer. Alezya didn't feel apologetic at all; she felt angry she was treated like this.

This public humiliation had become almost a daily ritual. However, she knew nothing good would come out of talking back to him; it would only make him even madder. So she bit back her emotions, her words clogging her throat, and kept her head low enough that he wouldn't see the bitterness on her face, nor would she have to face his.

"Our people are already struggling, yet my own daughter thinks she can act as she pleases! Do you think you can get away with your shame if you keep acting as if nothing happened? I can barely bring myself to face the other clans anymore, how dare you act like you did nothing wrong?!"

Because she had done nothing wrong. Instead, Alezya was furious that her father made her feel ashamed and acted like the fault was hers. Like she had any fault at all...

"You should be grateful we didn't kill you, and yet you're determined to let that creature live! If you had any compassion for your family, you'd get rid of that monster and cower in shame! You should be begging me for forgiveness!"

Alezya lowered her head even more and bit her lower lip even harder. She kept telling herself she had done nothing wrong and she would not be sorry. Weeks and months of hearing those horrible words again and again had built her up to become formidably resilient. She had always loved her family, but it was getting harder and harder to keep doing so. She hated her father right now.

"Dishonoring your own clan, your own father! Thank the gods your sisters are already married and have accomplished their duties as women, or you'd be the end of us all!"

Alezya did not feel happy for her older sisters at all, nor did she feel sorry for them. They had long been married off to men from other clans and were fulfilling their roles... the one role she had failed at.

"...If I had known, I wouldn't have saved you for the son of the Exkiu Clan," he kept on grumbling. "You deceived us all with your looks, while you brought absolute dishonor to us all, and forever disgraced their future leader! You should be too ashamed to even walk amongst your people! A vixen like you!"

Alezya hadn't asked to be the prettiest of her sisters, nor for her father to "save her" as a present for political match-making with another clan. A man she had only met a few times had become her future husband, while she was just a prettily wrapped present. For a long time, she had tried to act the part, convinced herself it was for the sake of her clan. She had gone through a whole nightmare and her own sacrifice to make her father happy, to make him proud, to make everyone content, and the result... had led to this.

"Things are hard enough with those wretched demons and their hellish dragons! The clans are barely surviving, and now I can't even count on my own blood to protect and serve her clan! We're all going to starve or be killed, and this is your fault!"

He slapped her.

Alezya didn't try to resist or dodge. She didn't cry from the burning pain on her cheek. She had been waiting for this. As painful as it was, this violence marked the end of her father's sermon and her release. He wouldn't openly beat her in front of the rest of the clan, not with so many eyes watching. Most of them probably thought she deserved this, but her father couldn't risk the shame potentially reaching other clans. She kept her head low, listening to his heavy panting, praying he was finally done. The worst part was that he always did this with many eyes around, yet nobody ever stood up for her...

"Go," he hissed, "and don't you dare leave this cave again."

With a heavy heart, she simply walked away.

She ignored the food on the ground, the eyes following her, and the deep, bitter injury in her heart. Tears were pooling at the corners of her eyes, but she blinked them back; she didn't want to show them how hurt she was. Her feet quickly took her deeper, much deeper into the mountain's intestines, to where there was more wind and less sunlight. There were also fewer humans along the way. Their mountain was so large that her whole clan could live scattered within it, and the families could always find a new corner in which to settle. If her clan had ever been big enough to find it crowded, that was far too long ago to remember. Now, their number was declining, and there was more and more space for everyone to share. Space was the only thing they never ran out of, besides snow.

Alezya finally reached her little corner. She had been forced to relocate herself far from the others' eyes and scrutiny in a little, secret space she had found for herself. She had to crouch down and almost get on all fours, cramming herself into a tiny tunnel, and climb up before reaching a half-open cave. It was one of the worst possible places to settle, with a large hole that let the wind blow in on a poorly protected corner of the mountain. It was a small space and far too open to the cold winds, but it was all hers, and one place her father could never get to. Alezya had tried covering the gaping hole with a large piece of leather she had sewn herself, but it wasn't enough to keep the little space warm. As soon as she stepped in, she ran to the small pile of furs on the side, the best-protected area. She had piled up as many snow cat and bear furs as she had been able to gather under, inside, and around a little basket.

"Lumie?" she asked, her heart beating fast with worry.

A joyous squeal greeted her, immediately calming her down.

Alezya smiled and leaned over the little basket, meeting the baby girl's gorgeous fair eyes. The baby was nestled in her little basket as she had left her, holding on to a tiny piece of wood Alezya had carved for her. As soon as she recognized her face, Lumie dropped her toy and extended her little, chubby baby arms to her.

"Hello, my little snowflake..."

All the grief and anger forgotten, Alezya grabbed the fur surrounding the baby and carried her against her chest, feeling the baby girl's temperature. Thankfully, it hadn't dropped too low. Lumie was alright, she seemed to have woken up not too long ago. With relief, Alezya kissed the baby's forehead and lifted her up so they could be at eye level. Lumie extended her little hands to touch her mother's cheeks and babbled some more of her cute but mysterious baby language.

"I missed you too," Alezya replied in a whisper.

Now that she was awake, the baby felt a bit hungry. She was no longer a newborn, but still a toddler, and very much in tune with her needs. Her cute smile turned downwards, and she made sure her mom saw how unhappy she was.

"I know, I know…"

Gently, Alezya rested her back against one of the walls of the cave and positioned her baby so she could feed on her breast. As soon as she began to eat, Lumie relaxed, happily drinking her milk. Alezya let out a faint sigh, both worried and relieved. At least her baby was safe for now, but for how much longer? She would not be able to keep her hidden in this cave forever.

As Lumie kept drinking, Alezya gently pushed back a little strand of hair from her face.

She couldn't understand why her family and people couldn't see the baby like she did… like a treasure. She was just different, but she was still her precious child. Yet, she was treated like a monster… simply because of her appearance.

Lumie's hair was snow-white. Her skin was white. Her baby was just born entirely white, with her eyes as pale as the shimmer of frost clinging to morning grass… Even her tiny eyelashes were as white as little snowflakes, something neither Alezya nor her people had ever seen before. Her own skin was a tawny beige, and already amongst the lightest of her kind. She thought she had seen all the colors among her people, from the Xihen with their skin as dark as tree bark, to the Leito and their famous golden skin tone, but in no other clan had she ever seen people with skin as white as the snow.

She couldn't understand how it came to be. No matter what her father and everyone else thought, Alezya knew she had been with no other man than the one she had been betrothed to. How could she forget all those horrible nights of pain? She had tried her hardest, just to make them all happy. And yet, not a single person had believed her innocence when the child was born. No one believed the heroic, revered son of the Exkiu Clan was Lumie's father. Worse, they couldn't even believe she was the child of a man from any of the clans.

So, as her mother and the only one to scorn, Alezya was deemed a traitor who had probably lain with some demon. That was the only explanation they could come up with…

After a while, she had learned not to care for their opinions, or for the friends she had lost. Alezya had learned to ignore the glares, the whispers everywhere she walked, the names they called her. Just when she should have been the saddest, she had found incredible strength in her new role as a mother. It was hard, and it still hurt at times, but all of those painful things were nothing compared to ensuring Lumie was safe and sound.

Alezya had never dreamt of becoming a mother. She had gone through puberty with her duty as a woman of the clan hanging above her head like some sentence and had not been given a choice in which man she would be betrothed to. Making her father happy and serving her clan was good enough for her. She had convinced herself, repeatedly, that her sisters and all women probably went through the same nightmare every night, laying in bed with their fiances and husbands... and despite everything else, she was relieved not to have to go through that hell again.

Her whole body would always shudder uncontrollably every single time at the mere thought of her ex-husband. Lumie had come almost like her savior, sparing her mother a lifetime of pain...

While she was lost in her thoughts, Alezya's stomach grumbled.

Lumie, who felt and heard that, giggled, making her smile. Her mother wiped her little mouth, as her daughter was done eating, and changed her position, putting the toddler more comfortably on her lap. Then, she took out a little bag of berries she had saved. She would have been foolish if she hadn't suspected what her father would do to her findings, for the hundredth time. She gave one to Lumie, who happily ate the extra snack, her fair lips taking on the red color of the fruit as she munched on it.

Alezya smiled and started eating some herself. She was glad she had always been a good climber. Who would have known she'd be left caring for herself and a child on her own...? Most women preferred to become good at cooking or knitting early, as their husbands would come to be the ones responsible for providing the food, but Alezya had always loved going out berry-picking, learning to spot herbs, and taking care of the herds. Perhaps she had known that lifestyle would never make her happy...

Suddenly, a large growl from outside resonated throughout the mountains.

Alezya hurriedly put Lumie back in her basket and jumped to her feet, running to the opening of their cave. Quickly, she put up more of the fur or leather curtains, doing her best to block it all; their cave went back to darkness. She grabbed a full bag on the side, swung it over her shoulder, and walked back to Lumie, pulling her basket close to her. In her tiny cocoon, the baby girl had her eyes open wide, looking a bit worried about the sudden change in lighting, unsure of what was going on.

Her lips were twitching, but she hadn't decided if she should cry or not yet. Alezya put her index to her lips.

"No, my snowflake. Hush..."

As if she'd understood, Lumie brought her fruit back to her lips, her eyes riveted on her mother. Meanwhile, Alezya stared at the opening, tense.

The sound came again, louder this time. She retreated to the back of the cave. The growl came from afar, but it was loud enough to echo throughout the whole mountain, like a storm above their heads. No doubt all the clans had retreated to the depths of their caves or hid in their tunnels, silent and listening. She suppressed a shiver, waiting and listening. It was hard to say how far away the beast was, for its size and the noises it made were confusing. That fearsome sound came again, and she pulled her baby's basket even closer, silently praying as she held her breath. She waited.

After a while, when no more growls had been heard, she relaxed a little. She waited some more, still nervous, yet nothing but the wind was to be heard outside. Alezya let out a faint sigh. That was the most dreadful sound of all, the one that came from the sky, like thunder ready to strike the flanks of their mountains at any given moment. Except that it wasn't thunder, nor as rare. It was a much more terrifying creature that freely roamed the sky, frightening them on an almost weekly basis.

It was a dragon.

Alezya had seen that dragon with her own eyes more than once.

It was an enormous, ghastly, and dark creature that appeared in their sky, first looking no bigger than a bird of prey, until it got closer and grew much larger than anything she'd seen. And she didn't want to see it from any closer.

The creature was already horrifying enough to witness in person, but the stories she had heard about the monster it served made it even more fearsome. The clans had been at war for centuries with the Dragon Tyrant that lived down there, long enough for them to fear, loathe, and envy their enemy's homeland. The same vast continent she loved to look upon and contemplate was in the hands of blood-thirsty men, who only answered their leader: a monstrous creature, half-human and half-dragon.

Even worse, that monster could summon and command an actual dragon, sending the mythical beast to strike their mountains, to rain fire, death, and destruction upon them. The stories were all about the same, told over and over so that every child knew them by heart. Tales of centuries of humiliation, but bravery and resilience. How the different clans had been forced to always hide deeper and higher in the mountains to stay safe from the flying monster, a flesh-eating creature that could come from the sky or the land. Dozens of men had been sent to the border to try and fight back, to win some land for their own, but they had never won. The clans only grew larger with the hope of one day winning against the enemy, while fewer and fewer returned.

The fight was generations old and desperate, but nevertheless endless. The clans scattered across the mountains were many, but they were getting along with each other less and less, fighting over resources and backstabbing one another for survival. And yet, at each gathering, most always stubbornly agreed to keep the fight going in the lower lands. Despite the many, many years of defeat, it was their intimate and deepest belief that one day, victory would come.

A young woman like Alezya had never been allowed to get close to the battlefront, but she had seen it from afar once or twice; it wasn't a sight she wanted to witness again.

The men from the ground were so many, she even wondered how the clans hadn't all been wiped out already. Like the others, she knew there was a fearsome man-dragon leading them, with inhuman strength and cruelty, but she hadn't even spotted his shadow; if he was worse than his men, she was glad she hadn't. She only wondered why her people were still alive when they were faced with such imperishable monsters; the only reason she could find was that the people from the ground had no interest in conquering the mountains... and they had already conquered everything else. At least, as far as her eyes could see on clear sky days, the land was either deserted, used for farming, or occupied by their villages.

Alezya had often contemplated those villages, squinting her eyes as hard as she could to try and get a glimpse of the other side. If she had been able to live down there, with everything she needed for a peaceful life, perhaps she would have never cared about climbing up some tortuous mountain either...

"Ma..."

She turned her eyes back to Lumie, who suddenly seemed a bit bored and impatient.

Her mother smiled and grabbed the little toy she had made, handing it to the baby to hold and play with. Lumie was already fifteen months old, but luckily, she was a bright baby and growing up just fine. Alezya was quite proud of herself for having managed to raise a baby by herself for so long... All her sisters had a community helping them in the clans they had married into, while she was left to manage all on her own.

The first nights, she had cried along with Lumie, not knowing how to calm her baby. When she was sick, she'd had to beg the Healer for help, again and again, until the old hag agreed to give her some advice before sending her off to find and try every natural remedy she could. Several times, she'd tried to ask one of her cousins for advice, but most avoided her and her white-skinned child like the plague.

By now, Alezya had learned two things: one, she could only rely on herself, and two, her daughter was much more resilient than she thought. Lumie had survived every fever, learned to cry to alert her mother when she was hungry, and could stay on her own for longer and longer.

This was the hardest part for Alezya: not having anyone who could watch over Lumie when she had to go out. She had taken the baby out with her a few times, but Lumie cried every time she was outside of the cave and exposed to the daylight.

After a while, Alezya had come to believe her baby was a child of the moonlight, who could only come out when the sun was gone and the night was peaceful. Sadly, the nights in the mountains were rarely peaceful; the dragon wasn't always around, but the snow cats were good at climbing and attacking both the unattended herds and imprudent climbers. Alezya didn't fear the snow cats, but she couldn't risk exposing Lumie to their claws and fangs.

Thus, she only took her child out sometimes in the evening, or held her on her lap while they both looked out of the opening of their little cave, their home, and into the wide, wide landscape of the continent. At least now that Lumie was older, she could leave for longer periods of time. When her baby was a newborn, she'd exhaust herself going back and forth to watch her child, try to find food and then run back whenever she heard Lumie cry from afar. Alezya sometimes wondered if her baby was calmer than most toddlers her age to quietly support her mom. At least to her, it felt like this part of motherhood was getting a bit easier, thankfully.

Once she had eaten a bit more, including a piece of dried meat from her food supply, Alezya decided to curl up next to her baby and catch some sleep.

She had woken up early to sneak out before Lumie woke up and escape her father's surveillance. It was getting a bit harder every time, with their clan sentinels watching out for her. More than once, she had been caught and beaten up for disobeying the Clan Chief's orders. Her father had a hard time hitting her himself in public, but he had no issue letting his minions do it. She had to be even more cunning each time she went out to gather food for Lumie and herself; the baskets her father frequently knocked over were both decoys and ways to try and bribe her place back into the clan.

Alezya knew the real reason he hadn't banished her to some remote, deserted, and inhospitable mountain like their traitors was that she was still bringing in significant amounts of food. She was sure every single berry spilled earlier was already washed and carefully stored away. She only needed that much for the clan to ignore the rest of it hidden in her pockets and the bags around her belt. The small amounts she managed to smuggle to her space were not only feeding them on the daily but also slowly piling up to be an emergency supply for Lumie and herself.

Alezya was always preparing herself to leave.

She had seen people banished for less than this, and she was constantly gauging the situation, trying to evaluate how close her father was to simply getting rid of her. She was both curious and worried that it hadn't happened yet. Even if her father had missed his chance to kick her out as soon as the baby was born, she had given him plenty of occasions by disobeying him. He was a bit more furious each time, so she couldn't understand why she was still allowed to come back... Something was going to happen.

One day, one way or another, her father was surely going to do something about this situation. His pride as the clan's Chief was hanging in the balance, and he certainly couldn't afford to lose face in front of the other clans. The shame of disappointing the Exkiu Clan was already bad enough, but with another gathering of the clans coming up, Alezya just knew something was going to happen to her. She could feel it like the treacherous wind getting calmer before a snowstorm.

For now, she was still fine and safe, and she managed to fall asleep next to her child.

As usual, she slept until late in the day and woke up to Lumie's voice right before sunset. Yawning, Alezya sat up, glancing at her little daughter in her basket, who immediately smiled at her mom.

"Hi again, my snowflake," she whispered.

She left a little kiss on the baby's forehead, who responded happily to it.

Then, Alezya took her out of her basket, changed her diaper, and threw the nasty contents away through the opening. She always loved to imagine it would land on someone's head somewhere below... perhaps one of the sentinels if she was lucky. Although, in reality, it was more likely to just hit a hare in some inhospitable flank of the mountain. After that, she washed the cloth, hung it in one corner of her cave, and grabbed Lumie to sit her on thick bear fur, laying the baby's toys in front of her.

Every single one of them she'd made herself, from a little stuffed ball to the little pieces of carved wood. It wasn't much, but the baby was once again understanding of her mom's limited means. Lumie could entertain herself for hours with those simple things, sitting up on her own and making sounds as if she spoke some secret language.

Meanwhile, Alezya liked to position herself so she could watch her daughter, but also lean against the opening of their cave, a leg hanging above the cliff, to look outside at the sunset sky. It wasn't just at the sky.

Often, her eyes would drift down to the land below, and her mind would be filled with questions about those villages, the people living there. She'd get lost in her imagination again, wondering what it's like to live in the land of dragons and hot skies. To live on the ground, on flat and snowless lands.

"Perhaps we should leave, Lumie."

Her daughter babbled happily at her name, unaware of her mother's dilemma.

Alezya had thought about it, many times.

What if she got down from this mountain?

She knew of no other clan that would take a woman with a child like hers, and she wouldn't be able to hide long in any other mountain either. There was no way up, so why not try to go down?

She'd seen the war, the endless war against the dragons, but what if she could get past the battle?

She glanced farther down, at the steep edge of her cave. Far, far below this edge she was sitting on, there had to be some way down. Her clan only knew of a few paths down those mountains, and all of them led to the battlefield. That was because their mountains were on a secluded, cornered end of the continent. What if there was another way out? In the farthest mountain of the Leito Clan, she knew they were surrounded by the sea... Has anyone ever tried jumping down? To leave their fate to the raging waves and see if they survived?

She would have seriously considered it if she didn't have Lumie, and if she was capable of swimming...

"Alezya? ...Alezya, are you there?"

She frowned at the familiar female voice.

Alezya quickly grabbed the little circle of wood and wool she had finished not long ago; it was very unsophisticated construction, but it was sturdy and heavy enough to place around Lumie to prevent her from going anywhere, a simple playpen. Alezya checked that the little baby-proof construction would stay in place, put a quick kiss on her daughter's forehead, and squirmed back out of the entrance. She was always nervous to be called out there. She imagined one day, she'd find her father at the end of the tunnel, perhaps with some of his men, ready to beat her up and end her...

Luckily, there was no bad surprise this time. As she climbed out of the last bit of her tunnel, she found her cousin standing there, looking a bit nervous, her fingers and foot tapping restlessly and her eyes watching the surroundings. "Zenia." She sighed. "What is it?"

Her cousin turned to her, frowning at Alezya's appearance.

Of course, she still looked a mess from her outing, the beating from her father, and going back and forth in a tight, dusty, and impractical tunnel. Compared to her, Zenia was a perfect-looking lady of the clan: her long, leather dress was spotless and elegantly covering all of her limbs, and she was wearing several little decorations, trinkets, and jewels her husband had gifted her. Even her hairstyle, a heavy braided bun, was showing off a new wooden piece.

"I need your help," she announced honestly. "The Healer is out of that flower she uses to calm down Perick's fevers, and no one knows where to find it... but you know, right? That purple one?"

So that's what it was: they needed her help. Alezya was a good herb-picker, and the best at remembering which herb or flower could be used as food or medicine. More importantly, she was good at remembering the best spots to gather them and the areas where they generally grew.

Whenever the clan would run out of one herb, having exhausted all the natural supplies they had found last, they would struggle to find it again. The mountain was too tortuous and quick to change to remember all the spots; one good area could be covered by inches of snow the next day, or all eaten by hares.

Alezya knew exactly what plant her cousin was in dire need of; it was one of their most efficient fever-reducing medicinal plants, the Huankin...

It was also a pain to find. That plant liked high and sunny spots on the edges of the mountain, the hardest ones to reach. It would be dangerous to get them.

"Please?" her cousin insisted.

"That old hag is such a hypocrite! The last time Lumie was sick, I had to beg her for over an hour to take care of her, with her saying it was a waste of her damn herbs! And now, she has you send me on errands?!"

"Please," Zenia begged. "I know that old woman is a pain, but this is about my son! He's really ill again, Alezya. That old woman didn't want your help, but I don't care, I just want my son to be better. ...You're a mother too, you understand me, right?"

Alezya immediately glared at her cousin.

"Oh, so now I'm a mother too? Weren't you the one who said I shouldn't have had her, that I should have just gotten rid of her and waited for another child?"

Her cousin went a bit white. Alezya could see she was genuinely panicked and worried, which meant her little cousin truly was sick again. Still, she couldn't help but be bitter; Zenia was barely better than anyone in this clan, only using their blood relationship when she needed her.

"I-I'm sorry for what I said," Zenia mumbled. "I was just... I was thinking of you, Alezya. You know we used to be so close... If it wasn't for that child, your life would be so different now. You're so stubborn... You know I'm not evil, I was just trying to help you out, even if you didn't like my words. Plus, I didn't have my own child then... Please, I'll apologize and beg all you want, but my son is trembling with fever and the Healer has nothing for him. You know that old hag would rather let him die than ask you for help! Please!"

Alezya sighed, looking elsewhere because she couldn't endure her cousin's teary eyes. It was true she and Zenia used to be close. Very close, even. She had often felt closer to her cousin, who was a year younger, than to her sisters.

They had also been betrothed to their respective husbands the same year and been pregnant around the same time... although the outcomes had been very different. Zenia was perhaps one of the few women in their clan who seemed to have chosen her husband and loved him. They were both once their fathers' favorite daughters, but while this had allowed Zenia to choose her future husband, Alezya's reward had been to be betrothed to the most promising one.

Once again, her father's greed had been her downfall.

"...Fine. But promise me you'll watch Lumie for me."

Her cousin took a slight step back, looking horrified.

"W-what? You want me to watch her?"

"What am I supposed to do with her while I look for that herb?" Alezya retorted with an angry tone. "I'm risking my life out there, I could be gone for hours and Father will be furious when I get back. Can't you watch my baby for me in exchange for your son's medicine?"

"B-but if others find out..."

Zenia looked terrified, which made Alezya even madder. They all knew what she was enduring every day just for keeping her child alive, yet everyone was using her without an ounce of pity.

And now, her cousin was probably terrified to be punished too or scared of the child somehow.

"Hide her," Alezya said. "Father will kill her if he finds her, so please, just watch her and hide her while I'm gone. You can do that. Your home is the most secluded, and I'll be back before your husband comes back from the hunt. Zenia, you know I'll be gone for a long time to find that flower for you. Would you leave your son alone for that long?"

Her cousin immediately shook her head, honest at least.

Right, Alezya thought. Zenia was stuck to her baby all day, she would never leave him for as long as Alezya was sometimes forced to leave her daughter on her own. This was a risky choice, but there was just no alternative. At the very least, she believed her cousin would be a decent enough person to not do anything to Lumie and take care of her for a short while. She would also be too scared of the consequences to not hide her from the Clan Chief... and she really needed Alezya to get those medicinal herbs for her son. The fact that she had arrived so late and looked so nervous showed that she had hesitated and waited before coming here, but now her son was probably truly ill.

"A-alright," Zenia mumbled, "b-but please, make sure you come back as soon as you can. If Uncle finds out... or even my husband, I'll be in big trouble..."

Alezya knew her cousin would be in no trouble compared to her. Lumie's life was hanging in the balance.

"Who's with your son now?" Alezya asked.

"I left him with our grand-aunt," Zenia whispered. "I-I'll be careful about your daughter, I promise."

Alezya nodded, but she didn't consider her grand-aunt much of a risk; the old woman was mostly deaf and mute. She actually liked the old lady, who had a funny and unpredictable personality. Their father's aunt was one of those women who had never had her own children despite being married several times, so she had helped raise those of others instead.

Now that her husband was gone, she wasn't as respected as the elders, just a forgotten old relative, convenient only when it came to watching the children.

Once Zenia promised no one else would know of or see Lumie, Alezya went back inside to gather her things and those of her baby, and came back out to hand her to her cousin. Zenia tried hard not to show her feelings, but she couldn't help opening her eyes wide and awkwardly taking the baby girl in her arms.

They made sure to hide Lumie under a large piece of clothing, and curled her against her cousin's chest; if no one checked, they'd just assume she was carrying her son, who was the same age and about the same size.

"...She's quiet," Zenia noted, a bit surprised, glancing at the wide-awake Lumie.

"She's a good girl," Alezya said. "Now go, quickly. The sooner I'm gone, the sooner I'll be back."

Her cousin nodded, and Alezya put a quick kiss on the baby's forehead. She watched Zenia walk away with her, worried. Then, without losing a second, she fastened her bag around her body and hurried toward the closest exit. Alezya was in a hurry to go; the faster she got that flower, the faster she'd be able to get back to Lumie...

At that time of the evening, she knew exactly where the men would be guarding the flank of the mountain; she wouldn't have been so good at sneaking out if it wasn't for the very, very regular habits of the watchmen. Her father had put a very tight schedule in place so that anyone who would go missing during a storm or get in trouble during a hunt would be looked for immediately. Luckily for Alezya, all men on duty were eager to follow the schedule and please their leader, and no one had ever tried to change it. Thus, she knew exactly where which man was supposed to be and when. It was only a matter of minutes for her to find an opening, sneak out, and climb out of sight, far enough from her clan's watch.

Alezya already had a few ideas in mind as to where she could find that flower, but not all of those would be easy to get to.

At first, she tried a couple of the usual spots, but they had already been sought out; she got angry while finding out that the herb-picker before her had been an idiot and dragged the whole plant out of the ground. If roots were left, this place could have given more flowers in a few weeks time...

Annoyed, she quickly moved on to the harder places: those that required her to really use her climbing talent, where most of the others in her clan wouldn't have been able to get to without a lot of effort and life-threatening risks. As familiar as she was with the mountain, the Goddess of Rock could soon turn out to be a mortal, unforgiving enemy.

Alezya was trying to progress fast and efficiently, taking the smallest, calculated risks. Luckily, the fourth spot was a bit better for her: she found a few flowers that had been left untouched by the weather and fauna. Relieved, she picked them swiftly and proceeded to move to her next spot.

She was moving quickly, but no matter what, moving around the mountain was still quite the challenge; sometimes, she could just walk, but most of the time, she was climbing dangerous uphill peaks, using all of her muscles to not fall to her death. None of the women who went out there could have done what she did in clothes like her cousin wore. Compared to Zenia's, Alezya's outfit wasn't made to be attractive. The skirt had been ripped at a mid-thigh length, and she wore tight-fitting leather pants underneath, which were perfect for climbing. She had altered them herself despite her poor sewing skills, using wool for a warm inside and thick yak leather for a sturdier outside. She didn't care about her looks, only about what she could accomplish on her own. Handpicking herbs in risky places was one skill she hoped to keep relying on. Anything that could help keep her tenuous spot in the clan a bit longer would do...

With a heavy sigh of relief, Alezya reached the fifth spot, the hardest one. It was a little platform on the side of the mountain, which sheltered a nice gathering of herbs. Alezya sat there to catch a break while quickly picking every herb she recognized. She was grateful she'd been a bit faster than anticipated, but she still had to be quick; this was the snow cats' hunting time, and she didn't want to run into them. Plus, the climb had still taken a lot of time, and she was incredibly worried about Lumie. As much as she tried not to, she couldn't help but worry something would happen to her baby without her around. Leaving their cave was always a dilemma... The temperature was starting to drop too. Now that the sun had set, it would quickly and progressively get worse. Alezya was used to going out after sunset, but it was still the most dangerous time.

There was one more danger she was well aware of and trying not to think too much about. She hoped it was gone for the night; all she asked was that the monster stay away from the mountain for a bit longer that night...

After a glance in her basket, she knew she didn't have enough flowers yet. Those would be quickly used, and she didn't want to have to make this trip again. Hopefully, she could collect enough flowers that by the time they'd need it again, they would have regrown in the other spots.

Alezya was running out of ideas of places to look though. Because the clans were so fiercely territorial and mistrustful of one another, risking herself on a mountain other than their own was twice as dangerous, so that option was out. Her only other way was to get closer to the top...

It was a dangerous climb, but not impossible.

Without hesitating much more, she kept climbing up. The main risk was running out of places to hide. She wasn't as familiar with the higher regions of the mountain as she was with the middle ones. It was the most treacherous part, constantly covered in snow, with almost no proper trail. No inexperienced climber would be able to take that route, and even for Alezya, it was a challenge requiring all of her focus. She knew not a single rock could be trusted, and she had to double-check every corner she stepped or pulled on. Her fingers sometimes had to dig deep until she could find the rocky surface underneath. She had to move carefully and slowly to not trigger an avalanche that could bury her in seconds, yet be fast enough to not let the cold bite her to death. Chills were already spreading through her body as her outfit wasn't warm enough for this height. She kept going, thinking of how Lumie and the other children would need that flower. She had lived through worse challenges, but always knew the risks taken. While she was willing to sacrifice herself for her baby girl, she was also well aware she needed to survive for her sake.

This way, Alezya kept herself focused and determined, gritting her teeth through the cold and continuing her uphill climb. She was high enough that her father's men were of no concern anymore, only finding more of that flower as quickly and safely as possible. She kept an eye out for her surroundings, but the growls of the beast would be heard long before it would be seen. Or so she hoped.

Finally, after a few more minutes of climbing, she found what she had been looking for: a little plateau, a spot where she could stop and inspect. That flower liked to grow under little areas protected from the wind and snow like these, and sure enough, after pushing some of the snow out of the way, Alezya spotted some of that familiar purple shade.

She smiled in relief, and as she could sit and take a break, she carefully unveiled more flowers. Luckily, they had just been covered by snow not too long ago, so they were still perfectly fine. There were plenty of them too. That dangerous trip had been worth the risks...

Alezya quickly collected them, making sure to leave what it needed for it to regrow some more later as she'd keep that place in mind for emergencies. Now, her basket was full enough. Those flowers grew in patches and were of medium size too, luckily for her. The Healer would be able to get enough medicine from all of these.

In a way, Alezya was doing this more for the children of the clan than for her cousin. She may have been resentful toward the adults, but as a mother, she couldn't bring herself to make the children suffer for their parents' mistakes. She didn't care about her cousin's hypocrisy or the Healer being cruel; she was able to find a good reason to do this despite them. Hence, with her basket full, Alezya came down that plateau, feeling genuinely glad. She had found the flowers quicker than she'd feared, and it wasn't late either. All that was left was going back down. She didn't even try to rush, instead making sure to have a smooth and safe descent.

Except that she didn't have as much time as she thought.

While she was changing rocks to step on, a faint spot of color appeared in her peripheral vision. She would have mistaken it for the setting sun, or one of its glowing streaks, if she hadn't already watched it fall behind the horizon.

At first, Alezya thought she'd dreamed it.

However, it flashed a second time, this time out of the corner of her eye, and a chill immediately ran down her spine. She turned her head, worried already. She had never seen anything orange flying in the skies, but her gut feeling told her it was no bird, no star. She could tell. That thing was far, but it was big... monstrously big. It was like a burning fire in the dark skies, both beautiful and terrifying. After forcing herself to look for a couple of seconds, just to be really sure, she felt her stomach drop.

It was a dragon.

Rather than staying frozen by fear, she moved quickly, her head full of questions.

What was going on? She'd never seen that creature as orange before, was it the same dragon? Or a new one?

She was trembling at the idea of another dragon flying in those skies. One giant beast was already terrifying enough! The one she had dared to peek at a few times was definitely black as coal, so what was happening? Had her clan seen that thing too? It was like a bright fire illuminating the night sky, her father's sentinels wouldn't have missed it...

Right now, she had to focus on her own safety and hide as quickly as possible. From the size of it, she hoped that thing was far away, but she was still hanging on the side of a mountain, vulnerable and exposed.

It was the worst situation possible.

Alezya accelerated her descent, trying to stay careful while getting back down as fast as she could. It would mean nothing to escape a dragon if she was to break her neck...

When the growl suddenly thundered, she froze, stifling a scream.

She had been out once or twice when the dragon had appeared, but never this close! This was all because she had to go out so late and so far. She couldn't even believe she was in this situation; It was like her worst nightmare had come true.

Fighting back tears, thinking of her daughter, she hurried down, trying to calm herself by breathing steadily.

With a bit of chance, that thing hadn't seen her, or it was too far away. She was wearing light-colored clothes in the midst of a lot of snow, perhaps that would be enough to hide her from that creature.

Another growl suddenly filled the skies, and Alezya stopped, closing her eyes hard to suppress the tears and fear. She wasn't going to die now. She had a daughter to care for. She waited, listening. The dragon sounded... different. She'd heard it plenty of times before, and this time, the growls were higher-pitched, stretched longer. It was a little like thunder compared to the sharp crack of lightning.

Maybe it was just her fear making everything worse, but something about it felt new. And somehow, more terrifying.

When her feet reached another plateau, she stopped to catch her breath. She had gone down faster than usual and was a bit lost, not on the same path she had climbed up. Her palms hurt, but that was a minor detail. She tried to figure out which area of the mountain she was on, where the closest opening was. She knew she'd reached the area her clan lived in, but she had to find an entrance to the inside of the mountain, quick... She tried to brush away some of the snow around her to find a familiar spot. She was trying not to think about how close the dragon could be by now, or how scary it was when she couldn't hear its position...

There! She recognized her clan's markings on the rocks, telling her exactly where she was. The closest opening was only seconds away, she just had to get down to the next plateau and make her way down on the left. With a gleam of hope, Alezya forced herself not to look back and quickly moved. She was so close to safety!

She took one step down, and then she heard it.

A flap of some very, very large wings that couldn't belong to a bird. Alezya's blood went colder than the ice around her. It was close.

A chill ran down her spine and she closed her eyes, trying hard to convince herself not to move and not to look back. How close could that thing be? How big was it? She felt the air freeze in her lungs.

She could jump down to the plateau. It was risky but doable. Then, she'd be right in front of the opening, and one step away from safety. She had to decide. To stay still, or make the jump. She tried to calm down.

Her only objective was to get home safe. She trusted herself to make that jump, she didn't trust the dragon to not try and kill her. ...She had to move, fast.

Alezya took a deep breath, visualizing the jump, doing everything she could think of to increase her chances. She shifted her weight to her right foot, moved her shoulders forward, and then...

Then, a gigantic paw suddenly appeared on her left, and violently pushed her back against the mountain.

The air left her lungs before she could scream.

She felt her right shoulder brutally hit the rocks while the strange heat of large scales rubbed against her left one. She shivered, and unable to resist, turned her head to see the beast.

The orange dragon was right there, staring at her with one of its eyes.

It was a big, dark gray eye, shiny like obsidian, polished as a mirror. She could see herself in it, while well aware of the gigantic iris moving. The beast's breathing was sending wide waves of hot air against the flank of the mountain, making its whole body slowly move along.

Alezya tried to choke down a cry of pain or fear.

That thing could eat her at any second, and her mind was blank with no idea what to do. Tears were just forming in her eyes as if her body knew before her the fatal outcome of this.

After a while of her staring into the dragon's eye and the dragon staring back, she started to come back to her senses. The pain was numb, manageable. The fear too. Her will to survive was starting to take over, and her gaze hardened.

"...Let me go," she suddenly mumbled through her lips.

The dragon answered with a strangely weak growl, but enough to make her whole body shiver in fear.

Still, Alezya bit her lip and repeated herself.

"Let me go, Dragon," she hissed.

She had no idea if it could hear her, let alone understand. It sounded like it was listening, but she had no clue what that gigantic monster could be thinking of its prey trying to order her freedom. It didn't matter.

Right now, Alezya was gathering all of her bravery to stand against that predator, to not give up.

"...I have a daughter," she muttered. "I have a baby girl, and without me, she won't have anybody. If you kill my child's mother, I swear, Dragon, I will curse you, your parent, and the next ten generations after you."

The dragon growled, a bit louder, but this time Alezya didn't flinch.

She just glared back, as if defying it. She was scared, but she was even more scared for her daughter's life. She just knew Lumie would be condemned without her, and she couldn't have that. She would have died to protect her baby, but this time, she had to survive.

"Release me," she cried, both an order and a supplication. "Release me, Dragon."

The orange dragon didn't move at all, but it strangely moved its head, as if tilting it. ...Was it actually listening?

Alezya's heart was beating fast, hoping, praying she could survive this.

She decided to try to move. She was pinned against the mountain, the dragon's palm against her, but its claws were dug into the rocks. She could move a bit. She tried to wriggle her way out of its clutches, slowly but surely.

The dragon growled a bit but, strangely, it didn't move, only watching her do so. The tiny human in its grasp trying to free herself was perhaps entertaining, Alezya had no idea. Moreover, she quickly found out it was worth nothing: she was tightly held, the bit of movement she could make was useless. Frustrated, she kept pushing against the warm orange scales, trying to get even an inch closer to that entrance; the dragon was taking its time before eating her, and she wasn't going to stop trying in the meantime. This time though, it seemed as if the beast understood what she was doing.

Without warning, it slowly lifted its paw that was holding her against the mountain, which meant Alezya wasn't its prisoner anymore, but also that she was now losing all ground to support herself on.

When she realized her imminent fall, her reflexes took over: she grabbed the dragon's scales in front of her, leaned forward, and pushed herself toward the platform. It was the messiest jump of her life, and without relief, she landed brutally on some solid, lean platform. Thankfully, her fall was completely harmless due to the thick layer of snow.

There, Alezya spun herself to face the dragon again, her instincts telling her not to turn her back to it. It hadn't moved. For some reason, the orange dragon had just seen her jump out of its grasp without reacting, still watching her with that paw hanging in the air just inches away from her. Alezya slowly stepped back into the entrance, watching for any sudden movement, but it didn't come.

The dragon just stared at her, its expression indecipherable.

She heard it growl when her body reached the safe shadows of the tunnel, and it leaned its head farther. Worried it might change its mind, Alezya retreated farther into the tunnel, where it was so narrow and far from the opening the dragon couldn't reach. She heard it growl again, a bit louder this time.

Alezya shivered and turned around, running away from that opening. She heard another furious growl, but she was already far away.

It took her a couple more minutes to stop running, and she actually fell on her knees, all strength leaving her body.

"...What was that?" she mumbled to herself.

She had no idea what had just happened.

For the dragon to have let her go made no sense at all. That thing had her in its clutches and it didn't attack? What in the world?

Alezya felt like she had dreamt the last few minutes. It felt so surreal, how close she had been to that dragon and survived. Something was odd in that new creature's attitude. The fact that there was another dragon was already weird enough, but for it to spare a human...?

She didn't believe for a second that her begging had worked, or that this beast could be capable of pity. Perhaps it was smarter than they thought, but then why spare a clanswoman instead of having a meal...?

She took some long, deep breaths to calm herself down, and unloaded the basket of flowers from her bag. Sadly, it had been partially crushed by the dragon's claw. Her basket she had spent ages weaving was badly damaged, and she had lost about a third of the flowers she had struggled to gather... Well, so be it.

She wasn't going to go out there anytime soon, not after this. Right now, all she wanted was to see Lumie again and hug her.

That was all she needed.

Tired, slightly shaking, but glad to have survived, Alezya walked back into the tunnels leading to her clan's living caves.

The few people she crossed paths with gave her confused glances: her appearance wasn't usual. The clothing on her shoulder that had hit the rocks had ripped, and had a visible bruise, with even a bit of her skin grazed. Her hair had become a mess, she had snow covering a lot of her clothes, and her lower lip was bleeding from how much she'd bit her dry skin. From the pain on her right cheekbone, she could guess another bruise was there. However, Alezya couldn't even feel mad, she was just so relieved to have survived her encounter with the dragon, her pain was nothing compared to the death she had foreseen just minutes earlier.

Still in a daze of disbelief over what she had lived through, she let her instincts take over and guide her body back to her cousin's home, another cave, to get Lumie back.

She heard the cries of her nephew long before she arrived. The baby was screaming his lungs out and had cleared all the nearby tunnels. Her cousin was walking in circles, nervously trying to calm him down until she spotted her.

"Alezya! Finally! What took you so long?"

Alezya answered with a glare, fed up with this errand already, but her cousin didn't even seem to notice. Instead, she almost jumped to grab the basket, immediately showing disappointment over the content.

"...That's all you could get?"

"I had more," Alezya retorted angrily. "I had a basket full, but that was before I almost got killed by a dragon!"

Her cousin's expression immediately sank.

"...What? The dragon spotted you?"

It did more than spot her, but Alezya didn't feel like correcting Zenia.

"Yes. And it wasn't the usual black dragon, it was another one. ...An orange dragon."

"Orange?" Her cousin frowned. "...There's never been word of an orange dragon. There used to be a silver and a yellow one a while ago, but orange?"

"I don't care whether you believe me or not, the spotters will have seen it too. Where is Lumie?"

"At the back," her cousin simply pointed behind her.

Alezya walked over quickly, inviting herself into her cousin's living space. It was much more spacious than the hole she and Lumie had to hide in, at least ten times bigger. Her cousin had a large living space, a pretty kitchen, and even a full area for her baby.

She found Lumie there, sleeping in a large basket on a fur bed. Alezya immediately relaxed at the sight of her daughter, safe, sound, and peacefully asleep. She leaned over her, finding relief in the soothing sight of the baby girl's sleeping face. Lumie had no idea of the troubles her mom had gone through, and that was alright.

Alezya carefully lifted her to not wake her up. The baby made a grouchy sound, but immediately grabbed her clothing, and went back to sleep on her shoulder. Alezya put a kiss between her white curls.

"Good girl, my Lumie."

She carried her back to the exit, where her cousin was still lamenting over the flowers.

"I hope that's going to be enough," she purposely said aloud.

"I hope for you," Alezya coldly retorted, "because I'm not going back to fetch more."

"This is about my son's life!" Zenia exclaimed.

"And I'm the one who risked mine to save him. Next time, if you care so much, you or your husband go and face a dragon yourselves. You're welcome, by the way, Zenia."

Without adding another word, she walked out of there, carrying Lumie. She was more than fed up with her cousin's hypocrisy. Even if she knew she had done this more for her nephew than for her cousin, Alezya was pissed at her lack of gratitude. Zenia was like everybody else in this clan: they only cared as long as they found a use for her.

She walked away, carrying Lumie and glad she was done with this. At least her conscience was clear. There was enough to make medicine for her cousin's child, the rest would depend on the Healer's skills.

She walked all the way back to her cave, carrying Lumie, feeling tired, but relieved. This time, she kept the large opening tightly closed.

Just thinking about her encounter with the dragon was enough to make her shudder all over again. While putting Lumie in her little basket and taking off her clothes, she kept replaying the scene in her head. None of it made sense. The dragons had never spared one of their fighters, despite facing them at the front almost every single day. The fact that this dragon was orange too...

A new dragon?

It had been a while since she had spotted one other than the black dragon. There used to be two more, a silver and a yellow one, fighting their people when she was younger, but now, it was only the legendary black dragon left... or so she'd thought. She didn't dare glance out to check often enough, maybe that orange dragon had been around longer than she thought?

It couldn't be good. She hoped Zenia would mention it to her husband. As much as she disliked him, their clan's safety was still tied to hers. Alezya hated relying on anyone else, but this was too important to ignore. Alezya knew all too well she and Lumie would have a hard time without a clan. If they were ever chased off this mountain, they'd literally have nowhere to go. She couldn't think of a place to establish herself, it would take days to gather everything necessary for their survival, and all the resources were already fought over by the different clans. She just couldn't afford to leave, or she would have done so long ago.

Alezya carefully began washing herself, taking care of her injuries as she discovered them. Most were caused by her climb up the mountain more than the dragon though. A lot of grazed skin and bruises, mostly.

She took from her own batch of medicinal herbs, those she knew how to use, to treat herself preemptively. It was the way of the Northern clans to consume medicine before they got sick. They believed that no herb was wasted if it could prevent one from falling sick and needing twice more later. She knew herbs to prevent infections, to strengthen one's body before the cold months, and even ones to eat before meals to prevent stomach aches while eating hazardous foods. Alezya had learned mostly by experimenting herself or secretly spying on the clan's Herbalist. She even collected herbs whose uses were still unknown, hoping to find new medicines by herself, and carefully recorded any new species she found. She had even made her own mortars and pestles, two out of stone and one out of wood. What was once a young girl's hobby had become an important survival tool for her.

Once she was done cleansing her wounds and putting some herbal medicine on them, she focused on her clothes. She was probably the worst embroiderer out of all the women in her clan, but she knew just enough to stitch up the ripped fabric. She got to work, cursing that dragon for damaging her only outfit and all the times she stabbed her own fingers.

Still, Alezya kept replaying the scene in her head, unable to understand how she was still alive. It was as if something within her had deeply changed after meeting a dragon face-to-face and surviving.

Somehow, she felt as if she'd been given a second chance at life. She left her clothes to dry in one corner of their cave and wrapped herself in one of those large furs, around Lumie's little basket, putting her hand on her daughter's round belly.

She couldn't find sleep for a long while; the image of that dragon's mirror-like eyes stayed engraved in her mind.

The sun was already high in the sky when she woke up to Lumie's hungry cries. Mechanically, she sat up and placed her baby against her to drink, grabbing their last berries for them to share as breakfast.

Alezya grimaced as each movement uncovered some muscle soreness from the strain of her climb the previous day. She dared to open the hole, peeking outside. It was a clear day, no clouds and no dragon to be seen. Yesterday's events felt unreal; she would have even thought it was all a dream if it wasn't for her injuries.

"Alezya!"

Her father's voice.

She just darted a glare toward the entrance of their cave, but Lumie started crying, afraid. She'd better get there and see what he was mad about this time. The sooner this would be over, the sooner her daughter would be able to calm down. She placed Lumie in the little pen and got dressed, ignoring the repeated calls of her father growing impatient.

Strangely, she had never felt more confident to face that man. What was an angry man compared to a dragon...?

Still, as soon as she crawled out of their refuge, she felt her nervousness come back. She had to be careful, for this wasn't just about her, but she had to watch out for Lumie's safety at all times as well.

Alezya quickly walked toward her father's voice, its echoes almost way too easy to follow. Something felt wrong when she got there, though.

Not only was her father waiting for her, but the clan's Herbalist, a few of the elders, and her cousin's husband, all of them with dark expressions on.

"I've been calling for you for a while!" her father angrily greeted her.

"Well, I'm here," Alezya retorted with a glare.

She took him by surprise with just that.

Usually, she wouldn't have dared to look him in the eye for so long. Instead, not only did she glare back, but she did the same toward all the people around. Alezya had no sympathy for any of them and they had none for her either; she didn't owe it to them to act polite or anything.

She was even more tense as she knew this kind of gathering was highly unusual and felt threatening.

"What is this about?" she asked first.

"We heard you said you saw the dragon last night?" said one of the elders. "An orange dragon?"

"Didn't the spotters see it too? Why do you need to confirm it with me?"

"They did. However, they were careful to hide and only saw it from afar... They saw it attack a woman."

So that was what they were all curious about.

The spotters had seen the scene, they'd seen her survive, and no one could explain it. No wonder all those elders felt uneasy and suddenly wary of her; Alezya's experience was completely unheard of.

She crossed her arms, nervous about what they were going to do with that information.

"And?" she asked coldly.

"Was that woman you?" Her father squinted his eyes.

Alezya directed her glare back to him. She could see him thinking deeply about this, probably wondering how he was going to be able to use her next. She knew she had to be careful with her answer; she couldn't predict their reactions to this unheard of situation. She was already trapped.

"...So what if it was me?"

He slapped her.

Alezya took it silently despite the painful burn on her cheek. Instead, she didn't hesitate to turn her glare back to him, making her father even more enraged. He could keep hitting her all he wanted, she wasn't going to back down so easily. Not when she was being cornered like this.

"Answer our questions, girl," hissed one of the elders.

"I am no girl," Alezya retorted. "I have a daughter of my own."

"You're an unmarried wench," scoffed another elder.

"This unmarried wench still won't answer unless I know what the hell you want with me," Alezya retorted, fierce. "Yes, I survived after that dragon attacked me. What of it?"

Those men all exchanged glances. Of course they would be surprised. The dragons and their masters were the clan's archenemy, why would one have let a Northern clanswoman go? Alezya was as baffled as them, but after being able to survive the previous night, she hadn't thought too deeply about it. As if she could possibly ever understand a dragon, a creature akin to a living deity...

"Why did that dragon let you go?" one of the elders sternly asked her. "What did you do?"

"How would I know?" she retorted, growing impatient. "I barely managed to escape, how would I possibly know what possessed that dragon to let me live? It's not like it talked or anything!"

They exchanged glances, annoyed with both her tone and her answer, or lack thereof. Although, she could tell they were strangely cautious.

With her tone even more rebellious than usual, her father should have already hit her once or twice more by now. Alezya could endure the beating, but those men acting differently than expected were making her nervous.

"What did you say to it?" Zenia's husband asked. "Did you say anything?"

"I told that dragon I had my child waiting for me, and that I'd curse it if she became an orphan! What's the use of this? I doubt it understood a word I said, perhaps it was just fed up! What's the point of your questions anyway? I was lucky to survive, why does it matter what I said?!"

Some of them exchanged glances, making her even more nervous. Why did it matter what she said? She had answered thinking it was completely irrelevant, but she realized she had been wrong. What did those men know that she didn't? She didn't like this at all.

"...Just as we thought," said one of the oldest men. "This is another sign from the gods."

Alezya squinted her dark eyes. A sign from the gods was precisely the sort of nonsense those people often used to justify forcing their ways regardless of others' opinions. She didn't give a damn about the sign from the gods, for she believed the gods couldn't possibly be bothered with these petty people. But she got even more nervous. She didn't think anything they were going to say next was going to be good news for her.

"We've never had someone survive an encounter with the dragon," muttered Zenia's husband.

Alezya glared at him. She regretted ever saying anything.

Of course they'd twist it for their own gain. She should have known better than to trust her cousin, even for the clan's sake. No doubt her husband had been the one to snitch the identity of the woman the orange dragon had spared. He probably hadn't even thought twice about it.

"This will be perfect for the next clans' gathering," nodded her father. "We can prove our willingness with the sacrifice, and use this to turn things around."

"What are you talking about?" Alezya asked, growing nervous. "What sacrifice?"

"You should be grateful for this opportunity," one of the elders told her. "Your ex-husband would most likely be willing to take you back if you prove your willingness. This is a unique position you will be in, a small sacrifice for the sake of the clans. You could erase all your mistakes and start over, child. We are being more than benevolent already, considering your past offenses."

Whatever they were going to promise her, Alezya already knew she was about to get offered some deal she was going to hate. She glared at her cousin's husband. This was their fault! She had been kind enough to look for medicinal herbs for their son at the risk of her own life, and it hadn't even taken a day before they sold her out!

"Grab the child."

"W-what?" Alezya mumbled, all blood leaving her face.

They wanted Lumie? For what? Her mind was going numb as she was starting to piece it together. Her father looked at her like she was some foolish insect and a very stupid one at that.

"Give us that creature you call your child," he insisted. "If the dragon spared it, it's all the more reason for us to sacrifice it to the gods. I knew there was something off about that wretched spawn, and now we get to use it for our clan's sake."

"You should be grateful, child. With this sacrifice, your willingness to help your clan will be considered, and we will plead your case to the one that was once your husband."

This had to be some sort of nightmare. Sacrificing Lumie? And to go back to that monster they called her husband, no less? Alezya felt like a piece of the mountain was cracking under her feet.

"...You can't be serious?" she muttered. "You'd sacrifice a child...? Because of some stupid things I said to a dragon?"

"A woman does not need to know such things," said one of the elders, "but the dragons are intelligent creatures. Our records prove they are capable of understanding words. Whatever the reason was for that orange dragon to spare your child, it's all the more reason for us to get rid of it. Why are you so surprised? Sacrificial rituals are common."

"Yes, with beasts and criminals!" Alezya retorted, now furious. "No one's ever been mad enough to sacrifice a child!"

"That creature is an abomination," her father hissed.

"She is my child," she retorted immediately, her anger even more palpable than his.

One of the elders rolled their eyes as if she was just being difficult. Those mad men were seriously talking about sacrificing a child as if it was a natural thing!

"You'd gain your place back in the clan," said her cousin's husband, looking dumbfounded. "Alezya, this might be your only chance! Your crime would be forgiven!"

Alezya glared at him even more. She had committed no crime, and she certainly didn't give a damn about her place in the clan.

Those were obvious lies. How could she go back to where she was, after everything that had already happened? After being treated like this by her father, in front of the whole clan, for months? There was no going back. And even if there had been a chance she'd believe that lie, she wouldn't have cared. There was nothing in this world that would possibly make her give up her own child, and certainly not to a bunch of men who were going to sacrifice her. She didn't know how much of that crap about the dragon they actually believed, and Alezya was far from being stupid.

Their real reason wasn't to piss off the dragon, it was probably to make themselves look good in front of the other clans. Showing they weren't afraid to burn a baby that was believed to be of some stranger's blood was just to curry her ex-husband's clan's favor.

And Alezya wouldn't let them have their way.

"No."

A single word, that had barely left her lips, but she had already made her resolve. No, she had decided a long time ago. No matter what happened, it was Lumie and her against the world. Against this insane, cruel world. Some of the elders sighed and turned around, visibly already bored with this situation. Her father, however, just went red.

"What did you just say?"

"I said no," she hissed. "You're not having my child, and you're not going to sacrifice her, Father."

"How dare you–?!"

He raised his hand, but Alezya didn't flinch.

She stood there, facing him, with anger in her eyes and not even batting an eyelash at the promised violence that was coming her way.

He slapped her, violently, but this time, she stood still. Despite her ear ringing, despite the pain on her cheek. She immediately raised her furious eyes back at him. This was her way to tell him. He could hit her all he wanted, it wouldn't be able to break her. He could beat her all he wanted, he could hit her again and again until she was on the brink of death, but she would not, she would never, ever abandon her child.

"...You're a foolish woman," he muttered. "Just like your mother. But your disobedience stops here, Alezya. If you don't grab that thing and bring it to me, someone else will. This is my clan, this is my mountain. You may defy me, but you won't be able to hold on to that creature. I was going to show some benevolence to you, but you persist to defy me. Fine. There are two weeks until the gathering. One way or another, I'll have that creature by then."

He turned around and his eyes fell on her cousin's husband.

"You. Spread the word. Whoever brings me that thing will be rewarded. Whoever helps her hide that creature, however, will be treated like traitors and punished."

"...Understood."

She knew there was no use trying to talk to her cousin's husband or to anyone else in the clan, for that matter. Alezya had months to see how quickly they could turn on her for their own benefit.

There was no one that would be on her side. No one. She was already trapped. That's why she knew she had to escape.

Chapter 2

"...Commander?"

The man carefully stepped inside the tent, nervous. It was dark inside; nobody had bothered to light a flame. He carefully stood a step away from the entrance, suppressing the terrible urge to leave this place. He waited a couple of seconds for his eyes to adjust to the darkness until he located the silhouette of a man, seated at the opposite end of the tent, immobile as a statue. He tried to control his breathing and not gulp down that knot of fear inside his throat. After a couple more seconds, he noticed the faint shine of the blade spinning where the man sat. A shiver ran down his spine, and the urge to run away got even more pressing. Still, he chased this thought away from his mind, trying to act bravely.

"A new unit of recruits arrived at the North Camp this morning, Commander. Around a hundred men arrived from the Capital for reinforcements and training. I am their representative, Captain Dajan, sir. This is our first time in the North Camp and an honor, Your Highness. We are setting up our tents and we will take our posts around the camp shortly. My men and I will join the camp's daily training schedule as soon as tomorrow."

The man waited for a response, but only a heavy, scary silence followed. He hesitated for a few seconds. Was he supposed to stay until dismissed? Or run out of there, as his whole body was screaming at him to? He dared to raise his eyes again, looking for a response. That's when he spotted them. Two dark green emeralds shining in the dark. It was like crossing paths with a dangerous, mortal snake, and realizing it was already too late. The man shivered irrepressibly in his armor, regretting his mistake instantly. He knew he wasn't supposed to look him in the eye!

"M-my apologies, sir!"

"...Get out."

The voice sounded like a beast's thunderous growl from deep inside a cave. Suddenly, the tent felt a whole lot bigger, and the poor Captain a whole lot smaller. His feet refused to move at first; his legs had gone numb from sheer fear. Embarrassed, he tried to force his feet to move after a huge effort and kept his eyes riveted on the ground. Leave, he had to leave. Immediately. Quickly, before he got killed. Or eaten... He finally managed to move his right foot, then the other, and he stumbled back with shaking legs and that fear screaming from the back of his mind for him to get out of there. He tried hard not to fall, not to turn his back either, and after vaguely remembering to bow again before stepping out, he finally found the tent's curtain and kicked himself out of there. He didn't even take two steps outside before he tumbled into the snow, falling on his knees and wetting his pants all the way to his thighs. He was drenched in a cold sweat, and out of breath for some reason. He'd never been so grateful for fresh air. The cold shiver down his nape wasn't going away, and even as he tried to get back on his feet, he felt weak in the knees.

"You fool."

He looked up. A man with a pockmarked face, thin lips, and an annoyed expression wearing a pale blue leather outfit under a thick black fur coat was looking down at him. If he hadn't been so busy being scared, he might have thought the man looked funny, with just his head popping out of the thick fur coat. The man looking down on him raised a thin eyebrow, while his fingers drummed on the little notepad he was holding firmly.

"Who are you?" he asked as if he was already annoyed by the answer. "Which unit do you belong to? I told them a hundred times not to bother the Commander in Chief without warning me first. Why did they send you? Are you looking to die, soldier?"

The questions were fired quickly, one after the other without much room for him to answer until the man with the notepad was done. Once he finally stopped, his fingers still dancing along his notepad, the Captain forced himself to stand back up, feeling embarrassed. His legs were still trembling a bit.

"Th-they couldn't find you, and someone had to warn the Commander about the new recruits, s-so... I'm Captain Dajan of the new division..."

"You moron," the other one answered right away. "The Commander doesn't care about new units arriving at the camp, the higher-ups played you... They're going to hear from me! Either way, don't bother him again. You're lucky he let you walk out without twisting your neck, Captain Dajan."

The man's expression sank. What kind of cruel prank was this? After everything he had heard about the Wild Prince, how could he make a fool of himself and get on His Highness' bad side from his very first time meeting with him?! Seeing his expression, the man in blue sighed.

"Don't fret over it. If you're lucky, the Commander in Chief will have forgotten your face already. Try to do your best on the battlefield, and maybe you'll be more than a bothersome rat to him."

The man nodded.

"Thank you for your advice. Y-you are the camp's Grand Intendant?"

"You may call me Intendant Tievin. In the future, don't bother His Highness again. Come to me if needed. You might be able to survive longer if you do."

"Don't you... fear the Commander? I heard even the generals are cautious around him..."

The man sighed as if the answer to the question was obvious.

"I have been by His Highness' side for ten years. Of course I am afraid of him, but I am certainly the best at handling his temper. Newcomers like you should just make yourselves small and stay out of his way. ...Morons."

Captain Dajan nodded and showed a resolute expression that made Tievin raise an eyebrow again. That young man seemed more earnest and unwavering than most. A lot of men were sent to the north with selfish dreams of honor and battlefield achievements and only had one objective: to stay out of trouble. This one at least seemed to have some respect for the Commander in Chief.

"I understand! I will make sure myself and my unit become valuable elements to this army, so even the Commander in Chief won't be upset with us!"

Tievin nodded and watched the young man go. So eager, so young... and so stupid, he thought. It wouldn't be long before that spirit would die down, as they all experienced. Most men who came here became disappointed after a while. The fights weren't as often nor as thrilling as most thought, the weather was worse than harsh, and the food was not that good either. Plus, there was little to no entertainment around. Glory couldn't be achieved in just a matter of months, and there were plenty of men who had gone from being as hopeful and enthralled as Captain Dajan to being wrapped up in utter resentment and boredom. This could only be expected. Those soldiers were unknowingly caught in a struggle between the Imperial Palace and the North Army that only a handful of people knew about. In other words, pawns.

The Intendant combed his long, black hair twice before stepping toward the tent. He frowned at the darkness of the place before entering. He did not need to look around for the Commander. Not only did he know where he was sitting, but there was no need to cross his fiery green glare.

"...Good morning, sir. It seems like the Emperor sent more souls to get lost here with us. Again."

Tievin did not need to look up to feel the burning glare on him. Still, he was used to it, and instead, only kept his eyes down on his notes.

"This is the last unit expected to reach the North Camp this month since we're already at full capacity. ...Commander, those men are going to need something to do here. Like everyone else."

A long silence answered him. Tievin didn't even try to suppress his eye roll; luckily for him, he was one of the few who could make that kind of disrespectful gesture in front of the Prince and still get away unscathed, all limbs attached.

"Sir, I won't take care of this for you this time. Unfortunately, this is something only the Commander in Chief of the North Army Camp is entitled to do. Me stepping in won't work this time, the generals won't allow it."

This time, he glanced up. This was it. That heavy, numbing sensation of danger. Luckily for him, Tievin knew this killing intent wasn't actually directed at him, but at some unlucky souls out there, who were probably shivering already, if they had any half-decent instincts. Were the generals going to be able to keep their necks? It didn't make the situation any less scary for him, but it was a good way to convince his body not to run away from that place, not yet. He forced himself to breathe, only to be disappointed with the smell of a place that hadn't been aired out in quite a while. He had to convince His Highness to get out of there...

"Alright," he said. "I know we both love the sound of my voice, so I'm just going to continue this monologue, as usual... I did need to let Your Highness know that your dragon was spotted again."

This time, he clearly felt the tension increase in the room. Tievin could never tell if he should be glad to have the Commander's attention, or if he wasn't just unknowingly walking a very thin line that could sever his head from his neck at any time. Hard to say, but so far, he'd managed to stay alive.

"Kein was sighted above the mountains, probably hunting. He disappeared before dawn though, so that's... another issue you might want to look into."

He waited as if there was a chance for him to get a response, but none came, as expected. He sighed. At least the hardest part was done.

"Alright," he mumbled. "Since we're both obviously enjoying this very much, I'm just going to continue... The generals' latest report mentioned six attacks from the Northern barbarians within the last ten days, which is not an unusual rate, but they have definitely been more vehement than normal. It seems they were trying to capture some of the men, but so far, we only have a few victims to account for, and all the bodies were retrieved. We still do not know why they are so set on taking them alive, and the units that were captured the previous time still haven't been recovered. They might... find it nice if Your Highness went to free them...?"

Tievin waited, for the sake of it, his eyes going around the floor at his feet for a few seconds, before he answered himself.

"Right, they are probably dead already; may their souls rest in peace. Let's move on. It's not like anyone's ever returned anyway. Not that we should perhaps try to retrieve our men, but, really, who cares? Not Your Highness, clearly..."

He dared to glance up to see how his foolhardy words were perceived, but again, only the darkness answered. He sighed. Sometimes, he hated this position... He glanced at his notes and immediately regretted his short-lived bravery. The next thing on the list was definitely going to put his superior in a foul mood. After a hesitation, Tievin very slowly took a little step back, preparing himself.

"Next, you received a letter... from your family."

"I'm sure I told you to burn them all," the Prince's voice suddenly thundered, making Tievin jump.

"You did, sir, but a letter from the Imperial Family is not something that someone like me can freely dispose of..."

"I said to burn it!"

Tievin had to gather all of his strength and self-control to not leave the tent running. It was one thing to know the Prince wouldn't kill him, it was another to wonder how many limbs he could lose if he pressed him any further. He took a few seconds to carefully think of his next words, as well as taking a deep breath to calm his nerves.

"Did you consider that maybe, this letter might come from your older sis–"

"If you mention my older sister or brother again, Tievin, not even the Emperor will be able to save you."

Tievin immediately pressed his lips together, sealing his mouth firmly before he actually lost something, probably his life. He waited a few seconds and then nodded.

"...That will be it for today, then," he muttered.

He suddenly felt movement in the tent, but in this darkness, it was hard to tell what was going on. He heard the sound of clothes, metal, and heavy, angry steps. His only reflex was to freeze where he stood and wait. After just a handful of seconds, a large figure walked past him and furiously flipped the tent's opening before disappearing. Tievin waited a couple more seconds in complete silence before he finally let out a sigh.

"I swear I'm going to die young and lose my hair before that," he grumbled, nervously combing his long black hair. "No, no, no hair loss. Think about the money. Think about how much you're paid to endure this horrible temper of his... You can do this, Tievin. If Father endured thirty years by their side, you can do this for a few more years..."

He took another deep breath and then forced himself to exit the tent.

It blinded him for a second to suddenly be back in the bright light of the day after the darkness of that tent. Two soldiers who were standing guard by the tent ran to him.

"The Commander in Chief just left toward the Northern Forest," one of them reported to him.

"Send three units with him... no, behind him. Tell them to not bother him, just clean up the mess if they can."

"Should we tell them to hunt with the Commander...?"

Tievin scoffed.

"They can try, but then you might want to warn them they are at risk of losing a limb. For the smartest ones of the bunch, tell them to simply collect whatever the Prin-the Commander leaves behind. We can always use more furs and leather... Make sure to do a rough inspection of the surroundings while you're at it. The Commander's presence will probably chase any of those barbarians out of the woods and back into their mountains, so capture them if you see any. Who knows, it might not be too late for an exchange..."

"What about... the dragon?"

Tievin grimaced.

"If you think that thing is near, stay behind the Commander. Never, ever get between him and his dragon. And don't run, either. It excites that stupid thing. Make sure someone reports to me as soon as the Commander is back."

"You're not coming along, Grand Intendant?"

Tievin glanced at the man as if he'd said something completely stupid.

"What for? To get drenched in inches of snow and watch the beast butcher whatever crosses his path? No thanks. I'm going to go to my tent, work, and finally have my breakfast."

"You haven't eaten yet, Grand Intendant?"

Tievin sighed but turned around with no intention to respond. No, he hadn't. He would have been an idiot to think it was smart to have anything in his stomach before confronting the beast... He slowly walked back to his tent, taking a detour to inspect the camp. Things were rough, as usual. The winter was getting into its worst part, meaning the snow was piling up, the prey was getting harder to hunt, and the men were getting restless, exhausted by the biting cold. The good part was that they would look forward to the next fights, anything to provide them excitement and a good occasion to warm up these days. Tievin took note of a tent that needed to be repaired and then glanced back at the mountains behind them. Those things were like a long stone wall they had pushed as close to as they could, but the North Army could go no farther as the tribes would fight fiercely. What had the Emperor thought, to send his reckless brother here? Although he had been there to listen to this nonsense order, Tievin himself was still confused.

Pacify the north. That was the only order the Emperor had given his younger brother. It was an order, a punishment, and a challenge all at once. A way to send his troublesome younger brother away from the Capital, to the cold, bitter north where the Wild Prince would be able to fight and kill to his heart's content. And kill he had. In just a couple years' time, the North Army had gone further north than ever before, forcing the Northern barbarians to hide in their mountains and only come down for desperate attacks against the camp. Now, it was like they were trapped in the fight, both opponents stuck where they stood. The barbarians wouldn't leave their mountains, and the North Army couldn't risk going up. The Prince had pushed the North Army as far north as he could, but what could possibly come next? Hence why Tievin thought the Emperor had given him a cruel order. There was no easy way to end this battle that had already taken place for centuries. The mere word "pacify" could mean a lot of things, so it was up to the Wild Prince to come up with a means to end this war. Either that or they would stay stuck in the north forever... What a scary thought. He shivered and resumed his walk. Perhaps that impossible dragon would somehow manage to kick the barbarians out of their mountains, who knew. If only that wretched thing could be tamed...

Tievin went back to his tent, and by the time he got there, he was freezing and mentally complaining about the cold. He couldn't help but think his father had somehow punished him too by sending him to this hell of a place with the Prince... As soon as he was back, he tried to get the fire going again and wrapped himself in new, dry fur coats before sitting down to have breakfast while going through the paperwork. Still, they weren't short on materials or provisions, and wouldn't run out any time soon. The Prince had made sure they were well stocked before the worst of the snow arrived. The Northern Forest was full of creatures that had roamed freely for decades, and thanks to the long hours Kassein had spent hunting to his heart's content, they had enough fur, leather, and meat to trade and use. Whatever they couldn't use here was sent to the closest villages and sold for what they couldn't hunt or find. The mere presence of the Prince in the Northern Region had improved the quality of life of all the nearby villages. He didn't keep anything he didn't need for himself, nor sought merit. He always did a lot by himself without requiring assistance, and he didn't order the men around needlessly. He was extremely cold and unforgiving, but he wasn't unfair. This, among other things, explained why the Wild Prince was popular despite his horrible temper. He was both feared and respected by his men and the locals, a necessary quality for whoever was in charge of the cold north. In the North Army were only the best soldiers, or the worst people. It wasn't rare that criminals were sent here to serve their sentence, by fighting without pay for the length of their punishment. They were clothed, fed, and provided shelter, but their lives belonged to the Wild Prince. Due to that, it took an inflexible man to lead the camp, nip rebellions in the bud, and maintain order. Fights were common within the ranks, but no one was stupid enough to do anything to provoke the Commander in Chief. They knew there was never a second warning.

Thanks to that, even frail and harmless Tievin could carry out his tasks with relative safety. As the closest aide to the Prince, he was an untouchable weakling whom even the generals respected, and he was content with that. In fact, although he couldn't carry a sword, he was somewhat respected for the simple fact that he could endure the Wild Prince's temper.

A couple of hours passed while Tievin was holed up in his tent, finally able to warm up a bit. He had one of the largest tents in the camp due to his status, with plenty of room to himself, but most of it was occupied by paperwork, account books, and chests filled to the brim with documents. One table was buried under his collection of fur coats, as he had no shame changing as soon as the previous one was soaked by the snow. They didn't dry fast enough either, so he had conscientiously saved a few. If he was going to suffer in the north, he should at least do his best to make his stay as comfortable as possible... Comfort was the best. This precious little pile of warm, nice, and fluffy coats he had bought was probably his most cherished belonging here.

"Grand Intendant," a man called to him from outside. "He's back."

Tievin sighed, but put down his pen. He got up, stretched, and carefully selected another coat before going out.

"I'm listening," he told the soldier while they began walking in the snow.

"No injuries to report, sir. As you instructed, three units followed the Prince and returned. Do you want the hunting list?"

"No, I'll go and see what he brought back once it's all... taken care of."

Tievin hated the sight of blood, so he usually waited until the soldiers were done cleaning the hunting trophies and organized everything before he went to see it for himself.

The Wild Prince went hunting so often that some units of men had become almost specialized in taking care of his prey upon his return. In a matter of a few hours, no matter how many, they would be carefully skinned, the fur washed, the meat set aside for the camp to have within the next couple of days, the bones would be washed to be sold, and the claws and fangs would also be put aside. Nothing went to waste. Although most of the Empire didn't have any need for fur given its warm climate, the regions most north had begun to take a liking to those, and they were popular in the area. Tievin was also responsible for making sure they could still use those while keeping them at a high selling price. While some fur could be put on the soldiers' uniforms or used as extra blankets, there were still too many most of the time. Thus, he had spent some time making sure those would become a trend in the Capital as well. Now, the supply was matching the demand, so the Commander's hunts were also a nice source of income for the North Army, which was vital.

Sadly, no matter how wealthy the North Camp became, it wasn't enough to bring a solution to this war. The soldiers may have been more comfortable, but they were still stuck in the coldest region of the Empire to fight a battle that never ended.

"Any sightings of barbarians?"

"Just from afar this time, sir. We spotted a few of them, but they were on high outposts in the mountains, watching us. None came down to fight, though, and they disappeared before the Commander was done with his hunt."

Tievin wasn't surprised or pleased with that information. The barbarians had learned to recognize the Commander in Chief, and stayed away whenever he was close. They knew they didn't stand a chance if he was there, so they would stay hidden in their mountains, and only come down if some of the North Army's men were visibly alone.

He sighed and crossed his fingers, thinking. Was there a way to end this war? It was like fighting an invisible enemy. The mountains were a nightmare to climb, there were far too many, and they were mostly unexplored by the Empire. The bits they knew had come solely from watching those barbarians. They figured there were a few hiding posts the barbarians used, and they could travel from one mountain to another quickly. From their attire, they'd also realized there was likely more than one tribe, half a dozen at least. Moreover, there was no telling how many people were actually hiding in those mountains. The only map they had that was possibly accurate had been drafted long ago by one of the Prince's ancestors, a predecessor who'd been in charge of the north just like him. It was enough to understand that there were more mountains than their eyes could see from down here, and possibly a lot more barbarians hidden in them. Hence, the status quo was persisting to this day; even for someone like the Prince, it would have been madness to go into those mountains they knew nothing of, to fight an enemy on their own territory when there was no telling how many of them were hiding up there. The only way that made sense would have been with the help of a dragon, but that too was impossible.

"Alright," he said. "What of His High–I mean, the Commander?"

"He's gone to the training grounds..."

Tievin let out a loud sigh. That meant he hadn't had enough of hunting, then. If he was in the training grounds, there had to be a few poor soldiers trapped with this monster to entertain him... Poor lads. He couldn't understand why some of them still considered it some honor to cross swords with such a beast. He waved his hand as if to chase some annoying fly.

"Fine, let him have his entertainment. Just send someone to let me know when he goes back to his tent. Ah, and send someone to clean in there while he's out. It smelled worse than a snow leopard's den in there."

"Yes, sir."

"What about the dragon?"

"There was no sign of the dragon since last night, sir."

"Fine, fine. You can go."

After the soldier left, Tievin returned to his tent and sat down again, absently tapping the tip of his pen against a parchment, lost in thought. That damn dragon... At least they knew it was still around, although it was hard to say what it was doing. That beast was never too far from its owner, anyway. It would have saved them a lot of time if that thing could actually be used against the tribes, though. Was that why it kept roaming around the mountains? Was it hunting, or simply just making rounds to reflect its owner's intent? The tribes were clearly afraid of it, but how could they not have been? There was no telling if the dragon had actually attacked some of them. Several times, it had come back covered in blood, but there was no way of knowing if the blood was human or from some animal, as it didn't bother to bring back the bodies...

If only the Commander had proper control of his dragon, then maybe this endless war would actually have a possible outcome. But was that the Emperor's real intent, though? Once again, Tievin couldn't grasp the Emperor's objective.

Had he really sent his younger brother to fight an endless war just to get him away from the Capital, as many believed? As someone who had grown up relatively close to the Imperial Family like Tievin, this didn't make much sense. Anyone could tell the brothers didn't get along, but this seemed too cruel and unlike the young Emperor. What was the Emperor truly hoping to accomplish by sending the Wild Prince here? Tievin had been there the day the Emperor and his younger brother had fought. It was like all the other fights: Prince Kassein had always been difficult since he's known him. The Fourth Prince was short-tempered, violent, and hard to understand. His dragon was even worse. The two of them had caused countless accidents within the Capital, almost always resulting in terrible damages. More often than not, it had been caused by the two of them fighting. The Wild Prince and his untamable dragon, the chaotic duo feared by all. The Imperial Family had spent over a decade trying to pick up after them, trying to be understanding. This time though, it seemed like it had been one too many. The Emperor had banished his younger brother to the bitter, cold, and abandoned Northern Region, and Tievin was sad to know it was to the relief of many. The Wild Prince hadn't earned his moniker by mistake... although the dragon was the wilder one. Perhaps sending them north was so they'd stop destroying the Empire, but then, why this order to pacify the north? Trying to kill two birds with one stone?

"Grand Intendant!" a voice suddenly shouted from outside the tent. "The dragon! The dragon's here!"

A cold shiver ran down Tievin's spine. That damn dragon, right when he was thinking about it! He grabbed a fur coat and ran outside, just in time to witness the large shadow flying over the camp and, right after that, hear its loud growl. Everything around them trembled under that thunderous growl. Tievin caught a glimpse of the situation around: the soldiers were running out of their tents, grabbing weapons, running in all directions, and trying to decide what to do.

"Where is the Commander?" Tievin shouted for anyone around to answer.

"At the training ground!"

"Evacuate that area! Order all soldiers near the training ground to get as far from there as possible! Evacuate what can be and protect the nearby tents to reduce damages! Any valuables should be moved to safety! Immediately!"

"Yes, sir!"

As soon as they were given orders to follow, the soldiers sprang into action. The units spread out and split into groups with the efficiency of those who hadn't just witnessed this once or twice. The truth was, all of them knew that a dragon attack was on a different level than battling barbarians, and while some were scared, most were also excited for action. The newest recruits were the only ones panicked, but they followed orders anyway. If anything, some seemed excited to witness a dragon from up close, their eyes scouring the sky to spot the bolt of fire-colored scales. There wasn't much time for them to just wait and watch, though. Soon enough, another growl was heard, and violent gusts of wind shook the camp. Tievin had to protect his eyes with his fur-covered arm as the camp was suddenly caught in a massive winter storm.

"Keep moving!" a general shouted. "Don't stop!"

Only Tievin stood still at the entrance of his tent; he was completely resolved with the fact that he wouldn't be of any help anywhere, not when he could barely stand his ground at each blow of wind. Unlike the soldiers, he didn't wear any armor and wasn't near heavy enough to be able to resist the snow from the mere flick of that beast's gigantic wings gusting his way. He crouched down, trying to hide behind his tent, while the soldiers kept running, shouting orders, desperate. Soon enough, booming growls resonated loudly, and the ground began shaking. It was no earthquake, but a mere echo of the fight going on in the training grounds at the same moment. Tievin felt glad he hadn't followed His Highness there; he would have been on the frontlines of a terrible display of violence, man against dragon. He had seen it enough, and had no intention to witness it again if he could avoid it. There would be nothing to see but rage, blood, dust, and more rage. It was savage, ruthless, and merciless. It wasn't a fight common mortals could even understand, and it wasn't something a weakling like him wanted to even be near.

"Keep moving!" he shouted, noticing that everything had gone a bit too quiet around. "Don't wait until it's over!"

He knew it was tempting for the soldiers to watch and witness this incredible battle between two beings akin to gods, but they couldn't afford it; the damages would only be greater if they waited to act. Soon enough, the stomping of boots in the snow around him resumed. He sighed, and proceeded to crawl, hiding behind his tent. Although it happened quite often, he could never get used to those skirmishes between the Prince and his dragon. In what state would he find the Prince this time? The dragon wasn't holding back because it was facing its owner... No, it was more accurate to say it wasn't holding back precisely because it was facing its owner. There had been instances before of Imperial Dragons being hostile toward their owners, or hard to control, but this dragon was truly a rageful beast like no other. Never had someone witnessed a dragon so determined to attack its owner, and not be afraid to kill them. It didn't make sense. A dragon's life was tied to its owner. If Kassein died, his dragon wouldn't survive long. A dragon that had lost its owner could survive a few years at best, from what they knew. The ones who had survived the longest were the dragons who had been cared for by other members of the Imperial Family after their owner's passing. The previous Emperor's golden dragon, Glahad, was probably the one who had survived the longest, as it had been taken care of by Empress Shareen herself. Since she had no dragon of her own, Glahad had stayed by her side until her nephew, the current Emperor, had taken the golden throne. As soon as Prince Kassian, now Emperor Kassian, had been crowned, Glahad died in the following days, leaving Kassian's silver dragon, Kian, to replace him as the Imperial Palace's dragon. But no one would be insane enough to care for a dragon who had killed its owner... So what was that mad dragon trying to accomplish? Was it simply crazy, as some believed? The Wild Prince and his wild dragon. What a problematic pair... Though he did believe it was cruel, Tievin didn't blame the Emperor for sending them away.

"Sir, I think he's gone!"

Indeed, the snowstorm had calmed down. There was still some snow flying around them, but it was nothing like the previous blows. Tievin sighed and got back up, trying to wipe some snow off his shoulders and limbs. He glanced around; the camp had been covered by a thick white coat, as if it had snowed three inches.

"Get started," he said. "I want a full report of the damages, all the snow cleared as fast as possible. If anyone is injured, send them to the medical tent and give me a list of all those who check-in. Do not let any injury go unexamined. Make sure the inventory is done twice, and once everything is ready, call the generals to my tent for a review of the evacuation process."

"Yes, sir. Where are you going...?"

"Well, someone has to verify if he's alive," groaned Tievin, who had started walking toward the training grounds.

He didn't even bother to check any of the damages on his way there; he knew the soldiers were so used to this, the reports would be detailed enough. Many had already begun repairing what could be, pulling the debris out of the way, swiping the snow off the top of the tents or out of the main alleys. He crossed paths with a few new recruits who were carried to the medical tents; their curiosity had almost cost them their lives. As he got closer to the training grounds, the damages caused by the fight became more apparent, and he couldn't help but shiver. How violent that brawl must have been to cause this much destruction in just a matter of seconds... Many tents had collapsed or had been wrecked, and wooden pillars that had taken days to install and secure had been torn off their bases like twigs. Even the wall that they had built over weeks with the sturdiest wood had an entire portion blown away. This was problematic, making Tievin frown despite the soldiers already at work in that area. This wall had been made to protect them against possible night raids from the barbarians. With so much of that wall destroyed, it would take days before they could restore it to its previous state, days where they would be exposed... Well, the men were going to be excited for night patrols.

The closer he got to the epicenter of the brawl, the more wreckage was around him. No soldier had actually dared to get close to that area yet, and he couldn't blame them. There was absolutely nothing in this place that had been able to survive the battle. All tents had been blown away, everything around looked like it had gone through the worst storm of the century. The snow had receded from his knees to his ankles as everything had been swept away from the area. The training grounds were nothing but a simple circle delimited by some wooden barricades, a few weapons arranged in rows, and some benches, but none of that was where it used to be. In fact, it was hard to recognize the area at all. It was as if they were deeper in the forest, where the Commander usually hunted. Except that nothing living would have chosen to stay here... Tievin began scouring the area with his eyes, looking for the Commander. No matter how many times this happened, every single time, he couldn't shake that feeling in his stomach, the nervousness that maybe, this time, the Prince might not have made it.

He finally located him just a couple of minutes later. A bit relieved, he walked over, only to witness the extent of his injuries. The dragon wasn't pretending to harm its owner, that was for certain. The snow all around the Prince was dyed crimson, in such a large range that most humans probably would have been dead, or close to it, if they'd lost that amount. Not their Commander in Chief, though. The man wasn't just alive, he was awake. He was lying on his back, still breathing heavily, small wisps of mist escaping his lips.

"You're alive," Tievin simply said.

A faint growl answered him. Tievin glanced up. No sign of the dragon anywhere. That beast had just come down to brawl with its master and flown away as soon as it was done... He could never understand what was going on in the head of that crazy dragon. He glanced down. From the sight of him, the Prince had endured a lot again. It wasn't just the snow; there was dried blood all over him. Luckily, his body was already healing at the incredibly fast rate that was characteristic of Imperial Dragon owners. Irony had it that it was the orange scales of his dragon that were appearing all over to patch the large wounds caused by that same dragon. Tievin had seen enough of those to know the dragon had put its claws deep into its master's chest, bit him over and over, and injured every single bit of skin it could, like an enraged beast. The depth of those injuries was perhaps the most incomprehensible part; there was no doubt that the dragon was genuinely going for the kill. Every time, the Prince survived, but not by much. It was a miracle he wasn't missing any limbs yet.

Tievin stood still by his side while the Prince's body slowly, and most likely painfully, healed up. The fights with his dragon were happening so often that this crazy beast had managed to leave some permanent scars on a body that could heal itself at an insane speed. There was apparently a limit to how much the Dragon Blood running through the Prince's veins could heal, and the proof was on his skin. The same places had been attacked over and over again, so much that his body had lost the battle, and instead of healing him perfectly, he was covered in orange scales or deep scars. Tievin knew that even when one had lost their dragon, the scales would still heal a dragon owner. Would the orange scales have stopped protecting Prince Kassein if his dragon had a say in this? Or was it enjoying being able to harm its owner again and again?

"...Who won?" Tievin asked with a dull tone.

The Prince didn't answer. Well, if both the Prince and dragon were still alive, one would have thought it was even, but in Tievin's opinion, being able to survive a dragon's murderous intent was a victory for the Prince. Seeing that the dragon wasn't in the area anymore, the Prince had probably dealt enough damage to that beast to convince it not to come back too soon for another round.

"I see." He sighed. "Well, it might take a while to repair the damages, so I hope it won't be back anytime soon."

As always, the Prince didn't bother to answer him. In fact, he had closed his eyes, looking exhausted. Tievin didn't really blame him, and simply stood still by his side, watching the injuries get reabsorbed and his breathing calming down. Soon enough, some soldiers finally came to the training ground.

"Sir, shall we call a doctor?" one newcomer asked, horrified by the amount of blood.

"No need," said Tievin. "Stay away, just take care of the area. Quietly."

Although a bit surprised, the men nodded and started sorting out the debris, piling it up, and noting the damages, silently as asked. Tievin tightened his coat around him, internally protesting against the biting cold. The Prince had most likely fallen asleep to recuperate, and he would stay by his side all through that nap. Unlike common mortals, those with Dragon Blood didn't fear the cold, so sleeping on a mattress of snow was probably as good as any other for him. He wouldn't allow anyone to touch him, let alone move him, so he might as well nap here until his injuries were healed... For some reason, standing by the Prince's side while he was like this was one task Tievin always took on. Making sure no one disturbed the Imperial Prince's rest and that the soldiers would carry on their tasks was his duty, even if he had to stand and shiver in the cold for hours...

Tievin was reading the list, only his arm out of the thick fur coat to hold the parchment. He was back in his tent, in a chair put as close as possible to the fire without the risk of burning anything. He was still shivering a bit, but his expression was stern.

"Good job," he said once he was done reading, turning to the General standing there. "Is that all?"

"Yes. Luckily, no one sustained life-threatening injuries, and the newcomers learned a good lesson about getting too close to a dragon..."

"Morons," Tievin grunted. "Anything else?"

"A rough first estimate is that the damages will take about a week to be repaired. Naturally, the defense wall is our top priority, but the construction units are quite hopeful. We have enough wood stored and as per your recommendation, we had planned a few more extra panels in case such a thing happened, so it shouldn't take too long to replace the damaged parts."

"I see. Make sure to establish twice the usual number of night patrols to compensate, and put some men on surveillance duty as well. It will be bothersome if the barbarians notice our defenses are down... No, they most likely already noticed. Just make sure they don't get the wrong idea and use it to attack us."

"Yes, sir. The other generals and I have already begun working on a defense strategy."

Tievin nodded and flicked his eyes to the next piece of parchment. The estimated cost of the damages was about what he had anticipated. Thankfully, the camp was already used to this. It would mostly cost them in manual labor to replace everything that was broken, as most supplies could be found in the area, except for the new tents they would have to order. And they had no shortage of men with free time on their hands.

"Once you've confirmed the list, send it back to me for approval and have some men ready to go to the nearby villages to purchase what is needed," said Tievin, handing one piece of parchment back, "and have the medical unit give you a list of their own needs as well; we might as well replenish everything that ought to be... Any news of that bothersome dragon?"

"No, sir. The last reports are that it flew north after the fight with the Commander in Chief."

"Good. That crazy beast might go annoy the barbarians and make them stay hidden for a while, that would save us some time. And the Commander?"

"He's still in his tent, sir."

"Alright. Don't be stupid and send anyone to him yet, I'll bring him dinner..."

"Understood, sir."

Despite being one of the five men with the most power in the camp, the experienced soldier knew that the whole camp wouldn't be functioning if it wasn't for Tievin, the Grand Intendant. While they could handle training the men and organizing the daily schedule of the camp, it took someone highly educated like Tievin to do all the paperwork, take care of the finances, anticipate any needs, and watch over the supplies. Tievin and Prince Kassein had arrived together at the North Camp, and the whole army had seen drastic changes applied ever since. What was a simple outpost of defense against the occasional barbarian attacks before had now turned into a fully functioning army camp. They had conquered as much ground as possible in a matter of months, and made it so that the army camp that was previously relying on the nearby villages could now survive in the cold north by itself. Instead of focusing on battle, they had turned some of the units into construction units, supply surveillance units, supply management units, catering units, hunting units, and so on, everything the camp needed to function like a whole village without any exterior help.

This wasn't so much by necessity as it was the Prince hating to request any help from the Capital. The less he had to ask anything of his Emperor brother, the better his mood. Thus, every single soldier understood that there was no task too small to be undertaken for the well-being of the camp. If it had been a different Commander from a different era, perhaps this would have almost been perceived as the first signs of a rebellion; the Prince's army was growing to be self-sufficient and independent from the Empire, and strong enough that it could probably take a small city in a matter of hours. Luckily, it was common knowledge that the Wild Prince had no such ambition. This was a man with no desire for conquest; he had even abandoned the once-legendary Onyx Castle to live in the bitter cold of the most northern part of that region instead. He was acting more like a man who had exiled himself than a prince looking for rebellion.

Tievin was an essential part of the North Army precisely because the Prince had little to no desire to lead anyone. Both of them had been sent here against their wishes, and both were doing what was expected of them: the Commander in Chief led the North Army, the Grand Intendant managed it. As long as he wasn't required to lift a sword, Tievin could be content with that, and Kassein only gave the bare minimum of attention to the paperwork that did require his approval. The only reason the duo had taken the army this far with this little ambition was because they both effortlessly excelled in their own occupations.

"You may go now," Tievin dismissed the General with a movement of his hand. "I'll finish reading the report and go for an inspection tomorrow morning."

The General left, leaving him alone. It was getting too cold for him to put a toe out, except when he'd bring food to the Prince. In normal circumstances, he'd have put his tent close to the Commander in Chief for convenience, but convenience didn't weigh much in the prospect of being close to a potential dragon attack. Thus, Tievin had put his tent as far as possible from all the places the Prince visited daily, in a quiet corner near the forest. Quiet and safety were the best, especially as it kept him not far from the camp's kitchens.

He finished reading the parchment, taking notes about this and that, and when he was done, he put it on the pile of priorities. His tent smelled like parchment paper because of the numerous piles sitting in every corner. Even his bed was only taking a small corner of it, while his desk sat in the middle, facing the fire and surrounded by more columns of paperwork. The only other furniture was the two chairs, one behind the desk and one in front of the fire, and the shelves that held more paperwork, ink bottles, and spare feathers. He didn't have room for any guests to stay, and his precious bottle of wine was saved for his personal use, hidden on top of a shelf with a little box of biscuits for the days when the paperwork got too overwhelming. As he stood up, changing coats for the fifth time today, his eyes went to the one letter that had remained unopened. The one with the Imperial Seal. He sighed. Not even he dared to open it, but he also didn't have the guts to burn it. Thus, he took it and put it in a box by the chimney that contained two dozens of similar letters with the same seal. The Prince strictly and stubbornly refused any contact from his family. The Emperor was using a different type of letter and seal for Imperial Orders, so those had to be a family matter. They could have come from one of the Prince's siblings or his parents, yet they were all the same to him. Since his exile to the north by the order of the Emperor, he had never opened any of them. Even Tievin, who was perhaps the one closest to the Prince, couldn't tell if it was out of anger, resentment, or shame. Prince Kassein was a difficult man to understand, and no one was daring enough to push him for answers.

Gathering all his willpower, Tievin walked out of the tent, immediately slapped by gusts of frosty wind. He grumbled and began walking in the snow, keeping his precious coat tight around him. It was cold enough already by day, but the temperatures fell even lower during the night. Windy nights were the worst, and they were always cautious to never put the soldiers on evening rounds two nights in a row as it was hard to endure for anybody. Even with his boots, scarf, hat, and thick coat, Tievin found himself shivering all the way to the kitchen and then to the Prince's tent. Many times, he'd considered having a soldier do this instead of him, but there was no way. Especially after a brawl with his dragon, the Prince was unapproachable by almost anyone but Tievin. Most soldiers were replaceable, after all. He wasn't.

"D-dinner," he announced between his chattering teeth as he stepped inside.

As always, this place was in the dark and not lit by any fire, but it was still better than being exposed to the cold outside, and after taking a faint sniff, Tievin noted that it had indeed been cleaned earlier that day. Despite the lack of response, he put the tray down by a table near the never-lit fireplace and walked to the darkest corner of the tent. He could only locate the Prince by his faint breathing and once his eyes adjusted to the darkness, he spotted him on his bed, an arm over his eyes. He glanced down. He smelled like blood, but the scales were mostly done healing him. They hadn't worked their magic fast enough for the sheets to be saved, however. He'd have to send someone to change them whenever Kassein left his tent the next day...

"Because the defense wall was damaged, we will have to increase the night watchers," Tievin said. "The damages are about as bad as usual, which means it'll take a week or so for the repairs. Your dragon was spotted going north, so hopefully it's gone to hunt in the mountains and will stay out of sight long enough. We will also have to send men to the nearby villages to buy what needs to be replaced. I expect the tribes will notice and look to cause trouble once they have. A preventive attack to dissuade them might be a good idea."

"...Tomorrow morning," the Prince grunted.

Tievin frowned.

"So soon?" he asked. "...Are you sure? It can probably wait a bit. They won't notice until–"

"I said, tomorrow morning," Kassein grunted, suddenly moving his arm to glare directly at the Grand Intendant.

Tievin immediately averted his eyes, nodding.

"Tomorrow morning, it is," he sighed. "I'll inform the General to have a few units ready for a raid."

At least, a few men were going to be thrilled about the news. Most of them were dying for any kind of action that didn't include facing a dragon, and the hunts weren't enough to entertain soldiers who spent the rest of the day cutting wood or peeling potatoes... The raids in the mountains, hunting for barbarian warriors to convince them not to dare get down from their mountains was the real thrill. The main issue was that they would have to be ready to go first thing the next morning, as Kassein woke up early and would not wait for them. He was a Dragon Prince; he could definitely do those raids by himself and come back unscathed. Tievin nodded; he had no doubt he could find a few units of soldiers crazy for action that would be fine with waking up at dawn to follow their leader. Despite the risks, despite the biting cold and how dangerous those mountains were, the men would definitely be excited for this. Fighting barbarians was their reason to be here, after all. Tievin briefly finished reporting what he had to and then left the tent, leaving the Imperial Prince alone. He wasn't worried about him; the Commander in Chief would be healed by the next morning for sure, and even if he wasn't, fighting with the barbarians was probably nothing compared to an actual dragon...

Protesting the cold once again, Tievin found two soldiers that were still out and had them send one of the generals to his tent. No way was he going to chase after people in this cold! Luckily, it didn't take long for a general to present himself in his tent; meanwhile, Tievin was already back in his chair and wrapped in yet another fur coat. Explaining the situation took no time either, and as expected, the General was just as excited as his men for some action. He promised he'd have half a dozen units ready before dawn, and Tievin chased him out. The General was definitely going to work tonight to prepare his troops for the raid, but not him. He needed his sleep, and while he didn't care for the raid, he too would have to be up the next morning to watch them go, check the details of who was going with what, and be there when they would get back. Tievin was getting a headache already. If only the Prince had agreed to let him rest a bit and focus on the repairs first! There would be a lot to be reported to him the next day, and even after those partaking in the raid were gone, he was going to be busy all day long supervising the repairs after that crazy dragon had made such a mess...

The next morning, he did not enjoy being woken up before dawn. A soldier had to call him four times before Tievin extracted himself from his cozy, warm bed and pile of soft furs. He grumbled, but got ready in a hurry anyway; the Prince wouldn't wait for him to leave. Once he got out, with his favorite snow leopard fur wrapped around him, carrying his notepad, he was escorted by two soldiers to where those participating in the raid were preparing. It was at the edge of the camp, not far from the destroyed barricades. As the General had promised, there were men gathered in more than half a dozen units. A regular unit was composed of six men, yet from what Tievin could see, there were over forty men there. He glared at the General.

"A lot of them insisted," he explained. "Plus, I swear these men are among our best, and deserve to be there!"

"Fine," Tievin grumbled, "but any deaths are on you, General Kauser.

And I want a detailed list of every soldier sent, their units, and details."

"You'll have it, Grand Intendant."

Mad. They were all mad and in a hurry to go and get themselves killed... Tievin glanced around, but the men were visibly excited indeed, all gathering their weapons, packing up, and exchanging cheerful laughs. A lot of them would be disillusioned once they had achieved that raid. The mountain was much more difficult than it let on. To start, they would have to climb narrow, unstable paths just to get to the first plateau. It was going to take them over an hour of difficult walking uphill, and they would have to actually climb some parts. That was just the easy part. After that, the mountain wouldn't give them any breaks and they would have to split up, as every way was too narrow and certainly wouldn't allow forty men. The quickest and strongest would be able to follow their Commander in Chief, but the unlucky ones would be on their own if they met any danger. And the danger wasn't just the barbarians; they could also meet other dangerous mountain inhabitants like the snow leopards, raptors, or rarer, mountain bears. There was also the risk of slipping and breaking their neck on a sharp rock, if the rock that'd kill them didn't actually come from the sky after some landslide above them. Really, Tievin couldn't understand those men's hurry to meet their deaths... He glanced up at the mountains and shivered.

"Grand Intendant," one of the men suddenly hurried over, "I need to report: the Commander's dragon was sighted above the mountains."

Tievin frowned. That crazy Kein was still roaming up there? That couldn't be good... He glanced toward the mountains, but where they stood, it was hard to see anything. The mountain stood like a wall, and they were at the very foot of that natural monument, way too close to see anything past that rock wall.

"When?"

"Last night. We're not sure if he's still in the area; the watchers last reported seeing the dragon a few hours ago."

Tievin hesitated. Should they call off the raid? It was going to be even more dangerous if the dragon decided to attack... This time, even the Prince could possibly be in danger. What if it decided to attack while they were on some climb? Even a Dragon Prince would have a hard time healing from a fall on some rocks far below, let alone all the soldiers who would be in danger by staying by his side; those men would stick to their Commander at the risk of being caught in a battle between two beasts. He glanced around; no sight of the Commander yet, but if he followed his usual sleeping schedule, he'd be here soon. Could he convince him to give up on the raid? Tievin looked up once more. He couldn't hear any growls in the skies above. Perhaps that mad dragon was simply on the hunt to replenish its strength after a hard battle? After all, it had probably been injured like the Prince was, and even that crazy dragon couldn't be in a hurry to attack again so soon...

"Commander."

The General greeting their Commander took Tievin out of his thoughts.

As expected, Kassein didn't even stop to greet his men. He walked past them, with only a black fur cape over his shoulder and his long sword attached to his back. There were still orange scales largely visible on his body, making Tievin think he wasn't fully healed yet. Not that this was going to be enough to stop him, of course. He quickly walked over, strutting quick small steps through the snow.

"Commander," he said, out of breath just from keeping up. "Your dragon was sighted in the heights of the mountain last night."

Kassein didn't answer. He kept walking toward the mountain, gathering all the eyes of the men around him. One could read the sheer, honest, and pure-hearted admiration in most soldiers' eyes. Those were young men who had come to witness the greatness of a fighter with the Dragon Blood, a son of the legendary War God who could rival his father for the title. It had been ten years since peace had been instilled with the Eastern Kingdom, where the Prince's sister, Princess Cessilia, had become queen. Coming to the north was now the only way for men to obtain true military merit, as no security or patrol duty within the Empire could be compared to an actual battle. Not only had those men chosen to come here, but they were all desperate for some action, anything that would help them elevate their status and rack up military achievements. Coming back alive from a raid against the barbarians was already worthy of praise, but boasting of having fought by the unapproachable Wild Prince's side was an honor they would go on to gloat about for years. From that perspective alone, all those young soldiers were absolutely ready and willing to wake up before dawn, get out in the blizzard, and risk their lives on tortuous mountains. It didn't matter how harsh, cold, or ill-natured the Prince was; his strength and achievements were enough to have them lining up in his shadow.

Thus, even the mention of the Prince's crazy, blood-thirsty dragon possibly flying above their heads during the raid didn't slow them down; they got in tight ranks behind their Commander in Chief and marched. Tievin rolled his eyes.

"Alright, I'm guessing you won't be calling this off then," he grumbled. "I'll await your return, hopefully with all those men alive. I hate having to write bad news to their families, so please, at least try to make sure most make it..."

Tievin stepped to the side. Despite his best wishes, it was rare that all men who accompanied the Prince returned. There have been a few that had slipped and killed themselves, some who were attacked by barbarians and didn't make it, and those who had just disappeared with no way to tell what had happened to them. The mountain was that cruel, but they were still willing to go.

Thus, he stood next to the General and watched them go, following their Commander toward either death or a battle that could change their lives.

The men that followed Kassein only began to struggle after the first hour. They weren't weak by any means; they were young and followed the camp's rigorous training day after day. No new recruits were ever sent on the raids, as it was far too dangerous. Only those who had been in the north long enough to roughly know what to expect were allowed to go. The truth was, there was never enough preparation. Even the few men who were on their second or third raid with the Prince found the path unrecognizable; snowfalls, landslides, and wild beasts always shaped it differently within a matter of hours. A whole portion could have disappeared overnight, forcing them to take a different route, or to climb over some risky gap. Luckily, the first portion was the easiest, as they didn't have to watch for dangerous predators this close to the camp. This was just the beginning, though.

As soon as they reached the first heights, things began to get really difficult. From walking in lines or two by two behind their leader, they went on to struggle even keeping up behind him. In some portions, there was no path at all, and they were just progressing as they could in the snow, among rocks, and in a way that was getting more vertical than flat. There came the real climb, where they had to press their bodies against the ice-cold mountain, tighten their grip, and move quickly so as not to be snatched by the void beneath. The worst part wasn't the cold biting their faces, the rocks cutting through their clothes and gloves, nor the exhaustion of carrying the heavy equipment; it was knowing this was just the beginning. The mountain was incredibly tall and it would take a long while before they even reached the first plateaus where they could actually spot the barbarians. No doubt they would find them; the mere sight of one soldier of the Empire was enough to prompt them to run out of the caves they hid in and attack. This was a territorial war, and any intruder had to be killed. Soon enough, the soldiers began scrutinizing their surroundings at any chance they got, standing guard while their peers crossed a difficult section, and counting and recounting the members of their unit to make sure none were left behind. It was tragically common for someone to be left behind and disappear before the others could notice. Whether they were taken as prey by a beast, killed by the enemy, or had fallen silently to their death, no one could tell. The only way to prevent such a horrible loss of a comrade was to watch over one another and keep going.

The only man who didn't take such precautions was the Commander in Chief. No matter how many times they saw it, all men were equally baffled by that man's strength and speed. The mountain was like a training ground to him. He could run, climb, and jump without being slowed down by any of the elements. It wasn't just because he was carrying less equipment or because his armor was the lightest. His fingers were like claws against the mountain, perforating the rocks like they were butter, with arms so strong that his feet barely needed to touch the ground to support his whole body. An eye watching this from afar might have found his movements as smooth and precise as the snow leopards in the heights. Those big, tight, and firm muscles were enough to cause all his men to watch that superb figure with envy, and make them swear internally they'd devote themselves to even more training as soon as they went back. It also pushed them to try harder to keep up and merely chased away any ideas of giving up. All of them had worked hard to deserve a spot in this raid, and they were not going to turn around so easily. Moreover, it would have been suicide to go back on their own, so that wasn't even a real option; no one wanted to be the one conceding defeat, not when they hadn't even spotted and fought a barbarian yet. Hence, no matter how hard it was to keep going and even keep up with the Commander, none of those men dared to utter a single word of complaint. Kassein wasn't slowing down for them, so it was up to them to match his pace while not risking their lives. He wasn't so kind to help them out either, and receiving any help from the Commander would have been shameful as well; there was a tacit agreement that helping their peers was fine, but no one shall bother the Commander in any way.

Kassein barely glanced back no more than a couple of times; his men were loud enough that he could tell how far they were and how much longer they'd last before they had to take a break. Normally, he wouldn't have bothered to wait for them any time they stopped to catch their breath after a more strenuous part than usual, but it wasn't just about taking a break; it was slowing down to listen. Tievin's words hadn't fallen on deaf ears, despite his lack of response. If Kein was around, he had to watch out for his dragon more than for the barbarians, beasts, or any landslide. Because of the wind, even his enhanced hearing would have a hard time catching the sound of a wing flapping before it got too close, and it might be too late by then. The dragon's loud growling was usually the best and easiest way to locate it, but no one could guarantee the predator wouldn't attack without warning... The scales on Kassein's chest were still painful, stretching the nearby skin and slowly building over the deep wounds. With every reach for the next rock, he could feel the pull on his skin and his muscles complaining from the strenuous exercise so soon after a harsh battle. His body's protests weren't something the Prince ever listened to.

This pain was nothing. Nothing compared to the betrayal he had endured back home. The glare of his older brother, fed up with him, and the sadness in his mother's eyes. The disappointment on all of their faces. His anger, that no one could tame nor understand. The shame of one Wild Prince and his mad, blood-thirsty dragon wreaking havoc, the only one amongst his seven perfect siblings. No wonder they had sent him away; he couldn't bear to stay with the rest of his family either. The echoes of his argument with his father still haunted him, even after all these years. He couldn't understand. He could never.

"Commander! Barbarians incoming!"

He glanced up and immediately took out his sword. Those barbarians had definitely waited for them to be in a difficult spot to attack, but he wouldn't let them have their way. Before they got to them first, Kassein jumped up like a beast ascending a hill, ahead of his men, closing the distance between him and the enemy in a matter of seconds. He saw in those barbarians' eyes that they'd realized their mistake too late; when cornered, a beast was even more dangerous. He killed them in one blow, his long sword in one hand, the other holding on to the mountain, his body crouched against the rocks and above the emptiness. His men cheered from below as the bodies fell, but he didn't care.

Kassein jumped back down to his men, taking the lead again while they were all excited about that first blood. There were only two barbarians just then, but no doubt there were more ahead. Those people rarely attacked blindly and without backup. It was always like this: at first, a few would try to attack by surprise, singling out some of his men to kill them if possible, before cornering them into an area where it would turn into a full-on battle. Thus, it was vital that Kassein and his men quickly found an area where they could all stand and get ready for the next attack. He kept going ahead, taking out assassins when possible and watching out for their surroundings.

"Sir! The dragon!"

Kassein glanced up, having heard it a split second prior too. An orange streak flashed in the sky, and as if it had waited to be seen, Kein furiously growled. Kassein glared at the beast before it disappeared again in the heights; this was horrible timing... Strangely though, he was sure his dragon had seen him, but it wouldn't attack. Instead, he could hear more of Kein's furious growls, not far from their location. As if the dragon was after something else, fighting another battle nearby. Kassein heard more barbarians too. They were shouting, moving quickly in the nearby area. This was unusual for their enemy; their common strategy was to be as quiet as possible and then attack all at once when ready, but right now, they were making a lot of ruckus when they were still too far. As if something else was going on. Was his dragon fighting the barbarians elsewhere? That would have explained it, but something felt amiss. The barbarians were shouting from different locations around the mountains, as if they weren't localized in one area as usual. Or had they scattered because of Kein? He had to check.

"Commander!"

He didn't wait to see how many of his men would follow and keep up. He rushed, climbing even faster, following the shouting and his dragon's growls. Perhaps it was his dragon blood urging him to find his dragon and see what was going on with crazy Kein this time. Perhaps it was just the thrill to witness something unusual in those mountains, to surprise those tribes they understood little of, but he felt the urge to just go, quickly. He had to see what was causing those barbarians to get so riled up. He climbed higher and faster, getting rid of any enemy that appeared on his way. None of them could survive more than a handful of seconds before his sword swung through the air and dyed the snow crimson. He didn't have time for a clean kill either; blood spilled over him as he didn't even wait for the bodies to fall down. He could hear some of his men behind him, trying to catch up, panting and calling him. He didn't wait for them; there was something happening ahead, and he had to hurry.

Kassein finally climbed to a cornice that was good for him to stop and take a peek at the situation. From this height, he was still only about a third of the way up the mountain he was on, but it was enough to glance down and see some of the nearby valleys. There was definitely something going on. He spotted a handful of barbarians running down the closest mountain. They had visibly come from different areas, but they were all headed in the same direction. He tried to glance farther down, see what it was they were after, but soon enough, another of Kein's growls pulled his eyes back toward the sky. His dragon was flying above the area like a vulture with its eyes set on its prey. Kein growled, a high-pitched, scream-like growl, and then suddenly dove. Kassein followed his dragon's movement with curiosity for once since he wasn't the prey. Kein attacked one of the barbarians; the man screamed right before he was torn apart by the dragon. Were those men simply running away from the dragon? Why go down, then? He had seen enough of those barbarians to know they had a hundred hideouts in the mountains. Moreover, they were all shouting something, which sounded pretty much like madness, given that they were the targets for a dragon that was far from deaf... Kassein glanced back down just to check on his men. They had also found a small plateau to stop and were visibly resting. Since they were all gathered on a flat area, they should be fine. One of them suddenly spotted him, pointed his finger, and called him, but Kassein didn't have time to wait. He jumped down. Following a mountain slope that was taking him in between some deep valleys, he tried to find another cliff to stop on. His men were on the other side of the mountain now, but it wouldn't take him long to find them again.

Just as he was hesitating between going farther down or trying to climb to the side of the mountain, he spotted them. In a crevice, four barbarians. All the others were clearly headed the same way, but he understood why Kein wasn't able to attack them: they were in a tight crevice in between two mountains, a spot that would have been hard to access for the dragon. This shouldn't have been so frustrating for the dragon to act like this, though; he had plenty more to hunt elsewhere. But as he kept watching, it became obvious that Kein was trying to get to that area. The dragon would growl, dive, but his claws could only reach some cliff above them and scatter the snow. Kassein stared at the tiny group again. That's when he realized something was off: someone was lying on the snow, but trying to fight off one of the men. He squinted his eyes, confused, when he realized it was a woman. One of the men suddenly grabbed her long, black hair, pulling her head back, and he suddenly felt his anger rising. For once, he finally understood what his dragon wanted.

He jumped again, heading right for that area. He glanced up just once, as Kein furiously growled and once again, attacked one of the barbarians heading there as well. Kassein ignored his dragon and kept going down. He was going so fast it was almost a free fall; he only caught the rocks once in a while to slow his descent, or jumped to a small cliff just to jump less than a second later. He didn't have to think much about it; seeing a man pulling on a woman's hair like this, the way the four of them were surrounding a woman lying down, their stances, he just didn't need to understand much more. He hurried, feeling the same restlessness and impatience as his dragon did.

He could hear Kein growling nearby, but for once, he didn't have to watch out for his dragon's attack; just temporarily, they were on the same side. In fact, he could even feel his dragon's silver eyes on him, warning him to hurry up, or else...

Kassein kept jumping and diving, regardless of his body aching. He scratched over the scales he already had, scraped his finger's skin, and disregarded his own safety completely while hurrying down. Even for one with the miraculous Dragon Blood, a fall from a mountain to crash on rocks below could be deadly, but he wasn't one to care much for his own safety, not when he had something on his mind. Thus, he kept going at a crazy fast pace, much faster than the men who were running opposite to him to get there too. Why were so many men after one woman? Were some of them coming to her rescue? That was unlikely. From their attire, he could tell they were all from the same tribe. Moreover, they kept shouting, and the one answering them was one of the three surrounding that woman... His dragon growled and took down one more man right when Kassein was finally getting there. He jumped into the crevasse, taking all the men by surprise. They all recognized the enemy at once, though. The one who had been pulling the woman's hair let go immediately and they all pulled out their weapons: curved blades and strange, two-bladed, pointy daggers. Kassein felt the anger rise as he was now close enough to see the situation under a clearer light: the woman was heavily injured, while none of those men were. She wasn't unharmed, yet they were. All the blood on the snow belonged to one person, and as the man had let go of her hair, her head had fallen down against the white ground as if she was too tired to keep it up. Her eyes were open, but they were those of someone clearly exhausted, almost unconscious. It only fueled his anger more.

The three barbarians attacked, but just like their peers trying to escape a dragon, they had no chance. Kassein swung his sword one, two, three times, one neat movement for each kill. Everything went quiet around him for a few seconds. And then, Kein growled above his head. He glanced up, but as expected, his dragon could only fly in annoyed circles above them, its tail swishing the air. Its big size wasn't an advantage in irregular spaces like this. Still, Kein soon resumed hunting the barbarians coming their way, so Kassein knew he probably wouldn't have more enemies to face.

He cleaned his sword, and slowly walked up to the woman. She had fallen unconscious while he was busy killing those men, her body lying still in the snow. From one glance, Kassein could tell a bit of what had happened; her hands and feet were the most injured, bleeding all over. She had probably gotten hurt while trying to run from those men. He glanced up and realized she had likely not chosen to trap herself down here, but fallen off that cliff right above their heads, into this small crevice. This explained why most of her injuries hadn't been caused by those men's weapons... Still, she was in bad shape.

Kein growled impatiently again and Kassein glared back. The dragon was probably done with its hunt, and didn't enjoy waiting... Kassein sighed, put his sword in its sheath behind him, and walked over to the woman. He couldn't help but stare at her face; she looked young, but her eyes, nose, and lips were reddened by the cold. Tears had drawn faint lines on her face, and even unconscious, she was slightly frowning. From the pain? Kassein got down on one knee, and very gently, put his arms under her legs and shoulders. She was lighter than he had anticipated, but she groaned as he lifted her; she had definitely broken a few bones from her fall. Her long black hair fell off her shoulder as he got back up. She had really pretty hair, black as a crow's feather and smooth as silk, like he'd never seen before. In fact, it was the first time Kassein had ever seen a female barbarian. From her clothing and skin color, she was definitely one of those barbarians, so why had those men chased her? Would this be considered taking her away from her people if he took her back with him? Either way, he didn't have a choice. None of her people had come to her aid, far from it, and if he left her here, she'd die of the cold and blood loss in a matter of hours. Her feet were so severely damaged, all he could see was blood dripping from her wrecked shoes.

Kassein didn't hesitate much longer before climbing out of the crevice carrying the foreign woman. Because she was so light, it wasn't too hard for him to get back, although he had to move much more slowly and carefully than before. It took him a little while to find his way back to his men, and all along the journey, he felt Kein hovering over his head. His dragon had gone surprisingly silent ever since he had picked up the woman, but Kassein could feel it watching like a hawk. This got him quite nervous, but this was also the first time he and his dragon had been in the same vicinity without trying to murder each other; nervousness made sense.

"Commander! Where did...?"

His men's questions died as soon as they noticed the woman he was carrying. They exchanged glances, visibly all confused, but none dared to protest or question him about this unprecedented situation. The woman's horrible state and the way Kassein was carrying her gently spoke volumes already.

"We're going back," Kassein simply said.

Although they had all waited for this raid to battle some barbarians, none of them voiced their disappointment. Instead, they quickly gathered into formation again and followed their leader. They also quickly noticed the large shadow that kept hovering over them, and while they were frightened the first few times, they quickly stopped reacting to it, leaving their questions suspended on the way back to the camp. Kassein didn't glance at his dragon again; he was solely focused on that woman and bringing her back as quickly and safely as possible. Was she even going to make it? She looked too weak and in critical condition. This prompted him to hurry back even faster, and he reached the camp in half the time they had needed to go up. They weren't expected back so soon either; the sentinels had to run to go get Tievin, and by the time he arrived, Kassein was already marching into the camp, gathering curious eyes around him.

"Wha-... What is this?" Tievin exclaimed as he saw the woman in

Kassein's arms.

"Call a doctor," the Prince simply said.

It was an order this time, not a request. Still dumbfounded, Tievin gestured impatiently for a nearby soldier to go and fetch the closest medical unit. As he was still moving his hand, the large shadow suddenly flying above them caused all the men around them to panic.

"Dragon! Dragon incoming!"

But Kein landed with a loud growl and, to the men's surprise, with no visible intention to harm its owner. The men hesitated, swords drawn, and directed all their eyes to the Commander in Chief for an explanation, or at least an indication as to what to do. Kassein was standing there, still carrying that woman, only slightly turned toward the dragon. It was a surreal scene. The dragon and the Prince stared at each other for a long time. The dragon growled in a menacing manner, but didn't move. It was just showing its fangs as Kassein was squinting his eyes at it, the two of them completely still in this strange stand-off.

"Your Highness, the medical unit is on their way."

"...To my tent," Kassein simply hissed.

He turned his back to the dragon and began walking toward his tent. Tievin's jaw dropped, but no sound came out. He glanced at the still-growling Kein, and after a few seconds of trying to make sense out of this situation and failing, he sighed.

"Yes, sir."

He hurried after him.

Chapter 3

She had to leave.

As quickly as possible, and as far away as possible.

Alezya still had no idea where she could possibly escape to, but she was certain of one thing: she couldn't stay here, or Lumie would be killed by those madmen. She was willing to endure any hardship but that.

She tried to think fast and hard. Her father and his men were still standing there, but her cousin's husband had already left to spread the word. Soon, her entire clan would be hunting her and her daughter down. Alezya knew all too well that no one would be slowed down by the idea of harming a defenseless child. Those greedy bastards would be too enticed by whatever her father, the richest man of their clan, had promised. Even without that, no one would be on her side. If she wasn't useful anymore, she had to disappear. She was already a hindrance anyway, an embarrassment that had brought shame to the clan with her failed wedding and her "evil" spawn. There didn't even need to be a reward, they would all be too willing to help her father. Nobody would miss her, except perhaps those who found her herb-picking skill useful.

That was it. Her father had just officially decided she was of no use to the clan anymore, and therefore decided to kill her.

Alezya didn't even consider handing them Lumie for a single second, but she did know they would think she could possibly be willing to. Those people took so much pride in their clan and thought so little of her that they might believe she was willing to do such a horrible thing for her own survival. She could use that.

"I-I'll get her," she cried.

She didn't even need to fake the tears; the whole situation was more than enough for her to cry about, although they had mistaken her tears for sadness when they were actually fueled by sheer anger.

Even worse, her father suddenly smiled, a smug, irritating smile that made her hate him even more if possible.

"Good, Alezya. You're finally an obedient child."

She didn't respond to that. She just acted like she was defeated and broken-hearted. She was, but she still held onto the hope that she could save Lumie, one way or another. Every single one of her thoughts was hell-bent on pulling together a plan, anything that could work to save them both. Even if the chances were slim.

She turned around, and walked away, biting her tears back, aware of their stares and steps following her.

Thankfully, they couldn't follow her as she slowly crawled inside her hole. As soon as she entered, Lumie's happy coo greeted her, breaking Alezya's heart a bit more, but she didn't have time for that. She had to act quickly.

First, she pushed a huge rock that she had been saving for such a case in front of the opening. She couldn't remember when she'd had that thought, but the idea of needing to block their cave opening someday crossed her mind, and thus, she had begun digging a rock from the wall of their cave, a rock big enough to block the entrance. That thing was big and heavy, and she had to make it roll all the way to the passage with a lot of effort.

This would block anyone from entering after her, but it was also preventing her from going out this way. It didn't matter; she could only leave this place with Lumie, and she wouldn't hand her over to her father. They had to leave the only other way: their window.

Next, Alezya quickly grabbed everything she could, once again feeling thankful she had already anticipated such events. She had hoped many times it wouldn't come to this, but there she was. She had to act fast and think even faster.

That opening was terribly dangerous, but it was way too late to worry about that now; they had no choice. She had to tell herself they'd make it, and think about the next step. Once they climbed down, where could they run to? Her entire clan would be after her once they realized she was fleeing. Not only that, but she would have barely more than a handful of minutes before one of the watchers caught sight of her and snitched to her father. Thinking she would be able to flee unnoticed was just madness, so she had to consider she'd definitely be spotted sooner or later. Alezya had to decide what direction they would take that would increase their chances of survival.

She had already thought about that before too. She knew no clan would accept a pariah like her, but she had to believe some of them would have mercy on a woman and her baby. All the clans knew the mountain was cruel and merciless to its inhabitants. Could she find refuge with a clan that wouldn't sell her out, even temporarily?

She knew there were more clans up north, clans that didn't like her father, and would be happy to find a reason to piss him off. Would sheltering his daughter and her baby be a good enough reason for them to help her?

She didn't have time to think about the scenario any longer. The priority was fleeing this clan, disappearing into the mountain, and getting herself close enough to another clan. She knew her plan was sheer madness, but it was the only one she had. If she handed Lumie over to her father, even for a second, she'd never see her baby again.

"Ma..."

"It's alright, my snowflake," she whispered, putting a kiss on Lumie's head.

Her baby was still sleepy, as she often was in the middle of the day. Alezya silently hoped it would prompt her to stay still during their escape... It was going to be a long and difficult run. She took Lumie and quickly wrapped her in some thick fur and a leather blanket.

Then, she put on the bag she had. Just a few useful things, but Alezya was confident she could find more supplies wherever they went, and her priority was to be fast. Her only valuable item was her mother's medallion, the only memento she had of her. She had never dared to wear it in front of her father, but this time, she tied it on a leather string around her neck.

Last, she wrapped Lumie against her chest, making sure to secure her and have her head protected too. If she was going to climb with her baby in front, she had to be sure Lumie wouldn't be scratched. It wasn't the safest way, but her father's men had bows... Lumie being scraped by the mountain would be better than risking her being killed by an arrow.

Alezya paid particular attention to the way she tied her daughter to her chest. There was a reason she had strapped Lumie on last, another part of her plan that she really hoped she wouldn't have to use... one that made her throat tighten. She had to hope for the best, but prepare for the worst.

"Alezya!"

Her father's angry voice.

It had taken just a few minutes for her to get ready, but patience had never been her father's thing... and he might be starting to realize she had fooled him. She hoped he would be unsure for a bit longer. Any second won would be precious, and possibly decisive.

Carefully, Alezya slowly got closer to the window. She pulled the cloth that was covering it, took one last glance at the place that had been their home for over a year, then slowly stepped out, cautious like never before. She had looked down so many times, she already had a rough idea how to start, but she still couldn't go as fast as she wished she could. Falling to their death would put a tragically early end to their escape. Alezya began her descent carefully, keeping an ear out for any more of her father's shouting or the sentinels.

Thankfully, it was still early in the day, so not many would be out yet; hopefully, less chances for them to be spotted. While climbing was something she'd done all her life and could do without thinking, Alezya's mind was still busy weighing their chances, playing every possible scenario, doing the math over and over again in the hope of finding some miracle solution she wouldn't have already thought about before.

But she just knew nothing would be easy. Easy was an option that had disappeared ever since she'd become a mother.

For a while, her hopes remained high as she was going down, quickly and still unnoticed, farther and farther away from their cave. Perhaps a few minutes passed while her descent was steady.

She couldn't really tell, she was too focused on securing her grip, stepping on steady cliffs, and glancing back down once in a while to be sure they were headed in the right direction. Alezya had never felt so thankful for her experience in climbing, allowing her to move quickly despite this area being almost completely new to her.

"There! Catch her!"

Her blood went as cold as the snow around her. She didn't even glance up; the voice's echo gave her a rough idea of their position, way too close for her liking.

She kept moving, faster, but still careful. She couldn't afford to slip, she couldn't risk it with Lumie there... She took slow breaths and kept going, ignoring the ache in her body, the strain from so much effort, and the fear. How much longer? She couldn't stop. She had to keep going.

The first arrow broke far above her head, but the sound made her panic. They were already shooting, and she was in a completely exposed area! If it had been just one second earlier, that arrow would have hit her right in the head. Alezya glanced down, with that feeling of urgency that completely redrew the risk rates. It was still too early to jump, too risky. Just a bit more though, and she would get down a familiar slope. She could do this.

She kept going, forcing herself to go fast and ignore the second arrow that hit a rock right above her hand. She had to pretend no one was aiming at her, or she'd lose her focus. Her heartbeat was like a battle drum in her chest, pressing her to keep going, take any risk that felt takeable. She could endure the pain, the cold. She could handle anything as long as Lumie survived this...

"Look out!"

For a second, Alezya lost her focus. It wasn't the man's scream, but the furious growl that had followed it, so loud, so sudden, and so close that she had loosened her grip in fright, just for a second. She fell.

She kept her hand up in the air, the other around Lumie, desperate to grab something; it was a reflex she'd mastered after falling several times on purpose, one she knew could save her life. Her arm got brutally grazed once, twice, three, four times before her fingers finally grabbed onto something. The violent strain of her whole weight pulling down her arm made her muscles ache, but she didn't let go. Alezya caught her breath and glanced up. Her arm had caught on a tiny cliff, but this thing wouldn't be enough to support her for long. She looked at Lumie; her baby had woken up, but she seemed more shocked by the sudden situation, too shocked to cry yet. Alezya immediately smiled at her gently to calm her, pretending as if everything was alright. Luckily, that was enough.

Lumie was visibly confused, but without knowing what emotion to display, she simply stayed neutral, her big, curious eyes opened wide and staring at her mom for more clues.

Alezya didn't have more than those few seconds to care for her though. She glanced up, and now that Lumie was fine, she used her other hand to grip on with both arms before assessing the situation. She had fallen far below her previous position, which was a good thing for now, at least. No sign of the archers anymore and to her relief, no dragon either. She let out a faint sigh. That dragon had scared the hell out of her... She glanced down. She wasn't far from the slope! Almost right above it, to be exact. Her hopes came back.

She felt the pain before she heard the arrow crash. She winced and almost lost her grip. Her flank sent a wave of acute pain throughout her body. Alezya tried hard not to cry out from the pain, not to worry Lumie, but it was hard. She could feel exactly where the arrow had drawn a sharp line on her flank, ripping the clothing to get to her flesh. The arrow hadn't stabbed her but flown by, but it had been sharp enough to cause damage. It stung, and she knew she had to be bleeding. She bit her lower lip. She had to get out of range.

Alezya glanced down at the slope. It was a bit too far on her left, but it was doable. It was one hell of a jump, but not too crazy. Perhaps crazy was the kind of action she needed to save herself and her child right now... It wasn't just about the archers or her clan anymore, she now had a dragon to watch out for as well. She just had to take the risk. She took a deep breath, wrapped her arms around Lumie, and leaped off the cliff. She didn't have the luxury to close her eyes and wait to see where she landed; she squinted as much as she could to protect her sight. Her body brutally hit the slope, and she started to tumble. She rolled down, as anticipated, following that long descent, the natural slope quickly taking her farther down the mountain. It wasn't a smooth ride by any means. Her body was being battered by the rocks hitting her along the way, the uneven ground rocking her body and bruising her all over. She was doing nothing, but it was strenuous just to endure being jolted around and stay focused on protecting Lumie, so she gritted her teeth and waited.

She only realized she had closed her eyes when everything stopped moving. She had ended her fall much farther down the same slope in an area she had only been a handful of times. Luckily, this was one of the rare areas covered by a few pine trees; she'd be safe from that dragon, just for a bit.

Alezya caught her breath, and with difficulty, pulled herself back up. Lumie was fine, thankfully, but her eyes were opened wide. She probably wondered what the hell was going on after this wild ride... Alezya ignored the pain and forced herself to smile at her baby as if this had just all been some funny game. Lumie hesitated, but replied with the cutest smile, already reassured. This broke Alezya's heart a bit more.

Her body was aching on all sides, but she had to keep going. She knew it wouldn't be easy, but carrying Lumie on top of the pain was getting really difficult. Alezya surveyed their surroundings, already nervous again.

It didn't take long for her to hear her father's men shouting. They were awfully close already! They weren't fast climbers, but they also didn't have a child to carry. She felt mad that all her risks had only bought her this little time. Still, she had to keep going.

She wasn't too far from the area she had been aiming for since the beginning, one that several clans shared as a farming space and brought their livestock to. That was her best hope; another clan that would understand her father's madness, that they couldn't abandon a woman and her child. Anyone who could help them...

Putting her arms around Lumie, she resumed her course, running through the pine trees. She was heading farther south now, to an even lower ground. Alezya ran as fast as she could, thankfully this area was less snow-covered. Her feet were painful but steady, and she could almost run normally without sending waves of snow flying around her.

She kept an ear out, and she could hear them belt out about chasing her, who had just spotted her, where that wench was going. A horrible thought began creeping in her mind. They were too close. They knew where she was. She would soon reach the edge of the pine forest and be fully visible from above again. No matter how fast she ran, she wouldn't make it to the common grounds without them catching up to her. At least, they'd get there before anybody else did.

They wouldn't give up on catching her, and she and Lumie were going to get dragged back, or worse...

Tears began to stream down her cheeks at that painful realization. No, perhaps she already knew in her heart. She had entertained the thin hope that they would both possibly make it, but she just knew better. Perhaps hope had given her extra bravery for the first part of her journey, but now came the time to face reality. The cruel, painful reality.

The two of them weren't going to make it. She couldn't outrun her father's people. They wouldn't draw another clan's attention soon enough to be rescued, and even if they miraculously did, another clan wouldn't dare openly oppose her father and risk a battle between clans. Not for a repudiated woman and her fatherless child.

Alezya kept running, her tears flying behind her. She hated herself for even thinking what she was thinking, but again, the truth was there, right in front of her eyes. She was no fool, and she wasn't mad enough to risk the infinitesimal chance; she'd be taking them both to their deaths.

Alezya kept crying, her jaw trembling, but her mind was still there to help her sort out what to do next. Lumie. She had to save Lumie, no matter what. As long as her baby made it, everything would have been worth it, even her death.

She couldn't outrun her father's people, but she could buy herself time. No, she could buy Lumie time. If she could get them to chase her, far enough from Lumie, then maybe, someone would get to her baby first and take her away.

Alezya shivered, not because of the cold, but because of how mad and desperate that plan was, even to herself. She kept thinking, again and again, but she could see no other option than this horrible one.

Worse, time was pressing her, as she could hear her clansmen getting closer and closer. Now that it was a running race instead of a climbing one, she was losing ground quickly. She had to make a decision or her hesitation would end up killing them both. Alezya kept crying, not only from despair and sadness but out of anger at how unfair this situation was. She couldn't believe there would be a world where the gods were so cruel, they'd push her to do this. She had to abandon her own child for her sake.

Lumie's short life had been a long list of compromises, settling for less than she had deserved and surviving. Why? Just what had her child done that was so wrong for her to have to endure all this?

She'd always done everything right. Alezya had followed all of her father's demands since she was born, she had been married to a stranger under his orders, endured countless nights of pain to follow customs, and bore a child. What had she ever done wrong to be pushed to such a tragic end?

If there were any gods out there, they were cruel. Even crueler than the beast flying above their heads.

As she kept crying, Alezya knew she had to end things quickly. The longer she waited, the harder it would be, and the fewer chances Lumie would have. She had already ventured far enough into this unclaimed territory.

She kept looking around. She had to find an area where she could hide her baby. Somewhere big enough to contain a child and hide her, somewhere that would be protected from the winds and possibly beasts in the area.

Alezya shivered again but tried to get that thought out of her head. The snow leopards were nocturnal, they wouldn't be out so soon... and not when there was already a much bigger predator in the area. She just needed to buy her a bit of time. In an hour or so, the clans would all be up and more people would be out there. She could only hope things would go as planned then, at least for Lumie.

The second she had decided she'd part with her child, Alezya had already given up on her own life; in her eyes, it was a good bargain if it could give her baby a chance.

She finally found it. A perfect hiding spot, or almost. It came in the form of a dead tree, with almost nothing but its pathetic tree stump left, the original trunk lying on the side, a portion still attached and shards pointing up to the sky. Not losing a second, Alezya ran over.

It was a bit hollow, with a hole inside that would be large enough for her to put Lumie in. From the look of it, that tree had been torn apart by some very strong wind, a recent snowstorm perhaps. Either way, it was unoccupied, and she only had to dig out a bit of snow and debris before she found it deep enough.

Her tears wouldn't stop, but nonetheless, she untied Lumie from her chest quickly. No matter how heavy the sadness in her heart, she couldn't let it slow her down.

With trembling hands, she put Lumie down; miraculously, she had managed not to leave any blood on her child. Her baby noticed her mom's tears, and to Alezya's horror, she began crying.

"No, no, no! Everything's alright, baby. See? Everything's alright, my little snowflake..."

Alezya forced herself to smile through the tears. Nothing was more painful than painting a beautiful lie on her face, for her baby's sake.

She kept sobbing but smiled as hard as she could, like another torture she had to subject herself to. Lumie was crying a bit, but once again, she seemed utterly confused by the soothing words, smiling face, and her tearful mother's torn expression.

Alezya kept smiling at her as if everything was alright, as if her heart wasn't being ripped apart by this moment, shredded into painful shards that were killing her. With her fingers shaking, she took off her medallion and put it around her daughter's neck instead. Perhaps someone would recognize the symbol of her mother's clan. Perhaps someone good would find Lumie... All of her hopes felt like snowflakes in the wind, so fragile and ready to scatter into oblivion.

"Go to sleep, Lumie," she whispered. "Mommy will be back. Sleep, my little snowflake. Please sleep."

Mommy will be back were words that she had said a lot before, words that Lumie could understand, somehow. That meant Alezya would leave her alone, but she'd be back some time.

Perhaps she had indeed grown used to it, because her baby's eyelids seemed a bit heavier, and she calmed down. Alezya forced herself to keep smiling, patting her head as if Lumie was a good child for feeling sleepy. Her hand was trembling, and her heart felt painful like never before. She was glad Lumie was already in the trunk, and couldn't see her mother's entire body trembling from the pain, the blood dripping from her ripped shoes and her side.

Lumie was a smart girl, she'd have noticed something was wrong. She couldn't have that. Instead, Alezya soothed her like she always would, with a gentle little music coming from her lips, although she had to focus on uttering it from her trembling lips and through that painful knot in her throat.

All of her body was making her pay for what she was doing. She couldn't shake the horrible feeling that she was abandoning her baby, and she had to remind herself, again and again, that it was a bet for Lumie's survival. Lumie's life against hers. It was horrible, cruel, and heart-breaking, but it was the best bargain she could afford right now.

The last one.

"Sleep, my snowflake," she whispered to her dozing baby. "I love you. I love you so, so much..."

Her voice cracked on those last words.

Had she told her enough that she loved her? Had she made Lumie feel happy and loved enough, in what little time they'd had together? Had she hugged her enough, exchanged enough smiles with her? A horrendous wave of regret hit her. All those times she was out hunting for food, she wished she'd been by her baby's side. Every second lost was now like another blade piercing her heart.

A male voice nearby took her out of that black hole of thoughts. She was out of time.

She took a deep breath and sealed her emotions deep in her heart. She could keep crying, but she had to save Lumie. Making sure her baby was ready to nap, Alezya took a painful step back and glanced around. She found a piece of tree bark that was large enough, and she put it over Lumie's hole, like a lid on a precious basket. It looked a bit suspicious, but it was wood on wood.

Hopefully, that would protect Lumie from the cold more, and yet be unusual enough that someone would take notice.

"Catch her!"

Alezya stepped back, feeling like she was leaving her heart behind.

She dropped her bag, leaving it under another piece of tree bark, and without looking back, she began running.

Now a lot lighter, she could run fast, and as far away as possible. It was anger and rage that fueled her steps because everything else inside felt broken and hollow. She had to trick them. She had to take them far away, so far they wouldn't think of coming back to check that area.

They wanted to hunt her down like some prey?

She was going to make them run.

Perhaps because she had left behind everything she still had to lose, Alezya found herself faster than she'd ever been before.

She could run and not care about the risk. She could trip over a tree root and get back up without giving a damn about the pain. That was nothing compared to what she had just gone through. She kept running, heading south. She had to go south, for that was the one place most people didn't want to go. No one wanted to approach the area the Dragon Clan's people patrolled for they knew about their powerful fighters and their dragon.

Even as she ran past the line of trees, Alezya didn't bother to glance up. That dragon could have her if it wanted, but she was going to draw those bastards out and get them killed too if she could. As if it had read her mind, a loud growl echoed her thoughts.

"She's there! Grab her!"

They were getting closer to her.

No matter how fast she could run, Alezya was already exhausted, her body reaching its limits. She was leaving a trail of blood behind her, and her feet were burning, her shoes having given out long ago and ripped wide open, letting her skin be grazed by everything and anything she stepped on. She could feel the sting on her flank, her skin bitten by the cold everywhere her clothes had been ripped apart.

Her hair was no longer tied back, flying around her face. She hoped that would make her an easier target to spot; she needed those men to follow her...

"Catch that swine! Traitor!"

She was growing deaf to their shouts. She could hear the whole valley echoing like a large trap closing in on her. More people were joining the hunt. No one felt pity for her, the thrill of hunting a human down was too exciting for those heartless monsters. Alezya kept running, tirelessly.

No, she was tired, but she wasn't willing to listen to her body's complaints anymore. A desperate rush of adrenaline was the only thing keeping her moving.

A scream from behind her got her to glance back, just once.

The dragon. That same orange dragon she'd faced had just dove down and murdered a man, not a mile behind her. This time, fear grew in her. She had resolved that she'd die, but she still couldn't help but hope it wouldn't be a horrible and painful death. At least, the dragon seemed to make it quick. She heard a growl, and the beast jumped into the sky again, its furious growls resonating throughout the area.

Time. All she needed was more time and a bit more distance. To get as far as she could from Lumie, to drag them all out to where she'd finally be unable to continue... The ground suddenly disappeared under her feet.

Alezya realized she was falling when her body was still mid-air, and yet too late. She tipped over, getting a glimpse of what was to come before closing her eyes. This was the trap of an all-white environment. White, fresh, and immaculate snow was treacherous. The sparkling perfect white mane of snow, the one that was there first thing in the morning on a clear day, was blinding. Perhaps if she had been going a little bit slower or walking, Alezya would have noticed that the ground before her was uneven, that the snow was tipping downward. She would have stopped before the crevice that had suddenly opened before her.

It was now too late, and she fell, her body violently hitting the ground below just two seconds later. It wasn't a fall hard enough to kill her, but she felt her body screaming in pain. Because she'd fallen from an upright position, her legs were the first victim, and now the ones screaming in an unbearable wave of pain.

Alezya gasped for air; all of it had left her lungs the second her body hit the ground. Her only luck was that there was snow down there too. The few inches of treacherous white coating had softened her fall a bit, just a bit. Right now though, she was in too much pain to move, even with all the willpower she could muster. Her body was done obeying her nonsense, it was just subjected to too much pain to endure anymore.

Black and white dots were like bugs appearing in front of her eyes, warning her this was her limit. No, she had gone past her limits a long while ago already. Somewhere in her heart too, Alezya settled a bit. If this was the end, at least she was hidden a bit.

Perhaps they wouldn't find her?

Men shouting nearby proved her wrong. To her despair, it didn't take minutes before she heard the damp sound of someone falling next to her; unlike her, they had seen the crevice and jumped down there. She was still lying down, but with a heroic and last attempt at bravery, she struggled to get back up; all she managed was to get on her elbow and look up. She recognized one of her father's men; he was staring down at her with a vicious smirk on his face like she was some trash, some prey he'd managed to hunt down .

"There you are, you traitor!"

There was no need to answer that; no answer was expected.

Alezya knew she had lost, and she didn't have it in her to throw some bitter response. Instead, she stubbornly kept trying to move. It was strange, to know that she wouldn't be able to go anywhere, and yet to want to keep trying. It was like she had carved an intention with hot iron in her mind, and her body kept obeying mindlessly.

She could only move so little and drag the lower half of her body behind her, managing to crawl perhaps three inches.

"She's here!"

"That damn swine! Where did you think you were running to, you cursed whore?!"

Their insults fell on deaf ears, literally. Somehow Alezya's ears were ringing too much as more black and white dots had appeared, and she couldn't hear anything. If she did, she would have heard the furious growl of the dragon, somewhere above their heads, that got both men to jolt and look up in fright.

"That damn monster," one of them hissed. "It got three of us!"

"Let's grab that whore and just get home quickly. Where is her bastard?"

"That thing is not here?" said a third man who had just jumped down with them.

They cursed and looked around, but they wouldn't find Lumie there; that information should have comforted Alezya, but then again, she didn't hear it. Instead, she saw the dots getting bigger, and her head heavier. Her entire body was getting incredibly light, like she was about to float. A fourth man arrived in the crevice out of breath.

"That wretched monster got four of us!" he shouted. "It's not even hunting, it's on a rampage!"

"Tell us where you put your bastard!"

One of the men tried to grab Alezya, but by reflex, she fought him off. More exactly, he grabbed her arms and she used her hands to try and push him away. People about to fall unconscious cannot close their fists properly, and that was exactly the case for her. Her hands were just weakly trying to move around and keep that man away from her, but even as he held her up, her whole body felt way too heavy to move.

One of the men suddenly grabbed her hair, pulling it furiously.

"You whore! Where is that bastard?!"

The sudden movement hurt her neck, but at least, the other man let go. Alezya felt herself about to pass out, and she was sure she would not wake up from it. Either those men would kill her or she would die from her injuries, she had already given up on any hope of surviving. She was completely exhausted in every way and done fighting.

Her head was heavy, and if it wasn't for that man pulling her hair, it would have happily laid in the snow with the rest of her body, ready to give in to the soothing call of numbness. Somewhere above their heads, another growl was heard, and she found the strength in herself to wish that the dragon would just eat them all...

"Who is tha–Argh!"

Alezya was too tired to feel the sudden change of atmosphere around her. All she noticed was that at some point, the man had let go of her hair, and her head was now resting against the snow.

Finally being able to lie down was a relief she hadn't expected. She was so tired, she could gratefully pass out. But it didn't happen right away. For some reason, her body wasn't ready to fully give up yet. Perhaps she was too tired to even pass out. She felt herself in a strange state, like she was just a passenger in the broken vessel that was her body, observing a scene that had nothing to do with her.

Her eyes saw the sudden flashes of crimson that stained the scene around her, but her head didn't register the potential danger, or even that it was blood. It didn't matter anymore, as the darkness finally swallowed her.

Being unconscious is different from being asleep. There is no consciousness left, not even a single thought, nothing that happens.

That's why for most, unconsciousness feels like it happened only for a fraction of a second, for their mind is completely blanked out during the period they were unconscious. One doesn't dream, think, or even realize time passes. The body and mind are completely shut off.

Thus, Alezya couldn't have been completely passed out because very briefly, she had moments where she felt carried, her body moving independently from her will. Somehow, she found it incredibly soothing to be simply carried away by something that seemed incredibly warm and gentle. And then, she'd go back to the darkness, or what she thought to be death.

She didn't die. That was the first thought that came to mind as she gradually woke up.

Her body was sore and painful, that might have been what helped her wake up. Her stomach felt tightened by painful hunger too. Everything else was strangely comfortable though, something she hadn't experienced in a long while. During the time it took for her to fully regain consciousness, she was aware of being on something soft, and her whole body being surrounded by delicious warmth. She had grown so accustomed to the cold that this sensation felt eerie to her.

Her eyes slowly opened, and they felt horribly dry, a strange sensation that was pulling on her skin around them a bit. The place around her was so dark that she didn't need to adjust at all; in fact, her eyes were immediately drawn to the only source of light, a small fire flickering several steps away, its glow casting faint shadows against the walls.

She was too exhausted to move her head, but even in her peripheral vision, she could tell she was in some kind of human dwelling. There were wooden pillars with fabric running all around them, sheltering the large place. It felt strange for her to see a place created by man that could be as large as some of the natural caves that had been claimed by the wealthiest of her people.

The floor was even and covered by a patchwork of short fur rugs. There was some wooden furniture, although most of it was bare, and in a corner, a set of shiny plates that looked like battle braces, and several swords lined up. The sight of weapons should have alarmed Alezya, but she was too tired to move or even think of running away.

Not only that, but aside from the foreign environment, there was no one around. As she was lying on her side, she couldn't see what was behind her, but from the shape of the room, she could tell the bed she was on was against the wall of this habitation; thus, there couldn't be anyone. She was alone.

This allowed her some time to remember the recent events. As unbelievable as it seemed to her, she had survived. How, she had no idea. Had the dragon eaten everyone but her? She had a vague sensation that something had happened right before she passed out, but she couldn't remember what. Was she with another clan, then? She had never heard of a clan that had such habitations, but she knew there were a lot of clans up north that she knew nothing about... Perhaps they had established themselves in faraway plains? If so, she was far from the mountain she used to belong to.

Lumie. Her child suddenly came to mind, and she panicked in silence. A cold shiver ran down her spine at the realization.

Where was she? Had this clan found her too? Was she safe?

Not knowing if her baby had survived or not was a torture worse than any physical pain she could have endured. She tried to move, hoping to get up to find someone and ask, but her whole body winced in protest. She was badly hurt, and only now was she fully realizing just how badly. Everything hurt, literally so, and it was worse when she tried to move.

As she had tried anyway, her hand came into sight. It was covered in bandages, and smelled of something she didn't recognize. Alezya took a minute to try and stubbornly move her body, taking the full measure of what had been done to it.

All of her injuries were bandaged. She could even feel some strange paste on her lip where it had been cut. Her feet were the most painful of all, but she could tell they were also bandaged all the way up to her ankles and something cooling had been spread on her soles. Her flank was covered by bandages tightened around her waist too; she could feel them with each breath she took.

She wasn't wearing anything but her underwear, all her clothes were gone.

She forced herself to sit up a bit and the blanket fell from her neck down to her chest, just enough to cover her bare chest. It wasn't a simple blanket, but a sheet covered by two layers of thick fur.

No wonder she felt so warm all along...

Someone suddenly stepped inside the habitation, and all her hopes vanished like snow under the sun.

It was a man like she had never seen before. He was tall, dark-skinned, and most shocking of all, he had eyes of vibrant green. The color contrasted so starkly with his dark skin and hair that she was rendered speechless. It was both beautiful and terrifying to see a human being so different from any she had ever met.

She felt like a large beast had just walked in, a foreign species that she could only see as a dangerous one. He didn't have fangs or claws, but she could tell just by the sight of him; he was a warrior. His body was covered by a cape, but that large frame of his made it easy to guess the size of the muscles underneath.

Her questions died in her throat. She was on the other side, amongst the Dragon Clan's people. A wave of panic surged in her mind.

How? Why? Had she been captured, not rescued? She wasn't restrained, but her body was in no state to run anywhere anyway. She watched every one of the man's movements, feeling like prey in a predator's den.

He seemed surprised she was awake; his shining green eyes lit up and opened wider as soon as they met hers.

That man suddenly taking large strides toward her put Alezya even more on alert, and she forced her body to retreat as far as possible, by mere survival instinct. He seemed to notice because he slowed down before reaching the bed.

What was he going to do, now that she was awake?

Alezya was mentally preparing herself for anything. She'd seen so many men treat women like slaves, especially those they knew nothing of. If they weren't some other man's daughter or wife, they were disposable. This man knew nothing of her, nothing of her clan even.

She kept retreating, no matter how much her body screamed in pain, using her elbows to push herself back toward the edge of the bed, her legs pathetically dragging behind. There were only a few inches of difference from her initial position to when her shoulder touched the wall, but that was the best she could do to protect herself.

But then, to her shock, the man put a knee down.

It was the last thing she would have expected, for this foreigner to lower himself in front of her. She didn't even know what to make of this. What was going on?

She glanced toward the entrance he had come from, but realistically, she wouldn't be able to run before he grabbed her. No, she wouldn't even be able to run at all. The man was staring at her, making her horribly nervous. She wanted to ask what he wanted with her, where her baby was.

He spoke first.

"Kayf ha du sheyrkaha?"

She frowned. His tongue was strange.

She had never heard any of the Dragon Clan's people speak before. They spoke with guttural sounds, sharp like a snow leopard's claws. She could vaguely understand from his tone that he was asking her something, but what?

He waited for a few seconds for her to answer, but eventually gave up. Instead, his eyes drifted down, and as she followed it, she realized the hand that she was using to support herself had begun bleeding through the bandages and onto the sheets. A new wave of panic hit her. How was he going to react?

He stood up, his height scaring her even more, and walked to one of the shelves, presumably to get something. He was so tall that his head almost touched the ceiling of this place, but perhaps it had been made to fit his height. Why else would they have put such high pillars?

He returned with a roll of what she recognized to be the same thing she was bandaged with and a bowl of a mixture that smelled like what was on her injuries too. *No way,* Alezya thought.

That man was the one who had treated her injuries?

"Ti inkir banzifha."

She could understand nothing of what he had said. Was he talking to himself or to her?

He suddenly reached out his hand, but that only made Alezya jolt and try to retreat more. Her eyes went up to his hand, and that's when she noticed something on his forearm. It was orange, brighter than his skin, and it looked like scales.

Was that some tattoo? She had never seen anything other than blue or black ink on someone's body, but then again, he came from a different world... It seemed oddly real though. Was he some dragon worshiper?

Those were the exact same color as the orange dragon's scales she had seen from up close, and oddly similar too. She was getting a weird feeling from seeing those, like a memory scratching at the back of her mind, warning her.

"An la yadrahu ti."

Was he getting impatient with her? She was trying to decipher the man's expression, but he barely showed any.

If anything, his expression was rather blank, his fascinating green eyes riveted on her. She was confused as to why he was talking to her from this position; never had Alezya witnessed a man putting a knee down in front of a woman like that. It was odd, and she couldn't decipher his intentions.

He'd obviously treated her injuries, but why? Her clans and the Dragon Clan had always been sworn enemies, they'd killed a countless number of her people. She had never heard of them taking any prisoners.

Was that warrior acting like this because she was a woman? If so, what was his aim? Would he use her once she was healed? Sell her as a slave, or abuse her? The fact that she was naked, alone in a foreign man's habitat, and unable to communicate made her feel trapped. She wasn't restrained, but it felt like it.

He sighed but slowly got up again.

He walked to another corner of the enclosure, and returned just as quickly, carrying a jug. He was about to hand it to her, but before he did, he suddenly seemed to think of something. Still while looking at her, he slowly brought it to his lips and drank two gulps. Then, he handed it to her.

Alezya was confused. Was it custom for a man to drink before a woman could? Or was that his way to prove the water was safe...?

Alezya hesitated, but as if her throat had realized that water was within reach, she suddenly found herself horribly thirsty. With a trembling hand, she took it. He didn't react, but she couldn't help but keep her eyes on him while she drank.

It felt so good to finally drink... How long had she been unconscious? She couldn't tell. She just had a vague feeling there was still daylight outside, but the fabric walls were so thick, it was hard to tell. She only hoped it hadn't been too long. Every hour spent away from Lumie was too much...

She almost emptied the jug without thinking, and when she handed it back, the man took it without a word, putting it on the ground next to him. Then, he got up again, and this time, he grabbed a larger bowl, filled with water too. He hesitated, and then he drank a bit again. It was most likely to show her this was just water, because this time, he didn't hand it to her, but instead, gestured toward her hand with his index finger again.

"An yatani aheti biatik."

Did he think she could understand him, or was he just going to stubbornly keep talking knowing she couldn't understand?

He raised his eyebrows a bit and opened his hand toward her. It was like a large paw lying flat on the mattress, just inches away from hers.

Alezya glanced at that hand. She was still confused about those scale-like tattoos on his arm and that arm overall. But slowly, she was starting to realize he had no intention to harm her for now. In fact, he looked strong enough that he could very well have grabbed her hand and done what he wanted already.

After a hesitation, she finally gave in and showed him her bleeding hand. He took it, surprisingly gently, and undid the bandages. As soon as he touched her, she was shocked by how warm his skin was. For someone who had just come from outside, it was even stranger. Had he warmed up in such a short time? She'd been under a thick blanket, but how was the skin of that man warmer than hers?

She knew it couldn't be that she was wrong about the temperature outside;

she could feel the cold chill in the room wherever her skin was exposed, and it wouldn't have made sense for the place to be covered in thick, heavy fur rugs.

Still confused, she watched as he finished removing her bandages, inspected the worst injury, and began cleaning it with the water.

Alezya was getting more and more bewildered. He clearly knew what he was doing. This man was a healer? In the clans, it was always a woman's role. It was the woman's role to heal, nurture, and take care of others. No man would have cleaned her wounds and applied medicine like he was. Men couldn't be bothered with such things... Wasn't he a warrior?

She glanced again at the collection of weapons gathered in a corner. The way he applied the bandages neatly and with the right pressure over her wound clearly showed he had at least basic medical knowledge.

Alezya was utterly confused.

Once he was done with her hand, he glanced at the other, but the bandage had held on, no blood visible.

Then, he pointed toward the end of the bed. For a second, Alezya didn't understand what he wanted, but before she could react, he stood up and lifted the covers in one movement.

She panicked as she felt her legs exposed all the way to the thighs. He was some pervert after all! She attempted to move her legs by reflex to hide them again, but a wave of pain made her wince and cry out.

The man sighed.

"Aheti hatam dahilika. Imada yuhahil tankal?"

From his exasperated tone, Alezya could tell he thought she was stupid to have moved, and she darted a glare his way without thinking.

She was prepared to be hit or something for that glare, but instead, he just slowly shook his head and got back down on one knee.

"Ashu. Tarmilha klila."

What in the world was he saying? At least she knew by his tone he wasn't mad...

Alezya decided to stay still and wait as her body wouldn't have it any other way anyway.

The man pulled the bowl of water closer and slowly undid her bandages. Just him taking them off was horribly painful. She knew he was trying to move gently, but every single bone in her feet was making her pay for her mad race earlier. Was it broken? She'd never felt that much pain radiating from her ankles, so much so that she teared up.

She kept wanting to cry, but bit her lip not to. But her lip was painful too, and she just kept groaning more, her fingers grabbing the mattress helplessly.

When he had finally taken off all the bandages, she dared to glance down. From the pain, she was expecting her feet to be covered in blood and the bone exposed or something, but it wasn't half as bad. At least, not to the eye, because the state of those feet didn't match the horrible waves of pain.

They were cut, each foot with at least a dozen open wounds, but if they had bled, it had been cleaned already. Her soles felt like the skin had been completely scraped off, all of it burning at the smallest blow of air.

She forced herself to take long, deep breaths while the man kept touching her feet. Even more than the pain, Alezya was obsessed with that man's strange attitude. He was *washing* her feet?

She reddened even more than when she'd realized she was naked, or when her legs were suddenly exposed. A man was willingly washing her feet! Not only that, but he was doing it so gently toward a prisoner! What kind of mad situation was this?

Alezya covered her mouth, in utter shock. Somehow, his hands touching her feet felt incredibly intimate, and she had no idea what to do with herself. No one had ever washed her feet for her, no one had ever touched them since her own mother! Men didn't wash women, it was the other way around, and only between married couples! Did this man not know how humiliating this was? But he didn't seem to feel humiliated at all. In fact, he was taking care of her feet with so much caution and gentleness she was astonished.

They both remained quiet while he cleaned her feet, took off the weird paste, and reapplied a new layer before putting new, clean bandages on.

While she was still in shock, Alezya was first and foremost trying to withstand the pain and move as little as possible. It was soon over, and the man pulled the blankets and furs back over her legs and stood up. He was carrying the dirty bandages and cloths, and quickly walked out, leaving Alezya alone again.

Although she couldn't see them anymore, her eyes were still riveted on her feet. The pain was making her realize one thing: she wouldn't be able to move around on her own two feet for a while, no matter how hard she pushed her body. And this thought broke her heart more than anything.

Alezya was dying to go back for Lumie. Every instinct in her body screamed for it, even though a part of her knew it was probably already too late. The part of her that had been rendered cold, rational, merciless by life. Still, her heart couldn't stop circling back to that tree stump. To the hole she'd left her daughter in. That last vision of Lumie haunted her. ...Had she survived?

The thought alone made her stomach twist. She hated herself for even letting the darker possibility form, but Alezya wasn't naive. Not anymore. She had faced death too many times to pretend this couldn't end the worst way imaginable.

It was simple. Brutal. Two possibilities: either someone had found Lumie... or no one had. If it was the latter, if her baby was still curled up alone in that hollow, out in the cold... then it had already been too long. Alezya had been unconscious for hours. No child could survive that. Her breath caught, and tears slipped free before she could stop them.

The pain bloomed sharp and sudden, even worse than any physical pain that already harassed her. Overwhelming, numbing, ravaging, it felt too much to endure. Her heart ached like it was bleeding raw, burned, and crushed all at once.

Her heart had been left behind in that tree trunk, and right then, the only thing that prevented Alezya from shattering completely was a thin, lingering shred of hope.

The hope that someone had found Lumie. That her baby girl had cried, shouted to the world this injustice, and that somehow, some kind soul or even the gods themselves had heard her and intervened.

Maybe even that strange man. If they had saved her... maybe there was still a chance?

For the first time in what felt like forever, Alezya dared to believe. Dared to pray. Because the alternative was a void she couldn't survive falling into.

She had to pray. To all the gods she'd forsaken before, to all those who looked down on her and felt any pity. At some point, she realized she was crying. Silent sobs wracked her body as she curled in on herself, pressing her newly bandaged hand to her mouth. The shame hit next, hard and vicious.

What kind of mother was she? She should never have been one in the first place, not someone like her. Not someone so broken, so stubborn, so sure she could do this alone. What had that pride earned her? Nothing but the unbearable truth: she didn't even know if her daughter was alive or dead.

How could she not? Wasn't a mother supposed to feel it? Wasn't there supposed to be some sacred bond? But Alezya felt... nothing. Just emptiness. A hollow ache where certainty should be. It was the worst pain she'd ever known. And doubt was her last punishment, haunting her like a nightmare waiting to swallow her whole.

The part of her heart that had endured all the hardships, that had been beaten over and over, that had survived with difficulty, told her it was probably over.

It was the pessimistic voice, the one who knew she and Lumie had lived on borrowed time ever since they were alienated by the rest of her clan. Perhaps the most reasonable one, who knew the chances of a toddler surviving alone in the cold, in the middle of nowhere.

And then, there was the other part of her. The part of Alezya that still wanted to believe, because the alternative was a truth so unbearable, it threatened to crush her from the inside out.

The heart of a mother inside her, who desperately needed to hold on to that small, incredibly tiny chance that Lumie was alive somewhere, somehow, just so she wouldn't give up. She couldn't give up on her baby. Because if she gave up that hope... there'd be nothing left.

The man returned while she was still crying. Alezya hurriedly tried to wipe her tears, as she hated to cry in front of anyone, even more so this stranger. He didn't say anything this time, and instead, walked over. To her surprise, he was carrying a small bowl with a spoon in it, and still steaming food inside. Her stomach jumped in expectation. Her body didn't care for her mind's turmoil; she was starving.

"Kuha."

Eat it, or something like that. This time, this man's words were easy to decipher. Once again, he took a spoonful and ate it in front of her, before handing her the bowl.

Even if he hadn't eaten some before her, Alezya would have probably given in. Her body was just begging for food, and whatever was in there smelled good. She tried to recognize the food before tasting it; it looked like some sort of orange soup, with little chunks floating at the surface...

She tried just the liquid first. It was good, and even better, nicely warm. It had a slightly sweet taste, despite clearly being savory. She ate one of the chunks next. Some sort of vegetable. Another, brown piece. Meat! She was given meat? Why would they give precious meat to a foreigner, especially one who is most likely a prisoner? She was confused again.

To her surprise, when she glanced at him, the man was faintly smiling. ...That man was definitely strange.

He turned around, leaving her with the bowl, and went to take care of the fire. Then, he opened the entrance a little, exposing the room to the cold air from outside.

Alezya pulled the blanket over her a bit tighter. Because she needed both hands to hold the bowl and eat, she had to keep the blanket under her armpits and hope it wouldn't slide down. If that man was the one who had bandaged her, had he... seen almost everything already? She didn't care much anymore.

She kept eating, trying to convince herself she was going to need to heal fast if she wanted to go look for her daughter, ignoring the voice that was insulting her for filling her belly while her child's whereabouts were unknown. She had to be stronger than that voice, at least while she waited to know for sure. And then, she'd accept whatever punishment there was. But right now, she needed anything she could get to feed that last shred of hope.

At least that soup thing was good and filling. Since Lumie's birth, she'd only ever eaten rabbit meat—it was all she could catch on her own, and she hadn't been allowed to touch the clan's food. Her traps must have been bad, because she'd only managed to capture a handful of rabbits.

But the meat in the soup wasn't rabbit. The bits were thicker, and it was tastier, making her curious.

She finished the bowl, and the man walked over, taking it.

"Inkir?"

She hesitated. He probably asked if it was good, so she nodded, but to her surprise, the man left right away. This guessing game was going to be a headache...

Less than a couple of minutes later, he returned with the bowl full again. Alezya was stunned, but then she realized her mistake. More! He'd asked her if she wanted more, not if it was good...

Now that she thought about it, it was probably obvious she liked it from the way she had emptied the whole thing. He handed her the newly filled bowl, and she took it helplessly, feeling like an idiot. He'd given her a full portion again, with even more meat floating at the surface.

Was it really alright? She did have space for a bit more. Alezya ate, feeling obligated to finish it now that this had been brought for her. Most importantly, she mentally noted that *inkir* meant "more" or something like that...

She had a harder time finishing this bowl and had to eat slowly, but she loved whatever meat was in there. Perhaps that man was really rich to be able to afford some stranger two servings of such good meat. The tons of furs lying around might have meant so too.

Alezya vaguely knew the Dragon Clan was likely wealthier than most of the clans, but she had no idea how different the scale was. While she ate, the man took off his coat, and Alezya almost dropped her spoon.

He was covered in those orange tattoos! Most importantly, they were shining strangely for tattoos... or were they fire-colored stones? She was utterly confused. She'd heard of a clan that liked to put beads under their skin, but this was different; most of it was exposed, not under the skin...

It really looked like that dragon's scales were completely painted over his muscles. And she had seen few warriors as physically blessed as this man.

"*Mahi?*"

She raised her eyes, blushing to have been caught staring. The man had asked her something, but once again she was clueless. He grabbed the jug from earlier and pointed at it with his index finger.

"*Mahi?*" he repeated.

Water. *Mahi* meant water. Alezya nodded, more to confirm her guess than because she was thirsty.

He left, and sure enough, brought back water a few seconds later.

Mahi and *inkir*. She'd forgotten that other word when he'd brought her the food before, but at least her vocabulary was growing, and perhaps she would get to understand him and let him know what she wanted soon.

As someone who had the mind of a survivor, Alezya knew how to set her priorities despite the gloomy thoughts about her child.

Alezya had already made up her mind: it didn't matter if Lumie had survived or not, she would go and look for her. She had to know, and she wouldn't stop. She wasn't the type to just let fate decide her and her child's futures, and she had to know for certain. Even if it took days, weeks, months, or years, she wouldn't allow herself to grieve for her baby if she didn't know for certain what had become of her.

At least, that was one good reason to stay alive, get better, and go back. She ought to know. Hence, she ate her soup until the second bowl was empty and her stomach was full. Surviving in a completely foreign environment would at least keep her busy while she tried to heal. She still couldn't understand why that man was taking care of her, nor his intentions, but she was going to use him until she could go back.

As he saw she was done with the bowl, he took it away.

Based on the amount of light she saw as he lifted the flap of the habitation, she could guess it was the evening. So, at least several hours had passed since she'd parted ways with Lumie...

Was it the same day, even? She couldn't be sure, she had been unconscious with no notion of time. Alezya tried to think. From then on, she was going to act and plan as if Lumie were alive, and she could get back to her. The odds were put back into the corner of her mind; even if it was slim, she was going to focus on the hope and possibility that someone had found Lumie and saved her. If so, then there were two probabilities: either another clan had found her, or her father's.

Even if it was another clan, she couldn't be sure they wouldn't hand her back to her father if he claimed the white-haired and white-skinned child was theirs. If so, Lumie's chances were even slimmer... Perhaps he'd wait until the next council gathering to harm her?

Alezya tried to remember; she vaguely recalled her father mentioning when the next gathering would be, but she had been too preoccupied with getting Lumie to safety. Usually, she wouldn't be important enough to be told when the next gathering of the clans would be as she was never included. To be exact, no woman ever was. They didn't even allow the women-led clans to partake.

Anyhow, she had to retrieve her child before this council gathering was held. Knowing her father, Alezya had no doubt he'd have no second thoughts about sacrificing her child as he had planned to. Worse, if he had already mentioned the sacrifice to other clans, he would stop at nothing to get his hands on Lumie and avoid the humiliation of a man not living up to his words.

How long until that damned council gathering? A few days, maybe? She was sure she'd heard before that they often held it on the night of a full moon, as it was in an open area. She most likely had until the next full moon then. This was just one in an already hazy pool of possibilities anyway... but Alezya held on to what she could.

Would she be able to walk within a few days? Her broken feet were her worst nightmare. She couldn't be stuck at such a time! She'd expected to die; instead, she lived but was now unable to go and save her daughter. What kind of twisted fate was that? She let out a desperate sigh.

The worst part was, maybe she was doing it all for nothing... Either way, she had to do her best. Forcing herself to believe she could still save Lumie was the only thing keeping her together.

Alezya found herself tired once she was done eating and drinking; it seemed like her body had used the last of its strength just doing that. She laid back down, right when the man walked back in.

She hesitated. Perhaps this was his bed and he'd take it back?

He walked up to her, but to her surprise, it was only to pull the fur back over her shoulders. That gesture took her by such surprise that she didn't react at all. He didn't say anything this time, but he only glanced in her eyes once before turning around.

He went to the corner to grab one of the blades, a long one that was about the size of Alezya's leg, and came back toward her. He sat down against the end frame of the bed, near her feet, facing the fire. Then, he simply began cleaning and sharpening his weapon in silence. Alezya was still utterly confused by each of this man's actions, but at least, she didn't feel any malice from him anymore.

She hadn't even flinched when he'd brought a weapon toward her... She could genuinely feel no threat coming from him. In fact, she was deeply shocked at how she'd already grown to be less afraid of a man who looked strong enough to end her life in an instant. She'd grown afraid of men that were familiar to her, like her father, her once husband, or any other man of her clan, but not this foreigner?

She stared, still confused about her own thoughts. Despite his appearance, he'd been incredibly gentle and was able to do things no clansmen would lower themselves to like it was no big deal. That stranger was truly too different and always took her by surprise...

She kept staring, thinking maybe she was underestimating him. Men could be treacherous and surprisingly good at using a woman's feelings against themselves... but this was the back of the man who was going to spend his evening quietly taking care of his weapon.

Feeling a bit better, she slowly curled up under her blankets, allowing herself to drift into what would be, hopefully, a restful sleep.

Alezya woke up to male voices talking near her.

After a couple of seconds remembering where she was and what had happened, she opened her eyes.

The habitation was in complete darkness. She recognized the silhouette that was seated in the same position she'd last seen him at the end of her bed, and another man was standing by the entrance. It was obviously dawn outside, allowing her to partially see his frame, but he seemed skinnier than the warrior who had taken her, although he was wrapped in the thickest fur coat she'd ever seen. He seemed tall too, and she wondered if the men of the Dragon Clan were naturally taller than her clansmen. She'd only ever seen a handful of them from afar, so she had never noticed, but it wouldn't have been surprising. She thought the warrior was the tallest man she'd ever seen, but maybe this was the norm here... although the other one seemed remarkably skinny.

The two of them were talking in a low voice, and she realized the man standing couldn't sit down in front of the warrior to talk. He was just standing there in the opening, no matter how uncomfortable it was, showing their difference in status.

She had no idea what they were talking about, but she had a vague impression it could have been about her. Her eyes drifted back to the seated warrior, and this time, instead of his sword, he had a strange little bottle he was turning between his fingers. It seemed the two men were arguing from their way of speech, but the warrior clearly was the one to decide. The other man sighed.

She couldn't tell if they could see she was awake, given how dark the room was. Probably not; the man standing was too far and the warrior had his back turned toward her, so she was only at the very edge of his peripheral vision...

Alezya silently curled up a bit more under the sheets, closed her eyes, and kept listening. She couldn't understand a word of what they were saying, and her hopes were disappointed as she had thought to be able to learn at least a new word from listening. Their tongue was more guttural, with lots of sharp sounds and quick tongue clicks. It had something warm about it though. Especially the warrior's voice. It was like hearing a large beast purr when one would only expect growls...

She chased those thoughts to the back of her mind, feeling ashamed. How could she think such things at a time like this...?

It was clearly morning when she woke up again.

Alezya stared toward the open entrance, wondering if it had been two, three, or more days since she'd been brought here. The stabbing pain in her heart rose anew.

Once again, the thought of each second she'd spent away from her child broke her heart. It was out of sheer will and hope that Lumie was alright that she'd been holding on until now, pushing the darkest thoughts into a corner of her mind just to tell herself she had to hang on a bit longer...

The man had probably opened the fabric flap to air out the space, and it felt good to have some fresh, cold wind gently greeting her face, by contrast to the rest of her body still warm under the blankets.

There was a fresh layer of white snow from what she could see of outside, meaning it was probably a clear, blue sky day. The perfect white snow made her think of Lumie. She missed her baby so much already...

They had never been apart for this long since her birth. It felt like her heart had been ripped out of her chest and left somewhere. Her throat tightened a bit, and she hardly suppressed the urge to cry. Instead, she tried to focus on something else.

Soon enough, she noticed the little bowl that was on the small table next to the bed. Alezya forced herself to sit up, careful about her legs. At least her wounds were healing properly, it seemed. Whatever medicine that man was using was quite efficient... and all of her bandages had been changed again without her noticing. After months of living afraid of everyone, Alezya had learned to sleep lightly, an ear out for the smallest sound, so it was astonishing to her that she could have slept so soundly while someone moved her and changed her bandages.

She took the small bowl, full of still lukewarm food. There was some new foreign mixture at the bottom that smelled sweet with slices of fruit on top. It smelled good, and this time, she didn't hesitate before trying it. The taste surprised her. It was so flavorful and filling. The pieces of fruit were white, crisp, sweet, and a bit juicy too. They had visibly been cut in small chunks from a bigger fruit, and she wondered if the warrior had cut it for her, or if this was the breakfast all their people got... If so, they were lucky to be able to have that thing every day. She ate slowly, thankful for this.

While she was still busy eating, someone walked into the habitation.

Alezya expected the warrior, but instead, it was a tall, scrawny man wearing a coat two times too big for him. There was so much fur around him, all the way up to his neck, that his head seemed to be small and just popping out of a bundle of dark brown fur. He had long black hair, thin lips, a small nose, and skin strangely covered by hundreds of little marks. She was almost sure it was the man she'd heard chatting with the warrior a few hours ago... He stood at the entrance for a little while, staring at her with a deadpan expression.

Alezya wondered if she should put the bowl down, but really, she felt no threat coming from this man... or, to be exact, he looked like the weakest man she'd ever seen.

For a little while, he said nothing, just staring at her. And then, he let out a sudden and big sigh, as if he was annoyed. Alezya frowned.

He walked up to her bed, and she prepared herself for anything, but he rummaged through the depths of his coat, and suddenly took out a small little bottle, handing it to her. She was confused. He looked reluctant to give her something that just looked like... water? The bottle itself was really pretty though. She put her bowl aside and took it.

"*Ti. Shrib.*"

He spoke loudly and excessively clearly as if she was deaf, which annoyed Alezya. She showed the bottle and asked with one of the two words of their language she'd learned.

"*Mahi?*"

She wasn't sure of her pronunciation, but at least, the word and the context should have made her question clear...

She waited, expecting an answer, but the man just stared at her with that deadpan expression of his for a couple of seconds, before rudely rolling his eyes and turning around to leave without a word. Alezya had already decided she didn't like this man.

He left, and she was alone with that bottle thing.

Was she supposed to drink it? She checked it up close, and the cap had visibly been sealed. If she opened it, it would be obvious. Did he expect her to keep it to hand to the warrior when he came back?

But he could have just left it for him on the table... While she wasn't sure, Alezya decided to leave that thing aside and finish her bowl of breakfast first. Now she wished she'd been up when it had been brought; this thing ought to be delicious when hot...

"*Ti ha shribahu?*"

The man's voice took her by surprise; she hadn't heard the warrior come back into the habitation.

Alezya glanced up, and she realized he was questioning her about the bottle on the little table. She put her bowl aside and grabbed it, showing it to him. He walked over, and after kneeling in front of the bed like he usually did, gently pushed it toward her, his fingers only touching the bottle. With a little nod, he confirmed it was for her to drink.

"*Shrib.*"

Shrib. Drink, she guessed. Another word for her vocabulary.

Why was this bottle for her to drink? It was strangely small and preciously conserved, it couldn't just be mere water... Mistaking her hesitation, he took it from her hand and opened it, breaking the seal effortlessly.

Then, he handed it back to her without the cap. Alezya smelled it. It just smelled like nothing, like water... She touched it with the tip of her tongue. Just water? It had a very, very faint taste, something mineral maybe. Seeing how the man encouraged her with another nod, she gave up and drank it. It had to be something safe, right? It would have made no sense to poison or drug her now... She emptied the bottle.

It really was just water, or at least that was her deduction. Nothing strange about it, no alcohol or weird aftertaste or anything. When she finished it, the man seemed a bit relieved and took the bottle back. Why had the other man seemed so reluctant to give it to her? Alezya knew she was missing something there, but she had no idea what.

As the man stood back up to put the bottle away, Alezya felt the strange need to say something. She hadn't said a word since she'd woken up, but if she was to use that man to regain her health and get back to the mountains, she had to get him to understand her a bit. And she needed to understand him too.

"Thank you," she said, in her language.

The man, surprised, turned around and stared at her.

"Thank you," she repeated, still in her language.

There was no way to know if he'd understood, so she hoped to convey it through her emotion and expression. The man stared at her, confused for a few seconds. His eyes went to the almost finished bowl of food, on the jug of water that had been left on the table for her, on the blankets. Alezya faintly smiled. At least he was as bad at understanding her as she was understanding him...

The man suddenly walked over and kneeled down again in front of her. Every time he did that, she felt deeply uneasy and uncomfortable, but he didn't seem to care at all. More importantly, she was curious as to what he was going to do next. Was he going to ask her to repeat until he understood what she'd said? He stared into her eyes and suddenly said another word she'd never heard before.

"*Kassein.*"

She frowned. What was that word supposed to mean?

While she was still wondering, he suddenly gave her the answer by pointing at his chest.

"*Kassein*," he repeated.

His name. Kassein wasn't just a word, it was his name.

"Kassein?" she repeated.

He nodded, and another rare smile faintly appeared on his lips for less than a second. Kassein. She now knew the name of her savior. In a similar fashion, Alezya pointed at herself.

"Alezya," she told him.

"Aleshya?"

She frowned. Were the sounds foreign to him? Their tongues were so different. Still, she shook her head and tried again.

"Alezya," she repeated, insisting on the second part and how she moved her lips differently.

"Alezya?"

She nodded. It wasn't perfect, as his pronunciation was a bit too rough and used the back of his throat too much, but this time, the sound was right at least. The man seemed surprised with himself.

"Alezya," he repeated.

He seemed pleased to have finally learned her name too, and that made her feel strangely good. Thinking immediately about what she wanted to learn next, Alezya grabbed the bowl of the breakfast food she'd had and showed it to him. She pointed at the little bit of leftover.

"*Kuha?*" she asked.

She had remembered him saying that, and it either meant food, or eat, or something like that. He shook his head.

"*Taam.*"

"*Taam?*"

Taam meant food. She tried to mentally remember that. It was going to be hard if she couldn't write anything down, but she was going to have to learn and remember quickly. *Taam*, food. *Mahi*, water. *Inkir*, more. Then, *kuha* meant to eat?

"Alezya."

She turned to him, and he pointed at the bowl, and then her. For a second, she was curious about what he wanted, but then, she realized.

He wanted to learn it in her language? She hesitated. What for? Was he planning to use this later? Any communication between the Dragon Clan and her people was unprecedented, from what she knew... Was he going to tell his superior that someone could translate her people's language? Perhaps that was his aim all along?

He wasn't interested in her body, but in what she knew. If he learned her language, would he use it to dig up information to use against the clans? Alezya was surprised at how she felt herself still wanting to protect her homeland from the Dragon Clan after what she had gone through, but her instincts were flaring up at the surprising demand.

Why was she hesitating? She most likely wouldn't be welcomed back... but she didn't want to be a traitor. There were children up there. Families, women, and young ones as innocent as Lumie.

Lumie. She had to do anything to retrieve her child. That was the priority in her mind, and eventually, what helped her make her decision.

"Ruokaa," she finally taught him.

This word, he didn't have any issues repeating. There, she'd done it.

A small seed of fear was planted in Alezya's stomach at this moment. Was she committing a mistake by trusting a stranger? It wouldn't have been the first time she would be used and eventually betrayed by someone.

But what choice did she have? That stranger was the only way she was going to get back to Lumie. If she didn't show willingness, would he stop helping her? She knew it was a bit foolish after all he'd done for her, but doubting men had become second nature. She still felt nervous whenever he came close to her, when he was so near, his eyes on her.

However, he didn't ask her to learn more. Instead, he handed her back the bowl, gesturing for her to finish it. She quickly did, gulping up what was left in two mouthfuls. It really was good food. *Taam*, she remembered. Food.

"*Inkir?*" he asked.

"*Inkir*," she nodded.

She didn't know how long she'd been asleep this time, but she felt she had enough empty space for more of that delicious thing. The warrior didn't seem to mind fetching some for her.

As he left, Alezya sighed. This was a strange new reality to get used to. Something she couldn't quite feel at ease with yet, but that man was somehow making everything feel safer. She hadn't left the enclosure so far, but she was nervous about what she'd possibly find outside. How long would it take for her to be able to step out?

She felt better. ...She felt a lot better already, actually. Now that she was paying attention to her body, she noticed the pain that was previously radiating from every limb had somehow been subdued by quite a lot. Even her ankles were still aching, but not as badly as before.

Alezya was dumbfounded. Was it possible to heal so fast? Or had she slept a lot more than she thought? But no amount of sleep could prompt a miraculous healing. Her eyes suddenly went to the bottle, as if it all clicked. Was it because of that water she'd drank? What was that strange water? She couldn't be sure, but she had some gut feeling it was related. Did the Dragon Clan have such advanced medicine?

Just with this, a bit of hope reignited in her heart. If she had these kinds of means within her reach, then maybe she had more chances to get back to her baby than she thought...

Chapter 4

"...Again?" Tievin raised a judgmental eyebrow.

"She liked it."

As if it was enough of an explanation, Kassein filled the bowl again to the brim, and grabbed another apple for the woman. Alezya, he mentally reminded himself. Her name was Alezya. It was strange and a bit hard to say, but pretty. When she had spoken for the first time, he'd thought her voice was surprisingly soft and clear. It sounded like the gentle stream of cold water under the ice, like the sounds of a near-frozen river.

"I must voice my disapproval yet again, Commander," Tievin wrinkled his nose. "We do not know what those barbarians are capable of. She could be an assassin sent to kill you."

"She was beaten by her own kind," Kassein growled at the memory. "Did you not see the state she was in?"

"I did, and I do find it odd. They chased her close to the border with us, and left that woman behind. The barbarians we tried to capture previously committed suicide rather than be taken by us, but suddenly, they leave a woman in plain sight, right where you could potentially find her. It is odd."

Kassein didn't reply; most likely, he was done answering Tievin.

He turned around, heading back inside the tent. This time, Tievin didn't follow him. Instead, he watched the back of the Prince as he left, powerless. Was it really safe to leave this woman with him...?

His Majesty was like the rest of the men in his family: weak to women. More precisely, they had grown up admiring their mother, and watching their father, the almighty War God, be completely enamored with her. Not only that but every woman in that family was deeply loved and respected. No matter how cold the Wild Prince was acting toward his family right now, there was no way he would ever harm a woman, especially one that seemed as defenseless as this barbarian he'd brought back. Tievin sighed.

He couldn't help but worry for His Highness. When a man was stronger than anyone else, the only way to hurt him would be through his heart... and he knew better than anyone how badly Prince Kassein's had already been wounded.

"...Have one unit keep an eye on the Commander's tent," he ordered.

He had said his order without looking at any soldier specifically, but the men were used to obeying nevertheless. Several answered at once.

"Yes, sir!"

They left, most likely to inform a lieutenant a new surveillance guard would have to be established, while Tievin remained standing near the food distribution. He tightened his coat around him and finally drifted his gaze from His Highness' tent to the mountains.

...What were those barbarians truly thinking? Hard to tell. All their attempts at a peaceful negotiation had amounted to nothing. Those people were so different. It was the first time they'd seen a barbarian woman, and she was harmed right under the Prince's eyes? Somehow, he had a bad feeling about this. That woman was going to be trouble.

...All women eventually led to trouble.

"What about the dragon?"

"It's still, uh, resting, sir."

Tievin rolled his eyes.

First the woman, then His Highness, and now the damn dragon acting all strange too. That beast was parked near its owner's tent, clearly waiting for something.

The dragon had only moved from its spot to take its flight to go hunting and came right back after like an obedient dog. It had caused quite a ruckus inside the camp as most men had only seen Kein from afar. Tievin didn't even need to be informed of the dragon's movements; there were "ooh"s and "aah"s rising all around the camp every time the damn thing decided to fly up or land back here. He had felt relieved the first time Kein had decided to leave, only to be disappointed when the dragon had come back just a couple of hours later, belly full.

That thing was just as stubborn as its master, for sure... and even harder to understand. Tievin didn't care for the dragon as long as it miraculously didn't cause any ruckus, but he was quite annoyed by how it disturbed the camp. He hated anything that stood out and came to disturb what he'd worked hard to put in place. Most soldiers were both curious to see the orange dragon from up close and too terrified not to take a noticeable detour around it. Thus, the foot traffic around His Highness' tent had increased significantly, another major disruption in the usually well-oiled machine that was the camp.

Because there was an actual dragon lingering in the camp, somewhat tame for once, the news about the woman had died quite quickly. She had been there for two days now, but as most soldiers hadn't seen her, the talk about that foreigner had almost disappeared, compared to all the whispering about His Highness' dragon.

"Report the dragon's every movement. And make sure the men stop going to see it like it's some attraction. Anyone caught near the Commander in Chief's tent without a good reason will be put on night patrol. I don't care if one of you gets bitten; that might be a good warning."

"Yes, sir!"

Tievin poured himself a second bowl of food, forgetting all about how he'd protested about the prisoner getting another helping too, and left the food distribution area to eat inside his tent as usual.

On the way, he chose to walk by the Prince's tent... and just like everyone else, he saw Kein. Even for someone who'd grown close to the Imperial Family and their dragons, that was a spectacular sight. The large orange dragon was simply lying there, sleeping.

It was still early, and that beast had been out most of the night hunting. It was now peacefully snoring, like a dog happy with a full belly. Except that the dog was a scaled dragon taking up an awful lot of space... There already weren't many souls brave enough to put their tents near the Prince's, but now, thanks to the dragon, a large area had been cleared around Kassein's, and some tents had been promptly relocated for safety measures, and common sense.

That dragon was huge. The Imperial Family possessed a total of seven dragons, if one excluded the dragons of Queen Cessilia, Prince Darsan, and their children, who all lived in the Eastern Kingdom.

Out of those seven dragons, Kein was now undoubtedly the largest. The dragon had grown bigger than its own progenitor, the War God's legendary black dragon, and bigger than its sibling, Kian, the Emperor's silver dragon. The difference in size was mostly due to the fact that Kein was an Earth Dragon, and Kian a Water Dragon.

No one exactly understood why a dragon was born either way, but Earth Dragons had been the only ones known in the Empire until the War God and his wife, Imperial Princess Cassandra, had children, and six out of those eight children had been born with Water Dragons by their side.

Those Water Dragons were different than their peers; they had longer and slimmer bodies and were faster. By contrast, the Earth Dragons had thicker bodies and were stronger than their peers, but slower. Prince Darsan and Prince Kassein were the only ones who had been born with Earth Dragons, and theirs were the biggest ones once they'd grown to their adult size.

Despite knowing all this and having grown by the Imperial Family's side for a long time, Tievin could never not be afraid of dragons.

Those things were as temperamental as their owners, which was a way to say completely unpredictable and dangerous. Kein was the worst of all. The fire-colored dragon's humongous size only matched its horrible and indecipherable temper.

A few years back, when the Prince and his dragon were still young, their raging battles could somewhat be contained, but as Prince Kassein had become an adult and his dragon had reached its adult size, they'd gone on to cause an incredible amount of damage wherever they fought.

Seeing a beast that was akin to a natural disaster on its own sleeping peacefully was not giving Tievin the slightest bit of relief. Instead, he felt like he was simply watching the calm before yet another storm...

As if the dragon had felt him watching, it suddenly opened its eyes, prompting Tievin to jump back, almost spilling his food.

He froze, watching out for the dragon's movements. But Kein simply stared with its silver eyes as big as a man's shield. The dragon was three times the size of its owner's tent, but it had its body curled in a half-circle around it, like it was guarding it. Upon clearly spotting Tievin, it growled faintly, half-closed its eyes, and puffed out a cloud of hot steam his way. The hot air reached Tievin, making his body shiver.

...Was that beast just acknowledging his presence? Right, he was probably just another potential snack walking by.

With that thought in mind, Tievin resumed walking, although since he didn't dare not watch out for the dragon, he walked away weirdly, sideways. Any soldier passing by would find the Grand Intendant's strange crab-like walk funny, but he didn't care. His life was more important than his pride.

Kein waited until Tievin was out of sight, and then let out another bored growl. The soldiers kept walking by, thinking the dragon didn't see them, or it clearly didn't care. They were right about the last part. Kein directed its silver eyes toward the tent, and after another growl, closed them again, going back to that nice nap.

Inside the tent, Kassein stood still and darted his eyes toward the tent's entrance at the growl. Whatever had agitated his dragon, he knew for a fact it wouldn't move yet. For the first time in a long time, he and his dragon were capable of enduring the other's presence... and their thoughts were focused on Alezya.

Right now, that woman was finishing her bowl of porridge in silence. Kassein had been worried she'd refuse to eat, but she was clearly satisfied with the camp's food. She carefully ate every spoonful of the porridge, despite that injury on her lip.

Every time he looked at her, the sight of her injuries made his blood boil. Outside the tent, Kein growled faintly, startling her. Alezya glanced toward the side of the tent the noise had come from, before glancing at him. He didn't say anything and simply sat down on the tent's floor.

If anything, he had to prove to her she didn't have anything to be afraid of here. When he had first brought her to camp, she was clearly terrified, but she hadn't been scared like he expected one to be. In fact, her first reaction to him was solidly engraved in his mind. She had retreated to the edge of the bed like a cornered animal, but instead of shivering in fear and crying or begging, she'd shown her fangs.

That look in her eyes... She'd looked like a snow leopard ready to defend itself. Despite her injuries and the incredible amount of pain every movement must have put her through, she had still been strong enough to protect herself and try to get away from him. The defiance in her dark eyes spoke volumes... She was used to this. That kind of resilience didn't happen overnight. Not only was she feeling threatened by him, but she had felt this way many times before. Every movement he made put her on edge, and even now, he could tell she was watching him from the corner of her eye, if not glancing at him every once in a while.

It was incredible to witness such a slender woman, who had already been able to withstand this amount of injuries, still have the strength in her to defy him. Although the thought hadn't crossed his mind at all, if he were to try and harm her, Kassein was certain she wouldn't let him have his way without a fight. She had that amazing fire in her dark, doe-like eyes. That woman had the heart of a warrior.

"I'm glad you like it," he said.

Once again, she gave him that confused expression, like she did every time he spoke in his language. It was somewhat amusing to see her get frustrated every time he said anything.

Thinking about it, Kassein had probably spoken more with that woman in a couple of days than he did with anyone else in a week, with maybe the exception of Tievin. It didn't really matter that she couldn't understand; it was more about his willfulness to establish some kind of dialogue between them... any kind, really.

Like many times before, he couldn't understand himself, but he was curious about that woman, her actions, her reactions, and what she was hiding behind that strong facade.

It wasn't like she was as strong as she was pretending to be. He'd seen her crying. A lot.

Alezya cried in her sleep, and he heard her sobbing when she was alone in the tent. Her eyes had turned red, shiny, and puffy from all the crying. He didn't know if she realized how much she cried in her sleep.

When she woke up, her eyes would be dry, and she seemed tired, but she somehow did her best not to cry when he was there, as if she refused to show him her weakness. For that, he found her quite interesting too.

And at the same time, he was dying to know the reason for those tears. A part of him couldn't help but think it was mostly his fault. He'd taken that woman away from her homeland, and she was held in a tent, in a place she knew nothing of, and couldn't understand anything. And yet, she didn't act that scared of him to justify all the tears she shed.

He had a gut feeling there was something else. That woman was acting unusual, as if she was torn between two minds. A part of her was trying to be brave and face him, feisty even, but also, he had noticed she seemed incredibly vulnerable at times, almost... broken, as if she was ready to collapse at any moment. Her gaze would get lost and that light in her eyes would suddenly extinguish. It only lasted a couple of seconds, as every time, she seemed to get back to her former self after some thought.

He couldn't understand what was going on in her mind, but he was dying to know. Kassein couldn't understand why that woman was so fascinating. He couldn't even explain why he'd decided to save her on a pure whim that day. Perhaps he'd simply been raised in a way that he'd never stand by while a woman was being harmed.

Perhaps he'd simply done what felt right, but then, it wouldn't have explained his dragon's actions before his.

"Kassein?"

Her gentle, cautious voice brought him out of his deep thinking.

She was done eating, and handing him the empty bowl. He smiled faintly, something that he had rarely done in these past few years... No, the last decade. Why did that woman feel so different?

He couldn't tell, and truthfully, he didn't want to think too much about it. He took the bowl away, but he had no intention of going out yet, not when most of his men were up and roaming around the camp. He loathed other people's gazes, and they followed him everywhere he went. He'd had enough of that constant scrutiny. Perhaps it was a good thing his brother had exiled him to the north; he was fed up with the Capital...

"Barbarians! An attack!"

Right after that, a young soldier appeared at the tent's entrance.

He didn't dare enter, but he stood at the entrance and his gaze went to Alezya, visibly surprised to find a woman in the Commander in Chief's bed. She darted a glare at him, and pulled the blanket higher to cover herself, although he hadn't seen anything.

"Commander, there's a–"

"Get out," Kassein growled before the man could finish his sentence.

Realizing his mistake, the soldier disappeared in a hurry.

Meanwhile, Kassein had no choice but to grab his sword. For once, he was thankful Alezya couldn't understand them. She stared with big, curious eyes riveted on him, her breathing a bit faster, probably nervous and wondering what the hell was going on out there. He didn't say anything this time and left the tent without looking back.

It was probably for the best she didn't know...

Outside, the army was already moving. No doubt the men were excited by the prospect of another fight with the barbarians.

Kassein ran to the frontline, but without hurrying unnecessarily; they had been expecting an attack since the barrier was down, and this was the second one already. The men were ready.

The first had happened the previous night, just a little brawl with a handful of barbarians who had attacked under the cover of night. They had been caught and killed before they could set foot inside the camp.

The night patrol hadn't even needed to inform Kassein; he'd learned of this once all the action was over. This time though, he had time to get to the frontline, as the barbarians had decided to attack in numbers.

Although there was no doubt every soldier in the camp would have loved to partake in the battle, they had strict orders, and each their own duties. Hence, only about two hundred men were busy fighting, another hundred waiting behind them in case the fight didn't go favorably, and the rest of the camp was busy consolidating the defense, preparing to heal the wounded, or getting more weapons ready for use.

One of the generals was supervising the battle from on top of his horse, shouting orders at the top of his lungs, while Tievin, as always, stood carefully far from the battle, flanked by a unit for some reason. He looked incredibly bored watching the fight, only grimacing from time to time when the bloodshed was getting too much for him to witness.

On one of those occasions when he averted his gaze, he spotted Kassein running toward them.

"Commander," he greeted him.

Kassein slowed down as he reached him, although his green eyes were already scouring the fight.

It was obvious they were winning, or would be soon. The barbarians had lost the element of surprise, and would quickly be overwhelmed by the difference in numbers. Truthfully, they could have been wiped out already if it wasn't for Kassein's men's desire to enjoy the battle while it lasted.

"The attack began just a few minutes ago," Tievin stated with a bored matter-of-fact tone. "General Kauser's fourth patrol unit was the first one to spot them, so as per the rule, their units were the ones to partake in the fight."

Kassein didn't answer, his eyes just scouring the battlefield.

The fight was already well into its second half as the casualties were lying on the ground. From time to time, one of the evacuation units would run in to grab a wounded soldier to take them off the battlefield, often despite the wounded's protests. Only the bodies of the barbarians were left on the ground to redden the snow with their blood.

"...Shall we take prisoners?" Tievin asked, noticing the Prince's gaze.

The handful of soldiers guarding Tievin also glanced at him, curious to see if the Commander in Chief's orders were going to change.

He didn't answer. Instead, his eyes shifted to one of the fighters. At this very moment, one of the barbarians somehow managed to detach himself from the battlefield and having spotted him, ran toward Kassein while yelling and holding some axe-like weapon aimed at him.

Normally, there would have been orders given, and two or three men jumping in his way, but because that man was running toward the Commander in Chief, no one was brave or mad enough to stand in his path. Instead, they all watched as Kassein stepped forward, calmly grabbed his sword, and with one perfect, clean movement, swung his sword in the air. The blade had been sharpened so well that it cut effortlessly through the man's skin, flesh, and bones, and sent his head flying high.

It dropped down right in front of Tievin.

"Ugh," the Grand Intendant covered his mouth, barely suppressing a gag.

That answered everyone's question, and nobody raised the idea of taking prisoners anymore. They only witnessed the Commander in Chief running into battle, his soldiers carefully getting away from him and his deadly long sword.

Meanwhile, Tievin tapped the shoulder of the soldier closest to him.

"Y-you. Get that... that thing out of my sight."

The men guarding him were annoyed. None of them wanted to be there guarding that wimp... Still, one of them swiftly took care of getting rid of the severed head.

As expected, the battle quickly ended. No barbarian was spared, and truthfully, they hadn't shown any signs of trying to leave either.

They all had fought with the intention to kill and hadn't stopped even when injured. Despite the North Army leaving them a route to go back, none ever ran away. For some reason, they were resolute to come down to kill their enemies from the Empire or die trying. Not that the soldiers felt much pity; like every battle, there were casualties on both sides and this time again, they had to count their dead and gather the wounded.

While doing so, most couldn't help but steal glances toward the Commander in Chief. That man had nothing to envy of the legendary War God, in their eyes. Once again, he'd come out of the battle unscathed, with the highest count of kills despite joining late. And yet, none were so bold as to go up to him. Instead, they watched from the sidelines while the most cowardly of them casually walked up to the Commander in Chief, a handkerchief on his mouth.

"...Another victory," Tievin commented. "There are four confirmed deaths so far, twelve men in critical condition, and about fifteen sent to the medical tents for lesser wounds. All barbarians are dead."

Kassein's eyes were on one of the barbarians' bodies, and Tievin followed his gaze, although he immediately averted his eyes at the exposed entrails.

"They are from a different tribe than her, sir," Tievin said, his voice muffled by his handkerchief. "Their attire, weapons, and tribal markings suggest they did not come from the same tribe as that woman."

Kassein had noticed too. They had fought with the tribes enough by now to notice there were several of them, and some were quite different from one another. It didn't make him feel better, or worse. He simply wondered if her tribe was going to come for her, and if it was indeed her own tribe that had initially chased her... If so, would they try to save her, or finish the job? He put his sword away.

"Take care of the bodies."

He turned around and left, headed back toward his tent.

When he stepped back inside his tent, to his surprise, he found Alezya trying to stand up. She had one leg out of bed and was using her elbow on the bedside table to try and support herself.

Their gazes met, and she froze, visibly embarrassed to be caught. He rushed to her side. What was that mad woman doing, trying to get up by herself? She fell back on the bed, her face turning red, grabbing the blanket to cover herself.

"Why are you trying to get up?" he asked her, completely confused.

He'd left her with water, and she had eaten enough to be full for twice the time he was gone at least... So what was it? Was she trying to leave the tent? Why? To escape? He kept staring, but she was flushed red and avoiding his gaze. Seeing how she'd gone back to being cautious, her shoulders a bit up, he retreated one step, giving her some safe space.

Something was off, in the way she wouldn't look at him. It was not the attitude of someone who was afraid after being caught trying to escape, so what was it?

"Alezya?"

He was trying to figure it out, but this time, she wasn't answering or even looking at him. Instead, she kept turning her body away from him, her legs hanging out of the bed, her hand on the fur blanket covering her front... That's when he understood, from the way she held her knees awkwardly against one another.

He was an idiot! She had been lying in bed for two days, and she hadn't been able to relieve herself... and now she had drank quite a bit too. He internally called himself an idiot again and tried to think quickly.

Most men would do their business outside in a deserted area, preferably far from the camp, and clean after themselves, but they didn't have much to accommodate women. Thus, he just grabbed a bucket that was in his room and placed it in front of Alezya, and without saying a word, left the tent, now feeling embarrassed too.

He stood outside, trying to think. He hadn't realized there would be a few issues arising with bringing a woman inside a male-only camp...

There hadn't been a woman in the North Army since he'd taken it farther up the inhospitable north. Plus, a lot of criminals were sent under his command, and he wouldn't have been able to guarantee the safety of several women. But there was one, now, in his tent, and while he could guarantee her safety, it also meant he had to provide for her.

Kassein frowned, thinking long and hard. What else could she possibly need?

"Call Tievin."

A pair of soldiers who were just in the vicinity and pretending to walk by stopped in their tracks, surprised, and then realized they'd received a direct order.

"Yes, Commander in Chief! Immediately, sir!"

The two of them literally raced to wherever they believed the Grand

Intendant to be. Meanwhile, Kassein sighed and crossed his arms.

He'd grown up with three older sisters, so one would think he would have been more knowledgeable about a woman's needs, except that he had also grown up in the gigantic Imperial Palace, with dozens of servants taking care of him and his siblings.

Now, he felt like a fool for not realizing Alezya would have needed to go to the bathroom, probably much earlier. And they were in a camp, they had no proper bathroom either. The men were living among their peers and had gotten used to washing themselves using hot water basins in their tents and doing their business somewhere private. There had never been a situation where a woman came into the picture...

He and his siblings had lived in the north with their parents when they were younger, but that was ages ago, back when they still resided in the Onyx Castle, not so deep into the wild north.

When he had moved this army up north, to a wilder area, he'd never thought they'd one day welcome a woman...

He tried to think on his own what else she might need. Clothes could be arranged easily, they had no shortage of fabric within the camp.

His third older sister was a peculiar woman who needed a lot of things, but Alezya used to live in a mountain, not a palace, so there was no use comparing the two of them... He sighed.

"K-Kassein?"

He turned around, hearing Alezya call for him, probably meaning she was done. When he walked back inside the tent, she was back on the bed, hiding most of her body under the covers, and still red to the ears. Kassein did his best not to react and make her even more ashamed.

She'd left the bucket a few steps away from the bed, along with the little towel she'd used most likely to wash herself a bit. She could probably use a bath... It might be difficult with her injuries, but he knew no woman who would hate a bath, and she was probably closer to being fully healed now. He grabbed the bucket, ignoring the content, to throw it outside.

"Commander?" Tievin's voice called him from the outside, sounding a bit out of breath.

Much to his bad luck, the Grand Intendant had appeared right when Kassein was walking out with that bucket and its content.

"Hold this."

Without warning, Kassein pushed the bucket into Tievin's arms and walked away. Confused, Tievin looked down, and for the second time that day, he hardly suppressed his vomit.

He dropped the bucket out of surprise, which, luckily, fell bottom down in the layers of snow without spillage.

"Commander?!" Tievin protested out loud.

Meanwhile, Kassein had found another pair of roaming soldiers and ordered them to bring a hot bath to his tent as well as new warm clothes, the smallest size they could find in the camp.

Alezya wasn't particularly small for a woman, but she was very slender, and as a woman, she was still shorter than most of his men. Any male attire would look big on her, but he figured they'd find a better solution later. With that done and the soldiers gone to do as he'd asked, Kassein walked back toward his tent, finding Tievin with his lips pinched and an extremely upset look.

"Did I do anything to offend you, sir?" Tievin asked, with a higher-pitched voice than usual.

"No."

"Then. What. Is. This?" he emphasized each word, pointing at the bucket.

Kassein ignored him but grabbed the bucket, and stepped away from his tent to get rid of the contents a few steps away, washing it in snow. Luckily, his tent was isolated enough that he didn't have to go far to get this out of the camp's main alleys. When he came back, Tievin was still standing there, with his lips pinched in a thin line of disapproval.

"She made you wash... *that*?" he grunted.

Kassein didn't answer, ignoring him, and he only heard a loud sigh as he walked back inside the tent. In there, Alezya glanced up at him, and then, her eyes went to Tievin. She frowned slightly, looking wary of the Grand Intendant. Kassein found that funny, considering Tievin was by far the most inoffensive man of the camp...

"Introduce yourself," Kassein ordered him.

Once again, Tievin made a sound of protest, but after a while, he turned to the woman, back to his usual bored expression.

"My name is Tievin, Servant of the Imperial Family and Grand Intendant of the North Army."

Kassein wanted to roll his eyes. How was she supposed to get all that? As expected, Alezya was staring at Tievin with a confused expression.

He got her attention and then pointed at him.

"Tievin," he simply said.

"...I'd actually prefer she call me Grand Intendant," Tievin mumbled. "She's not exactly a guest, Commander."

Kassein glared at him, cutting off any more protest.

"...Tievin."

They both turned their eyes to Alezya, who'd clearly just tried pronouncing his name. Tievin sighed, but nodded.

"Yes, my lady."

No matter how much he would protest, Tievin had been well-raised in a family with high standards of education. As the son of one of the most prestigious Imperial Servant families, he'd been taught to act with politeness, courtesy, and decorum in all circumstances, and wouldn't get mad at a woman for calling him by his name instead of his title; it was the first rule of etiquette to not make someone else aware of their mistake and thus embarrass them. Especially considering Alezya couldn't understand their language, it was better she didn't believe Grand Intendant was his name, and she would be hearing Kassein call him Tievin too anyway.

Now that this was sorted, Kassein was back to thinking. The bath was on its way there, so were the clothes, but what next? His eyes went back to Tievin. Or, more precisely, to Tievin's coat.

"...Bring two of those here."

"W-what?" Tievin blinked several times.

"Your coats. Pick the smallest ones you have."

"Commander!" Tievin protested again. "Those are *my* coats!"

"Your coats that I hunted."

"Still! They're... They're part of my compensation!"

Kassein raised an eyebrow as if to ask, "Compensation for what?" but Tievin only seemed even more frustrated. *My compensation for being sent to suffer with you in this stupidly cold country,* was the thought Tievin really wanted to say aloud. Alas, after so many years by the temperamental Prince's side, he knew better than to retort back.

Instead, he took a deep breath in, and mentally calmed himself.

"...Yes, sir."

Tievin already didn't like this woman.

It wasn't even lunchtime yet, and he'd been forced to cradle a bucket full of her vile, unspeakable... bowel hell, and hand over two of his prized fur coats like some kind of fool. For *free*. He turned to leave in a huff, but not before delivering a long, squinty, thoroughly offended glare in her direction. To his dismay, she wasn't intimidated in the slightest. Much to Tievin's horror, she *dared* to glare right back.

Well. Not one to be out-squinted, Tievin narrowed his eyes even further, lips twitching in tight disapproval, and backed toward the exit with the confidence of a man too proud to admit he had no idea where the door was. He bumped into the tent frame. Stumbled. Recovered.

Then walked out backward, still facing her, stiff as a board, pretending the whole thing had gone exactly as planned... Kassein, who hadn't missed anything of the scene, suppressed a smile.

"He's a good friend," he said simply.

Alezya had turned her eyes back to him, but she obviously couldn't understand that. Kassein had felt hopeful after she'd easily understood basic words like food and water already, but now, he was wondering how long they'd have to keep guessing each other's words.

He had never been a very talkative man, and was even less willing to talk after being sent to the north. In fact, he found himself wanting to talk to this woman, even though he barely spoke a word to his men.

He couldn't explain why. He knew why he didn't like talking to his men; he hated their gazes, the thoughts he could read on their faces, their stubborn admiration for him when he felt like he deserved none of it. He hated how they sometimes resented him, sometimes praised him, and none of that ever to his face. Tievin was the one he'd known forever, and the only one who knew honesty was better, although risky. All those other men who judged him without knowing him were just pests.

Alezya, however, was completely different. Not just because she was foreign, and a woman. She was wary around him. She knew nothing of his past, and only judged him by his actions, by what she could witness herself. They were meant to be enemies, yet that woman seemed to be willing to let him show his true character. Kassein didn't care that she was scared or wary of him; those reactions were legitimate.

He'd taken her away from the one home she'd always known after something traumatic had visibly happened to her. Wariness seemed fair.

"Commander, we brought the bath!"

They had been quick.

Alezya, alerted by more male voices, had already retreated back in the bed and under the blanket, her eyes riveted on the entrance.

He'd noticed it before, but she seemed to be afraid of men, not just because they were foreign. There was something in her gaze that made it clear she didn't trust any of them, as if to say she knew their kind and had no trust in males.

Kassein couldn't even explain how he knew it was a gender issue more than one based on their homelands; he could just feel it. She'd reacted more surprised than she should have any time he'd acted kindly to her. Her dumbfounded and embarrassed expression when he'd washed her feet came to mind. She'd never had someone do that for her, and she couldn't believe he had. She despised males and she wouldn't let her guard down in their presence. Was it related to the ones who'd attacked her?

Kassein went out himself to get the bath, which was really just a large bucket filled with hot water, and carried it inside. It was extremely heavy, hence Alezya watched him bring that inside with big round eyes. He didn't sweat over it and just handed the towels to her. She quickly understood who that bath was for because soon, her eyes were riveted on that steam with envy. Kassein let out a faint smile and pointed at the water.

"Bath," he said.

She frowned, and this time, didn't try to repeat it.

He could tell she really wanted to clean herself as her eyes kept going to the hot water, and he couldn't blame her. He'd known one of his sisters to bathe twice a day, and though she probably wouldn't be so needy, Alezya had spent a long time stuck in bed, probably sweating out the light fever she'd had too.

He went toward the end of his tent. He'd received some luxurious items he seldom used, sent from the palace or given by the locals as thanks for chasing the barbarians away. Some were soaps with smells that he didn't like, too sweet and floral for a grown man.

He grabbed a handful and brought them for Alezya to use. He showed it to her, said "soap," and put it on the bedside table where she could easily grab them.

When that was done, he wondered if he should help her get in the water or undo her bandages. She could already move a lot better now. While he hesitated, he stood there, watching her. Alezya's eyes were still riveted on the hot water, and she faintly glanced up at him, looking unsure.

"Take a bath," Kassein finally said. "I'll be right outside."

She knew his name, she could always call him if she needed help.

Kassein gave her one last glance before he walked out and, as he'd said, stood right outside his tent. As it saw him appear, his dragon immediately reacted, growling.

"Shut up," Kassein growled back.

Kein wasn't having it, and growled some more, showing its fangs to its owner, its claws digging into the snow under it.

The few soldiers who'd been posted nearby all jumped back or quickly ran away, undoubtedly scared there would be another fight between the two of them out of the blue. It wouldn't be the case though.

Kein and Kassein glared fiercely at one another, but the dragon didn't get up, and Kassein didn't touch his sword either. The animosity was palpable, but they stood in this strange stand-off, neither refusing to stop glaring at the other. It lasted a while before Kein reduced its growling, and Kassein finally stopped glaring, his eyes going to the mountain behind their tent. The corner of his eye had caught something moving.

His dragon also turned its head the same way, alarmed, and stood up, flicking its huge tail with annoyance. They'd never seen movement from this side of the mountains, but it didn't mean there was nothing. It was hard to see anything because the snow covered every surface, creating a blanket of pure white.

While he kept inspecting the area, Kein jumped first. The dragon effortlessly began climbing the mountain, in search of whatever it had spotted, its large body causing another substantial ruckus as its claws dug deeply into the stone. Kein was, as usual, oblivious to its enormous size, and didn't realize that massive rocks were being detached from the mountain under its climbing, loudly hitting the ground. Kassein glanced at the landslide his dragon was provoking.

He hadn't been foolish enough to put his tent that close to the mountain, but it still caused an awful lot of noise and made the ground tremble in the area. His eyes went back to his tent, where Alezya was bathing. There was no way she hadn't heard that, but she hadn't called him. Was she alright? She hadn't collapsed in the bath or something, had she?

He tried to listen, but it was hard to hear anything with his imbecile dragon making such a racket. Kassein didn't care anymore about whatever they'd been searching for up there, he was more worried about that woman being silent despite the uproar. After one more glare at his dragon, he decided to walk back into the tent.

"Alezya?" he called her name as he walked in to try and warn her.

When he stepped inside, he saw her, half-standing in the middle of the bath, looking panicked. She turned her eyes his way, clearly surprised to see him. Kassein was stunned. She was naked, most of the bandages taken off and lying next to the bath on the floor, and her long black hair all around her, framing her beauty.

She was breathtakingly beautiful, and this vision hit him. It was like he'd walked into an impromptu moment, and caught some ethereal goddess bathing. He'd seen a bit of her body before, but then, she was heavily wounded, covered in blood and bruises, and he hadn't cared much for her silhouette. Well, she had a gorgeous one.

She had a long, slender body, but larger breasts that a lot of women would have envied. Her long ink-like hair was down to her thighs, enveloping her body and enhancing her superb figure.

As Kassein took his eyes back to her face, he realized she was glaring, and he suddenly realized he'd been staring too much.

He darted his gaze elsewhere immediately, ashamed.

"S-sorry," he mumbled.

He hadn't pronounced that word nor felt so ashamed in a long time, but the image of Alezya standing naked was carved into his mind, and wouldn't go away. He tried to focus on something else, like the fire in the tent, but his feet were solidly anchored there, and he didn't turn away.

"I just came to check if you were alright," he finally uttered, feeling like a moron.

He hadn't felt this awkward in ages. Not just because he'd caught a woman bathing, or seen her naked, but because for the first time, the sight stirred something deep inside.

He had never found himself like this, so shy, so uncertain, and so... tempted. Something about Alezya's beautiful appearance humbled him inexplicably. Still, he tried to regain his composure quickly and chase that strange state of mind away.

He heard the water move around and glanced to see that she had sat back in the tub, her body submerged all the way up to her neck. She was still glaring at him though. He sighed and stepped out of the tent, mentally kicking himself out of there; she was alright, that was all he'd come to check.

When he stepped out, Tievin appeared in his field of vision, the Grand Intendant's eyes on the orange dragon climbing the mountain and making a full-on natural disaster out of it. He was carrying two of his coats, as instructed, and approached Kassein with his eyes still glued on the dragon.

"Dare I ask what's going on with that dragon of yours?" he sighed.

"No."

Kassein took the coats from him. He may have been reluctant about it, but Tievin had still picked two small coats that were soft and thick enough for Alezya. Right behind him, the soldiers from before were also carrying some clothes, just as he'd asked them.

Kassein put the coats back in Tievin's arms to check what they'd brought. The pants would still be too large for Alezya, but the tunic was long and should be fine.

"Her previous clothes?" he asked Tievin.

"I had them thrown away, of course. Didn't you see what state they were in?"

Kassein was a bit annoyed, but he couldn't say Alezya's previous clothes were salvageable. From what he'd seen, they were ripped, soaked, and stained with blood beyond salvation. Still, they could have kept them to take her measurements. He let that idea go.

Clothes were still clothes, they'd find a solution eventually. The men had brought a pair of shoes that could fit, but he wasn't sure her feet were in any state to wear those yet. Kassein took the clothes and sent them away. That was when he heard her call him.

Already? Did she finish in a hurry because she was worried he'd intrude again?

Kassein stepped in, Tievin following behind him. Alezya was out of the bath, seated on the bed, and wrapped in a large towel, busy drying her hair with another one. From the color of the water, that bath had been long overdue... Tievin frowned upon seeing that too.

Kassein walked up to her and put the clothes next to her on the bed while Tievin left the coats on the side.

"I'll get someone to take this out..."

"No," Kassein stopped him. "I'll do it."

Tievin froze, surprised, but Kassein didn't want other men walking into his tent; he hated anyone coming in, and he didn't want more men to see Alezya and risk scaring her.

Ignoring the Grand Intendant's stunned gaze, Kassein moved to grab new bandages for her wounds and that medicinal paste he'd made.

"Do you need me for anything else, Commander?" Tievin eventually sighed.

"...See that she gets new underwear," Kassein said, glancing at the old one Alezya had left on the bed.

It was dirty, of course, but that was the only thing they couldn't replace right away. Noticing the two men's eyes were on it, she blushed and took it away, but Tievin nodded. He'd had enough time to see it and guess the size.

"Understood... I'll get her some from the village."

Tievin already hated the idea of a trip just to get a woman new underwear, and probably some proper clothes while he was at it, but that would be better than having the clothing unit fabricate female underwear or clothes. Otherwise, he could already hear the kinds of rumors that would circulate within the camp. Those soldiers could be worse than old widows when it came to gossiping at times, especially anything that involved their Commander in Chief...

Moreover, it would be nice to go south for a bit, and he did like to go shopping and spend his hard-won money. With that said, Tievin left, planning to go right that day. The camp could do without him for a few hours, and he was more than happy to leave while that dragon was going on another rampage. Who knew what would be left of that poor mountain when he'd come back...?

With Tievin gone, Kassein and Alezya were left alone in the tent, and he noticed she did relax a bit once Tievin was gone. He brought over the bowl of medicinal paste he'd made and showed it to her so as not to alarm her.

"I need to put this on your wounds," he calmly said, putting a knee down in front of the bed.

Like before, Alezya reacted shocked, and nervous to see him seated underneath her, but he didn't leave her room to protest. He gently took her ankle and began spreading the ointment.

He felt her flinch; it ought to hurt a bit. Her skin and injuries looked much better though. Now cleared of all the dry blood and dirt, it was much smoother and the injuries and cuts clean. Her skin was healing fast, little scabs had appeared here and there to try and cover the open wounds. It smelled nice too. The soap that had smelled too floral for Kassein was now wonderfully adorning Alezya's skin, and it tickled his senses a bit.

He realized his fingers had paused a bit longer than normal on her ankle, and he looked up. She was staring at him, and faintly blushing. Alezya wasn't like most bashful young ladies though, averting her gaze and acting shy. Instead, she wasn't afraid to stare at him, with an inquisitive, confused gaze, her cheeks a bit red.

He quickly withdrew his fingers, and went back to the ointment, applying it quickly where he ought to. When he got close to the areas her towel covered, he stopped and put it aside. Then, he grabbed the bandages and began covering her feet again, careful of his movements and grateful to have a reason to hide her skin away.

He was feeling much more mindful of the way their skin touched, and Alezya's reactions. Sometimes, it was just a very faint flinch, but he couldn't help but wonder if it was because of the pain, or the contrast between their body temperatures. He tried hard not to look up again, focusing on bandaging her feet properly.

Suddenly, another loud growl was heard from outside, and Alezya jumped in fright. Kassein glared at the area of the tent behind which he knew Kein to be still wreaking havoc.

Either his dragon had actually found something or had begun hunting for the fun of it; it was just being annoyingly rambunctious and scaring Alezya.

Kassein ignored it and finished bandaging her wounds he could access. Then, he pushed the clean clothes toward her, making a gesture, so she knew it was indeed meant for her. Alezya nodded, but her eyes kept going toward the back of the tent nervously.

Kassein sighed, but anyhow, she had to get dressed. Even in his tent, it wasn't so warm that she could stay like this for too long.

Thus, he grabbed the dirty, old bandages and lifted the large water bucket to take it outside. Using the time he was outside to give Alezya some privacy to finish getting dressed, he spilled the dirty water in the snow a few steps away from his tent and got rid of the blood-soaked bandages.

Two soldiers came to pick up the now empty bucket and take it away, giving him curious glances. He'd visibly not taken a bath yet, as he still had some blood on him, so they had to be wondering who had used that in the Commander in Chief's tent.

Neither dared to ask it out loud though, so they were left with no choice but to leave, their gazes shifting to the noisy mountain behind the tent. Kassein also turned around to see what kind of rampage Kein was still on.

His dragon was just jumping and climbing on the mountain, digging into some area with its tail swishing around like it had found something to play with. For a while, Kassein just stared its way, until the dragon picked up on his gaze. Kein stopped moving and glanced back, glaring immediately at its owner.

The dragon growled and jumped back down in a few hops. Its heavy body brutally and loudly landed on the ground, shaking the whole area. Kein stood facing him, visibly upset.

The only reason the dragon wasn't growling louder was the prey caught between its fangs. A dead snow leopard was trapped there, its blood dripping down the dragon's maw and on the snow.

Kassein clicked his tongue.

"What's that?" he growled at his dragon.

The dragon growled back as if it was equally pissed at him.

They both stood in another stand-off, but the anger was rising slowly. The dragon raised its shoulders and lowered its head, its silver eyes riveted on Kassein. Because he'd joined the fight before, Kassein's sword was still hung on his back, ready for use. He lifted his hand, threatening to take the handle.

Kein's growling got louder.

Then, a yelp coming from the tent got both dragon and man to suddenly turn their heads. Kassein didn't wait more than a second to lower his hand and head inside; that was definitely Alezya's voice.

He walked inside the tent, mentally fortifying himself in case she was naked or almost naked again. This time, however, she wasn't; in fact, Alezya had already finished dressing herself, except for the coat that was still next to her on the bed.

Kassein walked up to her, wondering what was wrong, but she had her eyes on the entrance and was visibly nervous, not in pain or anything.

"What is it?" he asked when he reached her.

"*M-mike ha menissa bahira?*"

Kassein was stunned. This was the first time Alezya had tried to actually speak to him, and in her own language too. He was so shocked, he forgot her scared expression for a moment and just stared at her.

He hadn't understood a word of that, naturally, but hearing her use her mother tongue was making him strangely happy.

"Can you repeat that?"

She looked at him and noticed the strangely happy expression on his face. She got impatient, and pointed at the door, visibly running out of patience and not in the mood to indulge him.

"*Kassein! Mike tyo ho?*" she insisted.

Kassein followed her finger, glancing at the entrance. She was probably getting nervous because of Kein's growls.

She'd seemed fine when his dragon was still at a distance, like when it was attacking its stupid mountain, but now, it seemed fair that she was nervous about the growls heard right outside the tent. He sighed.

After a hesitation, he grabbed the coat, and gently put it over her shoulders. Alezya was surprised, but she didn't fight it.

Then, he paused, but offered her his arm. That gesture got her very confused once again. She glanced up at him.

He could tell she was nervous, but he waited, patiently.

After a while, she finally put her hand on his arm, just below a patch of orange dragon scales. Her skin felt fresh compared to his... He did his best not to react to it, and instead, he gently moved to slide his arm under hers, putting it behind her back, while his other arm went under her knees to lift her up. Alezya gasped, surprised to be carried like this.

Still, she held on to him by reflex, gripping his fur cape so as not to fall; not that he would have let her fall, of course. She weighed less than he'd thought; even the fur coat on her shoulders seemed heavier than the woman herself.

He glanced down at Alezya to make sure he wasn't holding her in a way that was hurting her more, but to his surprise, she just seemed completely flustered. She was blushing, and avoiding his gaze. ...She was embarrassed to be carried like this?

Kassein suddenly found himself a bit shy too, and stopped looking at her. Instead, he walked outside, giving her a glimpse of what was going on out there, as well as her first breath of fresh air since he'd brought her to the camp.

Alezya immediately yelped a second time, and held on even tighter to him, frightened. Unfortunately for her, Kein had been waiting right outside the tent.

While Kassein had gone inside, the orange dragon had moved to stand right outside the tent's entrance, its snout and blood-covered maw and fangs the first thing Alezya had seen. Now, she was absolutely terrified, and shaking in Kassein's arms.

Interestingly, though, despite her desperately holding onto him, Kassein found her once again surprisingly brave, as she still had an eye on Kein, rather than hiding her face and completely turning her back on the dragon like most people would.

She was still terrified though, as anyone would be when a blood-covered dragon stood inches away from them.

"Back off, you imbecile."

Kein growled in disapproval, showing its fangs even more.

Stubborn as always, the dragon hadn't let go of its prey, and the dead snow leopard had half its body dragging in the snow, coloring it red under them. If it wasn't for all the blood from the fresh hunt, maybe Alezya wouldn't have been so scared, but his dragon wasn't looking its best like this.

"You're scaring her," Kassein retorted to the dragon's growls.

This time, Kein calmed down a bit. Its silver eyes shifted slightly, and although it wouldn't stop growling, the dragon very slowly backed away from the two of them, its large paws leaving huge holes in the snow.

It also lowered its body, half-crouching in the snow. The dragon that should have towered above them was now at Kassein's eye level.

It growled a bit, but this time, its growls were less threatening, and more like a heavy, loud, but peaceful sound, like an echo inside a rock cave. Kassein redirected his eyes toward Alezya, who was still shaking.

As soon as the dragon had moved its silver eyes toward her, she'd looked away.

"Alezya."

He gently called her name, as if to tell her it was alright. She looked up at him, obviously still scared and confused, but she had already understood. After taking a couple of seconds to gather her bravery, she turned her eyes back to Kein.

Once again, she didn't just stare at the dragon with nothing but terror in her eyes. In fact, as he watched her, Kassein found that same defiance she'd shown with him. As if she was daring the dragon to attack them.

That woman was truly something, he thought. What kind of woman didn't cower in the face of a dragon? He'd seen warriors run away without a second of doubt when Kein had appeared in the sky, but that woman could withstand the dragon's gaze and glare back like so? He pinched his lips in a faint line, hardly suppressing a smile. She was truly something.

Kein suddenly growled, making Alezya jump, and retreat a bit, her body leaning against Kassein's shoulder, the only way she could back away from the dragon.

"Behave," Kassein warned him.

This was not something his dragon would normally be willing to do. By now, the two of them should have been tearing each other apart, soaked in the other's blood, and wreaking havoc on this place. The fact that Kein was almost calmly growling and staying still like this was already a miracle in itself. Kassein could guess the gazes of some dumbfounded soldiers on them, although they were all standing at a careful distance.

"Alezya."

He called her again to get her attention back on him.

There was a strange satisfaction anytime she reacted to him saying her name which he couldn't quite understand. Still, her eyes went back to him, although she was obviously reluctant to stop watching the dragon.

Kassein gestured at Kein with a little movement of his chin.

"Kein," he simply said.

He hadn't expected to be introducing his dragon already.

Once again, Alezya had that slightly confused expression, and her eyes went to the dragon, frowning.

"*Kein?*" she repeated.

The dragon immediately reacted to her saying its name.

Kein lifted its head and tilted it, its silver eyes clearly on Alezya, causing her to be scared again.

"...*Kein,*" she muttered. "*Dryagaan.*"

Another word from her language. Kassein had no idea what it meant, but from the way she'd said it, she was perhaps trying to match his dragon's name with her vocabulary.

Meanwhile, his dragon reacted to its name again, letting out a short growl. It tried to approach again, but slowly this time. Alezya didn't yelp or scream as the dragon's warm snout approached her, sending hot whiffs of air her way. Instead, she froze and stared, nervous but trying to hold it all in. Kein approached its snout so close it almost touched her, and then, it lifted its head, as if to show the prey still caught between its fangs.

The poor state of what had once been a beautiful snow leopard was absolutely gruesome. Kein suddenly opened its gigantic maw and dropped that thing at their feet.

Then, it stepped back and pushed the dead body toward Kassein's feet, although it was obviously staring at Alezya.

"...Are you for real?" Kassein grumbled. "In that state?"

Kein immediately furiously growled back at its owner, its silver eyes clearly shifting target. Between them, a confused Alezya had her eyes on the dead body.

After a couple of seconds, Kassein sighed and gently let her down, making sure she didn't step in the blood. If she'd been able to stand in the bath, she could probably stand a few seconds on the snow.

He made sure she was stable on her own, although he still held her firmly by her waist in case she stumbled or something; he didn't trust the state of her feet. Alezya did struggle to stay up, but that was most likely the fright that had left her legs weak.

Moreover, she did look at the dragon and its "present" for her, but slowly, her gaze shifted to their surroundings. It was her first time seeing the camp herself, so Kassein let her look around, take in the environment.

She looked at all the tents scattered around, the few soldiers who'd stopped to watch this strange scene, and farther away, the snow-covered forest. Then, her eyes turned toward the mountains. Like a large rock wall, the mountains this woman had come from were now standing tall before her, at an angle she'd most likely never seen them from before.

Kassein watched Alezya's expression intently during this moment.

And that's when he saw it, again. Her tears, pearling quietly at the corner of her eyes, and that unspeakable expression on her face. There was despair, hope, sadness, and longing in her eyes, and it broke Kassein's heart a bit. ...At first, he'd thought she missed her old home, but no.

There had to be something else. Somebody else. She was missing someone. He knew the signs all too well.

She kept staring at those mountains, scouring them for a sign, clearly looking for something. It had to be someone very important for her to look up so long when there was a gigantic beast right in front of her.

"...Alezya?"

He'd called her gently, but she jumped, her watery eyes going back to him. She was clearly distressed and a bit embarrassed to have cried in front of him from the way she awkwardly rubbed her eyes.

Kassein grabbed her wrists to stop her before she undid her bandages, and looked into her eyes, with a serious expression.

"You need to go back up there, don't you?"

Of course, she had no idea what he'd just said. She just stared at him with a lost expression, a bit upset. After a hesitation, Kassein followed his impulse to put his hand against her cheek. If she seemed surprised by his gesture at first, Alezya didn't push him away. Instead, she kept her dark eyes staring at him, listening to his words.

"I'll help you go back," Kassein promised. "I'll help you go back up there, to your people."

He didn't know what had happened to her, but if she wanted to go back, he'd help her.

Suddenly, Kein growled furiously behind her, its claws angrily digging into the ground. Its violent burst of anger made Alezya jump, but Kassein immediately stepped between them, shielding her with his body.

Kein wasn't calming down this time. The dragon stood back up, furiously growling and going on a rampage where it stood, sending snow flying and making the ground tremble. Still, for once, it didn't try to attack Kassein. The Imperial Prince stood perfectly still between his dragon and Alezya, glaring back as if daring the dragon to attack.

After a while, he turned his back on the dragon, and picked up Alezya again, taking her back inside. There was no reason to let her witness any more of his dragon's madness nor let her stand in the cold, especially now that he'd made up his mind to send her back.

They got back inside the tent, and he gently put her back down on the bed; Alezya didn't seem to mind the end of her short break outside, she still looked a bit sad and distraught.

At a loss of what to do, Kassein put water to boil on the fire; that was what his mother had always done to appease tensions, and he must have picked up that habit after all.

Then, he went back to Alezya and sat down in front of her, him on the carpet of fur on the floor while she sat above him on the bed.

"When Tievin comes back with new clothes for you and you feel better, I'll take you back to the mountain," he said.

"...Tievin?" she said.

He chuckled faintly. She was most likely repeating the only word she'd recognized from his sentence. He nodded, but didn't explain any further; he didn't have the heart to.

Instead, he simply waited for that water to boil, in silence, his eyes down on her injured feet. He'd given her some of the sacred water from the Lake of the Imperial Palace, so of course she was healing fast. She'd be a lot better in a matter of days... and he hated himself for regretting helping her recover faster.

While he was lost in some dark thoughts, Alezya's hands appeared in his field of vision. To his surprise, she was moving toward his forearms with a curious expression. He didn't react and watched, curious as to what she was doing, until her fingers reached his skin.

A faint shiver went down his spine, but he did his best to stay still. She glanced up at him, her expression hard to decipher this time.

It was like she was worried, or asking for his permission. As he didn't react, her eyes went back down to his skin, and he realized what she was going for: his scales. Most of his body had been covered all along by the fur cape, but as he sat, his arms were revealed, and Alezya was frowning at the orange scales. Her fingers finally reached it, and she frowned even more, glancing up at him with questions in her eyes.

"*Dryagaan?*" she asked in a soft voice. "...Kein?"

Her index finger pointed toward the entrance of the tent.

She had realized those were dragon scales, the exact same ones as she'd just seen on the orange dragon standing outside. He nodded, but she only seemed even more confused. Kassein sighed and took off his fur cape. He let it fall around him, and then, he also took off his armor, which could use a bit of cleaning, showing Alezya his bare torso. The woman blushed slightly, and her eyes widened in surprise.

There were a lot more scales visible on his chest, scattered across his massive body, some fainter, some more visible, a bright orange.

She gasped in shock. Her eyes went back to the entrance of the tent, then to his torso, then back to him again, as if she was just now making all the right connections. Kassein grasped her hand and pulled it so her fingers could freely touch his scales.

He tried hard to suppress another shiver when her cold skin met his.

"Kein," he nodded once her hand was on the scales.

Alezya left her mouth open, speechless. She blinked a couple of times, her eyes scouring his body, completely impressed or shocked.

As if to prove himself even further, Kassein took out a small dagger from his hip. Alezya pulled her hand back, a bit worried, but he put the blade against where his skin was intact, on his forearm which was usually protected by a metal sleeve. In front of her eyes, he cut himself.

Alezya gasped, and grabbed his hand, pulling the hand with the dagger away from his skin to stop him. Kassein was already bleeding though, and as her eyes went to the injury, she witnessed for herself the incredible phenomenon. The vibrant orange scales seemed to sprout right out of the injury and quickly covered it all.

It happened in a matter of seconds, and after a little while longer, the orange scales themselves faded, melting back into his skin to leave it flawless. Alezya was completely stunned, staring at where the injury had disappeared. Her grip on his hand with the weapon lessened, and her eyes slowly moved, from his forearm to the rest of his body, as if evaluating the large patches of orange scales again. She hesitated, then pointed her finger at his chest.

"...*Dryagaan?*" she muttered.

Kassein wasn't sure what she meant, but the question didn't seem to be actually directed at him. It sounded more like she was having a hard time believing what she'd just seen. She opened and closed her mouth again. Her eyes were still on the scales as if she still couldn't believe it.

Kassein took her hand and gently pressed it against his torso again, to let her feel them. He couldn't feel the temperature difference as much when her skin was against the scales, but nevertheless, that contact made his stomach do a loop. Perhaps he'd taken her hand to touch him for something more impure than his scales... He let go, but her hand stayed on his torso a couple of seconds longer, and their eyes met.

That's when he realized she was as flustered as he was.

The water bubbling over making the fire sizzle caused them both to jump.

Alezya took back her hand, and Kassein got up to take the pot off the fire. An awkward silence took over the tent as he prepared two cups of hot water, each avoiding the other's gaze.

Alezya had retreated back on the bed, although she'd kept the fur coat around her shoulders. Kassein had considered putting his clothes and armor back on, but after one look, he realized it was too sullied already. He gave Alezya her cup of water and put his aside. It was a bit too hot for her to drink yet, so she just held it between her hands and watched as he used the remaining hot water to quickly clean the blood off of himself with a cloth.

Her gaze on his half-naked body was perhaps even worse than when she'd touched him earlier. Since when did a woman's eyes have this kind of effect on him? He did his best to ignore it, putting the dirty clothes aside and briefly cleaning his armor before putting it back on.

His fur cape was the most blood-stained, so he just left it aside, knowing someone would come and pick it up to clean later. Once all that was done, he realized he wasn't sure how to act in front of her.

He grabbed the cup as the hot water couldn't burn him and drank it quickly. He knew she was still seated on the bed and staring at him, but the lack of communication between them was getting more and more frustrating...

No, he shouldn't think about it too much. She'd be back in the mountains soon anyway. Why was he so bothered?

"...I'll be going outside. Call Kein if you need me."

"Kein?"

Outside the tent, his dragon growled softly in response.

At least she now knew the name of his dragon... although he highly doubted she'd understood the rest of his sentence. Kassein sighed and walked out.

He walked past his dragon, which didn't miss the chance to furiously growl at him, but he ignored it. Kassein just wanted to get away from his tent, and from those frustrating thoughts he had.

He walked deeper into the camp, crossing paths with several men surprised to see him up and roaming.

"C-Commander? Are you going for a hunt?"

He was annoyed that he'd sent Tievin away. At least when the Grand Intendant was there, he didn't need to report every single one of his movements nor give orders to the men.

Still, he ignored them all and kept walking, headed for the forest. He had thought about going up into the mountains, but every time he did, Alezya's image came to mind. What if he ended up attacking someone who was important to her this time? What if he already did, and she wasn't aware?

He'd never thought twice about the Northern people before. They had pushed every attack, fought back when they were attacked, and that was all there was to it. No need to think about it too much; he didn't need to think when his brother gave him the order. After all, Kassian had only wanted to get rid of him by sending him here. He'd pushed the army as far as he could, but he didn't care enough to actually try and invade those mountains.

Why would he? It would be sacrificing more men, and Kassian would use that against him too. Kassein only tolerated the deaths he could justify. But now, he felt like he couldn't justify any of them anymore.

He walked alone in the forest, ready to hunt anything that came his way. Those woods that had remained untouched by humankind for decades were still full of life, and it didn't take long for him to come across the first hares.

He ignored the smaller prey though. He'd only taken his sword and a small dagger, and he didn't need anything from skinny snow hares. He was looking for the real challenge, the current masters of the area, the ones topping the food chain. The snow leopards.

Those felines were numerous and had propagated as much as they wanted without a natural enemy to stop them. They did fight once in a while with the wolves or bears in the forest, but because of their agility, the felines could climb the mountain for safety and come back down to the forest to hunt when the prey up there got scarce.

The other bigger creatures didn't have that luxury, and would sometimes move south to avoid those dangerous predators. Kassein's capes were usually bearskin, for they were wide enough to cover his whole body. He didn't care much for snow leopards usually, but right now, he was on the prowl for one. His dragon had inspired him, perhaps.

As predicted, he soon encountered one. A young male, it seemed, roaming alone and fully aware there weren't many that could defeat it from the way it strolled carelessly. It froze on sight as soon as its eyes met Kassein's though and it began growling, a warning for the stranger.

Kassein scoffed. The snow leopard wasn't completely foolish; it was growling furiously, ears down, its fur standing on end and its tail curled under it.

"You alone?" Kassein asked, glancing around for the rest of its family.

Snow leopards often hunted in groups, but after scouring their surroundings, it became clear this young male was on its own.

"...Got kicked out by your family too?" Kassein muttered.

The beast growled even more. Somehow, it seemed aware of how dangerous the male human was, for it didn't dare turn its back on him.

All the better for Kassein though; it would have been bothersome if his prey ran away. He slowly got closer, and the feline hissed, beating the air with its paw, all claws out, warning what would happen if he got too close. That didn't stop Kassein. Soon, he stepped too close, and both human and beast jumped at each other. The fight only lasted a couple of seconds. Kassein's movements were brutal, merciless, and precise.

The snow leopard's body fell silently to the ground.

Unlike his dragon, he had done a neat kill with only one strike, and barely any blood on the fur, much to his satisfaction. Moreover, this was a pretty one; snow leopard's fur could vary from white to gray or yellow, with gray or black spots. This one didn't have any yellow; it was only white and light gray with dark gray spots.

Satisfied and calmed down, Kassein picked up his prey and made his way back to the camp. He took long detours to hunt some more, following animal trails and paw prints, only because he didn't feel like going back so soon. He'd have heard Kein's growls if Alezya had tried to call for him, but his dragon remained quiet.

When he finally came back to the camp, it was much later in the afternoon, and several men were eagerly waiting for him at the edge of the forest. They all opened their eyes wide at the large amount of dead prey he was carrying.

When he stopped in front of them, Kassein let down the snow leopard and three white foxes at their feet, and separately, let down three deers and a large black bear's body.

"C-Commander, you hunted all those by yourself?" one of them exclaimed.

"He only had his sword too..."

Kassein lifted his eyes at them, and the men immediately shut up, some even taking a step back from their Commander's glare.

"Make those into a cape," he said, pointing at the snow leopard and white foxes.

"F-for you, Commander?" another asked, confused.

"Is it for the lady?"

The soldier who spoke was one of those who'd seen Alezya earlier, and instantly made the connection. Kassein's green eyes went to him, and the soldier swallowed his saliva and nodded, more to avoid his leader's gaze than anything.

"I-I'll make sure it is made soon, sir!" he said.

Without answering, Kassein walked away from the little gathering, already fed up with them. He hated crowds, and he hated the way those men looked up at him.

As soon as he'd stepped away, he heard them exclaiming out loud about the superb kills or the amount of meat they'd eat for dinner. Dinner. He realized he hadn't brought lunch for Alezya. Was she hungry? He hadn't seen time pass while he was out hunting.

He walked across the camp, usually quieter at this time of the day. The tribes wouldn't attack when the sun was so high in the sky, any attack the camp would see coming. Most units had heavy training in the morning, so the afternoon was their only rest time, where they could play games in the tents, chat while doing their chores, or simply walk around the camp. Some went hunting, while others gathered at the training ground to fight for fun or train some more.

A lot actually went there in the hope their Commander in Chief would decide to spar with them too. That was often his preference when the days got too long and he didn't know what else to do with himself.

Fighting was easy and didn't require thinking. Most of all, he hated when he had too much time to think. To remember.

That day in particular, most of the men were busy helping with the repairs at the entrance of the camp, so things were quieter than usual.

He crossed paths with almost nobody when he reached his tent. Nobody saw him slow down before getting to his own tent. Kein was out there, lying down and taking a nap. His dragon opened an eye upon feeling his approach and showed its fangs with a very faint growl, but Kassein ignored it.

He stepped inside the tent, mentally braving himself, and immediately feeling foolish for it. What was he nervous for...? He could defeat bears and snow leopards, but he had to be mentally prepared to face a woman?

Still, he walked inside and looked for Alezya. He found her standing again, although she was using the furniture next to her to help her stand.

She'd walked across the tent and was standing next to the chest where he kept his clothes and weapons.

He glanced toward the corner that was mostly his armory. A quick count told him there was one small dagger missing. So that was why she'd been walking around his tent... He scoffed. He wasn't upset that she'd taken a weapon for herself; in fact, he was just admiring her a bit more for looking for something to defend herself with. That woman was definitely resilient, he'd give her that.

"Kassein," she simply said, as if she needed to acknowledge his presence.

He took a deep breath and walked over.

She didn't seem particularly wary of him, as her body language didn't change much from him coming closer to her. If she was flustered he'd found her there, she was concealing it well.

"Are you hungry?" he asked her.

She frowned.

"Food?"

She immediately nodded. She had learned that word before, so at least they could use that. Kassein directed his eyes toward the weapons, and immediately, Alezya's attitude shifted slightly. She was worried he'd notice what she'd done, but he didn't want to pretend he didn't know.

Thus, he walked past her and took one of the small daggers; he had plenty of those and he'd sometimes have to leave them behind. He showed it to her.

"Dagger," he simply said, clearly showing the weapon.

Alezya stared at him, visibly confused. She knew he knew, and she didn't understand why he wasn't mad. At least, that was his take.

Kassein repeated the word again, and she bit her lower lip. He stood, wanting to stop her from doing that; her lip was already injured, what was she harming it more for?

But before his thumb reached her lip, Alezya took out the small dagger she'd taken, as if to confess, and handed it back to him.

Kassein chuckled, realizing that maybe she'd thought he was asking for it back. He shook his head, and gently pushed her hand with the weapon back toward her. He pointed his index finger at the weapon, then back to her.

"Your dagger. Alezya's dagger. You can keep it."

She stared at him, still a bit confused, or maybe surprised by his willingness to let her take a weapon for herself. But he smiled at her faintly and turned back to head outside of the tent.

Somehow, that confusion in her eyes made him happy. Why was that? Another mystery. Still, Kassein walked out of the tent to go and get food. The soldiers he walked past seemed surprised to see him again, and he did realize he'd been going out a lot more...

Usually, all his food was brought directly to his tent, while his only outings were to hunt or climb up the mountains, and never more than twice a day, so his men seldom had a chance to see him unless the barbarians attacked, or he decided to hit the training ground. This was a rare sight that left a lot of them dumbfounded.

Their gazes annoyed Kassein even more when he'd just come for two bowls of meat soup. Thus, he hurried back, ignoring them all to bring the warm food back to Alezya.

The woman was back on the bed, sitting with her dagger still in her hands. She lifted her eyes up to him when he walked in, but she didn't try to conceal the weapon. Instead, she just put it aside and took the bowl of food. He'd thought this before, but she was too skinny. Did the tribes not hunt enough? The men he'd fought were all of decent size for their height, though.

The scene of Alezya being attacked came back to mind. Was she starved by her own kind? She ate with the appetite of someone who knew to appreciate food, not unnecessarily slow and gracefully like the women who usually tried to seduce him. He preferred that. He'd always hated the decorum of the Imperial Palace...

He sat down on the floor and began eating too, the two of them enjoying the food in silence.

"...*Ruokaa*," he finally said, suddenly remembering that word she'd taught him.

He glanced up at her to see her surprised eyes.

As if to confirm, he pointed at the meat stew in their bowls and repeated that word again. She smiled and nodded.

Then, they simply resumed eating in silence. Kassein's mind wasn't at rest, however. He kept trying to think, glancing toward Alezya and her injuries, the bandages on her feet right next to him.

Was it really a good idea to send her back? She'd been hunted once; what if it happened again? What if he couldn't save her this time?

Outside the tent, his dragon growled, upset. Kassein knew he had to be more reasonable than the beast that mirrored his true feelings.

He had to when it was clear she wanted to go back. Her sad eyes on the mountain couldn't deceive anyone. Moreover, if she wasn't happy about going back, she could always let him know the next day, while they were heading there. She'd have the entire journey back to change her mind...

For now, he was just hoping she'd rest and get better. He hoped Tievin wouldn't come back too soon with those undergarments and whatever else he would have found for her, and he hoped his men wouldn't make her coat too soon.

However, Kassein knew a coat and underwear wouldn't be a good enough reason to hold her back. He hated even more that he felt like he needed a reason not to send that woman back to her people.

Despite all this and the dragon raging outside, he hardened his heart and decided they'd go out the next day to send her back. The next day, at dawn.

The sooner he sends Alezya back to her people, the sooner he'd be able to forget her.

Chapter 5

The silence between them wasn't awkward, but it was unsettling.

That man, Kassein, had a dark expression in his eyes that she didn't like. He'd cleaned himself before going out, and he'd come back covered in blood again. Was that animal blood? Or...?

For some reason, Alezya wished he hadn't fought against her kind. She was an outcast of her clan, but she didn't hate most of those people enough to wish for their deaths. Perhaps she was too kind, or perhaps she was holding on to the last bit of respect she had for them to not completely despise them. It was still her homeland, after all.

And, most importantly, she hoped someone had found Lumie. A kind clan, one that would have protected her. That was what she hoped, the thought she was holding on to.

When she'd caught a glimpse of the mountains earlier that day, she'd felt subjugated with pain again. She only wanted to go back for Lumie. She loved the mountain itself, but aside from her baby, there was nothing and no one waiting for her up there. All she wanted was to retrieve her baby, and then...

She stared at Kassein again.

That man was hard to understand. He had an aura of anger, fear, and death surrounding him at all times, yet he was kind to her. Maybe it was because she was a woman as he didn't seem kind to anyone else.

When they'd briefly gone out earlier that day, she'd seen many, many more men, and it was clear they all feared him. Those men seemed to fear that man as much, if not more, than that gigantic beast outside.

She shuddered, just thinking about the size of the creature. The dragon. The orange-scaled dragon, with its silver eyes and blood-covered face... That beast was the most terrifying creature she'd ever seen. And yet, the dragon had acted like... like some animal bringing her an offering. It had killed a snow leopard just like that! With the size of those claws, it could probably kill a human in just one movement.

She ate a piece of meat, once again grateful for the juicy bit that filled her. She was already so much better. No matter how much she feared that man, Kassein, and his dragon, she was much better thanks to them.

She still couldn't understand exactly how those two were connected. Kassein was the only man she had ever encountered who wore orange scales like the dragon. And those were real scales. As crazy as it seemed, the scales on his arms were absolutely real... It sounded insane, and yet, she'd witnessed it with her own eyes.

Even if it had been a miracle of the gods, it was a strange sight to witness and believe. In the few hours she'd been awake and with him, that man had changed everything she knew about his kind.

She'd experienced more luxury and comfort in two days than in the last twenty years of her existence, even back when she was still her father's favorite daughter, her clan's cherished beauty. She was eating meat-filled meals and sleeping in a large, warm bed with a thick mattress. She was protected from the wind, cold, and snow by some habitation that was as big as some of the biggest caves she'd been in and had soft, thick fur carpet on every inch of the ground. She had taken a bath with hot water, and washed with those little things that smelled incredibly good. She had changed clothes, had been given coats, and all her injuries were taken care of by their medicine with fresh, new bandages every time.

Alezya was shocked at how much wealth was spent on her, and she couldn't tell if that man was just so wealthy he didn't care, or if she was somehow given special treatment. She had always known the Dragon Clan was wealthy, but to this extent?

A part of her knew that this was mostly that man, Kassein's doing.

He was obviously someone important here. He hadn't let any of the other men approach her, and he was almost the only one she'd interacted with. And he was a strange man himself.

He washed her feet and carried her. He had given her his bed and a bath while he'd washed himself with just a cloth. Even in wealthy families with a loving couple, she knew the man always bathed before the woman, and the wife would use the same water later. But she'd been allowed a bath all for herself when the water was still clean and steaming hot. Moreover, he hadn't bathed himself? Perhaps things just worked differently in the Dragon Clan, but she was still shocked by everything.

Most surprisingly, he hadn't tried to touch her. By now, with all those displays of kindness and consideration, any man of the clans would have said he'd done enough to be entitled to some compensation. He had gone to far greater lengths than any man would to please a woman and make her his fiancee, or just take her to bed...

Yet, Kassein hadn't touched her, hadn't even tried anything with her.

She almost would have preferred if he'd acted like most men, brutal and entitled. The fact that he was so kind to her was unsettling, and distracting.

Alezya didn't want to let her thoughts linger anywhere too far from her baby. In fact, as kind as Kassein had been, all he did only added to the guilt that was piling up inside. How could she be so comfortable when she had no idea what her baby was going through? How could she stay there, be healed and cared for, when she was being the worst mother of all, unable to protect her child?

Every second that passed, she thought of Lumie.

She missed her so much, her heart ached non-stop. She hoped her baby was alright, fine and safe, somewhere, so much. She wanted to throw all of this away, she would have renounced every bit of this kindness and luxury if it had brought her daughter back. Sadly, she knew she needed all of it. She needed to get stronger and healthier, soon. Whatever miracle Kassein had used to make her recover so fast, she was grateful, for it made her hopes to go back soon rise.

He had said something earlier when he'd caught her looking at the mountain. She wasn't sure what, but she had a feeling he was about to send her back. At least, that was what she'd deciphered in his attitude.

No matter what, she'd go back the next day. She had to. If her feet kept healing at the pace they'd been all this time, she'd be fine to walk and climb the next day. And she couldn't wait any longer than that to find out what had happened to her child, and also, what was going on with her clan. Something was going on, she could tell.

It had been brief, but she'd definitely recognized two of her father's henchmen spying on them from the mountain behind Kassein's habitation. It had only been a split second before the orange dragon had suddenly started tearing up the ground, distracting her, but she was sure she'd recognized their faces. Her eyes were so good that she'd been able to read their expressions, and neither had seemed shocked to see her, nor to see the dragon down there, rather quiet instead of killing humans.

Something about the fact that two of her father's henchmen had seen her was very unsettling. Why? Why would her father have bothered to send two of his men so far to spy on her?

That mountain was quite a distance from their clan's territory, and very risky to be in, given the proximity to the Dragon Clan people. Even if they'd known she'd survived, why would they bother to check up on her? Were they looking for Lumie? Did her father's pride justify sending two of his men to such a dangerous area...?

There was no way that was the only time they'd spied on her; how else would they have known where she was? This place was very wide, with many habitations like Kassein's, some a lot closer to the mountains and with safer areas for spying. But right when she'd come out, two of her father's men had been there.

No, they ought to have known she'd been taken to that place, which meant they'd probably seen Kassein save her. Did they hope to get something from her?

Perhaps that was it. Her father would never say no to information about their worst enemy. If he had Lumie, Alezya wouldn't think twice about trading any intel he wanted for her child. Not only was any price worth her baby's safety, but after she'd spent a couple of days here, she was now certain their clan could never win against Kassein's. Her father was delusional to hope he'd ever win against the Dragon Clan...

Either way, she could use that. If her estimation of the number of days that had passed was right, the council gathering in which her father had planned to sacrifice Lumie shouldn't have happened yet. Which meant, if he had Lumie, she had to be alive.

That was only one possibility though. Alezya was still silently praying every second she could that someone good had found her baby, that Lumie was safe and sound, just waiting for her mom to return.

She internally swore she'd never allow herself to part from her baby again once they were reunited.

"Alezya?"

She glanced up at Kassein, who was staring at her with a concerned expression, and realized she'd begun crying. She wiped her tears, mad at herself that she'd let her emotions show.

As unbelievably kind as he'd been, she didn't want him to know what she was going through. In fact, she didn't want to let him in more than she already had. She was infinitely grateful for everything he'd done for her so far, but she didn't want to get attached and she didn't want him to know anything about what was truly going on. Despite all this, she knew better than anyone how men could suddenly turn from kind to cruel overnight. Even like this, when he was gently getting closer to her and putting his hand on hers, she didn't want to rely on him any more than she'd already done. He couldn't ask, and he couldn't understand.

Even if he'd had the language for it, he wouldn't have understood the pain she was going through. He looked like a strong man, with no one relying on him to survive. She was all that Lumie had, the only one who could protect her child, and she'd failed. She'd failed as a mom.

Alezya kept silently crying, neither acknowledging nor pushing away Kassein's hand on hers.

Her feet still hurt when she stood, but she didn't care about the pain; it couldn't compare to that of losing her child. She would have gone back bleeding without a second of hesitation if she'd been sure she'd make it to Lumie.

Except that she knew her own limits. She was feeling good enough to stand now, but Alezya knew the mountain wouldn't be so kind. The climb would kill her if she went back now, but she just needed a bit more. Just a bit more time, and she'd be fine to go back.

She couldn't understand the miracle by which she was healing so fast, but that was the miracle she needed. She only wished she'd healed even faster.

Every minute was too precious to lose, and yet all she could do was be there, eat meat, and hope that would help her journey back, giving her the strength she needed to go back to her child.

Kassein was still looking concerned for her when voices outside made them both look in that direction. He gave her another glance before standing up and going out. Alezya let out a long breath, forcing herself to calm down. She wiped her tears and took deep breaths, trying to suppress the sadness deep inside.

She had to be strong. She couldn't allow herself to fall apart, not now. There was still hope. If Lumie was alive, she had survived so far. Yes. She had to believe her baby was fine and just waiting for her. That was the only thought she needed for now.

"Alezya?"

Kassein had returned, carrying something. He put a leather bag next to her on the bed and gestured very simply for her to understand that it was for her. What was it this time? He took her empty bowl from her, and left again, confusing her.

She opened the little bag. Undergarments! They were different from her own, but they were obviously meant for a woman. She immediately felt grateful. She was used to living scarcely, but putting dirty underwear back on was far from comfortable... Now she understood why he'd left.

She quickly cleaned herself again using the water from the washing basin and changed into them. Not only that but there was also a new pair of leather pants, also meant for a woman, a pair of shoes, and some gloves, also her size. They were incredibly well made and comfortable, with rabbit fur inside and leather outside.

She was at a loss for words. This was too much... She didn't need to wear the clothes here, but they'd surely be a huge help when she had to climb her way back.

She kept them next to her and wondered if she was supposed to take the bag too. She could always put food supplies in it... Would Kassein let her take dried meat?

She glanced toward the entrance. She could hear male voices talking, and she recognized the voice of the skinny man from earlier, the one called Tievin. He and Kassein's voices were audible for a while, although she had no idea what they could possibly be talking about...

After a while, it sounded like they walked away from the way their voices gradually diminished. Done with her food and getting dressed, Alezya hesitated. She was curious to go outside and check if those men were still spying... She probably wouldn't risk anything by going out, right?

Kassein hadn't chained her nor specified in any way that she shouldn't go out. She'd been completely unrestrained, except for her injured feet. She couldn't hear the growls from before, either. Did the dragon go away?

Despite being nervous about facing the orange dragon again, Alezya forced herself to ignore her doubts. She put on the shoes, grimacing as they rubbed against her wounds, but it was bearable. Then, she put on the thicker-looking of the coats and walked outside with great difficulty, one agonizing step after the other. The soles of her feet felt like the flesh was exposed, burning at each contact, and her ankle was still weak, sending painful protests at each movement. Still, Alezya stubbornly carried her body outside. She hesitated only a handful of seconds before pushing the curtain that was the entrance.

For the first time, she ventured outside without Kassein by her side.

At a quick glance, the man with the orange scales was nowhere to be seen, but there were a handful of men in sight. Most seemed busy with something and didn't even notice her. Alezya didn't want to be noticed, so she quickly stepped away from the habitation and turned around to look at the mountain.

Before she could set eyes on the mountain though, something else came into her line of sight, something far too big and too significant to ignore. The orange dragon.

She'd been mistaken to think it was gone simply because she couldn't hear it. The dragon was still there, its humongous body surrounding the place she'd just walked out of. Alezya gasped and immediately covered her mouth.

Even if it hadn't heard that, the dragon was already watching her. Although it was hard to say, with its pupils as large as silver trays, she could feel the beast's stare was on her. It let a hot whiff out of its nostrils, and as soon as it moved, Alezya took a step away, unable to hold it.

The dragon's head moved toward her and sniffed a couple of times. Then, it let out a soft growl.

The fact that she couldn't move, frozen by fear, combined with the dragon's apparent calm, forced Alezya to stand still for a few seconds.

At least, during those seconds, she was somehow able to breathe and calm down a little. The dragon wasn't going to attack her, or it would have already. She was no expert on dragons, but she knew most beasts didn't stay lying down when prey was right in front of them, and that dragon's humongous body was still lying in the snow with no visible intent to attack.

Even if it did, her body stood far enough from its fangs that she'd have time to move before it was up and she was within reach... or so she really hoped.

"Stay... still."

She had gathered all her courage to utter those two words, with no idea if that dragon would understand or obey them. Still, it was a bit reassuring to her that Kein, if that was really the dragon's name, remained still and calm. She forced herself to push the fear away, and finally moved her eyes from the dragon toward the mountain.

Immediately, her hawk-like gaze found them. Two silhouettes, perched high in the mountain, higher than before. She glared at them. What did they want? Why stay posted there, just to check on her? If they already knew she was alive, why would they stay there?

Just then, she saw one of them draw a weapon, and she stepped back. They were aiming at her.

Alezya didn't have time to think before a loud growl echoed throughout the area. Kein too had noticed the intruders, and was not happy to see them either.

Something flew by Alezya's cheek, and a sting immediately followed. She grimaced, but before she could make sense of it, the earth trembled beneath her and violent gusts of wind knocked her off her feet.

Her body hit the snow painfully, and she had just enough time to open her eyes to see the orange dragon taking off, its wings throwing layers of snow around below it.

She covered her eyes, trying to protect herself.

"Alezya!"

Less than two seconds after that, Kassein appeared next to her, shielding her. She had no idea how he'd arrived so fast, but she could hear many voices around them, his men visibly unsettled by the dragon, or perhaps they'd seen the clansmen too.

Kassein helped her up. The snowstorm provoked by Kein had died already, while the dragon was furiously attacking the mountain.

That's when Alezya started to piece things together. She touched her cheek, feeling the cut there. Kassein's green eyes were on her injury too, frowning again.

She ignored it and looked around. She found an arrow, planted in the ground right next to where she'd been lying moments ago... and that wasn't all. Her heart dropped.

"*Alezya? Ku ti bikhyan?*"

She didn't listen to him, she actually barely heard him.

She fell down on her knees and dug the snow around that arrow to reveal the object attached to it. Her heart sank even lower when she confirmed what it was. Her mother's necklace.

There was no doubt. It was one of a kind, the only necklace she had of her mother's, the one she'd left with Lumie before parting with her.

Next to her, Kassein seemed to be shouting orders to his men, but she didn't care; she didn't care about anything but the precious necklace she was clenching, held tight in her fist. She darted her glare back to the mountain. This was a message. They had her daughter. They had Lumie, and they wanted her to know.

Which meant they wanted her to come back, the gods knew for what. She tightened her fist around that necklace. She hoped the dragon got them. She hoped Kein caught her father's men and ripped them to pieces.

For a long while, Alezya was too mad and upset to move.

She didn't care about what was happening around her, she didn't care for all the men sending her glances, running in all directions, drawing weapons, and pointing fingers at the mountain.

All she could feel was the grasp she had on her necklace.

Her father had Lumie. That thought was horrible enough to send shivers down her spine, and yet, it was an incommensurable relief. They'd found her daughter and sent her this, which meant chances were high that her daughter was alive. Alezya found herself in a strange state of mind, overwhelmed by relief, and yet more angst rising than ever before.

She remained still, trapped in her thoughts. What did her father want by sending her this? Why had his men waited until she was alone to send her this? There was something bigger at work here.

There was no need to let her know her daughter was with them and still alive if Lumie was to be sacrificed soon. Why would her father send her this, knowing she'd come back for her daughter? After he had driven her to leave and almost gotten her killed, what could have gotten him to change his mind?

"Alezya."

Kassein's voice took her out of her spiral thinking.

She realized things had calmed down around them and nodded faintly as she stood up, trying to regain her composure.

It seemed like he'd sent most of his men away, and the dragon, Kein, was already back. To think she hadn't noticed the large beast coming back spoke volumes about her state of mind...

In fact, she felt a bit faint. Without thinking, she grabbed Kassein's arm to hold on, and he caught her before her legs gave out.

Effortlessly, Kassein put an arm under her and, while saying something to Tievin, who had run over with him, he carried her back inside his habitation. Alezya felt on the verge of passing out until she was sat back down on the bed. The chaos had been left outside, and it helped her calm down a bit.

Moreover, Kassein hadn't let go of her, his hand still holding her forearm, as if he was worried she'd pass out any second.

"...She's alive," Alezya finally muttered.

It was as if she needed to say it herself to believe it. The thought hit her, and she chuckled nervously. She began crying while smiling, which was strange, but a perfect reflection of her state of mind.

"She's alive," she repeated, now sobbing. "My baby's alive."

She broke down in tears, covering her face with her hands, her shoulders shaking. It still felt unreal, and yet, she'd never been so grateful.

The tiny string of hope she'd been holding on to all this time was now a thick rope she could use to climb back up. The confirmation that Lumie was alive was all she'd needed, and now, she had it.

She kept crying, unleashing all the emotions she'd managed to restrain so far, feeling a distraught Kassein's hands on her arms.

Of course he was confused. He had to be. She moved her hands down to only cover her nose and mouth and smiled at him, her smile carrying to her eyes. She wanted to let him know she was fine.

At least now, she was. She put her hands down, grabbing either side of the bed next to her, and smiling between her tears.

"Lumie's alive." She smiled. "She's alive, Kassein. My Lumie."

She needed to share her joy and relief, although he probably understood nothing of it. He simply stared at her, still completely confused. Aware she probably looked a bit crazy, Alezya wiped her tears and forced herself to calm down.

Despite the joy, she also couldn't completely ignore everything that was still waiting ahead. Her child was far from safe yet, and the fact that it was almost certain she had survived was a big relief, but it didn't mean they were done and out of harm's way. But if her father had kept her alive, that meant there was a way. He wouldn't have waited for Alezya nor let her know he had her child if things were as simple as wanting to kill Lumie during the council gathering as he'd planned to.

Just that thought was enough to give her all the hope she'd been needing to carry on. She was going to go back and find a way to keep her baby safe, no matter what. No matter what her father wanted in exchange, she would do it. Absolutely nothing could be worth more than her baby's safety. Nothing.

Just as she felt that wave of relief wash over her, Alezya stared into Kassein's green eyes. It was like her heart had suddenly warmed up with the perspective of seeing her little girl again.

Suddenly, she felt grateful, incredibly grateful to him. If he hadn't saved her, she wouldn't have had a chance to see her baby again. She wouldn't have survived long enough to get another chance to see her daughter. Both she and Lumie would have been condemned.

She had felt nothing but guilt for all he'd done for her before, but now, she was truly overwhelmed with gratitude. He'd taken in a complete stranger, a woman meant to be his enemy and he had healed her, fed her, and made sure she was safe all along. Kassein was the one man who'd made it all possible. He'd been kind, and much more.

Without thinking, she leaned forward to put her arms around his neck and hugged him.

She felt him freeze, probably even more confused now. Alezya was well aware she ought to look crazy, suddenly hugging a complete stranger after crying and smiling so much out of the blue. Still, she felt the need to hug him, just this once, to let him know how grateful she was. How much she'd come to trust him and his kindness.

It lasted a few seconds before she released him. He was still completely stiff, and after a little while longer, she began to worry she'd stepped over some invisible line she shouldn't have crossed.

"Kassein?"

She called his name, but he didn't answer.

Instead, he suddenly stood up, stepped away from her, and walked out, leaving her there, utterly confused. Alezya waited, for a bit, but there was no sign of him coming back.

That's when she started to really get anxious. Had she done something wrong? Perhaps she'd unknowingly broken some custom of theirs?

Now she regretted her impulsive move. She'd been so overtaken by her emotions, she hadn't thought straight and just jumped at his neck...

She was feeling foolish. She sighed and took off her coat, leaving it to dry at the end of the bed. She hoped Kassein would come back so she could apologize.

However, he didn't come back for a long time after that. Alezya waited until late, but only that man, Tievin, came much later to bring her some food for dinner.

As he stepped inside, she tried to ask him.

"Kassein?"

He glanced at her, and instead of answering, just shrugged and walked out.

Now she was upset. Did he not know, did he not care, or did he just not want to tell her?

She was tempted to go out and look for him, but it was now dark outside, and she was wary she'd face the dragon again. Although she had survived three out of three encounters with it, she didn't want to push her luck and relive the experience again.

Thus, she ate in silence, feeling strangely lonely... She was listening for any sounds, any signs of Kassein coming back, but even long after she'd finished eating, nobody came to take the empty bowl away.

She sat on the bed, straightened her clothes, laid the coats on the bed, and combed her long hair with her fingers, thinking.

She had barely parted with her necklace since she'd gotten it back, and now that she was staring at this precious thing she'd set down on her lap, the darkness and loneliness were letting some dark thoughts creep in. What if she was wrong? What if her father didn't have Lumie, what if he'd only found the necklace?

No, it didn't make sense. She was sure she'd attached it tightly around her daughter's neck. It was her only memento of her mother, the most prized possession she had, and the one thing she valued most after Lumie. This little necklace couldn't be a decoy either; it held the symbol of her mother's birth clan, the Lumiata, and it couldn't be copied easily.

Moreover, this pendant was old and bore the same imperfections she'd always known it to have. She knew it was definitely the necklace she'd left with Lumie...

Then, what could her father possibly want? The only thing she could think of was intel on the Dragon Clan. If his men had seen her here for quite some time, maybe the madman had decided that information about the enemy was more important than a child's sacrifice.

Her father was obsessed with his pride and maintaining his status in front of the other clans. Under the pretense of safekeeping peace with alliances and betrothals, the council gatherings were usually a way for those men to prove their clan was more worthy than the others, to show off their wealth and how powerful they were, and to prevent future wars. Since everything was so scarce and each clan desperate for survival, wars happened anyway, but the clans carefully chose an enemy, and anyone who'd shown weakness at the council gathering was vulnerable.

Those gatherings were nothing more than a show to display wealth they didn't have, show off new weapons they'd invented, gloat about the amount of prey they'd killed, and pretend their mountain was the biggest, most comfortable one.

Her father's clan's prestige relied a lot on their proximity to the Dragon Clan's people. He pretended they were at the forefront of the fight against the Dragon Tyrant and its people, and would once in a while show off a weapon they'd supposedly gotten from the men they'd killed.

The pathetic truth was that they rarely fought, and mostly hid. So, perhaps seeing his daughter actually last behind enemy lines had given her cunning father some ideas. She wouldn't have been surprised; information that could be used against the Dragon Clan was considered far more valuable than anything else, for it was most of the clans' impossible dream to one day be able to get down to those lands to access more food and living space.

With that thought in mind, Alezya looked around the space she was in. They'd been right on one thing: the Dragon Clan was far wealthier than their clans. She'd experienced so much good food and had eaten more meat in two days than the wealthiest people of her clan ate in a week. She'd never seen a more comfortable living space, nor enjoyed so many furs to protect her from the cold. Not only that, they had enough to gift her two coats without thinking about it. She'd never had enough money to buy a fur coat... Fur was expensive enough, but the price easily tripled with the craft to turn it into a piece of clothing. The ones she did have were all from her mother, or what she'd been given prior to her wedding that she could keep, and since she couldn't buy any, the bits of fur she'd been able to hunt by herself, she'd used them all on Lumie.

She quietly washed herself with that good-smelling thing again, wondering what face her father would have made if he'd seen what luxury she had been living in after she had just survived certain death. She had been numb to most of it in the pain of losing Lumie, though.

One thing her father would never, ever understand was how she would easily trade all this to get back her child, without an ounce of regret.

In fact, the only thing she hoped was that Lumie would get to experience such wealth one day... Her hand stopped moving.

What if, after whatever deal her father wanted to make, she came back here with Lumie? If the clans didn't want her, why couldn't she try again in the Dragon Clan?

If she was honest with herself, she'd always dreamt of a new life down here, in a world she'd only ever been able to stare at. She'd hoped to be able to join another clan, one that was hostile to her father, but maybe, this was even better. She didn't care about being labeled a traitor, she had been wearing that one for a while now.

Now that she'd seen and experienced the Dragon Clan for herself, it didn't seem that crazy anymore to come here with Lumie for a second chance. From what she'd seen, these people weren't as bad or barbaric as the clans had painted them to be... although most of her interactions had been with Kassein.

She let out a faint sigh. She'd have to leave him; no matter how kind he was, no man in his right mind would want a woman who'd already been married and had a child with another man. Moreover, there was no telling how he'd react to Lumie. Her baby was different, and she had yet to see anyone react positively to her unique appearance.

Tired, Alezya chased all those thoughts away. She was thinking too far into the future, making too many conjectures.

She finished cleaning herself up, and slid into bed, wearing only her new underwear and tunic. The fire in the middle of the habitation was slowly dying, but she was afraid she'd do something wrong if she tried to take care of it herself since she didn't know how they made their habitations safe despite it. She assumed that strange channel above it was the key.

She glanced toward the entrance, but there was still no sign of Kassein. In fact, she couldn't hear anything but the gentle wind blowing the snow around. She curled up under the covers, grimacing a bit at her painful feet. She had to leave the next day, so she hoped they would heal as much as possible during the night. She would have waited longer for Kassein, if she wasn't so eager to recover, and leave to see her daughter again. Still alone as the habitation grew darker, she couldn't find sleep. Too much had happened, and everything was too quiet.

After a while of hesitation, she opened her lips.

"...Kein?"

She had barely whispered that into the dark, but a soft growl answered her from the other side of the fabric behind her, making her smile. The dragon was still there, at least. This crazy, dangerous creature was suddenly a little bit of a comforting presence surrounding the place.

It also made her believe Kassein would eventually come back. She didn't want to leave without at least saying goodbye to her benefactor.

Just like that, Alezya gently drifted to sleep.

More tired than she'd let on, she didn't hear Kassein come back inside, and she didn't even wake up when he removed the heavy, fire-colored gear and set his sword aside.

He fanned the flames of the fire a bit, made sure the habitation was sealed shut except for the hole the smoke escaped through, and then, he finally went to lay on the fur rug right next to the bed Alezya was sleeping on.

He had just closed his eyes when she opened hers, perhaps woken up by the sudden proximity.

With no idea they'd missed each other by a handful of seconds, she stared at his large figure sleeping beneath her. So he had left her his bed indeed and was sleeping on the floor. She watched him sleep for a little while with mixed feelings.

She was still nervous about what she'd done wrong, and a bit sorry. She hoped he'd be up when she left the next day. She wasn't sure what he understood of all this, what he thought of it.

Perhaps he thought she was crazy, and was just helping her out of the kindness of his heart. It still baffled her how such a powerful man could act so kind and humbly toward a foreign woman. Was he like that to all the women he knew? If so, the Dragon Clan's people were far kinder than she'd have ever imagined.

But she couldn't help but think that Kassein had been especially kind to her. He hadn't let other men approach, yet he hadn't staked any sort of claim on her.

It was strange, a bit unsettling, and yet it made her feel safe and grateful. But Alezya tried not to think about it too deeply and blew her feelings away. She couldn't get over how stiffly he'd reacted to her hugging him, and it made her embarrassed. She'd been foolish. Perhaps she'd misread the way he looked at her all along... It would be too late to know now. She had to leave, so those questions would perhaps never be answered. Alezya drifted back to sleep, with a bit of a heartache.

The next morning, she woke up first.

She felt refreshed, but her heart was still heavy. Now that she was faced with the prospect of going back, she felt nervous to face her father again. She wanted to see her daughter so bad though and confirm that she was fine that she couldn't hesitate.

While Kassein slept, she quickly got dressed. She must have made a bit of noise though, for Kassein slowly woke up just as she was almost done and making the bed. Their gazes met, and she found herself blushing before she could control it.

"Kassein..."

It was frustrating that she couldn't have him understand her with words, but even if she did, she didn't know what she would have said.

Thankfully, he didn't seem upset at all. He nodded and slowly got up, quietly stretching his impressive figure; rarely had she seen such an imposing man.

Since he was half-naked again, she could see there were far fewer orange scales than the previous day and more human skin. So those scales were really healing him...

She was still completely shocked at the phenomenon, but that only made her even more curious about the scars he did have. Some were atrocious and made her wonder if her people had done that. She wouldn't dare ask, however.

She simply waited as he got dressed, including his hard plating and his sword, wondering how to tell him she was leaving.

"Alezya."

To her surprise, as soon as he was done, he walked up to her first and handed her something. She opened her hands to receive the small object, curious as to what it was.

It was a long and thin piece of fabric, one she'd never seen before. It was incredibly smooth, but surprisingly cool to the touch, and without any imperfection like one would expect in something made with leather or wool. From a closer look, it seemed to have been woven somehow, but at such a tiny scale that the naked eye only saw a smooth surface. The color was vibrant too, a rare purple color that could never be so dashing in the wild, except for gemstones.

She was shocked to be handed something that seemed so rare and precious, and a long string of it too! She glanced up at him, confused.

Was this a gift for her? What was she to do with it? Did women of his kind wear it on their clothes, or as an accessory? It was undeniably pretty, but she was clueless as to what to do with his gift, and she feared offending him again.

To her relief, Kassein smiled and took it from her. Then, he gestured for her to turn around, and she did, feeling a bit nervous, wondering if he was to put it around her neck.

Alezya almost jumped when she felt him touch her hair.

She'd never had a man touch her hair before! A woman's hair was sacred, and only women could touch it, except for one's husband!

Still, she battled with her instincts to stay still, well aware Kassein couldn't possibly know about that.

Now she was curious as to what he was doing. Married women could tie up their hair, but since her own marriage had been annulled by her kind, she couldn't be seen with her hair up, or she'd risk another beating.

She wondered what the elders would think of her letting a Dragon Clan man do her hair... but she kind of enjoyed it. Despite his large hands, Kassein's fingers were very gentle, not pulling at any point, just combing through and moving the strands in a mysterious way. It made her nape feel a bit hot, and blood rushed to her cheeks again. Alezya tried to ignore those feelings again and stay still.

Moreover, it felt like Kassein knew exactly what he was doing, and she could feel him quickly move through her strands, combing it here and there with his fingers, and tying the long strand of that strange fabric in it. When his fingers finally left her hair, she couldn't help but let out a faint sigh of relief.

Then, he stepped back, and she was free to touch and feel what he'd done. Just from what she could visualize, it ought to be pretty.

He'd braided the sides while leaving the rest to hang loose, with a pretty, butterfly-like knot binding some of her hair together at her nape. Her hair wasn't too tightly done like a married woman's hairstyle, but it wasn't as free and loose as her people would expect from a rejected woman either. It was in some strange area in between, out of the norms.

She liked it. The idea that such a vibrant, unique thing was adorning her hair made her feel ten times prettier. She felt guilty for feeling so when so many things were going on, but it made for a wonderful parting gift from him. She wished she had something to give to him, but the only thing she owned was her mother's necklace, which she wanted to give to no one but Lumie.

Alezya turned back around and smiled at him, hoping to convey how grateful she was. Kassein nodded, but he quickly avoided her gaze again, making her feel dejected. Instead, he went to the fire and began cooking something in a pan.

Eggs! The biggest eggs she'd ever seen too. What kind of animal did those come from...?

She'd been lucky enough to find eggs twice before, but those were about three times the size of the ones she'd found! They were much bigger than most birds she knew, except for rare vulture eggs. Although she'd hoped to leave as soon as possible, her stomach immediately begged for a taste of those before she went. She'd need the strength after all.

Even worse, Kassein brought out something she assumed to be bread, but a different bread from the type she knew. Everything was done cooking in a matter of minutes, and soon, a plate full of eggs, bread, and fruits was pushed into her hands. Alezya sighed, but she resolved herself to eat nonetheless, knowing she'd need the strength, and guilt wouldn't do her any good.

Moreover, she didn't know when she'd have her next decent meal, as she wasn't foolish enough to expect a warm welcome once she got back. It would even be a miracle if her life wasn't harder than before, after what she'd pulled... although she was going there blind about her father's intentions. She only hoped Lumie had been properly fed all this time. Her father couldn't be bothered with taking care of a child he didn't acknowledge, so she silently prayed the clan's nannies or her cousin had at least fed her decently.

With those thoughts in mind, her breakfast had a taste of guilt, but it still filled her stomach well. Kassein was still silent and avidly avoiding her gaze, which was beginning to upset her quite a bit.

He still didn't look at her when they were done and he took the plates away. Unwilling to press him, Alezya simply put on the coat, hoping it was fine for her to take it with her.

Then, she resolved to call him, to let him know her intentions.

"Kassein?"

He finally turned his green eyes to her. She smiled, but her heart wasn't there. She showed him the entrance, with a determined expression, hoping to convey what she wanted to say.

To her surprise, he seemed to understand right away and nodded. He grabbed his large cape, and strapped it on his torso, obviously getting ready to go out. Probably to gauge how her walking was that morning, he gestured for her to go out first with his open hand. Alezya nodded and took the few steps to the entrance.

Much to her relief, she was fine to walk on her own. It was still painful, but not nearly as much as it used to be, and she could easily endure it to walk. The climb should be fine too.

As she was the first one out, Alezya glanced around. It was very early, but this place was already busy. She saw lines of men pass by, all of them running in tight formation at the same pace, clearly for some sort of training. A lot of them spotted her and lost focus while turning their heads, losing the pace they were supposed to follow or making the ones behind them stumble. She chuckled, but a quick shout from their leader running beside them got them back in formation.

Other men were busy with what ought to be daily chores, some moving large buckets of clothes with a grimace, or pulling carts around. She could hear the clatter of weapons in the distance, but the calm atmosphere suggested it was some sort of training.

Alezya felt a bit melancholic; while well aware she was an intruder in a man's world, her curiosity made her feel unsatisfied she hadn't been healthy enough to explore more of this foreign world.

"Alezya."

Kassein had walked ahead of her, and much to her relief, he seemed to be headed toward the mountain too.

While she nodded and followed him, Alezya couldn't help but think about his attitude again. Did that mean he'd just been waiting for her to get healthier to send her back? Or had he understood her intent from the beginning? ...Or was it because she'd hugged him the previous night?

She couldn't get her faux pas out of her head. It was even worse to think she was going after making that mistake, leaving things unresolved between them. Although she knew she most likely wouldn't be coming back or seeing him again, Alezya felt unsettled.

The two of them remained quiet during their walk through the camp, and that silence felt heavier than anything that could be explained by a lack of vocabulary.

Soon enough, they reached the far end of this place, close to the foot of the mountain, and Alezya saw for the first time the large wooden walls that separated their worlds.

There were a lot of men working on some damage that had been done there, and most were seeing her for the first time, unable to not stare. She tried to ignore them, but she did step closer to Kassein, a bit nervous.

That other man was there too, Tievin. He was wearing a different coat again and that bored expression, with his nose a bit red. He asked some questions to

Kassein, judging by his tone, but the latter didn't bother to answer. A couple of times, Tievin glanced her way, but she didn't know what he was thinking. He walked with them for a little while toward the barrier, speaking to Kassein the whole time despite him not answering.

Then, when they reached the wall, standing a few feet away, he shouted something. Much to Alezya's surprise, several men ran over, and like a rehearsed choreography, they grabbed large ropes and pulled. It took a few seconds, but the wooden panel in front of them was gradually lifted.

She opened her mouth, shocked. That was such impressive engineering! The barrier stood firmly to protect them, but they could lift it anytime with the strength of twenty men thanks to those large ropes...

When she realized her own people's main defense was simply using their expertise of the mountain to hide, it hit her again that they'd never win against the Dragon Clan. Her father's dream of conquering these lands was just laughable. Even if she spilled everything she'd seen for Lumie's sake, it would take her clan decades to compete with the Dragon Clan, and this made her feel a little bit more hopeful.

After exchanging a glance, she and Kassein walked beyond the wooden wall, which shortly closed behind them. Things got a lot more tense and silent from then on. Alezya glanced up at those mountains which had been her home her whole life.

They felt much taller and imposing when she was looking at them from down here. Now that it was time to go back, the only thing that was pushing her forward was the prospect of seeing Lumie again. Otherwise, she wouldn't have been foolish enough to go back. After what she'd done, she knew all too well that things were bound to get a lot worse for her than being treated like a pariah.

"Alezya?"

Kassein gently calling her name got her attention. He was standing ready, waiting for her to make the first move to go back. She nodded, and quickly followed him.

In a sense, she was grateful he was taking her back, as she imagined he'd escort her at least part of the way. Before, she would have been worried it was too dangerous for him, but now that she'd realized who he was and what his body was capable of, she knew she needn't worry anymore.

Moreover, they'd chosen to go back in the early hours of the day, which might be the safest, when the sunrise was blinding a good half of the inhabitants of the mountains. With the snow, people would avoid looking at the large white area, and with a bit of luck, the arrival of two people wouldn't be noticed too soon.

It felt strange to walk toward her home with Kassein by her side, walking just one step ahead of her. She could tell he was keeping a protective stance, expecting to be attacked at any minute.

What kind of man was ready to stand in front of the enemy's daughter to protect her from her own kind? He probably didn't even understand what situation she was in, and yet, he was acting so selfless.

This made her a bit happier and braver as they began climbing. Even if she wasn't wanted up there, maybe she'd still have a chance with Lumie here. This was a thought she'd nurture once she knew what her father possibly wanted with her.

As they were getting closer to her home, and deeper in the mountain, she began to get nervous. What if her father just wanted her back to kill her? If that was the case, then Lumie was already gone, and that necklace had just been a trap.

The mere thought of her baby girl being gone from this world was enough for Alezya to accept her fate; as a mother, she wouldn't allow herself to live happily when she'd failed to protect her own child.

She knew she wouldn't have the will to. How could she? Lumie was all that she had. Even now, she was returning to the most dangerous place for herself, purely for her little girl's sake. She knew the risks.

There wouldn't be another chance to escape, and she would pay the price for what she had done.

"Alezya."

It was Kassein who spotted one of her father's men first. Alezya glanced up, and she saw them too.

They were perched far above in the mountain, looking down at them. The fact that they were merely watching and didn't react to being seen meant that they had indeed expected her return.

She and Kassein were still far from the closest access to her clan's location, but Alezya had no desire to endanger Kassein further. If her clan had seen him, she couldn't imagine they'd welcome him in any way.

As he resumed walking, she grabbed his arm. His green eyes met hers, looking a bit surprised, and she shook her head. *You shouldn't go any farther,* was what she wanted to convey, and she hoped he understood that.

They stared at each other for a while, and Kassein glanced up again. He seemed conflicted, but Alezya was resolved not to let him proceed any farther. She couldn't predict what was ahead, but she wouldn't risk endangering that man who'd been so kind to her.

Still holding his arm, she walked in front of him, placing herself between him and the path ahead. They hadn't gone too far from the camp yet; there was still about two-thirds of the path to go, but she would continue alone.

Still looking him in the eye, and with a heart heavier than she'd expected, Alezya put her hands on his torso, and gently pushed him. She was doing her best to smile, to convey her gratitude for all he'd done for her, but her feelings weren't there. She felt sad, and sorry. Sorry because she could see the confusion in his eyes. He hadn't thought to part with her so soon.

To her surprise, he put a hand over hers on his chest, staring at her with a frown on. The language barrier between them wasn't enough to stop all that his eyes were trying to convey, and Alezya's heart ached a little bit more. Once again, she forced herself to smile and hide how scared she was to go back, how upset she was to part with him. Her own feelings were beyond what she'd thought them to be, but after years of being mistreated, there was no way she wouldn't have been touched by Kassein's kindness. To have been able to rely on someone, even if it was just for a few days, had been one of the best feelings she'd experienced in a long time.

Still, she had to let go of those thoughts, and push him away. She couldn't tie Kassein to her fate any longer.

"Alezya."

She shook her head as he called her name, and looked down to avoid his eyes. She had to go, she couldn't waste another minute when Lumie was waiting for her mom to come back. Kassein knew nothing of who she was, what she'd been through, what she was about to face.

This time with him had just been a short, bittersweet respite she'd enjoyed, but now, it was time to get back to reality.

She took a step back. Kassein was still holding her hand against his chest, but she slowly took it back and separated from him.

"I'm sorry," she muttered. "Thank you for everything, Kassein."

Unable to look him in the eye again, she simply turned around, and walked away, beginning to climb up the mountain.

It was hard not to look back, but she knew her heart would only break a bit more. If he had already walked away and back to his world, it would have been painful. If he was still down there, staring at her, it would have been even worse.

Alezya swallowed her tears and feelings, still shocked at how heavy they were, and kept climbing up stubbornly. She couldn't keep any lingering feelings. It was unlikely they'd see each other again; moreover, she had to focus on Lumie now. Her daughter had been without her mom for far too long, the longest since she'd been born.

Those thoughts made Alezya climb even faster. Had she been fed well? Did she get proper sleep? Did she cry a lot? Had she been sick?

The more she brought the sweet face of her toddler to mind, the more she was in a hurry to see her again. Alezya kept climbing, feeling the mountain welcoming her back despite the circumstances.

She easily found her way back, the fresh morning snow not causing her much of an inconvenience to find her familiar and safest climbing spots, and the paths she could walk on were all free of any recent landslide. Her return was made strangely easy by the elements, adding to her unsettling feeling. She was grateful for the thick coat around her, for it was the warmest piece of clothing she'd ever possessed and was efficient in keeping the snow out of her inner clothing.

She felt her hair still firmly held by Kassein's present and the knowledge of that beautiful fabric being there made her feel a bit stronger, as if the memory of him was there to support her.

Alezya finished her climb, feeling more confident and determined than ever. She had no idea what was lying ahead, but she was more ready than she'd ever be to face it.

Alezya spotted the closest entrance to the caves that led inside the mountain her clan resided in almost too soon, in her eyes. She stopped and stood on the little cliff, taking a deep breath.

After a hesitation, she glanced back, but from that spot, she couldn't see the place where she and Kassein had parted ways or, more accurately, where she'd left him. Thus, her eyes drifted to the little area she knew his people resided in. It seemed so small from up there, although she couldn't see all of it from that flank of the mountain.

The men were reduced to little ants moving around, their wooden border to a thin line, and their habitations the size of her pinky nail. There was still no sign of Kein the dragon, and she wondered where the beast had gone. Even if she never went back down there, she was now confident that if she ever saw that orange dragon again, she would never be half as scared as she used to be. At least, she had that.

Still, she couldn't let her memories linger for too long. She walked in with a dreadful feeling. Lumie. She was going to see and hold Lumie again; that was all that mattered.

She'd only been gone for a handful of days, and yet everything seemed different. Despite walking through those familiar stone walls, Alezya felt like a complete stranger. The sounds of her clan's people getting started with their day couldn't have felt more foreign to her.

She already knew she didn't belong to this world anymore; she was only visiting because of circumstances she couldn't avoid. She'd only come back to get her daughter, that's all she knew for certain. What would happen once she and Lumie were reunited, she couldn't tell. She was scared to think of what her father had in store for her. Truth be told, she was terrified to face that man again. After what she'd done, she was expecting the worst punishment she'd ever faced. No matter how strong she was, she couldn't help but fear the pain. She only hoped he wouldn't kill her, and the beating wouldn't be so bad that she'd be too injured to care for Lumie or make the right decisions. Perhaps they'd have to flee again, which was very likely.

The first people she crossed paths with all seemed shocked to see her, so much so that they stopped whatever they were doing to stare. As she met more and more of them having the same reaction, Alezya gradually realized they'd thought her dead. For some reason, her father hadn't let the rest of the clan know about what had happened, or about her survival. To them, it was like she'd come back from the dead. Did only his henchmen know? It was even more puzzling.

Alezya wasn't surprised not to be greeted, but at least, none stopped her. She kept walking, the nervousness building up in her stomach. Never had those tunnels and caves felt so oppressing; she felt like she was walking in a snow leopard's den.

After taking another corner toward the largest cave, one of the guards finally acknowledged her presence with a disdainful look.

"He's waiting for you," he simply said, making a head movement toward the next area.

Alezya didn't answer and kept going, even more nervous. Of course her father knew she was coming back, he ought to have been informed. But the fact that he was waiting for her was nerve-wracking.

When she finally walked into the clan's main cave, she was surprised to find it mostly empty. It should have been busier than that at this time of the day, but right now, there were only a few of her father's men, the elders, her cousin's husband, and, dominating them all by his position and seated on top of a rock while they were all on the fur-covered floor, her father. That was all.

The fact that no woman was present puzzled Alezya. They only sent the women away when they were about to make important decisions. Despite feeling cornered, she came forward and stood in the middle of the circle they formed, ready to face them.

Getting Lumie back was all she wanted.

"...Daughter," her father greeted her, with a sarcastic tone. "You're back."

His strange attitude made Alezya even more worried he was about to reveal something bad. Him calling her his daughter when he'd considered her like a thorn in his side all along was the strangest thing too.

She'd have preferred his usual fit of rage; at least she knew what to expect with those...

"Where's my daughter?" she asked, her voice hoarse.

"She is alive," her father said.

"I want my daughter," Alezya insisted. "Right away."

"You're in no position to make any demands," one of the elders scolded her.

Alezya scoffed, putting on a scornful expression.

"Aren't I?" she retorted, trying to put some confidence in her tone. "Since you kept her alive and summoned me back, it feels like you're expecting something from me. If that's the case, you won't get anything until I have my child back."

"You little-!"

But her father raised his hand, cutting the older man off. There truly was something odd afoot, Alezya thought. He would have been the first to slap her for her arrogance.

The vicious smile he showed didn't help ease her worries.

"As I said, your child is alive and well. Your cousin and the nannies have been taking care of her. I can assure you."

She had a hard time believing a word of his, but Alezya darted her eyes at her cousin's husband, who nodded to confirm her father's words.

She felt a bit relieved. They wouldn't have dared to come up with such a lie, or at least she hoped so. Nevertheless, she had to be sure. She couldn't act weak and compromise on Lumie's safety.

"I want to see her," she insisted. "With my own eyes."

"You will," her father nodded, "but first, we have questions for you. We know where you were all this time."

Of course they knew.

Perhaps her father had meant to intimidate her with that accusatory tone, but Alezya truly couldn't care much about what he thought. Her child's life had been threatened and she'd fled, why would she have felt apologetic on top of that? She owed them nothing, and certainly no loyalty. She wouldn't even have been standing here if it wasn't for Lumie; she hadn't come back for any other reason.

She didn't answer her father, waiting to hear what he wanted to know. She could guess most of it.

"No one has ever set foot on the enemy's territory and come back alive," he continued.

"And unharmed, at that," one of the elders added.

Alezya darted a glare their way but quickly came back to her father. She still didn't speak. If they wanted answers, they had to stop using their slithering ways to corner her and actually get to it.

Moreover, she wasn't sure she could control the nervousness in her voice, so she would rather use it sparingly.

"My men have been watching you," her father continued, his eyes narrowing. "Not only were you taken to their habitations, but you spent a long time with their leader. That man and you stood next to the dragon, and yet you were unharmed."

Alezya could guess her father was dying to know how she'd achieved that. She stood still, waiting, making her father even more impatient.

"...Tell us," he pressed her. "What happened down there? How did you manage to stand next to that man? What did you learn?"

She took a deep breath.

"It seems like you didn't hear me the first two times, Father. I want to see my daughter."

"You insolent bitch!"

There it was. His facade hadn't held up long, and he was already back to the furious glaring and calling her names.

Alezya didn't flinch; she'd expected as much. Moreover, she knew she had the upper hand and she wouldn't let them bully her into thinking otherwise. He could beat her and insult her all he wanted, she wouldn't give them a shred of information before she had Lumie. As her mom, she couldn't be weak now and hand them the bit of information she had like that. She had to be stronger, she couldn't afford to fail her again.

"If you dare show insolence again," one of the elders hissed, "we'll kill that thing you dared to give birth to!"

"Then I'll kill myself too," Alezya immediately retorted, "and none of us will get what we want."

She'd said this in such a cold and composed voice, they immediately understood she was dead serious. Her father's eyes were murderous, but he didn't get mad anymore; he knew Alezya would not back down.

He took a deep breath to calm himself and glanced at her cousin's husband.

"...Go get her," he said, as if the words were burning his mouth.

Much to Alezya's relief, her cousin's husband left. As soon as he was gone, her father looked back at her.

"Now. Tell us-"

"I'm not telling you anything until I see my child," Alezya cut him off, empowered by her win.

As if she'd trust his words so easily. It should only be a matter of minutes before her cousin's husband came back anyway, and she wasn't going to give them anything until she confirmed for herself that Lumie was fine. Her father wasn't so happy about her strong refusal though.

He glared at her even more, but it was one of the elders who translated what most of them thought.

"You're a disgrace to this clan," the older man hissed. "You should be grateful we didn't banish a depraved witch like you! It should be an honor to serve this clan, but you keep being nothing but an arrogant slut! The gods will punish you for being such a wretched creature!"

"The gods let me give birth to my child and have kept both me and her safe so far," Alezya scoffed. "Not only that, but I faced a dragon three times and survived. What do your gods say about that?"

"You women have a way," another one hissed. "A wretched, sullied woman will only get tainted more. It is obvious how you got the enemy's favor. Shame on you for using your body, and for refusing to serve your father's cause!"

Alezya wanted to laugh. Of course, in their mind, the only thing she could have done to earn anyone's kindness was prostitute herself. They were already so convinced she'd slept around during her marriage, what else could they have had in mind?

Not only that, but they could all see the expensive-looking coat she wore and the shiny fabric in her hair. In their eyes, the only way for a woman to ever earn those was to actively curry a man's favor. Though it was true she'd been gifted those by Kassein, she knew it said more about his character than it did hers.

Finally, her cousin's husband came back, and much to her relief, he was carrying Lumie. She'd never been so grateful in her entire life. Her daughter was well and sleeping in his arms.

Alezya immediately teared up, overcome by incommensurable relief. She looked fine, her little body gently moving along with her breathing, her mouth in a cute little "o" as it always did when she slept. It had only been a few days, but Alezya felt like it had been forever since she'd seen her child. Had she grown a bit? Was her white hair a little bit longer?

She cried silently, covering her mouth with a trembling hand. She didn't care if they all saw how shaken up she was, she was a mother first and foremost. She gasped, trying to control her breathing, and took a step forward, but her father suddenly extended his arm between her and her cousin's husband, who was standing next to him.

Alezya's expression fell.

"You've seen her now," he said coldly.

"Let me hold her."

"No."

"Let me hold her!"

Her father suddenly took out a knife.

Alezya's blood went cold, while he smiled viciously.

"We may not kill her, but your daughter might get hurt if you don't start behaving, Alezya. I know you're a tough woman, but I'm not sure your bastard is as strong."

She felt absolute fury. How could he use her child to threaten her?! Her eyes went to Lumie, devastated. They wouldn't even let her hold her child for an instant! She was finally seeing her after so long, and yet they had to stay several feet apart.

"If you hurt her..." she hissed.

"I certainly will if you don't learn to behave," her father retorted. "Your daughter has been fine until now. What kind of mother would you be if you caused her harm with your stubbornness?"

Alezya had never wanted to kill a man so badly, but there she was, seriously considering throwing herself at her father's throat. Perhaps she would have if she hadn't been so unsure her movement would get both her and Lumie killed.

Thus, she was only able to stand there, trembling with rage, her eyes full of tears and her head full of murderous thoughts. She swore that she'd kill that man someday. No one ever deserved to be treated like that by their kin. Regardless of any blood bond, that man couldn't ever be called her father again. Alezya mentally severed the last ties she had felt to him. She had tried, hard, to keep an ounce of respect, to try and understand where he came from, but that was all gone. A man threatening to harm a child to have their mother do his bidding was nothing but evil.

She moved her eyes back to Lumie, and she'd never felt so heartbroken. The short happiness of seeing her alive and well had been completely shattered. She couldn't even hold her. She couldn't touch her, smell her, feel her body warmth against hers. She wanted Lumie to feel her presence so badly, to know her mom had come back for her. She wanted to tell her she'd never meant to abandon her. That no matter what, they'd find a way to escape, together.

But all that stayed locked up, choking her with tears. Then, her eyes went to her cousin's husband, and she was surprised to find him looking almost...

sorry. Not only that, but his eyes went down to Lumie, and the way he was holding her properly, gently... He had taken her from somewhere without waking her up too.

When their eyes met again, he spoke, in a neutral voice.

"...She's been well," was all he said.

And yet, that was enough to procure Alezya with a minimum of relief. It wasn't about his words per se or how he'd said it, but from the meaningful look in his eyes. She didn't know exactly what had happened, but now, she had a feeling that her cousin's husband had somehow changed. Lumie wasn't a nuisance in his arms, she was a young child. He was a father too, and a better one than her own.

Perhaps he and his wife caring for Lumie during that time had softly changed his mind. Either way, it was a small relief, and perhaps what prevented Alezya from completely falling apart.

She redirected her tearful eyes to her father, glaring at him.

"What do you want?" she hissed.

He smiled, satisfied to finally see her submit.

"You make foolish decisions, but you remain a smart woman. You've already spent time with our enemy, and gotten close to their leader. That arrogant bastard, his family, and their dragons have been our nemesis for generations. At each council gathering, there is nothing the clans want more than his demise. We have been waiting for far too long for a chance to strike back. Luckily, Daughter, you have opened a path to our victory."

Alezya was surprised. No woman was ever included in the council gatherings, so she wasn't aware of how much they actually knew about the Dragon Clan as the information was never openly shared.

It was her first time hearing that Kassein was part of a family related to all the dragons they'd seen before. She had always assumed their enemy, the one they called the Dragon Tyrant, somehow owned all the dragons and always sent them to attack.

But from what she'd seen in the camp and what her father's people had probably been spying on for a long time, the dragons didn't just belong to the enemy, they were actually bound to them. Kassein was obviously bound to Kein, which is why they shared those orange scales; her father's people had probably figured as much too. Did that mean they had seen other people from Kassein's family that had the same peculiar common trait with the dragons? Was there someone tied to the black dragon, somewhere? And one tied to that yellow one? Kassein was obviously the leader of that place, but then, where was his family? Had her people seen him with his family and their dragons, hence they knew all this?

She had known her father and all the clans had been spying on the Dragon Clan for a long time, but she'd never realized how far they'd actually come with that information.

"Rejoice," her father smiled. "You will be the one to carry out our plan and will be able to regain everything that was yours if you succeed. Your honor, your daughter, your place within the clans. Even better, you will be adored as the woman who made our victory against the Dragon Clan possible."

"I've heard that one before," Alezya coldly said, not impressed, "and you are a delusional man. Even if I have been able to survive confrontations with the dragon, I am in no way capable of tricking that man or harming either of them. I only survived because they showed pity. I haven't seen any weakness, and their numbers are far greater than you think."

"Oh, I already know that. But our plan will not rely on any immediate attack. No, we have been patiently waiting for an opportunity, and today will only mark the very beginning of our greatest plan yet. We've fought their kind countless times, and we've never won. It is obvious our only strategy can rely on information and preparation. You're right; we will never have the numbers. Even if we rally all the clans, we'd barely be able to fight that monster, his dragon, and his men on equal footing. But we're not counting on that. I am counting on time, and evening our chances. And our chances will only ever be equal to them if we too have a dragon on our side."

Alezya scoffed.

"Have you finally gone mad? Do you expect me to rally a dragon to your cause? Perhaps you want me to capture it and deliver it to you? Do you even hear yourself?"

"You're the one who's not hearing," her father retorted. "I told you our plan would take a long time. It may take a couple of decades, but it will all be worth it. From what we know, those people, their family, are the only ones bound to those dragons. One child, one dragon."

That's when the truth finally hit her. No, perhaps her mind had refused to even understand such a horrible design. She couldn't believe it, and her mind went numb for a couple of seconds, her ears ringing. Even for a despicable man like her father, it was such a horrible, wretched plan. She felt sick just thinking about it, and yet, she had to confirm.

She wanted to be sure of the horror he was suggesting.

"You want me... to conceive a child for you?" she muttered. "For you to use... their dragon?"

"You're saying this like it's impossible," her father chuckled, "but their leader is already pleased with you. He gave you such presents, and let you approach his dragon. A cunning woman like you will have no issues opening your legs to get what you want from him. After all, it wouldn't be your first time carrying a monster, would it?"

"...You're mad," she muttered, in shock. "You all are! You think I'll conceive a child for you to use for your designs?! You think I'll stand by and watch you use my child for your gain? I'm not just some cow you can breed and use the offspring for! First, you threaten me with my child's life, and now you want me to carry another one? For you to use against their own genitor? Have you all gone absolutely mad?!"

"What you think of it is irrelevant," her father retorted. "As a child of this clan, it is your duty to sacrifice yourself for the sake of your people. You've already seduced their leader with your cunning ways, it shouldn't be long before you bear his child. Weren't you so willing to get your daughter back before? All we're asking is a child for a child. As soon as we've confirmed you're pregnant with that monster's seed, we will give your bastard back to you. Isn't this a fair trade, given all the shame you've brought upon this clan?"

"I don't give a damn about your pride! Those are children we are talking about!" Alezya shouted. "Actual babies; young, defenseless children that you're all willing to use for your gain? You're not just insane, you're the most vile people!"

Her shouting woke up Lumie, who began crying in her cousin's husband's arms. Alezya's heart broke. She'd made her daughter cry, and she couldn't even go to console her!

She exchanged another glance with her cousin's husband. She had rarely if ever interacted with him, but she remembered his name was Suolk. As Lumie was crying, he began rocking her a bit, bouncing on his feet to try and ease her a bit. As he was one step behind the circle, none of the other men had their eyes on him nor did they notice him patting the toddler's back.

A bit reassured, Alezya turned her burning eyes to her father. He was still very much annoyed with her.

"This is a war," he said. "Sacrifices ought to be made, and a child that will allow us to have a dragon will be our best weapon against those people. Your opinion is irrelevant, Alezya."

"...I won't do it," she said. "You can't ask me to do that."

"Oh, this is not a request, child," he retorted. "This is an order, and you're a fool if you believe you have any choice. You want your child back? Then you'll come back here pregnant. The only thing that's up to you is how long that will take. The more stubborn you are, the longer you'll be away from your child."

"...I'm not going back," Alezya cried. "Not to do such a thing."

"You will."

Chapter 6

He watched Alezya's figure for a long time as she gradually disappeared into the heights of her homeland. Kassein didn't take his gaze off her, not until she was completely out of sight.

Only then did he let out a heavy sigh and turn around. It was a lonely trip back. He'd never minded being alone before, but now, he was hating it. It was so early in the morning, the land was just waking up and only the birds had begun their day, singing cheerfully somewhere above his head. It was a rare beautiful day, the opposite of his current mood.

He didn't linger, tracing the path in the snow back to the camp.

He knew he was being observed. Not just then, but these days, he felt constant gazes turned toward the camp. It wasn't completely new, but it sure felt like a lot more than before. Perhaps the tribes were getting bolder after seeing that one of their women had survived a few days in the camp, but they were still keeping a distance, and Kassein didn't like it at all. He still didn't feel good about letting Alezya go back either.

She had supposedly gone back to her people, yet she hadn't seemed that happy to go, although her determination was there. He wished he had accompanied her further to understand what was going on. Being sidelined was the worst feeling...

He tried to brush those thoughts away as he reached the camp with a heavy heart. She was gone now, and she wasn't coming back.

His men welcomed him back, but their greetings fell on deaf ears. Tievin raised an eyebrow, scouring the plain behind him with narrowed eyes, but didn't say anything, and slowly walked behind him for a little while until they were alone.

"Did you see anyone from her tribe? Did they come to collect her?"

"No."

Kassein's cold, annoyed tone conveyed how he felt about it.

If a woman had been missing, why had none of them come forward to retrieve her? If one of his sisters had been taken away, he would have stopped at nothing to get them back. Where was her family? They knew she wasn't dead, it was definitely her tribe that had been spying on them. So why were they acting so cryptically toward her? What was the meaning of that necklace they'd sent her? Alezya had seemed completely overwhelmed after getting it. Why? He'd only gotten a glimpse of the symbol, but he had no idea what it was.

Something just didn't feel right with her attitude, and he couldn't shake it off. She didn't seem forced to go back, so why did it feel like it?

"Commander?"

From his tone, it was the second or third time Tievin had tried getting his attention. Kassein turned an annoyed glare to him, but it wasn't enough to discourage him.

"I was asking if you still need that cape for the lady to be made. From my understanding, it is unlikely she'll be paying us a visit again. The soldiers in charge were asking. Also, I'm sure you already know, but we've noted more spies in the heights. What shall we do about them? Your dragon doesn't seem to want to bother himself with them. Of course, we could-"

He didn't get to finish his sentence as Kassein's eye caught a shadow behind him and brutally pushed Tievin out of the way, sending him flying far to his left.

Tievin landed face first and mouth wide open in the snow before realizing anything had happened or was happening to him. He couldn't see anything, but he did hear the deafening growl of a furious dragon above his head. His first reflex was to get his head out of the snow, spit some out with disgust, and cover his head while trying to look up.

He was right under Kein's wing, although the dragon was moving too much above him for its shadow to be stable.

Tievin panicked and began crawling in the snow to get as far away as possible. The dragon was even more violent than usual, and he could hear Kassein groan loudly in response to its growls as the two fought.

The sounds of flesh ripping and sword meeting scales were not reassuring either.

"Grand Intendant!"

A handful of soldiers came to his aid, several hands grabbing the Grand Intendant and pulling him away from the fight; this was only made possible because neither the dragon nor the Prince actually cared about Tievin being in the area. They were dueling each other, everything else was an annoyance at best, collateral damage at worst.

After much difficulty, and once they were a safe distance away, Tievin managed to get up, still a bit in shock, while the soldiers gathered around him, pressing him to keep retreating, a lot of them shocked.

"W-what do we do, Grand Intendant?"

"Shall we intervene? At this rate, the Commander will-!"

Tievin raised a hand, signaling them to shut up.

He was watching the fight, now from a reasonably safe distance, and just like the men, he was starting to realize this one was much more violent than usual. The Prince and the dragon were trying to slaughter each other in a storm of snow and blood.

No wonder the men were so panicked; it was hard to believe Kassein would survive this. Tievin was starting to genuinely worry too. Until now, both Prince and dragon had seriously tried to kill one another, but the attacks were short, and the dragon that had missed its chance to succeed in one go would often give up quickly.

This was worse, much worse than before. For some reason, Kein seemed determined to try and kill its owner for good. Neither dragon nor prince was giving up or holding back. They had been mad before, but this was pure rage. The sheer chaos of that duel was hard to witness and believe, even for the most experienced of the men.

Tievin hesitated, as he had never had to face this kind of situation before; He was just there to do some damage control and see that no one else was injured. This time, Kein had chosen to attack right at the entrance of the camp, thankfully away from any tents and in a large, unoccupied area that usually stood as a battling ground during the tribes' attacks. This was almost the exact same spot they'd fought in just a couple of days prior, so it only had a thin layer of snow. Now, all the snow was quickly getting tainted a dramatic red.

Tievin tried to think as calmly as he could, given the situation.

It was foolish for Kassein's men to try and attack the dragon; Kein had killed before, and it couldn't be stopped from killing one of them when it was this out of control. There was no way to get in between the Prince and his dragon without someone else getting hurt.

If this had been in the Capital, one of the members of the Imperial Family and their dragon would have intervened, but there was none here. The fastest horse wouldn't reach the closest of them before a couple of days at least, far too late. If this went on, there would be neither prince nor dragon left.

He watched, feeling helpless, with three dozen men behind him waiting for orders.

"Oh, by the gods," he eventually grumbled. "Somebody get me a crossbow and a boot."

"A-a boot, sir?"

"Hurry!" he insisted, annoyed.

Within a few seconds, somebody handed him a crossbow and half a dozen boots were handed out without more questions asked, although they were definitely raised in most minds.

He grabbed the closest one, put the head of the arrow inside, and aimed, boot first, at the dragon. He took a deep breath and shot. The first shot completely missed, flying far to the right, but Tievin just grabbed another arrow, another boot, and tried again. This time, he hit Kein right on the cheek.

The dragon growled furiously and turned its head toward the group, but at least it had left its owner alone for a second. All the men around Tievin froze or ran away, even if they had one foot bare in the snow.

The dragon's silver eyes met Tievin, who felt his voice and the very bit of bravery he'd mustered up for this moment leave his body.

"S-stop," he mumbled. "...P-please."

Kein snarled at him, but obviously, the dragon had been taken out of its murderous frenzy.

Still, the amount of blood on its face was worrisome, coupled with the fact that all around it, everything was strangely quiet. Wherever the Prince was in that chaos, he was not showing any sign of life.

Just as Tievin was getting worried Kein might release more of its fury, the dragon turned its head toward the mountain instead. It seemed to be listening, and then, it suddenly flew off.

As soon as the dragon was in the air, the men all ran, leaving Tievin's side to look for their leader. The poor man let out a long sigh of relief and prayed for his legs not to let him down completely, all strength having left them. After a couple of seconds, he walked through the crowd and chased them away with orders that his hoarse voice only made half convincing.

He finally saw Kassein, lying in a pool of his own blood. His first thought was to thank the gods as the Prince was still alive. Considerably injured, but alive. He was on his flank, half of his face in the blood, his breathing making little ripples under him.

"Go away. Stop watching." Tievin chased the men away with his hands like flies.

When he finally stood alone by Kassein's side, he sighed.

"This seems to have been a close one, sir. It might be time to take Kein's unruliness ser–"

"You stink."

Kassein had barely groaned those words, but it made Tievin pinch his lips.

"I need... a dry pair of pants. Since you seem alive, and alive enough to be unaccommodating, I'll leave you here, Commander. I sincerely hope that mad, mad dragon of yours doesn't come and finish you off in the meantime. I'll come back when you're, hopefully, in a better mood. And me with clean pants."

He turned around, and after giving orders for no one to approach Kassein, he hurried back to his tent to change.

For some reason, he didn't trust that Kein was gone for good at all. Something was different this time, and neither the man nor his dragon were acting normally. Tievin hadn't had time to truly think while their brawl had been happening, but it wasn't just Kein.

He couldn't shake off the feeling that the Prince was acting oddly too. He'd seen it when he'd walked back into the camp after returning that woman to her people. That expression on his face was one he hadn't seen in a while. One that had taken a long time to disappear. The soldiers here didn't know the Prince, so they had no idea. Only Tievin, who'd been by his side since childhood, knew how complex the Prince's personality was, how tortured he could be under that cold, hard facade. He couldn't understand why his dragon had gone mad, but he did pity the Prince's circumstances a bit. He hadn't been too happy about a woman coming to the camp, but now, he realized that woman might have been the best thing that had happened to Kassein in a long while.

It spoke volumes that the Prince and his dragon had been able to stay together in the same place for several hours, a couple of days even, without so much as making a scratch on each other, and the second that woman was gone, they were back to trying to kill each other.

As he stepped out of his tent with new, clean, and dry pants, Tievin looked up at the mountains. He'd always thought women brought nothing but trouble, and he was still thinking that. But perhaps, just perhaps, that particular woman could have brought something good into the Prince's life. Now that she was gone, he was anxious about the days ahead.

With a lot of worrisome thoughts in mind, Tievin began walking back toward the spot he'd left the Prince. With his incredible regeneration capacity, he had no doubt that the Prince would be able to get up soon, unless the dragon came back for another round.

"Sir!"

A man ran up to him, which Tievin recognized as that new Captain, Dajan. The newcomer began walking beside Tievin, visibly nervous.

"Sir, I need to report that the dragon was spotted nearby. It seems to have gone toward the mountains."

"Toward the mountains?" Tievin repeated, feeling uneasy. "Anything more precise than that?"

"We're not sure yet, Grand Intendant. It suddenly... dove between mountains and out of our sight. We thought it was hunting, but it hasn't come back yet. Sir, should we prepare some protective measures around the Commander in Chief, just in case? If the dragon comes back, I'm worried that-"

"You'll just put more people between the Commander and his dragon, and it won't end well for any of them," Tievin scolded him.

"But, the Commander's life-"

"The Commander has survived ten years with an insane dragon trying to kill him daily. Sacrificing men will not end the problem. Just keep monitoring that stupid dragon. Let's-"

He stopped talking as, right ahead, they had both noticed the large figure now rising in the sky. In a clear blue sky, the sudden appearance of an orange dragon couldn't be missed, and Tievin rolled his eyes when someone shouted about the dragon being spotted. Next to him, Dajan went livid.

"Commander!"

The Captain ran ahead, and Tievin didn't try to hold him back.

He had already warned him. Moreover, he was more focused on something strange in Kein's behavior. The dragon wasn't flying like usual.

Earth Dragons usually flew with their bodies parallel to the ground, their limbs as close to their bodies as possible to ease the weight their wings had to carry.

But Kein was flying with his paws strangely hanging out unevenly, and as it got closer, Tievin realized the dragon was carrying something.

"Don't tell me..."

Tievin hated running more than most things, but he still accelerated to a quick pace to get to where Kassein and Dajan already were, bracing themselves for whatever was coming.

As he'd predicted, the Prince was already able to sit up, although his current state was worrisome. The right side of his face was covered in blood, making his appearance more gruesome than usual. Just like everyone else, he had his eyes up toward the silhouette of his dragon coming toward them, although a lot of that view was cut off by Dajan and a handful of his men standing in front of him, prepared to protect him.

At that moment, Tievin felt that Dajan was a righteous idiot; the kind of soldier who was too eager, too honorable for his own good, and would get himself killed out of foolish bravery someday.

Still, bravery was admirable.

"...Out of the way."

Dajan looked back at Kassein's imperious voice.

He was about to protest the Prince's order, until their eyes met, and he understood he had no room for refusal. He gestured to his men, and instead of lining up in front of the Prince, they formed two groups on either side. They were out of Kassein's line of sight, but still close enough to be ready to protect him.

At that moment though, neither Tievin nor Kassein cared about the men anymore. Both of them had their eyes riveted on Kein approaching; this time, the dragon clearly wasn't coming to pick a fight.

"No way..." Tievin muttered.

Kassein had realized a second sooner.

The Prince's dark expression fell into surprise, and he moved forward. With painful groans and Dajan rushing to his aid, although he was pushed away, Kassein managed to get back on his feet as his dragon was landing just steps away from them.

Kein was growling already, but this time, the dragon seemed unwilling to fight. In fact, it curled its body like a block of scales, baring its fangs to warn off the men. Even its wings were used like shields between its treasure and Kassein's men.

"Move," Kassein groaned.

They weren't sure if he was talking to his dragon or his men, but the latter moved a bit more out of his way. The dragon only growled even more in warning though. Tievin was following closely too, curious as to what was going to happen next. It was the first time he witnessed Kein seeming so nervous around his human counterpart. The dragon was acting like a trapped beast, unable to move and left to growl and guard itself.

Once Kassein stood in front of it, although visibly in pain and bleeding, the dragon seemed even more nervous.

"I said move," Kassein hissed.

The dragon growled, but this time, the Prince wasn't having it. He stepped forward and pushed Kein's wing out of the way despite its furious growls. That's when they saw her.

Still partly held by one of Kein's claws, Alezya was lying there, unconscious. Kassein almost fell to his knees next to her, pushing his dragon off of her angrily.

"What...?"

The words got caught in his throat.

Tievin was shocked too. Alezya had come back in a worse state than she'd left. He was no doctor, but it was obvious her injuries hadn't been caused by the dragon's rough carrying. She had a lot of bruises on her face and on her arm, as if she'd tried to defend herself from whoever had repeatedly hit her. There was blood on her temple, and the wounds on her feet had been reopened enough to bleed again. One of her shoes was gone, and the other was ripped open. Her coat was nowhere to be seen either. She was just wearing the inner layer of clothes, far too thin for her in this weather.

"Dajan, call the medical unit," Tievin muttered, shocked, "...and somebody, get her a coat!"

Things started moving quickly around them, but Kein, Kassein, and that poor woman were the only ones completely still.

Kassein was hugging Alezya in his arms, his eyes full of shock, incomprehension, and anger. Kein seemed to have completely forgotten him too, the dragon whining and pushing Alezya's legs with its snout, looking worried, its body surrounding the couple.

Tievin glanced toward the mountains. What had happened? There was no way His Highness had left that woman in an unsafe area. If she'd returned to her home, why did Kein retrieve her in that state? Tievin had spent enough time watching battles to know those injuries were caused by someone, not any beast; although, to cause such harm to a woman, they had to be worse than a beast. Not only that, but the darkness of those bruises was just wrong. And they had been separated for what, just about an hour or so?

Kassein was holding that woman in disbelief, shaking with anger. Tievin could understand that; he'd just made up his mind about returning that woman to her people, and now this... Her current state was sickening and impossible to understand. Why? Why was she so badly beaten up? What had happened, what had she done to deserve this?

The medical unit finally arrived, and Kassein and Kein reluctantly let them approach, although neither left Alezya's side. Tievin watched the whole scene from a couple of steps away, listening to the medical unit's quick diagnostic, his lips closed in a thin, annoyed line.

Something wasn't quite right here. That woman had been desperate to go back. Why return to people who'd treat her this way not just once, but twice? Had she run into a tribe other than her own? But who would beat a woman up to this point for no reason, and leave her like this?

He knew the Prince ought to be having the same thoughts now, just perhaps not as cool-headed. He was dead silent, but the anger was visible in the Prince's body language alone and the burning glares he sent to everyone around.

The medical unit had to be extremely careful with each of their movements, explaining and justifying themselves, while trying to give that woman immediate medical attention. Her state wasn't too bad physically, or at least not as bad as it looked. Her bruises would heal, and her feet would eventually too. Under all the blue, red, and black though, her eyes were puffy and wet. From her state, one could tell she had cried a lot. Over what? Because she'd been beaten up?

When she very briefly regained conscience, for just a few seconds, she muttered something, a faint sob, and cried silently, closing her eyes again. Kassein and Tievin exchanged glances, both equally clueless.

"...Let's bring her to the Commander's tent," Tievin finally muttered.

Alezya didn't open her eyes for over an hour.

During this time, the medical unit did their best before leaving the oppressive atmosphere of the tent, while Kassein remained by her side. Once again, Dajan and his unit proved their worth by establishing a perimeter around the tent without being asked and watching the surroundings.

At first, it seemed they did so by a belief that the barbarians would attack from the mountain all of a sudden, but Tievin soon realized they were more dedicated to keeping people and rumors away.

Most had seen Kein return, but few people knew the dragon had brought someone back with it. While there was no telling what that information would do once it got around, he silently agreed it was better to keep it concealed for now. It had been acceptable when it was clear that the woman's stay was temporary, but now, there was no telling how long she'd stay this time. There weren't just good men sent to the North Camp, there were some criminals sent here and assigned to the hardest units as punishment for their offenses.

While it was usually easy to keep them in line, Tievin didn't want to give those rascals an opportunity to cause problems. The in-fighting at the camp could be dealt with easily, but if anything were to happen once word spread that a woman was residing there...

He couldn't guarantee things wouldn't take a darker turn. Not because he was worried about Alezya's safety, but because he knew what an angry dragon could do, and had no doubt Kassein could do much worse. This was nothing but trouble; it would happen sooner or later and would be hard to explain to the Emperor if he ever turned an eye to this area.

While thinking of all this, Tievin kept an eye on the Prince and Alezya. She was back in his bed, lying with cold compresses on her injuries, visibly enduring the pain in silence, half unconscious.

It wasn't clear how much she realized was going on. Sometimes she'd open her eyes, meet Kassein's, and start crying silently, then close her eyes again. Even for Tievin, it was gut-wrenching to watch. The Prince was sitting against his bed, recovering from his own injuries. He was gently holding her hand, his face close to hers, the fingers of his other hand combing her hair gently.

She had lost that silk ribbon he'd gifted her too, Tievin noted with a faint sigh. Did she get robbed of all the things they'd gifted her? That silk ribbon was the only item Kassein had that was a proper gift for a woman. Purple was the color of the Imperial Family, so Tievin guessed he'd gotten it from his mother or one of his sisters perhaps. It wasn't such a big deal that this woman had lost the item; purple silk was no rare find back in the Capital, but it was a bit sad that she had no idea of the significance of this gift before she'd lost it.

Tievin stayed there in silence, watching the scene of those two stuck together. The Prince wasn't letting go of that woman's hand and he was barely acknowledging anyone who walked into the tent. It was Tievin doing all the sorting of sending that person back or letting that one in if they were useful, mostly the medical unit bringing new cold compresses to change the ones on Alezya's face. Tievin couldn't help but feel sorry for the bruises on her face the most; women relied a lot on their appearance, and whoever had attacked her obviously had no regard for hers.

Luckily, it didn't seem to deter the Prince one bit, only fueling his anger. From the outside, they could even hear Kein growling at whichever guard was foolish enough to come too close, or pacing around the tent, sometimes trying to take a peek inside. The dragon was rendering all the other people posted outside useless.

"What could have happened...?"

Kassein's words had been pronounced late into the night, so faintly that Tievin had almost believed he'd dreamt it. By then, he'd sat down on the chair next to the fire, but the Prince hadn't changed position once, nor had he shifted his gaze away from Alezya.

That woman was now asleep, although she'd sometimes sob and get a bit agitated in her sleep. One of the older men from the medical unit was there, as he'd just brought over some fresh compresses and medical herbs. He was only bringing in the materials, though. Kassein hadn't let anyone else treat or touch Alezya once she was laid on his bed.

"It seems like she is not welcomed back in the tribes," Tievin said with a neutral voice. "Her injuries can't possibly be accidental, and she seems pretty shaken too. At first, I thought she could have encountered another tribe and been robbed, but the display of violence on a woman makes little sense for robbers. My guess is that she was exiled."

He wouldn't dare voice it in Kassein's presence, but since the medical unit had confirmed she hadn't been sexually assaulted, Tievin had become more doubtful about the reasons for her beating. It wasn't just a robbery gone wrong;

someone capable of harming a woman to that extent wouldn't have passed up a chance to do worse, was his thinking. The fact that Kein had brought her back so wet and cold meant she'd probably been abandoned somewhere, or else the dragon wouldn't have come back without her attackers' blood on its scales.

And he'd already looked, but it didn't seem like the orange dragon had attacked anyone else but Kassein that day.

"She wanted to go back," Kassein muttered. "She was the one who wanted to go back up there. She told me where to split up. Why? Why, if she knew she wasn't safe..."

"It will be hard to tell what happened, sir," Tievin said. "Communication with her would give us more clues, but at the moment... I fear this might take time. Luckily, she will be safe here. If you plan to let her stay, I can have all the arrangements made soon enough. It isn't proper for her to continue sleeping in your bed."

"No. She stays with me."

Tievin pressed his lips in a thin line, but he had expected this.

Truthfully, he had several reasons for which he found it improper for Alezya to stay in the Prince's bed, but he wouldn't risk his neck to point them out.

He took a big breath, mentally sorting out the priorities regarding this woman. He could understand the parts the Prince was stubborn about, and he supported him to a certain point. However, as his aide, Tievin knew there were things they'd have to sort out.

"Commander, I need to point out that this woman staying in the camp will require us to make some preparations. This camp was never meant to welcome a woman, even less so a foreigner. I understand you will be unwilling to make the Imperial Palace aware of this matter just yet, but this is no small matter. Those tribespeople are unpredictable, and they just proved it to us once more. I do not believe a woman would end up in this state willingly, but I still believe there is something odd about all this."

"Get to your point."

Tievin let out a faint sigh. Of course, the Prince wouldn't want his older brother, the Emperor, to be aware of what was happening here.

In fact, he wanted nothing to do with him so much that Tievin had mentioned "the Imperial Palace" rather than saying his name out loud.

However, they couldn't act too carelessly, or it would be detrimental in the future. Tievin was worried that if some things were learned too late, Prince Kassein would alienate his own family even more.

"Have you considered... asking for help–"

"No."

Tievin hadn't even finished his sentence, but Kassein had answered firmly with a tone that wouldn't allow another similar suggestion. He suppressed the words in his mouth. Perhaps it was too soon, or he'd find another way. There was always another way. Although his relationship with his older brother was the most complex, the Prince still had six other siblings, loving parents, and uncles and aunts who would no doubt come to his aid if he ever asked for it. The hardest part would be, of course, for him to ever actually ask for anyone's help.

For now, he was unwilling to confide in anyone or to allow anyone near Alezya. Something was definitely shifting, and for once, Tievin couldn't predict where that would lead them. He just hoped this woman wasn't going to increase the wedge between the two brothers even more.

He remained silent for a few more seconds, then announced he was going back to his tent, the soldier from the medical unit quietly following him, leaving the two of them alone.

The tent fell completely silent after they'd left.

It was late, but Kassein didn't feel sleepy at all; he felt angry. He hadn't felt so infuriated in a long time. If he weren't so worried about Alezya's state, he would have immediately gone after whoever had done this. Truthfully, he was ready to burn the whole mountain down. But she had a fever, and with her injuries so visible, making her suffer so much, he felt bound to her side. He couldn't entrust anyone else to watch her, and he couldn't leave her alone in his tent. He knew Kein had gone on a rampage in the mountains about an hour ago, and he didn't care. For once, he felt grateful for his dragon's madness. He only wished he'd been up there too, going after whoever had done this to her.

Her injuries were hard to look at, not because of their appearance, but because he could imagine the pain she'd gone through. From the bruises on her arms, she'd tried to protect herself, and yet her head was covered in bruises still. His blood boiled even more, thinking how quickly this must have happened.

There hadn't been much time from when they parted ways to when Kein brought her back. Did her people attack her as soon as she had gotten back? Why? Did she know this would happen? If so, why had she chosen to go back anyway?

Kassein stared at the tears that had dried on her cheeks. He hated not knowing. He hated that they'd made her cry and hurt her, and he hated that there was nothing he could understand about all this. He wished she could explain why she'd gone back, why she'd risked all this.

However, right now, what he wanted most was for her to be at peace and safe. He'd protect her. He wouldn't make the same mistake twice.

He sighed and readjusted his position against the bed. He didn't want to sleep; he wanted Alezya to know she was safe now. Whatever had happened to her, he wouldn't let it happen again. Perhaps Tievin hadn't realized, but Kassein didn't just want to keep Alezya in the camp; he never wanted to let her go back.

Still, his Intendant's words stayed in his mind. He hated asking for help and he certainly didn't want any from Kassian. He'd be the last person he'd ask help from, ever. And anyway, what could his older brother help with? He'd be the first one to send Alezya back to whatever hell she came from.

Even if it wasn't his older brother, Kassein didn't want to ask for help from his family. If one of them knew, they would all know, and it would only be a matter of time before the Emperor was aware. He didn't want that, he didn't even want his parents to know what was happening here. He liked being left alone, he liked that the North Army was his refuge, the one place he didn't feel watched. He'd been sent here as a punishment, but now, it had become his best excuse to ignore them. He hated his family's suffocating concern and the more distance he put between himself and them, the better. And this was the farthest place from them he'd managed to get to.

Still, there might be another option. Someone else he hadn't considered before... He turned his eyes to the fire, thinking. That might not be the worst idea. Out of all the people he knew, only they could help Alezya, and they wouldn't snitch either, as they wanted their family's attention even less than he did.

The hardest part would be finding them; he hadn't seen them in months, had no idea where they were, and they most likely didn't want to be found. If it was for him though, he knew they'd come. He turned his eyes back to Alezya. He was still reluctant to bring anyone to the camp, but Tievin's words did hold some truth. If she were to stay, Alezya would need help.

By the next morning, at sunrise, Kassein had made up his mind. He'd barely slept, but his mind was clear, and he was now determined.

He waited until one of the medical unit soldiers showed up at dawn, visibly surprised to find him still seated by the bed and awake.

"C-Commander, did you not sleep at all...?" the man whispered.

Kassein didn't answer and instead, stood up.

He glanced at Alezya as if to be sure she was still there. Her tears had dried, and at last, she seemed to be getting some proper rest.

She'd only woken up a couple of times during the night to drink medicinal herbal tea and gone right back to sleep. He could tell something was weighing heavily on her heart, but for now, he was happy to let her rest. He was annoyed that he couldn't do more, but she had already drank the only bottle of lake water he had, and he wouldn't get another one without going back to the Imperial Palace, which was a hard no.

He stepped out of the tent, stretching his sore limbs. The only issue with scales appearing to heal him was that they were stiff and often reduced his mobility since they were not as stretchy as his actual skin. He hated the sensation of dryness they gave him, but he had to ignore it, for he knew it was only temporary. The weather outside was beautiful again, with a clear sky and the first streaks of sunlight over a fresh, white coat of snow. Kassein wasn't moved by that beauty; he only walked up to his dragon.

Kein was lying beside the tent, and the dragon was awake. It glared at its owner as soon as it saw him, although it was too lazy to lift its head. Only a few swift flickers of its tail, throwing waves of snow left and right showed its annoyance. Kassein planted his feet before his dragon, glaring right back down at it.

"Find them."

Kein answered with an annoyed growl and moved its head in another direction, very obviously ignoring his order. Kassein took a deep breath, trying to stay calm. He'd expected this much; it was only fair his dragon would be as reluctant to leave Alezya as he was.

"It's for her sake," he said.

The dragon growled a bit louder, darting a glare back. It wasn't fully convinced yet and was still grouchy. Its tail movements had doubled in speed. Kassein crossed his arms.

"Should I ask someone else, then? Who? Someone from the palace?"

The dragon furiously growled, springing to its feet. Kassein didn't flinch when the fangs came an inch from his face, only keeping his green glare on the dragon. The two of them were in an odd stand-off, the handful of guards on watch staring in nervous awe.

"The sooner you go, the sooner you'll be back," Kassein said.

Kein let out another couple of annoyed growls but finally decided to move. The dragon stepped past its owner, not without purposely bumping into him with its huge body and, after a couple more steps, finally took off. Kassein turned around to watch. The orange scales were particularly striking in this cloud-free sky, and the dragon stayed visible for a long while before it finally flew far enough to the west.

Although Kassein didn't care about sending his dragon away, he hoped Kein wouldn't take too long to find them. He needed the help more than he was willing to admit.

"Commander? May I ask where Kein went off to...?" asked Tievin, appearing tired, wrapped in another coat, and staring curiously into the distance.

He'd definitely noticed the dragon had taken an unusual direction, west. Kassein sighed and walked back to the tent.

"I followed your advice."

Those four words rendered Tievin speechless.

He stopped walking behind the Prince, blinked twice, and looked around as if to find someone to confirm he wasn't the only one who had heard that. The two men posted at the entrance of Kassein's tent glanced at him, confused about this situation, and didn't say a word. While Kassein had already walked back inside, Tievin glanced at the sky.

"Ancestors, be proud," he sighed.

Then, he stepped inside the tent. He didn't need to ask; from the direction Kein had taken, he knew who Kassein had sent his dragon to find, and while he was surprised by his choice, he found it to be a good one.

"I'll organize everything for their arrival," he said, glancing over to Alezya. "Also, since we're out of the Lake water, should I send someone-"

"No."

There it came again. Tievin took a deep breath, bracing himself for another tough discussion.

"Sir, for your safety–"

"I said no."

"But I can send–"

"If you send someone, my mother will know."

Tievin so badly wanted to roll his eyes. Gods forbid the Prince's mother found out he'd used up all his vials... Still, with such a strong refusal, he didn't dare press the matter further. Instead, he took a mental note to find a way to send someone to retrieve a vial without the Prince or his family knowing. It wouldn't be an easy feat, but his most important job was to ensure the Prince's safety. He'd rather have the Prince be very, very mad at him than risk his neck back in the Capital... and his father's wrath.

"I understand," he said. "Then, I'll just take care of the accommodations."

He left the tent. At least, with some luck, he would soon have someone else to help him convince the Prince... and Kassein was definitely going to have to be more flexible with that person here.

"Get them to have the breakfast ready early, and add some extra meat to it," he told one of the men guarding outside. "...And tell them to double the surveillance rounds."

Tievin still couldn't shake off the feeling that Alezya's arrival at the camp would stir things up badly with the tribes. There was something wrong about this whole situation, and his gut feeling had rarely been wrong. For once, he didn't like that the Prince's dragon had left the camp.

Perhaps he would have felt much safer with Kein around. Hopefully, the dragon would return soon, and it would be enough to double the manpower in the camp. At least the soldiers would be happy to have some serious business to get to...

Despite Tievin making sure breakfast would be ready early, Alezya only woke up a few hours later. Once again, she looked a bit confused and shaken up. She looked pale, her cheeks hollow, and her eyes red.

She kept glancing around as if trying to put the pieces together. She didn't seem wary of him, thankfully, but she did look completely confused as to where she was. Kassein knew she probably didn't remember much about being dragged back to the camp by Kein, nor her feverish night. Thanks to the herbal medicine they had though, her fever had subsided already, and she was left looking restless and nervous.

"Alezya?" He called her name gently.

She nodded and managed to show him a weak smile. It didn't make him happy at all. He only hoped she knew she was safe here.

Since she seemed stubborn about sitting up, he helped her, grabbing the pillow to place it behind her. She kept glancing around the place and nervously tried to comb her long hair with her fingers, but her left arm was badly hurt, and so were the fingers of her right hand. It was hard for her to move either one very much. He placed his hand gently on her wrist to stop her from doing that.

"You're safe here," Kassein whispered.

He gently moved to take her bruise-covered hand, grabbing her attention. She nodded again as if she was trying to persuade herself.

"What happened?" Kassein asked.

This time, he looked at her arm, pointing at the bruises with a frown.

Alezya's dark eyes went to them, then back to him, and she shook her head with that sad expression. Whatever had happened up there, she didn't want to talk about it. Had she been rejected by her tribe, then?

Strangely, Kassein found her to be in better spirits than the first time he'd found her. The first time, Alezya's expression had seemed hollow, empty, as if she had almost given up on life. This time, although she was physically harmed again, she somehow seemed to be in a better mood.

Perhaps because she'd returned to him? He chased those selfish thoughts away, and sat beside her legs on the bed, facing her.

She definitely looked more serene.

"Food?" he offered her, handing her the lukewarm bowl.

She chuckled weakly, recognizing one of the few words she'd learned. Kassein almost dropped the dish. It was the first time he'd seen the hint of a genuine smile on her face... and it was beautiful.

While he was hypnotized by that new expression on her, Alezya nodded and took what he was handing her, her eyes lingering on the meat. She took the spoon, but her hand was so injured, she barely had the strength to hold it and lift it up to her mouth. Her bruised fingers kept trembling in their bandages, the spoon shaking so much it was almost painful to watch. Kassein helped her, not taking the spoon from her but patiently supporting her hand instead until the food passed her lips.

Alezya grimaced, probably because she had reopened the cut on her lip. Maybe the food being lukewarm wasn't a bad thing after all...

She ate silently, clearly unbothered by his presence. The two of them just focused on feeding her, in a quiet, peaceful atmosphere. Kassein wouldn't say it aloud, but he felt much better now that she'd returned.

Meanwhile, Tievin came back.

"Tievin," Alezya said, either to acknowledge his presence or because she was glad she remembered his name.

The man bowed politely.

"Good morning, my lady," he said, before turning to Kassein. "Sir, new clothes have been prepared for the lady. Her cape you ordered isn't finished yet, but it should be shortly. I prepared another coat in the meantime."

"My dragon?"

"It hasn't been spotted since, sir. It might take a while before it returns, I'm afraid. I've ordered the men to reinforce the barricades just in case."

Tievin seemed to hesitate, darting a glance toward Alezya despite knowing she wouldn't understand his next words.

"I need to let you know, some of her... people have been sighted again, in the heights. Should we do something about this, or let them be?"

Kassein tightened his fist, and a cold chill ran down Tievin's spine. The Prince was in no mood to let those people be, not after the state they'd put her in, twice.

"Is it her tribe?"

"We think so, sir, but we haven't been able to confirm because of the distance."

Kassein took a deep breath. He was fed up with those people. If they wanted to exile this woman, they should leave her be, once she was gone. What were they spying for? He didn't believe it was a coincidence, and it made him even more annoyed.

"...Make sure they stop spying."

"Understood."

Tievin left, most likely to go and give the men orders that they were now allowed to shoot the lurkers. The archery units would be delighted, although they might not be able to get them all. The height was considerable, but anyway, Kassein would send his dragon to finish the ones hiding in the highest and hardest spots once Kein returned. His main goal was to keep those people away from Alezya this time. Whatever reason they had to force her out of her mountains, it didn't give them any right to keep spying afterward. Perhaps they didn't know she had survived, perhaps they were only spying on the camp as their enemies all along, but he didn't care. Alezya's safety came first, and that meant none of the tribespeople would be allowed near her again.

At least, not until he knew what had happened.

"Kassein?"

He immediately turned his eyes to her. Alezya looked hesitant, so he tried to wait and let her speak. She glanced around, clearly trying to think. Was she trying to remember a word she'd learned from him?

"Water," she finally spurted out in his language.

"You want water?" he asked, grabbing the pitcher.

But she glanced at it and shook her head, looking around again. She pointed at the fire, the pitcher, and then to herself. Kassein was slightly confused, trying to put the pieces together. Then, she glanced around again, but she visibly couldn't find what she wanted. The charade was growing frustrating for both of them. But she got his attention again and rubbed her skin. That's when Kassein understood.

"A bath? You want to bathe?" he asked.

Of course, there was no way for either of them to be sure, but he realized what she'd been looking for. He put the pitcher back down and stood up, going to find the little basket with the soaps. He pulled one out and brought it to her.

Much to his relief, Alezya's eyes lit up, and she nodded. She wanted to bathe, which wasn't surprising, given her state. She'd been found covered in sleet and blood, carried around in a dragon's dirty claws, and spent most of the night sweating a lot. Kassein gave her a nod, leaving the soap with her, and walked out to order a bath to be brought to his tent.

"Bath," Alezya repeated to herself as he returned, trying to memorize the word.

Kassein smiled, not saying anything, and he took the bowl again, helping her finish breakfast while waiting for the bath to be brought. This time, he didn't personally carry it into the tent; three men from Dajan's unit did it. They came, put the basin full of hot water down, and left just as quickly, trying hard not to stare or let their eyes linger.

Coincidentally, another man brought over the new outfit for Alezya, as Tievin had mentioned. Another coat had most likely been taken from the Grand Intendant's collection; he was the only one wearing such thick and fancy coats in the whole camp, while most soldiers had to make do with capes over their armor and thick layers underneath.

As she was impatient to get herself cleaned, Kassein helped Alezya up, but it got him more worried. She could barely stand on her own, and her arms were still weak and most likely painful. Once she stood next to the large basin, he hesitated. Could he leave her to bathe on her own?

"Kassein?"

She gave him that look, that she was clearly waiting for him to leave to undress, like before. He hesitated, but he had a feeling he shouldn't go away, not when she was in this state.

After a couple of seconds, he sighed and took off his armor, leaving it next to the bed, and went to sit facing the door. He wasn't leaving, but he clearly wasn't intending on peeking. He sat with his legs crossed, hands on his knees, waiting. For a couple of seconds, he didn't hear her move, and he guessed she was surprised he didn't leave. But he couldn't. She may not like him being there while she was bathing, but in her state, he didn't feel safe to let her bathe alone, and there was no one else he could trust with this. It took a little longer, but finally, she let out a faint sigh and began undressing.

Kassein had underestimated his own reactions. He'd seen her naked before, so he didn't think he'd get tense when he was not seeing her naked body, but he'd been wrong. He could hear the sounds of fabric coming off her body and falling to the floor; it was strangely more enticing than anticipated. He could hear her breathing, the light sounds she made, and exactly when she entered the water. Knowing that she was naked, right behind him, made him feel strange, tense, and bothered.

He silently got mad at himself and the poor control of his own emotions. It became harder not to turn around when he heard her hiss faintly. She had a few open cuts that would sting upon meeting the hot water. Still, he anchored himself to the ground and waited. After a few more seconds, he heard her sigh. The hot water had to be a relief for her sore body. Now that he knew she was seated in the basin, it became easier for him to breathe, although his heartbeat wouldn't stay steady.

Perhaps because of the hot water, the room felt hotter and steamier. He forced himself to stare at the entrance and focus his thoughts elsewhere too.

"Ah!"

He turned around at Alezya's shout, worried. He caught her with her arm hanging mid-air, seemingly having dropped the soap. Her fingers were having difficulty holding on to it, or so he guessed.

Their eyes met, and although her body was still submerged in the water with the basin covering it from Kassein's eyes, she blushed helplessly and covered her chest. Kassein sighed. He had to do something about this, or else this would take hours, and for his own sanity, he probably shouldn't endure that.

He stood up, despite Alezya giving him that defying stare again. It made him smile. She had that expression of a defiant, cornered feline again. He didn't linger though and walked around the place to find some of the clean bandages meant for her injuries. To her surprise, he used it to cover his eyes, and just two layers were enough for him not to see anything anymore.

He put down the bandages, and using his spatial memory of the tent, walked up to the bath. His knees hit it first, and he got down, finding the soap quickly. Then, he took a deep breath, and put his hand in the water, almost immediately touching Alezya's skin. Both stopped moving.

He wished he could see her expression at this moment. He heard her breathing a bit louder, but she didn't move. Slowly, he began moving the soap along her skin. He couldn't see her injuries, so he deliberately moved slowly. Was he the only one with that strange clenching down in his stomach?

It was nerve-wracking and made him ridiculously tense when he wished he was cool-headed and composed. She moved, and he resumed washing her, guessing he was on her back. He could hear her move a bit in the water, while he made mechanical movements, having to guess which part he was touching. Although he couldn't see it, his fingers brushing against her skin, making him guess the curves he'd only caught a glimpse of before, was akin to torture. He had a hard time thinking straight, mentally forcing himself to stay calm and keep stroking her skin with the wet soap. Alezya being so silent made it impossible to guess her emotions.

He heard her breathing, her motions in the water, and felt her move just an inch or less away from his hands. Everything she did kept him on his toes, and he was nervous to hear or feel more. The prospect of her being naked, just there where he could touch her, was a lot more complicated and hard to endure than he'd anticipated. He was no child; he was a man with the reactions of a man, and Alezya was easily stirring up those emotions in him, making him feel like a clueless, awkward fool.

"K-Kassein..."

He realized they were done. He dropped the soap in the water, stood up, and retreated away from her. He ripped the bandages off his eyes one second before walking out of the tent.

The cold air hit him like he'd burst a bubble and stepped back into reality. He glanced around, his eyes adjusting to the sudden brightness and ignoring the surprised looks of the men who'd been guarding the tent. His heartbeat was still going miles a minute, despite forcing himself to slow his breathing and calm down. He stood there, ignoring the confused stares on him, glancing around the camp like a hawk looking for prey to attack. None of the nearby men dared to utter a word, and quietly stayed focused on their tasks. It had been a night of heavy snow, and a cold, frosty blizzard had begun, so they were busy, most shoveling the paths from one camp area to another. He glanced up, but there was still no sign of his dragon amongst the clouds, and if he did return, he'd be hard to spot in the now gray sky.

He glanced back up at the mountain; there was no way the tribes could spy anything from the heights in this blizzard, and the archery unit might have already persuaded them against coming any closer.

Braver than his peers, Captain Dajan stepped forward, shouting above the wind.

"Sir, the heavy snow should last a while, but we're taking care of it. Is there any order you'd like us to execute or relay...?"

"No."

There was no need. The camp knew how to function regardless of the weather, and there was no such rule that bad weather would cut short the training or lessen their tasks either. If they were that weak that they'd complain about a bit of snow, those men wouldn't have been sent there. It was annoying, but not a problem. At least it looked like it'd keep the men busy for a while.

Kassein didn't feel like explaining why he was waiting out there, so he just stood up, trying to chase his interaction with Alezya from his thoughts, while at the same time wondering if she was going to be alright dressing by herself. Maybe that was why it was taking a while, but he could hear movement inside, and she hadn't called for him. He simply had to give her time to do things.

He clenched his fists as soon as he thought about her injuries again. Why? Why had they done this to her? What had she chosen to go back to? Did she know she might be harmed? Had she chosen to go back anyway? He'd spent hours taking care of her and focusing on healing her, but now that he was away from Alezya, those questions were back to haunt him. He hated that feeling of being powerless. He couldn't attack the tribes without knowing exactly what had happened, and he couldn't know what had happened unless he found a way for Alezya and him to communicate. His only hope was for Kein to return soon with, hopefully, someone who could help...

Finally, he heard her call him. Kassein took a couple of seconds to prepare himself before walking back inside the tent. Somehow, she had managed to dress by herself, which explained why it had taken a while. She was still slightly blushing when their eyes met, and both looked away, a bit embarrassed by the previous events.

Worse, with that weather, they'd both be confined in the tent for a little while, even if she'd been in a state to go anywhere, which she wasn't. To give himself a few seconds to regain his composure, Kassein took care of the fire in the tent. It was hard to maintain with the sleet outside that was trying to come through the chimney and wet everything, so he had to add some wood and vent it, a bit of smoke made the tent hotter and their eyes itchy.

For a few minutes, neither of them said anything, but he could feel Alezya's eyes on him, even as he had his back turned. It made him even more self-conscious. What was she thinking? Was she disappointed to be back here after failing to go home? Or was she glad they had reunited?

His emotions were caught in a fierce battle inside his head, and meanwhile, he had no idea how to react. He hated being so clueless and uncertain, it wasn't like him.

"...Kassein?"

He had ignored her for too long.

Even with the lack of communication, she was bound to find it odd that he'd kept his back turned to stare at the fire. Kassein took a deep breath and braced himself. When he finally looked at her, it was clear he'd made Alezya nervous too.

She was looking at him apprehensively, which only made him feel worse. He had been so certain he wanted to keep her here, but now, his own willfulness felt childish, and he wasn't sure what was right anymore. Even if he'd known how to talk with her, Kassein would have probably failed to put his conflicted emotions into words. He knew what he wanted, and he understood his heart all too well, but he wasn't sure it was right, nor that it wasn't his own selfishness misleading him. He didn't know what that woman wanted, or what had happened to her, and being in the dark was nerve-wracking. He hated his own immaturity. It was like having his older brother's words thrown in his face again.

"It's alright," he finally said, more to say something and reassure her than anything. "As long as you're safe..."

He glanced at her, and went to sit down next to the bed on the fur rug. He didn't want to sit on the bed. Somehow, he felt he couldn't be that close to her. But he did put his hand on hers, mindful of her injuries.

This simple, small gesture seemed to comfort her a bit, and Alezya faintly smiled at him. That smile was like a dart to Kassein's heart. He was afraid to be mistaken, and he was afraid to let his emotions mislead him. He sighed, and leaned against the mattress, staring at her. At least she was back. The gaping hole in his heart had mended a bit with her presence.

Looking a bit reassured, Alezya laid back down on her flank, leaving her hand where he was holding it and curling up her body so that her face was just inches away from his. She pressed her weak fingers around his hand a bit. For a while, neither of them said anything. They were just staring at each other as if trying to decipher the other's gaze, in a strange silence, with the snowfall in the background like white noise.

Kassein had only ever felt at peace in the midst of a battle, where his thoughts could be drowned out by the sounds of violence and chaos around him.

Yet, in here, confined with that woman, he felt more at peace than ever before, staring into her dark eyes. Neither of them was going back to sleep as it was the middle of the day, but they had nothing to do or say to break the silence, a silence that wasn't awkward. They were simply there, finding comfort in each other's company, holding hands as if that gentle, trustful grip could wordlessly carry their feelings to the other.

He wished he could read her mind. He wished he could have asked her all those questions that haunted him.

Alezya was holding onto his hand, as if looking for comfort too, her eyes looking straight into his without any fear; that wasn't something he was used to, but he did find solace in her gentle gaze. He found that woman fascinating. She could be surprisingly brave at times, and sometimes, she looked incredibly vulnerable.

It made him think about something his older brother had told him before: "*You never care about anyone but yourself.*" Back then, Kassein had thought that was untrue and got mad as a result. Yet, right now, while looking into Alezya's eyes, he was beginning to doubt if he had ever known what it was to truly care for someone. He loved his family, but none of them really needed his protection, his care. He was the seventh in a family of eight children, with a difference of over ten years with his older siblings. None of them had ever needed him like Alezya did.

Kassein was woken up by a light stroke on his cheek. He wasn't used to getting touched in his sleep, and his body reacted to it right away, grabbing the hand. He opened his eyes just as Alezya winced in pain, and immediately let go.

"Sorry," he muttered.

He must have sent the message across because she shook her head with a slight blush and a guilty expression. She was embarrassed to have been caught caressing his face, but as soon as the surprise had passed, Kassein grabbed her hand and put it back against his cheek. He wanted to show her it was alright; he hadn't meant to push her away and was now afraid she'd gotten the wrong message. As he pressed her palm against his cheek, Alezya blushed a bit more. The sudden contact felt incredibly intimate, and he felt his own heartbeat quicken. He liked her fresh skin against his, and that soft flush in her cheeks. Kassein's stomach leaped.

He wanted more... He wanted her to touch him more.

He wanted to touch her more.

As he stared into her eyes, gawking at her reactions, he very slowly turned his head until his lips reached her palm. He held her hand pressed against his face, and with his green eyes riveted on her, he kissed a small square of her skin. Alezya shivered slightly but didn't avert her gaze. She was breathing more heavily, and he could guess her heartbeat had accelerated too. Kassein was trying hard to read her, looking for the slightest sign of fear or disgust, but there was none. There was hesitation and doubt, perhaps, but she was looking right at him, not shying away, although she did look shy as he held her hand. His gaze went from her eyes to her lips.

The sight of that cut on her lower lip cooled his ideas like snow in the sun. She could barely eat properly; what was he thinking about?

Kassein sighed and let go, Alezya's hand falling slowly back on the mattress. He stood up and walked away from her, trying to regain his composure and chase away the image of her chapped lips lingering in his mind. He felt like a shameful animal, lusting after a battered woman. With no idea what else to do, he took care of the fire and put water on to boil, keeping himself busy with anything that would help him avoid looking back at Alezya.

"Kassein?"

Her voice calling him made him stop right in his tracks. He hesitated.

Of course, she was confused by his erratic actions. What was he thinking? Nothing he should be proud of, that's for sure. He'd gotten carried away by that single stroke on his cheek, and unknowingly, she'd encouraged him to pursue his reckless desires. It hit Kassein brutally, but the truth was there. He desired this woman. And he hated himself all the more for it. It was a messed up situation, and he knew all too well it was unfair. She was in no state to refuse him. Worse, she possibly felt indebted to him. Kassein hated that.

"Commander."

Tievin calling him from outside was a welcome intervention.

With a valid excuse to leave the tent, Kassein stepped out without looking back, only feeling sorry for ignoring Alezya like this.

He just didn't have the courage to glance at her right then.

Wrapped up tightly and visibly hating every single snowflake falling on his coat, Tievin was standing outside and seemed surprised when Kassein joined him. He glanced toward the tent but didn't dare voice his question.

"Your dragon is in sight," said Tievin.

He was right. The snow had calmed down while Kassein had fallen asleep, and on the horizon, Kein's orange silhouette could be seen flying toward them. Finally.

Kassein had never felt so relieved to see his dragon come back, even more so as he noticed it wasn't alone. A smaller, slimmer dragon was flying next to Kein, and each dragon was carrying a human silhouette too.

"Get ready," Tievin said to some of the soldiers nearby.

Whatever they were supposed to get ready for, the soldiers nodded and hurried away. By the time Kein landed in the snow a few paces away, two soldiers had already made it back, carrying sets of thick clothing and fur boots, and stood waiting patiently. Kassein had his eyes riveted on the silhouette riding Kein. When his orange dragon growled angrily at the sight of him, he ignored it and walked toward them.

"He lives!"

The woman on Kein's back greeted him with a snarky smile, and effortlessly jumped down, landing elegantly in the snow.

She was tall, sporting a sleeveless leather outfit, with her skin tone the exact same color as Kassein's. As she stood up, she slid her long braid over her shoulder nonchalantly, and with a little amused spark in her dark green eyes, she patted Kein, who gave her an affectionate growl.

One of the soldiers rushed over to offer her the thick clothing, but she just took it without a second glance and walked over to the other dragon.

The second dragon landed more elegantly, its long body making a soft sound on the snow. It was dark gray with ash-colored scales and small black eyes shining like onyx jewels. As soon as its four paws were dug into the snow, it turned its head around to watch the female human on its back get off.

The first woman helped her down, and immediately wrapped the fur cape over her shoulders, then proceeded to help her put the fur boots on right away as she was still wearing basic leather shoes that would be wet in no time. They smiled affectionately at each other before walking over to Kassein and Tievin.

"Good day, Your Highness, my lady," Tievin greeted the two of them with a slight bow.

"Hello, Tievin," said the second woman with a gentle smile. "Your Highness."

She was a very pretty woman. She had beautiful black eyes, slender traits, and an oval face circled by an impressive mane of black hair only held by two thin silver bands. She seemed even smaller once wrapped up in a fur coat and standing next to Kassein and the other woman, who was almost as tall as the Wild Prince. Those two hadn't greeted anybody yet and were just staring at each other. The woman with the high and long braid was staring at Kassein with a smirk, her arms crossed.

"You sent Kein and didn't even come to get me yourself. What kind of trouble did you get into this time?" she scoffed.

"...I need help," Kassein hissed.

"Help?" she repeated. "Did I just hear you ask for help? What happened to the Kassein I knew, who'd die before he asked anyone for help?"

"Kiera," the other woman called her with a little scowl in her voice.

"Oh, come on," she chuckled. "I'm summoned by my brother after well over a year without any kind of news from him. I should get to tease him a little now that he needs me..."

"It's not for me," he retorted.

"Color me curious," she said, tilting her head. "I do hope you didn't make me cross half the continent during a blizzard for nothing!"

"We're happy to see you well, Your Highness," said the other woman, speaking on behalf of her partner.

Kassein glanced at her and finally gave her a faint nod of acknowledgment. "Lorey."

She smiled back politely, but Kiera wasn't having it. She sighed.

"Come on, Kassein, what is it? If you called me of all people, it means you're in some trouble that you can't tell the others about, right?"

Kassein let out a faint sigh, annoyed at his older sister's acumen, but he still turned around to guide them to his tent. Just like him, his sister had no need for winter coats, so the soldier who was still carrying one followed, unsure what to do until Lorey took it from him with a polite smile, causing him to blush. Then, with one look from Tievin, he quickly left the small group of four to go back to his tasks. While the siblings walked ahead, Lorey walked alongside Tievin, a few steps behind.

"How have you been, Tievin?"

"As well as one can be in this area of the Empire, my lady," he said, wrapping his coat a bit more tightly around him.

"I feel you," Lorey smiled. "I miss the heat of the south already. But I'm happy His Highness called Kiera for help... Is he really in a lot of trouble?"

"...I am not quite sure," Tievin sighed. "You shall see for yourself in a minute."

His words left Lorey curious, and she glanced ahead at the two siblings. Despite an eight-year age gap, the two of them were so similar that they looked like twins. She had always thought that the Prince looked older than his real age, and she found it even more true now that he had reached adulthood. He held a very stern, serious, cold demeanor, while his older sister was more youthful and carefree. Kiera was very tall for a woman, almost as tall as her brother, and quite toned too, with large shoulders and long limbs. They had the same very defined jaw, and amongst all their siblings, Kiera and Kassein were also the only ones to not have their father's black eyes nor their mother's pale green eyes, but a mix between the two, a mysterious dark green. Seeing the two of them walk together made Lorey smile; the pair hadn't seen each other in a long while, but Kiera hadn't hesitated a second before hopping on her brother's dragon's back to see what he needed her for.

Finally, they reached the Prince's tent, and he seemed to tense up a little before the entrance. Kiera raised an eyebrow.

"Kassein, what kind of mess did you get into this time?"

"...You'll see."

Lorey and Kiera exchanged a glance, both curious, while Kassein led the way into his tent. When they walked in, they were surprised to find a woman there, in what ought to be the Prince's bed, staring at them with a confused and nervous expression.

Immediately, Lorey knew that woman wasn't from the Dragon Empire. Her skin color, her silky black hair, her eyes, and everything about her felt foreign. Kiera slapped her brother's shoulder.

"You animal!"

"I haven't touched her!" he protested.

"I can confirm, Your Highness," said Tievin, clearing his throat while the siblings glared at each other. "The Commander in Chief has merely been caring for this tribeswoman for the past few days. He graciously left her his bed out of concern for her health."

"What happened to her?" Lorey asked, who had immediately noticed the bruises and bandages.

"We don't really know," Kassein admitted, still rubbing his arm. "I found her in the mountains; some of the tribespeople were attacking her. They were about to kill her..."

"And you got involved?" Kiera guessed. "Gods, you're so much like Dad... So you saved her? And then? She's been here all along?"

"No. I did send her back to her tribe yesterday morning. At least, I tried. We parted ways in the mountains when she decided to, after sunrise, but just an hour later... Kein brought her back, and she... looked like this. Worse than when I left her."

"Gods," Lorey muttered, shocked. "Her own people did this to her?"

"Twice," Kassein insisted, glaring at his sister.

"How awful..."

Alezya was staring at the four of them, legitimately confused about what was happening and who the two women were. Her eyes kept going between the four of them, frowning and nervously pulling the blanket to her. After a little while, Kassein went to sit next to her legs on the bed, not too close.

"...Her name is Alezya," he said while looking at her.

Alezya stared at him once she heard her name, understanding that he might be explaining the situation to those women. Then, he turned back to his sister.

"That's all I know so far," he explained, "but I am not sending Alezya back to her people. Not after they did this to her."

Kiera noticed how he was looking at that woman and let out a long sigh, massaging her temples.

"...Kassein, did you just make me travel half the continent to help you seduce a tribeswoman?"

"To help her," he retorted. "You're the one who knows foreign tribes more than anyone else."

"I know Western tribes, not the Northern ones! ...And you do realize Kassian would rip your head off for this?"

Kassein glared furiously at the mention of their older brother. Meanwhile, Lorey ignored the siblings' banter and approached the bed. With a gentle smile, she got on her knees to face Alezya, and talked to her.

"I'm Lorey," she said, putting a hand on her chest. "Lorey."

Alezya nodded, and put a hand on her own chest, mimicking her.

"Alezya."

Lorey smiled.

"*Niu ga walashiu bilka?*" she then said, using a different language.

But Alezya only frowned, clearly not understanding her.

"Looks like she doesn't speak the Rain Tribe's language," Lorey said.

"No. Her language is entirely different," Kassein declared. "The one word she taught me isn't like anything I know."

"What did you learn?"

"...Food."

A few seconds of silence passed, during which Lorey suppressed a chuckle and Tievin looked elsewhere.

"...That's it?" Kiera scoffed. "Wow, Kassein, no wonder you needed us. You really know your way with a woman, don't you?"

"How long has she been here?" Lorey asked before they could argue again.

"Just a few days," Tievin answered, his eyes on Alezya. "We tried to conceal her existence in the camp so far. I am afraid the rumors will spread quite hastily now that she's back."

"You mean Kassein did whatever he wanted, and you tried to deal with the damages, like always," Kiera sighed. "I don't... Kassein, if Kassian hears about this..."

"He doesn't need to know," her brother angrily retorted.

But Kiera wasn't convinced. She crossed her arms.

"That's why you called me, isn't it? You knew I was the one who wouldn't snitch to our big brother about you taking one of the enemy's women. ...Dara told me what happened in the Capital, Kassein."

"Of course she did," he groaned.

"I am not going to blame you," Kiera insisted. "I'm sure the family berated you enough already. But this... Having a tribeswoman here is not going to help your case. If things get worse with the Northern tribes because of this..."

"Worse? What exactly could get worse?" Kassein angrily retorted, standing up. "Kassian already exiled me here. What kind of result do you think he expects? This was never about the tribes! He doesn't care what I do here as long as I stay out of the way. Out of *his* way."

"That's not true," Kiera said more calmly. "You know he cares. We all care about you, but–"

"But he got rid of me the second I became a nuisance," Kassein hissed. "The Emperor sent his troublesome, irresponsible brother as far away as he could the second I became a hindrance to his pristine reign, and everyone was satisfied. You're the first to come here in two years, Kiera. Don't tell me everyone isn't relieved with me being away."

"You're the one who isn't answering anyone's letters! Sadara said you haven't even been talking to Mom!"

"Don't you dare mention her!" Kassein suddenly roared.

He then burst out of the tent. Kiera sighed, glaring at the door, but her gaze then went to Lorey, who was glaring back.

"What?" she said under her partner's accusatory stare. "You know I didn't say anything that wasn't true!"

"...Did we come here to help or not?"

After a few seconds, Kiera rolled her eyes. As always, Lorey was the voice of reason. She looked at Alezya in the bed next to her.

The tribeswoman seemed worried, as she probably had no idea what had suddenly triggered Kassein to shout and leave. Her dark eyes were lingering on the tent's entrance... In fact, her eyes were really stuck to where Kassein had disappeared seconds ago. That's when Kiera realized.

That tribeswoman wasn't just here against her will, or because she had no other choice. She felt safe here. Kassein and that woman might have gotten closer than she initially thought. Her brother hadn't opened his heart to anyone in ages, and yet, it was clear he and that foreign woman cared about each other. Deeply.

The truth was, he would have never called for help if it hadn't been for someone else's sake... for that woman's sake. It wasn't just that Kassian had cast their little brother away to these mountains; Kassein himself had chosen this exile. He'd stopped answering their letters, and put up walls that no dragon could cross, not letting anybody in. Until now.

After a little while, Kiera turned to Tievin.

"Do they still try to kill each other?"

She did not need to mention who this was about. Lorey turned her eyes to Tievin too.

"...It has become rarer since Kein brought this woman here," he admitted.

He preferred not to mention that they had very nearly murdered each other just a day ago when Kassein had briefly sent Alezya back. Kiera, of all people, would understand what was implied. She turned her eyes back to Alezya, staring at that woman. Then, her eyes went to Lorey, and she eventually shook her head, before walking out. Tievin let out a heavy sigh.

"It can be tough serving the Imperial Family, can't it?" Lorey smiled.

"Stubbornness is their most troublesome family trait," he declared, "but, dare I say, the Commander is most likely relieved you and the Princess came."

"She's happy too. She missed her little brother."

Tievin and Lorey exchanged a complicit glance, and their eyes turned back to Alezya. She was still visibly confused to be left with those two, but Lorey smiled reassuringly.

Outside the tent, Kiera found her brother just a few steps away, glaring at the top of the mountain. Kein had begun scouring the heights with menacing growls again, flying around and scanning for enemies like a bird of prey.

"We're not alone," she commented.

"They are watching her. We caught them spying several times."

"Curious. The tribes have never acted so boldly before..."

For a few seconds, the two of them stood side by side, trying to spot the origin of the stares that triggered their instincts. Kiera's dragon, Kiki, had also taken flight to accompany Kein, seemingly more curious to inspect the mountains than feeling like hunting. After a little while, she uncrossed her arms and turned to the camp. Some of the soldiers close by opened their eyes wide upon seeing her, a striking female copy of their Commander.

"We will help you," she finally said.

"...Because of her?"

"Because I believe Kassian was wrong."

Kassein finally turned to her, shocked. His sister sighed.

"He's always been harsh, and I believe he's been so with you too. It got worse when he took the throne and gave up on that woman... I'm not saying what you did was right in any way, and you already know that, but you're our little brother. He shouldn't have just sent you away. That's not how our family solves things."

Her words took Kassein by surprise, so much so that he had nothing to answer for a while. Kiera looked up at Kein.

"I'll help you," she said again, "as long as you don't tell the family I'm here too."

He nodded.

"You know I have no reason to."

Kiera smiled and gave a faint punch against his shoulder.

"The bad apples stick together," she chuckled. "Come on, let's get started. I am not letting that poor girl sleep one more night in your stinky tent."

Chapter 7

The relief of knowing that Lumie was alive and well felt like a faraway, too short-lived dream that had been caught up and devoured by the subsequent nightmares.

Lying in a bed of pain, Alezya relived the painful memories, over and over. She was aching everywhere, but the worst lay in her memories.

She had been separated from her child, again. It just felt like a nightmare on repeat, a loop of torment she just couldn't get out of.

She cried, silently, painfully. She had no escape, no way out of this madness, no way out of this horrible, gut-wrenching plan her father had imposed on her.

This time, her protests had been met with the worst beating she'd ever received. She had tried to refuse. She had tried, so hard, to voice and shout her anger at her father's evil, disgusting plan. She had shouted from her guts how abominable he was, he and his monstrous plan. She had screamed until they'd hit her face to shut her up, until they'd knocked her to the ground, and kicked her some more.

It was even more horrifying that this scene had happened in front of Lumie's eyes, under her baby's shocked cries. Lumie's terrified screams still haunted her. Alezya hoped her cousin's husband had taken her baby away at some point, but she couldn't remember how that violent scene had ended; she'd passed out before that. She truly hoped Lumie hadn't been forced to witness it for too long, but she truly couldn't tell. She'd already lost sight of most of what was going on since her head had violently hit the ground, but then it was all a blur, an agonizing blur of pain and helplessness.

She had a vague memory of her body being dragged and thrown out of the mountain. She had a faint impression of the familiar cold ground under her, shuffled in waves of fresh snow, and then, seconds later, while she thought she'd passed out, or died, something had grabbed her. She'd been taken away from the cold ground, and lifted up by something rough, but warm.

Then, at some point, she had found herself in Kassein's bed, again.

It was as if the previous events had been but a fleeting nightmare, but sadly, they weren't. It was real, she knew all too well. She was certain from how her face and body hurt, way more than before. She was certain from the way her father's diabolical plan haunted her, like a sentence.

Worse, Alezya was certain because Kassein was furious. Absolutely furious. She felt even more sorry. After all the time he'd spent caring for her, they were back to square one, with her intruding on his bed and needing his care and benevolence, again. He ought to be lost, or to think she was mad. He probably found her troublesome, at least.

Alezya knew she hadn't been gone long, and felt ashamed to be back so soon, and in that state. She knew it probably made no sense to him, no sense at all. And yet, Kassein was by her bedside again, caring for her, guarding her, feeding her, and patiently waiting as she healed from her wounds. His kindness was almost suffocating, especially since Alezya was growing more aware of him, and her father's horrible plan kept resurfacing in her thoughts.

Every time she caught a glimpse of his dark green eyes, she couldn't help but think about it. He wanted her to have a child with Kassein, a child he'd then plan to steal from her. Worse, she'd never see her daughter again if she didn't go along with that horrible scheme... It was her father's curse and warning to her.

His voice still echoed in her mind, more oppressive than any of those nightmare-like memories, far worse than any of the pain she'd endured; she'd never be granted to see Lumie again unless she came back pregnant... Alezya wasn't just heartbroken from having been separated from Lumie once more; she couldn't believe she'd have to betray Kassein to see her child again. She didn't want to believe it.

But it was all too real. Her father had shouted at her, again and again, as he was beating her, that she'd never be allowed to come back and see Lumie until she was pregnant with his child.

Alezya had known her father was horrible from how he'd treated her, but she couldn't believe a single person could have that evil of a heart to wage children in a war.

Her children.

When the pain had retreated a bit, leaving her a few lucid moments lying in the dark on Kassein's bed, Alezya had even found herself cursing at those gods she didn't believe in anymore.

Why? Why her, why her children?

Why to a man as good as Kassein? Why would the gods, if there were any, impose so much suffering on her? Was there a plan from above, as her mother had once taught her to believe?

Alezya had thought about it. She had tried, like someone looking for a light in the dark, a thin strand of hope in the midst of all that pain and despair. As horrible as it was, Alezya had thought about it, or she had tried. Could she do this? Could she go along with her father's despicable plan if it was for Lumie's sake?

One look in Kassein's deep green eyes had told her everything she needed to know. *No.*

No, she would never be able to. That man was too good, and there was no way she wouldn't love another child she'd give birth to as much as she did Lumie. She would never hate *his* child. Kassein had been good to her, so good it almost hurt.

She could feel her own heart growing weaker in his presence every time their eyes met. At times, Alezya wondered if it wasn't just her own wishful thinking, making it look like he possibly liked her. But if she was wrong, what could explain the long hours he spent by her side without asking anything in return? How he slept on a fur rug while she was in his bed? The way he gently took care of her, how he looked at her?

The bath, earlier... She'd felt her heart make a loop several times from how close his fingers had been to her skin. And she had been so glad he didn't see her embarrassed self, her shameless blushing. How could she be having such thoughts in her situation?

She shouldn't have the luxury to think about this. About a man, in that way. She couldn't afford to think about romance or desire, not when she had so much else to think about. Lumie. She had to think about how to save Lumie in a way that wouldn't require sacrificing another child... or conceiving one. And yet, Alezya cursed herself, for she couldn't seem to think straight whenever her eyes met with Kassein's.

Her emotions were long out of control, and she was afraid she couldn't trust herself near him. He was too nice, too caring... He was unlike any man she'd ever met before, and he was breaking the walls she'd erected around herself. He was feeding a hope she shouldn't have let grow in her heart, as it was only adding to her inner turmoil and torment. The way he'd kissed the palm of her hand... She knew that moment would haunt her for a long time.

However, right now, she was feeling nervous again.

Who were those women who had shown up? Alezya had been thunderstruck by their abrupt arrival. She couldn't have foreseen that she would feel so threatened by two women suddenly appearing, yet here she was alone again, with her thoughts spiraling. When had those two women arrived, and why?

Alezya was pretty sure those women hadn't been in the area before, as their clothing suggested. From what she'd seen of them, one had to be related to Kassein, as they were too strikingly similar not to be related. But if he had brought his sister or relative here, who was the other one? She bore no resemblance to him, but they clearly knew each other. They had been near each other with that proximity of people who were comfortable with one another, not strangers. She wasn't a subordinate either for she hadn't acted as wary as other people in his presence. She hadn't bowed or stood still at the entrance of the habitation. Lorey, she was called.

Alezya hated herself for feeling so threatened by another woman of whom she knew nothing. Except that Lorey was beautiful. Really, really beautiful, with her big dark eyes. Graceful and kind too. A kind beauty that she hadn't expected had suddenly appeared. Until now, she had thought she was the only woman in this place, the only woman near Kassein.

Why did she hate that another woman had come while she didn't mind his relative much? Alezya knew the answer, but she didn't like how easy it was to read her own pathetic heart.

She waited alone, unsure of what to do next. She hated that they had all gone out and she was trapped here, too injured to move. Her body was aching, but her mind was aching even more to be out there, to see what Kassein and those women were up to. She had never wanted to leave this place so much to peek outside.

She could hear the dragon, and at some point, she wasn't sure if there was more than one creature growling, which made her nervous. Another dragon? Or was that merely an echo? Alezya was so curious that her body had begun leaning forward toward the entrance when that woman came back. Lorey. Her heart sank.

Why? Why was she allowed to freely come and go inside Kassein's living space? Alezya didn't say anything and just watched as Lorey laid out on the bed what she had brought: new clothes, all clearly female clothing. There was a set of undergarments, a dress on which some fur had been sewed, a set of small gloves, and some thick pants. Some of the fabrics were foreign to Alezya, but she could tell all those were meant for a woman in a cold setting like this.

Not only that, but Lorey also put down a pretty comb for her and a headband that looked like her own, a simple silver half-ring.

Then, she smiled as if this was a gesture of goodwill. Alezya nodded, with a half-smile, but she couldn't help but feel conflicted about those "presents." Where had those come from? Were those Lorey's? She hated how tormented her heart was by the apparition of one woman.

Where had Kassein gone, and why wasn't he coming back? She was growing more nervous and couldn't relax. The pain was keeping her on edge, but not nearly as much as the worries that grew inside her mind.

Not long after that, a smaller basin of hot water was brought in with small, smooth cloths, and to her surprise, Alezya realized that Lorey was here to help her clean and change. That woman wanted to serve her? Was that why Kassein had brought her, to take over in taking care of Alezya? Perhaps he had realized that it was unfitting of him, a male warrior, to be taking care of a woman...

Once again, she felt her heart fall a little. If the other woman was his relative, was Lorey a servant? Or was she a friend his relative had brought to help him take care of Alezya? Had he told them some bothersome woman had appeared, and she had brought a woman to save his pride? Or had his clan heard of this mad situation, and decided to set things straight, unable to bear one of their warriors' pride defiled like this?

Either way, Alezya decided to stop letting those doubts sour her mood. She had to set her priorities straight, and the first one was that she had to heal. She wanted to heal and stop being some dead weight, incapable of helping Lumie and relying on Kassein.

She accepted Lorey's help, convincing herself that this was the proper thing to do to begin with, and focusing on the moment to calm down her thoughts. She had to stop that spiral of nervousness and worry... Alezya slowed down her breathing and focused on what they were presently trying to do: clean her up. Her injuries hurt a lot, but Lorey was kind and extremely gentle with each of her movements.

She patiently helped Alezya undress and washed her with hot water and that nice-smelling thing, being mindful of her injuries and making sure to gently smile often as if to reassure her.

After a bit, Alezya realized she genuinely wouldn't have been able to dislike such a kind and patient woman, even if she wanted to. And she didn't; she refused to turn into a jealous, bitter creature. She wanted to get off that dangerous, dark path before she'd turn into something she hated. She had seen some of her half-sisters, who had always been quietly jealous of her beauty, rejoice over her fall into disgrace instead of helping her. Alezya refused to be anything like them.

In fact, she hoped she could make allies with these people, especially now that there were women here. Unlike her half-sisters, her mother's clan had shown her what women, if they were all tight-knit, were capable of. Her mother had come from one of the only clans that were women-led, a rare matriarchy amongst all the other male-dominated clans. They weren't recognized by the other clans, and often ignored, but it hadn't kept them from doing well and being a peaceful, thriving clan of their own.

Alezya only had faint memories of it from the few times she had visited her mother's clan when she was much younger. She had never gone back after her mother had left, and she wasn't even sure where this clan was located. But she only had good memories of it, with images of women freely speaking, laughing, and gathering together. She wished she knew what had happened to her mother's family, but she had never been allowed to go and visit them after her mother had left. She only knew they were far, a dangerous journey she hadn't even considered for her escape with Lumie. But perhaps, after this was all over, finding them wouldn't be such a crazy idea. They would welcome a woman and her baby, she was sure of it. Or her babies. If she ever did get pregnant with Kassein's child, went back to her clan, and managed to escape with Lumie, then...

"Alezya?"

She was taken out of her thoughts by Lorey's gentle smile. She was done washing her and was presenting Alezya with the bandages and paste to re-apply to her injuries. She helped her back to the bed, and then, Lorey carefully tended to her injuries, obviously somewhat experienced.

This was the right way, Alezya thought. A man like Kassein shouldn't have lowered himself to a task that was a woman's job, to begin with... She tried to ignore the pinch in her heart as Lorey finished bandaging all the injuries that ought to be and presented her with the new clothes to help her put them on. Alezya nodded with a slight blush and, with Lorey's support, got dressed.

Those new clothes were even more comfortable and fitting, and she guessed that the fabrics ought to be more expensive. There was a sort of wool she'd never seen before, and the undergarments were made of that same thin and cool fabric that Kassein had gifted her before for her hair.

Once dressed, she already felt a lot better. Lorey was now helping her rebandage her hands when the other woman came in. She was definitely nothing like any other woman Alezya had met before. First of all, she was tall, almost as tall as Kassein. Alezya had decided they ought to be siblings, given the striking resemblance. She was the tallest woman Alezya had ever met, and Alezya herself was considered rather tall amongst her own people.

Moreover, she was muscular, which was also highly unusual. Not as much as the men Alezya had seen out there or her sibling, but she was still the most impressively fit woman she'd ever seen. She didn't seem to mind the cold, as her incredibly defined arms were showing under the black fur cape she had put on. She had put on the same shiny protective coverings that the other warriors in the Dragon Clan wore, but hers was bronze-colored. It covered the shape of her chest perfectly, as well as arm and leg braces. That woman was a female version of Kassein, except for her long brown braid and softer, rounder face shape. Was she a warrior too? Was there such a thing amongst the Dragon Clan as a female warrior? Perhaps that was why she was leaving Lorey to take care of her... or perhaps Lorey was her helper of some sort.

Alezya still thought their customs were most likely different. Still, she hoped Lorey hadn't come here to assist Kassein like she perhaps already did his sister. She tried to chase those thoughts away, annoyed at her own pettiness. The two women exchanged a few words, and Lorey suddenly turned back to Alezya, while her hand was pointed toward the other woman.

"*Kiera,*" she said. "*Ha ku Kiera.*"

Alezya gave them a faint nod. Kassein, Kiera. Even their names sounded similar; that woman was definitely Kassein's sibling. She couldn't tell if Kiera was older or younger though. Perhaps they didn't have much of an age difference. They probably had the same mother, given how alike they were. The woman gave her a faint smirk as she looked Alezya up and down. Then, the two women exchanged in their odd language again, although Lorey was still busy helping her with the bandages and re-applying paste on her injured hands.

As soon as she was done fastening the dressings, she smiled again at Alezya, leaving her alone on Kassein's bed, and went to stand next to that woman, Kiera.

Kassein suddenly walked in, taking Alezya by surprise. She found herself unconsciously holding her breath, both relieved and shocked to see him again so soon. For some reason, she'd expected, and feared, to see him less now that those two women had appeared...

Unlike Alezya, the two other women must have expected his arrival, because neither of them reacted to it. It was only her blushing and feeling flustered, while they just watched with perfectly composed expressions as he walked up to Alezya first. He had barely glanced toward nor talked to them, making Alezya feel a bit relieved... and once again hating her spiteful self. She tried to chase those thoughts away, focusing on the happy leaps of her unsteady heart instead. He was acting the same toward her, wasn't he?

She stared at him as he walked over naturally, overly conscious of each of his movements, and their eyes met for just a second. His deep, green eyes were the same... He immediately put a knee down next to the bed, his face a bit below her eye level. Kassein was so tall that even with Alezya sitting on the bed, she wasn't much higher than him. His eyes went to her fresh bandages, as if double-checking that Lorey had taken good care of her, but Alezya only felt all the more embarrassed.

Why was he kneeling in front of her? And in front of other women too? Wouldn't his sister find this undignified? Alezya nervously glanced at the other two, expecting them to protest this ridiculous situation any second now... but neither of them seemed about to jump in and tell him to stand up. At least, not yet. Lorey had a gentle gaze over them, while Kiera, with her more serious attitude, had her arms crossed and was staring at her brother, but she didn't seem mad. Her intense stare made Alezya nervous. She grabbed Kassein's forearms, trying to pull him up and have him stand up before his sister got truly mad...

He noticed her gaze and glanced back. With one word from him, both women left, Lorey with her smile still on, but his sister rolled her eyes... making Alezya even more nervous. Her eyes kept lingering on the entrance. What if she truly got mad after this? What if she reported this to their clan's elders?

"Alezya."

Pulling her out of her thoughts, Kassein gently grabbed her attention and her hands in his. Alezya looked down. His hands were so large and warm on hers... They were even bigger than her thighs, and yet, he was holding her hands so carefully, mindful of her injuries. His body heat soothed her a bit.

She was a bundle of nerves ever since she'd seen Lumie. Her snowflake was still up there, waiting for her mom, needing her mom. And this man's gentle, insanely caring hands were her only way back...

Alezya felt choked up. She didn't know what to do. She wanted Lumie back, and she wanted her baby safe with her. She would have done anything for that, but this awful plan? She let the tears out, feeling sorry for Lumie, for herself, and for Kassein who probably thought she was insane. He had to. How else could he have understood her crazy actions otherwise...?

Alezya shook her head and lowered it, embarrassed to be crying.

She had been a mess and now, she couldn't even fight to hold back those tears. She was tired. She was tired of being her clan's pawn and watching her child suffer for it. She was tired of being such a bad mother, incapable of protecting Lumie properly...

Kassein's hand took her by surprise. She felt his warm, large hand gently cupping her cheek, and she looked up to meet his concerned green eyes. He had gotten so close, for a second, he took her breath away. He looked concerned, his dark, straight eyebrows furrowed, his green irises riveted on her. She didn't want him to be concerned for her, she didn't deserve it.

For a second, Alezya wanted to push his hand away and shout how bad of a woman she was, how wrong he was for caring for her.

She lifted her hand, with the intent to push his away, but... but before she knew it, she was pressing his palm against her cheek even more and closing her eyes, finding comfort in this warm hand. Her heart was too weak, too battered to push the one hand that wanted to console her away. Even if it was just for a bit, she needed this. She needed Kassein's gentleness.

As she didn't push him away, but instead leaned against his hand to cry silently, she felt Kassein's thumb gently caressing her other hand.

Nothing mattered but the two of them, in this place, with the sounds of her quiet crying and hectic breathing.

For just a moment, Alezya wanted to imagine the world had paused to let her cry and seek comfort. She couldn't go on anymore if she didn't find one gentle hand in this world. What lay ahead was too hard, too much. She hated herself for not being able to protect Lumie, for being kicked out again, and for the cries of her baby that still echoed in her head. What had Lumie possibly thought, seeing her mom abandon her again?

Alezya couldn't take it anymore. She wanted her baby back now. She needed her little snowflake, in her arms, safe from this mad world of men...

"Alezya."

Kassein's whisper grounded her in the present again.

Alezya opened her teary eyes and pulled away from those dark thoughts and the ache in her heart. She saw his green, helpless eyes.

Slowly, he moved, and with his hand, guided her to put his forehead against hers, taking Alezya by surprise again. He closed his eyes, and she did the same, simply choosing to let go and go along with this. Both his hands cupped her cheeks now, and she held onto his wrists a bit tighter, as if silently asking him not to let go.

She needed him... Alezya finally accepted what she had pushed away all along. She needed Kassein. She needed his gentleness and his strength. She couldn't do this alone.

For once in her life, there was a man who was genuinely trying to help her, asking for nothing in return, and she wanted to accept it. His gentle, slow, and warm breathing, against her face, was helping her calm down. She was scared, and she wanted her baby back. She wouldn't be able to go against her father, not alone.

Whichever way things went... She would need Kassein's help.

And she wanted him. She wanted his large, warm hands to hold her, and never let go. She could prepare her heart. Alezya had done it before.

She'd trusted, and been disappointed, and even if her sore heart wanted to believe Kassein wouldn't turn out like the others, she wanted to believe that even if he did, she would survive. As long as she had Lumie...

Yes, as long as she had her baby, she could endure anything. But she wouldn't be able to survive without her little snowflake.

Slowly, after a while passed in this position, the two of them silently holding on to each other, she calmed down. Alezya was clinging to his thick wrists, until she didn't need to anymore, and released her grip a little. Her crying had stopped, her breathing had slowed down, and her heart was under her control again.

She opened her eyes, and Kassein did the same, pulling his head back an inch to look at her. She tried to gather a weak, half-hearted smile to tell him she was alright.

She wasn't ready for what he did next. Still holding her face between his hands, Kassein slowly moved to press his lips against her forehead.

His kiss took Alezya's breath away, and from his mouth on her forehead, a wave of warmth spread throughout her whole body. Something in her awoke, something she'd thought was long extinct... Her heartbeat quickened, and Alezya felt the blood rushing to her cheeks and to her extremities. His lips... Alezya felt almost endangered by them, and the sensations they provoked in her.

Suddenly, she felt all too aware of Kassein's presence, in a different way. Of his large body, his warm hands, his hot breath... his thick lips. She was so shocked by her own thoughts, it took her a second to mentally slap herself out of it.

Thankfully, Kassein's lips left her skin, and he didn't seem to notice her turmoil, as he pulled his hands too, and gently helped her move into a lying position. Alezya was desperate to hide her troubling thoughts from him and let herself be manipulated like a doll, obediently lying down as he pulled the blankets over her.

What was she thinking? *What was she thinking?!*

How could she harbor such thoughts...? Had her father's horrible plan gotten to her? She was troubled beyond words by Kassein's kiss.

Maybe he hadn't even thought much of it, maybe it was a custom in his world. Maybe this was just a meaningless gesture toward a woman he found all too pathetic...

Alezya's heart was in for a tumultuous race again in her chest. She could barely dare to look at him again, and she awkwardly tried to wipe the remains of her tears off her face as an excuse to hide her shameful eyes. It was only getting worse. Now she felt too aware of his bare skin... and the sensations in her stomach. Was it because he'd acted too kind to her? Was she merely troubled by his disarming kindness, too inexperienced to resist?

Kassein didn't seem very aware of her trouble, thankfully for her. Or perhaps he thought her blushing was on account of the crying.

Once she was tucked into his bed again, he simply sat next to it.

Except this time, he didn't just put his back against the far end of his bed but sat right next to where Alezya's upper body was, facing her, dangerously close. Not only that, but he also put his arm on the mattress and held her bandaged hand.

He probably didn't think much of it, but it took Alezya a little while to steady her heart again. She tried to slow down her breathing and focus on Kassein's hand holding hers. Her hand was pale and bandaged, while his was warm, large, dark, and in some areas, punctuated by orange scales.

She wondered if his dragon was still outside... She hadn't heard it growl in a little while now. Or had Kein gone with the sister? She still couldn't believe she actually knew a dragon's name... nor that she had seen one up close. Kassein's thumb gently rubbing her hand brought her thoughts back to the present moment.

Finally, she felt safe enough to look into his green eyes again. He gave her a faint smile, and leaned even more against the bed, staring at her. What an odd man... A warrior who let a foreign woman have his bed, and simply sat beneath her. Who was content to hold her hand for as long as she needed it... A madman, she thought.

She wondered how different her life would have been if she'd been promised to a man like Kassein. Would he have believed her, if she'd given birth to *his* all-white baby...? She wondered how Kassein would react to Lumie if he ever saw her. Would he think she was an abnormal creature too? Would he suddenly feel disgusted by her if he knew she'd been married and rejected? No man she knew would willingly take a "used" woman...

She pushed those thoughts aside to focus on her and Lumie's survival. She was safe with Kassein, and Lumie was safe as long as her father believed she could bear another child. What was she to do now?

For once, Alezya felt thankful for the language barrier between them. If it wasn't for that, she would have had the difficult choice of whether to tell him the truth or not... Would she have confided in him, telling him the whole truth and asking for help, if she could? Or would she have kept it all to herself and acted like she hadn't been married before, like she wasn't part of some horrible scheme for her daughter's sake?

"...Kassein," she muttered.

She got his attention, and he slightly lifted his eyebrows, staring at her even more intensely.

How she wished she could read into those deep green eyes and know his thoughts. She held on to his hand, a bit tighter. *Don't let me go*, she wanted to beg him. Let me trust someone, one more time... but Alezya couldn't believe her own hopes. She knew she didn't have that luxury, for if she was wrong, Lumie would be the one to pay the price, and she couldn't have that. What was she to do? Use Kassein, like her father wanted? But she knew she'd have two children to protect, and she didn't want to flee, carrying the child of an innocent man who'd shown nothing but kindness to her.

Moreover, she knew nothing of his world, and if she was honest, she knew too little of him too. Once they got closer, if they got closer, would he simply let her go?

She couldn't abandon Lumie, so she would have to go back, no matter what. And once she got back, what would she do? Her father would only use her like some vessel while she grew his revenge plan in her womb? She tried to think of a way, any possible way she could fight back and protect her child, or children. It was insane to plan as far ahead as having to protect a child she'd conceive with Kassein, but Alezya knew she had to think about it now. She knew that her father wouldn't be fooled, and he'd definitely have the clan's Healer confirm if she was pregnant or not. He was definitely not going to take her word for it. Alezya knew he would check, and she couldn't think of any way to possibly fool them. They wouldn't allow her back until they were sure she'd accomplished her part of their horrible plan. Whether she would lie with Kassein or not would have so much weight on Lumie's fate.

Worse, she knew it wasn't madness nor that far-fetched, not with the way Kassein looked at her, cared for her... and yet, she knew how dangerous it would be to fall in love with him. Her own heart was barely listening to her anymore, would she be able to do anything if she gave in to him even more? Her only certainty was that she would never, ever abandon Lumie.

But what of Kassein? What would she do if they got any closer than this? She would potentially put him through so much... and he had no idea. He couldn't have known she was some viper sent by her father to use him... Could she be that cruel, that selfish? She was so desperate to protect Lumie, and yet, her heart was already aching for him. She couldn't possibly protect them both, and she refused to leave her fate in his hands either. She'd been deceived by men too many times, she couldn't believe in him so easily. Alezya knew how kind Kassein was now, but the man she had been married to had once been kind too... and she didn't have it in her to take any more risks.

And even if, by some miracle, Kassein truly was as good of a man as he'd been acting all along, would he be willing to take on all the risks that would come with it? Did she have what it would take to protect him too?

"Alezya."

He had simply whispered her name, but without knowing, Kassein made her heart ache even more.

Why? Why was he so kind and caring? Things would have been so much simpler if he was just another heartless brute... Alezya let out a long sigh. Her head ached a bit, and she felt sore in various places. She moved her body closer to the edge of the bed, closer to him, holding on tight to his hand. *Just don't let go*, she wanted to say. But she didn't have the words for it...

Should she give it a try? Just to learn a bit about his world. She despised that her hateful father would have seen an opportunity from it, while Alezya was just trying to find ways to survive. Somewhere in her heart, there was a faint hope that maybe, just maybe, that man would be the solution to end her suffering.

And once again, she shut that down. Hope was ever so quick to disappoint. She let herself drift to sleep while staring into Kassein's eyes, wondering if that man had any secrets of his own.

She awoke later, and the pain in her leg had gotten worse.

Alezya grimaced and tried to glance around but from how dark it was, she could only assume it was nighttime. She painfully moved, trying to massage her leg or find a position where it wouldn't hurt so much. She turned and found Kassein asleep beneath the bed again. So he hadn't gone to sleep anywhere else...

Alezya was relieved. She had feared the other women's arrival would change things, but for some reason, he still found it suitable to sleep beside her on that fur rug. Not only that, but he seemed peacefully asleep, using his arm as a cushion, his body on its flank, turned toward the bed.

Had he fallen asleep while looking at her too? She leaned over the edge of the bed, ignoring her sore body, trying to stare at him. He seemed so peaceful while sleeping... probably the sleep of someone who feared few things in this world. Alezya wouldn't have been able to sleep so deeply if it wasn't for her body being exhausted. She'd spent the last two years on edge, desperate to protect Lumie, keep her from any harm, surviving while being ostracized to gather food and other things they needed to survive...

 She let her thoughts drift toward the mountain again. Was Lumie alright, in her cousin's care? Zenia and Suolk could probably provide better for a child that wasn't their own than Alezya had for her own baby... She felt guilt choke her up again. Her baby was probably living a better life now that she was a hostage of their clan than while she'd lived with her mom since she was born.

She felt the tears come up again, and she chastised herself for it.

She had to stop crying... The crying would solve nothing. She needed to get stronger, for Lumie's sake. She needed a plan. She needed her baby back. Her father wouldn't give her child back until he believed she was pregnant with Kassein's child. She didn't care what would happen to her, but she needed Lumie to be safe, and out of her father's reach.

"...Alezya?"

Kassein had opened an eye. He found her eyes over him, and she greeted him with a faint smile. Ignoring the pain, she extended her arm, and boldly caressed his spiky cheek with her fingertips. His skin was so warm... How could he be so warm while sleeping on the floor? Did that have to do with the dragon, like the scales on his skin? Someone like Kassein surely wouldn't have had any issue keeping a child safe from her father, Alezya thought. But could she really trust Kassein?

Either way, she had to make her father's spies think she was going along with the plan. She was already sleeping in his habitation; it wouldn't be so hard to show she was close to him. At least for now, she could trick them into believing she was playing their game...

He put his hand over hers on his cheek and closed his eyes again.

He seemed tired, and she found him looking a bit childish like this. She wondered if he was younger or older than she was. He didn't seem very old... but it was hard to tell, with his kind. She wasn't familiar with the people of the Dragon Clan, and they were so different in so many ways.

Soon enough, Kassein's breathing eased into a peaceful sleep again, still holding her hand. The position wasn't too painful for either of them, so Alezya didn't feel like taking her hand back. In fact, the warm touch of Kassein's skin was soothing to her too. She really wished she'd never have to let go of that hand... She had to get better, soon. She had to understand him and his world better.

Their hands still linked, Alezya laid her head down on the very edge of the bed, an eye on him, and fell back asleep.

The next morning, Alezya woke up all alone, and thankfully, not due to any pain but naturally. It clearly was the morning... How long had she slept?

She felt rested, and a whole lot better. Kassein was gone, and his spot on the floor was cold. The habitation was empty, but things weren't quiet outside. She could hear activities going on, the voices of men, and the faint wind against the fabric walls.

Alezya took a little while to sit up and assess the pain throughout her body. She was healing, and faster than the norm again. What kind of medicine did the Dragon Clan have that she could possibly recover so fast? Was it really fine for Kassein to be wasting their medical resources on her? Back in her clan, herbal medicine was one of the most valuable things she could exchange... but maybe here, they had plenty of it, enough that he could use some on one of the enemy's women...

She let out a faint sigh, stretching what she could, and taking a glance around. This place was now familiar, familiar enough for her to feel completely safe to wake up in. Kassein hadn't even gotten mad at her for stealing a weapon! She still felt guilty when she thought about the tiny blade she'd hidden under the pillow, but it seemed to be of little consequence. To think she'd been prepared to risk her life for a theft he thought nothing of...

She glanced at the bed, where the thick furs were stacked up, only one having fallen off during her sleep. The comb Lorey had brought for her was still lying at the end of the bed, and she grabbed it. Even that was a beautiful item, something she wouldn't have dreamt of owning back in her hole in the mountain.

Slowly, she began combing the ends of her hair, noticing how messy it had gotten while she slept. She hadn't been able to properly care for it in a while, and it was long too. Those other two women didn't wear their hair loose, did that mean they were already committed? They had their hair at strange lengths and in strange hairdos... perhaps it meant nothing here. After all, Kassein had touched and arranged her hair, so he probably had no idea of the significance of it.

She blushed a bit again upon remembering his fingers in her hair.

He seemed to like her hair... With this in mind, Alezya combed her long black locks twice as meticulously. A few years back, she was considered the beauty of her clan, but she hadn't been able to afford to pay much attention to her appearance since Lumie's birth. She had probably lost the shine of her prime years...

She felt a bit dejected when she thought of women like her cousin, who could afford to spend time, herbs, and effort on their appearance. Being a single mother hadn't allowed her to spend any time being a young woman. Alezya chased those thoughts away and put the comb down.

Now that her hair was a bit better, she checked on her injuries and rearranged her bandages where she could; her hands were still injured and painful. She had used them to try and protect her head... She shivered, remembering how half a dozen men had unleashed their wrath on her, beating and kicking her against the floor. She could have died, and at the time, she had genuinely thought she would. Her flank had taken a lot of the damage too, but the bruising was already fading... and her headache was mostly gone. What kind of sorcery did Kassein's people have that she could heal so fast?

"Alezya!"

She glanced up at the feminine voice and spotted Lorey as she stepped in with a little tray of food. Again, Alezya couldn't help but feel that twinge of jealousy for her to be waltzing in so casually... But Lorey clearly didn't expect to see the male warrior for she walked straight to her bedside and put the tray aside. Her warm smile made Alezya feel guilty of her bitter feelings again; that woman showed her nothing but kindness, and she was already helping her out, checking her injuries and changing the bandages carefully.

"Lorey," Alezya said, hoping to greet her somehow.

Lorey seemed a bit surprised to hear her name but gave her biggest smile yet and a big nod. Then, to Alezya's surprise, she began talking.

She was talking too fast in their strange language, and Alezya couldn't understand any of it, but it didn't seem to matter. It looked like Lorey had decided to chat with her anyway, perhaps to make her feel a bit more comfortable, or perhaps in an attempt to befriend her? Alezya tried to listen while the young woman helped her with her bandages, cleaning and dressing them again. They truly had a lot of clean water and bathing items to spare for her... but Alezya took it all gratefully, feeling a bit happy to become more and more presentable every day. When they were done washing her, she presented Lorey with the comb she had left.

"Thank you," Alezya said, showing how she'd been able to comb her hair.

Lorey smiled again, and having clearly mistaken her, took the comb and moved to sit behind her on the bed. Alezya was frozen in shock for a few seconds. She hadn't had another woman comb her hair since her wedding ceremony! But she didn't do anything to stop Lorey.

In fact, she felt a bit emotional. It was like when she was young, and her mother would gently help her comb her long black hair... The older ladies during her wedding had mercilessly pulled and been completely inconsiderate of the pain they inflicted on her, but Lorey was as gentle as one could be. In a matter of minutes, she was not only done combing her hair, but she had also braided a few strands and arranged them around the silver headband she'd given her the previous day. Alezya felt grateful upon touching her newly arranged hair... and a little bit prettier.

"*Ti jib ha kuha,*" Lorey then said, pointing at the food.

"*Kuha!*" Alezya repeated, happy to finally recognize a word.

Lorey seemed surprised by her sudden excitement but presented her with the food.

"...*Taam,*" Alezya said, remembering it meant food.

Lorey nodded encouragingly. She then began gathering the used bandages around the room and cleaning up a bit while Alezya ate.

It was more of that soup with the chunky bits she liked. What kind of meat was this?

"Lorey," she called her. "*Taam?*"

Upon Lorey's confusion, she tried to point at the chunky bits in the soup, having isolated a couple on her spoon. Then, Lorey smiled.

"*Lehma,*" she said.

"*Leh-... Lehma,*" Alezya repeated, trying to imitate the guttural sounds.

Lorey smiled and nodded. Then, she came back, next to Alezya, and showed her the little cup of fruits on the side.

"*Atiwut,*" she said.

Was that their word for berries? *Atiwut,* Alezya mentally repeated. She really hoped she was going to remember these things... *Lehma* meant meat, or perhaps that specific type of meat. *Kuha* was to eat, *taam* was food... She remembered *inkir,* for more. What was the word for water again? *Mahi,* or *shrib*? One of those two?

"*Shrib?*" she asked Lorey, pointing at the jug.

Lorey took the jug and tilted it to point at the content, more precise than the other two.

"*Mahi,*" she said.

Then, she pretended to drink from it.

"*Shrib,*" she said, mimicking the action of drinking again.

Alezya enthusiastically nodded. She was starting to get this, and Lorey seemed only too happy to help her out. Maybe it wasn't insane to try and learn their strange language. Maybe it wasn't insane at all, but on the contrary, her best chance.

"Alezya?"

She looked up at Lorey, wondering what she wanted. To her surprise, Lorey pointed at the water, then at her. Did she want her to drink?

"*Mahi*," she repeated. "*Lorey, mahi?*"

She then pointed at her lips, and that's when Alezya understood: she wanted to learn her language too. Alezya hesitated. She was apprehensive about teaching Lorey or anybody else. Was it because she was nervous to teach her language to a foreigner? Or because she felt she would be betraying the clans if she did so?

...What if the Dragon Clan used this against them? She couldn't even understand why she felt so loyal to the people up the mountain. Perhaps because this wasn't just about her own clan, but about all the people that lived up there. She had that heavy feeling that at this precise moment, if she began teaching the Dragon Clan their language, she might be the first one to topple their fate... and she wasn't ready to take on such a responsibility.

Lorey seemed to notice how troubled she was by her simple question, and gently put a hand on her knee, giving her a compassionate smile.

Then, she got up, and resumed her tasks again, not insisting any longer. Alezya was a bit grateful for that. She felt bad refusing Lorey when she'd already learned a few new words herself. She silently resumed eating, mentally repeating the words she had just learned to remember them, while Lorey seemed to be cleaning around or after her.

After observing her for a little bit, Alezya couldn't help but notice that Lorey was mindful of Kassein's place, and not daring to touch too many of his things either. She would wash or throw out the used bandages, take care of the fire and take out the extra ashes, rearrange the furs on the bed, or clean the dust off the fur rugs outside, but she didn't touch any of the weapons, nor attempt to rearrange the mess on the table at the other end of the room.

In fact, she carefully only took care of anything that had to do with Alezya but didn't dare touch any of Kassein's belongings, nor venture into his private space. This realization made Alezya a little happier and rid her of the jealousy she had felt toward Lorey. It was hard to hold any negative feelings toward a woman who was acting so selflessly kind toward her. Alezya couldn't help but wonder what her status actually was. She was too beautiful not to be married already, but she didn't know the signs of a married woman in the Dragon Clan. What of Kassein's sibling? Was she married too? It was Alezya's first time seeing a female warrior, so she wondered how different their customs possibly were.

"Kassein?" Alezya asked as she had just finished eating.

Lorey raised her head from the fur she had been busy cleaning off at the entrance and smiled.

"Kassein, Kiera, Tievin," she listed, before pointing outside.

So the other three people she knew were all together? Alezya wanted to go. She wanted to get some fresh air, out of this place, and see what Kassein was doing when he wasn't with her.

"...Kein?" she asked.

This time, there was no dragon growl to answer her, but Lorey gave her an amused smile for some mysterious reason. The young woman put the fur back on the bed, and took the tray away, but only after glancing to see if Alezya had finished it all. And she had, much to Lorey's satisfaction, it seemed. She took it out but came back too quickly to have taken it anywhere, confusing Alezya.

Next, she walked to the bed and helped her up.

After a minute, Alezya realized: Lorey was actually preparing her to go outside! She gave her a new fur coat, a brown one which was a bit too long for her, but nicely soft and warm. Then, Lorey put on a similar one. It didn't seem like Lorey's coat was tailored either, making Alezya wonder from whom they were borrowing these. Those coats were too small to belong to Kassein and clearly weren't made for women. Then, she remembered the tall but scrawny man. Tievin. He seemed the right frame for these coats...

With Lorey's help and arm under hers, Alezya realized she was already fine to walk, and more than happy to. The two young women left together, and Alezya was greeted by a beautiful, blue sky.

There was nothing more beautiful than a snow-filled landscape on a sunny day, and for the first time, she was able to take a proper look around. There were lots of habitations like Kassein's, but his seemed to be much bigger and a bit isolated from the others... probably to mark his higher status, she thought. Directly on their right, a young man dressed in warrior attire suddenly exclaimed something. Had he been guarding the place? He was carrying the tray that Lorey had just taken out. Seeing that he was bowing, Alezya turned to Lorey for help, as he seemed to be addressing her, or both of them.

"*Dajan*," Lorey said, pointing at the man. "*Dajan.*"

"*D-Dajan*," Alezya repeated.

The man then replied something enthusiastically and stood back up, confirming that was his name. Much to Alezya's shock, he not only answered but bowed his head again respectfully. Another warrior bowing to a female prisoner and a woman! She glanced back nervously at Lorey, but the other woman didn't seem shocked at all; she only replied something to Dajan before she pulled Alezya along as they left.

She was still completely confused by the Dragon Clan's strange customs. Or was she missing some information? Perhaps Lorey's status was higher than she'd thought? If she was some clan's matriarch or a chief's wife, it would have explained things a bit, but that didn't seem to be the case...

Alezya was getting more nervous now, wondering if she was going to make a mistake that would get her killed. Kassein had seemed to have the higher status here, but now that she was out in their clan, she was getting worried she'd had her initial beliefs all wrong. She kept looking around and back at Lorey for cues.

For one, the other woman seemed perfectly at ease and unbothered, which might mean Lorey was safe and exempt from showing respect to the warriors. And there was nothing but male warriors around. They were all wearing more or less the same uniform, or various combinations of it, and were all busy with different tasks.

Alezya noted some of their protective coverings were different colors, and others wore a specifically colored band around their arm too. Maybe some signs to distinguish them within their clan? It was such a big clan, after all...

There were a lot of men, but neither she nor Lorey seemed to be expected to bow in their presence. Instead, some of the men greeted them, and Lorey was the one acting like she had a higher status. Some didn't raise their heads from their tasks or gave them some curious glance, but no words were exchanged.

Alezya was utterly confused by the dynamics of their clan. Women were free to walk amongst men, didn't even have to greet them, and the men wouldn't come to them either? Back in her clan, no unmarried woman would have been allowed to walk alone, and she would have certainly been punished for walking by a warrior without so much as greeting them...

After the first few nerve-wracking paces, she decided to try and relax, and simply keep up with Lorey instead. The men truly didn't seem bothered by their lack of politeness, only curious to see them. Whether it was because of Lorey's beauty, or simply because they were women walking freely, the pair was gathering a lot of stares.

Alezya noticed that whenever a warrior in heavier gear barked orders, the others quickly returned to their tasks, avoiding eye contact. Did they have ranks among their warriors? There were so many people, all men, but unlike her clan, where warriors were only distinguished by their victories and accomplishments, something here felt different.

She saw both young and older men, some weighed down with thick protective wear, others not, but there was no clear pattern to their hierarchy. Some young ones seemed to hold authority, while others, dressed as warriors, were assigned tedious labor, like piling wood, shoveling snow, carrying supplies. In her clan, such tasks would have been left to those of lower status.

These people were strange, their structure unfamiliar, and Alezya tried to take it all in, nervous about making a mistake later on.

"Kiki!"

Lorey's sudden exclamation got Alezya's attention, and to her surprise, the snow ahead of them suddenly moved on its own.

Initially, Alezya was utterly confused by the little waves of snow, until she realized that something was moving under the fresh coat. She barely held a gasp of surprise once she spotted the dark gray creature slithering a few steps away in the snow.

At first, she only saw a few gray scales emerge, and then, its whole body surfaced. It was so different from Kein the orange dragon that, for a minute, she had wondered if it wasn't a different creature altogether.

But no, that was clearly a dragon, although its body was different. It was thinner, smaller, and longer than its peer, with a snake-like form, rather than Kein's bulky structure. Its head surfaced, with shining black eyes, a long snout, and a mischievous spark in its eye that made it not half as scary as Kassein's dragon. The fact that it was playing around in the snow helped too.

Alezya watched, shocked, as the new creature came up to them, before taking a detour to make an excited circle around the two women. If it wasn't for Lorey holding her arm, she might have jumped back, or been way more terrified.

But the incoming dragon seemed to be merely playing around, and when it dove before resurfacing again to face Lorey, she was granted a good look at it. The dark gray color surprised her too, for this was her first time seeing a dragon this color, and she'd never heard of an ashen-colored one either. Yet, this creature had the same scales, the same thinner limbs, and similar wings too. It was definitely another dragon...

Then, coming from farther ahead, she much more easily spotted the large orange dragon also coming at them. Unlike its peer, Kein could hardly hide its humongous body in the snow as the dark gray one did.

Instead, the orange dragon was stomping in their direction, its chunky paws dipping in puddles of snow that melted immediately under its steps.

Alezya would have once again taken a few steps back if it wasn't for Lorey standing completely fearless next to her. The woman then unlocked arms with Alezya and even crouched down to pat the head of the dark gray dragon before it dove back into the snow. It was playing in the layers of snow like one would in shallow water.

"Kiki."

Lorey had spoken while Alezya's eyes were still on the incoming Kein, so she'd lost track of what she was possibly talking about. Just then, the dark gray dragon resurfaced, just in time to playfully bite Kein's leg, making it growl, and then dive again.

Lorey chuckled, pointing at the moving snow.

"Kiki. Kein ay Kiki."

"Kiki?" Alezya repeated.

Kiki was the name of the dark gray dragon?

She watched as Kein, confused and annoyed, glared at the moving snow before resuming its stampede toward them.

There was something utterly terrifying about seeing a creature twice her height and four times her width rush in her direction, but Alezya summoned every inch of her being into not moving as Lorey did.

Thankfully, Kein stopped right in front of her, its huge silver eyes on her.

The dragon looked positively terrifying, and yet, every time she met it, she felt a bit less terrified. In fact, its warm and fire-colored body facing her had something reassuring about it. It growled, but it wasn't a warning growl; instead, it was a deeper, smoother sound, almost like a snow leopard's purr... She could feel hot air puffing out of its nostrils and onto her face, warming her up effortlessly.

She glanced to the side and saw Lorey was petting the other dragon again. The smaller one was acting like a happy dog around her, perfectly submissive and tilting its head excitedly under her hand. Alezya glanced back at Kein. The orange dragon had its eyes riveted on her, looking almost excited, but still. Was it possible that... this terrifying creature was expecting the same of her?

"K-Kein?" she uttered as if trying to confirm.

The dragon replied with another deep growl, and even, to her surprise, lowered its head a bit toward her. There was no way... was there?

Alezya took a deep breath. She had genuinely thought this dragon would kill her a few days ago. What was she doing now...? She raised her trembling hand and, mentally preparing herself to lose her limb, approached the dragon's head. Before she finished her movement, Kein suddenly moved forward, and her fingers met the hot scales without warning, making her jump in surprise, and take back her hand. Kein growled in protest and approached even more, scaring her into taking a step back.

Next to her, Lorey chuckled, and gently came to her aid. She grabbed Alezya's wrist, and slowly guided her hand back onto the dragon's head. Alezya could barely believe it when her fingers touched the hot orange scales again, and Kein growled in response. It was incredibly warm under her fingers, like a hot log...

Alezya felt a wave of unique, excited sparks in her stomach about this unparalleled moment. She was touching a dragon! She was even *petting* a dragon! Her father would have been mortified to witness this...

She glanced at Lorey, almost glad there was someone to witness this, and the young woman gave her an amused chuckle as if this was normal for her. Indeed, Kiki seemed to be literally stuck to her, making little high-pitched growls around her legs to get her attention. Despite being smaller than Kein and its length against the ground, Kiki was still tall enough to reach their chests and kept dancing in elegant circles around them. When its body made another circle around them, it bumped Alezya and interrupted her contact with Kein, causing the orange dragon to growl furiously in indignation and snap at its peer.

For a second, Alezya was worried that she was going to be stuck in a fight between them, but soon enough, Kiki took an elegant dive into the crisp white blanket, and Kein was off to chase after the wriggles of snow. Alezya turned to Lorey for cues, but as the young woman seemed amused and not worried whatsoever, she thought this might be normal... until she looked around at the nearby men's expressions.

They were all stunned, with wide eyes on the bickering dragons.

No, Alezya realized. This wasn't normal, even for the Dragon Clan's people, and she had just had a privileged moment with the orange dragon... which made her feel all the more happy about it.

"Alezya."

Lorey gently called her before wrapping her arm around hers again and pulling her to resume their walk. She realized they weren't just strolling around and taking the paths of shoveled snow, but had a precise direction in mind. Soon enough, they reached a habitation that was far bigger than the others, even bigger than Kassein's. Alezya nervously wondered to whom could a place that was four times larger than Kassein's belong. Maybe their Clan Chief? The archenemy of her clan...?

Upon entering though, she realized she was wrong; this wasn't someone's living space, but a communal area like her clan had in the largest caves of her mountain. It was large, but crowded, with lots of warriors loudly cheering, and Alezya suddenly felt nervous to be surrounded by so many men. She would have rather faced Kein again... Lorey didn't seem to mind, however, as she pulled her through the crowd. Once again to Alezya's incomprehension, the men were letting them through, only giving them surprised glances when the two women walked past.

Thankfully, they soon breached through the crowd and Alezya could finally see what the fuss was all about; in a large open area, Kassein and his sister were facing each other with weapons. If she was shocked to see a man and a woman fighting against each other, Alezya's questions were soon obliterated by the sight of Kassein's half-naked body.

The blood rushed to her cheeks as she was instantly mesmerized by the warrior's impressive figure, his superb muscles shining wet with sweat dripping down to his leather pants. She had caught glimpses of his body before, but now that she was seeing it, exposed in plain sight, it was just impossible to ignore. Not only that, but he was panting heavily, his dark green eyes shining with excitement, and his black hair stuck to his skin from the heat. She found it almost impossible not to stare, especially as he hadn't noticed her arrival, and everyone around was watching the fight.

"Lorey," a bored male voice called out.

Alezya hadn't even noticed the presence of Tievin next to them, and she realized Lorey had purposely walked up to him. He lifted an eyebrow at Alezya and then turned back to Lorey to chat with her. Even if she'd wanted to understand their words, the clamor around was so loud that Alezya probably wouldn't have caught much of it. Not that she minded much; she turned her eyes back to the sibling duo as soon as she could.

It looked like they had arrived while those two were merely catching a short break as they began moving again, throwing themselves at each other, blades first. Alezya was stupefied by the violence of this fight; it was as if they didn't mind hurting each other, and after a few seconds, she realized they truly didn't. With a superb movement, Kiera inflicted a wound on her brother's arm, lacerating his skin with one of her two blades. Alezya gasped, worried for

Kassein, but then, she witnessed the orange scales that immediately bloomed on his skin to cover the wound.

She took a closer look at his sister, and that's when she noticed Kiera also had scales on her body; just like her brother, she had taken off her top except for a leather bra, and thus, Alezya could clearly see the ashen gray streaks of scales shining on her dark skin.

She waited for a bit, and sure enough, when Kassein's blade slashed her shoulder after a wrong move on her part, the dark silver scales formed in a matter of seconds. Those scales were exactly like Kiki's... Did that mean Kiki was Kiera's dragon? Did the dragons truly have their own owners, allowing this sorcery that healed them?

Alezya was both confused and amazed. She kept watching the match, feeling as excited as the cheering men around, although she kept quiet. She didn't even want to blink and miss a split second of this. She knew nothing of fights, but she could tell this one was amazing.

The siblings' moves looked like a mortal, dangerous dance with one another, and they weren't holding back nor giving the other any chance for a mistake to slip by. Their movements seemed so brutal and deadly; they wouldn't actually risk inflicting serious harm upon the other, right? But then again, with their amazing healing abilities, how far did they have to go for them to inflict any wound that would seriously harm the other...?

She kept watching in absolute awe, trying to absorb every bit of the incredible match, but every time, Alezya found that her eyes would inevitably drift back to Kassein. She was mesmerized by each of his movements, and the impressive strength demonstrated by his body. Her throat went a bit dry, and her stomach a bit funny, thinking that those same hands that carried such a big sword had been the ones to gently caress her just the night before...

It was hot in there, but her blushing was getting embarrassing, and Alezya nervously patted her cheeks. She was just remembering her bandaged hands when she caught Lorey's amused eyes on her. She had been caught staring... Alezya reddened even more and averted her gaze.

"Kiera! Kassein!"

Alezya was not only shocked that Lorey had dared to interrupt the battle, but on top of that, despite the ruckus, both Kassein and Kiera actually heard her, immediately turning their eyes her way and lowering their weapons.

When Kassein's deep green eyes found her standing next to Lorey amongst the crowd, Alezya could only burn up even more. She internally cursed Lorey for calling out to him when she wasn't ready! Even worse, now both he and his sister were walking in their direction, drawing every single set of eyes to them.

Their arrival had gone relatively unnoticed because the warriors' eyes were on the fight, but as she, Lorey, and Kiera were the only women there, and with her being the foreign woman, she was especially standing out. After nervously peeking around, Alezya regretted it immediately and began to feel instinctively scared, having so many curious men's eyes on her. Then, Kassein arrived, obliterating everything else. At least, her fear had drained the blood away from her face for a bit, and she wasn't blushing like a young maiden anymore...

That was until he came close, facing her from mere inches away.

He said something to Tievin, who handed him a piece of fabric to wipe himself with. But Kassein only quickly wiped the sweat off his hand right before putting it on her cheek. Alezya's blushing immediately came back, and now, she was torn between seeking comfort and protection in this hand or pushing it away in a desperate attempt to get the attention away from her...

Then, Lorey said something, and Kassein briefly glanced in her direction before looking around at the men gathered here. They had stopped cheering when the fight had been stopped, but now, all the warriors around seemed to be shrinking under Kassein's stare. He didn't say a word, but after a second of heavy silence under his glare, all the men moved at once, rushing to get out. Alezya was shocked by the sudden stampede toward the exit, but the other three didn't move, only watching with amused or bored expressions as the place emptied in a matter of seconds. What had Lorey said?

Alezya was confused until Kassein's eyes got back to her. He gave her a faint smile, his thumb rubbing against her cheek. She found herself blushing again, as they were still not alone, and this felt way more embarrassing in the daylight, away from his room... but she didn't hate his touch. Far from it. It was as comforting as Kein's warm skin under her fingers...

After a hesitation, she shyly put her hand over his. His sister rolled her eyes and said something, Tievin answering. Alezya glanced their way as the other three exchanged, but Kassein still kept his eyes riveted on her, and she was all too aware of them. If she could understand them, at least she could have tried distracting herself with their conversation, but now, she was absorbed by Kassein's warm gaze, and his gentle hand on her cheek. He then looked down at the coat covering her and asked something to Lorey, who replied with a calm expression. Alezya was a bit annoyed at herself for feeling glad he'd barely looked at Lorey all along...

Tievin said something, which made Kiera burst out laughing and slap his shoulder. But the poor man did not have the siblings' constitution, for he almost fell forward from that. Alezya tried not to laugh at his stumble and watched with compassion as he grimaced and painfully massaged his shoulder upon standing back up.

Then, Kiera did something that shocked Alezya even more: she put a quick kiss on Lorey's lips before turning around and walking casually back to the center of the space, calling her brother. Those two women had just... kissed? Alezya was utterly confused. Was that a greeting between women in their clan?

She was still bewildered, but her attention was soon called back to Kassein's dangerously close presence. He was still staring at her with that warm, troubling gaze, despite his sister calling him for the second time. Then, he gave her a faint smile, and took his hand back, turning around to resume his fight with Kiera. Alezya was left there, still speechless. Tievin then said something as the two siblings resumed their fight, both looking even more excited than before.

As Alezya wondered what he'd said, Lorey gently nudged her toward a bench on the side. She had Alezya sit next to her, while Tievin stood to the side, but this time, Alezya decided not to be surprised anymore by their strange customs. She was going to have to adapt quickly if she wanted to survive here. She wouldn't go as far as kissing a woman's lips, but she could overlook their completely off-throwing differences of status.

From what she had seen, Kiera and Kassein stood at the top here, Lorey behind them, the warriors next, and then, Tievin... No, perhaps Tievin was above the other warriors despite not being a warrior himself, seeing as how he hadn't been kicked out. Or did he have a particular status? Maybe as the clan's counselor, or like an elder?

She couldn't tell, but right now, he was standing next to them, so he was at least below Lorey... so she would be safe, as long as she remained mindful of these four.

With everyone else gone, the place felt much bigger, and the siblings didn't hold back either, using the entire space for their fight. With no one blocking the view, Alezya could finally look around the place and distract herself from Kassein's dripping figure.

The floor was flat and clear of any snow, replaced instead by an inch of some dry, thin soil that would fly around under their steps. It wasn't rock-solid, but more like something slightly soft on the surface, fitted for a practice fight and potential falls. This was definitely some training area, and she saw some weapons lined up on a rack on one end, both wooden and metal swords, bats, and sticks of all sizes. The roof was also higher than in Kassein's habitation, a large piece of leather or something of the like stretched over their heads.

Then, she heard a grunt and turned back to the fight. Kiera had managed to make her brother put a knee down and was taunting him, judging by the snarky tone of her voice and her expression. Just as Alezya was getting a bit worried, Kassein darted a glance her way.

...Was his sister reprimanding him for his attitude toward her? He quickly turned back to the fight, jumped back on his feet, and fought back. Kiera immediately lost her smug expression for her brother's attacks were relentless and merciless, rapidly pushing her to a corner of the area. She began to frown and fight back with similar anger, but Kassein was pushing her and gaining more ground. They didn't look to be playing around anymore, and Alezya felt like the fight's tone had changed drastically...

Then, just as she thought Kiera was going to lose or seriously get hurt, they stopped. Alezya wondered what had prompted them to suddenly lower their weapons, but then, a man's voice came shouting from outside. Next to her, Lorey jumped to her feet too, and Tievin ran past them to the entrance, the siblings catching up quickly behind him. In a matter of seconds, all three were outside, and Alezya followed.

"Alezya!"

Lorey had tried to hold her back one second too late. She stepped out of the training area, and right away, a flock of the Dragon Clan's warriors ran past her, all headed in one direction. She turned her black eyes toward the mountain, and she saw it: a group of people coming down toward this area, people that came from up there...

Her heart jumped in her chest. Lorey emerged right behind her, but Alezya ignored her and marched toward the crowd. Kassein's warriors were fighting another clan! In one glance, she knew it wasn't her clan; their clothing and weapons were different, and they had markings on their faces, a custom her people didn't have.

Her relief was short-lived though. She knew that clan, and she had seen those particular markings before. She watched helplessly as the fight happened too far from her to act; she had lost sight of Kassein and his sister, but she had no doubt they were in the middle of the violent battle.

And the Dragon Clan was easily going to win this one. She'd seen these fights before. Perched in the heights of her mountain, on a day she happened to find herself on the right flank of it, she had witnessed for herself another clan's warriors being wiped out in a matter of seconds... and the very same was going to happen here, no doubt.

Even worse, Alezya could witness as some of the Dragon Clan's warriors were literally standing by, gawking at the battle and looking pissed they wouldn't have anyone left to fight themselves...

Their numbers were so great, the attack itself was a mass suicide.

It left her feeling torn apart. She knew some clans would try their luck against the Dragon Clan, sending some warriors to test them, and the survivors were always left to flee if they so wished. Those attacks might have seemed desperate to Kassein and his men, whose victory was certain, but Alezya knew those men had come to sacrifice themselves for honor, and a greater goal: information. Information against their biggest enemy was considered one of the highest currencies among the clans...

She glanced up, and sure enough after a couple of seconds, her trained eyes spotted a couple more people spying from a high, safe hideout in the mountains. Had that clan launched an attack ahead of the upcoming council gathering? Some clans had no choice but to try and gather information to exchange for food or medicine...

She turned her eyes back down. The fight was ending soon...

That's when she saw it. A man's hand amongst the fallen close to her. One of the other clansmen had fingers missing...

A chill went down her spine. She got closer to the next body, despite Lorey's protests. That body had missing fingers too.

Criminals. That was how most clans marked the criminals, by cutting fingers off so they wouldn't be admitted into another clan after their crimes. Petty thieves had one finger cut off, but two or more fingers cut off meant they'd committed more serious crimes.

So that clan was sending their criminals to fight? Then, they weren't expecting them to return? Now that she paid more attention, none of them were attempting to flee...

Something was off. This wasn't the clans' usual technique. Criminals wouldn't bring back any information!

"Alezya?"

For the first time, Lorey was sounding nervous behind her, and the men around were eyeing Alezya's actions, uncertain of what they were supposed to do about her. Then, Tievin appeared and began talking, ignoring that she couldn't understand a word he said.

Alezya ignored him all the same, just approaching the corpses without fear. It seemed these had been the first to die, for Kassein's warriors had already pushed the rest of the attackers back to the edge of their territory. One had an arrow planted in his neck, and the other had been slain by a sword ripping his body open from shoulder to gut.

Alezya wasn't one to be scared or horrified by such a sight. She had seen bodies before, from unlucky watchmen who had been half-eaten by predators overnight or those she had found, long after they had fallen to their death in some forgotten crevice. When she'd been lucky to catch one, she had also learned to butcher her prey herself. She didn't have a constitution that made her repulsed by blood, gruesome sights, or death.

Thus, she had little qualms about inspecting the dead bodies, ignoring the confused glances her actions were gathering. She was following some gut instinct, knowing something was wrong about a clan sending criminals to attack with no hope of return...

That's when she saw it.

Pulling a sleeve, she found the cross markings on the man's forearms. Someone had made crosses on that criminal's forearms and waited for them to heal... or show signs of disease.

Alezya gasped, and then covered her mouth, jumping back. They had sent infected people! She was about to shout when she realized they wouldn't understand no matter which words she used.

In her despair, she turned back to Lorey and Tievin.

"Lorey!" she called her.

The young woman exchanged a confused glance with Tievin before they both walked over, trying to understand her actions. With trembling hands, Alezya pulled the sleeves of the corpses, showing them similar marks.

That didn't need much more words, for when Tievin's eyes fell on the discolored skin and white bumps, his eyes opened wide, and he jerked back, his sleeve covering his mouth. Lorey was slightly braver, as she pulled Alezya away from it with her.

Then, Tievin shouted something over the ruckus, and all eyes turned to them. Alezya hoped they were going to do something about it, and quick. The men were shouting, and a second later, Kassein and Kiera came running over, both covered in blood, their weapons in hand.

They stopped right in front of the trio, and for a second, Kassein's eyes were filled with anger as he saw her. Alezya thought he was mad at her, but then, his glare went straight to Lorey, and she understood; she wasn't supposed to be there, to have seen the fight...

"Kassein!" Alezya tried to get his attention away from Lorey and onto the matter at hand.

His dark green eyes went back to her, and she pointed a trembling finger at the corpses. Tievin began speaking, quickly and nervously, most likely explaining the situation.

To Alezya's shock, Kiera walked fearlessly to the bodies to examine them. She lifted their wrists, noticing the signs of disease too, and grumbled something to her brother. Then, Kassein nodded and turned to his men, and began shouting what Alezya unmistakably understood as orders. All their warriors began to move as one; those who weren't in the fight stood back, and those who were grabbed the bodies, pulling them all toward the edge of the camp.

That's when Alezya understood: they were splitting themselves between the potentially infected people and those who had stood far enough from the fight to be safe. Then, the Dragon Clan's fighters all began taking off their outer gear and clothing, and throwing them on the pile of dead bodies. Alezya realized the fight had already ended just moments ago.

Just as she wondered what they were going to do, Kein and Kiki suddenly came flying in, their silhouettes flashing above the battlefield, causing the nearby warriors to move even farther away from the scene. Both dragons had different objectives though. Kein landed right before them, turning its back to Lorey and her, and immediately began growling at the pile of corpses. Kiki, on the other hand, hadn't stopped and was running toward the mountain with a furious, high-pitched growl that echoed Kein's.

Then, Kiera walked up to them, and before Alezya could understand, she and Lorey were suddenly grabbed and mounted on the dragon's back, brutally thrown against a mass of orange, warm scales. Even worse, and much to her horror, Kein took off. She'd had no time to prepare herself, but suddenly, the ground was jumping away from her. She would have screamed in fright if her voice hadn't been stuck in her throat.

The last sight she caught was Kassein's eyes, half-anger and half-worry, turned toward them as he got smaller. Then, Kein flapped its wings, turned in another direction, and took them away from the battlefield.

Alezya couldn't even grasp what was happening; she was flying!

She was flying and was merely held by Kiera's strong hand, her body inelegantly thrown across the dragon's back. It didn't last long, thankfully for her panicked heart. They landed brutally, and she was dragged off the dragon's back just as helplessly as she'd been thrown over it.

For a second, she genuinely wondered if they were angry and about to kill her off or something, for the last sequences of sudden actions had been so unpredictable and scary. She had known Kiera was strong, but she hadn't been prepared to be suddenly passed and tossed around like a lifeless doll!

Fortunately, she soon found ground in Lorey, who grabbed her hand. While Alezya caught her breath and tried to steady her beating heart, she realized the two other women were hurriedly talking, a nervous tone in their voices. She wondered what was going on and, more importantly, where they were. She took a look around. It looked like they were in the mountains, but not anywhere she knew, and she hadn't paid any attention during the trip to have any idea of the direction they had taken.

Moreover, this place was cold, but strangely... steamy? There was white steam all around them.

Not staying any longer after dropping the three of them off, Kein left without warning. Was it going back to Kassein, Alezya wondered. Not letting her watch the dragon's flight, Lorey guided her on a smaller, rocky path that Kein couldn't have landed on, and Alezya decided to trust her and follow her. It wasn't as if she had any other choice, as Kiera was following right behind them, closing the walk.

Thankfully, they arrived at their destination not long after, and Alezya's jaw dropped. Hot springs! They were in the midst of a hot springs area... and a large one too. No wonder it felt hot and steamy around there. She had been in a similar place, a very long time ago, while with her mother's clan. Alezya didn't have any time to reminisce about some happy memories when Lorey turned to her and, without warning, began to help her undress.

After a moment of shock, she finally understood: they wanted her to bathe and get rid of the disease! She nodded and began undressing herself obediently, taking over Lorey's hands. To her surprise, as soon as she showed she'd undress by herself, Lorey did the same, and Kiera was pulling off the lower half of her battle gear without any embarrassment too. Although she'd been eager to comply, Alezya now felt a bit self-conscious; she hadn't been in such an intimate environment with other women in a long while...

She slowed her movements and averted her gaze, until Lorey was the first one naked and to dip into one of the hot baths, with a relieved smile. Only then did Alezya feel a bit more confident, and followed after in the hot water.

At first, she grimaced a bit upon the sting of the hot water on her injuries, but this soon eased, and she relaxed naturally. The water was very hot, maybe a couple degrees away from unbearably hot... and quite pleasant, once she got used to it. Lorey smiled but quickly insisted on helping her rinse her hair and rub her skin. Then, Kiera joined in, and all shame gone, the three women got busy rinsing their bodies with hot water.

Alezya tried to take her thoughts away from there to lessen her embarrassment. Was Kassein alright? He had been exposed too, and he had stayed back there... Were they the first ones taken out of the dangerous area because they were women? How would they deal with the bodies?

She was still in shock at everything that had just happened. She knew the other clans always tried to attack the Dragon Clan, but to resort to this?

This was inhuman. To use criminals and disease? Had the other clans approved of this? Were they even aware that such underhanded methods were being used? If they were, how could they have let it happen...? She had been raised to respect the warriors above everything else, those who were praised for their honor and willingness to die for their clan. But this was... different, and odious. She wouldn't stand for it. She knew that whichever clan had sent those men would have seen her actions too. If she was recognized as the woman of another clan, they would know there was a traitor who had foiled their plan.

Had she unwittingly stood with the Dragon Clan and triggered a war between two others? Alezya sighed, and while Lorey carefully helped her rinse her long black hair, she closed her eyes before diving her head underwater to try and drown those thoughts.

Things were just getting more and more complicated every minute she spent with the Dragon Clan... every minute she spent with Kassein.

Chapter 8

Standing with his arms crossed, Kassein was staring at the pile of burning bodies, clothes, and armor with a frown.

"The tribes are getting bolder," Tievin commented with a soulless tone.

Kassein didn't grant him a response. His anger could be felt, silent but deadly, and surprisingly efficient at keeping the surrounding soldiers' heads down on their tasks. If anything had gone wrong, the outcome would have been much worse. If it wasn't for Alezya letting them know that those men were infected, they would have had a disease ravaging their ranks... Another team would have cleaned after the battle, doubling the number of men possibly infected. The bodies would have been dragged back outside the wall, as usual, to let their tribe have the opportunity to get their bodies back if they wanted to. But this...?

He and Kiera would have most likely been spared thanks to their Dragon Blood which made them resistant and immune to most common diseases, but his men would have been at risk. Lorey, Tievin, and Alezya would have been exposed.

He had gotten too complacent. The endless victories against the tribes had made him soft. Or was it since Alezya's arrival? No, she had fueled his anger more than anything. To think they dared to do such a thing to her, twice, he had no second thoughts about harming them back. But to think they wouldn't be afraid to spread disease amongst them...

He took a deep breath, trying to keep his anger under control.

"...Why aren't they back yet?" he groaned.

Tievin raised an eyebrow before checking the sky.

"I sent Kiki with towels and clean clothes a little while ago," he said, "but you know how Princess Kiera is... If they are enjoying themselves, the ladies might stay longer. ...Isn't it a good thing, Commander? It leaves you more time to take care of things here. Without hindrance."

Kassein glared, and Tievin looked down. He'd better not name which one he thought of as a hindrance... however, he was right. Kassein had been in a hurry to send them to a safe place to take care of things here. All the men who had partaken in the battle had been isolated and sent for a thorough washing, the bodies were being burned a few paces outside the camp, and another unit was busy double-checking the area where the battle had occurred to make sure they hadn't missed anything.He hadn't even kept one of the bodies for the medical unit to examine; he didn't want to take the smallest risk, not with his men...

He felt even more furious when he imagined what would have happened if his brother had come to hear of this. Ever since he'd taken the North Army all the way to the edge of the continent, he and the tribes had been in a stand-off, but despite the almost daily battles, he had few deaths to record and more men who were joining their ranks than the ones he lost. His army was growing at a steady pace.

He wondered if his brother ever got worried about what he could do with such an army under his command...

He turned around, heading back toward the camp to let the pile burn. Kassein didn't even let his men outside; it was too risky for them, and there was no point in guarding a pile of burning bodies, thus the unit who had come along walked back past the wall behind him, and they closed it again. He heard a few of them let out a faint sigh of relief once the wood touched the snow, closing off their camp.

"Sir," said one of the soldiers, smartly addressing Tievin rather than their Commander in Chief, "the units who took part in the battle are now all done cleaning themselves and the quarantine zone is ready for them. As instructed, the medical unit has been installed nearby to keep them under watch for the next two weeks."

"Well done," Tievin nodded. "Make sure we keep an accurate record of all of them, and the progress of their health if there is any. No one is allowed out of the quarantine zone until they have gotten the medical unit's approval, or it will be considered treason."

"Yes, sir. General Herken already said he would take full responsibility for his brigades being involved!"

"Good."

The soldier bowed and walked away. Tievin tightened his coat around himself with a tired expression. He wished he'd had the luxury of extending his bath too, like the ladies, but he didn't. Instead, both he and Kassein had hurried through a thorough washing to get back into overseeing the aftermath of the battle and making sure no mistakes were committed. The Commander in Chief's hair was still wet, and Tievin couldn't suppress a shiver every time he saw his bare torso exposed to the wind. Those dragons and their immunity against the cold...

Kassein had changed completely but only bothered to put on clean leather pants and a fur cape, under which he was naked. The point of the fur cape over his bare skin, Tievin didn't really understand. Perhaps to avoid the gazes of the soldiers who couldn't help but gawk at the orange scales on his skin...

The orange scales got Tievin looking back toward the mountains.

If he had doubted the Commander in Chief's silent anger, one just had to take a look at his dragon. After dropping the three women at the hot springs, Kein had come back for a vengeful attack on the tribes and was still going at it. The echoes of his furious growls were now reverberating between the mountains and all the way to the camp, where the men couldn't help but send nervous glances, despite the dragon being far away. Tievin even felt a little bit sorry for those tribes. An attack from one of them had triggered the dragon's anger to hunt them all... Those people better stay hidden for the next few hours.

This got him thinking about Alezya, that woman their Commander had been guarding so stubbornly. Another reason Tievin had suggested Kiera's presence was that his sister would be much more efficient at convincing the Prince on any matter regarding that woman, and he had been right. She had been the first to raise some doubts about that woman, voicing what Tievin wouldn't have risked his neck for.

Now, he hoped the Commander in Chief would perhaps be a little less blind and deaf to the risks of keeping that woman amongst them...

Although, it would be more difficult after she'd proven herself on this occasion. Tievin himself was quite confused. He had been wary of her, but that woman had been so quick to reveal the enemy's wicked scheme. Had her morals prevailed? Or did she not care about a tribe that wasn't her own? Or had she been worried for her own safety? If the tribes acted independently from one another as he'd theorized, this woman surely was only one tribe's doing, and the others probably cared little for her. She had quite literally risked her life to warn them about the disease, but perhaps this had all been to save herself first and foremost.

Tievin glanced at the Commander in Chief's perfectly still figure.

His dark green eyes were back to glaring at the mountains in the general direction his dragon was still wreaking havoc. It was clear he was getting a bit more smitten every day with that woman. While Tievin could understand a young man his age would easily find himself disarmed by the sudden presence of a woman after years of being exiled in the north, he could only see this was all going to be too troublesome... There was a reason women weren't usually allowed here. More than one good reason, even. Several very good reasons.

"Your Highness, the tent for Her Highness and Lady Lorey is also ready, and their belongings have been moved," Tievin said. "M-may I suggest again—"

"No."

Kassein's firm rebuttal tone had Tievin pinch his lips together to hold back his frustration.

"I am just saying, for a lady's comfort, it might be better for her to—"

"No."

Tievin mentally prayed for himself. Was there any way to change His Highness' mind without risking his neck? He wasn't foolish enough to attempt a third time, but really, how long was that woman going to be staying in the Commander's tent? Not only was it improper for her to be sharing his accommodations, but the soldiers were starting to talk. No matter how much he tried to do some damage control, men confined in a military camp could be worse than bored widows when it came to gossip!

Tievin had hoped that Kiera would put some common sense into her brother's head, but she hadn't even commented on the situation, nor seemed to be alarmed by it. He massaged his eyelids. Really, he was now starting to wonder if he hadn't made a terrible mistake in suggesting His Highness summon assistance. Now he was going to have to deal with the actions of two of them...

"Double the people guarding the wall, and have men surveying the mountain at all times," Kassein suddenly said. "I want reports on everything that happens up there, any sighting of them."

Tievin frowned. The Prince had never been this interested in whatever was going on in the mountain. He barely even cared about the attacks, unless he needed to relieve his nerves in battle...

He glanced at the mountain.

"Yes, Your Highness. Although, thanks to your dragon's intervention, I doubt any of them will show themselves for a while..."

Kassein didn't answer, but just then, Kein happened to appear in between two mountains, flying with what looked like some impatience.

Tievin almost felt sorry for those tribes, but at the very least, that dragon was finally getting slightly more useful than problematic. The orange beast was now just most likely attacking any human or animal who didn't have the survival instinct to crawl into the nearest hole, having turned its wrath into a hunting game.

Kassein didn't stare long at his dragon but turned around to walk further inside the camp, Tievin following behind him.

He knew all too well why he wasn't willing to let Alezya out of his tent, and why, right now, he was pissed that his sister was keeping her away for so long. Not only that, but he was pissed at Lorey for having brought her out. Even if she was still healing fast thanks to his last vial of Lake water, she was still hurt. And she was a woman in a camp full of men. Men who hadn't seen a woman in a long time... Hungry dogs.

"Which brigade failed to warn of the attack early?" he asked.

"Th-the twelfth brigade's fifth and sixth units, sir," Tievin said, glancing down at his notes. "General Sazaran's. They weren't supposed to be the ones in charge, but apparently, they were assigned to replace the first and second units after causing a ruckus during lunch. They might have been not as... dedicated as they should have been. I need to mention it is one of our problematic brigades, sir. Sent half a year ago, mostly on forced military duty. They are on their third warning for this week alone."

In other words, they were criminals sent here because their crimes were too severe to ever allow them back into society. Most did not last long, either dying in service or breaking under the brutal conditions. A few might still cling to foolish hopes of redemption, but units like these were made up of the worst men, those who treated their punishment with defiance and spread their disdain for the rules to others. Usually, the generals assigned them to the most miserable tasks until they either broke or fell in line. Some, however, remained troublesome.

Moreover, Tievin would never have the guts to voice it out, but Kassein had gotten slightly complacent since that woman's appearance, and some might have seen this as an opportunity to push the limit a bit further... at least until now.

"...Sazaran's gone soft," Kassein groaned.

Tievin wanted to remark each general had more brigades under their command than they could possibly handle correctly due to the constant inflow of new recruits, but seeing which direction Kassein had taken, he held his tongue. The Commander in Chief was now taking the route to the training grounds, and Tievin could easily guess he intended to tackle that issue himself.

"You," Tievin grabbed a unit that was walking back with shovels. "Have the twelfth brigade's fifth and sixth units be summoned to the training grounds immediately. Make sure General Sazaran is informed as well."

"Yes, sir!"

The men left immediately to execute his orders, while Tievin let out a faint sigh. Well, maybe Sazaran would have a bit less on his hands after today... In most cases, he would have tried to relieve Kassein's anger and made sure to dissuade him from killing or mutilating people, but those units were almost entirely made of criminals, and Tievin had very little pity for them. No one was sent to the North Army for small crimes like petty theft, illegal gambling, or tax fraud. The Central Army, stationed in the Imperial City, usually handled more problematic but victimless offenses like merchandise trafficking, bribery, and forgery. The men sent north were those whose crimes were too severe to be allowed back into society, but not proven enough for execution. Murderers, rapists, arsonists, wife-beaters, kidnappers, and human traffickers.

Men whose fates had teetered between execution and exile, spared only because of insufficient witnesses, contested circumstances, or lack of prior offenses.

Tievin didn't feel an ounce of pity for them.

None of them would ever live normal lives again. Their only options were to survive as part of the North Army's workforce or die. Those units were tightly controlled by their superiors, kept busy with the worst tasks from dawn until dusk or throughout the night. They were sent with no expectation of return, which meant no one cared how they ended. Either they behaved, or they risked their lives. Those already on their third warning for failing to stand watch properly had long since pushed their luck past the point of no return.

Following Kassein, Tievin quickly double-checked his notes. He always carried a notepad filled with the latest reports, and reviewing the ones he had gathered recently only reinforced his opinion. Good riddance. There wasn't a single redeeming character among those units, and it wasn't like Sazaran hadn't tried to keep them in line. He let out a quiet sigh. At least His Highness would relieve his nerves and kill some time before the women returned.

"Which one's worse?"

"That would be the sixth, sir," Tievin answered right away. "Poor Sazaran already asked them to be removed from his command twice, but we had to follow the rules."

Luckily, the General was about to have his wish granted, and two fewer units to watch out for. Kassein took out his large sword from his back as he entered the training area for the second time that day. Naturally, a unit had quickly cleaned the area behind him and his sister, thus the place was perfectly ready and the sand on the floor had been raked and leveled for the next training session. Unfortunately, they'd soon have to replace it with fresh sand.

Kassein walked toward the end of the arena, unclasping his cape as he moved. Without warning, he tossed it in Tievin's direction, the heavy fabric nearly dragging the poor man off balance as he caught it with a grimace. Why wear the damn thing if he was just going to take it off...?

He kept the thought to himself. Adjusting his grip on the ridiculously heavy cape, Tievin hauled it along as he made his way to a nearby bench behind Kassein, where he'd be out of the way. By the time he perched himself down, Kassein had already settled, resting one hand on his sword and the other on his knee.

Setting the cloak aside, Tievin pulled out his notepad, flipping through the piled-up reports. If they were going to be here for a while, he might as well make use of the time. It didn't take long; General Sazaran arrived, along with the entire twelfth brigade. Tievin raised an eyebrow; the General wanted to make this an example, then.

"Commander," the General greeted Kassein more ceremoniously than usual.

While Kassein didn't reply, Tievin noted the attitude of the rest of the brigade. It was easy to spot the fifth and sixth units; they were the only ones stupid enough not to greet Kassein, but instead, they were playing around with arrogant attitudes. Tievin rolled his eyes and went back to his notes while the General took charge.

"Units One and Two, guard outside the training area. Nobody comes in without permission. Units Three and Four, to the sides. Units Seven and Eight, make sure nobody leaves this place without my order. Everyone else to the sidelines."

All the units obeyed quickly, and Tievin realized most of them had no idea what they'd been summoned for. The General had been smart not to make it too obvious. Moreover, Units Five and Six were still acting up as they were the last to get to the sidelines and were being loud and rambunctious under the General's glare. Those from other units who had actually spotted the Commander in Chief though weren't laughing at all. Instead, they rushed to their posts with pale faces.

"Units Five and Six!" Sazaran barked. "In the arena!"

He was met with a disordered wave of laughs, taunts, and protests. If they mostly did what they were told, those men were also making sure to act up and do it in the most annoying way possible. Tievin shook his head. Sazaran ought to have been internally celebrating...

"Units! Draw your weapons!"

This time, there was a hint of confusion in his men's eyes, as even those on the sidelines had to take their blades out. Once again, the twelve men gathered on the training ground didn't obey, or did so by playing around with their weapons. Then, Sazaran turned around and bowed to Kassein before exiting the training area, walking up to stand next to Tievin, hands behind his back.

"Happy to be relieved of the circus?" Tievin asked without raising his eyes from his notes.

"Some criminals do not deserve redemption," Sazaran scoffed under his beard.

"Indeed. Especially when they don't bother to even try and earn it..."

"Garbage, the lot of them. This place wouldn't be half the shithole it is if only His Highness stopped dumping this kind of trash on the Commander in Chief..."

Tievin didn't bother to remark on the blasphemy; he agreed with Sazaran. He couldn't help but feel that the Emperor was testing his younger brother by sending so much trouble their way. They both turned their gazes to the arena as Kassein finally stood back up, facing the twelve men. They had all stopped laughing, suddenly rendered nervous about facing the Commander in Chief while everyone else was on the sidelines.

"Attention, all units!" Sazaran thundered, causing Tievin to grimace and cover his ears. "Today's training is a deathmatch! Forfeiting is not allowed! All units, you have the order to kill anyone who attempts to leave the training arena until only one victor is left!"

There were a few seconds of heavy silence as the actual meaning of his orders sunk into those men's heads. Units Five and Six were the only ones on the sand with the Commander in Chief. Suddenly, all the other units felt all the more grateful to have been ordered to stand on the sidelines, and some even instinctively took another step away from the line of sand. Those twelve men were about to die, there was no doubt about that. The ones condemned were also starting to realize how bad their position was. They glanced around at the stares of the other units, and then faced the Commander in Chief.

"This... This isn't fair!" one of them finally uttered. "We're going to die!"

"It's a deathmatch," Kassein retorted with an ice-cold tone. "If you kill me and everyone else, you can survive. Unit Five first."

Tievin smirked. So he wanted to make sure the sixth unit knew what was coming to them... Indeed, he was in a foul mood. Those men knew their chances were naught. They could possibly kill the others, but the Commander's presence annihilated their chances of survival. A few of them glanced to the sides, but their chances of running out of there weren't much better; there were twice the number of men ready to greet them with swords, and they had done absolutely nothing that would make the other units want to save them, quite the opposite.

"W-we... M-maybe we can take him, all of us! There are twelve of us! L-let's get rid of this bastard!"

There were a handful of half-convinced cheers, more to try and summon the bravery they didn't have than anything. Then, someone began running, sword first, toward Kassein, and the bloodshed began.

Tievin suppressed his vomit and quickly raised his notepad to block his view. He had little doubts about the outcome, and he hoped to keep his lunch down. Instead, he turned to Sazaran. Unlike him, the General had his eyes riveted on the fight, nodding at intervals as if he was watching an interesting scene and mentally giving points.

"Sazaran. Your opinion on the Commander's recent... acquisition?" Tievin asked, trying to speak not too loudly so Kassein wouldn't hear, but loud enough for Sazaran to hear him above all the screaming and shouting.

"The woman?" Sazaran scoffed. "What of it? The Commander's a young man. Good for him!"

"She's going to bring trouble," Tievin insisted. "She's a foreigner. An enemy."

"So what?!" Sazaran shrugged, seeming annoyed to be distracted. "Nothing the Commander in Chief can't handle. Plus, Princess Kiera is here, isn't she? What are you scared of, Tievin, you chicken!"

Tievin rolled his eyes. These brainless animals...

"...The men are talking, for sure," Sazaran said after a while. "A woman in the camp is a first... Frankly, we should worry more about the trouble on the inside than the outside. I'm not mad to be rid of those animals, but they aren't the only ones. We're not doing charity work here. Nobody would blame the Commander in Chief for taking a firmer hand on his troops!"

His words had Tievin smirk.

The issue wasn't about Kassein being soft, but him lacking any interest. He had been sent here as a punishment and decided to stay because he refused to go back. Having to lead and take care of an entire army was just like a side dish on his plate. He didn't care for it, just like he cared very little about actually conquering those mountains. In fact, that woman was the first thing he'd shown any interest in for months...

Just then, there was a damp sound of something landing in the sand a few feet away from them, and Tievin made the mistake of peeking. He almost threw up again and quickly hid behind his notepad.

"...How bad is it?"

"We're going to need a big order of sand," Sazaran chuckled. "The Commander in Chief is in particularly good shape today."

Tievin rolled his eyes.

"Just let me know when he's done..." he grumbled.

It didn't take long, fortunately. After many screams, grunts, and shouts, everything suddenly seemed to fall into a half-admirative, half-horrified silence. Still, Tievin wasn't foolish enough to lower his notepad just yet. He watched as Sazaran left his side to get on the sand, declare without surprise the Prince as the winner, and then start scolding his troops. That was Tievin's cue.

He grabbed the Commander in Chief's heavy cloak and took a large detour around the sand to get through the crowd of soldiers and find Kassein to follow him out of there. Although he did his very best to avoid looking, it was clear the sand had taken a crimson color, and the horrified gazes of the other soldiers convinced him to keep looking in the opposite direction until they stepped out. The training area was going to take a while to be cleaned, but that wasn't his problem. Sazaran would have his men do it... He doubted any unit would feel like going there after the word spread, anyway. And no doubt it would spread pretty quickly.

Those men had been executed as an example, although a lot of it was also the result of Kassein's frustrations. Every time the Prince was pissed, there would be blood spilled. That was the rule and the main reason everyone was smartly staying out of their way as they crossed back through the camp. That, and the trail of blood dripping behind him too...

"...Are they back yet?"

Tievin, who was struggling to keep up behind him while carrying Kassein's humongous cape on top of his notepad, blinked a couple of times, before realizing who he was talking about.

"N-not that I know of, Commander."

He wanted to ask how he would possibly know better than Kassein when they'd been together all along, but it wasn't worth dying today.

Instead, Tievin gestured quickly at a unit that was passing by with wide-open eyes at their Commander's gruesome, blood-soaked appearance.

"You take this," Tievin said, pushing the heavy fur cloak in their hands with a sigh of relief. "Was Her Highness spotted? And her dragon?"

"Th-the women aren't back yet that we know of," they replied with a dry throat. "N-neither is the Commander's dragon..."

"Fine. Take this to the Commander's tent, and have someone alert us as soon as they're back!"

"Yes, Grand Intendant!"

Tievin didn't need to repeat what had been said, for he was sure Kassein had heard it all already. Instead, his hands now free from that heavy piece of clothing, Tievin hurried behind him, catching up to a safe distance of a couple of steps between them.

"Your Highness, may I suggest you... get cleaned up before the ladies return?"

Kassein stopped and looked down as if he'd only just now realized he was drenched in fresh blood... Tievin sighed.

At the very least, having women in the camp would get a few of those animals to finally exert some basic hygiene. Soon enough, he ordered another unit to bring a hot bath to the Commander in Chief's tent. Kassein kept glancing at the skies, and Tievin silently prayed that his sister would come back before he ran out of patience... He could imagine the ladies would want to take their time and enjoy their baths, but even in his eyes, it had been quite a while since they'd left. Tievin chose not to voice it out and instead, act as if this was to be expected.

He might have had his doubts if it had been anybody else, but Princess Kiera, the Emperor's younger sister, had cultivated quite a reputation since childhood as the most unpredictable member of the Imperial Family. Even when she was young, she'd taken the habit of escaping the safety of the Imperial Palace on her own with her dragon, finding every opportunity she could to escape her caretakers' watch and disappear, at first for a few hours, and as she grew up, for several days. Her whereabouts were more often unknown than known, and it usually took one of the dragons to actually find which corner of the Empire she'd gone if she even stayed within the borders...

Now that she was an adult, her entire family had quite accepted the fact that Kiera couldn't be tied down to anywhere, and only visited home whenever she felt like it. As a child though, it had been quite problematic.

The Imperial Family counted eight children, and it was an exceptional sight to see them all in one place, mostly because Kiera had a genuine talent for disappearing. Tievin, who had been raised alongside them, had a front row seat in witnessing the countless number of times Kiera had been brought home by one of her older siblings' dragons, or been escorted by the Imperial Guards after she'd been caught stealing with other children in the street.

As she'd grown up, her family had seemed to be less and less bothered by her carefree spirit and accepted that she was more often gone exploring the world than safe at home. Moreover, when she did return, she spent most of her time training with her older siblings and father, making her one of the best fighters in the Empire and confirming that very few things on this continent could actually harm her.

Thankfully, she'd dropped the stealing habit... or perhaps she'd gotten good enough at it not to get caught anymore, Tievin wasn't quite sure. He had no idea how the dragons were able to find the Imperial Family members no matter how far they were, but he was quite sure Kiera would have been capable of disappearing for entire weeks if it wasn't for the family dragons chasing her to bring her back home.

Thus, her disappearing with her companion Lorey and that foreign woman wasn't as worrying as it should have been. It was mostly Kassein being quite annoyed with it, and for his nerves' sake, Tievin did hope she had intended to return that day.

"...I'm going on a hunt," Kassein grunted after he was clean and changed into a new set of clothing.

"You just bathed, Your Highness," Tievin said, hardly suppressing his eye roll.

Kassein glared back, meaning he did not care.

Tievin sighed but shrugged. The only way for the Commander in Chief to exercise patience was while he was keeping himself busy, and hunting seemed like a better option than slaying more of their soldiers...

Kassein left with his weapons, leaving Tievin alone to stand in the camp, glancing at the sky again. He really hoped Kiera would soon remember her brother was not as patient as the rest of her family with her antics...

At least, with Kassein gone and such nice weather, Tievin had no trouble keeping himself busy around the camp. While his superior was gone, he collected reports, interrogated the medical unit, rearranged the night watch's shifts, refused or agreed to new orders of clothing, and ordered for more snow to be shoveled out of the way. Since no more sightings of Kein were reported, he assumed both dragons had now gone to Kiera's side. This meant the Prince wouldn't return from his hunt until he heard the dragons come back to the camp as it was hard to miss Kein's loud growls.

It was later in the afternoon when he heard news of Kein returning and, sure enough, the orange dragon appeared in the sky with a loud growl. Tievin was confused for a bit as he only saw a couple of silhouettes on its back. The dragon landed heavily a few steps away, and Lorey and Alezya got down, both looking refreshed.

"Thank you for sending the clothes, Tievin," Lorey said as she helped Alezya down.

"You're welcome. May I ask where Her Highness is...?"

"She had Kiki take her to her brother once she realized he'd gone hunting. You know how she loves to compete with her brother. They'll be bringing us a nice dinner, I hope."

Tievin nodded. Not having the siblings around for a little longer was not something he was going to complain about... His eyes drifted to Alezya. That woman looked a bit better, with rosy cheeks, her wounds bandaged anew, and in clean, fitting female clothes.

"I don't recommend you two tour around the camp alone," Tievin said, going back to Lorey. "I can escort you ladies, but as you know, we also have quite a number of ill-reputed people living here. It wouldn't be smart for young women to go around without an escort."

Tievin didn't consider himself much of an escort, but without Kiera and Kassein by their side, he knew he'd lose his head if he let those two explore without ensuring their safety first, and he could summon a couple of reliable units to escort them within the minute.

"Thank you, Tievin," Lorey said with her usual kind smile, "but I think we'd better rest in a safer area until Their Highnesses return. Actually, would you be kind enough to provide us with what I would need to paint?"

"Paint?" Tievin repeated, confused.

"I want to teach Alezya our language, or at the very least, the basics of it. She only knows a handful of words, it ought to be frustrating for her. It would be better if she could communicate with us, at least a minimum."

Tievin wasn't too comfortable with that idea. That woman was a foreigner, and she belonged to the enemy. Her intentions were completely unknown, and the Commander in Chief had already been quite bewitched by her without Alezya speaking a word of their language... Would he get even more unreasonable once she could use her tongue to seduce him too?

"Tievin," Lorey tilted her head, calling him with a firmer tone. "I'm just going to teach her some basics. I doubt she'll be able to master the intricacies of our military strategies or the layout of the Empire within a couple of hours."

Tievin turned his eyes back to her. He didn't trust Alezya, but he did trust Lorey. Just like him, she'd grown up close to the Imperial Family, and in many ways, she was quite impressive herself. She was smart, well-educated, loyal, and most importantly, she was able to bring some sense to Kiera, which was a feat in itself. Despite being the Princess' companion, she'd never shown an ounce of arrogance, nor any want to rise above her station. Just like him, she was fully committed to serving the Imperial Family, although for a different reason.

"...Fine," he said, briefly glancing again in Alezya's direction. "Let's go to my tent then, I have all the supplies you might need."

Lorey gave him a thankful smile, and he turned around, guiding the two women to his accommodations. So it began, he thought to himself. More trouble...

They reached his tent, and after giving Lorey the supplies she needed, he let the two women find a spot for themselves near the fire, sitting on cushions to face each other. Tievin simply went to his desk after hanging their coats. While he did want to get some work done from the comfort of his tent, he also wanted to be within ear's reach to assess for himself what that woman learned of their language. He'd barely heard her talk all along and was quite curious to see how quickly she'd be able to learn their language. After all, this situation was completely unprecedented. No tribesperson had ever tried to learn the Empire's language, and the opposite was also true. Both camps had been at odds for as long as the Empire had existed, it seemed. The tribespeople hadn't even let the Empire see one of their women until now, for some reason.

Tievin didn't like changes, and he liked even less when something unprecedented happened. And it had all happened because of one woman, to boot. Trouble, trouble...

Thankfully, he soon realized that, as Lorey had said, Alezya was still far from mastering their language. Lorey had some drawing talent, and she used it to teach Alezya what she could. Instead of going for the grammar or teaching her to form full sentences, she was more dedicated to increasing the woman's vocabulary through images and gestures. While Tievin read and annotated his reports, he listened with one ear as she taught her like one would have a child. To eat, to drink, to sleep. Water, food, fire, bed, bath, clothes. Sky, snow, mountain, forest. Man, woman, child, dragon, bird. Me, you, us, them, and the numbers, one to ten. Soon enough, Tievin stopped listening, feeling bored and trying to focus on his work instead. At least, it appeared that Alezya was genuinely trying to memorize it all. Lorey was a patient teacher too, repeating without end the words Alezya had trouble remembering or enunciating.

"...Why isn't she trying to teach you too?" Tievin asked when the two women had stopped for a bit to drink.

"I tried asking her, but she's reluctant to."

He frowned.

"She's learning our tongue, but she won't teach you hers?"

"She's nervous," Lorey defended her. "Tievin, she's in a foreign land with foreign people, and she doesn't understand why we're kind to her nor what we want from her. She's afraid."

"She's ungrateful."

"She'll open up," Lorey insisted. "If we give her some time to. She was beaten and exiled by her own people, twice. You can't expect her to suddenly open up to complete strangers about the ways of her people."

"You're too trusting of people," Tievin sighed.

"If one woman could lead to our ruin, the Empire would have collapsed long ago," Lorey chuckled. "Moreover, this isn't the first time Kiera and I have dealt with foreign tribes. When we explored the west, do you have any idea how many times we were greeted with arrows and spears? We have actual dragons obeying the Imperial Family's will, Tievin. If I were Alezya, unable to check our intentions, I'd be worried that you'd destroy my home if I did or said anything wrong. That young woman has experienced enough trauma already, give her some time."

An actual dragon was guarding the tent right then, for they could hear Kein snoring right outside Tievin's tent, although it had already been established Kein wasn't a menace to Alezya. If there's one thing Tievin was grateful about that woman's presence for, it was that this mad, havoc-wreaking dragon had finally been somewhat subjugated... for now.

"...And what does Her Highness think?"

"You'll hear it from her," Lorey replied. "I don't speak for Kiera."

Tievin didn't raise any more protests. Only in a private setting like this did they allow themselves to call the Prince and Princess by their names...

"Lorey?" Alezya suddenly called her.

"Yes?"

"...Kassein?"

Lorey smiled kindly.

"Where is Kassein?" she translated Alezya's question for her. "Kassein and Kiera are gone hunting. Hunting."

She mimicked the act of hunting, and whether she understood that or not, Alezya gave her a little nod, looking satisfied with that answer. The two of them resumed their "lesson" and Tievin resumed his work while they waited for the Imperial siblings to come back from their hunt.

Tievin wasn't so worried now that he knew both siblings were together; he could easily guess Kiera would taunt her younger brother into a competition, and they wouldn't return until they were both satisfied, which meant it was definitely going to take a while.

Moreover, those two hadn't seen each other in years, and despite their eight-year age gap, they'd always been quite close. With seven siblings, it was always hard to fully identify the dynamics of each relationship, but Tievin could confidently say Kiera was one of the siblings Kassein felt closest to, notably because of her honest, blunt, and outgoing character. She had also been away while his relations with his family had deteriorated, so she didn't play any part in the downfall that had led to his exile... which explained why she was the only member of his family Kassein had felt comfortable asking for help, although he'd never explicitly said it.

Tievin was silently congratulating himself for having pushed the Prince to seek help when they heard Kiki's particular, high-pitched growl in the distance.

They all turned heads and, after putting their cloaks back on, left Tievin's tent to go and meet the returning siblings. Just as Tievin had anticipated, they'd been at it for a while, and it was dusk when Kiki landed, making happy hops around Lorey. The two siblings hadn't flown back, but they'd left the dragon to carry their biggest prey, and the result of their hunt was now lying in the snow, two impressive lines of dead animals that garnered the attention of many soldiers around.

"Did you win?" Lorey asked, walking up to Kiera, who put an arm around her.

"We got hungry before we could settle on a result," Kiera pouted, glaring at her brother, "but I would have..."

Kassein didn't answer her; his eyes were already riveted back on Alezya as she walked up to him. For the first time, there was a hint of excitement in her eyes, despite the pain of her injuries still giving her an awkward walk. When she reached him, Kassein grabbed her elbows to help support the young woman facing him.

"Kassein," she said with a pretty voice.

"Mh," he nodded.

"Kassein," she repeated. "Kassein, man, dragon."

"...What?" He frowned, surprised and confused.

"Kassein, man, dragon," she repeated, pointing at a line of orange scales at the base of his neck, one his sister had caused earlier.

"I taught Alezya some of our language while you were gone, Your Highness," Lorey explained with an amused expression. "She's learning fast."

Kassein turned back to Alezya, who was waiting for his reaction, her eyes shining with what looked like pride and expectation, like a child waiting to be praised. After a bit, he finally seemed to relax and chuckle.

"Yes," he said. "Man-dragon."

He caressed her long black hair, making Alezya blush even more. Standing on the sidelines, Tievin rolled his eyes. To think His Highness would look like this over a woman mastering a two-year-old's level of language...

"What are you waiting for?!" he barked at the soldiers standing nearby. "Do I have to carry these to the kitchen myself? Chop-chop! You should be happy, we have plenty of meat for dinner thanks to Their Highnesses! Now take it and scram!"

It didn't take any more for all the soldiers to start grabbing whichever prey they could and scatter.

Meanwhile, Kassein turned back to observe Alezya, checking on her. She looked much better after the bath and an afternoon with Lorey. She didn't seem to mind his hand on her cheek either, only responding to it with a shy pinch of color on her cheeks. Her hands were warm too, so they'd probably spent the afternoon inside. He didn't like her being out here though. Even if Lorey and Kiera were here now to get some of the attention too, he wasn't fond of the men being aware a foreigner was here.

"Let's go back," he told her, wondering when she'd be able to understand all of his words.

"Oh, stop hiding her in your tent, Kassein," his sister protested. "It's a very nice evening. Let's have dinner by the firepit."

She'd used a tone that didn't leave room for refusal, and she also turned around, pulling Lorey with her before he could protest. Kassein glared at his older sister but quickly gave up. With an arm around Alezya's waist, he guided her toward the firepit, Tievin following behind them.

There was an area that was the army's main eating place. Although it wasn't used every day due to the more often than not poor weather, the area was a nice plain with no tents nor trees, just a bare patch of land at a crossroad, where a large fire pit was constantly kept going or reignited when needed. As most of the day had been very fine, it was now a big roaring fire, and the men had already reduced the layers of snow to a couple of inches and gathered the tables in a chaotic arrangement around the pit. There was no real order, just one brigade after another having brought their tables and lined them up, forming rows of them like streaks around the fire, for quick access to the roasting meat.

While a lot of them were already busy drinking and chatting loudly, many heads inevitably turned upon their little group's arrival. Kassein tightened his arm around Alezya, glad he'd put his cloak back on and that his large figure hid her a bit. After being apart all afternoon, he felt somewhat reluctant to let go, even for so much as a minute...

Luckily, his sister, who didn't care for mingling with the soldiers either, brought even more attention to herself with her bronze armor and tall frame. Not that she seemed to care for any of the pairs of eyes lingering on her or Lorey though. Instead, she was walking ahead, guiding the five of them and the dragons to a little hill that overlooked the area a bit farther than the gathering, and both Kiki and Kein quietly settled themselves in the snow.

This area hadn't been swept by the soldiers, and to avoid getting wet up to their chins, they quickly sat down on the dragons, except for Tievin, who only hesitated a second before he turned around and went to grab a chair for himself.

Kassein glanced at Alezya, gauging her reaction. She seemed to now be more relaxed around the dragons, although her amazement while watching Kiera help Lorey climb Kiki was still palpable. Her eyes kept going from one dragon to the other, perhaps comparing the two, or surprised that they agreed to be used as warm benches. Kassein then took her hand and guided her to climb and sit on his dragon so that she was seated between his legs, a bit lower than him, with her shoulder against his knee. This way, she could be mostly protected from both the wind and the men's stares by his cloak and Kein's body. Although she seemed unsure about sitting on Kein's foreleg, Alezya was now opening her hand on the orange scales with a faint, amazed smile. His dragon was chunky enough that it didn't mind her nor Kassein's feet, and quite the opposite, was happy to have its huge head next to her, keeping one silver eye on her. Kiki, on the other hand, had thinner limbs on top of being generally smaller, and Lorey and Kiera sat side by side on its back. Tievin summoned a pair of soldiers who'd been walking by a bit too slowly and had them bring food to the little group.

"Did you two have a good talk?" Lorey asked while they waited, her eyes going from one sibling to the other.

"Even if my brother was the chatty type, which we all know he is not, hunting isn't an activity that leaves much space for chatting, love," sighed Kiera. "So no, unfortunately, I haven't been able to properly ask him what he's been up to."

Kassein didn't respond to that, and luckily, the soldiers returned in a timely manner, bringing bowls full of food before leaving again. Kassein looked down as Alezya seemed to inspect the content of hers with a spoon. He smiled behind his index finger as she immediately went for the chunky bits of meat first. He'd hunted more tender meats on purpose.

"Kassein," Kiera grabbed his attention with a more annoyed tune.

He darted his dark green eyes back to his sister.

"You could at least answer Mom's or Sadara's letters," she said. "Do you know how annoying Dara is when I go home?"

"You're saying that as if you went home often yourself," Lorey chuckled.

"At least I give them some news!"

"Only because Adda doesn't leave us unless we give her a letter to bring back home."

"Sadara only uses her dragon like a bloody messenger bird, anyway..."

She stopped talking for a bit as she filled her mouth with meat on a skewer. Kassein glanced down, catching Alezya staring at his sister with a confused but curious expression. Not used to meat on skewers? Or was it his sister's terrible table manners? She hadn't reached for one, focusing on her bowl first, but now, she seemed quite interested.

"Alezya," he called her.

There was always that tingle of excitement whenever she reacted to his voice and her name, and sure enough, she turned her head back to him with those big black eyes full of curiosity. He took her bowl to hold it for her and handed her the last half of the skewer he'd started right before. Alezya took it, and after inspecting it, she ate it like she'd seen his sister do, using her teeth to rip the meat off the skewer. He could tell right away she liked it... Then, attracted by the smell, Kein sniffed in their direction, turning its big orange head and making Alezya stop eating. Kassein pushed his dragon's snout away with his boot and an annoyed click of his tongue. Kein had already been brought a full bear to eat on its own, as did Kiki, and the two dragons were already stupidly trying to steal each other's prey despite having the exact same meal. Except because of the humans on their backs, neither could use more than one paw and their heads without getting scolded, making them growl in frustration.

"*Tsk.*"

They all turned heads, surprised, as Alezya had just imitated his tongue clicking. She blushed to be having all eyes suddenly on her and turned to Lorey as if hoping she would explain what she'd just done.

But Lorey just smiled, amused.

"It looks like she was curious about that habit of yours," she chuckled.

"For goodness' sake, don't let her pick it up," Kiera groaned. "I already get scolded a ton by Mom when I do it... I swear between that and her stubbornness, we all got the worst of Grandma's traits."

Tievin couldn't agree more. The tongue-clicking was a mere sound, but it was enough to terrify anyone who'd worked in the Imperial Palace long enough to know it was a warning, and a bad one at that. The current Emperor's grandmother used to click her tongue every time something annoyed her, and it had been passed down the Imperial bloodline like a unique curse word...

"...Anyway," Kiera said after filling her mouth again, "what are you going to do about her?"

Kassein glared at his sister, not liking how she was pointing at Alezya with her skewer. Kiera already had terrible table manners, but she was also painfully blunt at times.

"What do you mean?" her brother asked with a warning in his deep tone.

Kiera wasn't one to be impressed by her younger brother, but between them, Alezya had stopped eating, and her eyes were going from one sibling to the other with the fear of someone who couldn't understand what was going on. Lorey had stopped smiling too to eat silently, letting those two deal with one another.

"You know what I mean, Kassein," Kiera retorted. "You need to know what her deal is. She is not supposed to be here. Let alone the dragon's dung heap of problems that are not going to fail to drop if Kassian hears about this, you still have the whole tribes' situation to figure out."

"She was kicked out by her tribe," he hissed. "She's not with them anymore."

"She is still a foreigner," Kiera replied, way calmer than him but firm in her tone. "You can't ignore that you do not know her intentions."

"Did you not hear me? She was–"

"Kicked out, yes. But why?" His sister waved her skewer. "Why would they kick a woman out? Have you ever actually stopped to give it some thought? Kassein, you've been living here for years now, but you have never seen a woman from the tribes before, have you? No one in the Empire has, not that we know of. Whatever happens in those mountains, they don't usually kick their women out. They don't even let them in our sight, but all of a sudden, that woman was thrown out and within our reach, twice. Even if she was indeed exiled, didn't you ever wonder why? What could she have done to warrant such horrible treatment? There are few criminals that we punish this severely in the Empire, Kassein. The tribes might be very different from us but I am pretty sure they aren't savages who collectively beat women for no reason, or just for the fun of it."

"...What are you implying? She's not a criminal."

"That's exactly my point, you don't know that!" his sister exclaimed. "I'll concede she's not any kind of fighter, judging by the little amount of meat on her bones and how she's scared of her own shadow. But you saw it earlier. She didn't flinch at the sight of blood and she wasn't scared by dead bodies, open skulls, and exposed guts. She approached a fight without batting an eyelid to inspect a bloody corpse. That's not the reaction of someone who's never seen such things before."

"...She's scared of men."

Both siblings turned their heads to Lorey, whose calm tone had taken them all by surprise. Even Tievin, who had quietly listened to the siblings' arguments, raised an eyebrow.

"What?" Kiera said, confused.

"Alezya is scared of men."

"Men," Alezya repeated, recognizing the word.

Lorey gave her an encouraging nod and smile, before looking up at Kassein.

"She's far more wary of men than she is of blood or dragons. Only you and Tievin seem to have earned her trust. Every time a soldier comes near, she shows signs of nervousness."

As if to prove her words, a soldier just happened to be bringing more food to them. The man was keeping his head lowered in respect, so he didn't notice all the eyes on him when he dropped a new plate full of meat skewers between the two dragons before leaving with an empty one, hurrying to get out of their fangs' reach. Kassein's eyes went to Alezya. Sure enough, she'd stopped eating to keep an eye on the man coming near, looking a bit stiffer and her fist clenched slightly tighter on her second skewer. Only after he'd left did she seem to relax, and actually notice all the eyes on her.

"See?" Lorey said with a calm tone to reassure Alezya. "And this is when you're nearby, Kassein. When you were gone earlier and we crossed the camp, she wouldn't let go of me and acted wary of anyone we walked near. She couldn't possibly know some of your men are criminals. I think whatever happened to her, she's developed a fear of men, or at least, some defensive instinct."

Kassein didn't say anything, his eyes riveted on a confused Alezya.

After a second, he left his position for a second to bring her a skewer and one for himself. She waited until he sat back behind her before taking her first bite, her eyes going to the dragons, whose bickering seemed to intrigue her. More meat had been brought for them, and the duo was back to their shenanigans, trying to steal each other's food.

"It could be a result of being beaten up by them," Kiera finally said.

"I don't think so," Lorey replied. "One doesn't develop a fear of men after being beaten up by a handful she knew. She'd hate and resent them, but she wouldn't associate the foreign soldiers with those who attacked her. No, I have a feeling that her fear of men comes from a place deeper than that."

She looked at Kassein as if there was some more serious meaning that she was implying. He frowned slightly, his eyes going to Alezya.

For the first time, he finally understood what his sister and her partner meant by saying he didn't *know* Alezya. He only knew what had happened to her recently, and he was getting to know her, but... that was it. He didn't know anything about her past, and he didn't know what her personality was when she actually had a voice. So far, she'd been dependent on his protection and care just to ensure her survival. ...Was he making her dependent on him? Would she have acted the same if she had been in a position where she didn't need him? If she had been born in the Empire, if he wasn't a prince exiled for his crimes...

Kassein's thoughts were quickly spiraling, and it was Alezya's hand on his knee that eventually brought him back.

She had her big black eyes on him, full of questions. Strangely, seeing her nervously scrutinizing his reactions brought him a bit of self-assurance. It didn't matter what could have been, for none of it reflected their reality. Whatever had happened to her in the past, in the present moment, Alezya was here with him, and somehow, she relied on Kassein rather than fearing him like she did other men. If it would take time for him to actually get to understand and know her, he was alright with that.

There was already a lot said between them, not with words but with their gazes and actions. That was enough for him... for now.

He brushed Alezya's shoulder with his thumb to reassure her, and then glanced up, ready to show his determination to Lorey, but to his surprise, that woman already had a faint smile on her lips.

"...This woman aside," said Kiera, "you still have the matter of the tribes on your hands. Have you made any progress at all?"

"I've pushed the army this far and taken back most of the land," Kassein grunted. "What else do you expect from me?"

"Kassein," his sister protested. "Are you just going to stay like this? Kassian is–"

"Don't. Say. His. Name," he hissed, glaring again.

His sister responded with just as much anger, dropping her spoon back in her bowl.

"Do you intend to stay exiled here forever?" she insisted. "You know they're all missing you out there!"

"They're not," Kassein said. "Don't give me that crap, Kiera. If any of them missed me, they'd have come here a long time ago. Nobody's even visited the Onyx Castle in years."

"Because they want you to have it, you stubborn brat! Now that Kassian's the Emperor, of course Mother and Father want to remain near the Capital! We knew they'd end up there eventually! Most of our siblings are there, and our parents aren't getting any younger. Ever since Cessi and Darsan moved to the Eastern Kingdom, except for me and you, the other four live in the Capital. Do you know Grandmother even said I could have the Diamond Palace since I'm the only one interested in the west? She's getting too old to travel between the two palaces and she's already made it clear who's going to inherit hers."

"Get to your point."

"Our parents aren't getting any younger, Kassein. You need to stop your tantrum and fix things with our older– with Kassian. Yes, you can glare but I'll call him by his name if I want to! ...I don't know about Kassian's stubborn ass, but Father wanted *you* to have the Onyx Castle. I'm sure of it. Who else? Sadara's definitely staying in the Capital, and both Sepheus and Shenan are on their way to becoming scholars. You're the only one left who would be fit to inherit it."

Kassein didn't respond this time, only looking pensive. His eyes went back to Alezya. She was paying attention to their conversation, visibly nervous from not understanding what he and his sister were arguing about. Kassein sighed.

He really had no answer for that. He wasn't as optimistic as Kiera was about their parents' hope for him, if they even had any left.

"...I doubt it," he finally muttered.

"Kassein. It's our childhood home. You should be happy they want you to have it!"

"It's an old abandoned place collecting dust and snow right now."

"It was still our home," Kiera insisted, with a gentler tone this time. "...Do you remember? When we were kids, every time we had to go to the Capital for Imperial duties, we all couldn't wait to go home, back to the Onyx Castle. Despite having a whole wing to ourselves, we never felt at home in the Imperial Palace. That place was too big, and our rooms were too far apart. We'd refuse to sleep apart and gather in one bed... and Sepheus cried his eyes out every time we had to leave the older ones behind because they weren't coming home with us. Still a crybaby, isn't he?"

Finally, a faint smile appeared on his lips.

Growing up with seven siblings sure made for a lot of memories. They all had different personalities, different hobbies, and different aspirations, but they'd truly grown up as a tight-knit little tribe. Kassein, being one of the youngest, didn't remember as much as Kiera did. Only Sepheus was younger than him, by almost two years, while their older siblings were over ten years older than him. They had always admired Kassian, their oldest brother, Darsan, the rowdy second-born, and Cessilia, their gentle older sister. However, now, Cessilia and Darsan lived far away in the Eastern Kingdom with their families, and Kassian was busy with his duties as the new Emperor.

"Those were the good days," Kiera reminisced with a smile. "The Imperial Palace workers would always brace themselves whenever we were coming... Did you know? The servants secretly called us the Terrible Three."

"Who was the third— Oh. Darsan."

"Of course," Kiera chuckled. "Darsan the Destroyer, me who was always running away, and you who would always get into a fight with one of us, or with your dragon..."

Kassein's mood soured immediately, and his sister bit her lip, realizing her mistake too late. Even Lorey gave her a little glance, but Kiera already knew her mistake. She shook her head.

"What happened wasn't–"

"It was entirely my fault," Kassein retorted, closing his eyes as the anger inevitably surged. "Don't patronize me."

"I am not patronizing you. Sadara told me all about it."

"I bet she did."

"You made a mistake, yes. But the way Kassian sent you away was not—"

"He did what he had to do to protect the Empire," Kassein grunted. "He got rid of his murderer of a little brother so the people wouldn't riot against him and the Imperial Family. I didn't commit a mistake, Kiera. It was murder."

"It was an *accident*, Kassein," Kiera sighed.

"If anybody but the Emperor's younger brother had done it, I'd have been sentenced for life."

"Nobody but one of us could have provoked such a thing!" she exclaimed. "Do you even hear yourself? Why are you so hell-bent on being wrong? You're always like this! You may blame Kassian for being harsh, and yes, he was, but you're the one punishing yourself beyond reason! Why the hell are you always like this?! Yes, you committed a mistake, a huge one, but you're not the criminal you're trying to pass for! Nobody asked you to stay here for years on end and ignore the whole family!"

"Kassian exiled me—"

"He said you should go to the north and not come back until you've pacified it. He never said to ignore all of the family's attempts to hear from you! If it wasn't for Tievin and the generals keeping them informed, they wouldn't even know you're still alive! You are always so quick to bicker with everyone, but you didn't put up a fight when Kassian gave you that impossible task? Why?! Why the fuck are you always begging to be treated like you're some horrible monster?!"

"Didn't you hear the part where I actually killed someone?"

"It was a fucking accident!" Kiera shouted. "Darsan's provoked dozens of accidents, and he got lucky nobody ever died from their injuries! We all learned to fight and kill as soon as we were able to hold a weapon! We are paired with bloody dragons, the top predators on this continent, and as if it wasn't enough, we're raised and built to be killers! Father and Aunt Shareen killed countless people before they were our age! Even Grandma did so, and without a dragon! It may have been for extenuating reasons, but they meant it! You caused an *accident*, Kassein, and you meant none of it! It's even a miracle it didn't happen sooner with that mad dragon of yours!"

All the shouting had now drawn a lot of attention to their group, with many heads turned and ears curious to grasp what was going on.

After a few seconds of silence, Lorey gave a little nudge to Kiera's knee, who suddenly stood up and got down from her dragon, taking big angry steps toward the fire.

"Who's the idiot who's been grilling the meat?!" she growled aloud as she walked away. "How dare you ruin my hunt?!"

That was enough for all heads to turn right back to their plates, hoping to stay out of trouble. Even if their argument had been somewhat defused, Kassein had lost his appetite. He got up, angry, and left.

After a second of hesitation, Alezya put her bowl of food down and followed after him. Lorey sighed.

"He's not really mad," Tievin commented when he estimated his Commander's ears were far enough.

"This isn't about his sister," Lorey replied.

She stood up, put her bowl down on Kiki's back, and quickly followed after them.

It took Kassein a little while to realize Alezya was painfully trying to catch up to him, her injured legs aching in the snow. He stopped and turned around, finding her panting and grimacing in pain a few steps behind. He sighed, his anger immediately cooled down by her presence.

He felt like an imbecile, having not noticed her... He had expected that she'd stay behind with Lorey to finish her meal. He walked up to her and, unable to witness her struggle any longer, picked her up in his arms.

She blushed, surprised for a second, but quickly regained her senses and wrapped her arms around him. He glanced down at her. It looked like his fight with his sister had made her nervous, and now, she was staring at him with a more concerned than shy expression.

He let out a faint sigh.

"...I'm alright," he muttered, rubbing his thumb against her waist.

He hadn't managed to gather a smile this time, not even a fake one. Alezya hadn't understood and was just staring at him, trying to decipher his emotions...

"Your Highness."

He glanced back. Lorey was also coming up to them, but she hadn't run like Alezya had, instead walking elegantly in the snow. Kassein frowned, wondering what his sister's partner wanted with him.

He was prepared for her to lecture him or something, but instead, Lorey's eyes briefly went to Alezya.

"...There's something I have been meaning to tell you," she whispered.

For her to be speaking in a low tone surprised him the most. He glanced back at the firepit further behind her. Kiera was still busy loudly chastising his men over their poor meat-roasting skills... while being brought copious amounts of alcohol as a bribe.

"You waited until Kiera couldn't hear?" he guessed.

Lorey gave a little nod.

"Yes... This is about what she said earlier, about Alezya."

Noticing her name, Alezya seemed more curious than before, her eyes riveted on Lorey with a slight frown. Lorey kept going, ignoring Alezya to stare at Kassein with a more serious expression instead.

"I didn't want to mention it in front of Kiera, as she's already suspicious of your protege's intentions. Truthfully, I do agree with some of her points. It is hard to know what has happened to her before... but I do not think Alezya bears any ill intention. Not from what I've seen in the bit of time I've spent with her, anyway."

"What's your point, then?"

"Truthfully, I am saying this out of concern for you, Your Highness. I do like Alezya, but she has a past, and not everything about it, obviously, will be safe and pleasant to uncover. I think you should be prepared for it, Your— ...Kassein."

He frowned. Lorey was the type who always carefully respected the rules in the presence of anyone but Kiera. She was well aware of their difference in status. Despite having grown up close to the Imperial Family, like Tievin, she was careful to respect the protocol in all circumstances.

This was one of the extremely rare cases where she didn't, and Kassein felt like this was her attempt at showing genuine concern. As if she was a friend or even a sisterly figure. After all, just like Kiera, she was a few years older, and she wouldn't have done anything behind his sister's back if she didn't genuinely believe it was for his sake.

"...I understand," he muttered. "I know."

"No," she said. "I'm not just spouting this out of the blue without a proper reason."

She tightened her arms around herself and glanced back, before taking another step closer.

"...I don't think Kiera noticed," she whispered, "but when we bathed earlier, and when I washed her, I noticed stretch marks on Alezya's body."

"Stretch marks?" He frowned. "...What of it?"

"This is just me making an assumption here," Lorey whispered, "but... they were the same kind of markings a woman who's been with child would have."

"...With child?" Kassein repeated, stunned.

Lorey slowly stepped back.

"As I said, she probably has a past we know nothing about. I thought it would be better if you could fully prepare yourself for it."

Kassein was speechless, too shaken up to speak. A child? Alezya had been... pregnant before? He wasn't an ignorant man. Even if he hadn't been there or too young to witness her pregnancies, he knew his mother, who had carried eight children, had such marks too. This was the kind of mark that happened if a woman carried a child for several months...

"Good night, Your Highness," Lorey said, going back to her usual gentle tone. "Good night, Alezya."

"Lorey," Alezya said, acknowledging some form of greeting too.

She turned around and left, probably to go back before Kiera grew suspicious of her absence. Kassein took a second before he moved again, slowly resuming his route to his tent.

He was lost in his thoughts. Lorey's revelation had hit him hard, shaking him to his core. If it was true, if she'd had a child... Did that mean she had a family back there? Was that why she had been so insistent on going back? If she had a family, why had she been rejected by her tribe? And what had happened to her child?

...What of the father of the child? Was he waiting for her?

He heard his dragon growl loudly in frustration somewhere behind him, but he didn't turn back to check. With Kiera and Kiki back there, Kein shouldn't go overboard... and Kassein knew he was more shocked than angry. He just wanted answers, now. Kiera had been right all along. He knew nothing about her. Maybe it was all his own wishful thinking...

He finally walked into his tent, and for a second, he wondered what he was doing. Was it even right for Alezya to sleep here? Still, his legs carried them to his bed anyway, and he put her down, still in a strange daze, and put a knee down to help her take off her cloak without thinking.

"...Kassein. Kassein!"

He looked up. Alezya had been calling him, and he'd just now realized. She put her hands on his cheeks, looking worried. Was he acting out of it? He sighed and closed his eyes.

Regardless of her past... He wanted to believe the woman she was now. Her gestures, her gazes. Everything she gave him, he'd take it as it was. After a couple of seconds, he put his hand over hers and re-opened his eyes, looking deep into those long, big, dark eyes of hers. She looked worried, scrutinizing him for clues.

"...Is it alright to want to believe you?" he whispered.

"Kassein," she whispered again.

They both lacked the words, the language to tell each other everything, everything they wanted to know, and everything they wanted to hear. It was cruel, and it was helpless... In the distance, his dragon growled again. Kein would take off and go to vent their frustration elsewhere.

Alezya glanced up.

"Dragon," she said in his language.

"Kein," he nodded.

"Dragon, sky."

"Yes."

How much could she learn of their language, and how fast? He didn't care for Kassian's opinion, or even Kiera's. He wanted to understand Alezya right then and there.

He let out a long sigh of frustration, but also to relieve the tension in his body and heart. Then, gently brushing off Alezya's hands, he stood up, hung up the cloaks, and went to re-ignite the lazy fire. The day had been good, but one couldn't predict when the next snowfall would occur and the temperature would drop again. This offered him a few seconds to turn his back to Alezya and catch a break from those black eyes.

Lorey's revelations had shaken him to his core, and once again, when in doubt, he hung on to what he knew to be true.

Alezya needed him. Her tribe had cast her out, attacked and hurt her. Even if a family was waiting for her back there, she'd need help getting back... but was there a family? What had happened to the child she'd carried? ...Was the child even still alive? Why wouldn't they be with their mother, then? Kassein felt even more frustrated.

If she had a partner, a husband, why hadn't he helped her? Why hadn't he come down from the mountain to retrieve the mother of his child? Was he dead? ...Or had the child's father taken them from her?

Alezya looked young, around his own age. Could she have suffered such a terrible loss? Her days and nights of crying came back to his memories. She'd been desperate to go back... Now things were starting to make sense.

He took a deep breath in. If she had a family she longed for, she deserved to reunite with them. He could bury his own feelings for her sake. He wanted to ask... If there was a child, there was a father. If so, maybe he'd been so horribly mistaken. It ached. His sore heart ached already, a pain that no Dragon Blood would be able to heal.

And still, he was more resolute than ever. He had to know.

When he turned around, however, and saw Alezya lying on the bed, looking nervous and watching his reactions, his willpower broke down. He walked up to her, and with slow movements, helped her get under the blankets. It was early, but she needed the rest, and his heart needed the night to strengthen and gear itself up for any answer. At dawn, he would ask.

Once she was under the blankets, giving him confused glances, Kassein turned around, took off his armor, and lay down on the fur rug right next to the bed, like usual, staring at the ceiling above. He wished he'd stayed to drink with his sister. Getting drunk would have been nice, rather than letting so many questions harass him most of the night...

Alezya ought to be way more tired than he was, for a while later, and while sleep still avoided him, he heard her shallow, sleepy breathing.

Kassein was still lost in his confusing thoughts, imagining every possible scenario, trying to figure out which parts were true, and all the possibilities he might have to prepare himself for.

He couldn't help but find himself worried about Alezya's child; not because they might exist, but because they would be separated from their mother right now, and perhaps in danger... Was that why she'd been so desperate to go back? But what of the child's father? Had she loved someone else? Was there someone else...?

His downward spiral was interrupted by a faint cry. Kassein frowned, and got on his elbows, glancing at Alezya's sleeping figure. She wasn't peacefully sleeping anymore. Instead, her thin brows were furrowed, her breathing hectic, and her hands were clenching her pillow. Tears appeared in her eyes, and she was whimpering something unintelligible.

Kassein waited for a couple of minutes, hoping it would pass, but it only seemed to get worse. He grabbed her hand to hold it before she pressed on her injuries despite the bandages, hoping his warmth would soothe her a bit.

"Alezya," he whispered, caressing her hair.

She woke up silently crying, and visibly disoriented. He saw her eyes quickly glance around the place behind him, before going back to him.

As soon as she seemed to figure out where she was, and with whom, Alezya's breathing eased down a little. She tried to rub her tears, but the fabric on her hand was dry and harsh, making her skin redden. Kassein took over, using his thumb to gently wipe away the tears from her eyes.

His other hand was already holding hers, and Alezya's tightened around his a bit. This was enough to make his heart falter again. ...Would he be able to let go when the time came? Kassein clenched his jaw, feeling angry at himself. He was too selfish. He'd always been...

"Kassein," she muttered, pulling him out of his dark thoughts.

He turned his attention and eyes back to her. Alezya was frowning faintly again, and holding his hand tighter than ever. Was she confused by his actions?

Or still affected by the nightmares that haunted her?

He couldn't think of anything to say that would soothe her, so instead, he kept his elbows on the edge of the bed, held onto her hand, and caressed her hair.

For a while, they remained like this, staying together in silence. The camp was completely quiet in the midst of the night, not even a breeze howling above the tent. Alezya wasn't showing signs of falling back asleep.

Instead, she was holding onto his hand, her eyes looking up at him, still teary, but much calmer.

That woman wasn't afraid to sustain his gaze, which fascinated Kassein. All his life, people had lowered their eyes in his presence, as if afraid to trigger a beast. Only people in his family were able to look directly at him, and in the last few years, their gazes had shown more disappointment than he could endure. Alezya reminded him of a snow leopard again, when those felines were cornered and refused to go down without putting up a fight... except now, there was no fight to be had.

Instead, she trusted him, or so it seemed. She clearly wasn't afraid of him anymore.

Finally, a faint smile came back to Kassein's lips. He'd be alright...

Whatever she decided, whatever it turned out Alezya needed, he'd be able to comply with it. At least, that's what he wanted to believe.

"Kassein," she muttered again.

He tilted his head, wondering why she was calling out his name this time, but to his surprise, Alezya moved on the bed, retreating toward the end of the tent, and pulling him along...

It took a couple of seconds for Kassein to understand. She wanted him on the bed with her? His throat dried up a little, and his heart wavered dangerously. He knew she trusted him, but this much... He hesitated a bit, leaving her to pull and stare at him with intent in her eyes.

It wasn't that he hadn't understood, but he wasn't sure he could go along with that request of hers. His resolve he'd spent the last few hours trying to build seemed to be dangerously fragile now. But Alezya's wet eyes eventually won him over again.

After a faint sigh, Kassein climbed on the bed.

He pulled the fur blankets over her, while he lay on top. Not only did he not need them, but he preferred having some kind of barrier between his and Alezya's bodies, even if it seemed ridiculous by the way they were now lying next to each other. Trying to calm down his roaring heart, he put an arm under her pillow and watched as she closed her eyes and got closer to him, nestling her face against his shoulder like she needed that refuge... Their hands were still bound together, and to Kassein's surprise, she seemed to quickly fall back asleep as soon as she'd found the right position against him.

He wasn't so lucky, as his whole body was way too aware of the woman lying beside him to let him rest. Instead, he had to look down at her long raven hair sprawled behind her, on top of the piled-up furs, all the way down to her legs, while the top of her head rested right below his chin. He'd never paid much attention to women's hair before, but Alezya's was truly uniquely smooth, and a beautiful black color. It reminded him of the scales of his father's dragon.

He couldn't peek at Alezya's sleeping face, but he could feel her shallow breathing against his skin... Was she soothed by his body heat? Hers was pretty cold, and perhaps he'd underestimated how cold the place was. It was hard to tell with a higher body heat than most humans.

She was still holding onto his hand, and he didn't want to move, afraid he might disrupt her sleep after she'd already been awoken once. If she hadn't, he would have liked to caress her hair or her back while she slept, but knowing that she'd found some peace in his embrace was enough for now.

...For now?

Kassein closed his eyes, sighing. His sister was right, he was still a brat. He may have the body of a grown man, but he was only eighteen.

He wondered if Alezya was much older than him. She seemed younger than his sister for sure, but if she'd had a child already, he guessed she had to be at least his age. He wasn't sure how young women could conceive, but Alezya looked young either way. It was only her eyes that showed a strong and mature mind, forged by the need for survival. Lorey was right; he truly didn't know anything about her.

Kassein forced himself to close his eyes again, trying to strengthen his heart and mind for the questions that would have to be asked the next day.

It was a good thing that Alezya was learning their language.

He hoped she would teach him more of hers too. He wanted to learn everything he could about her, not just force her to absorb their culture for survival purposes. No matter what, he hoped she'd know she was safe with him. It didn't matter what she turned out to really need, in the end.

For once in his life, he wanted to be there, a safe haven for someone.

Chapter 9

The next morning, Alezya woke up feeling better than she had in a long time. The warmth covering her body was like a gentle cocoon she felt reluctant to get out of. She slowly opened her eyes, remembering how she was in Kassein's habitation... but the view that greeted her wasn't the fabric walls. Instead, a wall of dark skin, just inches away from her face, took her by surprise.

She blinked, quickly waking up as she was trying to figure out her situation and how she'd gotten there. After a second, she realized she was still on Kassein's bed, but Kassein was on the bed with her. Her heartbeat quickly picked up to a racy pace as blood rushed to her extremities.

She vaguely remembered having had another nightmare about being beaten up, Lumie crying, and then... and then, Kassein had been there to comfort her. He'd held her hand and caressed her hair, his warm hands soothing her effortlessly.

Alezya tried to calm down. He was close, but he was snoring, and she was now pretty sure nothing had happened between them. In fact, her lower body was tightly trapped under the blankets, and Kassein's arm was stuck under her pillow. Still, she had been so bold!

She vaguely remembered she had been the one to invite him onto the bed, a mix of guilt after so many nights of him sleeping on the cold, hard floor and her need for his gentle embrace after that horrible nightmare...

Alezya was shocked at her own actions; she'd been half-asleep, but still, even if she'd been dead drunk it wouldn't have made it much better for her to have Kassein come in bed with her!

Very careful with her movements, she glanced up to take a peek at his sleeping face. Thankfully for her poor nerves, he seemed deep asleep. His torso was moving very slowly with his breathing, and he was snoring, sounding like his dragon's growls... which, actually, she could hear right this instant. Alezya turned her head back to the wall of that habitation and realized she could indeed hear

Kein's growls matching its owner's. Was the dragon's snoring synchronized with its master's? It was a bit cute.

From the faint light in the room, she could guess it was at least dawn, and although Kassein's embrace was definitely warm and comfortable, she didn't want to stay longer and risk facing him when he woke up. For a second, she considered pretending to sleep until he woke up, but with Kassein's arm stuck under her pillow, he wouldn't be able to get up until she got up. Could she even get out of there without waking him up?

Luckily, they'd already unlocked their hands in their sleep, their fingers resting just an inch apart. She tried to move her legs slowly, gauging how much room she had to move under the blankets, but luckily, it seemed her thin limbs could sneak out of there without making too much movement. She took a silent breath in and slowly sat up, making as little movement on the bed as possible, watching out for Kassein's response. He truly was deep asleep, because he didn't flinch while she snuck her legs out of the layers of fur blankets, his snoring not missing a beat. It made her smile a bit.

Soon enough, Alezya was free of the blankets, and on all fours on the bed, ready to climb away. Instead of risking stepping over the Kassein mountain, she slowly crawled to the end of the bed and finally took a step out onto the cold floor. She let out a faint sigh of relief as she stood up, and glanced back.

At least now his large sleeping figure seemed to be getting a proper deep rest... That bed had clearly been made to fit his frame, for with her gone, there was plenty of space left for him. Alezya took a second to stretch, grimacing at her still sore limbs, as she was now sure he wouldn't wake up so easily. Then, she silently walked over to grab one of the cloaks hanging up and slipped into the thick fur boots she'd been given the previous day. There was a bright streak of sunshine sneaking into the habitation, and she was mindful not to direct it Kassein's way as she lifted the curtain to get out.

It was another bright, cloud-free day outside, thankfully.

It didn't seem like it had snowed overnight either, for the snow was the same level as the previous day, if not a bit lower. Alezya had been right in that it was dawn, the sun still rising and blinding her on the horizon.

She found herself smiling at the first streaks caressing her face. She loved that moment of the day, when she could witness the sky taking shy colors of pink and orange. She took a couple of steps in the snow, enjoying the early silence. She'd never known this place to be so quiet... and that's when she realized it was too quiet.

She turned at the corner of Kassein's habitation and found herself facing Kein, the dragon's big silver eyes staring wide open at her.

"Morning," she whispered, hoping her low tune would convince the dragon to keep it down too.

The large orange beast slightly tilted its head, but at the rear, Alezya witnessed its tail sweeping waves of snow left and right... Was that a good sign?

Alezya was shocked at herself and how unafraid she now was to stand inches away from an actual dragon. This beast had terrified her and all the clans for years, and now, it was wagging its tail and letting her stare right back into its eyes, those eyes she was so sure were going to be her end just days ago, during their confrontation on the mountain. That all felt so long ago now.

With a confident smile, she raised her hand, and sure enough, Kein was happy to let her caress its orange scales. Although rougher, the dragon's skin was as warm as Kassein's, and she smiled at the thought. The dragon let out a growl, and Alezya wondered how loud of a growl it would take to wake up Kassein... It was probably better not to rile Kein up too much.

She stopped and turned around, tightening the cloak around her. She'd hardly been alone at all during the past few days. While she enjoyed having someone as kind and caring as Kassein or Lorey watching out for her, she couldn't help but feel she also needed some alone time.

It had been just her and Lumie since her baby was born almost two years ago, and Alezya had spent most of her time alone, trying to avoid her people... Suddenly being forced to stay with so many people around was a bit suffocating for her. That morning was just what she needed, with its silence and the clear sky, both refreshing and soothing.

Happy that her legs and feet were also up for it after a good night's sleep, she began strolling away from Kassein's habitation. She heard Kein behind her, and soon enough, the dragon's head was keeping up inches away from her shoulder, following her quietly like some obedient pet.

Alezya was amazed by the situation, but not nearly as much as the few warriors whose paths she crossed. It seemed they had been appointed for some early morning tasks as they were all carrying wood or shovels, which they almost dropped along with their jaws as they witnessed the scene. The foreign woman walking around escorted by only a dragon seemed to be a truly stunning sight, for they all couldn't stop staring, some stopping right in their tracks just for their eyes to follow along.

While Alezya was uncomfortable with their gawking, she couldn't help but notice that none of them attempted to stop her. Even more surprising, they didn't even try to approach; on the contrary, they all carefully stayed away, or even turned back around or made some detours, as if they were scared to stand in Kein's path.

Alezya was slightly confused. Shouldn't the Dragon Clan be used to the dragon being around? Why did they all look so scared? Thanks to Kein's presence, however, she was able to take a long stroll around their territory, exploring it for herself.

While she'd gotten up very early, she wasn't the only one, and there was already quite a lot going on. She spotted a group of warriors training in ranks under another warrior's shouting, and some were running two by two, half-naked despite the cold weather. She tried to stay away so as not to disturb them or get in their way and just looked from afar, picking the quieter paths instead.

It was a strange experience for Alezya to wander in a place she'd only been able to glance at from afar. She knew there was a world beyond her mountains, but it didn't mean she'd ever thought she'd be given the opportunity to explore it... She'd thought that maybe one day when Lumie got older, they'd both be able to travel north to see the other clans, maybe reunite with her mom, and see the Northern Sea for the first time. But the south? The south was the land of dark tales, the land where warriors went and hardly returned; it wasn't a place a woman should have even been able to dream of visiting. It didn't seem real at all to Alezya.

Just a few days ago, she was fighting for her life, thinking she was bound to die protecting her daughter... but now, she was freely roaming in a land even the bravest warriors of her clan had only been allowed to step on at the price of their lives. Suddenly, everything seemed possible, as if fate had completely changed its mind. Either that or everything had become nonsense. Maybe she'd been hit too hard and was dreaming...

Alezya chuckled to herself. Sadly, everything was all too real, and she knew it. She wouldn't be fine until Lumie was, and right now, her baby was too far from her. Her heart ached as soon as she let her thoughts drift back to the painful memories of the last couple of days.

She stopped and held on to Kein's neck so as not to fall under the numbing pain in her chest. Lumie. Lumie was waiting for her mom. She prayed, all she could, that her cousin and her husband would at least take proper care of her baby. Zenia was a mother too, and Suolk had shown more kindness to Lumie than she'd thought him capable of in the brief moment she'd seen her baby in his arms... She could only hope they would be decent people, or that her cousin would remember how much she owed her for all the times Alezya had risked her life for herbs.

At least, her father wouldn't kill Lumie as long as he thought he could use her, but she didn't put it past that vile man to harm a baby. She had to find a solution, and quickly.

When Kein growled, pulling her out of her dark thoughts, Alezya turned to the dragon, patting its thick neck and feeling grateful for the comfort of its warm skin, until she realized Kein had growled at someone else. One of the warriors was bravely coming toward them, although his wariness of the dragon made him walk strangely to the side, like a crab. It took a second for Alezya to realize she knew that one.

"...Dajan?" she excavated from the back of her mind.

Dajan nodded and gave her a polite smile. So it was him. The warrior she'd been introduced to, for some reason... He kept glancing nervously at Kein, visibly unwilling to step any closer than where he stood. Then, Dajan's eyes finally left the dragon to look at Alezya and speak to her, a flow of words leaving his lips. She watched out for any word she might recognize, but none came up, not even Kassein's or Lorey's name. She frowned, confused as to what he expected from her, wondering if she was in trouble. It didn't seem so, judging from how strangely amicable that man was. She could tell he was making an extra effort to smile. After a few seconds of awkward silence, as she had no idea what or how to respond, Dajan glanced at Kein again, before going back to her.

"*Eh... Mahi? Ahra mahi?*"

Hot water. Alezya knew those words. Was he offering her tea?

"*N-nam,*" she nodded, remembering what Lorey had taught her the previous day.

Dajan gave her a big smile and turned around, running away to grab whatever she'd just said yes to. Alezya felt so strangely proud of herself. She'd understood one of their people! Without help! A bit excited by her little victory, she walked the same path Dajan had just taken while mentally studying the words Lorey had taught her the previous day. All were very basic, but she was confident she could make her basic needs understood thanks to that.

A couple of minutes later, she met Dajan again, and he was carrying a little cup he proudly handed her, obviously gathering every brave inch of his being to approach closer to the dragon and very carefully avoid looking anywhere near the orange scales. Alezya happily took the cup and realized that it was not tea. Dajan had just brought her a cup of hot water... Had he taken her word literally and decided to stick to the offer? Or was it custom for those people to drink plain hot water? She felt a bit reluctant to, but this cup was almost the first time she'd managed to ask for something for herself using their tongue...

Thus, she forced herself to take a sip, at least to make Dajan happy.

She suppressed a grimace. She really wasn't fond of unflavored hot water... and mentally took note for herself to look for flowers and herbs she could use to flavor it with later.

"...Herbs," Alezya suddenly muttered to herself.

Thinking of herbs, a crazy idea had just popped into her head. Ignoring Dajan's confused expression, she took a minute to think about it. It wasn't completely mad, but... it would be a big risk. Moreover, she didn't know if... Alezya suddenly turned back to Dajan, who jumped, surprised. She walked up to him, grabbing his wrist.

"Dajan, herbs? Uh..." She tried to remember, but she was sure Lorey hadn't taught her the word in their language.

Frustrated, Alezya glanced around, but there was nothing in sight she could use...

Then, she had an idea. She crouched down, and in front of Dajan's confused eyes, she emptied her cup right at her feet before putting the empty cup aside and diving through the melting snow. The hot water had helped melt a couple of inches, but the tips of her fingers still got red and cold by the time she reached the ground underneath all that snow.

She kept digging around, until, finally, she found a tiny, unique blade of grass that had miraculously survived. She stood back up and showed it to an utterly confused Dajan.

"This," she said, showing it to him. "Do you have any place with more of this?"

"*Eushib?*" he said.

Was that their word for herbs? Or grass? Alezya tried to think, getting frustrated by the language barrier, until she remembered she had even better, on herself. She undid the bandage on her hand and pointed at the remains of the greenish paste that had been applied there.

"This! Medicinal herbs! Do you have more? *Inkir?*"

"*Eh!*" Dajan exclaimed. "*Tibin eushib! Nam, nam.*"

"*Tibin eushib,*" Alezya repeated for herself.

Dajan gave her a sign to follow him and, after a brief hesitation, turned his back on the dragon and her to lead the way.

They walked for a long while, but even Kein didn't seem to mind, as if Alezya was walking it around the camp, only strolling away a couple of times to go and sniff the remains of a firepit, or another habitation which had something that seemed to pique the dragon's interest.

Still, Kein always came back to be her shadow, and even she was surprised at how little she minded the dragon anymore... unlike Dajan, who kept glancing back at their odd duo nervously.

This warrior seemed young, but he had shown more bravery than most of those Alezya had met until then. More kindness too. She couldn't bring herself to trust any man here but Kassein and Tievin. Anywhere she went without the dragon-skinned warrior, she could feel their stares on her... and it made her skin crawl.

She hated it. She hated not having a hideout she could crawl into and escape their gazes. Kassein was her only refuge in this place, his dark green eyes more efficient than any cave she could have crawled herself into. He kept all the others at bay, but without him, Alezya couldn't feel safe in this place.

Even right now, she was grateful for Kein acting as a bodyguard on his behalf, for she wouldn't have approached any man alone or dared to go so far away from Kassein without the dragon's protection. Dajan felt different from the other warriors, however. Unlike the other men, he didn't seem to stare at her like she was some exotic prize, and he was doing his best to put some respectful, calculated distance between them. It was easy to tell when one was purposely mindful of her, just like Lorey was. Hence, Alezya felt confident following him through the camp for a while, farther from the paths she'd already walked before.

It took longer than she'd expected, making her realize how little of this place she'd seen before, or how she'd underestimated its size. It was no wonder she had a hard time remembering the men she'd met already; there were a lot more warriors than she'd thought, too many for her to remember all those faces. Only those she'd interacted with stood out... or those who particularly creeped her out. There were a few that didn't try to hide their cunning gazes.

They made her shiver in disgust, and she tried to ignore them. If those warriors obeyed Kassein, she was probably safe, no matter how much they lusted after her... or so she really hoped.

She just made sure to keep a hand on Kein's warm neck as she walked and stuck close to Dajan.

After a while, he eventually brought her to face another one of those very large habitations, as big as the one Kassein had fought Kiera in. More surprisingly, this one was actually set near one of the mountains as if to protect its back from the wind, and there were more warriors guarding it. They gave the strange trio surprised glances, but Dajan said something, and they didn't stop her from entering after him... Only Kein was left behind with a frustrated growl. The orange dragon couldn't possibly fit in there, despite the place being extremely large indeed, as Alezya realized for herself upon stepping in.

She had no idea there could be such a place, and it took her a few seconds to fully analyze what she was seeing. Dajan was chatting, visibly happy to present the place with wide open arms despite her not understanding a word he was saying. She could only tell that *tibin eushib* kept coming back in his sentences. The Dragon Clan didn't just have medicinal herbs; they were actively cultivating them.

Alezya was stunned by the large square patches of soil covered in herbs, a lot of them she'd never seen before. They had built wooden squares and filled them with soil to grow those herbs, some even standing on wooden legs, or exposed to the sunlight; this habitation had been made so parts of its ceiling could be opened and closed to let the sunlight in! She wasn't just happy to find medicinal herbs, she was genuinely stunned by the Dragon Clan's ingenuity in growing them. Now she almost felt like a fool for keeping track of where the ones her clan used grew to go back to those with much difficulty every time. Their clan's Healer would have been green with envy at the sight of this.

Alezya wasn't just there to admire the plants, however. She quickly began looking around for the ones she recognized, and the ones she needed in particular. Still, she couldn't help but admire how well-kept and grown all those herbs were in this awful climate. She identified a few of the most helpful herbs she knew, used for fevers and headaches, and was almost annoyed at how many she'd risked her life for when they were now within her reach.

She kept looking around, followed by Dajan who was still chatting for some reason. That man clearly had no problem taking a foreigner to what was clearly a very important part of their clan's well-being. Was he going to be in trouble for showing her this? Or perhaps he was particularly trusting, or oblivious? Alezya was a bit confused, but she felt grateful. Thanks to his trust, she could look for the herbs she needed for her plan.

And soon, she found them. The first plant she was absolutely sure of, but the second one... She observed the plant, a bit flustered by the slight differences from the one she knew. The shape of the leaves was the same, a wide leaf with five points, but instead of being an all-green color, this one had strange pinkish borders. Was it because it was grown on the ground rather than on the mountain? Or could it be some poisonous difference...? It smelled the same too.

While Dajan wasn't looking, Alezya quickly put a leaf in her mouth, silently praying she wasn't poisoning herself. The taste was the exact same as the one she knew! This was probably safe to use. After all, the Dragon Clan also grew and used it... They wouldn't have bothered to cultivate something deadly. Quickly, she stole as many leaves as she could unnoticed, rolling them under the bandages of her forearm. When Dajan looked at her again, Alezya pretended to be innocently smelling the plants, or pointing at the most common ones. She hated being a thief, but this time, she had no choice. This was the best idea she had been able to come up with so far to protect herself and Kassein from her father's horrible plan.

Dajan gave her a proper tour of the place, and Alezya looked around for more herbs that she knew, wondering even more about the ones she had never seen before. Identifying herbs and their uses correctly was a life skill she had always been proud of, and now, she was dying to know about the ones that she was sure no one she knew had ever had access to.

She hadn't thought their clan would have such advanced knowledge of medicine. Their strength had always seemed to be in their numbers and warriors, and a part of her had always found them barbaric for that. Now, she was genuinely shocked about this new aspect of Kassein's people. She'd had no idea they had a similar knowledge of herbal medicine as her clan had, if not better.

It even made her wonder if the answer to Lumie's unique condition was there. She had never thought her child's uniquely pale skin color needed to be changed, but it was a fact that her baby couldn't endure the sunlight. Was there a miracle among those plants that would help Lumie suffer less under the daylight? If they had something that could make her baby girl's life a bit less painful, she would do anything to have it... Once again, Alezya swore to herself to learn their language faster so she could ask Lorey about it.

It seemed Dajan was really happy to show her around because they spent quite some time touring the square patches of growing herbs. Alezya tried to take note of as many as she could to remember them in the future, but while she did, another question came to mind: who was growing them?

The men outside were clearly just guarding the precious plants, but there was no one else in the habitation in charge of it. Did they have a healer in charge of this place? But she hadn't seen any woman around, or did the Dragon Clan warriors all know what those were? From Dajan's actions, it didn't look like it, for he didn't seem more enthusiastic about one kind of herb than another.

Alezya felt annoyed for feeling irritated about the prospect of another woman being in the camp once again... She already couldn't help but double-check Kassein's reactions to Lorey. There was a difference between how she wanted to act and what her willful heart made her do.

She'd felt happy about their proximity during dinner the previous night and how he didn't mind sharing his food with her, but then, Lorey had come to him to chat, and that discussion between them had made Alezya more nervous than ever... Some of the words she had recognized, in particular, had made her heart jump a couple of times. Woman and child. Lorey hadn't looked at Alezya, but she'd said her name. Worse, Alezya had felt Kassein's body stiffen unmistakably around her.

Now more than ever, Alezya was getting nervous. She had a feeling that Kassein knew, and it was making her feel scared.

What if she lost his trust and protection? Then, she'd really be considered a prisoner here. And all those men, and their stares... She shivered just thinking about it. She couldn't have that. She needed to stay safe, to get back to Lumie... and also, she genuinely didn't want to lose Kassein. She could betray him for her child's sake, but a part of her hoped she wouldn't have to lose him. Alezya knew her own heart all too well, and a silly part of her couldn't help but entertain some hope. He was almost too painfully easy to read. How would he react once he knew the truth? If he ever asked about Lumie, could she be honest? How would he take it...? She didn't want to think about it.

She shook her head and ignored Dajan to walk out of this place, seeking fresh air.

Once she stepped out, it wasn't enough. The stares of the men guarding this habitation made her uncomfortable, and Alezya hurried to Kein's side, where the dragon's warm skin would make her feel safe.

Only when she finally put her hand on the hot scales was she able to relax; she had a plan. It wasn't a full-fledged plan, and it was risky, but it was better than nothing... and if it worked, she might be able to protect both Kassein and Lumie. Quickly, she took some of the herbs, crushed them in her hand, and ate them. The taste was bitter, and the texture was hard to chew and swallow, but Alezya forced it down.

When Dajan appeared again, she asked him for hot water, worried the herbs wouldn't sit well with her stomach... She needed to get them to work. She had stolen enough to take them daily for a few days, but she'd need to come back to this place again. Would Kassein allow it? It hadn't seemed like a big deal for Dajan to bring her here, and now, she knew how to ask... *Tibin eushib*. Those two fateful words might be her salvation.

Dajan came back with the hot water, and Alezya was grateful to be able to wash away the awful taste of those herbs. She handed him back the cup, feeling a bit uncomfortable from the mix of herbs and plain hot water in her stomach, but grateful.

"*Shkran*," she thanked him in his language.

She was glad she remembered enough to be at least polite... She needed a few people around Kassein to keep a good opinion of her, at least.

Dajan smiled but kept the cup in his hands and stayed there, staring at her with eyes full of expectation. Was she supposed to say something?

Then, Alezya realized he was just waiting to see what she wanted to do next. She had come here, now what? She gave him an awkward nod and turned around to walk back toward the camp, Kein still stuck to her like an oversized dog. This time, the dragon properly walked side by side with her, Alezya keeping a hand on its warm neck.

It had been a little while since she'd gotten up now, and as the sun was rising in the sky, the camp was waking up all the same. They walked by a lot more men, and while Kein seemed to intimidate them, Alezya couldn't help but note how a lot of eyes followed her every move. Any woman with any sense of self-preservation could tell when she was lusted after, and right now, she felt like a piece of meat wandering amongst hungry dogs. A lot of the warriors turned their eyes as soon as they saw the dragon guarding her, but Alezya still couldn't help but feel their eyes on her back. All the gawking made her walk even closer to the dragon's side and hurry a bit.

Not all men could be as unbelievably kind as Kassein, she knew that. Had she been foolish to wander away from him? Only Dajan seemed completely oblivious to his peers' gazes, walking ahead of them proudly. Kein, on the other hand, began to growl in warning a couple of times when it noticed a pair of eyes lingering too long on Alezya. Never had she thought she'd one day feel so grateful to a dragon for making her feel safe...

When she first heard a sound like a whistle, she jumped in surprise, making the men laugh, and immediately regretted it. They were toying with her, and her reaction had encouraged them more. There was another strange sound of mouth, which irked her all the more.

Kein turned its head, but too late to identify who had done it, or perhaps the dragon couldn't associate the sound with any degrading meaning, because it didn't growl in warning. Alezya wished it had, for they continued. Someone else whistled, and there was another strange sound. It came from all around now as they had to go through what seemed to be a busy part of this territory, and the men were coming from all sides, emerging from habitations or on their way to somewhere else.

Dajan shouted angrily at the other men around them, having lost his smile, but his authority wasn't respected, for they kept going. Alezya was trying to ignore them, keep her composure, and walk while looking straight ahead, for Kassein's habitation was finally in sight, but it was hard not to let it show on her face. She was scared and angry. Those men were worse than animals, feeding off her fear and enjoying it...

Suddenly, they stopped, and there was a strange strangled sound.

She turned back and saw Kassein, absolutely furious, holding one of those men at arm's length, his feet wiggling inches away from the ground. All of the others had suddenly become mute and paralyzed with terror at the sight of their leader, lifting an entire man with one arm and crushing his neck in the process.

As if it had gotten a silent order from its master, Kein also started growling furiously, retreating its body closer to Alezya while its head was angrily turning around, the big silver eyes looking for prey. It was like those men were torn between running for their lives and witnessing what was to happen to their peer for his impertinence. Kassein hissed something in their language, his dark green eyes going around as if he were trying to remember the faces of all the men present. Alezya saw quite a few of them go extremely pale, and then, there was the sound of bones crushing. She turned her head back to Kassein right as he released his grip, the body falling heavily in the snow. That man was dead...?

She shivered. Kassein had just killed someone with a single hand... and crushed human bones with his mere grip. Even if she didn't want to, Alezya couldn't help but be struck at how dangerous the same hands he used to care for her were. And right now, this same man was holding a dozen men here, planted on their feet and paralyzed by fear with his mere presence. Or perhaps what he had said was keeping them from running away.

One of them suddenly made a strange yelp and began to run anyway. Alezya wondered why he was the only one and no others followed, but she got her answer straight away: Kein jumped and landed right on the man, its fangs finding the man's head immediately to rip it off.

She turned her eyes away a second before the bloodshed, but she saw it in the other men's eyes; it was awful to watch. All the men had gone dead silent, lowering their heads and very likely praying for their survival. Kassein hadn't even looked at her yet; his eyes were going around like a deadly snake picking its next prey. He had a murderous look in his eyes Alezya had never seen before, and it was... scary.

For the first time, it truly hit her how dangerous that man and his dragon were. She'd seen him fight before, but this was different. He was strong enough to hold a dozen men in their place to await their death or his mercy with his mere words. If they fled, his dragon would kill them. If they stayed, one of his hands was enough to crush their spines like twigs. Alezya lost her breath for a second, as she finally took in the full measure of the man she'd slept next to. Kassein was strong, and he could be merciless, even to his own men.

It was clear now: he was this clan's Chief, and everyone else was at his mercy. He was free to continue to kill those warriors until he felt like stopping.

"K-Kassein..."

He darted his eyes at her, and Alezya involuntarily took a half-step back. She'd never seen such anger in his eyes, and her instincts were screaming at her to get away from this dangerous beast. She hadn't meant to, but it was hard to stay still while looking death right in the eye.

She heard Kein growl, somewhere behind her, but was smart to keep herself from looking at what ought to be a horrible scene of death. She could hear the dragon still chewing and more bones being crushed, and she did not want to risk taking a peek at that.

Instead, she was focused on Kassein. He had definitely seen her recoil, and now he'd turned away, his eyes back on his men. Was he thinking she feared him now?

It took Alezya a moment to realize that she did.

But it wasn't something she could fight. It was primal, like prey recognizing that a predator could end them at any moment. She was weak, untrained, and wouldn't last long if it came to a fight against any man. He had just killed someone with his bare hands, and he could command a dragon like it was nothing. She couldn't fight that truth no more than she could deny that she should have been horrified.

But she could choose not to flee. Because she didn't want that fear to grow into something that would make him stay away. Because Kassein was the one man she refused to fear more than she had to. She didn't want him to protect her from himself. She wanted to be held by those hands and trust they'd never turn against her. She wanted to feel safe. Not because there was no danger, but because it was him.

It was madness, maybe, to want that kind of safety from someone like him. From the strongest predator of all. But she did. And it wasn't part of any plan to ensure her survival. It came from a desire stronger than the fear he inspired. It came from somewhere deeper, somewhere honest. She didn't want to fight it.

She feared a lot of things. She feared most men, the men Kassein could crush like they were nothing. And yet, a part of her wanted to be his. She still trusted that he was the one man who would never hurt her. Even if he was the last man she ever trusted again, her heart had already chosen him.

Right now, he was avoiding her gaze. Once again, she could read him easily, the way his forest-green eyes were looking away, a bit ashamed and a bit nervous of her gaze. How could she, a mere, weak woman, have this much power to make a man who terrified all others so cautious of her?

He slightly turned his back to her in an attempt to erect a wall of his own flesh between them, but it was no use. Alezya swallowed her fear and moved forward, stepping closer to him.

She refused to let Kassein think she was scared. He probably felt or heard her move, because his back stiffened; he had gone out without a cloak, his bare torso exposed to the cold without so much as a shiver. Had he been looking for her? Kassein said something, not addressed to her but most likely an order for all the men to scram, because they did. Dajan, with a man braver than the others, came to grab the body at Kassein's feet and take it away.

Neither Alezya nor Kassein watched any of the men leave; his stubborn gaze was on the snow ahead of him, and hers was riveted on his back.

"Kassein," she called him again when they were finally alone.

He kept his back turned to her, and for a second, she felt her stomach twist into a scared knot. Was he mad at her, perhaps? Was he going to be upset if she insisted?

Once again, Alezya reminded herself of her own promise: she wasn't going to be scared of him. Thus, she kept walking bravely until she could lift her fingers and touch his back. His warm skin which hadn't shivered under the ice-cold wind shuddered at her touch. Feeling bolder than ever, Alezya caressed it slowly, moving her fingertip between the scars.

Then, while he remained stiff as a wall, she took a step to the side to appear in his field of vision. His eyes immediately went to her, his brows furrowed with anger and confusion. He probably wondered if she was mad. Alezya thought the same; how else could she have been so bold to approach him in this situation? To get close to a killer, a predator still this angry? Yet there she stood, close to him like ignorant, foolish prey, looking up at him with her big dark eyes... She could read all of Kassein's confusion. Why wasn't she scared? Why was she approaching him when he'd clearly just killed someone right in front of her eyes?

Alezya wished she could tell him she didn't fear him, not nearly as much as she did those other men. She wasn't going to be afraid, no matter how many he killed; she'd seen more cruel things. Kassein was like a predator defending its territory, asserting his dominance; those men were the real monsters, who toyed with their prey for the fun of it.

"Kassein," she whispered his name again, standing even closer.

She could see his bare torso moving along with his tense breathing.

Now he was the one staring at her like he was apprehensive of her movements, of her words. There was something a bit exciting, to be the one responsible for making such a powerful man so vulnerable and cautious of anything she did. Kassein was staring down at her, utterly confused by her apparent fearlessness. His hands hadn't moved, and he was keeping them resolutely by his sides as if he was afraid to touch her after what he'd done.

Alezya was feeling bolder with each passing second. Her actions probably looked a bit mad to him, and she was sorry for that, but she absolutely wanted to let him know she wasn't scared, and she trusted him. After a hesitation, and when her heartbeat had jumped at the thought, she slowly got on her toes, and shyly pressed her lips against his.

It only lasted a second before she separated herself from him, feeling crazy and nervous to see his reaction. Kassein looked properly stunned and, if possible, even more confused.

He stared at her intensely, and Alezya felt her heart sink to her stomach at the realization of what she had just done. Had she really gone insane this time? She felt like she was slightly drunk because she couldn't explain how else she could have been that bold. Kassein's reaction seemed delayed, making her all the more anxious. Had she crossed a line she shouldn't have?

She raised her hand, maybe to caress his cheek or hold his shoulder, but Kassein grabbed her wrist before she could make up her mind. She jolted, surprised by the sudden movement, and her reaction made him let go immediately.

"*La*," she said, grabbing his hand back.

She wasn't scared. How could she make him understand?

She held his hand firmly, although hers was smaller in comparison, and pulled it toward her cheek, her eyes riveted on his. This time, after a few seconds, Kassein's expression seemed to relax a bit. There was still doubt in his gaze, but his brows relaxed, and slowly, gently, he deployed his fingers on her cheek.

Finally, Alezya thought. She slightly tilted her head in his hand, not breaking eye contact, and stepped a bit closer to him. She felt his strong arm wrap around her waist behind her cloak, holding her in his embrace, his warmth spreading to her body. She was safe in his arms. The same hands he killed with were capable of holding and caressing her so gently. There was something exhilarating about being so close to such a dangerous man, and yet completely safe from him, like she was with his dragon...

Slowly, she saw Kassein lower his face toward her, and her heartbeat picked up an excited pace again. He kept his eyes open, going from her eyes to her lips, gauging her reaction... and she didn't stop him when his lips met hers. Instead, she closed her eyes and sealed their kiss, her whole body firing up. His hold on her waist tightened, pulling her against his hot, bare torso, and Alezya felt her blood rush through her veins while butterflies bloomed in her stomach. Kassein was kissing her, a real, passionate kiss this time. She had nowhere to run from his thick lips on hers, and she loved that.

She pressed her hand against his on her cheek, and wrapped the other one around his neck, keeping him there with her. Kassein's kiss was slow, and a bit gawky, as if he was voluntarily holding himself back. He wasn't using his tongue, just kissing and plucking her lips, at a furiously slow pace. Now Alezya was the one growing impatient, her body heating up faster than she could bear...

"*Aqayir.*"

They stopped, Alezya surprised by Tievin's voice. She glanced back while Kassein was already glaring at the intruder. How long had... that man been here?

She blushed, hiding her face against Kassein's shoulder as his arm wasn't releasing her one bit. She'd thought they were alone, but Kassein didn't seem too surprised to see the scrawny man. Had he heard Tievin arrive?

Her blush deepened, what had just happened finally dawning on her. Since when was she so bold?! And that kiss...

She licked her lower lip very faintly. She hadn't expected Kassein to respond to her childish kiss with a passionate one. She could still feel the warmth of his lips on hers, and his torso being inches away from her face didn't help her cool down either.

Kassein and Tievin seemed to be arguing, the first one sounding pissed and the other one in his usual monotone tone, but Alezya didn't care for their conversation. Instead, she was trying to recollect herself, and it wasn't easy when she was still firmly held in Kassein's arm, with nowhere to run. S

he glanced to the side hoping to see something that would distract her, and her eyes landed on Kein. The dragon was busy playing with a bone it had licked clean... along with more in a pile underneath it. There was a lot of blood on the snow, but not a bit of human flesh or clothing left. Confirming that dragons could eat humans was quite an effective cool-down. Kein suddenly burped loudly, and she grimaced. Not the dragon's usual breakfast, probably...

While she couldn't understand what Tievin and Kassein were arguing about, Alezya could hear the latter getting more and more annoyed. Was Tievin pestering him about the killings, or about her?

She'd rather not know and avoided looking at him for that reason. That, and she was still ashamed to have been caught kissing their leader. As the dragon toying with human bones grossed her out a bit, she turned her head in the opposite direction, and this time, she could only look at the mountains... Those mountains were the ones above Kassein's dwelling, but they still made her think about her clan and the people her father had watching her.

Would they have witnessed her kissing Kassein? She hadn't done it for any calculated reason, but it might not be a bad thing if they had indeed witnessed it. It would make them believe she was complying with their plan... when she was, in fact, doing everything she could to counter it. The only part she wouldn't lie about was getting closer to Kassein. She felt guilty on the account of Kassein having no idea he was part of an evil scheme, but Alezya's feelings were sincere. She craved his warmth and kindness far more than his protection. For the first time since she'd been repudiated by the man who'd once been her husband, she felt the desire to seduce and be desired by a man.

His argument with Tievin was lasting a while though, and he was getting more and more annoyed and silent while Tievin was rambling... He wasn't going to seriously get mad at him, right? Tievin didn't seem like a nice person, but he looked essential to the Dragon Clan. At least, that was the only reason she could see for such a scrawny man to be there despite standing out like a sore thumb amongst all those warriors.

She shyly glanced up at Kassein, and half a second later, he happened to be glancing down at her too. Their eyes met, and a faint smirk appeared on his lips, while Alezya blushed and looked away. No, he definitely wasn't really mad at Tievin... but she was getting tired of listening to that man's monologue too. Instead of fighting Kassein's unmovable arm around her, she turned around in his embrace to face Tievin and smiled at him, making him finally stop his interminable speech.

"*Tievin*," she smiled. "*Taam?*"

He frowned at her. Either he could tell she was deliberately changing whatever topic he was on or he was annoyed to be cut off, she couldn't tell. He stared at her for a few seconds, with an empty gaze that reminded her of a fish on land.

She knew he didn't like her much, and he wasn't trying to hide it. Still, Alezya smiled anyway, trying to ignore that deadpan and annoyed expression of his. Tievin was nothing compared to the other men here, at least she was confident she would not have to fear him of all people.

Then, he rolled his eyes as if she couldn't see it, or he didn't care if she did, and turned around, taking a large detour around Kein. She felt Kassein chuckle behind her, and he put his chin on her shoulder.

"*Hungry?*" he whispered.

She nodded, happy to understand that word.

"*Mada huri hadu kuha?*"

This time, she was the one to roll her eyes. How was he expecting her to understand all that? She only knew *kuha* which meant to eat... After a second of thinking about each word he'd uttered though, she could only think of a handful of possible meanings, the most likely one was that he wanted to know what she wanted to eat. Was that it?

"*Meat,*" she answered with one of her favorite words in his language.

He finally released his grip a bit to step up next to her and look at her with a faint, amused smile. Alezya realized she had guessed right, and felt even prouder. She was really looking forward to learning more from Lorey now... The mere idea that she and Kassein would one day be able to have a proper chat was making her excited. There was so much she wanted to tell him, and even more she wanted to ask him.

After staring at her for a second, he leaned in, and pressed his lips against her forehead, softly but slowly. Alezya blushed like a young innocent girl, unable to stop the blood rushing to her cheeks and the warmth spreading throughout her whole body. Kassein's arm around her waist was still holding her, and she wanted to lean against him even more, every bit of his warmth so attractive to her.

But she didn't, and instead, tried to control her emotions a bit. That kiss had changed everything between them... even Kassein's gaze seemed strangely more peaceful, as if some of his worries had vanished. While still holding her, he gently nudged her in the direction that Tievin had taken, and she wondered if they were headed to wherever the breakfast was served. She was hoping that Lorey and his sister would be there too because she was still unsure about finding herself in the middle of a group of men again, even if Kassein was there. He was holding her waist, and they were now walking side by side. She wished he'd put on his cloak so she could have partially hidden underneath it and been closer to him without it being too obvious.

Alezya felt a bit ashamed as her desires gradually came to mind. She found herself so foolish for wanting to be as close to Kassein as she could... and yet, she couldn't deny what she knew she craved. She was an adult woman with desires, and Kassein had made himself more than desirable, enough for her to desperately yearn for his touch. Was it against her better judgment? She had once desired a man, another man, and the result hadn't been pretty or enjoyable in the end... but she wanted to believe Kassein was different. He was kind, gentle, and understanding, some words she couldn't associate with the one she had once been married to. His warm hands certainly couldn't be compared to the way she had been brutally handled by her husband.

Kassein was almost the opposite, all too aware of his inhuman strength and trying hard to control it so as to not harm her, while her ex had been weaker and yet very determined to assert his dominance. Alezya was almost mad at herself for comparing the two, but she knew it was also in her best interest to be cautious, the self-preservation part of her mind crying for her to be cautious and not trust a man so quickly again...

She wanted to though. She really wanted to trust Kassein. He was younger than the man she had been married to, or he seemed to be, and so far, the two had acted quite differently. Moreover, Kassein had been in a position of strength all along, and yet, he hadn't used it to force her to do anything. On that, the two couldn't have been more different...

She took a glance at him as they kept walking, letting her body warm up against his skin. Something had definitely changed between them since that kiss... although it was subtle. If anything, it had ignited even more hope in Alezya's heart. She wanted to believe, desperately, that Kassein would turn out to be different. The expression of sheer disgust of Lumie's father when he'd seen her was still carved into her mind like a horrible nightmare after she had spent hours suffering to give birth to her... Alezya didn't know if she would be able to endure the pain of such an expression a second time, not if it was Kassein looking at her in disgust this time...

Was she foolish to trust him? To want to believe again? Was she unconsciously setting herself up for more disappointment, throwing all caution to the wind? She had spent so much time picking up the pieces of her broken heart, and she had once sworn never to trust a man again. Why was she giving in again so fast, and to a complete stranger? Had she gone mad?

Suddenly, she thought of something and stopped in her tracks, getting his attention.

"Alezya?"

"Kassein," she called, her throat a bit tighter.

She bent down and grabbed some fresh snow in her hands to show him.

"Snow," she said in her language. "Lumie."

He frowned for a second, a bit confused by her sudden change of vocabulary, but nodded after a second.

"*Altha*," he replied. "Lumie. *Altha*."

Alezya smiled and nodded. He didn't know it yet, but this was so much more than just a word to her...

Oblivious to her inner excitement, Kassein took the snow off her hands and rubbed them gently, visibly more worried about warming them up. One day, she hoped he would meet Lumie.

She was still afraid of how he would react to her child, but Alezya found herself desperately believing in a future where he'd accept her daughter as he had accepted her. Just like she didn't see a ruthless killer in him, she hoped Kassein would see beyond Lumie's unique appearance and not treat her like some freak. He would keep her warm just like he was so determined to warm up her hands just now...

The mere thought of that dream of hers had Alezya tearing up. She couldn't help it; the hope was so foolish, and yet, she was desperate to believe again. How would she live on without hope? The only thing that mattered was for Lumie to survive, but if she was allowed to wish for the best possible outcome, she wanted Kassein to be a part of it. She silently told her beating heart to shut up and stop those foolish thoughts, but it was too late; the thought had bloomed in her mind, and now, she wanted to hold on to it...

Kassein was still warming her hands, pulling her toward the breakfast area. Luckily, he didn't seem to notice her tears; the sun was blinding anyway, so perhaps he had seen them but not thought much of it, for he smiled when Alezya awkwardly wiped the tears from her face.

They found almost the same gathering for breakfast as the previous night and, to her surprise, Lorey was already there, sitting on the dark gray dragon. Kassein's sister wasn't anywhere to be seen, but she heard her name mentioned between them, probably Kassein inquiring after her. Lorey answered with a polite smile. She was already holding a bowl of food in her hands and greeted Alezya with a smile. It made her wonder if Kassein's sister and her would notice... or if Tievin would be the one to mention what he had seen between Kassein and her. Would that be an issue? If she noticed anything between them, Lorey was graceful enough not to let it show at all, instead just politely chatting with the two men.

While Alezya was trying and failing to identify some of their words, Kein announced its arrival by stomping its huge orange paws in the snow, happily reuniting with the other dragon. The other dragon was reluctant to move and play, despite the orange dragon's taunts. It took a word from Kassein, answered by an annoyed growl, for Kein to settle down. The orange dragon turned its head back to them, stopping its silver eyes on Alezya for a second, before it sat down in the snow, not without a bit of attitude and lots of snow swept around...

This time, again, it decided to lay next to the other dragon and try to steal its food, and a concert of growls ensued.

"Kiki," Lorey called, patting the dragon's back.

For some reason, Kiki seemed to obey Lorey because the dark gray dragon let out a hot, pissed whiff at Kein, and turned its head in the opposite direction to eat in peace. Kein growled, trying to get its attention, but soon enough, a few warriors brought the body of a bear, and the orange dragon didn't wait for them to run away before it began devouring it. Just like the previous day, both dragons didn't seem to mind one bit about the humans sitting on them.

Alezya was still utterly shocked to be able to actually sit on a dragon's back! Not only that, but Kein's body was so huge, even if she just sat on its orange paw, her feet were barely touching the ground. Moreover, she loved to be able to lean against Kassein's knee. She was impressed that he was still half-naked, and apparently completely fine despite the biting cold. Even she felt a bit warmer by sitting between his legs, although she couldn't tell if he emitted more heat than her inner turmoil did...

Soon enough, Dajan himself brought her a bowl of food filled with meat. She had almost forgotten about him, and from his sorry expression, while holding the bowl, she felt like he was the first one remorseful about what had happened earlier. She gave him a faint smile as if to say she didn't resent him one bit; she had witnessed him speaking up for her, and that was more than enough in her eyes. Dajan smiled back at her, but unfortunately for him, he wasn't the only one mindful of Alezya's reactions; a hand appeared on her shoulder, and as he gazed up, the poor man went a bit white before quickly scuttering away.

Alezya glanced up at Kassein just in time to see half a second of his glare. She gave his knee a little nudge and a reprobating look. A bit childish, wasn't he? He shrugged and focused again on his food, a bowl having been brought for him as well.

Just like the previous day, Tievin didn't sit on either of the dragons, but instead, was pacing in the snow. He was reading something out loud, or telling Kassein and Lorey about the contents of his papers. Alezya didn't care for another one of his long monologues, but she was curious about what those words were written on. What did the Dragon Clan use to write? She ate while trying to take peeks in his direction, but Tievin was staying away from the dragons, and thus away from their trio.

Finally, someone cut him off, and it was Kiera, who arrived from a different direction, stretching with a satisfied expression on her face and a light layer of sweat on her skin. Just like her brother, she didn't seem to mind the cold at all, for she was only wearing a provocatively light layer of clothes, her chest covered by a skin-tight piece of clothing, leather pants covering her legs, boots but no protective coverings. The siblings were wearing almost the same outfit, if not for Kiera's chest-covering piece. This gave Alezya a better sight of that woman's impressive muscles.

What did a woman eat and do to get this strong of a body? She knew no woman of her own clan would have approved, but Alezya felt differently about it. In fact, she was quite envious of Kiera's strength.

If she had been stronger, she wouldn't have felt such humiliation...

"Kiera," she said, grabbing everyone's attention.

Kiera, who was talking to Lorey just before, turned her eyes to her with a surprised expression, and a faint frown.

"*Kiera, sword,*" Alezya said, annoyed at her own lack of vocabulary once again.

The woman frowned and glanced down at her sides as if she'd expected some weapon to be there, but nothing was hanging at her belt. Then, Lorey said something, and Kiera briefly looked at her before turning to Alezya. Alezya felt silly. How to express what she wanted?

She put the bowl aside, hoping Kein wouldn't move and spill it, and took out the dagger she'd kept concealed on herself. Absolutely nobody seemed alarmed to see her holding a weapon, which was slightly vexing, but Alezya turned to Kassein, showing him the dagger.

"*Alezya, sword,*" she insisted, tapping her chest.

Then, she pointed at Kiera again.

Everyone seemed confused, except for Lorey, who smiled and spoke, gathering everyone's attention again. Tievin replied something quickly, sounding annoyed, but the other three ignored him, their eyes going back to Alezya. Kassein put his hand on her wrist holding the weapon, and nodded.

"*Alezya sword,*" he repeated.

Alezya wasn't sure he'd understood her at all, but he took the weapon out of her hands, placed it on her lap, and put her bowl of food back in her hands. Now Alezya was confused again. Was he telling her to eat first? She held her bowl, unsure what to do or try next.

Then, his sister let out an exclamation, and the two siblings seemed to be arguing while eating their breakfast. As a last resort, Alezya turned her eyes back to Lorey, but as usual, that woman only gave her amused smiles, either by her confusion or the two siblings' bickering, while she ate in silence.

Alezya gave up and resumed eating. She would always have time to try and ask again later... or perhaps Kassein had better things to do than train her. Perhaps his sister thought it was nonsense, or Tievin was against it. Perhaps they hadn't understood her at all, really. Now, she hoped there would be another of Lorey's lessons that day because she had a ton of words she wanted to be able to say and understand.

They ate, the others chatting while Alezya enjoyed the warm food. At the very least, she was getting better, and far healthier, healthier than she had been in a while, actually. Her legs were mostly healed and barely hurt anymore when she walked. She felt stronger when she stood, and the meat was definitely helping her regain strength quickly.

She was enjoying a clan chief's feast three times a day now, and she couldn't help but be all the more proud to be treated so well by the Dragon Clan. Her father would have been absolutely enraged if he'd known how well his eyesore of a daughter ate and slept here...

She thought about the herbs concealed in her bandages again. Would she be able to hide them from Kassein for several days? It would be harder to conceal them when her bandages came off.

Did he even know what they were for? If they had so many medicinal herbs, it might mean that all of the Dragon Clan was well educated about their use, not just their Healer... whom she hadn't met yet. The intricacies of their clan's dynamics were still very confusing to Alezya; she still had no idea what Tievin's position was, for example. The other warriors seemed to take him seriously, so she thought he had some important position, although she never saw him working... and he didn't seem fit for any physical job. He only spoke a lot. Maybe he was some sort of leader counselor, but Kassein didn't seem to like to hear him out very much. Maybe he had been appointed despite Kassein's wishes.

Her father had mentioned that the Dragon Clan leaders were a full family blessed with dragons. Did that mean Kassein and Keira had a bigger family? Kassein seemed very young for a clan chief, but she hadn't seen anyone older than him yet who would be fit as a clan chief... but then again, their territory was far bigger than what she could see now. The land she had seen from her mountain extended far beyond the horizon. Even if they shared with other clans, she had no doubt the Dragon Clan was one of the strongest ones out there.

Kassein then said something with an angry tone, and Alezya recognized her own name as well as the word "men." Not only that, but Lorey and Kiera stopped eating, their eyes going to her briefly before going back to him.

Oh, no, Alezya thought. Was he telling them about what had happened earlier? How much of it had he actually witnessed? She glanced to the side to see Tievin's reaction, but the man seemed completely unbothered by the situation, back to his deadpan expression. Wasn't he going to say something? He had been the one to scold Kassein earlier, hadn't he?

Quickly, there was a rapid-fire between Kassein and his sister, the latter's eyes going to the men behind them. What were those two talking about? Surely, Kassein wouldn't do more than earlier, would he? He had already killed a man and let Kein eat another, that should have been enough! What if he lost his warriors' respect because he overprotected a foreign woman? What if his people rioted against him or something?

She had heard of clan chiefs being murdered for less than this, and now, Alezya was genuinely worried she might have caused irreparable damage to Kassein's standing in his clan.

But whatever they were chatting about, his sister was in on it, for their tones were the same, and her eyes riveted on a group of men.

The two of them suddenly stood up like one, clearly done with their food, and Alezya's blood ran cold. What were they going to do? She grabbed Kassein's hand.

"Kassein?"

But he didn't say anything, and instead, just put a quick kiss on her hand before brushing it away and leaving with his sister.

Alezya's head was spinning. What was going on now?

His sister seemed amused, giving him an elbow bump, but his expression was cold and determined. Alezya turned to Lorey for an answer or help, but the young woman was just calmly wiping her mouth and stood up next, giving Alezya a smile. She walked up to her, and as Alezya was done eating as well, she put her bowl aside and took her hand to guide her. She and Lorey walked past Tievin, but instead of following the two of them, he reluctantly went after the pair of siblings with a grimace... What in the world was going on?

Alezya was trying to peek, but she and Lorey were heading in a different direction, and the young woman had locked arms with her, making it difficult to glance the opposite way. Lorey seemed hell-bent on taking Alezya away from whatever the siblings were up to.

"Lorey? Kassein, Kiera?"

Lorey only replied with an infuriating smile and kept walking. Why wasn't she at least trying to tell her?

But Lorey kept quiet, and when Alezya tried glancing back again, her view was blocked by the two dragons that had gotten up and were following them. This time, Kiki seemed a bit more inclined to humor Kein, and the two dragons were playing around in the snow, snapping at each other and chasing after one another's tails like snow kittens.

At least with those two and Lorey, Alezya didn't feel too bad being away from Kassein and felt relatively safe. Still, she couldn't help but worry. Was she going to be Kassein's downfall within his clan? What if he broke some of their principles for her and lost all respect? At the very least, it seemed neither Lorey nor Kiera were too worried about it... and his sister had gone with him. That had to mean it was alright, wasn't it?

Helpless with all her questions, Alezya followed Lorey, surprised to be taken to a different habitation. It was another one, as big as Kassein's, but upon entering, she realized this place was vastly different.

Instead of weapons and furs everywhere, this habitation had more colorful fabrics hanging all around, more clothing hung up, and different weapons. All the furniture looked new too, not damaged and a bit dusty like the ones in Kassein's room.

Most significantly, it had a large polished surface that reflected like still water, surrounded by an array of small items.. It made Alezya think of her cousin's home, and she immediately understood this was most likely where Kiera and Lorey resided. There was even some silver and gold ornaments in a box, just like the ones Lorey wore, and a few weapons on the side, which could have been the right size for Kiera. So those two women lived here together... Had this habitation been put up recently? They had managed to make it so cozy in such a short time...

It felt a bit strange for Alezya to be in a womanly space all of a sudden. She had grown up with a lot of older sisters and was expected to act a certain way with other women, but since Lumie's birth, she had been shunned by all... No, even before that, since she had been married, she had felt the lack of a safe space to return to. It was the rule of her clan that she belonged to her husband since her wedding, but with her sisters all married to different clans, she had no female circle to go to, to confide in. The Exkiu Clan was even stricter when it came to what they expected from women, and although she'd benefited from the respect due to her husband for a few months, she had still felt like a stranger in a foreign clan. Her months married to him had been amongst the loneliest of her life...

She couldn't help but glance around, feeling strange standing amongst colorful fabrics, beauty products, nice scents, and ornaments again. When her eyes stopped on Lorey, she realized the young woman had let her tour around with an amused eye without saying anything. Alezya felt a bit embarrassed to be caught acting like this. Was Lorey thinking she was strange, or some uneducated kind of woman? But Lorey just kept that enigmatic smile on, and pushed one of the colored cushions in front of the polished surface, gesturing for Alezya to sit there.

Alezya nodded and sat facing the reflective stone. Only then did she get a glimpse of her appearance... and she was a bit stunned.

She had changed. Perhaps it was the fresh air from her morning walk or being able to bask in the sun for the last couple of days, but she found her complexion better than it had been in a while. Her dark circles were gone too, and all her injuries had been healing faster than she'd thought, leaving neat or no scars behind.

She even thought she looked a bit younger, all of a sudden.

She hadn't given a damn about her appearance since Lumie's birth, but with a few baths, some combing of her hair, and being able to sleep deeply and safely, she had already changed so much... That, and the generous amounts of meat had refilled her cheeks a bit too. The taste of her breakfast still lingered on her lips, and she was getting dangerously used to having a full stomach.

As always, she couldn't deny the pang of guilt that overtook her when she thought of all the luxuries she was enjoying while away from Lumie and with no way to check how her baby was. She could only hope, once again, that her cousin was acting like a decent human being in taking care of her baby. She knew Suolk was a decent hunter, more than capable of providing for his family, so she knew they wouldn't run out of food just because they had one more mouth to feed.

Her father also didn't care enough about Lumie to check on her or anything like that, so hopefully, they would be unbothered by him as long as Alezya seemed to keep going with the plan.

Her fingers naturally went to the bandages on her forearms.

The herbs. She just had to take the herbs for a few more days, and then, her plan could work. She could go back by the next full moon and, hopefully, fool her father and the Healer long enough to get Lumie out of there, one way or another. It didn't matter how fast her relationship with Kassein progressed so long as she gave her clan the illusion she was acting as expected. All they would see was that she slept in his habitation and stayed close to him. If her plan worked, she would return after a couple of weeks... and without her period. She had never tested that combination of herbs for herself, but she knew the effects they were supposed to have.

She hoped it would be enough to fool the Healer, at least for a couple of weeks. All she needed was to get Lumie out of there; Alezya didn't care what happened to her after that... but she knew who she wanted to entrust her baby to.

"Alezya?"

Lorey called her attention gently, and sat behind her with a comb. She showed her the object in her hands.

"*Mushti.*"

"*Mushti,*" Alezya repeated with a nod.

Then, Lorey began gently combing her hair, and while she did so, both women sat facing each other through the reflection in the polished stone surface, going through all the words Alezya had learned the previous day, plus a few more as Lorey showed her objects from her dwelling to add to her vocabulary.

It was hard. Alezya was getting frustrated each time she forgot a word, and the pronunciation was also complicating everything. She felt like every time Lorey uttered a full sentence, she was thrown on the side of a mountain to hang on to a cliff with one hand... and trying to grab the words she knew to make some sense and pull herself out of her ignorance.

Lorey was showing incredible patience, sometimes repeating words four or five times until Alezya got the pronunciation right, and repeating the same words over and over as Alezya went back to dig out what she'd supposedly learned the previous day.

If her teacher was patient, Alezya wasn't. She wanted to learn, and fast, and she was getting frustrated at her own memory for being so lacking at times. But slowly, she was learning. It wasn't a matter of days, but she trusted herself enough to learn the vocabulary that mattered fast enough.

She wasn't interested in how to say a ring, a necklace, or a comb, but she wanted to know how to say a sword, a mountain, or running. She already knew how to say "baby" and their word for snow. She could translate Lumie's name in Kassein's language, and it meant a lot.

"Lorey," she called her friend, remembering something from earlier. "*Aqayir?*"

Tievin had called Kassein that, but it wasn't his name. Was that his title here? Was that their word for a clan chief?

"*Kassein Aqayir,*" Lorey nodded.

"*...Kiera Aqayir?*"

"*La. Kassein Aqayir.*"

So it was a title only he held.

"*Kassein ku judun Aqayir.*"

He was a warrior *Aqayir?* So that probably meant some sort of special warrior title... Alezya had learned their word for warrior, *judun,* just earlier. Or at least, it seemed to be the word for their warriors. *Aqayir* had to mean some sort of leader, still. She already knew he had the highest position here, but it was interesting to learn the exact word they used for it. It made her think of something.

"*I am Aqayir child,*" she said, using the words she knew. "*Me.*"

"*Alezya is Aqayir child?*"

Alezya nodded at her surprised expression.

"Lorey Aqayir child too?"

"No. Kassein and Kiera Aqayir children."

So it was as Alezya had expected... It was some sort of inherited title.

"Aqayir dragon man?" Alezya asked, glad she had learned the word for dragon early on.

"Yes. Kassein and Kiera father is man-dragon Aqayir."

"Father... and mother?"

"No. Kassein and Kiera mother no dragon."

So their mother was a normal person, without the dragon scales or a dragon? For some reason, that made Alezya a little happy.

So their clan chiefs weren't just picking a partner amongst people with a dragon, it was just something that ran in their family. It had been a worry of hers that, in their world, all clan chiefs had dragons and they partnered each other up, like how the clan chiefs married their daughters to other clans' heirs in the mountains...

"Alezya mother?" Lorey asked.

For a second, Alezya had been worried Lorey was asking if she was a mother, but retracing the conversation, she realized she wasn't asking about Lumie, but about Alezya's mother.

Alezya hesitated and then slowly shook her head. She wasn't sure about her mother's whereabouts.

She knew her mother's clan lived far away from her father's, but her mother had become a strange taboo in her family, and her father refused to talk about her. If he did, it was to say how she had "abandoned" her.

Her mother had been her father's third wife and the last after she'd given birth to Alezya. Something had happened, something that had made him forbid Alezya from mentioning her mom ever again or asking for her. She was young when her mother left, not even ten years old, and she hadn't been told why her mother had suddenly left. She didn't know why she had been left behind or what had caused her mom to leave without a word... All she could hope was that her mom had returned to her clan safely and was happy now. But even as she tried to believe that, the questions had never fully left her. Why hadn't she taken her? Had she wanted to?

Alezya forced her fingers to relax and shook her head again. There was no point in thinking about it now. Her mom had never seemed happy while with her father, and after learning the harsh realities of marriage herself, Alezya couldn't blame her. It felt foolish for her to even trust a man again, after what she had gone through... and yet, every time she let her thoughts drift toward Kassein, she couldn't help but find her heart heating up and her stomach doing little flips. Was it so easy to fall for someone? To lose all reason to her emotions? She didn't want to be emotional, not when she needed to stay clear-headed for Lumie's sake. But Alezya could already tell she was too far gone. Kassein had penetrated her defenses and ignited a hope she shouldn't have had.

Even if she did dare to believe... She had to be sure. She had to be certain he would not harm Lumie. He wasn't like her ex-husband; he didn't have to recognize the child as his own. All that mattered was that he treated her fairly. Even if she was made a prisoner to the Dragon Clan, it would make her better off than up in the mountain, where she was selected for some nonsense sacrifice... but Alezya had to lay the groundwork to ensure her daughter's survival. The Dragon Clan clearly wasn't safe; her bad experience this morning proved it.

It didn't matter though, so long as she had Kassein and his dragon's protection. If she could ensure, somehow, that Lumie would also be under their protection here, then all would be fine. It didn't matter what sacrifice she had to make, what she had to do. So long as Lumie would be safe, that was all she could ask for...

Chapter 10

His sword was getting rusty.

Kassein inspected it; he didn't mind making those men suffer after what they'd put Alezya through that morning, but he hated when his weapon wasn't as sharp as it should have been. Upon closer inspection of the blade, he could spot a few dents where his excessive strength had probably broken the metal. The blacksmith wasn't so bold as to voice it out, but it was clear they were upset about Kassein's brute force damaging their carefully crafted weapons at an increased, unnatural rate. If anything, he would rather blame the crafters. He couldn't remember his siblings' weapons nor his father's being damaged so easily. Did they craft lower-quality weapons here?

"I think we missed one."

He glanced back at his sister, standing a few steps away from him with her fists on her hips and a frown on her face.

"What?"

"I'm counting the bodies," she said. "I think we missed one... The count isn't right."

"Tievin?" he called with an angry tone.

"W-well, from what I've been able to tell," he stuttered behind his notepad, "I-I think Lady Kiera might be right. Although I do need to point out, it would be a lot easier to tell if I could count entire bodies instead of limbs..."

He had been avoiding looking at the bloodshed around the siblings, but for once, Kassein wasn't the only one responsible for it. Kiera had been the first one infuriated by those men's attitudes and had gotten overly excited to be given the chance to fight, or more like slaughter, some real people for the first time in a while. His sister was a proper savage when it came to fighting, causing as many injuries as she could on the enemies' bodies until some bled to their deaths. One could tell she was used to fighting many enemies at once; she liked to inflict a string of incapacitating injuries first and only go for the kill later. He wondered if the absence of her partner had helped in unleashing her violent nature; she probably didn't dare to be this cruel in Lorey's presence...

"Pieces of shit," she hissed, finishing off a man who was still moving with a clean slice of her blade. "Those fucking rapists should be executed on sight, not sent here... I'll never forgive Kassian for refusing to strengthen the law."

Kassein scoffed. On that, they agreed. But their brother was too worried about what his precious politician friends thought...

Kassein checked his appearance; this time, he'd been a bit more mindful of the bloodshed and not staining himself as much. The blood didn't get higher than his forearms, but that could be washed away. He was getting annoyed with having to clean himself every time before seeing Alezya again. He couldn't touch her with his bloodied hands...

Kiera was the one covered in blood, while he'd managed to remain mostly clean. Nothing a bit of snow wouldn't wash away.

"That was all of them?"

"I think so. Minus the one we missed..." said Kassein, glancing around.

He had been dying to murder those bastards since earlier, and only Alezya's presence had kept him from going on a rampage right away. He had carved their faces into his mind and rounded them up the minute she and Lorey were out of sight to give that scum what they deserved.

Even Tievin hadn't objected for once; he was never against less criminal mouths to feed around the camp.

"I'm not too worried about Lorey," Kiera said, cleaning her sword while she walked up to him. "She can defend herself, and Kiki's never far away. But your girl, you do need to teach her how to use that dagger. This kind of shit is bound to happen again now that the soldiers are aware of her. You have more criminals here than can be found in the Capital. You'd better start tightening the discipline if you don't want to have to kill a dozen of them every new moon."

Kassein silently agreed. It wasn't that he had been negligent until then; he just didn't care. He felt as exiled here as those criminals had been, and so long as they didn't cross the line, he didn't care what happened to the prisoners sent here, in the middle of nowhere, where they couldn't harm anyone anymore... until now. Now, Alezya was here, and Lorey too. That made two people who were far more vulnerable than regular soldiers and possible targets for the worst of that scum to prey on. He couldn't just act passively anymore, for there would be direct consequences to his lack of involvement. He turned to Tievin, who straightened like a stick.

"...Summon all the generals, brigade captains, and unit captains. I want every single leader from every corner of the camp at the training grounds."

"When—"

"Now."

Tievin went a bit pale, but Kassein didn't care.

He watched until the Grand Intendant helplessly turned around and scurried out of sight. Only then did Kassein start cleaning his sword with the fresh snow, while his sister stood before him.

"I'll teach her too," Kiera said.

"I thought you said I should do it."

"I have a feeling you'll get distracted during the lessons," she scoffed. "Moreover, she's clearly not a fighter. There is a big difference between training someone to kill and training someone to defend themself. I've already done it with Lorey. Plus, your girl's growing on me a bit."

Kassein couldn't help but raise his eyes from his sword to give her a threatening glare, but his sister replied with a click of her tongue.

"Nuh uh, not to me, little brother, unless you want me to discipline your ass... Keep your bloody dragon-sized jealousy in check, you know I'm not interested in her that way. I'm taken already, remember? I meant she's an interesting girl. Not a girl, really, she's a proper woman, and far from stupid too. She's not afraid of Kein anymore, but she keeps in mind he's a dragon, not a pet. She was careful enough to use your dragon as her bodyguard too... She's smart enough to learn our language quickly, from what Lorey said. She nicked your dagger too, which was a smart move for her own good. Something I respect."

He wouldn't mention it to his sister, but there was one more way Alezya was impressive.

She had snuck out of bed without him noticing... It was true he'd spent most of the night awake and unable to sleep, but for someone to move around him without waking him up was a first. He'd always been hyper-sensitive, and no one had ever been able to sneak past him unnoticed.

For Alezya to have been able to do so, even if he might have been slightly more relaxed in her presence, showed that she had an impressive stealth skill... which made him curious how she'd come to cultivate it.

"...But?" he said, sensing his sister's unvoiced protest.

"But, I'll remind you to think with your head, if you know what I mean. If you're anything like the men in our family, you will tend to be unreasonable when it comes to your... love interest. Be careful, Kassein. We do not know those people, and there are reasons we've been fighting them for centuries. She might be different, but she was raised there. We still know nothing of her. So curb your dragon, because I won't be enough to stop the bloody chaos if shit goes wrong..."

He knew it all too well; Kiera meant that both as a figure of speech and as a real warning. His dragon was problematic; it had been for a lot of years, and they all knew that if Kein went on a rampage, Kiki or Kiera couldn't possibly stop it... Kiki was a stealthy dragon, but in terms of brute strength, Kein was stronger by far. It could rival most of his siblings' dragons, even his older brothers'. Last time, Kassian's dragon, the silver dragon Kian, had barely managed to stop and subdue Kein...

If anything happened here, Kein's attempts to kill him would be nothing in comparison. He could handle his own dragon attacking him for he had his

Dragon Blood to protect him and abnormal strength, but normal people like Lorey, Tievin, or Alezya would be the first ones at risk...

He took a deep breath. He had to keep his emotions under control. He wouldn't let another "accident" happen.

"I know," he finally said.

Kiera let out a faint sigh, clearly trusting him for now. They both knew there was little that could be done anyway; until they could communicate more with Alezya and understand where she came from and why, things would be at a standstill there.

Kiera kept glancing around with a frown now that her weapons were clean and back in their sheaths. Some soldiers had already come to clean the area, but she didn't care for them. She was looking more broadly at the camp as if she was seeing this place for the first time.

"I can't believe you pushed the North Army this far... Isn't it a pain to go back to the closest village?"

"We're far enough that they can't cause incidents there," he retorted, "and we send people there now and then. The journey isn't that long."

"That's still, what, half a day with a good horse? And you don't have many horses... Why, by the way? You're not breeding them or what?"

"We were not breeding them fast enough," Kassein scoffed, giving her a meaningful glance.

Kiera's jaw dropped.

"Fucking Kein kept eating them, you mean?! Your dragon's a bloody nutcase!"

"Has been for a while," Kassein groaned. "Glad you finally noticed."

"I thought you had him under control by now! He... He's been following your girl around like a trained pup!"

Kassein let out a grunt.

He hadn't told his sister that Kein had only started acting docile since Alezya's arrival at the camp. Everyone in the camp knew, and that was partially why his men were utterly confused at the previously untamable dragon acting so tame around the foreign woman, but he hadn't realized Kiera didn't have that insight. Thus, although it was thoroughly humiliating to him, he told her the truth; that up until Alezya's appearance, he and Kein had been trying to murder each other almost daily.

His sister listened, baffled, looking more stunned with every sentence.

"And you're saying, when you tried to take her back up there..."

"We fought again," he admitted. "Right away. He almost killed me, until Alezya was... harmed again. In fact, he probably only let me live because he went to get her back."

"...Wow," his sister scoffed after a beat. "Your dragon really is crazy."

Kassein didn't have anything to answer to that. He slowly got back up after cleaning his hands and sword in the snow and put it in its sheath.

A part of him felt almost grateful to his dragon for making it so he might not be able to live without Alezya. Even if Kein was a mad dragon, Alezya being the only thing keeping his dragon from killing him wasn't the worst outcome... that is unless she tried to leave again. She hadn't attempted anything since, but every time Kassein saw Alezya's eyes linger on the mountains, that fear gnawed at his insides.

They had kissed, and she seemed to enjoy his touch, but how could he be sure whoever she'd left behind wouldn't tear her away from him again? He wasn't a fool. Kassein wasn't scared to admit his feelings for Alezya, but he was scared of what those feelings could provoke if unchecked.

It was all fine when she was near, when she was within his reach, but the second Alezya was out of sight, something inside unsettled again.

A dangerous part of him wanted to keep her here, bound to him, by any means. A more reasonable side, the side that his mother's kindness had raised, wanted to do anything he could to chase that sadness away from her eyes, forever, for good. But how? How would she have everything she could ask for down here when she'd left something up there?

"Kassein."

He turned his eyes back to his sister, who had her eyebrows raised.

"If keeping her here keeps Kein sane for now... then fine. Let's keep her here and teach her whatever she needs to be safe. At the pace she's going, she might even finally be able to properly speak our language soon, and then, we'll know what's going on with her people. Who knows, with a bit of luck, she might turn out to be the answer you've been looking for."

"The answer to what?"

"Kassian's order," Kiera sighed. "Pacifying the north?"

"Fuck Kassian's order," he grunted. "I don't care for the tribes, and I will kill anyone who has harmed her."

"Sure, sure... Nevermind, let's go. This has taken a while, and I reek. I need a bath... You know what, I'm going to go to the hot springs; I can't let Lorey see me like this. Let her know I'd love for her to join, yeah?"

Kassein watched his sister leave but remained behind for a moment, irritation gnawing at his gut as he took in the aftermath. That missing body still nagged at him, an itch he couldn't scratch, but there was nothing to be done about it now. With any luck, they had miscounted, or the bastard had been smart enough to run. Either way, he'd be keeping an eye out.

The events of the day would spread through the camp soon enough. No one would dare bother any of the women for a while, not after what they had witnessed. If they did, they would know exactly what awaited them. With that final thought, Kassein turned away from the bloodied scene and walked off, ignoring the nervous glances trailing after him.

This time, Lorey had taken Alezya into her tent, and as soon as he walked in, Kassein's eyes found her seated on a little cushion, her face already turned to him. She jumped to her feet as quickly as her injuries allowed and walked up to him. Every time he saw those black eyes looking up at him with a mix of relief and wonder shining out of them, it felt like something soothed him inside. Now that he knew he could touch her, hold her, Kassein's hands were helplessly drawn to Alezya's body, settling on her back even though he was dying to caress her entire body.

"Your Highness," Lorey greeted him politely, "may I ask where Kiera is?"

"Gone to bathe," Kassein replied without taking his eyes off Alezya. "She said you'd join her. The hot springs."

"I should do that, then. Feel free to use our tent with Alezya. We were practicing her vocabulary again; she's quite good!"

"See you later," Kassein said as a polite but direct way to dismiss her.

"Yes, Your Highness. Bye, Alezya."

"Bye," Alezya repeated, that faint blush rising to her cheeks like every time she spoke their language.

Lorey left, leaving the two of them together in a strange, hot-aired silence.

Kassein was still half-naked, and now, he felt all too aware of his bare skin, inches away from Alezya's face. She was looking up at him, but it felt too dangerous for her to be standing so close, alone in that space with him.

"Kassein," Alezya said, her voice sounding dangerously sweet. "Kassein Commander."

He raised an eyebrow.

"You've been hearing Tievin call me that all day, I guess," he said. "Did Lorey teach you new words?"

"Lorey, bye," she frowned.

"Yes, Lorey's gone," he said patiently, "but Lorey taught you new words. Man-dragon? Commander? Meat?"

Alezya's eyes opened a bit wider as she understood, and she gave him a firm nod before grabbing his arm with her hands and gently pulling him deeper inside the tent. Kassein followed suit as she sat in front of the large mirror and the space Lorey and perhaps his sister readied themselves.

Looking a bit proud, Alezya began pointing at random objects around her.

"Comb, necklace, pearls... Bracelet, lip balm... Candle..."

She pointed at many objects around the tent, immensely proud, although Kassein corrected her gently and patiently a couple of times.

They were seated on the plush carpets on the floor, but Alezya kept moving around and pointing at things while he remained still, his eyes riveted on her. She hadn't looked so animated often, but he was falling even deeper for that woman every time her eyes shone like this. The contrast with the heartbroken, terrified woman he'd picked up in the mountains made him all the more relieved that she finally seemed to find some peace here.

Every part of him felt the urge to protect her, shield her. Even now, they were sitting on the floor and not touching, but his entire body was turned toward her while his leg was raised like a shield between Alezya and the tent's entrance, his forearm resting on his knee. She felt safe with him, and that was enough.

She had seen him kill a man, and yet, she'd walked up to him, despite the fear in her eyes, to plant that kiss on his lips and convey everything he needed in that moment. She had no idea of what she'd unlocked with that simple kiss, but it had changed everything.

"Kassein," she called him.

He hadn't been paying attention for a while, and she'd picked up on it. She gave him a half-shy, half-annoyed pout and then pointed her finger at the mirror.

"Mirror," she said.

"Yes," he nodded.

Then, he gently grabbed her pointed finger, and pulled it toward him, keeping it raised to show her. He covered her small hand effortlessly with his own and smiled.

"Finger," he said.

"Finger?" she repeated.

He gently opened her hand and, one after the other, touched her fingers with the tip of his.

"Fingers," he said. "Five fingers."

She smiled and nodded; he remembered Lorey had mentioned she had taught Alezya the basic numbers the previous day. As their hands already touched, she grabbed his and touched Kassein's fingers, his hand far more coarse than hers.

"Kassein fingers," she said.

Then, she turned it around, his palm now facing the tent's ceiling, and pointed at it with a questioning look.

"Hand," he said. "My hand."

"Hand," she nodded.

It would have been quite an innocent discussion if it wasn't for the heated, tense silence around them, or the way Alezya faintly licked her lips, leaned closer to him, and put a lock of her ink-black hair behind her ear. How she kept going back to his eyes shyly, while his green irises didn't leave her.

In a surprisingly bold move, she kneeled even closer and, with her pale hand, followed the curve of his forearm, up to his bicep.

"Arm," he taught her.

"Arm," she repeated.

Then, both her hands covered his shoulders, his muscles tightening under her touch while his hand had quietly moved to hold her lower back.

"Shoulders."

"...Shoulders."

Her hands moved again, to his neck, and similarly, he moved his palm up to her nape.

"Neck."

"Neck," she repeated with a sharp breath.

Their eyes were now locked on each other's, with a mix of excitement, shyness, and unspoken questions floating between them. But there was also a playful twinkle in her eyes, as she moved her hands again, down this time, to his chest.

"Chest," he said.

"Chest," she nodded.

His hand was still on her nape, her slender neck effortlessly covered by his palm, his fingers intertwined with her silky smooth hair. Did that woman not fear the hand that had killed men right in front of her eyes earlier? How could she trust him so? She ought to understand he was the most dangerous man of all by now. If she feared men, what did she think of him? Did she trust him so much, despite everything?

The mere thought sent a dull ache through Kassein's chest.

Alezya, a foreign, fragile woman, trusted him far more than his family did. More than his brother did. Sure, Kassian had reasons to exile him, but... would his brother trusting him more have changed anything? Their older brother had turned into a sour, bitter man after his return from the east alone, ever since he'd taken the throne. They'd fought more often without their kind older sister to mediate. If anything, Kassein resented Kassian more than anybody else, and his brother was the reason he wouldn't go back to the Capital.

Maybe Kiera was right when she'd said he was sulking in the north, but Kassian had been the one to exile him there in the first place...

"Kassein."

Alezya's patient voice brought him back to her. Every time he was near her, the anger subsided to let in more questions he didn't want to ponder about. He let out a faint sigh and, aware that he probably looked like he was lost in his thoughts and neglecting her, he took his hand off her nape to bring hers to his lips, gently kissing her fingers. Her injuries were mostly healed, so she wasn't sporting as many bandages these days, but she carried the smell of medicinal herbs all the time. It reminded him of his mother, and how she also treated him kindly no matter what.

Did Alezya have a child too? Was that how she was capable of such patience, trust, and kindness with him, although she should have been afraid of Kassein and his dragon?

She gave him a smile, and moved her hand to his cheek, grazing his stubble.

"Cheek," he said, aware he hadn't spoken in a while.

"Cheek?" she repeated, her fingertips playing with the beard he hadn't bothered shaving in a while.

"No," he chuckled, assuming she was confusing the two, and pressing her palm against his cheek to correct her. "Cheek."

He touched her cheek too for good measure, and then, brought her fingertips back to his beard.

"Beard," he said.

"Beard," she repeated, struggling with the pronunciation of that word for some reason.

"Yeah, beard. ...Do you like it?"

He remembered his sisters and mother being quite critical of his facial hair and that of his brothers and father on the smallest occasion, although he hadn't been around the siblings' banter in a while.

Now he was curious about Alezya's thoughts.

"Beard?" he asked her again. "Yes? No?"

He let out a faint, rare smile as she squinted her eyes, visibly assessing his jawline. She had seen him with and without as he usually shaved every now and then. After a while, she shook her head and put her fingers on his cheeks.

"No," she said.

"No beard?"

"No beard," she nodded.

"Alright."

Under Alezya's confused stare, he let go of her hands and got up, going around his sister's tent to find water, a bowl to put it in, and some soap. Then, he came back to put it all on the small table in front of the mirror, sitting back in his spot next to Alezya. Quickly, under her amused eyes, he used the soap and water to wet and lather his beard, and then, he gave her a smile.

"Dagger," he said.

Alezya took out the one she'd taken from his tent and handed it to him, but instead, Kassein waited expectantly, until she raised her eyebrows, and shook her head.

"Kassein, no. Not Alezya. Kassein."

"No. I want you to do it. Alezya."

She frowned and shook her head again, but he grabbed her wrist and gently, using the mirror for reference, had her scrape the first inches of beard off his jaw. She gasped but stopped trying to pull her hand away as she realized she might hurt him. Kassein chuckled and kept going until he let go of her hand to let her do it. Very slowly, and after giving him an almost apologetic glance, Alezya slowly moved the dagger to keep shaving him, Kassein moving his chin up to give her better access.

He wondered if she realized that, even if she did cut him, he would only have a thin cut and his scales would appear, but there was something endearing about watching her so nervous to shave him. She kept her eyes focused on his jawline, while he kept his eyes on her and all the micro-expressions of her face.

Even from so close up, she was beautiful. Her skin was incredibly smooth, and of a color he'd never seen in the Empire; not dark like his father's nor as pale as his mother's, but instead, a warm but pale color that reminded him of the sand on the beaches of the Empire where he and his siblings sometimes went to play as children. Her eyes were uniquely shaped too, thin and long like a feline. When she was so close to him like this, he could see how they were not simply black, but instead, a rich, dark, and earthy brown color.

"Kassein."

She had caught him staring, and now, was giving him a disapproving look that meant he was distracting her.

"Green," she said.

"My eyes."

"My eyes?"

"No. Eyes. Kassein eyes, green eyes. Alezya, black eyes."

"Eyes."

"Yes."

She pointed two fingers at his eyes and made a motion down.

"Kassein eyes, no."

"You want me to close them. Close," he repeated, closing his eyes before opening them again to show her. "Open eyes. Closed eyes."

"Yes. Kassein close green eyes."

He smiled and obeyed.

A part of him felt ridiculously excited about being able to understand her, although their exchange was childish. With his eyes closed, he was even more aware of her fingers going around his jawline, touching his chin, and the blade that slowly but steadily grazed his skin.

The truth was, it didn't matter if she just went ahead and cut him, but he enjoyed how slow the process was and how careful she was not to hurt him. The only thing was that he couldn't talk, so for a while, they both fell silent while she shaved him, the only sounds being the blade and the water when she rinsed it.

After a while, when he was pretty sure she'd shaved it all, he heard her rinse the dagger, get up, and then quickly come back to wipe his chin and cheeks. For some reason, he kept his eyes closed like an obedient boy, until he felt her lips on his cheek. It had been brief, but his eyes jerked open to find her blushing.

"Kassein cheeks no beard," she said.

"No beard," he repeated. "...You like it? Alezya like it?"

She frowned, having not learned the words yet. He grabbed her hands and sprawled them on his cheeks.

"No beard," he said. "Do you like it?"

"Like?"

"Yes. Like," he said, trying to think how to bring the meaning across to her. "Alezya likes meat, Kein likes meat. Kein likes Alezya. Kiera likes... daggers. Kiera likes Lorey. Lorey likes Kiera."

He could see that cute frown on her face, but was she confused or trying to work it out?

"Alezya likes no beard," he said, making her touch his freshly shaved cheeks again.

"Alezya likes no beard," she nodded. "Likes Kassein no beard. Alezya... likes Kassein."

His heart stopped for a split second before it exploded in his chest. He swallowed something hard in his throat, and then, brought her fingers to his lips.

"You like me?"

"Yes," she whispered. "Kassein... I like."

He smiled against her palm and kissed it softly.

"Kassein likes Alezya too," he whispered.

She blushed.

The truth was, he liked her a lot more than his dragon liked meat, but they had yet to get to that part. Although, from the way her cheeks had turned an adorable shade of crimson, she knew it too.

After a beat, he put his hands around her waist, bringing Alezya a lot closer until she straddled his spread-out leg, on her knees and with her face above his, her hair falling around them like a curtain of black silk. Their breathing deepened, and while one of her hands steadied herself on his shoulder, the other moved from his cheek to his lips, her index finger tracing his bottom lip.

"Lips," he whispered.

"Lips?"

He gently took her hand and pressed a kiss against her fingers.

"Mouth," he said, before placing her fingertip on his lip again. "Lip."

Alezya drew in a breath, and slowly, came down to press a kiss on his lips.

"Mouth?" she whispered.

"No. Kiss," he smiled. "Alezya kiss Kassein."

Gently, he intertwined his fingers with her hair and pulled her down for another kiss, which he made last just a second longer before he reluctantly parted from her.

"Kassein kiss Alezya."

"...More," she whispered.

"More?" he chuckled, pleasantly surprised.

"More kiss," she muttered shyly. "Alezya likes Kassein kiss..."

His stomach roared with a burning fire as she descended on his lips again for a deeper, more passionate kiss.

He had not suspected such boldness from her, but he loved it.

He opened his mouth, touching her tongue for the first time, intensifying their kiss while his hands roamed her body. One hand he kept on her nape, laced with her hair and keeping her locked against his lips, but the other one explored her body, caressing her curves, her lower back, her thigh, and after a beat, swooping under her skirt to touch her skin. He felt her gasp faintly against his lips, and a chill shivered under his hand, but she didn't break the kiss, instead making it even more passionate with an awakened hunger to it. Kassein felt his body react to her too, and to the rising heat between them. He was all too aware of how she was straddling him, how dangerous their position was despite the layers of clothing between his crotch and the apex of her thighs.

And yet, when Alezya moaned against his lips, when she lowered her body ever so slightly, the fire roared louder, and her eyes flew open with lust filling them. He let out a groan and pressed her even more against his lips, his fingers reaching her underwear, only to find it damp. Alezya let out another moan as he caressed her through the fabric, and her body arched slightly, breaking their kiss. But his lips scoured south instead, leaving peppered kisses on her jawline, on her neck, while she leaned her head back and let out delectable sounds, lust-filled music to his ears.

His fingers pressed against the thin line of her lips, and another shiver agitated her.

"Kassein," she gasped.

His erection was painfully pressing against his pants, but he just cared about touching her, about the delightful reactions she gave to his fingers, how he found new colors in her as she whimpered above him.

Her skin felt as hot as his now, and she had closed her eyes, but he wouldn't have it.

"Alezya."

She replied with a soft moan, and he pulled her back to his lips, although her kisses were half destabilized by what he was doing to her, and his fingers gently pushed the fabric aside to touch her directly. How wet she was made him mad with desire. He had never felt such an overwhelming, desperate need to bring a woman pleasure. Every sound and movement Alezya made pushed him closer to the edge. Her voice, her heavy, hot breathing, the slight movement of her hips on his fingers, and how her lips lost focus against his as he intensified his movements, pressing a finger in and rubbing his thumb against the button above. She cried out again, and her febrile hand caught his wrist, but he didn't stop.

He knew she was close, and he wanted to take her there. Alezya was both tense and losing her strength, her hips sinking lower as he pressed deeper in, making her cry against his lips again. How he kept her against his lips while he unleashed chaos on her had her moaning helplessly and breathing harder any chance she could, her grip tightening on his shoulder. Something inside Kassein bellowed with the brass of a dragon, a part of him that found pleasure in seeing her so helplessly subjected to his touch, his lips, his grip on her nape. He waited until she could barely breathe anymore to release her lips, letting her moan out loud against his ear while his mouth kissed her neck instead.

"Kassein," she let out in a strangled cry. "Kassein..."

He watched, fascinated, as she lost herself to pleasure, her hips now shamelessly riding his fingers, her chest heaving loudly, her head held back and her eyes closed. She kept gasping out loud and letting out moans like frenzied music until her body abruptly tensed up, trembled in his arms, and her voice got cut off in her throat. He kept moving his fingers, letting her ride that orgasm to its full extent until her breathing eased, and then he slowly pulled out, watching her sink onto his lap. Alezya's head came to rest on his shoulder, her breathing tickling his neck, while he quickly cleaned off his fingers and pulled her clothing back where it belonged.

Then, as Alezya seemed to come back to her senses, he kissed her temple before she faced him. The look of utter disbelief, surprise, and confusion in her eyes wasn't what he'd expected, and for a second, Kassein feared he'd gone too far. Had he misread her at some point? Or crossed some boundary?

Then, he noticed her flushed cheeks, not as a remnant of her orgasm, but as genuine shyness. Something else came to mind, but it couldn't be. She had been with other men before. Surely she'd experienced pleasure before... right? But seeing her mildly panicked expression, and where her hand went to next, a wave of anger surged.

"No," he grunted, grabbing her wrist.

He'd stopped her fingers inches away from the bulge in his pants, and Alezya's eyes went to his with something that looked like panic, confusion, and... almost fear.

Kassein's anger was reaching a dangerous level, and sure enough, somewhere in the distance, Kein growled, echoing his fury.

Alezya's head turned toward the sound, albeit from outside the tent, before she turned back to Kassein with a faint panic.

"Kassein," she mumbled.

"No," he said, a bit more firmly. "You don't need to do that."

He was furious, but not at her.

He was furious at the bastards who had dared to treat her like this, to make her believe she owed him anything in return. Kassein was only too aware that Alezya had no way of understanding his anger, so he gently lifted her hand to his lips, and kissed it softly, lovingly.

He wanted to reassure her, to comfort her that she deserved this, all of what she wanted, and he'd never ask her for anything in return. She was a foreign woman in a strange land, with few ways to convey her words, and he was most scared she'd ever feel pressured to do anything to ensure her survival. He couldn't have that. He was the one who wanted to obey and provide her with anything he could.

He'd never felt such an agonizing need to care for somebody else before, but there he was, desperate to convey his devotion, to make her feel safe most of all. Since they didn't have the words yet for that, he gently caressed her, kissed her hands, her lips, and her cheeks until she seemed to calm down, the worry fading from her expression. Alezya was left staring at him with something soft in her eyes, and returned his kiss a bit more confidently than before, caressing his cleanly shaven cheek.

Another growl of his dragon came from outside, but this time, his sister's dragon growled in response.

"Lorey and Kiera are back," he told Alezya, who gave him a nod.

They slowly stood up, both in a strange daze, but he took the dirty bowl of water and her hand and guided her outside, just in time to find Lorey and Kiera hopping off her dragon as he tossed the bowl's contents in the snow. His sister's eyes went from Alezya to Kassein, squinting.

"...What were you two doing in my tent?"

"Teaching her words."

"Words? ...You sure you only taught her *words*?" Kiera scoffed.

Next to Kassein, Alezya's cheeks were flushed again as if she'd understood something in Kiera's mocking tone, and she looked away, standing almost a step behind him as if to hide herself from the two other women's eyes. Kassein gave his sister a smug smile.

"You—!" Kiera exclaimed.

"How were the hot springs?" he retorted.

"It's time for lunch." Lorey pulled her partner away before she could argue. "Let's go and eat. Nice shave, Your Highness."

Kassein let out a rare twitch from the corner of his lips, and his sister made a gross sound in response. He let Kiera and her partner walk away first before he turned to Alezya, putting another reassuring kiss against her temple. She was still blushing, but she gave him a little shy smile and followed him to the fire pit, her body sticking close to his as she wrapped her free hand around his arm to hold on to. They had all barely sat on the dragons again for lunch when Tievin arrived, out of breath and almost tripping on his long coat, looking at them dumbfounded.

"Commander?!" he exclaimed.

"...What is it, Tievin?" Lorey asked as Kiera and Kassein stared back at him in moody silence.

"Y-you asked me to round up all the generals and captains earlier? At the training grounds? ...Didn't you?!"

Kassein had forgotten entirely. He exchanged a look with his sister, who'd likely just remembered as well, and gave him an amused snort.

"See what I meant about thinking with your head?" she mocked him.

"You were there too," he grunted before wolfing down the remainder of his lunch and standing up.

"I'm not the one who gave the order." She shrugged. "Who cares if I forgot? You're the one who got sidetracked in my tent."

He answered with a scowl and put a kiss on Alezya's forehead before he stepped away.

"Keep Alezya with you," he told them.

"We will, Your Highness," Lorey assured him.

Then, he followed Tievin, who looked stunned that Kassein had forgotten all about his order. However, he obviously wouldn't dare voice it out loud, instead walking ahead with his notepad clutched to his chest and a stiffer walk than usual.

"It took me a while to gather everyone," he finally spat with a slightly haughty tone. "As you know, the camp is large, exceedingly large, Commander. And not all of your generals and captains are in predictable spaces, but still. They have been waiting for almost an hour now, sir."

"Not too long, then," Kassein retorted.

And under Tievin's flabbergasted expression, he walked inside the tent that covered the training grounds.

As expected, it had been cleaned since his and his sister's earlier bloodshed, but now, all three generals and the captains were gathered with nervous expressions, likely heightened by the unusual wait. As soon as he appeared, an ominous silence fell, and every single man in attendance straightened. Without Alezya, Kassein's expression had returned to casting that dark, threatening aura around him that had them all tense. Even as he sat down on one of the benches while they were all standing, they all felt like he was towering above them like a menacing storm cloud.

"What does it take for you to keep them in line?" he hissed in a low voice.

There was no need to mention who nor what he was referring to; the sight of him and his dragon having killed a couple men earlier in the most gruesome manner had probably traumatized the few onlookers enough for the gory details to have already toured the camp. An uneasy feeling crossed the ranks until one of the generals spoke up.

"It is difficult to keep some of the most troublesome units in check... Commander in Chief," Kauser argued. "Those men do not take orders well, and no matter how much we discipline them—"

"Why do you think my brother sends them here, Kauser?" Kassein hissed, his eyes suddenly filled with venom.

The generals exchanged awkward glances.

"Well, they are convicted..."

"This is their only alternative to the death penalty," Kassein growled. "There is no such thing as second chances. The only reason the Emperor sends them here is that he cannot be bothered to butcher the vermin himself. This place is the Empire's slaughterhouse, General. And I am the executioner. If anybody dares tell me again that this camp is at full capacity after the shit I witnessed this morning, I will slice their throat myself. You have gone fucking soft. All of you. Let me be perfectly clear. If someone steps a toe over the line, I want their foot severed. If someone talks back, I want their tongue nailed. If anybody so much as looks askance, I want their eyes gouged out. And if anyone disrespects any woman again, I want their fucking head severed and their limbs fed to my dragon. Have I made myself clear?"

He had drawled that last word with his ice-cold glare touring the crowd. This wasn't just a threat to the criminals sent there; it was for every single man in the camp. Suddenly, nobody dared to look him in the eye, and every single brigade captain was fascinated by the sand at their feet. Even the generals had gone a shade paler than usual.

"...Understood, Commander."

After a heavy, understood silence, Kassein left his generals to lead the rest of the meeting, and for once, he didn't oppose their requests for more expeditions to the mountains. If he wanted to keep his army in line, he needed to keep it busy, and after what had recently transpired, investigating the tribes some more seemed necessary.

Moreover, he had his own motives for agreeing to this, and the main motive was Alezya. Whatever she had left behind, or whoever she missed, it was clear her tribe was not letting her come back for it, and it wasn't something he was going to help her with if he didn't start to question what was going on up there.

"Are you sure you're alright with this, sir?" Tievin asked, scurrying behind him as they walked back.

"What?"

"W-well, that woman's tribe might—"

"Alezya," Kassein hissed, glaring back. "Her name is Alezya."

Tievin only paused for a second, taken aback by his words, before he cleared his throat.

"Of course, Commander. I-I meant to say, aren't you worried about... potentially getting into a fight with Lady Alezya's tribe?"

"For whatever reason, they kicked her out and left her for dead on that mountain twice," Kassein growled.

Getting into a fight with her tribe was certainly something he'd actually very much like to do. If given the chance, he was ready to kill every single man who had dared to lay their hands on her with his own bare hands.

Kassein was well aware that a part of him also wanted to personally fight the man she had left behind, if there was one, but he would never admit that out loud.

"I understand, sir," Tievin said.

Just as he finished his sentence, Kassein brutally stopped, and Tievin almost crashed into him, instead staggering and managing to catch himself before he did and holding on to his notepad.

"Commander?"

"...Where are they?" Kassein growled, glancing around the camp.

They had been walking for a while, but he hadn't caught sight of the three women. His sister wasn't the type to confine herself inside a tent while the sun was out, so he had figured they'd be somewhere outside in the camp, but those women were nowhere to be seen.

"You," Tievin called one of the men walking by. "Have you seen the Princess? Or one of the ladies?"

"No, Grand Intendant."

"...What about the Commander in Chief's dragon?" Tievin asked after a beat.

"Oh! He flew southeast a little while ago, sir. Along with the Princess' dragon."

Kassein had turned on his heels before the man was done talking.

He knew where Kiera had taken them already. His sister hadn't visited the north in a very long time, but like his older siblings, she had grown up in that region before his parents had moved to live in the Imperial Palace once Kassian had reached the age to be trained as the heir to the Imperial Throne. Aside from Cessilia and Darsan, who had both moved to the Eastern Kingdom ten years ago, Kassian and their other siblings had lived in the Capital until Kiera had taken off to explore the uncharted lands, and Kassein had been banished to the north.

He had pushed his army farther north to the foot of the mountains precisely to get away from the north of his childhood.

It was easy for him to find his way back to the land he had grown up in, but without his dragon, and since the same dragon had made it nearly impossible for the camp to keep horses around, it took him and Tievin a long while and a long, long walk to get to where the women had flown to.

The journey was nothing short of unsettling for Kassein.

He didn't want to go there, and he was also certain Kiera had gone there with Lorey and Alezya on purpose like one would lure an animal to a trap. He'd entrusted Alezya to Lorey, but he had forgotten how cunning his sister could be. Of his three sisters, Kiera was unpredictable at best and incredibly shrewd at worst. She would have been an amazing military leader if she was capable of staying in one place...

Still, Kassein marched stubbornly, each angry step taking him closer to his sister's trap, just because he wanted to be reunited with Alezya. He could almost hear Tievin's disbelief behind him as his Intendant did his best to keep up.

The dark stone appeared in the distance, and Kassein's chest tightened every time he saw the silhouette of that place. When he was a child, that mountain of dark stone had been his home. As an adult, it stood like a monument to his failures. Luckily for him, the Onyx Castle was far too small of a place to host his dragon; thus, he spotted Kein's orange scales somewhere farther away in one of the long stretches of deserted land that once held his mother's gardens, right outside the castle's walls. This place was almost as bad as standing inside the castle itself, but he pushed away the dread, focusing on Alezya instead.

"Ah, there he is!"

He replied to his sister's satisfied expression with a furious glare.

She was standing, playing around with a dagger she kept throwing in her hand, one fist on her hip, and watching him walk into the frozen gardens with a smug smile. Opposite to her was Alezya, also holding a dagger, the one she'd taken from his tent. It looked as if the two of them had been sparring, and Kassein's eyes immediately scoured Alezya's body for any injuries, but she looked fine, if a bit tired.

A few steps away, Lorey was sitting on one of the benches his father had built for his mother. He walked up to Alezya, immediately dropping his hands to her shoulders and letting relief fill his lungs again. As much as he trusted his sister with her safety, nothing could beat holding her in his arms for himself to be certain.

"Sorry we made you come all this way, Your Highness," Lorey said. "Kiera insisted—"

"I have no doubt she did," Kassein growled.

His tone was filled with so much anger that Lorey was taken aback, although his glare was on his sister, not her. Lorey had no way of knowing he would have never come to this place if not forced, but she immediately understood something was off, her eyes going to Kiera with a suspicious, questioning frown. His sister was not apologetic at all.

Instead, she kept throwing that dagger, watching her younger brother with her malicious eyes.

"I wondered if you'd come," she said. "Turns out you like this girl a lot more than I thought."

"Well, I hope you're satisfied," he hissed.

Kassein could feel Alezya's worried eyes on him, and he curled an arm around her waist. Although she couldn't understand their argument, she could certainly understand he was angry, and Kassein didn't want her to think it had anything to do with her, so he kept his angry eyes on his sister.

"Not really," Kiera tilted his head. "I was expecting you to be... I don't know. Angrier."

"Sorry to disappoint," he grunted.

Then, he turned around and gently pulled Alezya with him toward the garden's exit.

"When are you going to grow up, Kassein?"

He stopped in his tracks, glaring back at his sister. This time, Kiera had lost her smile, and instead, she stared at him with an annoyed expression.

"It's been years," she said. "Fifteen years since your dragon went mad, and you refused to set foot in the Onyx Castle again. I don't know what happened to you that time, but you-"

"What happened is none of your fucking business," he hissed.

"Your dragon went mad," Kiera retorted. "We had never had a dragon attack one of us before, not the way Kein tried to kill you. If Dran and Krai hadn't stopped him, you would be dead."

"I know."

"And you don't want to address it? To face the truth?"

"None of your damn business."

"My little brother's business is my business," she retorted. "...And what if Kein attacks Alezya someday?"

The mere thought sent a horrible shiver down Kassein's back.

Even more surprising though, was how Kein suddenly let out a furious, loud growl that made them all jump. Alezya stepped deeper into Kassein's embrace, but her scared eyes were now on his dragon while Kassein's had gone to hers. The fear in her eyes was something he never wanted to witness again.

"...My thoughts exactly," Kiera said after a minute. "You might not care about your dragon trying to murder you every chance he gets, but this isn't about you. Whatever happened fifteen years ago, it's about time you face it and find a way to tame your mad dragon. Or there might be another incident again, and this time, your precious tribe girl might be the one they find dead."

Kein growled some more in fury, but it had no one to direct its anger at, so the orange dragon kept unleashing furious growls at the sky, acting restless as if it was bound by some chains or caged. It was exactly how Kassein felt inside.

He felt suffocated, trapped between the agony of the mere thought of something happening to Alezya and overwhelmed by a wave of guilt he had ignored for so long.

He was vaguely aware of his sister and Lorey walking away to return to the camp, but he stood frozen, his feet stuck to the ground and his thoughts so chaotic he couldn't settle on one. He refused to think of that night. It still hurt too much, and there was nothing he could do to get rid of that guilt. And yet, Kiera had planted a horrible vision in his head, the image of Alezya's cold and motionless body, crushed under the stones of a collapsed building...

"...Kassein."

Alezya's gentle, cold hands on his cheeks snapped him back to reality. Her beautiful dark eyes found his, and there was so much gentleness in them that the chaotic noise in his head settled down.

"Kassein, alright?" she asked, showing off new words she'd probably just learned that day. "Hurt?"

"No," he managed to utter, answering both her questions.

He covered her hands with his, keeping them on his cheeks while he took a deep breath. He could feel how worried she was about him, and he forced himself to calm down a bit.

She was there. She was there, with him, safe and sound, and Kein wouldn't hurt her. His dragon had no reason to attack her... but the man they had killed also wasn't meant to die. That innocent man was at the wrong place at the wrong time, and his only crime was standing between Kassein and his mad dragon.

Kassein closed his eyes, trying to chase the image away, but it was carved inside his eyelids. Before Alezya, it was the first thing he thought of in the morning and the last thing that came to mind before he slept.

Another victim, another chokehold of guilt. He reopened his eyes, looking at her. She had no idea of the monster he was, and because she had no idea, she could look at him like this.

"...Come with me," he whispered.

He took her hand and pulled her as he turned to the castle and took the very step he'd refused to take for so long.

Since Kiera had already lured him into the garden, he was already knee-deep in the painful nostalgia of happier days before everything had gone wrong. The garden he and his siblings had run and played in so many times, the once luscious garden filled with his mother's plants and the smells of herbal medicine. The familiar darkness of the castle most of them had been born and raised in...

The gardens had an entrance at the back, and it was easy to find the heavy door that led them inside. Kassein hadn't opened or walked through that door in a very long time, and yet, everything was strangely just the same fifteen years later. It only felt... smaller. The Onyx Castle had always seemed like a mountain to his younger eyes, but now, Kassein was a grown man, and he was realizing how small this place was compared to the Imperial Palace. There weren't as many rooms, and the kitchen and the staff's rooms were even in a separate building.

It was unnecessarily tall, with each floor spanning higher than necessary, its structure strange with rooms scattered, spiral staircases, and uneven ceilings of carved black stone and onyx his ancestors had covered this place in.

The most unusual thing was the smell... According to the legends his parents had told them growing up, this place used to be a volcano, and the stone had been darkened by the ashes. Kassein had no idea how much was true, but he had never known the Onyx Castle not to smell like cold ashes. He didn't know if this place truly was a volcano because, from the outside, the Onyx Castle stood like a giant shard pointing at the sky rather than a mountain, and there was no record of it ever being a volcano. Just a misshapen oddity erect in the midst of the most desolate lands of the Empire, and yet, for years, this had been his home.

"...Kassein?"

He glanced down at Alezya.

They were standing on what served as the ground floor of the Onyx Castle, a round room with a high ceiling of onyx stones, two thin and tall windows on each side, and stairs going up. It seemed like she had merely called his name because she was slightly confused about the place because her eyes were scouring every inch of black stone with a mix of wonder, shock, and bafflement. She was still flanking him, and he changed their positions, offering his arm for her to hold on to as he guided her to the stairs.

"This was my home," he said, talking as if she could understand every word, just to fill the silence. "The Onyx Castle."

He made a large gesture around them before turning to her to make sure she had understood this.

"Onyx Castle," he said.

"...Onyx Castle," she repeated, although she visibly wasn't sure.

He gave her a nod before taking her up the stairs. They passed a couple of corridors, but he knew which room he wanted to take her to.

He ignored the room that had once been his parents', as the doors were shut anyway, and continued to another room nearby.

Their mother had always wanted to keep her children close, although the unruly architecture only allowed for so many children to be in the neighboring rooms. Thus, as more siblings were born, the older ones moved to other rooms, which they often shared until they all moved to the Imperial Palace. Being the second to last child, Kassein had only ever been in this room, the one closest to his parents. He pushed the door open, and sure enough, everything was as he remembered, with a thin layer of dust everywhere. There was a crib on one side, the crib they'd all been in, and a small bed on the opposite side.

"Baby," Alezya muttered, walking to the crib on her own with a look of surprise on her face.

Kassein stood at the doorstep while she inspected the wooden frame, her hand touching the cold little mattress. He wasn't sure what he'd expected to feel upon entering this room, but right now, he felt... nothing. A faint wave of nostalgia, perhaps, but that was it. This room felt like a memory, something that stood with the past, empty and cold.

He glanced over the room before he forced himself to take a step inside. Alezya's eyes turned to him, full of questions.

"This was my baby brother's," he said. "Sepheus."

He pointed at the baby bed. He couldn't explain they had all been in that crib once, but that was enough explanation for now. He then pointed at the small child's bed.

"This one is mine. Kassein's."

Alezya frowned and turned to the small bed.

"Kassein?"

"Yes. My bed. Baby Kassein's bed."

To his surprise, she smiled softly and walked to the bed, sitting on it. Alezya wasn't a particularly small woman, but the fact that she spread her arms to check that she could touch each end of the bed with her fingertips made it look charmingly smaller.

She glanced back at him, clearly amused that he had once been small enough to fit in this bed. He walked over and sat next to her, and with the two of them sitting side by side, they covered most of the bed.

He pointed at two large baskets in the opposite corners of the room, on either side of the door.

"This was Kein's bed."

"Kein's bed?" Alezya repeated, surprised once again by the size of it. "Dragon Kein bed?"

"Baby dragon Kein's bed."

Alezya looked absolutely shocked. Kein was now gigantic, but back when Kassein slept in that bedroom, his dragon hadn't been bigger than a large dog. She pointed at the other basket.

"Sepheus dragon. Seus bed."

"Sepheus?" she repeated.

He pointed at the crib again.

"Baby Sepheus bed. Like Kiera is my sister, Sepheus is my brother."

"...Three children?" Alezya frowned, using the few words she knew.

Kassein snorted, his first hint at a smile since he'd entered this place.

"Eight children."

Alezya gave him a suspicious glance, so he held his fingers for her to confirm. Her jaw dropped, and he chuckled, amused.

"Come."

It felt much easier to show Alezya around than if he had been alone. With him holding her hand more than she held his, he took her to each bedroom, teaching her the names of his siblings and their dragons. Their bedrooms still retained some of the personality of their last occupants; Darsan's bedroom was a chaotic mess, with a ripped rug, the remains of furniture he had accidentally broken and fixed multiple times over, and his dragon's very chewed-on basket.

He had been the only one allowed his own room because no one could endure his snores or the constant chaos that surrounded him and Dran's antics.

Kassian had shared his room with his nine-years-younger brother Shenan for a while, and it was the tidiest of all, with books perfectly lined up, many quills on the desk, and stacks of paper. Even their beds were made as if they would return the next day.

Next was the girls' room. Cessilia, Sadara, and Kiera had shared the biggest room of the Onyx Castle, with their beds spread unevenly but in a gentle harmony. Cessilia had the bed by the window with a desk next to it, Sadara's was in the middle of a wall with a trunk full of fabrics at its foot and some embroidery work lying on her bedside table, while Kiera's was in a corner, an unapologetic mess with a half-charted map of the continent lying above it. Their room was also full of plants the sisters had cared for in turns over the years, and surprisingly, some of them were still growing along the walls or in their hanging pots.

Alezya seemed to like this room the most, for she toured it curiously, inspecting the plants, Sadara's piles of fabrics, and Cessilia's desk until she stopped in front of the map above Kiera's bed.

Kassein's eyes had stopped on his oldest sister's bed. Cessilia's. The vines that surrounded the window were the same vines that led back down to the garden on the other side.

"...Kassein?"

Alezya seemed worried about his suddenly dark expression. She glanced at the window, and walked up to him, gently grabbing his clenched fists in her hands.

"My older sister, Cessilia," he muttered after a while.

Alezya turned her eyes to Cessilia's bed, having been introduced to the name seconds ago. Kassein swallowed the knot in his throat and kept talking.

"One night... she left her room to find her lover."

He unfroze his body from the floor he felt stuck on and slowly moved up to the window, his hand touching the vines that had grown since then.

"She used these vines to climb down to the garden," he whispered. "Dad had chased him out earlier that evening, banishing him... and he had forbidden us all from going after him. Cessilia didn't listen. She loved... She loved him. So she climbed down to leave her room while Sadara and Kiera were asleep. I wasn't asleep. Sepheus was still a baby, crying often, so I often stayed awake a little while after my mom had taken him to their room. I heard Cessilia climb down. I went out of my room and into the garden, and I saw her about to leave with her dragon."

The words were pouring out of him like an endless stream after finally breaking the dam that had held them back all these years. Alezya didn't interrupt him, her eyes instead focused on his tortured, pained expression. Kassein's fist was still shut tight, his eyes full of hurt and anger riveted on the vines and that window.

"...She asked me not to say anything. I could have. I should have. I had... I had never disobeyed our parents before. Never. But Cessilia was my older sister, and she had been so upset over that guy leaving... I thought she could bring him back and be happy again."

He was there all over again; that boy, under the rain in their garden, torn between making his older sister happy and disobeying his father. That day, he had made a choice, and he had regretted that choice every hour for the last fifteen years.

"She didn't reach him. Instead, she was found by..." his voice cracked, broken in his throat. "...She got hurt."

He could never forget the sight of his sister's body as they carried her back inside. Lifeless, covered in blood, unrecognizable. Never had his sister looked so fragile. Those monsters had captured her dragon and tortured her. They had cut her throat, nearly killing her before his father and older brothers had managed to save her just in time. But if they had been just minutes later...

Every time, the mere thought of having nearly caused the death of his older sister sucked the air out of his lungs. Worse, he had witnessed for himself how broken she had been for the following years. They hadn't heard her voice for a long time, and when she'd finally been capable of uttering sounds again, there was no stringing a full sentence together without stumbling on her words. And it was all his fault.

"Kassein."

Alezya's gentle voice pulled him back to the present. She caressed his cheek, and it was then that he realized he'd let a tear slip when she brushed it off his cheekbone with her thumb. She looked concerned, seeking answers in his sad, green eyes. He let out a long sigh and, once again, kept her cool palm against his cheek for comfort.

"It was my fault, Alezya," he whispered, glad to confess to someone who had no idea. "I'm a monster. I almost got my older sister killed, and because I couldn't face that guilt, I actually caused someone's death... Someone died because of me. Because I hate myself. Because my dragon wants to kill me as much as I—"

He didn't finish that sentence.

He knew what was wrong with him. How could he not? Dragons weren't mad; they were a reflection of their owners' emotions, a weapon when they got angry and a protector when they loved. But Kassein's weapon had been turned toward one man and one man alone for the last fifteen years. Himself.

Until Alezya. Until a woman had walked into his life and ignited his need to protect, making this one thing far more important than anything else. He leaned his forehead against hers and calmed his breathing.

"I need you," he confessed. "You have no idea how much I need you."

He heard her let out a sigh, and then, as if she'd suddenly decided on it, she grabbed his arm and pulled him out of the bedroom. Kassein didn't resist; even though she wouldn't have been able to make him move an inch if he didn't want to, he was completely fine being dragged down the stairs and back to the ground floor.

Alezya pulled him through the only exit she knew, back into the garden, but she didn't stop there. She kept pulling his arm beyond the garden and back on the main path where Kein was waiting for them, lying in the snow with a sulky expression.

Then, she turned around to him and put her index finger between his eyebrows.

"Alezya?" he asked her, confused.

She kept rubbing her finger there, and after a moment, he realized she was going at his frown as if she could smooth it away. That finally managed to make him relax a bit.

"There," he said, mindful of his expression now. "I'm not frowning anymore."

Still, she didn't seem satisfied and moved her hand to his cheek, getting on her toes to put a light kiss on his lips. That finally made him smile, and Kassein wrapped his arms around her, pulling her in.

"I'm going to need a bit more of that," he whispered before kissing her.

He wrapped his large hand around her neck and heard a faint moan slip out against his lips, making him intensify their kiss. Her mouth opened for his tongue, and he took everything she was willing to give him, hungry for any taste of her, every breath, every sound. Kassein kissed her fiercely as if they could chase his demons with the fire of that one kiss, as if he could bury his memories and lie on top of them with Alezya by his side.

They were alone in the middle of the quiet, snow-covered Shadelands, and for a moment, it felt as if they were alone in the world. She was smaller, but he was the one holding on to her for dear life.

Kassein kept kissing her lips, caressing the hair on her nape, and pulling her waist closer, never quite satiated no matter what he did. He wanted more, and the lust was becoming unbearable; he could barely contain that hunger coming from below that clawed at his insides and made every inch of his skin burn and tighten with desire.

Kein's heavy growl burst that bubble and split them apart. Kassein forced himself to take a step back, although his hands settled on Aleyza's waist, still too stubborn to let go.

"Let's go back," he said, pressing his lips against her forehead. "...It's getting late."

It had taken him an absurdly long time to walk from the camp to the Onyx Castle, as the sun had already begun to set, but at least they had Kein to fly back on since Lorey and Kiera had gone back with Kiki.

Gently, Kassein pulled Alezya along toward his dragon, but as they approached Kein's back, she froze, staring at it with confused eyes.

"Hop on," he said, suddenly lifting her off the ground.

She let out a yelp, clearly unprepared to get on the dragon's back, and held on to its neck. It only hit Kassein then that this was her first time properly riding his dragon while conscious.

For some reason, seeing her so confused and scared made him chuckle, and while she sat sideways in front of him, he wrapped an arm around her waist. Truthfully, it had been a while since anyone had mounted Kein, including himself. His dragon had been a raging beast that wouldn't listen to anyone for the last decade or so, but right now, it was as docile as a kitten, glancing back at Alezya with its curious eyes as big as silver plates.

"Get moving," Kassein growled.

His dragon retorted with a snort, and if he weren't holding on to Alezya, Kassein would have bet that his stubborn dragon wouldn't have thought twice about throwing him off. Still, Kein let out a big snuff into the cold air around them and, after a lazy stretch, stood, flapped its wings, and took off without warning.

Alezya's scream got stuck in her throat, and instead, she clutched Kassein's neck even more tightly, hiding her face in his shoulder, her nails even grazing his skin. For some reason, he enjoyed that but shut his lips tight to keep himself from letting out a smile. He waited until they were high up in the air, and gently patted her shoulder.

"Alezya, your eyes. Open your eyes."

It took her a second and a few nervous blinks before she opened her eyes. But she soon saw what he had meant to show her, and she opened them wide, stunned by the breathtaking sight of the sunset. They were flying high and in the best seat in all of the Empire to watch the gorgeous gradient of orange to blue coloring the skies and the clouds around. Alezya's lips parted in awe, and while she watched the sunset over the horizon, he watched her. The golden hour was lighting up her features in the most beautiful shades, showing off the unsuspected highlights of gold in her hair and the warmth of her skin.

The flight only lasted a few minutes, but for both of them, it had granted them the memory of the most beautiful sight they'd ever seen. When Kein landed, Kassein got off while carrying Alezya, both quiet and still in a bit of a daze. A bit unhappy about the woman getting off its back, Kein growled and pushed her hand with its snout until she gave a pat on its warm, orange scales.

"*Kiitso, Kein,*" she whispered to the dragon.

Kassein tilted his head, helplessly curious and even jealous.

"...Kitso?" he repeated.

"*Kiitso,*" Alezya corrected him.

"What does that mean?" Kassein asked, taking her hand.

But Alezya smiled, and just put a quick kiss on his raspy cheek.

"*Kiitso,*" she repeated.

Kassein frowned and glanced at his dragon as if it had any clue, but Kein was already sniffing eagerly toward the large fire pit, smelling the meat of dinner. Alezya suddenly turned her head too with an expectant expression.

"Meat," she said.

Kassein smiled.

"Yeah, I'm hungry too. Let's go eat."

They joined the rest of their party with Kein on their heels, and quickly, the men were smart enough to bring a large offering of meat to the dragon before it chose its dinner raw. Meanwhile, Lorey and Kiera eyed the two of them without saying a word as they sat on the orange dragon like before. Tievin was nowhere in sight, for once, but it wasn't a rare occurrence when it was already late and the evening was colder than usual. Kassein also moved to be closer to Alezya and shield her from the cold with his cape.

"Didn't stay for the night?" Kiera taunted her brother.

"Shut up," he growled. "You've done enough for the day."

She wasn't about to ignore his injunction, but Lorey elbowed her with a warning glance of her own, and she dropped it. Instead, they focused on their dinner, and Lorey took over the conversation, teaching Alezya some more words.

"...She's decent."

Kassein lifted his eyes from his food to glare at his sister.

"That girl," Kiera said. "I taught her some moves for self-defense with the dagger while we waited for you to turn up earlier. It turns out she has some pretty good reflexes."

"You think she learned before?"

"I think she's sharp and had to grow some reflexes," Kiera shrugged, glancing at Alezya. "But no, I don't think she'd ever held a weapon before. The good news is she should pick up enough to be able to defend herself soon. The language too. She's learning fast."

Their eyes went to Alezya and Lorey, as both women were chatting over the fire, visibly bouncing words back and forth for Alezya to remember through repetition. Kassein had noticed too. He hadn't been there for most of her lessons, but it was becoming clear that Alezya was starting to understand them and make herself understood, surprising him more often than not.

The truth was, Kassein knew he could have asked her questions about the life she had left. She knew the word for man and the word for child. He just hadn't gathered the courage to ask yet.

They finished dinner, split up from his sister and Lorey, and walked together back to his tent, Kein close on their heels.

The weather had gotten colder, and they were in a hurry to get back to their shelter, but the silence felt heavier than before. Kassein had wrapped an arm around her shoulder, mostly to shield her from the cold winds, but he was all too aware of her body against his naked torso. She was wrapped in a coat, but she might as well have been naked, for his skin was burning everywhere they touched.

When they reached his tent, Kassein steeled his resolve, remembering Alezya's earlier reactions. They had certainly reached an unexpected turn in their relationship, a point of no return. There was something burning between them, and it would only grow hotter when they were alone together in such a confined space.

As soon as the tent's entrance was closed behind them, the silence was deafening, with the only sounds coming from the wind blowing outside and his dragon's heavy puffs. The little candle he lit in the corner of the room was the only light source, casting a warm, orange glow over them, and when Kassein turned around, he was struck by the sight of Alezya, sitting on his bed, her big black eyes lifted to him.

He turned back around and took off his cloak. He wanted her. Of course, he did. He was a man with a warm body and desires, and he was alone with the most beautiful, fierce, intriguing, and fascinating woman he had ever met. His entire body was pulling him toward her, wanting to lay on the bed and finish what he'd started earlier.

But his head was elsewhere. His head was replaying what had actually happened earlier, how she had reacted, and how he hated her thinking she owed him anything. He heard her take off her coat and her boots, and as she undressed, he forced himself to take a deep breath before he turned around and joined her on the bed.

Chapter 11

Alezya was confused.

She lay in bed, in Kassein's arms, utterly perplexed about what had happened. It had been a very long day, and a lot had happened; not all of which she had understood.

Lorey and Kiera had taken her to a very strange mountain, the darkest mountain she'd ever seen, and that place had turned out to be Kassein's home. His childhood home, but for some reason, he didn't seem happy to be there at all. He had taken her around, showed her the rooms where he and his siblings had grown up, and then, one of his sister's beds had made him talk a lot with that pained expression of his.

Alezya hadn't understood it all, but beyond that, she had hated to see how deeply hurt he seemed to be. Kassein wasn't a man who smiled often, but there was something that had seemed far more painful than usual in his green eyes when he'd talked.

She wished she could have understood everything so she could have helped him more. She wasn't learning fast enough, although Lorey was doing her best to teach her. When they spoke to her with intention, she could decipher their meaning, but she was lost as soon as they began to discuss something a bit more complex. Like when Kassein had argued with his sister... He had seemed angry at her, and she couldn't understand why. Maybe because Kiera had taken her to that place?

But Kassein didn't have to show up; the three of them would have returned by the evening either way...

She let out a faint sigh and felt Kassein's arm tighten around her. His strong, warm torso sent a new heat wave down her spine.

Alezya frowned. He was breathing slowly in her neck, but she was wide awake and feeling slightly annoyed, if not upset, at him. Why had he gone straight to sleep? How could he go to sleep after what had happened between them earlier? She was so sure something more would happen that night that now, she just felt disappointed. It was torture and humiliating too.

The things he had done in Lorey's space earlier... Her entire body heated up at the mere memory of it. She had never experienced such a thing. A man pleasing her solely to please her. Her previous husband had always taken. Roughly, painfully, regardless of her will. She had always thought lying with a man was her duty as a woman.

When she had been with him, she had no one to talk to about it, and when she'd been sent back to her clan in disgrace, there was no one the pariah she'd become could have confided in. But she had heard her sisters and cousins recount different experiences. She had been too young at the time to understand, and when she had been old enough to, she couldn't associate the tales of pleasure they had told with the violence she'd experienced.

For years, she had wondered if something was wrong with her, why she couldn't experience the things they talked about... and, in one afternoon, a mere moment, Kassein had blown her mind in more ways than one.

She felt the heat rise again in her chest as her thoughts drifted back to the memory of his fingers and the ways he'd touched her, made her cry and writhe. Her husband had never touched her like that. He had never cared about her at all, and yet, as it turned out, it could be a two-way thing... and Kassein had caught her off guard some more by pleasuring her without expecting anything in return.

She was still stunned, and every day, this man baffled her more and more. She couldn't tell if he was a strange man, or if this whole world of his was the strange one. She had been harassed by some of his warriors before, but on the other hand, some of them, like Dajan, showed her respect a warrior would have never owed a woman.

Kassein, who was the mightiest warrior of all, commanding every space he stood in, had the highest status and should have the most rights over her, a mere woman, and a prisoner at that. But by now, it had become abundantly clear that she was no prisoner, and he obeyed no rule she knew. He was kind, protective, and considerate at all times. He never forced her to do anything, while her ex-husband wouldn't have thought twice about it. He gave her comfort over his own, fed her, healed her, cared for her in ways she never thought someone would ever again.

Every single time, it felt like Kassein was wrecking her world and proving all her expectations wrong.

Alezya let out a faint sigh and carefully rolled around to face his chest. He was a strong man, and she loved how his skin was always warm. There was no pretending anymore; she knew she was falling fast and hard. How could she not? A man showing her kindness when she was at her most vulnerable was bound to break all the defenses she'd built around her heart.

She laid her cheek on his arm, and sure enough, she felt his arm tighten around her again. She was still a bit bitter about him not touching her, but maybe she was missing something. She hadn't seen him all afternoon, so maybe he was tired. Not that she'd ever think a man like Kassein could get very tired...

Moreover, did she want him that badly? He had given her pleasure, but the more traditional way for a man to be with a woman was bound to be painful, so why was she expecting it? Why did she even want it?

It had nothing to do with her father's horrible plan; she didn't want to get pregnant and risk her father using that baby, and either way, she was sleeping in Kassein's home every night. Her father's spies couldn't tell what was actually happening inside.

If her plan worked, she would fool them regardless, hopefully long enough to get Lumie out of their clutches. She didn't need to sleep with him, but she wanted to.

Perhaps she was curious. Curious to see what it felt like to be with a man who actually cared for her. Perhaps she wanted to experience that thing her sisters and cousins had talked about, the senseless thing about sex between a man and a woman feeling good... because Kassein had already made her experience a glimpse of that. The first orgasm of her life... and she would never be able to forget how good that was.

Worse, she was dying to feel that sensation again, like an addiction threatening to take root in her body. The mere nearness of him, of those hands, was enough to make her blush and heat up. Alezya couldn't fall asleep, although she'd had quite a busy day with all that training with his sister. Instead, she found herself dreaming of a life she would have never thought possible, down here, with the Dragon Clan, with him, and with Lumie.

Her baby girl... Would he accept her? Alezya wanted to think yes, but she was terrified it might be her own delusions and that perhaps Kassein's attitude would change if he came to find out she had a child, an unusual child, with a different man.

She could tell he already had his suspicions. Every single time the word baby came from either of their mouths, something tensed ever so subtly. When she had seen that beautiful crib earlier... she hadn't been able to stop herself from imagining Lumie in it.

Would Kassein watch over her baby like he watched over Alezya?

She fell asleep with her doubts taking root in her heart, right next to the hope that had dared to blossom already.

The next morning, she woke up to the sounds of wind battering the sides of the habitation.

She could tell precisely where Kein had decided to lie because only one portion of the thick leather panels surrounding them wasn't shaking, the wind most likely blocked by the dragon's humongous body.

Alezya turned her head; they had moved in their sleep, and while she was now on her back, Kassein's arm was under the pillow under her head, his other arm around her waist, and his breathing was tickling her bare shoulder, his face buried against her neck. She smiled and turned to face him again.

She'd shaved him the previous day, but spiky little hairs were already sprouting back on his chin. Alezya bit her lower lip and brought her fingers up to caress the tip of the little spikes on his chin, right below those thick lips of his... Kassein's hand suddenly captured her fingers, taking her by surprise, and he smiled with his eyes still closed.

While Alezya blushed, he pulled her fingertips to his lips instead, pressing a kiss against them before weaving their fingers together and drawing her hand against his chest.

"Kassein," she whispered.

He answered with a deep rumble of his voice, clearly unwilling to wake up just yet. She smiled. He acted surprisingly childish at times...

So, she decided to act playful too, and lifted her body to put a kiss on his lips. This finally made him open his eyes, a dreamy green staring back at her.

She loved his eyes. They looked like the green of a pine tree in the spring: deep, dark, and vivid irises with hints of gold in them. His sister's eyes were a lighter green, and she wondered if all their siblings had green eyes. Her people all had brown or black eyes, and Lumie had been the first child she'd ever seen with such pale eyes.

Would he mind her baby's strange appearance? Was there anyone like her in their clan?

Kassein kept her thoughts from spiraling any further by pressing another kiss on her forehead, on her nose, and then on her lips. A tender, slow kiss that ignited something in her again. She could tell he only intended to give her a deep morning kiss, but the woman in her had been awoken by his attentiveness yesterday, and now, she craved more at every chance she got.

Much to her disappointment, however, Kassein ended their kiss and sat up, leaving the bed first. Alezya sat up too, staring at his back with a bit of a sullen look.

She could feel he had decided to leave the bed on purpose before it escalated into something else, and she wasn't happy about it. She watched him put water on the tiny fire at one end of the habitation, open the flap a bit to air it out some more despite the raging snowstorm outside, and everything he did, he looked like he was trying to avoid looking in her direction.

"Kassein," she called him, putting some anger in her voice.

This time, he froze and slowly turned to her. Now he had a naughty smile on as if her upset expression amused him, but Alezya wasn't amused at all. Instead, she was on her knees on the bed, the blanket wrapped around her chest, staring at him with a disappointed expression.

She had gone to bed wearing a very thin piece of clothing that covered her from her chest to mid-thigh, which was perfect when sleeping under thick covers and next to a body as warm as Kassein's.

Still, there were nothing but two thin straps holding it on her shoulders, and Alezya knew enough about men to know many would have given in to temptation while spending all night next to her wearing this.

"*Water?*" he asked in his language.

"*Kassein,*" she insisted, frustrated that she hadn't yet had the words to ask him a more direct question.

He sighed and brought her a cup of warm water. She still didn't understand how they could drink just warm water, but she drank it anyway because without him by her side, it was getting cold fast.

As he was near her though, she grabbed his thick wrist and pulled him back to the bed with her. Kassein let out another sigh but obeyed. Letting her hold on to his wrist, he leaned and put another kiss on her forehead.

"*Kassein likes me,*" Alezya said.

"*Yes.*"

"*I like Kassein.*"

He smiled. She moved her hand toward his pants, but he grabbed her wrist with his free hand and shook his head.

"*No,*" he said.

"*Why?*"

"*Because Kassein likes Alezya.*"

She frowned.

That didn't make sense. Was she missing something about their customs that prevented her from touching him? Was it because they weren't married, perhaps? She hadn't thought about it before, but maybe the Dragon Clan also refused two people to lay together if they weren't married...

Alezya found herself stunned at how disappointed she was. Did she want him that badly? Although she knew it hurt? Or was she curious about how Kassein was with a woman...?

"*Teach me,*" he suddenly said.

"*Teach?*"

"*You. Alezya's words.*"

Her language. He wanted to learn more of her language.

She had been reluctant to teach them, but now she was desperate to understand him, and for him to understand her. She needed them to be able to communicate if she wanted him to help with her plan. She wasn't ready to tell him about Lumie yet. She had suffered through too much from the last man she trusted and all the horrible things she had heard everyone she once trusted say about her child. Her trust had been shattered, perhaps beyond repair, and believing in a complete stranger wasn't easy.

The only thing about Kassein was that he kept exceeding her expectations, and he held none of the beliefs she had grown up with. None of the rules she knew applied to him, and she hoped that would be the same when he eventually met Lumie... because she had decided he was her baby's best way out.

She still held some hope in her mother's birth clan, but realistically, she hadn't seen her mother in a long time, had no idea how far they were, and they were the obvious choice; her father probably would look for her there first. He had sent Alezya like a prize, but he would never have expected a warrior of the Dragon Clan to be willing to accept Lumie.

Her father was a man who didn't have an ounce of Kassein's kindness and would never believe that a man so powerful would accept a woman another had rejected and a baby that wasn't his.

Alezya was ready to take that bet.

"I teach Kassein, Kassein teach me," she said.

He nodded and sat with his legs crossed, facing her.

Unlike Alezya, he clearly didn't need any blanket to cover his body, but he grabbed another of the fur blankets and wrapped it around her. She felt ridiculously bundled like this, but perhaps it was for the best if they were going to behave while within inches of each other...

So, despite all of her expectations, they spent the next few hours of the morning chatting, teaching each other the same words again and again.

Alezya had already learned quite a bit from Lorey, and while learning some more with Kassein this morning and teaching him her own language in return, she began to realize that the reason she could learn quickly was also that the Dragon Clan's language was somewhat easier in unexpected ways.

They didn't have different words to differentiate a female subject from a male one. Alezya referred to herself with the female version of "I" and used a different version of "you" if she spoke to a man or a woman in her language, but the Dragon Clan's didn't bother with that; it made no difference if a man or woman was speaking to a man or woman, the sentence was the same. It was the same thing when speaking about people who weren't there; they had the same words for she and her and he and him, although they used names more often.

When she tried to ask if Kein was female or male, Kassein snorted and shook his head.

"Dragon. Not male or female. Only dragon."

"Kiki too?"

"Kiki dragon too."

They used names more often when referring to people, and Alezya realized they hadn't been speaking to her by using their names over and over to make it easier for her to understand who they were talking about, but simply because it was their natural way of speaking.

The way they built their sentences also had the subject of the sentence at the beginning, while hers had it at the end. She could tell Kassein was struggling to keep up with the differences when using her language too.

He could remember the vocabulary, but building the sentences was a nightmare for him. He kept misgendering them and instead, reverted to using their names quickly because he was getting frustrated and confused.

It was a lot easier and funnier for Alezya than it was for him, yet Kassein was incredibly stubborn and doing his best either way. She could tell he was desperate to understand her, but they found more common ground using his language.

"*That word you used before*," he said.

"*What word?*"

"Ki-... Kisoo."

Alezya chuckled.

"Kiitso," she exaggerated the pronunciation.

"Kisto," he nodded.

"*No. Kii-tso.*"

At least they both struggled equally with pronunciation. His language used a lot more throat, while hers was about putting the accent in the right place and using her tongue more.

"Kiitso. *What does that mean?*"

"*Thank you,*" she said, glad she had learned his way of saying it from Lorey.

"*Oh.* Kiitso."

She smiled.

At least now, they could converse in complete sentences, and she could make herself understood for the most essential things. She still lacked a lot of vocabulary whenever the subject drifted into anything different and more complex, but she was relieved to have established some solid foundations for learning.

"*I'm hungry,*" she admitted after a while, as they had both skipped breakfast and spent all morning chatting on his bed.

"*Do you want meat?*"

"*There is more meat?*"

Kassein smiled and quickly left the shelter, wholly unbothered by the snowstorm. She grimaced as he ventured into the cold, wrapping the blankets tighter around her.

She was curious to know if anyone else from their clan was out there despite the horrid weather.

"You *taniyen* are built differently," she told Kein through the fabric, using their word for dragon.

Kein answered with a faint growl that sounded almost like a snort.

Alezya smiled. To think she had been absolutely terrified of the orange dragon only a week ago... Now, she found its presence almost reassuring, just like when those men had harassed her, and she knew they wouldn't dare do a thing while she was with the dragon.

She got up and, while waiting for Kassein, cleaned herself a bit, changed into one of the outfits that she could find, a large shirt that was probably Kassein's but was so big for her it covered her down to her knees and elbows, and gave a large opening that showed her shoulders a bit.

When Kassein came back, she was back on the bed, combing her hair, her lap covered by one of the fur blankets.

"*Meat soup,*" he said, raising two bowls.

He might not mind the cold, but his hair and shoulders were funnily covered by half an inch of snow, and all his clothes looked wet.

He put the bowls he had covered with a piece of fabric on the bedside table and went to wipe up the now-melted snow off his shoulders, putting Alezya through some silent torture as she had to watch, from afar, all of his glorious and wet torso.

She had never gone throat-dry because of some male body before, but apparently, Kassein had that power over her. So much so that she had to reach out for some more hot water and avert her gaze, desperate to contain the blushing that threatened to expose her.

She had it mildly under control when he came to sit on the bed, his abs flexing as he sat down and handed her the bowl. It was still hot by some miracle, and she wondered how he'd managed that. Still, Alezya didn't wait and immediately went for her favorite chunky bits.

They ate in silence, but it didn't feel awkward at all. Instead, it was almost comfortable, with the both of them bundled in the warmth of this place while the cold blew outside. Alezya guessed the storm had calmed a bit because the wind wasn't as loud, and she could hear Kein's snores more often.

"Kassein."

He lifted his eyes from his bowl, and she wiped some of the soup off the corner of his lips.

Kassein let out a faint sigh, put his bowl aside, and quickly grabbed her hand, pulling Alezya onto his lap. Her empty bowl got knocked off the bed, but neither cared.

Instead, Alezya put her hands on his shoulders, all too aware of the heat of his body, the too-thin piece of fabric between them, and his gaze looking up at her as she was above him.

There was something in the way Kassein looked at her that made her feel like the most beautiful woman in the world, his green eyes filled with something that looked like pure adoration. She cupped his jawline with her hands, her thumbs rubbing his spiky cheeks while she leaned in for a kiss. First, a quick, chaste one, and then, a more passionate, deeper kiss.

The way his warmth spread to her was intoxicating. It was like hot lava was poured onto her skin everywhere he touched, triggering a wave of warmth in her stomach. Even more shameful was the way her nether regions reacted, immediately feeling hot, ticklish, and bothered, begging to be touched too. Alezya gently rocked her body against his without thinking as they kept kissing, and the heat increased again when his hands ventured under the fabric.

She gasped as his hands cupped her butt, crawled up her spine, caressed her thighs. There was a snowstorm outside, but she was sweating, dripping with desire. His heat was taking her over like a fire, almost making her drunk on that feeling. She wanted *more*.

"Kassein," she whimpered against his lips.

He let out a groan and pressed her against him some more. Alezya shivered upon feeling the bump in his pants, tightening the leather against her thigh...

"Kassein," she insisted with a shake in her voice, almost begging.

His lips moved from her mouth to her neck, and suddenly, he laid her on her back with him above her.

A hot shiver ran through her spine as she was basically caged underneath him between his arms, but before she could kiss him again, Kassein moved his lips even further down, pulling on the shirt and pressing his lips between her breasts.

She gasped and arched her back in response. His hands moved to her hips, caressing up and down her legs, cupping her ass, rendering her crazy with their warmth. She didn't need any blankets or clothes, not when Kassein covered and caressed her like that. She was feverish, burning with desire, and willing to beg for more.

As Kassein's chin kept pulling on the shirt's fabric, she grunted and quickly grabbed the hem to pull it above her head, getting rid of it.

She heard him loudly gasp and, with a bit of satisfaction, caught him red-handed, staring at her breasts. That was one asset she felt rather proud about, and to see it had some effect on Kassein made her feel even more desirable.

He let out a heavy sigh, and his mouth went straight for the left one, making her moan audibly. She knew her chest pleased men, but she had never realized it could have them please *her* too.

The way Kassein licked, sucked, and teased her with his tongue was doing something to her stomach and lower region, and she heard herself breathe louder, unable to keep quiet as his other hand fondled the right one.

And then she realized; he had to feel it. He had to feel how full her breasts were, unused as they should have been to feed her daughter.

She blushed, waiting for him to react, but he didn't. His lips moved, kissing her breasts and ignoring the liquid that dripped slowly from them, or licking some of it. She didn't say anything, and neither did he.

He knew, she thought. He knew, and he didn't care.

Kassein kept fondling her, ignoring how wet his hands had gotten, ignoring the liquid that continued to flow until it was but a slow drip. And that was all the confirmation and relief she needed.

Her entire body was moving under his hands, unable to stay still, unable not to react to the ways he touched her. She had a hand gripping his hair and the other scouring his back, her fingers caressing his warm skin and finding some scaled scars.

She could have paused to wonder what had caused those if she had found any room to think at all, but her whole mind was completely subjected to his hands and mouth.

When his lips moved from her breast to her stomach, she gasped, wondering where his tongue was headed as it kept going down, past her navel, her waist, and then—

"Kassein!" she gasped, lifting her head from the mattress.

The burning gaze he sent her from between her legs could have set an entire forest ablaze.

"Kassein, no," she muttered, embarrassed but without conviction.

He ignored her protest and instead, gave a lick that sent a hot shiver throughout her entire body.

Alezya let out a moan, and without waiting, he buried his face between her legs and had his tongue moving against her lips, teasing her button, alternating shallow licks, heavenly kisses, and sucking.

There was nothing she could have done to stop the sounds that came out of her mouth as he was full-on eating her like she was his last meal.

Her body tried to move involuntarily under the excruciatingly sweet torture, but Kassein wrapped an arm around her leg and pressed a hand on her abdomen while the other held her thigh, his large palm pressing it against his shoulder. She had nowhere to escape from his obscene mouth nor his burning gaze, so instead, she tried to close her eyes, but it was almost worse with only the sounds.

Now she wished the wind had been blowing stronger because the sounds his tongue made were driving her crazy.

"Kassein," she whimpered his name again and again, her voice half-broken.

He kept going, his tongue relentlessly licking, sucking, diving, and even his stubble caressing her skin was too much.

She felt one of his hands leave her thigh while the other had his thumb move to press circles on her button, driving her even more insane.

Now, his thumb and tongue were working in unison, and she was feeling that sensation climbing up, building up in sweet tension. She glanced to the side and realized his hand was moving... He was touching himself.

This was what broke the dam. Something about Kassein pleasuring himself while pleasuring her made the last strand snap, and she exploded.

Alezya felt the sensation suddenly rage through her, taking her by surprise and overloading all her senses. She couldn't stop the throaty, short whimper that came out of her mouth, nor the violent trembling, nor the way it just poured over her in waves. It hit a violent high and then came down slowly, leaving her out of breath, numb, and exhausted.

She lay on the bed in a post-orgasmic daze, slightly out of breath, until she heard a low, short grunt. A few seconds later, Kassein moved back up the bed to loom over her again, and she hooked a hand around his neck to bring him down for a long, languid kiss, tasting herself on his tongue.

Then, Kassein put a quick kiss on her temple and pulled a blanket over her before he left the bed.

Alezya wished he'd laid in bed with her, but she was too tired to protest, so she just pressed her cheek against the pillows and watched as he picked up the bowl she'd knocked over to put it aside and began cleaning himself. He just used a wet cloth and some of that scented stone paste, but watching him trace every line of his naked torso was quite a delightful sight, and when he caught her biting her lip, he smirked, making her blush.

He then grabbed one of the blades and began shaving himself, although his beard had barely started to regrow. Was it because she said she liked him better without it?

She didn't miss a single one of his movements and watched him until he was done, rinsing the blade and his freshly shaved cheeks. Next, he put some water on to boil again and stepped out to throw the dirty water away.

She hadn't taken time to think about it before, but the Dragon Clan's habitations were a marvel. Kassein's was bigger than some of the caves her people lived in. Plus, they even had a hole to let the fire's smoke leave without killing them, but it was never windy or cold inside. It probably had something to do with the mountain shape of that structure.

"My father would kill to see this," she muttered.

Her voice got Kassein's attention, and he returned to her side, sitting on the side of the bed and combing her hair with his fingers.

"Tired?"

She nodded.

"You tired me," she smiled.

"Good."

There was something adorable about how proud he looked of himself, and she smiled. Their conversation wasn't perfect yet, but it was enough to understand each other now, and she loved that. She knew her pronunciation and how she pronounced the sentences were probably still awkward, but she was just grateful she could convey what she meant now.

"Talk to me," she said, *"or I'll sleep again."*

"You don't sleep?"

"No. I talk with you."

"Talk about what?"

She thought for a second. She didn't want to pry for information, she hated anything that could be something her father would want to know, but she was curious herself.

"Kein is your dragon."

"Yes."

"Kiki is Kiera dragon?"

"Yes."

"Your brothers and sisters. They have dragons too?"

"Yes. Four brothers and three sisters, seven dragons. With Kein, eight dragons."

"Eight dragons..."

"One sister and one brother have babies too. Babies have baby dragons too. Lots of baby dragons," he chuckled.

That was a scary thought. Her clan had only seen a handful of them, but as it turned out, there were at least twice as many dragons they didn't know about... although she couldn't help but be curious about what baby dragons looked like.

From the size of those nests she had seen in his home, they probably once were as tiny as snow leopard cubs.

"Father dragon too?"

"Yes. Black dragon."

So the legendary black dragon her clan had feared for decades was Kassein's father's. The other dragons all belonged to his siblings, then? Alezya couldn't believe she held such a piece of important information, and she'd gotten it so easily too. His clan's dragons had terrorized all the clans for generations, and now, she was beginning to understand where they came from...

"Black dragon is a mother dragon?" She frowned.

"Not mother. Egg."

"Egg?"

"Yes. Baby dragons are eggs."

Baby dragons came from... eggs? Like birds? It almost made Alezya chuckle. To think such a mighty, scary creature hatched from an egg like a bird.

"Alezya has brothers and sisters?" Kassein suddenly asked.

"Three sisters," she said. *"No brothers."*

She once had brothers, but they had all been killed or died young. Every time, they were her father's pride until he sent them to their deaths to fight another clan. She knew her last brother had been killed in one of the attacks against Kassein's clan, but now, she knew her father was the one responsible for this, more than any of Kassein's men. His pride always came long before any of his children's sake.

She had never felt close to any of her brothers because she was her mother's only child, and as a girl, she had been raised with her half-sisters.

When her mother had left, Alezya had lost the only person who had ever treated her like family, and she was far too young to remember enough of it.

Now Lumie was her family, and as always, her heart hurt whenever she thought of her baby.

"Alezya father? Mother?" Kassein asked, visibly eager to know more.

"...Father," she said. *"No mother."*

She didn't know her mother's whereabouts, and she wasn't even sure she was still alive.

If she was, Alezya hoped that woman was happy. She had been sad when her mother had left, but she had quickly become resigned to it as she had been to any of the clan's rulings. At the time, she was too young to understand what had happened and why, but as an adult, and after having been married herself, Alezya couldn't blame her mother for having left. Her father was so horrible as a father, she couldn't imagine the monster he was as a husband.

After her mother, either no clan wanted to give him any more of their daughters, or her father had given up himself. He would probably pick one of his nephews as his successor someday.

"Father and mother," Kassein said, *"and jinida."*

"Jinida?"

"Jinida. Mother of father."

His grandmother. Alezya smiled, amused that he even had his grandmother.

"My azyela," he said. *"Father, mother, sisters and brothers, dragons, grandmother. My azyela."*

His family. It was funny how the word he used for family was so close to her own name, Alezya. In her language, Alezya meant freedom.

"Alezya azyela?" he suddenly asked.

She hesitated for a second.

"...Lumie," she muttered. "Lumie *is my azyela.*"

"Altha?"

She turned her eyes to him, surprised. *Altha* was the Dragon Empire's word for snow. She hadn't thought he would remember the one word she had recently taught him. And suddenly, she found herself tearing up, and she nodded.

"Snow is my family," she whispered, well aware it probably didn't make much sense to him.

Kassein frowned as she couldn't hold her tears back and began crying. He moved to lie on the bed with her, wrapping her in a protective arm. He didn't ask anything else, but instead, gently hugged her against his warm torso and rubbed her back until her tears dried and she fell asleep.

When she woke up, Alezya found herself cold and alone. Without Kassein nearby, the temperature had dropped and the fire had been extinguished too.

From the bit of orange light that came in through the hole at the top, it was probably sunset. She pulled one of the fur blankets around her shoulders and sat up. Her eyes felt dry from her earlier crying, so she grabbed some water from the jug on the bedside table and dabbed them.

How long had Kassein been gone, and where to? His side of the bed felt cold, which meant he'd probably been gone for a while. She knew they had been holed up inside for most of the day, so she figured he probably had somewhere to be for his clan.

"Kein?" she called out.

But the dragon was gone too because she didn't get a growl in response.

Alezya sighed but forced herself to move, getting up to do a little bit of cleaning again, rearranging the messy blankets, and drinking a bit of water. She was hungry, but she wasn't sure if Kassein kept any food in here, and after having been caught once stealing, she didn't want to be a fool and try it twice.

She did know where they kept the medicinal ointment though, so she decided to check on her injuries and change her bandages herself this time.

There wasn't much to do, however, for once she had taken the old ones off and cleaned her wounds a bit, she realized there was almost nothing left that needed much treatment. Which was nothing short of a miracle, and she knew it. What kind of heavenly medicine did they have in this clan to leave her with almost no scars, and wounds that healed so fast it was as if they'd never happened? Even the bones she knew her father's henchmen had broken in their violence didn't feel as if they'd ever been cracked at all. The remaining scars were just perfect white lines, almost too pretty to qualify as scars. This was close to sorcery if she had ever seen it, and she knew quite a lot about herbs, which reminded her to take the ones she had nicked from their herb-growing space earlier.

She would run out soon, but she had enough for a couple more days, so she would be fine so long as she got to grab more and kept taking it regularly. She'd had her last bleeding about two weeks before her father had kicked her out, so she would probably be safe now... but she didn't have much time until she was expected to return pregnant. If they wanted her back before the next gathering of the clans, she had to return within less than a week.

All she could do was pray that her father would buy that she had spent every night since she'd come here with Kassein and that their clan's Healer would mistake her for pregnant. It had to work. All she wanted was to get Lumie out of there; nothing else mattered.

"Alezya."

She lifted her head, swallowing the last bit of herb as Kassein stepped back inside with a small smile. He was holding two new bowls of soup and some of those sticks with meat on them. Her stomach immediately growled in appreciation, making him chuckle, but she grabbed some water first to rinse the bitter taste of the herbs.

"*You saw Kiera? Tievin? Lorey?*" she asked.

"*Yes. Too much snow,*" he said. "*All in khamzil.*"

In their leather dwellings, she guessed. Alezya nodded. Though it wasn't nearly as bad as in the heights down here, even the Dragon Clan people probably didn't enjoy being battered by heavy gusts of wind and snow.

"*Kein gone too,*" she remarked.

"*Kein hungry,*" he shrugged.

So his dragon had gone to hunt, then.

She wondered if the huge orange dragon could still fly in this weather, but given its size, a bit of wind probably wasn't too much of a bother. Maybe more for Kiki, who was considerably leaner and thinner.

She took the meat as soon as Kassein sat with her on the bed, and like earlier, they ate together. She was starving, and although the meat was just lukewarm, it tasted like the most delicious food.

"*You like meat,*" Kassein said, watching her eat with a little smile.

"*Yes,*" Alezya nodded unapologetically. "*In the mountains, I only eat small meat.*"

"*Small meat?*"

"*Rabbits,*" she said, remembering the word Lorey had taught her the previous day, when they'd spotted a couple of them in the garden. "*Birds too. This is more than rabbits and birds.*"

"*This is better,*" he corrected her with the right word. "*The meat is dubbrun.*"

Alezya had no idea what kind of animal *dubbrun* was, but it was tasty. She finished her first stick of meat, and Kassein tried to offer her the second one, but she refused.

"*I ate with Kiera too*," he said, "*and you're hungry.*"

She realized he had split his meal in two parts to eat some of his dinner with her.

Now it made sense; a single stick of meat and a bowl of soup wasn't much for a man she'd seen eat vast amounts of meat so far... She gave in, and took the second stick while he ate his bowl.

"*More meat?*" he asked when she'd finished her stick.

"*No. Thank you.*"

"Kiitso," he repeated.

She nodded, but she was still pretty sure that she had never heard Kassein or any of the others use their word for "thank you." Maybe she lacked some cultural context there.

They finished eating while exchanging more words, this time translating more abstract concepts such as greetings or emotions. This language exchange had become sort of a special thing between them, and soon enough, they were back to lying on the bed together, Kassein's arm around her shoulders and Alezya's cheek on his torso.

This time, neither of them initiated anything; in fact, their chatting was somewhat fascinating enough that they talked late into the night and fell asleep like this.

The snowstorm had stopped when they woke up the following day. Alezya woke up first this time, and she found herself still in Kassein's arms, both of them almost in the same position they'd fallen asleep in, except that her body, probably attracted to his heat, had tried to climb Kassein's, leaving her with her leg across his and her arm around his torso. She would have been a bit more ashamed if she hadn't been so cold; even with the blankets covering her, Alezya could feel the habitation had gotten really chilly overnight, and her face sticking out of the blankets was cold. She shivered and curled up even closer to his body.

"Good morning," he whispered, using her language.

She smiled. His pronunciation wasn't the best, but she liked how his raspy throat made the greeting even sexier. She put a kiss on his shoulder and felt him tug the blanket around her, although she was already as covered as possible.

Because they had slept so much already the previous day and not done much, they were up early, as the light that came into the habitation was definitely that of sunrise. She could hear Kein's snores and some morning birds taking advantage of the dragon's slumber to get chirpy.

Alezya pressed her cheek against Kassein's skin as he combed her hair with his fingers, thinking of how they only had a few days left together. She hated it, but she had to return to her clan before the next gathering, and she had to get Lumie out of there... A knot of anxiety formed in her stomach, and maybe Kassein had felt her tense or something because he put another kiss on her forehead gently.

"*I like your hair,*" he whispered.

That made her smile. He touched, caressed, and combed her hair any chance he got. Her long hair was one of her favorite things about herself too, and she had noticed no one in the Dragon Clan seemed to have this very straight, very dark, and very long hair. Being complimented about it made her want to take care of her hair even more.

She kissed his jawline, again amused by his beard, which was protesting the frequent shaves by growing back spikier every morning.

"*Breakfast?*"

"*Breakfast,*" he nodded.

They got up together, cleaned up, and dressed to venture out, but almost nothing was done without them touching each other in some way.

Alezya let Kassein braid her hair, and although she was gutted she had lost that piece of fabric he'd gifted her, she was still content with the little string of leather he used to tie it this time. She stopped him from shaving himself, as she was starting to like the little stubble, and helped him put on each piece of his war gear, the arm braces, shoulder pieces, and his cape, even though he could have done all of it on his own.

As Alezya was about to step outside, he grabbed her hand and swung her back so that she collided with his bare chest, making her laugh.

"*Kiss me,*" he demanded.

She smiled. How could the mere fact that they understood each other more and could talk like this make her so happy? Those words of his were enough to trigger little swarms of butterflies in her stomach.

She cupped his face with her hands and got on her toes, pulling his face toward her to kiss him. He wrapped his arms around her waist, pressing her into his embrace.

She never wanted to leave this man. Alezya had never known so much bliss as the time she had spent with Kassein, and the only thing that prevented her from being truly happy was Lumie's absence.

No matter how hard she was falling for Kassein, everything was tainted by how worried she was about her baby. She kept reminding herself how Suolk and her cousin were clearly in charge of caring for her, how they had a child of their own and would know what to do, and how her father was not going to do anything so long as he needed Alezya to return pregnant... So much was hanging in the balance, but for her, nothing mattered but Lumie. She was only allowing herself to enjoy this, basking in the sunshine of Kassein's affection, because she knew she had to brace for the inevitable storm that was coming.

They stepped out of the leather shelter together, and she insisted on greeting Kein, who was waiting for them outside. The orange dragon had become such a companion to Alezya that she found herself patting its hot snout fearlessly.

She glanced up the mountain, but there was no sign of her father's spies. She redirected her eyes to Kein. Maybe she had the key to her plan right here. Her idea was a bit mad, but madder things had happened in the last few days.

With Kein in tow, they walked hand in hand toward the large fire pit his men had lit up again in the middle of the area. Many men silently greeted them, and those who did out loud, Alezya was glad she understood their greetings to their *Aqayir*. Her father would die of envy; no one in any clan had ever understood as much as she could now of their archenemy's language.

"*Good morning,*" greeted Lorey and Tievin, who were with Kiki by the fire, both already eating breakfast.

"*Good morning,*" Alezya greeted them in return, a bit proudly.

Lorey replied with a smile, and soon, one of the men ran to bring them food. Alezya could never get enough of the Dragon Clan's food, and as soon as they sat on Kein, she began devouring her fruits and eggs.

"*Where is Kiera?*"

Alezya didn't understand Lorey's reply, but from the little head movement, she guessed Kiera had probably gone hunting in the forest near the camp. Lorey added something else that ended with Kassein's name, and he sighed. He finished his food in record time, got up, and put a quick kiss on Alezya's lips.

"*Bye,*" he said, using another greeting she'd just learned the previous day.

"*Bye,*" she replied.

She didn't know where he was going but guessed he was meeting his sister because he left with a sullen expression.

Alezya heard a chuckle and turned back to an amused Lorey and, from Tievin's grimace, suddenly realized she had just kissed their leader so brazenly in front of them. She blushed helplessly.

"*Are you happy?*" Lorey asked, tilting her head.

"*...Yes,*" Alezya muttered.

"*Kassein looks happy,*" Lorey nodded toward the direction he had disappeared. "*He wasn't happy before.*"

"*Why?*"

"*His brother is angry,*" Lorey said, kind enough to use simple words Alezya could understand, "*and Kassein is angry with his brother too.*"

Alezya remembered the bedrooms and the one of his older sister... Was it about what had happened to his older sister? She was tempted to ask more, but Lorey wasn't Kassein's family, and she didn't want to pry when he hadn't pressed her for answers either.

"*Kassein is... thanks,*" she said, not knowing the word for "kind" yet. "*I thank Kassein.*"

Whatever argument that brother had with Kassein, Alezya already found it unfair; she had witnessed for herself how kind Kassein was, and she couldn't understand what a brother could have against this kind man.

Tievin hadn't said anything but was eyeing both women while eating his breakfast. Alezya had noticed that the scrawny man was reluctant to approach either dragon, and sure enough, when she put her empty bowl aside and petted Kein's neck, he opened wide, surprised eyes.

She smiled, a bit proud. She was getting closer to the orange dragon than many of the Dragon Clan.

"Alezya?" Lorey called her eyes back to her. *"Let's go? Where?"*

She frowned for a second before understanding Lorey was asking her what she wanted to do that day.

"Medicinal herbs," she said, trying not to act nervous. *"I like to see the herbs."*

She was glad she'd learned the word for herbs with Dajan and confirmed it with Lorey two days prior; Kassein's home mountain had an impressive field and lots of plants surrounding it, so Alezya had used this unique chance to act innocent and confirm the translation for medicinal herbs with Lorey during one of her breaks from sparring with Kiera. Lorey nodded, and they both got up, leaving Tievin behind while they made their way through the area.

With Kiki and Kein following them, it was clear no warrior would be foolish enough to approach them. While they walked, Alezya proudly told Lorey about the new words she'd learned from Kassein, using gestures to demonstrate.

She realized Kassein was an even kinder teacher than Lorey was, because the young woman gently corrected her pronunciation a couple of times, and rearranged her sentences so they were more fluid too. Overall, Alezya was still glad their language was fairly straightforward and didn't seem to have as many rules as hers. Moreover, she was trying to chat more and use it more to become as fluent as possible, and Lorey was kind enough to entertain her.

"Where are Kassein and Kiera?" she asked after a while.

"Aslayid," Lorey said, mimicking a knife gesture. *"They are getting more meat."*

Hunting, Alezya understood. She nodded.

They continued the conversation, Lorey using the topic to expand Alezya's vocabulary on activities like hunting, fishing, and herb picking with many gestures to be sure to convey the meaning.

"Dragons... They hear dragon words too?" Alezya asked after a while, her hand naturally resting on Kein's orange scales as the dragon walked by her side.

"Yes," Lorey nodded. *"But dragons... Dragons are dragons. Dragons aren't men. They do dragons. A dragon wants to hunt, it hunts. If a dragon is unhappy, it doesn't listen."*

"Kein is a good dragon," Alezya said, scratching Kein's scales and getting a growl of appreciation.

Lorey gave her a strange look.

"Kein likes Alezya," she just said, eyeing the dragon with a mixed expression.

Alezya wasn't sure how to respond. Was Kein really giving her special treatment, then?

She had noticed everyone around was wary of the dragon, and after she'd witnessed it eat actual humans, she could understand why, but now, Lorey made it sound like she was even more of an exception than she thought. She glanced back at the orange dragon. Was it too risky to bet on that dragon, then?

Strangely, she felt like she hardly feared the dragon anymore at all. It was still this humongous creature with claws and thick, sharp fangs that could eat a whole man in the blink of an eye, and yet Alezya felt safer by Kein's side than she did next to any man besides Kassein. She had seen how horrible men could be; at least the dragon's violence bore no evil to it.

They arrived at the place with all the herbs, and like last time, Alezya felt a bit excited to see so many of them cultivated in the same place. They had left the dragons outside as they were too big to enter, but they could hear them playing outside, probably causing mayhem in the snow.

"Do you like medicinal herbs?" Lorey asked. They had been roaming for a while, Alezya looking for an opportunity to snatch the ones she needed.

"Yes. I pick herbs in the mountain."

"The medicinal herbs here are Kiera and Kassein's mother's herbs. In Kalat Unshreik too. She likes medicinal herbs."

Kalat Unshreik. That was what he called that black mountain of theirs, the place Kassein and his siblings had grown up in.

Alezya was surprised. Their mom was some healer, then? She felt slightly impressed. It mustn't have been easy to make so many herbs grow in the same place in such a complex climate.

They kept examining, and Lorey began explaining what each herb was used for, using words and gestures to describe body parts and conditions so Alezya would understand.

When they reached the herb, Lorey said it was used for blood illnesses, and Alezya wondered if she knew this could stop one's bleeding. Still, she asked about a herb on the other side, and as soon as Lorey turned her back, she ripped some more leaves off and hid them.

When they left the leather dwelling a while later, she was certain she'd picked more than enough until she'd returned to her clan... which would be soon now. Every time she thought about returning to the mountain, her heart was torn between leaving Kassein and returning to Lumie.

She knew it couldn't be avoided, and yet, she was in pain just thinking about leaving him again. This would be the second time. How would he react? He would think she was insane...

"Alezya?"

Lorey called her out of her thoughts; they had stepped outside, reuniting with the two dragons, both wet from playing in the snow.

"What do we do?" Lorey asked, leaving her the choice.

"I want to see Kassein," Alezya said, without hesitating.

Lorey smiled, and they resumed walking together, the rowdy pair of dragons following them once again. These two acted particularly excited this morning, as they kept pouncing on each other, playing in the snow and causing waves of snow in their wake. It was effective at keeping any of the Dragon Clan's warriors away, but both women also got splattered with snow a couple of times despite the sky being clear blue that day.

"*Kiki, tawa!*" Lorey suddenly called the dark gray dragon after they got splattered a third time.

Alezya was getting slightly fed up with their antics too.

The weather might have been fine, but now she was getting wet through her coat. At Lorey's angry voice, Kiki immediately jumped away from Kein and seemingly calmed down, but Kein didn't seem to care. The giant orange dragon once again pounced on its sibling, trying to resume their game, although Kiki wasn't interested anymore.

Lorey turned to Alezya.

"*Alezya tell Kein,*" she said.

"*Tell Kein what?*"

"*Tawa.*"

Did that mean to stop or calm down?

She hesitated, slightly nervous; she'd never given orders to the dragon before. However, when Kein tried to bite the dark gray dragon's thigh, and its tail swooshed another wave of snow to the side, missing them only by a foot, she got fed up too.

"*Kein, tawa,*" she said, trying to sound as determined as Lorey.

The orange dragon froze and turned wide, large-as-plates silver eyes toward her.

Alezya had never felt as small as she did under the dragon's surprised, inquisitive stare. It finally left its smaller peer alone, but now, its attention was all on Alezya, rendering her quite nervous.

After a beat, the orange dragon suddenly settled down in the snow, still staring right at her. It laid down like it usually did to sleep, but this time, its head was still straight up, and its eyes riveted on her.

Alezya glanced at Lorey for support, and her companion was smiling, her hand petting Kiki's head.

"*See. Kein likes Alezya.*"

For some reason, that made Alezya blush. Did that mean Kein was really listening to her?

She put her fear aside to step toward the orange dragon and, with all the bravery she could muster, put a hand on its snout. Kein's tail resumed scooping little waves of snow left and right behind it, and the dragon let out a long, low growl.

"Good dragon," she whispered.

That got her another growl.

With both dragons calmed down and now docile, the two women resumed walking, Kein sticking behind Alezya, so close its head kept popping over her shoulder, while Kiki marched next to Lorey. They resumed chatting again, and this time, Alezya was curious to know what other words she could say that Kein would understand.

When she asked Lorey, her companion chuckled.

"Kein understands everything. But listens only to you."

"Kein doesn't listen to Kiera? To you?"

Lorey scoffed and glanced toward the orange dragon.

"Kein? Go away."

Kein replied with a sudden, furious growl that made both women jump, showing off its fangs and stepping closer to Alezya in protest.

After the initial fright, Lorey chuckled.

"See? A dragon does what a dragon wants. Kein wants to be with Alezya."

Alezya smiled and patted the dragon's neck until its growls settled.

Although she doubted Kein would actually attack Lorey, it was still quite scary to see and hear the orange dragon suddenly get mad at her friend.

"Lorey? What is word for dragon bird?"

"Bird?"

Alezya mimicked flying with her hands, and Lorey nodded.

"Oh. Baytir. Kiki? Baytian."

The dark gray dragon let out a high-pitched growl, made a little hop, and flew up without waiting, making little circles above their heads.

Alezya watched its majestic, fluid flight before she turned to Kein, who was also eyeing its peer.

"Kein."

The orange dragon immediately flipped its head back to her.

"Baytian."

Kein let out a faint growl, pressed its snout against her shoulder briefly, and then lay down in a stretch before it flapped its humongous wings and joined its sibling in a couple of flaps that scattered all the snow around.

Alezya was just speechless. She could order the dragon to take off and fly just like that. Lorey had no idea how much she had just done.

"More," she asked Lorey, trying not to sound too excited. *"Tell me more words for dragons."*

Lorey gave her a little surprised look, but she must have trusted Alezya because she did, although she didn't teach her anything that could be dangerous, like telling the dragon to attack.

Instead, she taught her words such as lie down, wait, growl, go down, take, and let go. Alezya had never been so determined to carve those words into her memory, and she tried every single one on the orange dragon, who, to her shock and delight, obeyed every single one of them, leaving her astonished. She could command a dragon. Not only that, but the largest dragon of all obeyed *her*. An indescribable feeling of power fired her gut, and this time, she knew her plan had better chances than ever to work.

By the time they found Kiera and Kassein, who were sparring outside for once with quite an audience, Lorey was done teaching her words, and Alezya didn't ask for more.

The dragons stuck in the vicinity, and that was enough to clear everyone else from the area; the Dragon Clan warriors suddenly scattered in different directions. Only Tievin remained, giving the women a brief, bored glance but staying at a safe distance as the dragons came to settle next to them.

Alezya didn't care for the scrawny man; her eyes were already on Kassein's sweaty, naked torso, her stomach doing a little jump in appreciation. It was hard not to look at his slightly panting mouth and not remember the things he could do with it...

"Alezya?"

Lorey was staring at her with an amused smirk.

Alezya blushed and remembered to close her mouth. Her companion chuckled while Alezya, eager to do anything to justify hiding her face, went to Kein to sit on its paw as usual, the dragon curving its neck toward her in the snow so she could pet it.

Luckily, Tievin began to speak, and although it was much too fast for Alezya to follow, it distracted Lorey, and they all turned their eyes back to the duel, the three of them watching the siblings spar for a while.

This time, Keira and Kassein had chosen a rather deserted area to spar, and coincidentally, it was close to that large wooden door leading into her clan's territory.

The wooden wall they had built between the mountains and them was massive, but Alezya was curious why they'd put such a large door when they rarely bothered to attack the clans and didn't fear them much.

In her opinion, a dragon felt like a good enough defense, but maybe the Dragon Clan had no idea of their own superiority.

She shivered, thinking back to the despicable technique one of the clans used to attack last. She hadn't heard anything about it but hoped they prevented the disease from spreading. She understood fights were part of clan traditions, but such schemes were downright disgusting and evil.

Her eyes lifted to the mountains behind the wall. She hadn't seen or ever interacted with many other clans, but she was glad hers was a bit farther away from the Dragon Clan; the closest ones ought to be struggling. She wondered where her mother's birth clan was. She hadn't heard or seen anything about them in years, and her father had prohibited any talk of the Lumiata Clan. Some clans were also non-sedentary, moving from one inhabited mountain to another, and she wondered if that could be the case for her mother. That would lessen the chances of them ever meeting again...

The sounds of the fight stopped, and she turned her head back to it; Kassein and Keira must have reached an agreement to stop because both of them were walking toward the trio watching, Kiera parting ways with her brother to get the water Tievin offered while Kassein walked to Alezya first.

His dragon let out a faint growl, but Kassein replied with one of his tongue clicks, and then reached her, grabbing her hand first.

"*You cold?*" he asked.

Alezya shook her head. A few minutes earlier, she had been cold and wet, but she was back to dry and warm after sitting on the dragon and being in the sun for a few minutes.

"*Fight with Kiera again?*" she teased him.

He nodded. She guessed that was the sibling's favorite way of interacting; when they weren't sparring, they were hunting, and she hadn't seen them exchange many words aside from their grunts and tongue clicks.

She used the sleeve of her coat to wipe the sweat from his chin, but he grabbed her wrist and put her fingers to his lips instead. It was hard for Alezya not to blush and be aware of the three pairs of eyes on them.

She couldn't remember how they had acted in front of the others before, but a part of her also felt a bit proud Kassein didn't care at all for them to see. He was so unapologetic about displaying affection toward her in the open, and that was something she'd never experienced or witnessed before.

Most warriors hardly interacted with their wives in public, let alone caressed or kissed them. There were no other women in the area besides Lorey and Kiera, so she couldn't know if this was normal in the clan or if Kassein was indeed just a different species altogether... but she certainly didn't hate it. On the contrary, Alezya barely stopped herself from diving into his arms, knowing how little time she had left with him. Instead, she forced herself to remain seated on the dragon, trying to reign in her feelings. She just took any sign of affection he showed like a breadcrumb, cherishing every moment, trying to act calmly and think about Lumie, her clan, and everything that awaited.

It was just a matter of days, Alezya kept repeating to herself.

She only had days until everything would go down, until she would have to leave Kassein and put her mad plan to work to save her daughter.

Kassein had to know she'd been with child now, but they hadn't talked about it. Either he chose to ignore the subject, was waiting for her to speak, or didn't want to hear it at all.

Alezya was scared of his reaction when everything came to light, but she prayed, every single time that man's unbelievably kind eyes set on her, that he'd forgive her. That, no matter how mad or upset he was, he would be the man he had been with her, and he wouldn't harm her baby.

A part of her was also counting on Lorey. Day after day, Alezya had begun to befriend that woman, and she could tell Lorey would never harm a child.

While Lorey didn't have authority over Kassein, it was clear he listened to her and respected her to some degree. A male warrior and leader listening to a woman's advice would have been unheard of back in her clan, but by now, Alezya knew the Dragon Clan was nothing like the others, and what seemed impossible in the mountains could be a reality here.

And for once, she was allowing herself to believe in such miracles.

Another day passed, and another, and then another.

Every day, Alezya indulged herself in Kassein's touches, learned more of their language from Lorey, and exercised her orders over Kein.

She was taking the herbs, and much to her relief, her bleeding hadn't come when it should have, proving her plan was well underway.

For some unknown reason, Kassein still stubbornly refused to have intercourse with her. He would touch her, caress her, and give her more pleasure than she believed possible, but he never let her reciprocate. While Alezya loved being so loved, she was also getting... frustrated.

From the way his body very obviously reacted to her every time, it wasn't a physical issue, so why? Did he not want her? Was he bound not to sleep with a woman he wasn't married to? The man was stubborn, and every time she tried to question him, he kept dodging her question yet insisting that he liked her. Well, she liked him too, and she wanted to show it to him if he'd let her... and she was running out of time.

As brokenhearted as she was at the mere thought of leaving Kassein again, she was also getting more desperate to have at least one night with him. She wanted that. She wanted to make love to that man, just once, so she would go back with that memory buried in her heart and no regrets left behind.

Alezya was now perfectly healed and healthier than ever, thanks to being able to eat her fill every day, something she hadn't experienced in months.

She could now wander around the camp on her own, so long as Kein accompanied her. The orange dragon had hardly left her side for the past few days and only went away when she was with Kassein. It was as if the man and the dragon had some agreement to take turns guarding her.

Whenever she was alone, Alezya actually enjoyed being able to walk around, near the forest, so she could think her plan over again and eye the mountains. She often touched her necklace as she did so; she had put her only belonging back on her neck the day before, and even though Kassein had frowned at it, inspecting the little pendant with his fingers, he hadn't asked about it.

In fact, he didn't ask her much anymore. He would frown when she looked at the mountains, caress her hair when she cried, and comfort her when her sleep got restless, but he didn't pry. Either he didn't want to know or didn't care. Or perhaps he believed she'd left it all behind for good and didn't want to reopen that wound... Not that it mattered anymore. Alezya was trying to make her peace with the fact that chances were slim that she'd see Kassein again once she left, this time for the last time.

It was hard. The happiness she was enjoying with him would never be complete, and it would soon be nothing but a sweet dream she would have to leave behind. She loved the man. She had come to that realization and accepted her feelings just as soon as she did, and she was content with that. But she would never be able to love him more than she loved her child, and that was the only truth. Lumie came first.

She had already been lucky to enjoy what should have been exile among the Dragon Clan. She had loved, healed, and even been allowed to hope, but she was a realist. Alezya forbade herself from entertaining any hope she would survive another meeting with her father. She was going to be captured, and as soon as they realized what she had done, in days or perhaps weeks, her clan would most likely kill her. That was an outcome she could accept, only if she could be certain Lumie would survive her and be safe.

All she needed was for her plan to work, for her sacrifice to make it possible for her daughter to escape. She had failed Lumie once, and her baby had survived by some miracle, but she had learned her lesson: they wouldn't both be able to make it.

"Will you miss me, Kein?" she asked the dragon, patting its warm head.

The orange dragon let out a gentle, faint growl that made her smile sadly.

She had learned to truly enjoy the dragon's company, and by now, she even thought she was pretty good at understanding its mood.

Kein understood her well too. Not just the many, many orders and words she had practiced on the dragon for her plan when the others weren't around, but even her moods. When she felt unsafe around men in the camp, Kein would growl and walk closer to her. When she was feeling at peace but sad, it would lie next to her until her mood passed.

Sometimes, Alezya even wondered if dragons understood her tongue. When she was alone with Kein, she would openly chat with it in her language, and most of the time, she felt like the dragon behind those large silver eyes listened and understood. Still, she was careful never to give it commands in her own tongue. She kept all her orders in Kassein's language, so her clan wouldn't understand any order she gave the dragon. Slowly but surely, she was preparing for the day she would go back and put her plan to use.

She would even sometimes ride Kein when she was alone, not making the dragon take flight but just enjoying the ride on its back and going around the camp like it was a horse, not an oversized man-eating beast...

That afternoon though, she was just enjoying a quiet walk with her protector by her side, all too aware that this was her last full day with Kassein.

It had come too soon, she thought with an ache in her heart.

Every day had felt pretty much the same in the camp, and for a while, she had allowed herself to forget about how close to her deadline she was getting, but the signs were there.

Two more clans had attacked Kassein's within the last three days, ahead of the council gathering, always with the same outcome.

The clans were getting desperate for any kind of information to bring to the gathering. She had spotted more and more spies in the mountains, keeping an eye on them and, for some, keeping an eye on her. She knew what they saw, that she slept every night with the enemy, and that she had hours left before she had to go back.

At times she wondered if her father's spies were confused by how well she was treated in the camp, allowed to wander around guarded by a dragon, cared for by a warrior, and fed like she was one of them. She had no doubt they would have plenty of questions for her when she returned, so Alezya had been preparing for that too.

"...Alezya."

Her gaze shifted from the mountains to Kassein, who'd appeared between the trees.

Alezya smiled, always surprised at how quiet a man his size managed to be. Kein growled at its owner's presence, but as usual, Kassein replied with a glare, and the dragon reluctantly walked away. Alezya kept her eyes on the orange dragon until she felt strong arms wrap around her, and Kassein's lips found her temple. She smiled and turned around, lifting her hands to his nape.

His skin was warm, as usual, and covered by a thin layer of sweat.

"*You fought again,*" she noted.

"*With Kiera,*" he nodded.

His sister provoked him daily, and Alezya had a hard time discerning the times they were training from the times they were genuinely dueling and trying to harm the other. Their fights were nearly as violent as the ones they had against the attacking clans, and the strength difference between the siblings and other warriors was like comparing a mountain to a hill.

Now, she no longer worried when she heard the sounds of a fight and merely checked if it was her own clan, but it seemed her father had chosen to bide his time until her return.

Which reminded Alezya her time with Kassein was coming to an end soon.

"I missed you," she whispered in her language.

Whether he'd understood or not didn't matter; she went on her toes to bring her lips to his. It was a gentle, chaste kiss, but it wasn't enough.

They exchanged a short, loving look before Kassein closed his eyes and went for more, taking her mouth with his, pressing his tongue against the seam of her lips. She let out a faint moan, and he kept pushing her for more, hugging her and moving her until her back pressed against a thick tree.

Alezya's body was heating up fast under his burning touch, and soon, she felt overdressed, pushing Kassein's cloak off his shoulder to touch his torso directly. His hands were caressing her nape and the curve of her back with a tenderness that didn't match the passion of his kiss. He was holding back again.

Frustrated, Alezya replied to his kiss with even more hunger, running her fingers through his hair and pulling him toward her until there was no space left between their bodies, only clothes. She could feel Kassein's body reacting, and she was desperately egging him on.

Emboldened by the prospect of their upcoming separation, Alezya drifted her lips from his mouth to his cheek, his jawline, his neck, his collarbone, down to his torso...

"*No.*"

It had almost been a growl.

Alezya hadn't even realized he'd trapped her wrists in one hand until he pressed them against his chest, gentle but firm enough she couldn't move them.

"Kassein," she whined again.

He ignored her, his lips taking hers again to silence her before he drifted to her neck. His warm breath against her skin, his gentle nibbling and sucking, everything was making her feel hotter and hotter, almost dizzy.

When his hands moved under her coat, Alezya couldn't suppress another moan, aching for his touch, for his warmth to touch her there, anywhere. She felt his fingers dig feverishly through the layers of fabric, opening her coat, lifting her dress, and pulling down her pants roughly.

Soon enough, his warm palm was brushing her thighs, making her gasp.

"Kass—"

His name didn't make it past her lips as he kissed her again, almost forcefully.

And she liked it. Alezya whimpered in pleasure as his kiss got more fervent, more pressing, more... beastly. Kassein wanted her. He was kissing her like she was a never ending craving, like he wanted to devour her whole.

She craned her neck as he towered over her, pressing her against the tree while his hand pulled on the thin fabric covering her mound. He was barely leaving her room to breathe, let alone talk, and Alezya could hear her own moans filling the air alongside his growls. She could feel his fingers, those thick, calloused, hot fingers assessing how wet she was, playing with her folds. There was nowhere to run, no room to move, as his whole body covered her, the tree trunk pressed against her back.

Alezya cried out and jerked forward when, without warning, he pushed a finger inside. Balancing herself on her toes, she leaned her forehead on his shoulder, her breathing hoarse, his heat filling her from the inside.

"Kassein," she whimpered. "Kassein... *Please.*"

He moved, rubbing inside, his thumb on her button, sending delicious sensations through her body and burning her from her stomach down. She felt his lips trail down her nape, nibbling her skin, spreading hot shivers down her spine.

She couldn't tell when her coat had left her shoulders, only that her dress was exposing enough of her nape for Kassein to kiss and graze with his lips. She had a hand on his nape, the other on his bicep, but she couldn't find the strength to do anything but hold on tight because his finger was driving her mad. He was stirring, rubbing, slicking in and out, and not giving her any rest. Alezya gasped against his shoulder, and next, she was crying out at the second finger spearing her.

And he moved again, not giving her a second to catch her breath, just filling her with shallow thrusts while she breathed hoarsely against his skin. She had no room to think, and she had no strength to resist when his free hand grabbed the hair at the base of her neck and pulled her gently to incline her head at the perfect angle for another kiss before his lips vanished.

Alezya was still breathing hard with her mouth open and her lips wet when she opened her eyes to look for him and saw the man getting down on his knees in front of her.

"No," she let out a panicked whisper. "Kassein, that's..."

But she had little voice left and even less strength. When his free hand slithered around her thigh, put her leg over his shoulder, and pressed her waist back against the tree, she couldn't stop him. His fingers hadn't stopped moving, keeping her center hot, wet, and bothered, but it got worse when his tongue joined the assault.

Alezya didn't even pretend to try and stop her cries; her stomach tightened, her legs trembled, and Kassein's tongue was sending hot waves of pleasure to her core.

She looked down, and she had never seen green fire, but Kassein's eyes were burning from between her legs, his gaze riveted on her and making it look like he was devouring her like a hungry beast. Alezya's hands gripped his hair, his hand on her stomach, and she held on for dear life while he burned through her, his fingers and tongue relentless, his low growls of pleasure driving her insane.

She tried, she really tried to hold it in, but suddenly, pleasure burst, violent like a wave crashing against the rocks, unstoppable and inevitable.

Alezya cried out, tears coming to her eyes, her entire body shaking violently, and something sparkling behind her closed eyelids. It lasted seconds, long, painful, mind-blowing seconds, during which Kassein's tongue didn't let go, sucking her orgasm to its very end.

When the wave finally retreated, all strength leaving her, Alezya slowly fell against the tree, out of breath, her legs giving up. She felt Kassein's strong arms catch her and his lips against her temple as she melted in his embrace.

Alezya woke up slowly, her entire body feeling languished, and she had no memory of getting back to Kassein's dwelling.

She sat up and found herself feeling clean, a new dress on but her legs bare under the covers. She was alone again.

She let out a faint sigh, but got up, refusing to waste another day. She had no idea how many hours she'd lost, but when she stepped outside of the leather shelter, her feet bare in the snow, a pressing feeling squeezed her heart. They were running out of time. She was running out of time with Kassein, and she didn't want to waste it.

The evening was cold, but she didn't care; barefoot in the snow, she stepped around the habitation, hoping to find Kein, but the orange dragon was nowhere to be seen either. She frowned; it was a nice day and now evening. Were they all at dinner?

She was about to step back inside to search for shoes and a coat when she heard something. She turned around, hoping to find Kassein or his dragon, but instead, a man stood there.

Alezya stiffened with the instincts of a woman who knew what danger looked like. He was clearly of the Dragon Clan, but she knew not all those men could be trusted like she did Kassein, and the way that man was staring at her was worse than a snow leopard sniffing prey; it was vicious. She took a slow step back, but a blade appeared in the man's hand.

He spoke, spitting words like a snake would venom, and although the only words she managed to grasp were *Aqayir* and *woman*, she didn't need more to understand what he meant.

"No," she breathed.

If she could face a dragon, she could face a man. Alezya refused to cower to that man, not when she had survived many hateful stares already.

She took another step back, quickly considering her options. Going back into the shelterwhen she knew it was empty would have been foolish; she knew better than to let a man trap her in an enclosed space. She had a vague idea of where Kassein and Kein could be, but no guarantee. How far could a dragon hear? What if they'd gone hunting and were away?

She took a shaky breath, and just as the man lunged at her, Alezya didn't give herself time to freeze or panic; she turned around and ran.

The snow was soft under her feet, and she was running too fast to feel the burn of the ice under her soles. She just needed to run, as fast as she could. This felt far too much like deja vu, but she didn't have time to care. Or think. She had to at least get to the firepit and get Kassein's attention. Behind her, the man shouted, and she realized he was running faster; she was running out of time.

"Kassein! KEIN!" she screamed, her voice echoing around the mountains.

She felt a hand grab her long hair, yanking her back so hard her neck almost snapped violently at the brutal movement. She should have taken her dagger, she thought, just as the sharp burst of pain shot through her scalp. She should have–

"Alezya!"

A sudden gust of wind forcefully threw her to the ground.

The pull on her hair had vanished, and just as she hit the ground, a large, heavy body of orange scales suddenly covered the sky. Out of breath, Alezya lay in the snow, trapped under Kein's hot belly, the vibrations of its enraged growls rolling above her. She was ensnared under a dragon, near being crushed, and yet, Alezya realized she felt somewhat safe. Safer than seconds ago, at least.

It didn't last long; she heard a man's screams, cut short by the horrifying sound of flesh being ripped, and then, gradually, the heat retreated. By some miracle, Kein stepped off without crushing her, and a gust of cold wind greeted her. Strong arms lifted her up, and suddenly, she was faced with Kassein, out of breath, his green eyes full of concern, his free hand cupping her cheek.

"Alezya?" he whispered.

"I… I'm fine," she managed, giving him a nod.

He let out a faint sigh of relief and pressed her face against his neck, holding her tight.

His warmth spread around her like a warm coat, chasing away the remnants of her shivering. She hadn't noticed she was shivering until then, but it had nothing to do with the cold. Her nerves were suddenly catching up to the situation. No, to what had almost happened.

Alezya slowly wrapped her arms around his neck and lifted her legs around his waist, and she didn't want to let go. They hugged each other, their breathing calming down together.

Whatever Kein had done to that man, it was over. She forced herself to focus on him. She focused on his scent, his warmth, the steady rise and fall of his chest. Everything had happened so fast, but as panic subsided slowly, more erratic thoughts came crashing through her mind.

That man had grabbed her, yanked her by her hair, like in her worst nightmares. What if Kassein had been too far? What if Kein hadn't heard her?

She exhaled a shaky breath, belated fearful tears springing in her eyes. She held on tighter to Kassein, like he was her lifeline. And Lumie.

How many more times would she have to survive before she could see her baby? How many times would she be scared into thinking she'd never see her again? Why couldn't she get a moment's peace? She shuddered, emotions washing over her all at once, waves of anger, frustration, fear, and, thankfully, relief. She had survived. And Kassein was here, holding her.

He'd saved her life, *again*. The one man she didn't fear; the one she could count on to protect her, comfort her, and chase the nightmares away.

Without another word, Kassein gently carried her, and Alezya didn't care where. She held on tight to him, her heartbeat going fast, her gaze going to the falling sun behind him.

Their last evening. Their last hours together. Tomorrow, she would have to go... but they still had a night together, and she was going to make it count. She needed him to know. Once, just once, Alezya was desperate to give all of herself to Kassein. And then, she would go back to being Lumie's mother.

They got back inside the leather shelter, and Kassein dropped her on the bed gently.

Alezya could almost predict everything that was going to happen next, because she had come to know this man so well: he brought her food, ate with her, took the dishes away, and went to boil some water for her. She didn't have to leave the bed, he just did it all. She knew he had probably cleaned her body and changed her as well while she was asleep.

It was the kind of man he was, and she knew exactly how lucky she was to have been with him. She wanted to commit it all to memory: his gentle movements, his strong but kind hands, his warm skin, his faint smiles, his deep voice, and those green eyes.

It was her goodbye, and he had no idea. She was about to break his heart again, and then leave him with the hardest thing she could ask of him, to take care of Lumie. That was, if her plan worked...

The thoughts that swarmed her mind brought Alezya to tears, and she couldn't stop them. Kassein noticed right away; he put the water on the bedside table and rushed to her side with a concerned expression, already scanning her for injuries. She let his hands hold hers, marveling again at the difference. His hands were bigger, rougher, darker. And they had become one of her favorite things in the world.

"Kassein," she whispered.

"Alezya?"

"*Kiss me,*" she asked.

He frowned, but of course, he obeyed, pressing a gentle, long kiss against her lips, before pulling back a bit, still unsure about her tears.

"*Touch me,*" she continued. "*Kiss me again. Like me.*"

"*I like you,*" he said, caressing her cheek.

"*No,*" she shook her head, bringing her teary eyes to his. "*More. I need... more. I need you. All of you.*"

"*Alezya...*"

"*Please,*" she croaked before he could stop her, pressing her forehead against his, her hands on his torso. "*Please, Kassein.*"

He must have felt that something was different because this time, he didn't try to distract her. He stared at her, his green eyes worried and confused, his hand cupping her cheek.

"*...Habi ti,*" he whispered.

"*What?*" Alezya frowned at the new word.

"*Haishun, Alezya,*" he repeated, gently pressing her hand to move it against his beating heart. "*Only Alezya. My amari. I habi you.*"

"*I don't understand,*" she cried, her heart choking. "*What does that mean? Kassein, I–*"

"*You,*" he whispered, pressing their foreheads together again. "*You. My amari. Only you.*"

He didn't explain, but he was showing her.

He cut off her words with another kiss, his hand cupping her cheek again. The other moved to her dress and pushed her up his lap. Alezya's stomach made a loop as she straddled him across the bed. She could feel him, his body aching for her. Something felt different that night. Perhaps it was her heart, and perhaps it was him.

As if he'd read her mind, he dropped his usual cautiousness, letting her take the reins. Alezya kissed him eagerly, trying to put all the passion she could into this. She got rid of her dress and pressed her naked body against his torso, her skin against his skin. The air was getting hot and heavy around them, but neither cared. Kassein was hotter, his kisses were hotter, and Alezya couldn't get enough.

"I love you," she whispered in her native language. "I don't want to leave you, I'll never forget you."

Weak tears kept escaping her eyes, and Kassein kept wiping them off, kissing her cheeks, caressing every inch of her body as if his hands were molding her curves. Alezya's hands dropped to his pants, and this time, he didn't stop her.

With tenser movement than usual, he took it all off, getting naked impressively fast for a man who'd acted so shy before... and Alezya couldn't hold back that gasp. She should have expected so, but he was big. Big, and hard, and aching for her already. He must have felt her hesitation or nervousness because Kassein gently pulled her chin up to gaze into her eyes while his other hand ventured between her legs, caressing her, his fingers touching her and assessing how wet and ready she was.

"*You fine?*" he whispered against her lips.

Alezya knew he would stop. She had that belief anchored in her heart: if she asked him, he would stop without hesitation, without her having to beg and cry for it. The monster that had been her husband had never stopped or slowed down. He'd ignored her pleas, her pain, and her tears and taken what was "rightfully his" every time.

Kassein was bigger and stronger, and yet she wasn't afraid of him at all; no, she wanted this. She desired Kassein, his hands, his gazes, his hot skin, his warm kisses. She wanted it all.

For one night, he was all hers.

And that was all she wanted for her last time.

Chapter 12

Something felt different about Alezya tonight.

Kassein couldn't stand the sight of her tears or how her body was faintly trembling in his arms. He wasn't even sure if she herself knew how fragile she seemed.

When he had seen her running for her life earlier, about to be attacked by that scum, his blood had fired up like never before. His dragon had been faster to attack, but given the chance, Kassein would have torn that criminal to shreds with his bare hands himself.

It was his fault. Kiera had noted the oversight; they knew one of them had escaped, yet he had been careless and left Alezya on her own in the camp. He should have never left her alone.

Now, he had been seconds away from losing her, and he knew he wouldn't have been able to survive that. Not now, not when she was already carved so deep into his bones, taking all the space in his head, imprinted on his skin. Not when he couldn't have a single hour without his thoughts drifting to her, not when his hands begged to be touching her every minute, every second.

That woman was his new religion, and he worshiped every inch of her. She was beautiful, strong but fragile, mysterious, and yet so expressive. He could read her eyes better than her lips, those black eyes of hers always carrying so much more than mere words.

He was trying to function like a normal man, to stick to his duty, to hide his agony, but he could never get enough of her. Every time she let him touch her, he felt like a man on sacred ground, begging for any moment she would bless him with her presence, her touch, her kisses.

Kiera made fun of how taken he was, but there was nothing he could deny; Alezya had completely bewitched him, and his sister could tease him all she wanted. He wasn't sorry for it.

He wanted her so badly; every kiss felt like heaven and hell, a maddening ache between torment and pleasure. He'd tried to resist. He had tried to leash his desire, to be patient, to be strong.

He knew Alezya had gone through hell, and he knew she had a past that had scarred her deeply, deeper than he could ever know.

He knew there was a child. Or there had been one.

Lorey had warned him, and now, the truth had come to slap him in the face. He knew what a woman's breasts being full meant, and he had seen women nurse before. There was no denying it anymore, and if he knew Alezya had a child, he also had to swallow the fact that there was another man. Her child's father.

If so, where was he? Why wasn't he with her? Why had he let her come to any harm at all? Was he dead? Was he missing? Did she miss him?

"Kassein."

Alezya's raspy, needy voice snapped him back to the present. It didn't matter that there was another man. It didn't matter how many other men there were.

Right now, Alezya was his, all his, and she wanted him. And when a goddess summoned a man, all he could do was get on his knees and worship. And Kassein did.

He caressed her, his hands cupping her perfect curves, following every line of her body, enjoying the coolness of her skin. She was naked on him, straddling him, and he just loved looking up to see her eyes riveted on him, deep and dark like the night sky. Her hair, which she'd kept braided all day, fell in raven waves around them as he pulled the tie off with a finger, embalming the air with that intoxicating smell of hers.

Her entire body was a marvel to look at. The almost subtle white marks on her thighs, belly, and breasts were like the stripes of a beast, scars showing how strong that woman was. Her body was a marvel, and he wanted to learn it all by heart, carve it into his memory.

Kassein just knew that he would never, ever get to witness anything more beautiful than this.

"You're so beautiful," he whispered against her skin as he spread kisses on her collarbone, neck, chest. "You're so beautiful, my moonlight."

He didn't care that she didn't understand; the moon and sun never bothered with the humans who worshiped them, and he didn't need her to acknowledge his overflowing love either.

She was there, she was abandoning herself in his arms, and he felt like that was all he'd ever need for the rest of his life.

Kassein had never been a greedy man, but all of a sudden, he found himself ready to conquer continents and fight armies for one more minute with this woman.

His lips kept devouring her skin like an addict looking for relief that would never come. He kissed every inch of her skin, and as he sucked, nibbled, and kissed some more, her skin was getting peppered with blossoming imprints, all shades of pink and red, ephemeral proof he had been there.

Alezya was panting above him, her body moving softly against his fingers, her hands holding onto his nape and shoulders. She was wet, so deliciously wet, he didn't want to stop playing with her. He loved the sounds she made every time he moved his fingers.

He'd never been a man to enjoy music, but her body was an instrument he wanted to play forever. His thumb on her clit made her whine, while his index and middle fingers coupled thrusting inside had her voice make a sexy, deep, and throaty rasp.

There was something addictive about knowing how to bring pleasure to this woman, and Kassein never wanted to stop; just watching her was almost enough to trigger his own release.

"Kassein," she gasped again.

He smiled against her lips, kissing her again, pressing his tongue against her mouth and feeling hers.

His Dragon Blood heightened his senses and intensified sensations, and at times, he knew he could be rough with his hands, his kisses, but Alezya never seemed to care. That woman didn't want him to hold back, and she wasn't afraid of the beast he'd been holding back all this time.

He was scared she had no idea how much self-restraint he'd exercised, and he was scared she wasn't ready for it, but right now, he could almost hear the chains snapping.

Her hand drifted to his cock, and this time, he didn't stop her. A grunt escaped his chest when she stroked him, her hand palming his length, and he almost bit her shoulder when she squeezed him slightly.

"Alezya," he grunted against her shoulder.

The fearless woman was gripping his length, making him groan and pulling on the last bits of his self-restraint. In response, his fingers accelerated inside her, drawing full-on moans with that perfect voice of hers.

"Kassein," she whispered, calling him to attention.

His fingers stopped, and she grabbed his wrist to push it away.

He shouldn't have stopped. His fingers were thick already, but his cock... His size was already worrisome enough, but if he lost his self-restraint on her, if he hurt her...

As if she could read his mind, she gave him a gentle, sweet smile and lowered her lips to his again.

Her kiss was slow but confident, almost reassuring. Alezya was taking control, and he was beseeched to surrender. He did; he let her slowly fall seated on him, and when she pressed his tip at her entrance, it took every bit of restraint not to impale her.

Instead, he focused on kissing her, eagerly, desperately, while letting her slowly lower herself, take him further in, expanding his world and wrecking it at the same time. It was beyond words. Kassein felt her hoarse moans, her tightness around him, her warmth, and every quiver of her body while she took him in, inch by inch.

That woman was brave, bold, and beautiful beyond everything. He felt his gut clench while she sat completely on him with a loud moan, his full length inside of her, and in that moment, it just felt... perfect. This was everything. Everything he wanted, everything he could have hoped for. Just him and her, united as one perfect fit.

"Are you alright?" his hoarse voice asked her.

Alezya nodded, leaning forward to take his lips again.

Kassein grabbed a fistful of her hair, pressing her against his lips, just as she rocked her body against his. He groaned, unable to hold it.

Alezya kept moving up and down on his cock, making them both groan, breathe hard, and hold on tighter to each other.

Kassein forced himself to keep his fist around her hair and his free hand caressing the curve of her back because otherwise, he knew he would just grab her hips and pound her, hard.

Alezya's voice was already enough to push him to just this side of crazy with her throaty moans and hitched breathing.

He kissed her neck and licked her skin, keeping himself busy with his lips on her, but there was no ignoring the mind-shattering sensations that came from thrusting inside that woman. How could one ever get enough of this?

She kept squeezing his length, taking him deep inside again and again, rewiring every cell in his body to yearn for her. His inner beast was suffocating by now, driven insane by desire, more desire. It was like having just a bite when he was aching to devour the whole thing. Those thrusts were so much, and yet, he wanted more. He needed more. He needed to bury himself deep in her, fast, hard, relentlessly.

Kassein bit his lip, and suddenly, he pounded his hips hard, upward, just once. Alezya cried out, and it didn't sound like pain. More like surprise, pleasure, awe. It was just once, just one second, but he was burning to do it again.

«Kassein,» Alezya cried. «Kassein. Kassein...»

She stopped moving on him, submitting the man to torture, but she grabbed his wrists and moved his hands to her hips as if she'd read his mind.

He lifted his eyes to hers, out of breath, mouth dry, and Alezya pressed one kiss against his lips.

"You," she muttered. "I want you, Kassein."

Even if he hadn't understood her words, her eyes spoke for her. Eager, pleading, almost begging, with those hints of tears...

This time, he snapped. No more restraint. Kassein let a proper growl erupt from his chest, and he grabbed a fistful of her hair, crashing her lips against his as she moaned helplessly.

Then, he toppled her over and barely took a second to adjust himself between her thighs before he pounded into her, hard.

Alezya let out a full-on wail and held onto his shoulders and neck for dear life. He pulled out almost completely, and then he gave another deep thrust. She cried deliciously under him, taking all his might like the brave goddess she was, even giving him another nod when he checked on her with a single glance.

And so he kept going, pounding, taking, thrusting with the hunger of a beast starved for years. He didn't need to think, his hips moved fast and hard, his ass flexing with each thrust, his legs rocking their bodies in a jerky rhythm, rough and brutal.

His elbows were needed to hold his weight above her, but his hands couldn't get enough of her either; he kept a fistful of her silky locks between his fingers, his other hand caressing up and down her body, holding her hips for a better angle.

His mouth was just as restless as his loins; grabbing her lips every now and then, but most importantly, he trailed along the lines of her neck, her collarbone, kissing and sucking every inch of skin he could like he'd die if he missed one.

Alezya's breathing and loud moans were filling the tent, in canon with the slapping of flesh, his grunts, and the creaking of the bed. It was relentless, it couldn't end, and a strong smell filled the air; it smelled like mating, sweat, and everything he loved about her. She didn't ask him to stop, she didn't push him to slow down. She took it all like a goddess, like she was made for him, like she was the one he'd been waiting for...

He accelerated, his grunts loud, her moans louder, again, and again, his hand finding her sensitive button, because he wanted her there too when he reached that peak, that brutal explosion of senses.

He jerked once, twice, and emptied himself with a long groan of relief, just as Alezya's body trembled, her voice muted, her eyes rolled back. It lasted seconds, perhaps a minute, until they both came back down, out of breath, in a strange daze. Their eyes met, and after a second, they smiled at each other, with a long, loving gaze that didn't need words.

Then, Kassein kissed her, gently, softly, before pulling out, Alezya shivering at the sensation.

"...Are you alright?" he whispered, peppering gentle kisses on her flushed skin.

She gave him a faint nod, although she was visibly spent. Her eyes were half closed, and if it weren't for her fingers lazily stroking his back, he might have wondered if she was asleep.

Kassein leaned on his elbow by her side, watching this woman in reverent awe. She was beautiful beyond words. She was completely naked against the fur blankets, except for that little necklace she'd been wearing, her hair splayed around her like dark ink, her lips wet and swollen, and her entire body was covered in his red marks like scattered petals. It was a vision dreams were made of, and she was real, all his, breathing under him and smelling like him.

He leaned against her, pressing a kiss against her forehead, caressing her hair away from her face.

"Thirsty?" he asked.

"I'm hot," she nodded with a chuckle.

Kassein smiled and gave her another kiss before he got off the bed, unbothered about standing naked in his tent. Quickly, he poured her some water and prepared a cloth to wipe them both.

Not only were they both covered in sweat from the exercise, but his seed was dripping from between Alezya's legs, and while some part of him felt a bit of pride in that, it couldn't be comfortable for her. Thus, he cleaned them both while she slowly sipped the water. Both of them were quiet, merely exchanging gentle kisses, lingering touches, and faint smiles.

When he came back to lie down with her, she nestled against his shoulder, neither of them bothering with the cover; it was far too hot in there. They didn't speak; there was no need for one language or the other.

Kassein felt more relaxed than he had felt in... a very long time.

For once, maybe for the first time, he felt like he was in a place he belonged, and that was by this woman's side. He knew his father's dragon had always known his mother would be his. He knew his older sister had fallen for her partner on sight, and so did his second older brother. Were dragons meant to mate for life? He didn't know if it was true, but every instinct he had yearned for that woman to remain by his side. Nothing else mattered.

As he felt her breathing slow down next to him, he trailed his finger along her spine softly, taking in every inch of her beauty. She was tired, but she still shifted in her sleep to cover one of his legs with hers, nestling her cheek against his shoulder and making him smile.

Aware his body heat wouldn't be enough for her through the night, Kassein pulled a fur blanket over her, but he couldn't find sleep. The adrenaline from their passionate lovemaking was keeping him far too awake.

It had just happened, and yet he wanted to replay that memory over and over in his head to keep every detail fresh. He had a faint smile on his face, something few people had witnessed in recent years. He was content, with everything he desired breathing against his shoulder.

He stole another glance down at Alezya. She was deep asleep, rightfully exhausted. He would have gone for a second and maybe third round, but the young woman definitely wouldn't have been able to endure that. Kassein brought her hand to his lips, kissing her fingers, but she was far too exhausted to feel it.

This experience had been... mind-blowing.

He'd never been with a woman before. It wasn't a secret, merely a fact. He had never found someone he had wanted to satisfy his teenage curiosity with, and when one grew up with a large number of siblings and a status that put him above everyone else, it was hard to look for partners.

Kassein had always followed his family until he had felt like too much of a third wheel with his parents and too useless to his older siblings. His teenagehood had been mostly spent trying to convince his older brother he wasn't just the "Wild Prince" everyone called him because of his mad dragon, to no avail. He had reached the age of eighteen with no other will than to find somewhere he would belong, and he had never found it until now.

He had been mad beyond words when his brother had exiled him to the north, yet now, he found himself grateful. What would have happened to Alezya if he hadn't been in the north? If Kein hadn't been prowling the area? If he hadn't pushed his army to set camp so far…?

Kassein let out another sigh. Perhaps he would never get his brother's approval, and perhaps he'd reached a point where he didn't care for it anymore.

He and Kassian were only close in name. That was it. It was almost ironic how the two children who had been named in the tradition, after their parents' own names, couldn't see eye to eye. His siblings had been named after ancestors and dead relatives, but Kassian and Kassein were the ones meant to be a testament to their parents' love: Kairen and Cassandra.

Sometimes, he hated how he could never escape the comparison with his older brother when they couldn't have been more different, born fourteen years apart with nothing to share. If he had his own struggles, Kassian had never shared them. His oldest brother was the perfect son, the one destined to be Emperor, the golden first child. Kassein was the second-to-last child, forgettable if not for the chaos in his wake, a disappointment when there had been no expectations.

And yet, he had finally found the peace he'd always yearned for, with one fateful meeting with a woman. The dragon that had been trying to kill him for so many years was now peacefully snoring outside.

While he was still at war with the rest of the world, Kassein was finally at peace with himself. And for one evening, that was more than enough to qualify as happiness.

He stayed awake for most of the night, his eyes remaining open in the darkness while he listened to Alezya's breathing. That woman slept like she had years of sleep to catch up on. She barely even moved at all, except for instinctively getting closer to the main source of heat, Kassein.

When the sun rose, however, he knew he would have to get up, or else his sister was likely to come and fetch him herself as he'd promised to train with her. Kassein extracted himself from the bed slowly and almost unwillingly, keeping an eye on Alezya's sleeping figure at all times while he got dressed. He couldn't get enough of how beautiful that woman was.

He couldn't even remember moving, his body drawn toward the bed again, where he gently pulled the blankets over her body and pressed his lips against her bare shoulder before he covered it.

"Kassein?" she stirred with that dreamy voice.

"Go back to sleep, my moonlight. I'll be back later."

"What does that mean? That word you called me…"

She sounded tired, and she wasn't even opening her eyes, her breathing still slow. Kassein smiled and pressed his lips against her temple this time.

"I'll tell you later," he whispered against her ear.

If she heard that, Alezya showed no sign she did.

It was more likely she'd fallen back asleep, tired as she was. Still, Kassein lingered over her for a couple more seconds, taking in the sight of that woman's sleeping figure under the gentle sunrise until he really had to leave.

Leaving his tent and the woman in it had taken superhuman effort, even for a prince with Dragon Blood flowing through his veins.

Kassein stood outside, basking in the sunlight for a few seconds, taking in deep breaths of icy wind. The previous night had felt like a rebirth, a new world of possibilities opening under his feet.

Now, he didn't simply want Alezya; he needed her. He needed that woman like most men needed air and water. Some part of him was already thinking about the next time he would get to see her, to touch her, to smell her, like this was his new way of measuring time.

Finally, Kassein willed himself to move, if only to glance at his orange dragon at the side of the tent. Kein let out a warning growl; his dragon didn't appreciate being bothered during its slumber and barely lifted its head from its curled position, eyeing Kassein with a nasty silver-colored glare.

"Watch her," Kassein hissed.

His dragon growled back, and finally, the young Prince left to meet his sister.

It was early in the camp, but men were already working, carefully avoiding his path, scattering like scared rats as he approached. Kassein didn't care much for his men at the moment, but he did glare around, looking for the smallest signs of insubordination. He wasn't afraid to spill blood if that was what it took for them to behave.

Eventually, he crossed paths with Tievin, who was already glaring at the snow like the fresh new layer was personally offending him.

"Your Highness," Tievin half-yawned. "Good day. There are quite a few matters that require your attention regarding the camp, if you have a minute. I've received numerous reports from the generals about sightings of the tribespeople, well, male ones, really, in the mountains."

"Kiera mentioned it too," Kassein spat.

Tievin stopped walking for a second, visibly taken aback.

Kassein's usual replies were dismissive at best, and grunts if he was in a bad mood. His sudden interest in the matter threw Tievin for a loop that had him blinking numerous times before he realized the Prince was now paces ahead. He ran to catch up, tripping over his long coat a couple of times, and cleared his throat despite how out of breath the exercise had made him.

"W-well, this is most unusual," Tievin fumbled. "According to my notes, at least five different tribes seemed to have launched attempts to attack us, which leads me to think something is happening. A-according to my predecessors' notes, there are also multiple accounts of such unreasonable attempts being more frequent in a regular pattern."

"A regular pattern?" Kassein frowned with a questioning look.

Tievin's jaw dropped again.

He had never managed to get the Commander in Chief this interested in any matter related to the camp before. He would usually delegate to the generals or tell Tievin to "deal with it."

The truth was, ever since his father, the War God Kairen, had stepped away from leading this camp, most things had been overseen by the generals sent here or, every now and then, some Grand Intendant like himself who merely relayed orders.

Kassein hadn't been much more willing; he fought, killed, and did what had to be done, not out of a sense of duty or interest in the position forced on him, but more so to distract himself. His brother had sent him here, and ever since, the Commander in Chief had been in self-imposed exile. For him to actually show an inkling of interest was a first.

Thus, Tievin found himself tripping over his coat again before catching up and straightening in his layers of fur.

"Yes, sir," he said with a higher-pitched voice than necessary. "I-I-I may have, and I mean, I *have* been taking most arduous notes and asking the most ancient soldiers here, and it does seem that those attacks become much more frequent ahead of full moons. The records of the previous intendants are quite ill-managed and show an obvious lack of accuracy and thoroughness, but nevertheless, I am willing to consider them fairly reliable when it comes to the attacks over the years..."

This time, Kassein was the one to stop and glance up at the mountains with a confused frown.

"The full moon?"

"Yes, Your Highness," Tievin managed to say, catching his breath as he spoke. "Full moons. There is nothing else of significance happening in the Empire on full moons except for the odd festival, but I'm assuming they might be of a particular importance to the tribespeople. Our records show them being interdependent as much as they seem to fight, so various tribes trying to attack us ahead of any specific event might be some kind of rite on their side. Quite the foolish one, I dare say, but it must be important if so many would risk their lives to make a scratch on our army. A lot more of them are sighted in the heights ahead of the full moons too. A significant increase compared to the usual, according to my own observations since we have been here as well as my most thorough predecessors..."

Kassein didn't like the sound of that.

The more he got to know Alezya, the more it was starting to dawn on him that the tribes had been an itch the Empire had never bothered to scratch. The Northern Mountains belonged to the Empire, according to every map he'd been shown as a child. The east had been split off as the Eastern Kingdom his sister and her husband reigned over, and the west contained miles and miles of unexplored lands Kiera and her partner loved to roam, only to report more tribes living there just like the one their mother was from.

But what about the mountains? When was the last time someone from the Empire had tried or been given a chance to learn their language? When had they last tried to climb those mountains and meet those people? Kassein had memories of him and his brothers riding dragons above those mountains. That was it. Alezya's home had never been more than a child's playground, a landscape at the end of the continent.

And now, there was something he didn't like about that, something in his gut that refused to settle.

"...When is the next one?" he asked Tievin, his green eyes scouring the mountains, trying to spot one of the tribespeople himself.

"The next full moon?" Tievin coughed. "W-well, it should start tomorrow night, sir."

Tomorrow night. What was this sense of foreboding that washed over Kassein?

He had been in the north for countless full moons before, so why did this one feel ominous? Was it because of Alezya? Was her presence pushing him to question the Northern tribes more than usual? Was the full moon important to her too? Was she familiar with the rites the tribes seemed to practice? It was more likely than not, although tribeswomen were never spotted before...

"...Capture them."

Tievin blinked, doubting his own ears.

"Your–I mean, Commander? Di-did you just say...?"

"I said capture them," Kassein repeated, his eyes still riveted on the mountains. "The next ones who attack, I want as many of them as possible made prisoners."

"May I ask why, Commander?" Tievin frowned. "I mean, we do have structures for retaining prisoners, but this is most..."

Kassein wasn't quite sure why he had given that order either. At least, not yet. He had the beginning of an idea, something that looked like it might later sprout into some bigger plan.

They had killed tribesmen for decades, centuries perhaps, without trying to interact with them. If he believed the tales he'd been told, his ancestors had tried, but the tribesmen had been set on trying to kill anyone from the Dragon Empire. They had never been capable of having any kind of dialogue due to generations-old hatred and a language barrier that stood like a wall between their civilizations... but Alezya was proof that things could change. That communication was possible, and perhaps, one woman had set the first stone to pave a very different future.

Kassian had exiled him to do some impossible task, Kassein had always been sure of it. ...*What if it wasn't?*

He had never cared about satisfying his brother's demand or proving him wrong. Kassein cared a lot more about the woman sleeping in his tent and what kind of future could lie ahead.

Would she be capable of loving a man who had murdered dozens of her people? Would she one day miss her tribe and go back? Would this desolate place ever be enough for her?

Kassein owned nothing but a mad dragon, but he stood, wishing to offer that woman the world. He didn't care for his brother's throne or his Empire, but Alezya deserved everything. He wanted to give her all that he had, everything she needed, anything she wanted.

"Commander?"

He ignored Tievin's questioning and resumed walking.

He was still due to meet his sister, but now, he didn't care about training. Instead, as soon as he found her in one of the clearings they had been using to train on the sunny days, he walked up to her with determination.

"Did a dragon take a dump in your boots?" she scoffed at his frown.

"I want to negotiate."

"I usually take a bribe first."

"With the barbarians."

His sister's smile dropped, and she glanced toward Lorey.

As usual, her companion was nearby, and she had been seated on Kiki's long body like it was a tree trunk, drinking from a cup. But now, her surprised expression was on Kassein.

A few seconds of silence passed, only interrupted by Tievin's loud panting. Lorey gave him a brief look, but it was Kiera who closed her mouth, blinked, and then reopened it first.

"Say what?" she spat. "With the Northern tribes? The ones who have been a pain in our Imperial Butts for generations?"

"...Is this because of Alezya?" Lorey guessed first.

Kassein gave her a short but firm nod. Meanwhile, his sister rolled her eyes back hard.

"Men in this family, I swear... Kassein, this is *madness*. Even for you. The Northern tribes don't give two dragon shits about listening to us, remember? Every previous attempt has been greeted by spikes. They'd probably enjoy dragon steak for dinner every night if they could!"

Her dragon rose its head next to Lorey and growled in warning.

"They couldn't... listen to us before," Lorey remarked. "We couldn't understand their language, nor could they understand ours. Alezya might be the first woman in centuries to learn."

"You know this isn't just about *language*," Kiera scoffed. "We have met many Western tribes, and most of them didn't welcome us with weapons or try to kill our people thousands of times. Look at what they can do to one of their own and a woman at that! How do you think they'll react to your big boots and your stupid-sized dragon?"

"Most of the Western tribes we met were intimidated enough by Kiki not to," Lorey noted, petting the dragon's head, "and they didn't have instances of meeting one before. It is easier to establish trust upon a first meeting than it is after centuries of fighting. The Northern tribes rightfully fear the people of the Empire. Your father and the previous owners of the Onyx Castle either let their dragon hunt there, killed them for sport, or ignored them. You cannot blame those tribes for being terrified and distrustful."

"But to have Kassein, of all people, try to establish a rapport?" Kiera said. "Kassein, even *our* people call you the Wild Prince. A Wild Prince who owns a damn mad dragon, to boot. And you'd be crowned King of Chaos and Destruction too if Darsan hadn't claimed that title for himself for an entire decade prior!"

"Kiera," Lorey called with an annoyed tone.

"You know I'm right! I've never been one to coddle my younger brother, and I won't now. Kassein, just because one woman was blind enough to fall for your moody charm and tight ass doesn't mean the tribes will be willing to let you set foot on their wretched mountains unscathed. These people want you dead and your dragon's ass on a skewer!"

"They can't kill me," Kassein stated.

"I know that, smart ass," his sister rolled her eyes again, "but it doesn't mean the tribes will be willing to let you march up their land, sit down, and break bread together!"

"...Maybe not *all* of the tribes," Tievin mumbled.

Three heads whipped toward him with interest. He cleared his throat, visibly uneasy, and took a step forward before realizing it brought him closer to Kiki, and took two steps to the side instead. Then, he tightened his coat around him, his eyes going down to his notes.

"What was that?" Kiera squinted her green eyes.

"Do you have an idea, Tievin?" Lorey asked more softly.

"I-I wouldn't call it an idea," Tievin admitted, "but I did... have some... *observations* regarding the tribes that I think may contribute to the Commander's idea."

"What observations?" Kassein asked before his sister could speak.

Tievin blinked at him as if he couldn't believe he'd heard that, and then, his eyes drifted back to his notes. He flipped through the pages, cleared his throat, put a hand on it, and then flipped through the pages again before he took a deep breath.

"My personal records show nine different potential tribes having interacted with us ever since we were first sent here," he suddenly spat out, talking fast. "Based on their diverse appearances, outfits, demeanor, weapons, tattoos, hairstyles, and other similar external signs, I believe that the tribes living in the mountains have significant distinctions between them, indicating they have evolved to live in rather secluded tribes that only interact based on necessity. This would be quite surprising given the limited resources and geographical territory they share, but I believe that there are rivalries that keep them from being a unified front and meshing together like many tribes living in the same area for centuries should normally have. This could be the result of notable differences in opinion, lifestyle, and beliefs. I did ask around the oldest residents of this camp as well as corroborated their testimonies with the records of my predecessors, and there is indeed a surprising amount of evidence that the-that *this* camp, and the North Army in general, has been attacked by the same tribes over the centuries, while other tribes that had been recorded have never attacked but only been spy-I mean, observing us. Before Your Highn-I mean, the Commander pushed the North Army to the foot of the mountains, it was much easier to record which tribes would come down to fight, and once again, tribes who engaged in fights with our troops were not necessarily the same ones that were found spying. Whether the tribes have significantly different goals toward the Empire or some of the tribes do not have the numbers to attack us is hard to determine. What I do believe, however, is that the tribes have always shown an undeniable interest in the Empire, and while we do have numerous records of scuffles between our troops and their people, the evidence we have does not corroborate with Princess Kiera's statement that *all* of the tribes would want you dead... potentially."

A long, stunned silence followed his words, which caused Tievin to try to shrink in his coat and his cheeks and nose to turn crimson. Eventually, Kiera let out an amused grunt.

"Ha!" she scoffed. "I always wondered what you *were* doing here."

"Being the North Camp's Grand Intendant includes many tasks, Princess Kiera," Tievin gave her an exasperated sigh.

"Guess all that paperwork and scribbling you do does have some use..."

"It's... It's amazing news, Tievin," Lorey said. "It means some of the tribes might be up to negotiations with the North Army, that's... that would be historical for the Empire. How come we've never explored that option before?"

Tievin glanced briefly toward Kassein.

"If I dare to make any conjectures, Lady Lorey, I would say that it is most unlikely that any of the North Army leaders have ever been very... *open* to suggestions," he mumbled. "...Until now."

Lorey bit down a smile while the siblings looked at each other; fair enough, whoever had been sent here before had probably never shown much interest in befriending the other side until Kassein.

"Anything else we need to know?" Kiera asked after a sigh. "Now that we're open to suggestions and bad ideas, apparently?"

Lorey gave her a scowl, but Tievin only let out a faint sigh.

"I personally believe His High-I mean, the Commander's idea might have higher chances of succeeding than we anticipate," he said. "Thanks to his predecessors and the hard work of many grand intendants before myself, we have a fairly accurate map of the Northern Mountains. Based on that map, the observations that have been made so far, and the current information I have collected on the tribes that have been spotted and interacted with, I have come to the conclusion that the Northern Mountains hold many more tribes than those the North Army has been interacting with for the past couple of centuries."

"...More tribes?" Kiera frowned. "We already knew that, didn't we?"

"It is the logical conclusion anyone who's taken a look at these mountains should have, yes," Tievin replied with a slightly annoyed tone, "but that also means that the tribes that had a number of negative interactions with the Empire in the past only represent a fraction of the Northern tribes. In other words, as Lady Lorey brought up earlier, there are some Northern tribes with which our people could potentially have a clean slate. Naturally, we should suspect that they will have an ill perception of our people if they have heard about us from the tribes that antagonize us or received some significant threat from our side..."

"Some significant threat?" Kiera frowned in confusion.

Tievin raised an eyebrow, and then, slowly, his hand emerged from his too-long fur sleeve to point a long finger toward Kiki. The dark gray dragon under Lorey was presently busy playing with a tree trunk, tearing it apart with joy like it was some toy.

"Oh," Kiera grunted. "Yeah, right... Well, fair enough..."

"We know the Northern tribes are terrified of the Empire's dragons," Lorey sighed. "Rightfully so. But that might not deter them from establishing some discussion with us, especially if Tievin's right and the tribes do not all get along. Strategically, some of them would likely benefit a lot from any kind of rapport with the Empire. We could trade resources, guarantee them safety from the dragons..."

"We could do that?" Kiera raised an eyebrow, turning toward her brother. "I don't mean the resource part. I don't think anyone's safe from Kein, except for one lady."

Kassein didn't answer. Kein had been under control for the past couple weeks, but that felt nothing short of a miracle, and it was all due to one woman indeed. If anything happened to Alezya, he couldn't guarantee his dragon wouldn't go back to its usual madness and murder any human it felt like. He let out a heavy sigh, but pushed that issue aside for now; Alezya was here, sleeping peacefully in his tent and under the orange dragon's guard, and that would be enough for now.

"Anything else?" he asked Tievin, ignoring his sister again.

This time, his Intendant hesitated, glancing at his notes, pressing his lips together and squirming under all his layers.

"Tievin," Kassein growled.

"W-well," Tievin swallowed. "We might need to uh... consider that Your High— I mean, the Commander in Chief of the North Army does not, strictly, have the authority to establish such a... an alliance...?"

Kassein's eyes darkened, prompting his Intendant to look down.

"I-I mean this from a t-tactical point of view," Tievin squeaked. "Establishing p-proper rapport with the Northern tribes would include a considerable amount of time, resources, and manpower to make the... the suggested trades happen.

The mere coordination of resources coming from the nearest village to here is already quite the task given how far the army is located compared to the past. The Onyx Castle itself is at a notable distance, and if we were to establish long-term relationships, we would have to consider many factors as well..."

"The north is too deserted," Lorey muttered. "...It's true. I mean, we've already seen it. It takes a while for anything to reach this camp, and you have to self-supply as much as you can because of how long anything takes to arrive, less we use one of the dragons. The villages surrounding the Onyx Castle aren't doing too well either; they're too far from the center of the Empire and the Capital itself. The Empire has lost interest in the north. The Emperor has established a great relationship with the Eastern Kingdom since Queen Cessilia's wedding, and there are already countless tribes the Empire has been establishing rapport with in the west since Empress Shareen began abolishing the slavery laws, but the north has been... left behind."

Kassein knew it all too well.

The north prospered for a short while during his childhood, when his parents lived there, and the presence of the War God as the unofficial local lord allowed trade to bloom. His family had brought the wealth the north needed to thrive, but now, things were different.

The Onyx Castle had been deserted for a few years, ever since most of his now grown siblings had scattered in the south, and his father had had enough of sharing their mother with the Capital; now, his parents resided mostly in the Diamond Castle, their paternal grandmother's residence, using her old age as an excuse to stay in one of the most beautiful places of the Kingdom.

Kassian had sent him to the north because there was no better place to exile a prince; it was as desolate as it was in need of a local ruler. Upon his first days of exile, even with the little interest he had in his brother's order, Kassein had definitely noticed how the north had decayed since his childhood. The Onyx Castle was abandoned, the staff had left, and the nearby villages had thinned and most likely lost a bunch of their residents to the south as well.

Tievin's words ignited something in Kassein's mind. Something he had never thought of or desired before. Something he wouldn't have ever dreamt of wanting, but... Alezya had changed everything.

He took a step to turn and glance around the camp. This was the north: a bunch of tents braving heavy snowfalls every day, ragged soldiers, and criminals living out their sentences. Miles and miles of forest full of prey and large mountains full of strangers. A few miles from there, there were villages, the Onyx Castle, and the first paths that led to the rest of the Empire. Long roads he knew the locals seldom took; the journey was too long, and the resources were all readily available in the area already.

The north was poor and harsh, but it was resilient. In fact, it was very different from the rest of the Empire, which was hot, dry, and wealthy. The north was forgotten, cold, and gaunt, but it was also resourceful, enduring, and independent. It was... waiting for a change.

"Kassein?" his sister called.

Kassein was already walking away, turning his back to the other three and heading into the forest. For once, he wasn't going to hunt but just to get away from it all, to think.

He had always been one to need time to think alone. If it had been possible, he would have taken a ride on the back of his dragon, but Kein was both unwilling and unavailable; the only thing he and his dragon probably agreed on was that Alezya came first.

So he wandered into the forest on his own, picking up on cues about nearby prey on instinct, hearing them run away from him, unaware that, for once, all creatures were safe from him. Kassein was merely walking, looking for the silence he needed to be able to think, for the first time in a long time, about his future.

He had never been one to think about the future too much. He was enough of a disappointment to his family in the present, and his future had never been promising. Where his siblings saw endless possibilities, all he could see was a dark tunnel. Trying to avoid his parents' disappointment, his siblings' concerns, and their people's fear. He was the Wild Prince.

He had been since that fateful night when his dragon had turned mad, and Kassein had spent his teenage years trying everything to get away from Kein's attempts at killing him. His father had kept his dragon bound for a while. His older siblings' dragons had kept Kein in check until he became too big for another dragon to contain. And then, the chaos had ensued.

His fights with Kein had happened everywhere he stood, no matter how far he fled to try and avoid his dragon. The incident felt like a horrible fate that had just been waiting to happen, terrible and unavoidable. There had always been casualties resulting from their fights, but none had been a human life until then. Other dragons had destroyed buildings, burned forests, and ravaged lands. His brother Darsan's dragon had even damaged a mountain and a couple of bridges.

But Kein had caused someone's death, and that was the one crime no one could forgive.

He was the family pariah.

The one disappointment in an otherwise perfect family.

All of his siblings were adored. Kassian, the perfect first son and heir of the Empire. Darsan, the rambunctious second son. Cessilia, the beloved older sister, so kind and graceful. Kiera, the free spirit, always flying toward new lands. Shenan, the young prodigy, always studying and probably set to become a renowned scholar serving the Empire. Sadara, the Imperial beauty, as beautiful as she was witty, adored by all. Sepheus, the elusive youngest child, their mother's favorite surely, always daydreaming.

And then... there was him.

Kassein, the one no one rejoiced to see or even hear he was around because they knew of his mad dragon.

He had never hoped to be more than ignored. The Empire didn't want him, and he realized that was a prevalent truth for a lot of the Northern people. Those who lived in the north were either too stubborn to move south or had been sent here because the Empire didn't want them anywhere else. People who loved this land dearly, and outcasts.

The north was like him: the Empire didn't expect anything from them anymore.

Kassein kept walking, ignoring how long and how far he had gone as his mind was building the foundations of a different future. He had this idea that seemed both insane and... right.

It felt perfectly right for him, for the future, for Alezya, and for his family. He kept thinking about what his sister had said days ago about the Onyx Castle, about their parents' wishes for him, about everything.

He tried to ignore his past to think about the future, a future he had only dared to start fantasizing about recently. Alezya had done that to his flightless life. She had come in like a violent, graceful, blinding ray of moonlight to show him the world that existed alongside him in the darkness. This place. The Onyx Castle. His army. The mountain tribes and the Northerners.

Kassein stopped walking and took a deep breath, closing his eyes for a second before he looked up at the skies through the thick pine trees.

There was nothing but silence surrounding him.

He had ventured deeper than ever before into the forest, where no sound could reach him.

He stood for a while, letting the cold bite his skin, and his thoughts wandered back to the camp, to his tent, where that one woman who had changed everything rested, hopefully still smelling like him. Kassein wouldn't have dared to have the ambition he had now just days ago, but he also didn't have anything to wish for.

Now, every time he thought about Alezya, about her deep eyes, her shy smile, her long raven hair, and her body in his sheets, he choked up a bit. His heart ached because he wanted to offer her the world, and he had nothing. He wanted to be the kind of man who'd provide for her, not some lowlife failure with nothing to his name. That woman was happy with a bit of warmth, some meat in her soup, and his care, but Kassein refused to let her be content with just that. He had already disappointed his mother, his father, and his siblings. He didn't want Alezya to join the long list of people who'd given up on him.

For the first time, he wanted more; he wasn't resigned to his fate anymore. He hadn't felt that kind of hunger in a long time, but now, it just wouldn't go away. He was considering another future, and in other circumstances, he would have been the first one to laugh at the idea.

Yet now, it didn't seem as mad anymore.

He wanted that kind of future for himself and for Alezya. For the north too, for the pariahs like him, for the Onyx Castle that had been abandoned with its memories, and, maybe, to prove his family wrong too.

Kassein spent a while in the forest.

He didn't know how long, but he stayed long enough that when he got out of that forest, his mind was made up for good. There would be no coming back from that decision and no giving up either.

This wasn't just about changing his own future, but that of countless lives as well. His brother was going to be against it. His family might not understand, and he could already hear Kiera saying something about madness. Again, he might prove his infamous title as the Wild Prince right... except that this time, he had a reason for it. That reason was Alezya, and that was everything he needed.

He emerged from the forest, exactly the same as he had been when he'd walked in, but feeling different. Surprisingly, it didn't take him long to find his sister; Kiera hadn't moved, and was pacing at the same clearing they should have been training at that morning. Lorey was gone, but Tievin was still there, seated on a tiny rock and shivering with his arms crossed and swallowed by the layers of fur.

He stood so fast upon seeing Kassein that he almost fell forward before managing to find his equilibrium and running a sleeve to wipe the snot off of his red face.

"C-C-Commander," his teeth kept clicking.

"I told him to wait inside, but he wouldn't," Kiera shrugged at Kassein's frown. "Where the hell have you been? And you come back empty-handed too?"

"I've made my decision."

"Oh," Kiera grimaced. "Spill it. How bad is it? Who's going to die today?"

Tievin's face immediately paled, but Kassein ignored them, turning his eyes toward the mountains.

"...I'll take the north."

His words lingered in the air for a few seconds, during which his sister frowned in confusion, her nose scrunched, while Tievin's mouth opened and closed several times, no sound coming out.

Without waiting for an answer, Kassein suddenly turned around and began walking through the camp. He ordered the first soldiers he saw to summon the generals for an urgent meeting and to relay the information that any tribespeople should be captured from then on, not killed.

The soldiers had just taken off when Kiera and Tievin caught up to him.

"What was that?" Kiera spat. "Take the north? Kassein, wait!"

He finally stopped in his tracks, turning to his sister with an unreadable expression. Kiera shook her head in confusion.

"What the hell? What do you mean you'll *take* the north? What does that mean?"

"The mountains, the Onyx Castle, the North Army, and all the villages.

I'll take it."

"Take it? What the hell do you mean, take it?!" Kiera exploded. "You're saying that like Grandma at the local market picking the fucking jam for her next brunch!"

"M-my lord," Tievin squeaked, a bit out of breath, "Commander, have you considered that... maybe your brother, I mean, His Highness the Emperor, might not be quite keen on the idea...?"

"I'll visit him," Kassein spat, before turning around and resuming walking.

This time, Kiera was the one who almost tripped over herself in the snow.

"What did you just-? Y-you? Visit Kassian? We're talking about Kassian, right? ...By the dragon's balls, did you hit your head in the forest or something? Eat something you shouldn't have? Mom did always say to stop eating random mushrooms..."

"I want a map of the Empire and all the reports you have on the tribes in the meeting tent," Kassein told Tievin.

"When, Comman-"

"Now."

Tievin nodded and ran off, doing his best to walk as fast as he could despite the snow reaching his ankles and his fur coats impairing him.

Meanwhile, Kassein was still walking toward the tent he used to confer with his men since Alezya's arrival, Kiera going ballistic on his heels.

"You've gone mad," she hissed. "You've finally gone mad. Kassian will tell you to fuck right off, Kassein! What do you think you'll accomplish? What even is your big plan here? I know we mentioned the tribes might be willing to listen, but it was a fraction of them! And it could take years to get to them! Those people don't want to negotiate with us; they hate us! And with all due offense, little brother, you're not peace talk material!"

"I'll take as long as is needed to convince them," Kassein retorted. "I plan to stay here. Kassian wanted me to pacify the north, and that's exactly what I intend to do. But you and Tievin were right, I can't be convincing if I have nothing to offer to the tribes. I need to be the real leader of the north, not some castaway pawn of my brother's. Father once ruled the north and made it prosper. I can do it again."

"Alright," Kiera scoffed. "Firstly, I'm going to need the 'you were right' part in writing, and I'm pretty sure Tievin would love to frame a copy of that too. And secondly, what in the dragon is going on with you? You couldn't even be bothered to actually rule this army three hours ago, Kassein! Your last act of authority was when your woman almost got-"

He stopped and turned with a murderous glare toward his sister. Kiera shut her mouth, but only for a brief moment before she returned his glare.

"You know I'm right," she hissed. "Your thick skull might not like to hear it, but it's a sister's job to be honest regardless of your dragon-sized ego, so I'm serving you the honesty fucking buffet, Kassein. You can't go and claim the entire north on a fucking whim. Kassian will laugh in your face and tell you to fuck right back off up here. And I'm not going to watch you drop that dragon dung on his carpet!"

"Good," Kassein retorted, "because I need you to stay here."

"Wha—? Certainly not! I did not agree to become your second or your replacement or whatever!" she shrieked.

"Someone needs to stay in charge and watch the camp while I talk to Kassian."

"You've got generals for that!"

"They can't contain Kein. And I don't trust anyone else with Alezya."

His sister's eyebrows shot up to her hairline before she blinked, twice, visibly stunned.

"You expect me to stay here to babysit your woman? Kassein! And why would I need to contain Kein? How are you going to get to the Capital, it would take weeks without a–oh, fuck no, you are not borrowing *my* dragon!"

Kassein didn't bother to respond.

His sister kept ranting behind him, but he ignored her, convinced he would get Kiera to agree to this later.

For now, he had just reached the larger tent they had been using to gather. The truth was, his generals used to come to his tent for such things, but he had forbidden any males but Tievin to set foot in his personal quarters since the first day he'd brought Alezya in there, so they'd had to relocate to another tent. This one wasn't that much bigger than any other tent in the camp, but no one lived in it, so it had only been used for storage, and it had been little trouble to add a few chairs and a round wooden table, pushing the stocked weapons and resources to the sides.

He stepped inside, pleased to see the generals already standing there, albeit looking confused, almost nervous. It was most likely he had interrupted another meeting they'd held without him, but Kassein didn't care.

"Commander," General Kauser greeted him, a drop of sweat going down his bald head. "What is going on? We were just told you meant to summon us all of a sudden..."

"Trouble with the tribes?" Sazaran hazarded, petting his beard.

"Princess," Herken, the oldest of the three, greeted Kiera as she stepped in after her brother, still glaring fiercely his way.

"You may want to sit for this one, old man," Kiera grinned.

The other two greeted her too, but her words made them considerably more nervous, all eyes going to their Commander in Chief.

Kassein decided not to wait for Tievin to arrive with his map to explain his plan, or more exactly, his decision, to take the north for himself. In a few words, he repeated Tievin's finds, Lorey's suggestions, and how he had decided to finally grant Kassian his wish, although he was going about it in a more selfish way.

None of the generals interrupted him, probably taken aback by how talkative he was all of a sudden, and even more so by the entire ordeal. They only stole glances toward Kiera, who rolled her eyes more than once but didn't interject. He didn't mention Alezya, but surely the generals had heard about the tribeswoman who had been residing in his tent and could guess for themselves how she had influenced his decision.

Kassein had just finished talking when Tievin stumbled in, carrying a rolled map almost as tall as him and a few more of his notes.

"G-Generals," he rasped. "I see the Commander has explained his... marvelous idea already."

He almost laid himself entirely on the table to unroll the large map. General Herken slowly fell into a chair, while the other two's eyes went between the map and Kassein, looking gradually more confused.

"...Are you serious about this, Commander?" Kauser asked. "This is... unlike anything you've done before."

"I'm still thinking he hit his head," Kiera groaned.

"Actually," Tievin cleared his throat, "this idea might be the Commander's best attempt at fulfilling the Emperor's order."

"...Are you rooting for this because if he succeeds, your father might recall you to the Capital?" Kiera squinted her eyes.

"My personal aspirations hold no influence over His Highness' decisions," Tievin whisper-hissed back.

Kiera scoffed and shook her head, crossing her arms before falling into one of the chairs and putting her feet on the table.

"Your Highness," Herken cleared his throat. "I do... appreciate your newfound interest in leading this army, but—"

"Watch your tongue," Kassein hissed, narrowing his eyes in warning.

He was not usually one to get offended easily, but now wasn't the time to let his generals insult him with thinly veiled sarcasm. Kassein was still a prince, the owner of a dragon, and the Commander in Chief of this army. Even Kiera raised an eyebrow at the General, her sullen mood redirected at him. She might not have been fully on board with his idea, but Kassein was her younger sibling, and no one was allowed to disrespect him in her presence.

She took out her little dagger and began playing with it, throwing the weapon in the air and catching it perfectly as an obvious threat.

"I-I mean," Herken cleared his throat, "I understand that Your Highness has a personal interest in obeying the Emperor's order that is fuelling your plan, but this endeavor is... We might be setting the foundations for several years of labor. No one has managed to reach out to those tribes before and establish any kind of communication. I doubt that is what the Emperor—"

"My brother's will is not my goal," Kassein retorted. "He told me to pacify the north. It can be interpreted many ways, but no one can say the tribes have made a scratch on our people since I marched this army all the way to the foot of their mountains. As far as the Empire is concerned, the north is pacified enough. And no one cares what happens north of the Onyx Castle but me."

That was a truth none of them could deny. The three generals exchanged looks, visibly at a loss for words, before Kauser gave a strong nod.

"The Commander's plan might take years, but it also could be a quick affair. Those tribes have been isolated for centuries, they might be eager to establish a rapport with the Empire. Grand Intendant Tievin's hypothesis might turn out to be the solution the Emperor has been waiting for all along."

"I still want to clarify," Sazaran lifted a finger off his crossed arms. "Commander, it sounds like you want more than... to establish rapport with those tribespeople."

Kassein nodded and leaned over the map. He traced a finger all the way from the northernmost tip of the Empire, all the way down to the forest that separated the Onyx Castle from the Diamond Palace, and then crossed another horizontal line from one coast to another.

"This will be mine," he declared.

"Commander, that's—"

"The north has been neglected by the Empire for too long. The Onyx Castle is empty, the Shadelands and its villages are struggling, and the land is full of resources no one has bothered to exploit. Every hunt I've gone on shows that the Northern Forest is full of prey and resources. The land is harsh and the weather harsher, but the locals are used to it. The Empire has no intention of taking back our army nor welcoming anyone moving from the north. The Capital is already overcrowded and trying to send its people east and west to remedy that. The west is full of land waiting to be explored and plenty of places for new villages to appear, while the Eastern Kingdom is more than welcoming of the workforce. No one gives a fuck about the north but us."

The generals all went silent.

They all knew Kassein spoke the truth and were probably even more surprised by how knowledgeable the Prince was about the current state of the Empire.

Kiera's lips curled into a quiet sneer; under his brooding charm, as she called it, her brother had been educated the same as all of the siblings, which is more than most nobles. Their grandmother and mother refused to have young princes and princesses who were ignorant and uneducated about the Empire their family ruled. Kassian wasn't the only one who had been trained from a young age to take over the throne; all eight siblings had shared the same teachers over the years, been taught the basics of politics, and sent to scour the borders of their Empire with their dragons.

Kassein was probably even more knowledgeable, as he had traveled all over during the years, going west to fight in deserted lands with his dragon, east to visit their siblings who had established their families in the Eastern Kingdom, north during their childhood in the Onyx Castle of course, and south when he had followed the family to the Capital.

Kiera might be considered the adventurous one, but she had mostly stuck to the busy streets of the Capital and explored the unfamiliar west; Kassein was the one who had gone everywhere and truly seen all the confines of the Empire outside of the Capital. The fact that her brother had acted so uninterested before had probably pushed his generals to think he was also ignorant.

They couldn't have been more wrong. There was one thing that Kiera had to admit, and it was that when he put his mind to it, Kassein could be one hell of a leader. He was also the one that their mother had declared to be the most like their father, the War God, and Kiera had to agree; whether they liked it or not, Kassein was more than fit to inherit the Onyx Castle and take over the north.

"Commander," Sazaran said, "I will absolutely follow you into any battle and any conquest you want to make. If you believe we can pacify those people, I will be right behind you up those mountains to fight or negotiate peace. However, we are men of the Empire before anything. I was made a general and sent to this army by your brother, the Emperor. If... If you were to take over the north, does that mean you would become its official ruler? The Onyx Castle has always stood as the helm of the Empire's Northern territories, and I agree those territories, the Shadelands, have been neglected ever since your family left them. But for you to take ownership of the north... I am your man in any war you want to start, Commander, but I also want to be sure of what this would mean toward the Empire."

"I will go and meet my brother in the Imperial Palace," Kassein said. "The Emperor will be aware of my intentions and decide for himself what will be done about the north. But know that I will not give up on any of it. This army, the mountains and its tribes, the Onyx Castle, the Shadelands. I will return, and it will be mine."

"But the Emperor—"

"My brother and I will find common ground," he retorted with a growling tone.

Kassein's furious green eyes were not accepting any more objections.

His mind was set, and while his brother would be far more complicated to convince than his three generals, he wouldn't leave the Imperial Palace until he got what he wanted. He had never wanted anything so strongly before nor been so desperate for it. He wasn't willing to say it out loud, but he might be willing to fight his own brother. Kassian might have been the Emperor and fourteen years older, but Kassein wasn't willing to change his mind.

"...This might be a historical change for the Empire," Tievin cleared his throat, "but not... unheard of. After all, the Eastern Kingdom was also once part of the original civilization that created the Empire, if we believe what history has uncovered in recent years. Perhaps this continent should become ground for more countries before the Empire starts to cannibalize itself."

"More countries might mean more wars," Herken muttered.

"Then you won't be out of a job too soon," Kiera retorted. "You three have spent years in this place. You're men of war in times of peace, you should be jumping at the opportunity. My brother intends to pacify the mountains exactly as planned. Be assured that the tribes that are unwilling to cooperate might need more... heavy-handed convincing."

Kassein didn't voice it out loud, but a part of him did hope that one tribe would resist: the one that had banished Alezya.

He had never been one to enjoy actual wars, but he had been raised by the War God; he knew wars could be necessary. If he was going to raise a country and trace a border between his brother's Empire and the north, he had to be determined to do what it would take.

He had no intention to become a tyrant, but he sure needed to conquer those mountains once and for all. The feud between the Empire and the Northern tribes had been going on for centuries already, and while the casualties had lessened during his father's time in the north and his, he had every intent to end them once and for all. The tribes kept losing men to meaningless skirmishes; they couldn't possibly wish for this to last for several more centuries rather than end it once and for all and offer their people the option to trace a very different future. He had seen how Alezya reacted to things as simple as meat, fur coats, and soap. The fact that such common things in the Empire were a luxury in her eyes meant that the tribes weren't living lavishly, far from it.

He couldn't imagine what life was like, holed up in their mountains for centuries. They probably had a very different way of life, but it didn't mean that the north couldn't benefit them and the other way around.

He could already envision it. A future where the tribespeople taught the people of the Shadelands about life in the mountains, and they taught the tribespeople everything the land they hadn't been allowed to set foot on for centuries could offer.

"Is that why you've given the order not to kill any more of them?" Sazaran petted his beard again. "What are we to do with the prisoners, Commander? Are they hostages?"

"We will start negotiating with the tribes," Kassein said. "We cannot do that by killing any more of them."

"What if they send more carrying diseases? They've had no issues trying to kill our men with the most vicious, vile means before..."

"If you see any sign they carry diseases, kill them," Kassein said. "Otherwise, isolate their men."

"How are we going to conquer the mountains without harming them?" Herken massaged his temples. "I don't think this will happen without a fight, Commander..."

"I never said there would be no fight. There are some tribes who will refuse negotiations, and there is one tribe, in particular, that I plan to conquer first."

Kassein had very little desire to let the tribe who had hurt Alezya get away alive. He wasn't sure yet if it had been her own tribe, but he definitely remembered the men he had seen beating her up, and he had every intention to murder each one of them himself.

Anyone he could find who'd had a hand in her suffering, he would personally see to their end.

"So what?" Herken scoffed. "We start keeping those tribesmen hostage one by one? We cannot decide to start negotiating with their people; we don't even understand their language!"

"Not true anymore," Kiera smirked. "My brother's new pet has been learning plenty during her stay here."

"Your concubine has been learning our language?" Sazaran raised an eyebrow.

"You let a woman learn our ways?" Herken barked. "Commander! Who knows what that—"

"You really should value your tongue more, old man," Kiera cut him off with a hiss.

The General froze, realizing his mistake half a second before it was too late. Kassein's burning gaze was on him, absolutely murderous. The older General slowly shrunk back in his seat, suddenly feeling an ice-cold chill down his spine.

"A-apologies, Commander," he mumbled. "But... that woman is—"

"Our key to establishing the negotiations with the tribes," Kassein hissed, his glare still pinning the old man down in his chair.

Another cold chill made its way around the room.

No matter how much the generals distrusted Alezya and her people, Kassein wasn't taking any objections, and none of them were brave enough to stand up to their Commander in Chief. He might have been young, but Kassein already had the body of a grown man and the strength of one who shared the blood of a dragon. The number of people who could possibly hold their ground against him in a duel could be counted on one hand and were all related to him.

"I have made up my mind already," Kassein said. "I will go to the Capital and talk to my brother first. Then, when I return, our army will get ready to march on the mountains. Train all of our men and prepare them for a long, possibly drawn-out battle. The mountains are vast and wide, and conquering them on foot will take a long time. We need to get ready for several trips."

"What about the tribes that refuse to negotiate with us, Commander?" Kauser asked. "As optimistic as I want to be about this, according to Grand Intendant Tievin, there are many tribes who are of different opinions from one another. What shall we do about the ones that will refuse to cooperate?"

"I will go with Alezya to meet each tribe first and open the negotiations," Kassein said. "I'm counting on the word spreading through the mountains. The tribe I intend to take down will serve as an example of what happens if they try to fight us. I can ignore the tribes that will stay indifferent to us, but those who are set on trying to kill our people will meet their end."

The three generals nodded in unison. Kiera had her eyes on her brother too.

There was a huge change coming. The best outcome was that all tribes would submit and be open to negotiations, but it was unlikely.

While some tribes had shown curiosity or indifference to the Empire, some had been openly hostile for centuries. The way that one tribe had treated Alezya showed that there also might be a case of irreconcilable differences in their way of life... but at least Kassein had every intention of showing that he would not forgive or turn a blind eye to women being harmed. Even without having witnessed Alezya's torment for himself, her brother had been raised to not let any of his sex get away with raising a hand to a woman.

And Kiera was all on board with retribution coming to the people who had almost killed a woman not once but twice. They had been literally trained for war, after all. Kassein offering those tribes to negotiate first was considered mercy, especially after they had let them get away with those attacks for so long.

In all the months he had been here, her brother had launched only a few attacks, and only after being provoked. Perhaps the tribes were going to understand that hiding in their mountains could only save them for so long.

Kassein dismissed the generals, leaving only his sister and Tievin in the room.

For a while, he only discussed tactical borders, how much of the territory his brother would be willing to concede, and how to proceed with their negotiations with the tribes based on Tievin's observations.

The camp's Intendant had actually done a great job of keeping track of the various attacks and, correlated with his system of identifying the tribes by their attire, they were able to narrow down two more tribes that might be next in line to meet their end.

"...How do you think she will react to you attacking her people?"

Kiera's question made Kassein freeze.

His hand, which had been spread on the map, tightened into a fist.

His sister shrugged. She hadn't moved from her seat while participating in their conversation, but her eyes were riveted on her brother.

Kiera was on board with his plan; she had interacted with plenty of Western tribes before to know that things would either go fairly peacefully or need some strength, and she wasn't one to oppose the latter when necessary.

Lorey was the peace advocate, and she was the strong-handed persuasion. In fact, Kiki had seldom killed humans because Kiera had no qualms about dirtying her own hands first when people deserved it.

They had run into plenty of awful people who were keen to underestimate two females; she had learned quickly not to be too sorry for killing murderers and rapists. It was the world their ancestors had lived in, where their mother had been made a slave, sold to be killed or abused, countless tribes hunted down for their people to suffer the same fate, and abusers could live wealthy lives fed by enslaved people.

Their parents had changed everything or, at least, they had set things in motion.

Their father, the War God and an Imperial Prince, had fallen for a slave and made her his concubine. Far from being satisfied with her belonging to him like a possession, he had freed her and married her.

Then, when his sister, Empress Shareen, had been the first female to sit on the Imperial Throne alone, they had started to undo centuries of damage, freeing slaves and promulging more laws against slavery.

Now, their older brother Kassian was still arguing every day against old men who wanted things to stay the old way and were very much against giving up free labor and young female slaves.

However, all of this was fairly recent, and many tribes still feared the Empire which had hunted them for centuries.

It had sometimes taken weeks for her and Lorey to convince a tribe to even talk to them, and that was with Western tribes who spoke the same language.

How long would it take for Kassein to have those negotiations with the Northern tribes who spoke a different language and feared him and his butcher dragon most of all? Alezya would be essential to his plan, that is, if he could convince her.

That woman wouldn't even teach them her language. How was she going to react to the idea of her lover conquering her tribe and more?

"I will talk to Alezya," Kassein muttered.

He didn't sound as convinced as when he'd talked to the generals, but that was fair; the young Prince was far more nervous about that woman than three old men.

Kiera massaged her neck. While his plan made sense in many ways, a lot of things could go wrong, and they were setting themselves up for a few months' worth of work, probably, if not years.

"Ugh, fine," she grunted after a few seconds.

"Princess?" Tievin raised an eyebrow, visibly confused.

"I'll help you," she sighed. "Truthfully, I expected Lorey and I to be out of here within a few weeks, but I'm guessing you're going to need some help with this mad plan of yours... and you probably could use some."

"I can do it fine on my own," Kassein said.

"By the dragon's balls, shut up and accept free help when you get it, would you?"

Kassein didn't add any more, but after a few more seconds, he gave the nod to his older sister.

If it had been a few weeks ago, his pride wouldn't have allowed for any help from his family, but now, with a clear objective in mind, he would gladly take Kiera's. The faster he was done conquering the north, the faster Alezya would be safe and at ease by his side.

That was all he wanted.

"What's going on?"

All three of them turned their heads to see Lorey, looking confused as she stepped inside the tent and glanced at the map sprawled on the table.

"Just planning to conquer some mountains," Kiera shrugged. "Why?"

"Conquer the mountains?" Lorey blinked. "...Really?"

Kassein gave her a stern nod, and when she turned to Tievin, the Grand Intendant sighed and summarized everything she'd missed in a few sentences, from their hypothesis about the tribes, Kassein's plan to conquer the mountains and claim the north as his own, the meeting with the generals, and finally, Kiera offering her help.

"I hope you don't mind, honey," Kiera sighed. "It looks like we're set to stay here for a while."

"I don't, but... have you guys seen Alezya?"

They froze, the tension in the tent rising noticeably, all eyes going to Kassein as his jaw tensed.

"...She was in my tent."

"She isn't anymore," Lorey announced with a sorry expression, "and... your dragon took off a little while ago too."

"Kein?" He frowned.

"You have another dumb dragon we don't know about?" Kiera rolled her eyes.

Kassein ignored her, feeling increasingly nervous.

He had told his dragon to watch over Alezya. While Kein had rarely listened to its owner's wishes in recent years, there was one thing they had agreed on, and it was Alezya. She came first, especially her safety.

Kassein knew his dragon wouldn't have left her, not willingly.

If Alezya wasn't in his tent, she wasn't with Lorey, and Kein had taken off... Was Alezya riding his dragon? If so, where to?

Kassein tightened his fist. He didn't like this. He felt a minimal amount of relief knowing that she was with his dragon, but to think she had left when he wasn't looking...

How long had passed since he'd left her in his bed? A few hours?

His throat tightened. Where could she have gone with his dragon? A dragon could cross from one end of the Empire to the other in a few hours... but he had to think Kein wouldn't take her too far from him.

Perhaps she just needed some fresh air or to experience a ride again. After all, the weather was fair, and there was a full moon that night... or so he was trying to convince himself, ignoring the ominous feeling gnawing his insides.

"Shall we chase them?" Kiera grimaced. "Not that I think it would be a great idea to chase your insane dragon, but..."

"Let it be," Kassein said half-heartedly. "...They'll be back."

Kiera raised an eyebrow that clearly meant she doubted it but didn't pursue the matter any further.

Kassein forced himself to take a settling breath in.

He and Alezya trusted each other. After what had happened between them the previous night... he felt like they were marked forever by some invisible, unbreakable bond. She was his.

It was in a dragon's blood to hoard his treasures, and he had no intention of letting her go. Wherever she'd gone, she'd come back to him, or he would go to her. Neither mattered. Once he conquered those mountains, Alezya would be free to go wherever she wanted, and she would still be within his grasp. The possessive feeling was sudden but not surprising.

Once again, Kassein had always known it was in their nature to be jealous and possessive, and he had seen his siblings and parents with their partners; he was almost relieved to have found his own half to feed that instinct.

"Are you sure?" Lorey whispered as if the other two couldn't hear.

Instead of replying, Kassein turned to Tievin with a determined expression.

"Do we have everything we need to meet with my brother?"

Tievin hesitated, making some mental checklist in his head that included some grimacing, and eventually, nodded with a heavy sigh.

"I'm afraid so, Your Highness."

"You are *not* taking my dragon," Kiera hissed.

Kassein didn't even bother to ask her and simply walked out of the tent, Tievin trying to keep up behind him while carrying his map.

"I-I need to make a stop by my tent, Your Highness," Tievin panted. "The journey will also be quite long, we haven't been to the Capital in a while, and you know how much I hate flying..."

Kassein didn't reply, but as he was clearly headed for his own tent rather than Kiki, his sister's dragon parked right outside the tent, Tievin took a turn and headed for his own, leaving his Commander to walk alone.

Kassein wasn't even sure why he was making a stop by his tent when there was no one waiting for him. Perhaps he needed to see for himself the empty bed, feel the heartache more deeply.

Even if he expected it, the heartache hit him profoundly when he stepped inside and confirmed Lorey's words. Alezya was gone again.

The bed was left a mess, the fur blankets spread around that still smelled like her.

He resisted the urge to go and smell it more deeply. The tent still smelled like her, like *them,* but it was now cold and empty. Where had she gone? Why? Was it about whatever or whoever she had left behind again?

The snow. She had said the snow was her family... Was that what she missed too much to stay with him? What was he missing?

She had seemed happier lately. There was always this melancholy about her, but it wasn't as bad as when he'd first found her.

Would she ever be able to be fully happy with him? To trust him enough to stay? To rely on him, let him protect her from whatever was haunting her? Provide everything she needed? Because he would.

Kassein had made up his mind. If she didn't come back, he would find her again. He wasn't letting go. She could run and fly as far as she wanted, he would always find her again.

Kassein left the tent, not needing anything to head to the Capital anyway, and moreover, his sister's dragon would fly faster if he went without wearing his armor.

As he headed back through the tents to find Kiki, he could feel the bustling his meeting with the generals had launched; there was some newfound excitement throughout the camp as the men were gearing up for the action they'd been hoping for.

Ignoring their stares, Kassein scrutinized the sky, hoping to find a glimpse of orange scales, but Kein was out of sight, and he had a feeling through their bond that the beast had gone to the mountains, carrying their heart with it...

He clenched his fists, and resumed his walk straight back to his sister's dragon, unsurprisingly finding it next to Lorey and Kiera outside.

His sister was sulking, her arms crossed, while Lorey was affectionately petting the dark gray dragon.

"When do you expect to return?" Lorey asked.

"As soon as possible. If Alezya returns..."

"We will watch over her," Lorey smiled.

He nodded and glanced at the skies again.

Kassein didn't want to leave, but he felt like he would only delay this if Alezya was here, and he didn't want to delay the inevitable.

It was almost easier to go while she was away and under his dragon's protection. Surely Kein wouldn't let anything happen to her... and Kassein would be back soon enough. In the best-case scenario, she would be back in the camp, waiting for him with Lorey and Kiera. If not, he would look for her. He would search every mountain, every cave, every crevice for her. And he would return with his brother's benediction to do so.

Truthfully, Kassein cared very little about his brother's opinion, but he did want to go about this the right way. For once in his life, he wanted to take a chance at making the right choice, the right decision, and being the man Alezya deserved, someone who could claim the north and rightfully own it.

He only had to wait a while longer for Tievin to return, quite neatly packed for someone with such little enthusiasm to fly. Lorey, who had taken to scouring the skies with him, smiled at Kassein.

"...I'm sure she will return," she said.

How Alezya would return, of her own volition or after Kassein had brought her back, was left unsaid and up for interpretation, but it mattered little.

As soon as Tievin was ready, they climbed the dark gray dragon, who growled a bit, visibly as annoyed as its owner was about this, but still got up and flapped its wings a couple of times, getting ready for departure.

"Kassein," Kiera marched to stand next to her dragon's head, staring up at Kassein.

"...Don't let Kassian get to you," she simply said.

There was a lot more meaning to her words, but neither of them said it out loud, and he only replied with a stiff nod. Then, she stepped away, and Kiki took off with an elegant flap of its wings.

Chapter 13

After leaving Lumie, leaving Kassein might have been the most heart-wrenching decision she had made.

He had given her everything she could have asked for and more.

There was just no moving on from the dream she'd been given to live with that man; Alezya knew it.

As soon as she had woken up, finding herself alone in the bed, covered in warm furs and Kassein's lingering scent, her heart had been more full and painful than ever. It wouldn't have been so hard if that man hadn't given her so much. She hadn't even taken a step out of his habitation, and she missed the man already.

She didn't know where he had gone, but she was certain he had spent more time in his bed with her than he usually did for she had felt his strong arms holding her all night long.

Getting up from the bed, cleaning his scent off herself, and putting on some clothes felt so hard that Alezya found herself choking back tears several times, despite rushing just in case Kassein returned. She had to get out of here and on her way back to her clan before he returned.

She wanted to stay here, most of her heart wanted to stay here, but no matter how much she loved Kassein, how strong of a hold he had taken on her heart, there was absolutely nothing in this world that could have made her not go back to Lumie. Her baby girl was the only reason she would leave the best man in the world and return to the worst of all. Kassein made her heart full and warm, but Lumie was her heartbeat.

She couldn't go on without being absolutely certain her daughter would be safe and well. She had made the mistake of leaving her baby's fate in destiny's hands once, and she wouldn't be making that mistake again.

This time, she was going to make sure Lumie would be fine, loved, and safe, no matter what. No matter what it cost her.

She felt endlessly sorry for Kassein, but absolutely nothing could convince her not to save her daughter before herself. Alezya was resolved to give up on happiness as long as Lumie's safety was guaranteed. She would bury her own chances at a happy future so long as Lumie got her own.

Thus, with her heart more painful than ever before, she ventured out of Kassein's home and into the cold to find, much to her relief, the faithful orange dragon waiting for her.

Despite the tears that threatened to spill any second, Alezya was happy to see the dragon and realize again how lucky she was to have made such a beast an ally.

"I'm going to need you," she whispered to the dragon, using her own language.

She had learned a lot of Kassein's tongue, and since it seemed like Kein could understand some of hers, she had taken to chatting with the orange dragon when on her own, all while practicing how to give commands in the Dragon Empire's language. Alezya had never thought she could feel so confident about directing a man-eating beast, but it was a deliciously empowering feeling.

It was her best chance. She had a plan, a mad plan perhaps, but it was a far better one than the first she'd put into action when she'd run away from her clan the first time. Things were so different now. She had Kassein and his dragon by her side, even if neither of them really knew, and they were her best chance, a chance she wouldn't have ever dared to hope for.

Feeling braver than ever, Alezya placed her hands under Kein's chin and pressed her forehead against the large dragon's head, between its eyes, closing her own as she felt its incredibly hot scales.

"I need her back," she whispered again. "Will you help me get my baby girl back, Kein?"

As if it somewhat understood, the dragon let out a low, long rumbling growl. Alezya smiled and walked around the dragon to climb on its back, acting with a confidence that felt new to her. Kein seemed to hesitate for a couple of seconds before the dragon eventually lifted its heavy body, standing up from the snow den its body had shaped in the last few days.

"*Fly,*" she said, using Kassein's language.

Kein growled, took a couple of steps away from the habitation to find the space to stretch its large orange wings, and then, much to Alezya's relief, took off. She had never flown by herself, and she had only done it once with Kassein, making this feel like madness, but it was happening.

It only took seconds for Kein's large body to get high above the camp, and the men's figures were reduced to tiny ants beneath them.

Alezya willed her lungs to take a deep breath as the insane reality sunk in. She was flying a dragon by herself. As much as taking his dragon and betraying Kassein broke her heart, she needed the little bit of empowerment it gave her.

For a couple of minutes, she let Kein take them wherever it pleased, but then, she tried to practice the words Lorey had taught her, directing the dragon left or right with a tap on the matching side of its neck, and much to her relief, it worked. Kein was acting incredibly docile, letting a woman that wasn't even a fifth of its size direct it wherever she wanted.

They quickly found themselves high above the mountains, and Alezya saw her home from a dragon's point of view, as well as the many other mountains she had only seen from afar and those beyond all the way to the sea.

There were so many mountains and probably about as many clans... She was the insignificant pariah daughter of a clan's chief, and yet, she probably was the first of those people to ever ride a dragon. All of a sudden, she held more power than any of the men who had looked down on her could ever dream of, and that was quite an amazing feeling.

Alezya's plan still had to come into play, and she took in another breath of fresh air before directing Kein again. Thanks to the dragon's formidable size, it would be hard for anyone from below to notice a human was riding it, and she didn't plan to let her clan see what she could have that dragon do just yet.

Thus, hoping the clans would have the usual reaction to hide inside the mountain, she spotted an isolated clearing for Kein to land in, close enough to her mountain that she could find her way home on foot and hidden enough that they wouldn't see her coming off its orange-scaled back.

While Kein landed obediently right where instructed, the dragon seemed upset about the human female getting off its back, and its orange head kept following her movements with nervous or upset little growls.

Alezya gave it a sad smile, petting its neck.

"Don't worry," she whispered. "I need you to stay close. Can you stick around for me until I call you?"

The dragon let out another growl, which she took as reassuring.

Now that she was back on familiar soil, fresh snow, and far too close to her home mountain, dread began to fill Alezya. She wished Kassein was there to hold her in his strong, warm arms, but instead, she pressed her palms and her body against his dragon, feeling the hot orange scales warm her up.

She was nervous. She'd had to go back twice before already, and each time had hurt more than the last. It was a cruel truth she tried to push aside, but deep down, she knew she might not survive this one.

Alezya let Kein's body warm her for a few more seconds while she gathered the courage she needed to go back. The dragon's near-unbearable heat and thoughts of her baby waiting for her finally willed her to pull away and turn in the direction she had to take.

"See you later, friend," she whispered to Kein, hoping the dragon would stick around long enough to enact her plan.

Alezya heard Kein's pained growls as she walked away, but the dragon didn't take off until a few seconds later, and while she was still a long way from home, she could see the orange body making lazy circles above her, no doubt following her hike with its curious silver eyes.

Thanks to the predator in the sky, none of the ones hiding in the mountain crossed her path while Alezya made it back to her clan's territory.

It was a long journey, but she didn't hurry, knowing she had hours until the nightmare began. She missed Kein's warmth already as her feet were numb from the bite of the snow, and although she was used to the pain from the cold, it was nothing compared to what her heart was enduring.

She kept Kassein and Lumie in mind, alternating between hoping one would forgive her and the other one was safe. She had been away from her child for too long, and she missed Kassein already.

She willed herself to keep going, thinking the sooner this would be over, the better, whatever the final outcome.

She felt like the same woman who had left this place twice, only stronger, bolder. And, if she was honest, loved. There was something immeasurably powerful about knowing that someone was waiting for her. Someone who loved her, adored her, and made her feel at home in his arms. Her father's spiteful words wouldn't hurt anymore; Kassein's love was like an invisible dragon-scaled shield she wore to battle.

Thus, when she finally stepped foot inside one of the familiar tunnels, she kept her head high as she made her way past the stone walls and back to the depths of her home clan.

It didn't take long for her path to cross with a sentinel, who took a second to recognize her and another second to realize she was alive. He might as well have seen a ghost because the man's eyes opened wide in shock, and he darted in the opposite direction without a word.

Alezya let out an involuntary grin. She probably was like some sort of vengeful spirit, coming back every time despite their best attempts to get rid of her. Since she had been sent to the Dragon Clan, most of her people had probably not expected her to be able to return so freely. Her father must have been the only one to wish for her return, although it was for the most selfish reasons. Even if he had sent her on some horrible mission this time, he might not have actually expected her to come back alive, and certainly not this healthy nor wearing such a nice, warm coat.

This time, she was the one in a position of power, and her father had no idea.

When Alezya emerged in one of their main caves, her father and some of his men were waiting for her, slightly out of breath as they had visibly arrived from another tunnel seconds prior.

She felt her stomach clench in anger, fear, and disgust. Every inch of her body wanted her out of there before something terrible happened again. The trauma of her past experience was lingering like a promised nightmare to strike again.

She stood steps away from them, unwilling to approach any further, taking in the men almost cornering her already while her back touched one of the cave's walls. It was hard and cold.

"She really returned," her father hissed with a victorious grin.

Alezya tried to keep a neutral expression. She hadn't seen her father smile her way in a long time, but it was all for the wrong reasons. He was expecting to be victorious, for her to return pregnant with Kassein's child, to be crawling back to save her daughter's life.

For some reason, Alezya felt the urge to cover her womb with her hand, although there was no need for it. It just felt gross to see her father stare at it like he was ready to gut her for his prize.

"Where is Lumie?" she asked, silently praying her baby was fine.

"Are you pregnant?" Her father squinted his eyes.

Alezya nodded stiffly. She was hoping the herb had worked, and she couldn't act too certain about her condition; she had only been with Kassein for a few weeks, and even if her clan believed she'd slept with him since she'd returned to the Dragon Clan, she would have gotten pregnant recently, nothing for her to be too confident about.

"Check her."

Alezya realized the Healer had just arrived at the end of the little group that had just come out of the tunnel. The elder marched toward her without an ounce of pity toward the young woman who had been sent like a slave to breed with their enemy. She grabbed and pulled Alezya's wrist out of her coat unceremoniously, and everyone held their breath.

Alezya silently prayed it would work. She knew how strong the herb was, but if anything had gone wrong, if her father had the slightest doubt, she and Lumie could be killed on the spot...

"She is with child."

Alezya barely suppressed a sigh of relief as the Healer turned to her father with a nod. Her maker didn't seem as confident, squinting his eyes at the Healer.

"...Are you certain?"

"It seems like it," the old woman shrugged. "But it is far too soon to be absolutely certain. We could confirm in a matter of weeks–"

"We don't have weeks," her father hissed back. "We need her pregnant already. The council gathering is tonight!"

He hesitated for a few seconds, his dark eyes on Alezya like he was trying to decipher her.

"She really only slept with their chief?"

The question wasn't directed at her but at some of the sentinels, who gave him a nod.

"She spent every night with him."

Little did they know Kassein only touched her on one of those nights.

Alezya felt grateful that her clan's men were far too narrow-minded to believe a man like Kassein could have spent nights with a woman in his bed without touching her, and even more grateful to Kassein for being the man that he was. She missed him already, and seeing men who were so different from him made her miss him even more.

They had no idea that there were men like him, warriors who did not enjoy abusing women. A man putting a woman's desires before his own was sheer heresy in their clan.

"She was only ever in his quarters or with him or their women," another sentinel added.

Her father nodded with a satisfied grin.

"...Good. We wouldn't want you to have *strayed* again," he spat.

Alezya didn't suppress her grimace. They still believed she had cheated on her ex-husband with whoever Lumie's father was. They would never accept that the precious son of the Exkiu Clan had fathered her oddly white child. It was far more acceptable for them to push all of the faults on her than to risk another clan's trust.

She didn't care any longer; Kassein had been the only man to touch her since Lumie's birth, and that was everything she wanted. Now that her clan was only seeing her as a vessel to carry children with his blood, they wouldn't risk another man touching her, which was a good enough outcome for her. Alezya never wanted another man but Kassein to touch her ever again.

"My daughter," Alezya hissed. "You promised my daughter back."

Her father ignored her, turning toward his sentinels.

"Inform the other clan chiefs that we have succeeded," he said, not hiding his grin. "All eyes will be on our clan tonight. Even if we have to wait a few months, all clans will be waiting for us to have a dragon!"

Alezya certainly didn't correct him.

She didn't know how the dragon eggs were made, but she was fairly certain it wouldn't come out of her womb. Baby dragons were far too big from the nests she'd seen, and she doubted Kassein's mother would have been able to bear eight of them. Her father probably expected her to come back bearing some monster or that a dragon would magically appear with her child, but there was no child to be born anyway.

She was glad she had managed to trick them, but now, she had to focus on her main goal: getting Lumie out of there.

The sentinel nodded and left, but Alezya kept her eyes on her father.

"My daughter," she insisted.

He rolled his eyes, before turning his hateful glare toward her like she was some eyesore.

"Your bastard is fine," he hissed. "You should be grateful your cousin agreed to take that shame upon herself."

A wave of relief crashed over Alezya's heart, almost making her lose her balance, and she was glad she could lean on the wall behind her.

Lumie was alive and still with her cousin. Her father would have happily broken her heart otherwise.

Days and nights of worry suddenly felt like they had all been worth it. She had refused to entertain the thought for more than seconds at a time, but if Alezya had returned to find her baby was gone... She would have probably followed her.

"I want to see her," Alezya said, hardly suppressing tears as the need to hold her baby became more urgent. "I want to see my child!"

"You do not give orders around here," her father hissed. "The child is staying with us until you give birth to the dragon."

Alezya's heart dropped. She had braced herself for this, but it didn't stop the wave of panic rising.

"You promised!" she shouted.

"I promised to give your bastard back once you give me a dragon," he scoffed. "We'll have to wait until you finish your part of the deal, won't we?"

Alezya let out genuine tears. She had expected this much, but it didn't make it any less heart-wrenching.

Thankfully, she had an idea. She had spent a lot of time, while confined in Kassein's shelter, thinking about her plan and how to save Lumie. She was already crying and desperate; she didn't need to act much of her despair. While two of her father's sentinels came to grab her, she began fighting them, her eyes on her father's retreating figure.

"You can't!" she shouted. "Father, please! I need my child! I need to protect her, or the dragon–"

She stopped herself as if she had said one too many words, biting her trembling lower lip. Her father stilled and turned back to her with a gleeful expression.

"Or the dragon what, Alezya?"

She went silent, now avoiding his gaze.

Her father slowly walked up to her, and grabbed her jaw painfully with his hand, forcing her to look up at him.

"Or the dragon what?"

"I-it will take her," she cried. "The dragon... It wants to eat my child."

Her father's eyes opened wide. Alezya shivered, more horrified by his greedy eyes than the thought of Kein near her baby. The man-eating beast wasn't nearly as frightening as the monster in human skin before her. Alezya hated that she had to dangle Lumie's life like a negligible treat before him, but there was no other way.

He stepped closer to her, and despite the men holding her arms and shoulders, Alezya jerked back.

"Eat your child?" He narrowed his eyes. "Why would the dragon want to eat your child?"

"I-I don't know," Alezya mumbled.

"Answer," he hissed, unconvinced. "You know something, Alezya. Don't you dare lie to me, or you will pay for it."

"I'm not scared of you," she retorted. "You can do whatever you want to me!"

She already knew he wouldn't. As violent of a man as her father was, his belief that she was pregnant far outweighed his short temper. He wouldn't risk harming his most precious piece of the bargain before the upcoming council gathering. However, he sneered, looking at Alezya like she was nothing but disposable vermin.

"I certainly can," he hissed, "and that goes for your little bastard too. Should I chop off her arm so you'll start to speak?"

Even if she had expected it, a lump of coal dropped in Alezya's stomach.

"You..." she huffed, furious.

"Speak, Alezya," he hissed. "The council gathering is tonight and we don't have all night. Start talking now, or I will have to see how much the dragon wants to eat your bastard myself."

Alezya swallowed with difficulty. She had expected it, but at least now, her father would think she was talking merely out of fear, under duress, and against her will. She averted her eyes, looking down at the cold floor, watching her tears drop near her toes.

Those were tears of frustration, but it worked fine to fool them into thinking she had lost the battle already.

"I-I... I understand them," she mumbled.

"What?"

"The Dragon Clan," she whimpered. "I understand their language. I heard them speak... m-many times."

"You?" her father spat. "*You* speak the Dragon Clan's language?"

"O-only a bit," Alezya replied, "but... just enough that I learned things."

"What did you learn?"

"The... Their dragon," she whispered. "I know why it didn't attack me the first time."

Her father's eyes opened wider. It was a mystery he had been dying to solve, that was for certain. No one had confronted Kein from as close as Alezya had and lived to tell the tale.

Strangely, she realized she still wasn't sure exactly why she had been spared on her first encounter with the dragon, but she had some idea. Perhaps Kein never meant to hurt those who didn't harm it or its owner. Perhaps it was reluctant to attack women, or perhaps it had understood Alezya's defiant words.

She could almost smile at the memory now, but thankfully, she was avoiding her father's eyes and still looking down, so he didn't see it.

"Why?" he pressed her.

"It... It smelled her on me," she mumbled. "Lumie. The dragon... It wants her."

"Your bastard? Why would the dragon want her?"

"I-I'm not sure," Alezya cried. "I-I think she's different..."

She had thought about lying and saying that it liked children better, but

Alezya didn't trust her father and his peers not to start throwing innocent children in the dragon's clutches. She was far more confident in Kein's ability to not harm children than the clan chiefs.

"I knew there was something strange about that bastard!" her father gloated, suddenly excited. "Dragon food. She is meant to be a dragon's offering! Then we will bring her to the council gathering..."

"You can't!" Alezya shouted, acting panicked. "Don't! Not her! You promised you would leave my child alone!"

"I have yet to see it with my own eyes," his grin suddenly vanished, his eyes turning back to her. "What else did you learn? You were down there for days... Surely, you've learned more."

"I won't tell you," Alezya cried with a defiant stare. "I won't tell you another word until you let me see my child. You can't sacrifice her. You don't know a thing about the Dragon Clan, and I won't say another word until I can hold Lumie in my arms."

She felt the burn of the slap on her cheek before she even realized he'd slapped her.

Alezya hadn't felt that kind of pain in a while, it took a few seconds for it to sink in, for her to comprehend it had been her father's hand.

Perhaps Kassein's gentle hands had made her forget for a while, but her body didn't. Acting with the response engrained by years of abuse, it began to shiver and scream at Alezya to get away from that man. Against her better instincts, she bit her lower lip and glowered at him.

"Speak," he hissed. "What else? How many men do they have? How many dragons are there? Is the black dragon dead? How do we kill them?"

Alezya remained silent. He slapped her again, but this time, she had been ready, at least mentally.

She involuntarily bit her lower lip deep because of the slap and felt blood pool on her bottom lip, a single tear sliding down her chin. Her cheek burned, but she didn't care. She just glared at her father, stubborn and quiet. She was keeping to her word: he wouldn't hear another word until she saw and held Lumie.

It was a huge gamble; either she had said too much or too little, but if she knew anything about that man, it was that his greed held no bounds, and she counted on it. Information was power amongst the clans, and surely, he was far too greedy for power to let this unique opportunity go. Even if he was aware Alezya was partly bluffing, he also knew she had spent far longer than anyone with the Dragon Clan, survived, and returned unharmed.

And he also knew there was nothing she wouldn't do for Lumie.

"Speak," he hissed again.

But this time, Alezya was certain she had him, and thus, she narrowed her own dark eyes in defiance. Her father slapped her again, but this time, there was more frustration and less conviction, and Alezya could take it. She could take anything her father threw at her so long as she got to hold Lumie again.

Finally, he gave her one last spiteful glare before turning to one of his men. "Get the child," he spat.

The man nodded and disappeared, and a wave of relief crashed over Alezya again.

"You will pay for your arrogance," her father warned her. "You and your bastard will pay, Alezya. Your only value to this clan is the dragon you're bearing. You will have a few more months to live thanks to it but trust me, you will pay for every fit of disobedience you throw."

"You can't harm me," Alezya retorted. "You can't risk me losing the child."

"I can harm your other bastard."

"Touch a hair on her head, and I swear I will stab myself. I will stab my womb and kill the child you want with it."

Her father stared in shock for a few doubtful seconds. A man like him couldn't possibly imagine that she would go as far as harming herself to protect her child, but Alezya would have done this and worse without a doubt. He had no idea how much she had already sacrificed for Lumie's sake. Harming her own body or taking her own life felt almost too easy in comparison. She would have never wanted to harm a child conceived with Kassein, but since there was no child, she need not worry about that.

"You belong to this clan," he hissed. "I am your Clan Chief, your only duty is to—"

"My only duty is to my child," Alezya spat back. "I stopped belonging to this clan a long time ago, Father, and we both know it. Only Lumie matters to me now. So bring my child to me unharmed, and I will give you the secrets of the Dragon Clan. Otherwise, you won't be getting anything from me."

Her father's fury was seeping out of him, but he could still see she was telling the truth; Alezya had been consistent about caring about nothing but Lumie.

She would have left this clan a long time ago for the way they had treated her if she hadn't had her child with her. She might have had better chances elsewhere, and little did he know that she now did, for certain. Kassein had cared for her far beyond what she could have hoped; it was for the best that her father couldn't conceive how blessed she would be to get back to the Dragon Clan. He might have thought she had run away and escaped somehow, but he would never know she had left unwillingly.

The second Lumie was away and safe, Alezya would be ready to go back to Kassein or die trying. But first, she had to get her baby out of there.

"Alezya?"

Her father stepped away, and she saw her cousin, along with her husband, carefully holding Lumie in her arms. Alezya's crying resumed as soon as her eyes found her baby girl's, and Lumie's clear eyes lit up in delight upon recognizing her mom.

It didn't even take a second before the little girl's arms were stretched toward her. Much to Alezya's relief, her cousin barely gave her father a glance before bringing her child to her without waiting for approval.

Her father stepped back as if the child carried some awful disease, glaring at Lumie with sheer disgust on his face.

"Mama," Lumie cooed, visibly delighted.

Her baby girl grabbed Alezya's long strands of raven hair first thing, and Alezya cried her first tears of joy in a long while upon feeling her daughter's body pressed against hers, the curves of their bodies melding together like they were always meant to.

"Oh, my Lumie," Alezya cried, holding her tight.

Lumie had grown quite a bit, but thankfully, she looked completely healthy and quite happy too. She giggled at her mom's hair tickling her skin and nuzzled herself in Alezya's neck as she was pressed against her skin.

"She's fine," Zenia whispered, a sorry look in her eyes. "She's been... really good."

Alezya lifted her eyes from Lumie for a second to look at her cousin. She hadn't seen Zenia in a while, and she was surprised to see that expression in her cousin's eyes, almost as if the other young mother looked apologetic. Her husband had a hand on Zenia's nape and was standing somewhat between the two women and their Clan Chief.

"You alright?" he asked in a whisper, his eyes landing on Alezya's nice coat.

She gave them a little nod, taken aback by their concern.

She had already sensed Suolk had been kind to Lumie the last time she had seen him, but now, it seemed like Zenia wasn't reluctant toward her daughter anymore either. Even if she couldn't confirm it, Alezya would have bet they had simply taken to Lumie's easy and cheerful nature. Her daughter was a good girl, easy to love, and sweeter than most.

She pressed a kiss against her baby's cheek, happy to still find it full, making her giggle.

"Mama," Lumie chuckled again.

"Yes, my snowflake," she whispered. "Mama is here. Don't worry, Mama will take care of you, my love."

After a second, Alezya took a deep breath and quickly took off her necklace to put it around her baby's neck.

"Alezya?" Zenia whispered. "What are you-"

"That's enough," their Clan Chief interrupted them.

Alezya's grip tightened around Lumie, but her cousin and her husband stepped aside, Suolk giving Alezya a nervous glance.

"You have the child now," he hissed. "Start talking."

"What do you want to know?" Alezya asked in a tight voice, her eyes on Lumie.

She didn't want to waste time on her father's glare when she had spent so little time with her baby lately. Lumie had changed from the last time she had seen her, and she wanted to take in everything, every little detail she could carve into her mind, every smile and giggle of her baby.

She was starting to look more and more like a little girl and less like a baby, and it made her heart ache. Subtly, Alezya opened her coat and pressed Lumie against her skin, praying that she would share her scent and Kein would be able to smell it. Her baby immediately relaxed, breathing hard against her collarbone, and Alezya leaned her cheek against her, holding her as tight as she could.

All exits from this place were blocked by her father's men, so there was no way for her to make a run for it. Although she was dying to get them both out of there, at least she could finally hold Lumie again.

"Their clan. How many are there? Is there more beyond the forest we don't know about?" her father pressed.

Alezya suppressed a smirk just in time, thanks to Lumie hiding some of her face. Kassein's clan was far bigger than her father imagined. She had seen their land when they had flown, and it was a large country with lots more people and homes. *Kalat Unshreik* too. That amazing mountain was more impressive, beautiful, and imposing than any she'd seen. Still, Alezya carefully put on a neutral expression.

"It's mostly what we see from above," she lied in a low voice. "There are a few more beyond what we see, but that's it. The men aren't as strong as they seem either. Only the best warriors get to fight. Others are young or old and train when they can, away from our eyes."

Her father squinted his eyes. Alezya didn't care if her clan went to battle with Kassein's; her people only sent their warriors to fight. If they believed it might be a war they could win, they would send the kind of men she hated the most, and they could all go to hell for all she cared. She had no doubt Kassein and his people could crush them, and Kein eat them all.

Still, her father seemed suspicious of her words and tilted his head slightly.

"They didn't seem to have any women down there. Why would there be no women if that was all their people?"

"Women are seldom allowed out," Alezya lied. "Most live in a nearby place but remain inside, away from the mountains, so our clan doesn't touch them."

"But you and two other women were allowed outside. And there were no children either."

"I was never left alone, and there was always a dragon nearby, wasn't there? There's a section at the back for women. The other two women and I were only allowed to move around because we belonged to their chief and were watched by their dragons."

She hoped the lie would hold, and she counted on all the blind angles her father's sentinels had of the camp, which she knew all too well herself from having watched the Dragon Clan from the mountain a few times. Plus, they wouldn't have believed that women could move around with no other company than dragons without that kind of reason...

She was using the differences between their cultures to twist the truth into one her father would be more inclined to believe. What else would he think? That she had walked around freely? That the dragon followed her for her protection, not as a threat? That she feared Kein less than Kassein's men? Inconceivable for her father. No, it was far more promising for him to think he could potentially defeat the clan that had plagued them for centuries.

"How did you learn their language?" he squinted his eyes.

"...It was fairly easy. Their language is simpler than ours, and they didn't mind speaking when I was there. They didn't think I'd understand at all. I simply listened and understood things."

"What could you possibly know?"

He wanted proof. He didn't want to believe the daughter he'd kicked out was so smart that she had learned another language. Alezya smirked.

"Their chief is called *aqayir*," she said. "It's their word for clan chief. They call the dragons *taniyen*, the fighters *judun*, and the weapons *dinjhar*."

She knew a lot more vocabulary, but those were the words that would surely get her father's attention more than meat or family.

"How do I know you're not making it up? You have a knack for lying, daughter."

"I can call the dragon."

Her father's eyes opened wide.

"...What?"

Alezya smiled through her tear-stained cheeks, a bit proud at the feeling of anger and disbelief that appeared on her father's face. Envy too, no doubt.

"I can summon the orange dragon," she said. "They have a word for when they're ready to offer it a sacrifice, and I know the word for it. Should I show you?"

Holding Lumie tight against her, Alezya turned around, trying to keep her expression calm.

This could be her chance. This could be her one opportunity to get Lumie out of there... As her father's men's grip had already lessened around her, she shrugged them off and pushed past them to walk through one of the tunnels, feeling half a dozen people following her. She shouldn't run; they would no doubt catch up to her before they got out if she ran. But to think she was headed outside with Lumie... and into the sunlight, Alezya suddenly remembered, stopping in her tracks.

Her faint idea that she might have a chance to get her baby out of there so soon and so fast died as realization struck her. She couldn't take Lumie out now in the middle of the day; the daylight would hurt her.

A knot lodged itself in her throat. She could have been so close!

But it didn't matter. She still had her point to make, and her plan could still work.

"Why are you stopping?" her father hissed.

"...We're far enough," Alezya muttered, pressing Lumie closer against her.

"I don't want my child too close to the dragon."

Or the daylight, she thought to herself.

It was laughable to think the sunlight was more dangerous for her baby than the orange dragon outside. But Alezya had to be careful; she couldn't have her father think she was too close to Kein. It was better if he still believed she feared the orange dragon. Still, she had a point to make.

Alezya took a deep breath, and after shielding Lumie's ear that wasn't pressed against her bosom with her hand, she shouted.

"Kein!"

Her voice reverberated along the walls of the tunnel, all the way to the entrance she knew to be after one turn, opening into a large crevice of the mountain.

She waited a couple of seconds and was about to shout again when a loud growl made them all jump. Everyone but Alezya took a step back in fright. There was a violent gust of wind and then a deafening boom. A ruckus as loud as a thunderstorm came from the other end of the tunnel, shaking the walls around them and even making the floor tremble menacingly. They heard furious dragon growls, claws ripping against stone, and the terrible forewarning sounds of boulders crashing.

Alezya retreated back into the cave, nervous as to how much damage Kein could do against the mountain in its frustration.

She could hear it growl furiously, trying to rip the mountain apart to get to her, and she felt grateful for the dragon's stubborn loyalty.

"*Kein, tawa!*" she shouted again.

The rumbling stopped, but they could all sense the dragon a few steps away, its growls quieting down. Its warm breath sent faint gushes of hot air down the corridor.

After a few more seconds of unbearable tension, Kein let out a long, low-pitched growl, and they heard it take off. Alezya let out a faint sigh of relief.

"Do you believe me now, Father?" She turned toward him with a triumphant expression.

Her father had gone pale and wide-eyed, staring at the other end of the tunnel with sheer confusion painted on his face. Clearly, he hadn't been ready to believe her.

"Wha—... How did you do that?" he grunted.

"I told you I learned a lot from the Dragon Clan by observing them," she muttered.

"Do it again," he hissed. "Call the dragon again!"

"No."

His glare could have burned, but Alezya didn't cower. She held Lumie a bit tighter in case he tried to hurt them and returned his intense glare, resigned to stay defiant.

"What?" he spat.

"I learned how to call the dragon by myself," she said. "You can't do it, and I won't do it and risk my daughter again."

"I could have you and your bastard child killed right this instant!" he shouted.

"Yes, Father, you could. But then you would have no dragon child and no way to call a dragon and impress the other clan chiefs," Alezya retorted fiercely. "Your choice."

For a few seconds, her father kept glaring at her, visibly furious but considering his options. He was still the cunning, vicious all-mighty man she had once known and been scared of, but Alezya was the one who had changed. If she could face a dragon without fear, she could sustain her father's glare.

His eyes turned toward the end of the tunnel, and he licked his lips.

"K-Kain!" he called, butchering the dragon's name.

They all waited, but there was no response, which brought a faint smile to Alezya's lips.

Dragons were stubborn, and Lorey had taught her that they were quite willful too. Kein didn't care for her father and wouldn't respond to a stranger's call. The little doubt she'd had was lifted, confirming how much power she held thanks to her connection to the dragon.

Her father looked passably furious, and he had failed to prove her wrong in front of some of his men, which added to the humiliation.

Alezya almost expected another slap, but he was standing a bit too far and didn't move toward her, only pinning her down with his infuriated eyes.

"...Make sure she doesn't leave until the council gathering tonight," he hissed. "Keep her and her bastard under watch."

Alezya's cousin, who had followed, gave her a nervous glance, but Alezya ignored everyone, only following when pulled back inside the mountain by her father's men. She was just glad he was letting her be with Lumie for a few hours. Perhaps it was because it would be easier to watch them both, but Alezya didn't care.

They would have until tonight, and then, she would be able to take Lumie out after nightfall, which was all she needed. Once she got her baby out of there, everything would be fine. Kein was staying nearby, she was sure of it. She silently prayed it wouldn't change its mind and go back to Kassein, but the orange dragon had more often followed her than been interested in staying by its owner's side, so she hoped it would be patient until the evening at least.

She and Lumie were taken to one of the clan's main caves, where many of her father's men could watch her. Apparently, since her first escape, nobody trusted her to be alone in a narrow cave... She probably knew that mountain better than most of them, but Alezya didn't have any intention of disappearing into one of the crevices this time.

Instead, she ignored all the curious stares, settling herself against the familiar stone, and took off the fur coat to cover herself while she fed Lumie for the first time in a while. The relief of seeing her baby girl fine and healthy was worth absolutely everything. Alezya's heart still ached for Kassein, but at least it was full thanks to Lumie's warmth against her chest. Her necklace was a bit too long for her tiny neck, and her little girl had grabbed the pendant, her chubby little fingers holding onto it.

For a while, the two of them stayed like this in their little bubble while heavily guarded by half a dozen men. People passed by, more of her clan finding excuses to come and see the madwoman who had truly returned, allegedly pregnant with a dragon's child. Alezya ignored them all; she only had eyes for the babe getting milk drunk against her skin.

She wished it had been safe enough to tell her about Kassein. About Kein the orange dragon, about the kind Lorey and the fierce Kiera. About that skinny man who was always funnily wrapped up in absurd layers of fur coats.

She wished she could have let her taste the things she had tasted and the herbs she had smelled. She wished Lumie had experienced the luxury of Kassein's home, his bed full of comfy furs, the meat in his food, the warmth that always came with his embrace...

Instead, she just took in the sight of her baby girl, unbothered by the political plots at play around her and slowly dozing in her mom's arms.

Alezya wished that Lumie could always remain this happy and unafraid.

She leaned over, pressing a long kiss on the baby girl's forehead between her white locks of wispy hair.

"Everything will be alright, my snowflake," she whispered.

She would make sure of it, no matter what. Lumie deserved everything and more. To grow up safe, happy, and loved. It shouldn't have been something they had to fight for, but life just wasn't fair like that.

Thankfully, Alezya had hopes, high hopes, that Kassein could and would provide it for her. Perhaps it was a grand delusion she had been feeding herself over the past few weeks, but after everything that had happened, it seemed like the most plausible of all of her crazy hopes. And she was still hoping she would make it out of this mountain and survive so she could be a part of Lumie's future. At least she would get Lumie outside, but what about her? How long would it take for her father to realize she wasn't pregnant, and what would happen then?

Alezya bit her lip, a cold shiver running down her spine. In the worst-case scenario, he would kill her. Or would he possibly send her back to try again?

This time, she wouldn't be so foolish to come back, and with Lumie gone, there would be no more bargaining chip... so it was unlikely. If there was one thing her maker wouldn't forgive, it was to have been tricked and humiliated in front of the other clans.

Alezya took in a shallow breath; yes, her chances of survival were slim. She could hardly see a future for herself after tonight, but she could still dream of it for a bit.

"You're going to be alright," she whispered to Lumie.

A hard knot formed in Alezya's throat as more and more of her clan passed by, all assessing her with the same mix of surprise, disgust, curiosity, and hatred at different levels. The worst was the looks they were giving her child.

All of them looked at Lumie like she was some aberration, a gross creature they could hardly look at, and Alezya couldn't help but worry again. What if Kassein reacted like the man she had been wedded to did? Her own father had rejected Lumie; what if Kassein found her just as repulsive?

Alezya forced herself to breathe slowly and remember every time Kassein had shown her patience, kindness, and compassion. His own men feared him, and yet, he had been nothing but tender with Alezya.

She pressed her eyes shut. She had to believe Kassein would be the same man she had learned to love. Otherwise, she might have given up on everything. Getting her heart broken by the same man who had healed it once would hurt far too much...

For several hours, Alezya waited while her clan got ready for the gathering. She was watched by many, but no one bothered to ask if she needed anything.

She and Lumie were escorted once when she reminded them they had basic needs, and her cousin's husband brought her some food, clearly the only one who had thought that she might need to eat at some point.

The meal felt quite lacking compared to the lavish meat chunks Kassein had been feeding her, but Alezya was now quite hungry, and she needed the strength.

"Maybe you shouldn't have come back," Suolk muttered, still kneeling in front of her while she ate.

"I couldn't abandon my child."

"...Is it true, what you said? You speak the Dragon Clan's language?"

Alezya assessed her cousin's husband for a second.

Despite the concerned expression he had on, perhaps he had been sent by her father to check if she still said the same things to someone she potentially trusted more.

Luckily for Alezya, she didn't need to lie on that particular subject.

"I do," she whispered.

He raised his eyebrows, stunned. Alezya's eyes went over his shoulders to the busy tunnels. There was some extreme tension, worse than what she remembered from the previous gatherings.

"Why are things so tense?" she asked him.

"The dragon's making everyone nervous," he muttered. "It's still in the area. Some clans have been sending messages to ask to postpone the gathering, but your father insists on maintaining it."

"He wants to use me to make a demonstration," Alezya scoffed.

It was just like her father to thrive on other people's fears. Her cousin-in-law glanced around, nervous about being caught chatting with her, but cleared his throat and gave her a faint nod.

"...Thank you," Alezya muttered after a second, "for taking care of her."

Suolk looked surprised by her words, and his eyes drifted to the baby girl dozing in her arms, most of her white-skinned body protected by Alezya's fur coat. He gave her a half-hearted smile.

"She's so close in age to my son... I don't know why your child is different, but after spending time with her, it's obvious she's just that, a child. As a father, I can't help but think... What if it had been my wife's? How would I have treated the child then?"

"You're a good man, Suolk. Zenia's lucky to have married a man like you."

Perhaps it was because he had come from a different clan, like the man Alezya had been married to. Most daughters were wedded to other clans, but women who were related to the man of power in clans or belonged to stronger clans often had the luck to bring their husbands into their clan instead of the other way around. Zenia's husband had been one of those cases. Suolk came from a different clan with, perhaps, a different culture.

He let out another sigh, glancing around nervously.

"I have to go," he muttered. "Do you need anything?"

She needed a lot of things, but none that her cousin's husband could give her, so Alezya shook her head.

"I'm alright."

"Alright. I... I will try to come and check on you again later."

"Will you be at the gathering?" Alezya asked just as he was about to stand up.

Suolk froze, frowning. He seldom attended the gatherings; he came from a minor clan and had married into theirs.

Suolk was one of those men who held little authority during the gathering, so he usually only attended for the sake of seeing his former clan. As a woman, Alezya had never been allowed to attend the gathering, but she had heard that more than a hundred men from different clans usually attended; it was a big affair for all the neighboring clans, and tonight's promised to be one of the most important.

It was going to be Alezya's first and, hopefully, her last. She had no doubt that her father was going to bring her, just as a demonstration, to show off his daughter that's supposedly pregnant with a dragon's child and, even more impressive, her ability to summon a dragon.

Alezya was counting on things going very differently from what her father had planned; she was going to call Kein, not because her father wanted her to but because she needed the dragon's help.

If things went well, she might get Lumie and herself out of there, but if they didn't, she had to prepare for the worst-case scenario. She had seen Kein attack and kill human men plenty of times, and she had no doubt the orange dragon wouldn't hesitate to attack again; she wouldn't hesitate either if things went down this dark route.

However, she was unwilling to get more people killed than necessary, especially people like Suolk who weren't as evil and greed-filled as her father.

"Alezya..."

"You should go," she whispered.

A few seconds of heavy silence passed between them, Suolk still staring at her with a vaguely confused, almost nervous expression. Alezya dismissed him by refocusing her attention on her baby until he left.

Her short talk with Suolk made Alezya ponder how many other good men were in those mountains, subject to the schemes of others.

Her father and her ex-husband had probably been the worst: raised almighty, filled with the belief that they were above others. Above women, especially. Their daughters and wives were their property...

Kassein wasn't like that. He had shown great respect to his sister and the woman that accompanied her. There were some men in his clan who had shown her disrespect, and he hadn't let it go like many clan chiefs would have. Perhaps being a chief was his birthright, but being a good man was his choice. After having met him, she was all the more a believer that some men just chose to be controlling, abusive, and greedy.

Alezya didn't realize she had dozed off until someone kicked her leg, startling her awake.

"It's time," one of her father's men hissed. "Get up."

It was strange to think that she had seen these men all her life, walked the same corridors as them, and yet, she hardly knew any of their names. They were her father's men, but she was his daughter, and there was a world between them. They would be allowed to marry women from other clans if they showed loyalty and bravery, while she was raised like a princess, untouchable, a precious trade prize. But she was like a possession; her name mattered far less than her father's.

Perhaps they had learned it when she had caused great shame and decided to forget it at all; Alezya didn't care. Her heart hadn't been with this clan in a long while, and now, it was set at the foot of the mountain with a man and his orange dragon.

Alezya didn't fight being escorted, if not jostled, through the tunnels, only holding Lumie a bit tighter against her chest and hiding her with the coat. She had never attended a gathering, so if anything, she was slightly curious to see how those things went. The men in her clan who were allowed to attend considered it a great honor, and it was such a big event everyone talked before and after.

The cave was bustling with energy, everyone excited about the upcoming gathering with the other clans. A lot of people had gathered to watch their warriors and significant figures leave; Alezya had rarely seen so much of her clan gathered in the same tunnels.

She spotted her cousin and her husband, holding their son tight in a corner, giving her nervous glances as they stood away from the marching crowd.

It took a few minutes for Alezya to realize how tightly escorted she was. She had been walking with a lot of men, but when they finally left the mountain through one of its lower tunnels, walking on a snow-covered path that was too narrow for more than a couple of people to walk side by side, she felt a man's hand tighten on her shoulder, and another grab her arm forcefully.

Alezya realized they were forcing her to walk as much as they were trying to prevent her from jumping. She glanced at the ravine a few paces on their right as they were progressing down the side of the mountain. Did they really think she would try jumping down? To save herself, or to kill herself? With her child in her arms? Alezya found that almost amusing, in a dark way, when she had never felt so far from hopeless.

She held Lumie a bit tighter, glancing at her child who was still wrapped tightly in the fur coat; she had no idea how long the journey would be, but her baby didn't seem to mind the stroll now that the sun had begun to set. Lumie was awake and quietly playing with a sleeve of the fur coat, gripping and frowning at it.

When she noticed her mom's eyes through the little opening, she beamed at her, making Alezya smile back.

"Keep moving," a hand brutally shoved her forward, almost making her fall.

Alezya glared at the man. She had barely slowed down to glance at Lumie, but the man behind her was giving her a haughty glare.

"You got something to say?" he smirked.

"No," Alezya retorted. "I was just wondering what humans taste like to dragons."

To her satisfaction, the man's smirk dropped, and his face visibly paled.

As if on cue, a large shadow flew over their procession, making everyone but Alezya jump in fright and try to dodge, either throwing themselves on the ground or against the mountain.

Alezya was more afraid of the sudden crowd movement than she was of Kein, and she threw her back against the cold stone, pressing Lumie against her while the panicked men shouted and pointed at the skies.

She even saw a couple of them trip and fall to their death several dozen feet below while some tried to push others to get back to the nearest tunnel. Alezya only held Lumie tight against her, her eyes riveted on the dragon's flying figure.

Kein wasn't menacing at all; the orange dragon was merely flying above them, almost looking relaxed, and she would have bet it had a silver eye on her.

She couldn't suppress a smile; Kein was there for her, watching her amongst the crowd of men. At the very front of their procession, Alezya saw her father's horrified eyes riveted on her.

"Make it go away!" he barked.

All eyes went from their chief to her, the only woman of their group, who was staring back at her father with the calmest expression of all.

"I can't," she lied. "I don't know the words for it."

Her father's face went red, visibly unconvinced or pissed. Before he said something, Kein took a little dive above them, covering the group with its shadow again before it flew higher again. Alezya could almost feel the orange dragon was curious about the precious cargo in her arms, and she couldn't wait to introduce Lumie to it.

"I wouldn't shout if I were you," she simply warned her father. "Dragons enjoy chasing scared and fleeing prey."

Alezya knew she could have made Kein attack the men around her then and there with just a word. The only reason she didn't was that she was afraid of another crowd panic that could cause her and Lumie to fall to their deaths.

This path was far too narrow for the dragon to land and far too dangerous to cause a commotion. She had already seen two men slip and fall to their deaths; she didn't want to risk being pushed and thrown too. She had to wait until she was fairly certain she could give her child to the dragon without risking their lives, and Kein staying in the vicinity pretty much guaranteed that at least.

After a few seconds of tension, and once they seemed more confident the dragon wouldn't attack them, her clan's men regathered, although she noticed a lot of them were trying to be closer to her, perhaps thinking she could give them some sort of protection.

The fact that her father had ordered her to call the dragon away was probably a dead giveaway of her unique relationship with the orange-scaled monster.

Alezya scoffed when she was grabbed by two more hands than before, and their group resumed its march, every single man terrified and keeping their eyes on the skies while she walked calmly, holding on to Lumie. Her baby began to babble, and as they kept walking and the sun set for good behind the mountains, Alezya uncovered her slowly.

She was hoping Kein would get to take a first look at her baby from the skies and recognize the precious human later.

It was a dark night, the skies cloudy, but now and then, the darker shadow of the dragon could be seen flying in the area. Kein was keeping its distance, flying high in the skies but never out of Alezya's sight, and she wondered if it was intrigued by all the humans moving down from their mountains, converging toward one single area. She had never been to a gathering, but she knew enough to know that they all met in a clearing that was somewhat at the same distance from all mountains and took several hours for all clans to get to. It was probably meant to keep a pretense of peace, as no one would be foolish enough to attack so far away from their home base.

There had been a couple of stories from times when bigger, larger clans had gotten into fights at a gathering, and almost every attendee had been killed or died before making it back to their clan; it was too far in the middle of nowhere to be rescued in case things went wrong.

The most surprising thing was that they had never been attacked by a dragon, but now, Alezya could fairly guess why. First, dragons were diurnal. She had noticed Kein slept when Kassein did and hunted during the day. More importantly, the dragons enjoyed the chase, and a gathering full of humans was probably the equivalent of a boring buffet... if they were even aware of it.

Gatherings happened every full moon, which left a fair amount of time between each, and Alezya realized that either the Dragon Clan didn't know, or didn't care. Otherwise, why wouldn't they have used it to crush all their enemies at once?

"We're almost there," her father's voice announced after a while.

Alezya had lost track of time, but by now, she was freezing, shivering, and grateful for the shoes she had taken. She had fed Lumie once already since they began their descent from the mountain, and her baby was back asleep, thankfully protected from the cold by the large fur coat.

Selfishly, Alezya had taken the thickest of them, a gorgeous white-gray one made of snow leopard fur, and she was surprised no one from her clan had tried to take it from her yet. Perhaps with a dragon at her beck and call, they had decided it wasn't worth the risk... A lot of them around her were also shivering under the ice-cold temperatures but trying to keep a strong facade.

Alezya tried to look around, but the night was dark and the surroundings unfamiliar; she had never ventured so far from her home mountain before. They were still in the heights, but now, they were following the line of a river that ventured between the various mountains, most likely fed by melting snow, and seemed to stream all the way to the edge of the continent. The area was flatter and far safer to walk as a group now, although they had to watch out for crevices. Alezya knew the snow-covered land was more treacherous than it seemed; a fresh coat of white snow could crumble at any moment to reveal a deep, neck-breaking crevice underneath.

For that, she was glad to be positioned in the middle of their procession, with her father's men inspecting the ground long before it was her turn to step there.

On the other side of the river, they soon spotted another clan heading in the same direction, and Alezya witnessed as her father greeted them with a stiff nod and a hand salute.

Their group had gone quiet, tense, and despite the sounds of their men in the snow, Alezya soon heard more coming from other clans who were arriving in the area. Inevitably, she felt the stares on her too.

She was the only woman in a large group of thirty men, not only escorted but also carrying a very noticeable white-skinned child. Lumie, now fully awake, was gripping her mom's dress and glancing around with wide, curious eyes no matter how much Alezya tried to shield her from prying eyes. While her baby was blessed with ignorance, Alezya was filled with nerves. No woman could be comfortable amongst this many men and not a single other woman in sight, but it was worse to know the ones she knew hated her. It was a strange thought to think the creature she feared the least was a man-eating beast flying in the skies above.

Although Kein was flying high and quietly, Alezya, along with men from her clan, glanced up every now and then to check where the orange dragon was. It was reassuring to confirm, every time, that the dragon was far enough that her clan wouldn't freak out and yet close enough that if she screamed, it would dive to their position and be there in a matter of seconds.

She held onto that thought and quietly kept following, her stomach filled with dread as more and more men gathered.

It was a strange sight to see so many different clans, some bearing physical markings she had never seen before, strange tattoos, facial piercings, different types of jewelry, clothing, and weapons. Some kept their heads tightly shaved and covered with tattoos, while others had their hair braided in impressive lengths and intricate designs. Some were half-naked despite the biting cold, and others were showing off magnificent leather and fur clothing. There was even a clan that held some sort of mountain wolves on leashes, their jaws held shut by muzzles. The sight of them made Alezya hold Lumie a bit tighter, feeling anxious with those strange pets near her child. To her surprise, she realized some clans did bring women with them.

She was taken aback for a few seconds; she had always been told that women were forbidden at the gatherings, but now she realized her clan might have just entertained that lie to avoid their women coming.

She counted three clans that had brought a couple of women with them, most likely important figures in their own clans as each woman was beautiful, clothed expensively, wearing ornaments or intricate hairstyles, and escorted by one or two men holding their arm or hand. She had expected the gathering to be full of awful men like her father, but that wasn't the case.

If anything, she was witnessing for herself how different the clans could be, and it was a shock.

They were now gathering around three large fire pits, each clan keeping a good distance from the other, many members whispering between themselves, eyeing the other clans as much as they were eyeing the roaming dragon above.

The clans genuinely had no trust in one another, Alezya realized.

There were a dozen different clans gathered there, but none seemed closer than the others, and all the men who had shown up were armed. Some who could see her among her father's goons were giving her curious glances, frowning at the white-skinned child they could see in her arms.

"Mama."

Alezya turned her eyes to Lumie, who was toying with the necklace again while keeping her big white eyes on her.

"It's almost over, my snowflake," Alezya whispered, pressing her lips against Lumie's forehead.

She had to hope her plan would work. She was almost there...

She was out of the mountain, with Lumie, and Kein was staying close. She nearly felt grateful to the clans for being so brave and maintaining the gathering despite the dragon nearby.

Now, all she needed was the right opportunity as soon as this gathering started. Alezya was barely suppressing the need to call Kein now, but she couldn't risk a commotion when two or three hundred men surrounded her. Moreover, she was slightly curious to see how the gatherings actually went down.

There was something so tense that she couldn't help but want to see what the other clans had to say, what else her father had lied about. It felt like something big was going on, something she shouldn't miss.

So she decided to wait quietly, holding her baby a bit tighter and making sure Lumie was wrapped in the fur coat.

"We shall start," an older man with a long silver beard that reached all the way to his belly announced, stepping into the triangle created by the three firepits. "Welcome to the gathering, dear friends, neighbors, and allies!"

After he spoke, a handful of men stepped into the same triangle, including Alezya's father—the clan chiefs, she guessed.

A few of them checked the sky before they spoke, and though it was still around, Kein wasn't showing any sign of coming down yet. One by one, they greeted the others, acknowledging each other with tense nods.

The tension was so palpable that Alezya had a hard time believing in their "friendship." Every clan was there because they felt the need to, this much was obvious.

The gathering started with pleasantries, with each clan mentioning how little the weather had affected them, their good hunting results, weddings, and births. It was all for show, as Alezya could tell, aimed to present each clan as far more wealthy and well off than they actually were. There were a few mentions of daughters and sons of age to marry, a couple of promises of marriage talk in a more private setting later.

Still, while the discussion went on, Alezya noticed her father spoke very little, instead keeping on a barely concealed smirk. She could guess he was dying to gloat and only biding his time for effect.

"Darak, Chief of the Deklaan Clan!" the silver-bearded man finally called him. "How unusual for you to be so quiet!"

"And for you to bring a woman," another clan chief, the one with long braided hair, frowned.

He was from one of the clans that had brought women with them, and because he resembled one of the women, Alezya guessed it was his relative, perhaps a sister or mother.

Craning her neck to see past the heads of the men surrounding her, Alezya inspected the faces of the other clan chiefs, and sure enough, several were staring at her. Some were frowning at the child in her arms or at her, but none seemed offended by her presence; Alezya truly realized her father might have distorted a few truths about the gatherings to keep women out of it... or perhaps to spin other tales to his advantage.

Alezya had always believed her clan was one of the strongest, or so she had been told since childhood. It might have been true in terms of numbers, but seeing the other clans, she definitely found that their people were lacking in other areas. Some of the other clans boasted warmer outfits, better-crafted items, improved weapons, intricate hairstyles, unique accessories, and so on. Compared to others, Alezya even thought her people seemed... unrefined. Maybe their obsession with war with the Dragon Clan had stalled their cultural growth.

Either that or their pathological misogyny, Alezya thought darkly.

"How dare you bring that witch here?! You said she was dead!"

All eyes turned toward a man behind one of the clan chiefs, and Alezya's blood instantly went cold, a shiver crawling up her spine.

Her ex-husband.

Vasilias, son of the Exkiu Clan Chief, had just stepped out of the thick crowd that represented his clan to point an accusing finger her way.

Either he hadn't seen her before or had not recognized her sooner, he was now looking absolutely beside himself with anger.

Alezya unconsciously took a step back, but she didn't shy away from his murderous glare. It felt strange to see Lumie's biological father after so long, but her body recoiled on instinct. How had she ever tried to love this man? How had she been so desperate to please him, to forgive and forget the animal he could turn into? Now, the only desire he ignited in her was to puke and crawl out of her own skin.

And then, she saw it.

The dark, unnatural veins twisting beneath the skin on the side of his jaw and neck, like roots of something rotten. A network of sickly scars, as if his blood had once turned to poison and never fully faded. He was still marked by it, and likely still suffering. His fingers twitched, as if resisting the urge to claw at his own skin, but instead, he glared at her, his hatred boiling over.

Alezya forced herself to hold his glare; she wasn't scared or ashamed. Instead, she returned his menacing expression like the witch they believed her to be. He could loathe her all he wanted, but Alezya refused to ever shy away from his glare again.

So what if she had been rejected by this man? She had been chosen by a *dragon*.

"You said that vixen was dead!" he insisted. "After how she humiliated me! After how she cursed me! I want her head!"

Alezya realized she now feared the man far less than she hated him, and it felt good.

It felt even better to know he hated her as much as she hated him as if it solidified her own hatred. He really thought she had cursed him, and she would gladly let him think it, because she had certainly thanked again and again the ashweaver spider that had gotten revenge in her stead.

All of the pain she'd endured made her stronger, and she could focus her hatred on two men: her ex-husband and her father. Witnessing the hatred seeping out of the two of them, Alezya wasn't ashamed to nurture the vicious desire to have them both dead. After all she had suffered, everything she had been subjected to by their hands, it felt like justice. It wasn't something she had dared to nourish before, but now that she knew what a good man was like, she knew those two deserved no forgiveness from her.

Either by her own hands or her command to a dragon, Alezya silently took an oath to end those two men. She had suffered far too much to find it in herself to ever forgive or forget the abuse she'd endured and worse, how they'd used her baby.

"You have no say in what I do with those of my clan," her father hissed, clearly annoyed by the interruption. "We annulled your wedding, that is enough."

"My reputation was ruined by that whore!" Vasilias insisted. "I want her head as an apology for insulting me! And my clan! And her bastard's too! I should have thrown that abomination off the mountain the minute it was born!"

Alezya squinted her eyes, imagining pushing *him* off a cliff instead.

Perhaps she could convince Kein to drop him from far higher than that. That sounded fitting.

She didn't say anything, but his Clan Chief whispered something to her ex-husband that had him shut up, although he still had a furious expression on. Alezya realized the Exkiu Clan Chief was no longer his father. Had the power shifted in their clan? Was that why they could tell him to shut up and stand back?

"I hope you'll forgive this affront, Vasilias. And as you know, I don't usually find it appropriate to bring women to such meetings," her father said, "but in some circumstances, it might be unavoidable. Necessary, even."

His words were met with a couple of sour expressions, as the clans who had brought women, and perhaps often did, didn't appreciate their meaning. Yet, all eyes were now on their Deklaan Clan, eager for an explanation. Very purposefully, he glanced at the skies, his dark eyes quickly finding the roaming dragon above their heads.

"See," he said, "as one of the clans closest to the Dragon Clan, it is part of our duty to continually bring more information about them, learn about our enemy, and find critical weaknesses they might have. Our historical position puts us at a unique advantage to study our common enemy and bring to the other clans critical information for our survival."

"Get to it, Darak," the Clan Chief with the braided hair hissed.

"Are you unwilling to hear about our discovery?" her father sneered with an arrogance beyond measure.

"I am unwilling to hear you ramble on for hours about your so-called advantage. You harass us at every gathering with endless tales of how important your clan is and your tales of success, and yet, the dragon is still in the area, menacing us all. You're not the only clan trying to defend our mountains, but I hear very little tales of your battles."

Alezya didn't suppress her smile.

She had expected the other clan chiefs to all be as greedy and arrogant as her father, but she was discovering a very different world.

In fact, as she looked around, she recognized clans that she had only ever seen from afar, other clans who attacked the Dragon Clan far more often than theirs did, and they all seemed in silent agreement with the braided-hair Clan Chief. Her father's arrogant words seemed to annoy more than they impressed.

He must have also noticed, but he only grew more arrogant as, for once, he did have the means to back his arrogance.

"Daughter," he called. "Come forward."

Alezya almost snorted. He hadn't treated her like his child in a long while, and it felt quite irksome to hear him remind her of their bond now of all times.

Still, she was pushed to the front with forceful shoving from various hands, the crowd splitting between her and her father. She was careful not to approach him from too close, instead staying a few steps behind the imaginary triangle created by the fires, and a couple of steps away from the crowd formed by her clan. Alezya's blood heated up; it was almost time. She glanced up, finding Kein easily with her eyes. The dragon was now completely still in the darkness, gripped on the corner of a mountain like a gargoyle. No one but her had spotted it, but she could easily find the familiar pair of silver eyes.

"This is my daughter, Alezya," he introduced her.

"We all know of your child," another of the chiefs said. "As if anyone would have forgotten the mess she made between your clan and the Exkiu Clan, after Vasilias' outburst. She's the one who turned out to be a witch and a whore after you boasted of her 'incredible' beauty for months..."

Alezya's spine stiffened; she hadn't even thought anyone else would have been aware of her or her sham of a marriage. She also truly didn't care that her father had oversold how pretty she was; it was probably not the least of the truths he'd bent for his benefit...

"Right," Darak sneered. "As you know, she was 'returned' to our clan after the birth of that... child. This is why, while she was no longer capable of being wed, she was still eager to serve her clan in other ways."

Alezya couldn't remember being eager to do anything for her clan in a long while, but she remained quiet while her father explained, far too excitedly, how he had sent her as an offering to the Dragon Clan, with the hopes of getting her pregnant with a dragon's seed. It was a very freely adapted version from the truth of Alezya fleeing with her child, being beaten between the mountains, and then being rescued by Kassein...

She noticed some of the clans seemed aware he was lying; many were whispering between themselves, eyeing her and her father and pointing fingers. She had always wondered if other clans had been aware of her people chasing her down the mountain, and perhaps, they had.

Either way, many seemed baffled, but more seemed genuinely eager to know more. Alezya noticed most eyes were on her father, but the female relative of the Clan Chief with long braided hair had her eyes riveted on her instead. Alezya returned her stare, wondering what that woman's life was like, and what she thought of standing there amongst all those men.

Meanwhile, her father was basking in the attention.

"We have succeeded beyond our expectations," he announced. "She is bearing a dragon's seed!"

There was a collective gasp, and most eyes drifted to her, making Alezya step back, grossed out by the sudden attention. There were many whispers, eyes drifting to her belly, disgusted expressions, and others who seemed genuinely impressed or curious.

One voice raised above the general surprise, however.

"That whore spread her legs for our enemy?" Vasilias shouted, glaring at her. "After cursing me, you sent that witch and her bastard to the Dragon Tyrant?"

"...Better *his* bastard than your child," Alezya grimly muttered.

She realized as soon as she had uttered her words that this was true; Lumie's blood relation to that man didn't matter anymore. Alezya had once been disappointed that he didn't want her, but now, she realized that it was a blessing. Lumie deserved a good father, a good man who wanted her. She could only hope Kassein would be that man.

Reeling in the undivided attention, her father's vicious smile spread even further, and he raised both hands to commandeer the attention back to him.

"That isn't all," he shouted. "Not only was she welcomed by the Dragon Clan, unsuspecting of our genius plan, but she has also learned a lot of their ways. It is a truly unique blessing that our clan has received the gift to *command* that dragon!"

He pointed his index finger at the sky, his words followed by incredulous silence.

After a while, someone cleared their throat, and a few laughs echoed around. Alezya wasn't surprised; she wouldn't have believed it either if she had heard those mad words a few weeks back.

A few seconds later, some people broke into actual laughter, generating waves of sneers, chortles, and grins. If there hadn't been some tension, surely a lot more of them would have been laughing much louder, but either way, her father was being ridiculed for his words.

Alezya suspected some who hated him were even making their laughter worse on purpose to infuriate him, and it worked. He tried to keep his expression neutral for a while, but eventually, fury and embarrassment took over and he spun around, glaring at Alezya.

"Call it!" he barked.

While no one paid attention to her, most men around were busy mocking her father; Alezya squinted her eyes at him in disbelief at what she'd just heard.

"You want me to call him here?" she muttered. "There's no space for a dragon that size to land without harming—"

"I know," her father hissed.

He wanted to make a point, Alezya realized, horrified.

She hadn't anticipated the clearing being too small and packed with people for Kein to land, but it hadn't been something she had even begun to think about until her father had given her the order. Alezya glanced around at the other people present, still amused and chuckling.

She didn't think she would care about anyone other than Lumie at all, but those other clans had done nothing to her. If anything, they didn't seem to like her father at all either... Her plan hadn't accounted for the other attendants of the gathering being innocent people. She'd expected them to be as cruel and hateful as her father and his goons, and she hadn't even expected women to be in attendance. If she called Kein, several of them would inevitably die, crushed by the dragon if not trampled by the crowd's panic.

Aghast, Alezya realized that was his plan; her father wanted to make a bloody statement by causing a few casualties. The worst part was that none of the clans would have much room to complain once they had demonstrated they could control a dragon.

Except that her father had no control over Kein, Alezya did.

"No," she retorted with an angry voice. "Have them clear some of the area first. If we—"

"I said call it now!" he barked furiously.

"What is this, Darak? I thought you could control the dragon, but it's all your daughter?"

"I am her Clan Chief," he hissed, his eyes still riveted on Alezya, "and she will obey me. Grab the bastard!"

"NO!"

Alezya barely had time to scream before she and Lumie were ruthlessly ripped apart. She felt a violent pain tear her scalp, and her legs brutally hit the ground as she was dragged away. Through her panicked tears, she saw Lumie being taken away by one of her father's henchmen.

"No!" Alezya shouted through the pain, seeing red.

"Call the dragon," her father hissed. "Perhaps that beast will finally get the sacrifice it wanted..."

"KEIN!" Alezya screamed furiously.

A furious, deafening growl shook the area less than a second later.

All eyes went up seconds before the men ran in all directions, raw panic spreading through the crowd like wildfire, except for her father, who watched in fascination. If he hadn't been so greedy or drunk on his power, perhaps he would have found it odd how willing his daughter had been to call the dragon who supposedly wanted to eat her child in a moment of despair.

Alezya tried to fight the man holding her by her hair, her scalp burning while she was doing her best not to lose sight of Lumie. Her baby was quickly moving away from her, taken into the panicked crowd, but all she could hear was Lumie's terrified cries and screams. She couldn't see her anymore, but her baby was bawling her lungs out, probably scared, more by the panic and the stranger who had just ripped her from her mom's arms than by the dragon flying above them.

"Lumie!" Alezya called in the commotion.

She felt the familiar gust of winds whisking waves of snow left and right, throwing many flat on the ground. There was mayhem around her, and yet, pushing through knees and snow, Alezya managed to get somewhat on her feet to get a glimpse of the situation.

Kein hadn't landed, and to her surprise, the dragon seemed unwilling to, its silver eyes scouring around the confused crowd of humans as if looking for where to go. The orange dragon wasn't willing to harm those humans, she realized. It wanted to get to her, but it wasn't sure which humans it could harm, or so it looked like to her.

She had seen Kein attack humans countless times, but now, she realized the dragon was far smarter than she had given it credit for; how else would it have known to spare humans at the camp but attack those who peeked out of the mountains? To suddenly attack the ones who harmed her amongst humans it saw every day? Lorey had told her many times how smart dragons were, but only then did Alezya truly understand.

The dragon was hovering just above the crowd of panicked humans, but soon, they would go from panic to revolt, and Alezya could already see many of them shouting orders, taking out weapons.

"The baby!" she screamed to Kein before remembering to switch tongues. *"Take the baby! Take the baby to Kassein! Baby, Kein! The baby girl! To Lorey! Please! SAVE HER!"*

Alezya, out of breath and still fighting the man who was trying to drag her, tried to see if Kein had heard her and hopefully understood her words. She saw the dragon's silver eyes move away from hers to scour the crowd, easily locating the little dot of white skin amongst them seconds later. Kein let out an angry growl at the sight of the crying baby, and Alezya's heart stopped.

What if it misunderstood her? What if Kein misunderstood her and attacked her baby?

It was already too late. She watched, terrified, as the orange dragon dove toward Lumie and the man who was holding her. Unable to endure not seeing what was happening, Alezya finally grabbed the man who had been pulling her, violently bit his arm, and as soon as he let go with a pained scream, ran away from him.

She ran just far enough to get lost in the crowd and locate the man who had taken Lumie. Surprisingly and thankfully, her father's henchman hadn't dropped her in his panic; instead, he was running away from the incoming dragon with a horrified expression stuck on his face. There was something nonsensical about running away from a dragon whose wingspan covered half the area, but the man still ran, holding the crying babe in the bundle of fur, Lumie's screams barely audible above the gusts of wind, the adults shouting, and Kein's grunts.

The orange dragon chased the man with annoyed growls, but as its claws came close, the man escaped by taking a different direction at the last second. Alezya could only watch from afar, but she was fairly certain the man would already be dead if that had been Kein's intent.

Instead, the dragon was chasing after its prey, not needing to see Lumie to know it had to follow the bundle of fur. Her heart pounding, Alezya witnessed what looked like the longest hunt in the world for a dragon. Kein tried twice to take the baby away, but every time, its claws somewhat missed their grip, closing on snow or barely scratching the man's clothes.

Alezya realized the dragon was trying to take the baby away without killing the human, and all of a sudden, she didn't care who died or who lived but her daughter.

"Kill him!" she shouted angrily, forgetting to switch languages. "*Kein, hunt him and take the baby away! Save the baby!*"

She would never have thought she would one day send a dragon to kill a man, but right now, she was thinking like the mother she was, desperate to save her child. Alezya knew they were out of time; the clans, who had also begun to realize the dragon was unwilling to kill, were gathering and beginning to throw weapons in its direction. They were too far to aim well but too close for her to think Kein would remain unharmed for much longer, and she did not want to try to direct a furious dragon.

As if it had been waiting for her order, Kein let out a deafening growl and dove even faster onto the man holding Lumie, leaving him no chance this time.

But, to Alezya's horror, Kein attacked head first, its large maw wide open, all fangs out.

"No," she whispered, far too faintly for the dragon or anyone to hear. "*No, Kein, don't hurt her–!*"

If the dragon heard her, it didn't stop its attack.

Alezya felt her heart sink in her chest as she watched, helpless, the dragon's mouth close around the bundle of gray fur. Blood flew, and a man's horrifying scream erupted.

Alezya watched, all blood draining away from her face, as the man who had held Lumie fell back, half of his arms ripped away and bleeding. Kein had ripped everything from his elbows to his hands away, and Lumie with it. Alezya felt nausea swirl from her stomach to her mouth, and she fell to her knees, numbed by the horror of what had just happened.

It was still chaos around her, but she had gone deaf, her vision tunneling on the dragon's blood-covered maw. Lumie was gone. Kein had just...

"No," she heard herself mutter. "No, no."

The dragon had stopped growling, and it took off, visibly searching for her and finding her in seconds. Alezya knew she should have crawled away, tried to retreat from the monster that had just eaten her baby, but she was stuck to the ground, incapable of moving. Not a single one of her limbs was willing to move, stunned by shock.

She still didn't move when Kein tried to land in front of her.

The orange dragon was flapping its wings, sending gusts of snowy wind left and right, its large claws a man's height away from the ground. Kein couldn't land, but it was maintaining its flight right in front of the shell-shocked woman. Then, slowly, it opened its mouth.

"No way..."

Alezya gathered just enough strength to get up and, with shock, peered inside the dragon's bloody jaw. A baby was crying.

Alezya almost couldn't believe her eyes and ears, but Lumie was there, still perfectly fine and wrapped in the fur coat, nestled on the dragon's tongue, right behind the barrier of bone-breaking fangs. The baby girl didn't enjoy being tossed around, and she was squirming and crying under the covers, but she was fine; Kein had simply grabbed her the only way he could to tear her from the man without harming her...

Alezya was in utter disbelief but relieved beyond measure.

She only had a second to enjoy this, however, as Kein brutally veered off, and she saw a man's blade stuck in the dragon's flank.

"No!" she shouted.

Just then, hands grabbed her arms and hair, pulling her away from the dragon.

Kein growled in warning, but Alezya immediately made her decision and shook her head as hard as she could, trying to catch its eye.

"*Kein, fly!*" she shouted in the Dragon Clan's language. "*Go! Take the baby to Lorey! To Kassein! Go! Fly away!*"

The dragon seemed hesitant to leave her, furiously growling at the men handling her brutally, and Alezya could have cried; she couldn't even forgive herself for not trusting the dragon seconds ago. Kein wasn't just willing to save her baby, it was reluctant to leave her behind.

She cried but did her best to smile through her tears. Lumie was safe, and she was going to be safe for good with Lorey and Kassein, and that was all she wanted.

"*Go,*" she insisted, "*and thank you.*"

Kein let out another long, low-pitched growl, and after a beat, finally took off.

While she was aggressively pinned to the ground, men shouting around her, Alezya silently cried tears of joy against the fresh snow, watching with one eye as the orange dragon fled against the night sky. She was gone. Her baby was going to be free.

"Hold her! Hold the woman!"

With Kein flying away, the clans managed to regain a bit of continence, getting back on their feet, regrouping in their previous positions, helping each other up, and sorting out those who had been injured in the stampede. In fact, most injuries had occurred because of their own panic and disarray more than anything Kein had done.

No one but the man whose arms had been bitten off had died, they slowly realized, which was a surprise as much as it was confusing. Alezya was hauled back up on her feet, although she was tightly held with her arms behind her back, and someone gagged her before she could get a word out. She found it laughable; they were terrified of her calling Kein back. Many were now watching her with horror, shock, and even fear.

"See!" her father suddenly gloated, looking ecstatic. "The dragon obeys the Deklaan Clan!"

"Not your clan," one of the chiefs spat angrily. "Your daughter."

Alezya realized that she was heavily guarded not because of Kein but because of all the other clans that now had eyes on her.

They had all witnessed that she had been giving orders to the dragon, and Kein had faced her for several seconds before flying off. They might not have understood her words, but there was little room to misunderstand what they had all witnessed.

Her father's expression gradually fell, transforming back from elation to annoyance.

"The girl belongs to my clan," he hissed. "She is my daughter, she obeys me!"

"If so then why not let the child speak?" the woman with the long braided hair spoke up with a vicious glare.

"She will speak when we need her to," Darak hissed, glaring at everyone who didn't belong to his clan.

There was more tension in the air than when Kein had been there; this time, every clan was glaring their way.

The dragon's attack and its wings had blown out two of the three fire pits, leaving the clans in a red glow, a dangerous semi-darkness. Even surrounded by men from her own clan, Alezya could tell the tension was so high, things were a spark away from exploding. Would the other clans attack hers just to get to her, the woman who commanded a dragon?

She could still see many eyes on her in the dark, and she guessed many were considering the idea. Some were probably trying to gauge their chances, or how likely she would be willing to help; unfortunately, despite her hatred for her father, his clan was still very much rallying behind him, pulling Alezya away from the other clans and silently promising to fight anyone who tried anything.

"...This is nonsense," the silver-bearded Clan Chief finally muttered. "If the girl can talk to the Dragon Clan, we should be negotiating with them!"

"Negotiating with the Dragon Clan?" another clan chief sneered. "Have you gone senile? They have been hunting us down for centuries! They are our enemy!"

"They will be our enemies for longer and kill more of us unless we take a chance to change things!" the older man retorted. "The girl can speak the Dragon's language, by the gods! This is unprecedented, maybe our one and only chance in centuries!"

A heated debate began between those who were for and those who were against, and Alezya watched, stunned.

Her father loathed the Dragon Clan so much that she had never considered that other clans might be more willing to befriend them.

Those who didn't constantly send spies and warriors to the other end of the mountains... Alezya knew for a fact that the dragons didn't need to eat humans, unlike what they'd always believed. They attacked them because they were enemies; there was a necessity and a benefit to attacking the clans who attacked them back. Alezya knew her clan and the neighboring ones, those who resided in the mountains at the edge, had attacked Kassein's clan many times, and sometimes even in despicable ways.

Yet, some clans had few interactions with the dragons over the last decades and were most likely eager to take a chance at a very different relationship, one where they would be free to travel between mountains without worrying about the threat from above... She watched in awe as the realization struck her that some clans loathed this ongoing war and were more than willing to take a chance to make peace with Kassein's clan.

"Does the girl know what the Dragon Clan wants?" one of the clan chiefs redirected the conversation to Alezya. "What do they want from us? What would it take for the dragon to leave us in peace? We cannot continue fighting forever or worse, until they decide to wipe us all out!"

She could feel many eyes turning in her direction, but Alezya was tightly bound and still gagged by her father's men, and she could hardly see anyone from the other clans with how they were grouped around her like a wall. She was only lucky to be rather tall for a woman and able to glance over some shoulders because she was given no chance to speak for herself.

"Whatever you want to tell the Dragon Clan will go through me," her father hissed. "I am the Chief of the Deklaan Clan, and from this day on, we're the only clan capable of negotiating with the Dragon Clan. Therefore, I strongly advise you all to think things over until then. For the future too. After all, she isn't only able to speak their language, she will soon bear one of their dragons as well... See you next time."

With those words and despite a few protests, her father turned around, gesturing to his men that they were done here.

Alezya was dragged along, quickly taken away from the gathering. She heard angry voices, but no one dared to attack; apparently, her father's threat had been terribly effective. Her clan marched, dragging her along without leaving her much chance to protest.

While most of his men were securing their retreat, watching their backs for attacks, her father was already scheming, telling some of his men how they would conduct business with the other clans from then on, leveraging Alezya's link to the Dragon Clan and the dragon he hoped to have in a few months' time.

"And the girl? What if she sends the dragon to attack us? Even if we tie her in a cave, there's a chance she'll find a way to call the dragon. If it damages our tunnels or something..."

"I know where we will keep her."

Her father's cold voice sent a shiver down Alezya's spine, along with a bad feeling.

She would have been a lot more alarmed if it wasn't for the fact that little could scare her now; Lumie was gone, and she was fairly certain her baby would soon be in the safest place in the world, with Kassein. Whatever her father did to her felt like a very small price in comparison to what she had earned today.

She could still seldom believe it, and while she missed her baby already, there was nothing that could make Alezya more relieved than the knowledge that her baby girl would be fine. That was all she could have hoped for, except that she wished she could have seen it for herself, the moment Kein would deliver Lumie to Kassein.

She wished she could have been there to explain, to apologize, even to beg him to take care of them both. She could only wish things would go well for her baby.

It was almost dawn when Alezya and her people returned to their mountain, and much to their collective relief, Kein hadn't reappeared.

Her clan had walked fast and taken detours to try and avoid the dragon's eye, but there was no beast flying above them. Soon, her father's men began to split, some taking the first tunnels back inside, but those who were with Alezya and her father didn't return to the heights.

Confused, Alezya had no choice but to let herself be dragged between icy rocks, only recognizing the area as a dangerous route she would definitely not have ventured in by night, and not even by day. She knew those were dangerous and treacherous, and when she remembered why, she foresaw her father's plan.

"Here."

She was violently pushed, and before she could stop herself in any way, Alezya fell through a thick layer of snow.

She closed her eyes, ready for her fall, and sure enough, she landed brutally several feet below. She winced and curled up, vicious waves of pain radiating from her left side throughout her entire body.

"Aren't you afraid she'll lose the child?" one of her father's men commented from above.

"She wouldn't. Those dragon bastards are nearly indestructible... If she truly is pregnant, I doubt she'll die from the cold either. Dragons don't fear the cold."

Alezya barely suppressed the need to shout back that she wasn't pregnant to curse them, but she held her tongue. If he found out, her father might just try to get rid of her, and foolishly, she was holding on to the hope of seeing Lumie again. Instead, she grimaced in pain, and her eyes found the thin ray of light coming from above.

The crevice was deep, narrow, and several feet under the ground. There was just enough room for about three humans to lie down there, and there was another crevice next to her, narrower, which seemed to go even deeper, and she shuddered, hoping the ice under her wouldn't break.

It was awfully cold. She shivered, and curled around herself, missing the fur coat Kein had taken with Lumie.

"How ironic," her father's voice carried well in the cave. "You might face the same end as your mother, Alezya."

"Wh-what? My mother?" She shivered.

"That foolish woman tried to disobey me too. She wanted to go back to her clan and leave me. I told her she was only allowed to leave if she left you behind. At first, she didn't want to, but eventually... So she left, the silly woman she was. She really thought she'd get to leave me, the Deklaan Clan Chief. Truthfully, I didn't mean to kill her. My plan was to trap her in a crevice just like this one and make her regret her actions until she agreed to come back and be the obedient wife she was supposed to be... It's too bad she killed herself from the fall."

Alezya felt as if a block of ice dropped into her stomach, colder than the wind prickling her skin. The horror gradually filled her in waves as she slowly took in her father's words. She had heard him, but it was so awful that it took her several seconds to really understand what he'd just admitted to. She shivered and realized her body was reacting much faster than her head, violent sobs shaking her.

"You... You killed her...?" Alezya's teeth chattered between her tears. "You killed my mother?!"

"She killed herself when she chose to leave me," her father spat, "and you should know better than to repeat that stupid woman's mistake, Daughter. I will make sure you're fed, but until that bastard is born or we need you, you shall stay here."

Alezya didn't say anything.

She only lowered her head, letting her hair fall around her face, hiding the hatred she was feeling for her father at that moment.

She tightened her fists until her nails drew blood. Anger dominated her pain. Never had she believed she could hate the man more than she already did, but there she was, proven wrong.

She was silently grieving for a mother she'd already lost once, and shivering at the horror of facing the same fate, dying in a cold, icy pit. It formed an unexpected resolve in her. Despite the painful protests of her body, Alezya forced herself into a seated position, drawing her knees to her chest and wrapping her arms around them.

It was cold, so cold that she wasn't sure she would survive more than a day in there. She was grateful for the sun rising, but there was no way she would last a night in this place... and Kein couldn't rescue her this time. The ice above her would crumble and bury her alive under the weight of a dragon. Her only hope was for Kassein to locate her, but within a day, it felt impossible...

She let out another tear, and then a full sob.

She tried to hold onto her memories of Kassein's warmth or Lumie's smiles.

Of delicious meat soups around a fire pit, of hot dragon scales, and a funny man in layers of coats. She wondered if they would look for her again... She had left the Dragon Clan twice. How could they forgive her and come look for her again after that betrayal?

"...I love you," she whispered to the silence, snow and ice surrounding her.

Then, she let out a shivering exhale, closed her eyes, and rested a wet cheek on her knee.

Chapter 14

A heavy downpour was plaguing the south of the Empire.

It had started almost as soon as they had flown past the Shadelands and left the Onyx Castle behind. Kiki was usually one of the fastest dragons, but the rain and her load of two adult men slowed her down considerably, and the sun had set behind the dark clouds by the time they landed in the gardens of the Imperial Palace.

Tievin was drenched, all of his fur coats rendered twice heavier than usual, and his teeth were loudly chattering. The usual green grass around the lake the palace surrounded was so saturated with water that their shoes sunk in by half an inch. Kassein unloaded their luggage, mostly Tievin's, while his Intendant tried to disembark, but the operation was rendered quite difficult by all his oversized layers. Eventually, he tripped and inevitably landed on all fours.

"By the mighty dragon," he grimaced.

He was still a bit green from the trip and looked seconds away from puking in the grass. Kassein didn't say anything, glancing around while his Intendant regained his continence and equilibrium.

He had forgotten how sad and boresome this place could get during the rainy season. There were a handful of servants nearby walking under the white stone arched pathways of the palace, and upon recognition, a couple of them opened their eyes wide before running inside, no doubt to warn the Emperor of the unexpected arrival. Kassein had thought it best to fly straight to the Capital without forewarning, not leaving any time for the rest of the family to try to come. He already didn't want to be here and dreaded running into anyone.

He hadn't set foot in the Capital in a long time now, and he certainly hadn't missed it. This place had banished him as much as Kassian had, making him feel unwelcomed, if not feared by the locals. Even the Imperial Servants, whose duty it was to literally serve the Imperial Family, didn't come out to greet him, only observing him from afar like an unexpected storm cloud from the safety of the archways.

Kassein glared back at them, slightly annoyed. He might not have been the most popular, but he was still an Imperial Prince, and Kein wasn't even around to give them a fair excuse to stay away.

"So improper," Tievin scoffed as if he'd read his thoughts. "The Imperial Servants' training seems to be lacking nowadays!"

He had said it loud enough that a couple of Imperial Servants heard it and felt compelled to go against their instincts and approach, albeit they made a noticeable detour around Kassein to come and grab the luggage.

Kassein couldn't help but notice that even Kiki seemed to be more easily approached than he was... He shook his head in resignation and moved to get inside the palace, Tievin two steps behind.

Everywhere he went, there was a mix of reactions, going from wide, stunned eyes to some servants swiftly turning around and disappearing out of sight. There was something unnerving about still being so feared after so much time had passed, but at least no one dared to stop him on his way to the throne room. Even the guards seemed unsure what to do, shocked to see him, nervous about his determined approach, and unwilling to stop a relative of the Emperor, even the least popular one.

The only thing to slow Kassein down was the feeling of dread torturing his gut as he got closer to his destination. Tievin was somewhere behind him, moving more freely after having shed the drenched layers and leaving his luggage to be carried by servants, but Kassein couldn't hear anything; it was as if everything else was tuned out, his being solely focused on the impending encounter.

The last time he had seen his brother had been a terrible moment, a memory he didn't even want to remember, but his head was forcing him to. The fury and disappointment of his brother. The harsh words that had echoed around the walls, giving him the appraisal he'd always known as the failure of the family, an Imperial disappointment. Kassein's throat tightened and his nerves tensed.

He could feel his spine going stiff as steel, his muscles tense, his hands sweaty, his mouth dry. He hated every bit of this, every step that took him closer to his brother. The only thing that kept him going, the thing that had prevented him from having Kiki turn around during the long hours of this journey, was Alezya.

He wanted to be that man for her. If he turned around now, he would never be the man she deserved. It was as simple as that.

Not easy, but simple.

He held onto the memory of her, of her smell, of her silky hair, of her smooth skin and shy smiles, as he reached the large doors.

He hesitated behind the threshold, so tense he feared he might never be able to take another step again. It was Tievin's voice that unexpectedly grounded him, snapping him away from his internal chaos.

"Is the Emperor inside?" he asked the pair of guards who'd been staring at Kassein.

"Yes, Intendant."

"Well then," Tievin said, with a tone that implied they should hurry up and do what they were here for.

The doors opened. Heavy, imposing, needlessly high.

Kassein hated those doors. They were meant to make people on this side feel small, like everything in the throne room. It was one of the largest halls of the palace, and it was almost empty. There was no furniture but the large throne at the end. There were stairs, but once upon a time, there had been proper chairs and soft carpets for guests to sit on. It looked like Kassian didn't invite many guests to sit down anymore.

Perhaps the place was rendered even darker by the raging downpour outside, but even so, Kassein found it a striking contrast with the warm hall of his childhood. He and his siblings used to happily barge into the throne room at all times of the day to bother their Aunt Shareen, the previous Empress. There was a seat his sister Sadara preferred for her needlework, next to the one Cessilia would read on for hours. There would be carpets covered with toys for him and the younger siblings, and servants would go in and out all day to help his parents tend to the eight siblings. Now, the place was bare, cold, uninviting.

It took Kassein a few seconds to recognize the place as it wasn't even lit by candlelight, but engulfed in the darkness of a gray evening instead.

And it was almost empty, except for the one lonely figure of his older brother. Kassian wasn't seated on his throne but on the floor, his back and head slumped against the large golden seat. He seemed to be asleep; one arm was on his bent knee while the other rested on his straightened leg. His hair had grown longer since the last time Kassein had seen him, reaching beneath his shoulders.

He didn't announce himself, but took in a deep breath, almost expecting to smell something odd in the air. Alcohol, perhaps.

"What are you doing here?"

Kassian's voice broke the silence before he opened his eyes.

Kassein's eyes were a dark green, a soft mix between his mother's and their father's black irises, but Kassian's were exactly like their mother's, green as emeralds.

Perhaps that made the irate expression on his face feel even worse.

"Long time no see, older brother," Kassein finally managed to utter.

"I asked you a question."

Kassian sounded in an even worse mood than the last time he had seen him, and that didn't seem possible.

Still, Kassein steeled himself for a hard conversation. He had left after an irreparable mistake and was coming back to ask a favor of the brother he'd left to deal with the horrible consequences; this wasn't going to be easy at all.

"...I came to ask you something."

"I wonder what it could be," Kassian sneered. "...How is the family of the man you killed, perhaps? Or how many of them did I have to look in the eye and apologize to in your stead? No? Then how is the widow, surely? How are his children growing without their father? How many houses have been rebuilt since you left? How many times have I had to apologize for your actions? How many of our citizens fear and despise us thanks to you? How–"

"I get it," Kassein interrupted him, his throat tight. "...I get it, Kassian. I'm sorry."

His older brother went silent for just a second, squinting his eyes.

"You're sorry? ...*Sorry?* You think being sorry begins to cover it?"

"...I would have apologized myself. I would have apologized and rebuilt those houses myself if you had let me–"

"How?" Kassian shouted. "How the hell would you have done anything but destroy? How was I supposed to trust you to rebuild something after all the damage you've caused for the last ten, no, fourteen years? How do you apologize for killing a man, Kassein? Tell me, where would you start?"

Kassein clenched his fists, taking in the verbal abuse.

He knew his older brother had every right to be mad, but it seemed Kassian was done, for he slowly stood up. Surprisingly, he had to lean on his throne to get himself upright, which made Kassein frown.

"Are you drunk...?"

"What I am, Kassein, is *tired*," Kassian retorted.

His tone was full of anger and sarcasm, but beneath it, Kassein felt something in his older brother's voice. Genuine tiredness, not just physical fatigue, but the kind of deep mental exhaustion that took a toll on someone's mind. And, underlying, something that sounded like... sadness. Or grief.

Kassein wasn't sure what to say; a part of him almost felt sorry for his older brother, stuck in this golden cage every day. Kassian was the firstborn, and he had been raised to become the Emperor since he was a child. In the year Kassein had been born, Kassian had already reached fourteen years of age and begun to train under their aunt.

Kassein could only guess the kind of pressure that would put on a boy's shoulders.

"...What do you want?" Kassian eventually asked, his eyes set on the rain outside.

Kassein took a deep breath, mentally preparing himself for the hard argument ahead.

"I want the north."

That got his older brother's attention. Kassian turned to him with a confused frown, studying Kassein rather than asking what he meant. Slowly, he took a couple of steps back and let himself collapse into the oversized golden throne.

"You want the north," he repeated slowly.

"From the tip of the continent to the Shadelands," Kassein said. "The Onyx Castle too. I know the north is of little interest to the Empire now, and the local villages need someone to–”

“How dare you,” Kassian hissed from the throne he was slumped on. “After all you’ve done, after everything, you have the nerve to come back here, unannounced, and ask the north from me?”

Kassein clenched his fist. Alezya, he had to think about Alezya, and how much she needed him.

“You wanted me to pacify it,” Kassein retorted, his resolve getting firmer. “You can’t oversee all of the Empire from this throne, Brother. There are things happening in every street, every city, every shadow, and you cannot control it all. Give me the north, and let me take it off your hands.”

Only a subtle twitch of the vein on his older brother’s temple and the tight fist on his armrest gave Kassian’s reaction away. His brother was furious, but he knew Kassein’s words held some truth.

More surprisingly, Kassian kept his ire silent for a few seconds, and surely, that meant there was more to it. Kassein exchanged a glance with Tievin, who looked nervous but equally confused. It wasn’t like Kassian to waver. It wasn’t like his oldest brother to flinch or let anything get to him. Since first taking his seat on the Emperor’s throne, his brother had become as cold as ice and as unyielding as a fortress wall. But this time, for the first time, they both noticed a crack in that wall.

“...Kassein?”

Kassein’s head whipped back to the entrance of the throne room.

Their youngest sister, Sadara, stood there in a silk nightgown, holding two cups, probably one for herself and one for Kassian.

“Oh my dragon!” she exclaimed, a genuine smile spreading on her face.

Ignoring all the tension in the room, she ran to them, shoved the glasses into Tievin’s hands, and jumped at Kassein’s neck to hug him.

It took him a second to recover from the surprise and hug her back. Sadara had always been the sweetest and quietest of his sisters, and she was also the closest to Kassein in age, being less than three years older.

When she finally released him, he could see for himself how she’d grown more beautiful while he was gone, with her dark skin that contrasted exquisitely with their mother’s green eyes, long dark brown hair, and full lips like their father’s. While Cessilia looked a lot like their mother, and Kiera was a mix of their parents, Sadara was a copy of their father, his very feminine double.

“I have missed you,” she whispered, ecstatic.

“I missed you too,” Kassein confessed.

“You too, Tievin,” Sadara smiled, taking the cups back from him.

“Long time no see, Your Highness. Your beauty has blossomed even more.”

Sadara gave him a tight smile but didn’t approach him. Kassein had always noticed how Sadara was wary of men outside of their family and hated anyone but her relatives touching her at all. His sister was twenty-one, but she had grown early into a beautiful woman, and she disliked the extra attention she got for it.

She turned her attention to Kassian, then back to Kassein, frowning as she slowly took in the tension in the room.

"What's going on?" she asked.

Sadara's arrival had noticeably shifted the atmosphere in the room, and she fixed her gaze on Kassian, who was staring at her intently as if they were having a silent conversation. Kassein realized he might have been waiting for his sister to come back for whatever he had interrupted with his arrival.

Still, he couldn't leave without Kassian's approval. Thus, he cleared his throat and, ignoring their older brother's glare on him, quickly explained his request to his sister. Sadara raised her eyebrows, glancing several times toward Kassian while he spoke.

Then, she gave him a faint nod.

"Kassian?" she pressed him.

His older brother hadn't said a word for several minutes now, and he looked annoyed by Sadara's presence. Perhaps he didn't feel like being as angry as before with their sister in the room.

"What an unexpected request."

This time, another voice had spoken, and they all turned their heads to find another of their siblings, Shenan, peering in from one of the arched windows. His dragon, Shan, was as black as ink and incredibly silent, which explained how none of them had heard it land nor noticed its rider eavesdropping before he spoke.

"How long have you been spying?" Kassian hissed, looking even more pissed at him than he was at Kassein.

"Long enough to hear the interesting bits," Shenan grinned mischievously.

He climbed over the window and let himself fall elegantly.

It wasn't always like this, but Shenan was now the sibling Kassein knew the least, mostly because he was the most self-centered and hadn't been around much when they were younger. All that Kassein knew was that he was the next in line until Kassian had children, since Darsan and Cessilia had left the line of succession to live in the Eastern Kingdom, and Kiera had also said she'd never be empress. That and his own interest in politics was why he was the third and last sibling who still permanently resided in the Imperial Palace. For the rest, he might as well have been a stranger.

Despite being dripping wet, he strolled elegantly into the throne room, his messy black hair falling to his shoulders in waves, his skin the darkest of them all, his eyes as black as his dragon's scales.

Strangely, Shenan always sported a long line of black scales on his face, a scar that ran across his nose and under his left eye to his ear. For some reason, that particular wound never seemed to heal, and Kassein had no idea how that strange scar across his brother's face had first come to be. Most of them had a hard time keeping up with his eccentric, unpredictable personality.

While he barely acknowledged Kassein's presence with a little amused smirk, his eyes were scouring the room as if looking for something around the empty space. Their older brother went even more still, his fists clenched.

"Where is that little snake you usually keep by your side, older brother?" Shenan probed, unafraid.

Kassein witnessed Kassian's expression crumble right in front of him.

It was like Shenan's question had broken a dam. His mighty, impassible older brother suddenly looked torn by so many conflicted emotions that he couldn't keep up the act anymore. Fury, shock, despair, sadness, and fury again. His fists went from clenched tight to furiously shaking, and his cold green eyes suddenly turned into a raging and misty storm.

Kassein was stunned. Whoever that "snake" was, they had somehow managed to make the ice wall crumble with the mere mention of them.

If he hadn't known the siblings would never harm one another, he would have been worried for Shenan, for he was the target of the Emperor's most murderous glare he'd ever seen, of which he'd been on the receiving end many times.

While Kassian was still choked up by his boiling anger, Kassein glanced around.

Now that he thought about it, there was something else missing from the palace. The place was strangely quiet, but in the distance, he could hear the faint bustling of the servants.

What he couldn't hear or see, however, was the creature that had accompanied his brother since his birth.

"...Where is your dragon, Kassian?" he finally asked.

Now Kassian's furious glare was on him, and Kassein knew he'd just poured more fuel on the fire. Something else had happened in the palace which made their oldest brother far more enraged than Kassein's request.

Made him more vulnerable too. Kassein had never witnessed his brother failing so miserably to dominate his emotions, which perhaps explained the odd lack of entourage and the alcohol he could smell from Sadara's cups. Kassian was the Emperor; why would he be alone in his ridiculously grand throne room?

No, his older brother was hurting, nursing a wound where no one else had hurt him before, and for once, Kassein could relate to the pain.

They were dragons; they hated to show anything had broken through their scales and penetrated their skin, but here they were, both carrying their bleeding hearts and desperate to stop the pain.

It gave him the push he needed. Kassein stepped forward.

"...I'm doing this for someone."

Kassian frowned subtly, his anger seeming to lessen by a degree.

Kassein hadn't wanted to let Kassian know anything about his real motives, but that was before he realized that behind his facade of the untouchable, impassible Emperor, his older brother was still a man who could bleed, hurt, and go through the same pains he did. Someone who could love fiercely and dangerously, someone who loved like a dragon.

"I can't protect her if I don't have the north," he continued. "Not the military camp, but all of the territories. From the Onyx Castle to the North Sea, I need it all. I want to rule the land she steps on, to protect her. I want to own every single mountain, so there's nowhere they can hide her from me."

Those last words struck a chord with his brother as Kassian's mouth ticked again. His eyes went to his fists, and slowly, he spread his hands, his long fingers gripping the edge of his armrests instead.

There was a long silence, during which Kassein exchanged another look with his siblings. When Kassian wasn't looking, Shenan had somehow lost his smirk and looked as surprised and confused as he was, but Sadara had a sorry expression riveted on the Emperor.

Whatever had happened to Kassian, she knew, and she felt his pain.

"...Did she run away from you?" Kassian asked with a strangely hollow, choked-up voice.

Kassein was surprised by how accurate his older brother's guess was, but after a second, he realized that, perhaps, his older brother actually understood him better than anyone.

"Not of her own will," Kassein confessed after a while. "She had to."

His brother let out a strangled chuckle that had nothing funny to it.

"Maybe she doesn't want to be found," he muttered, staring at the rain. "Maybe that's just your wishful thinking."

"It doesn't matter," Kassein retorted, his brother's eyes flying back to him. "...I'm a dragon, Brother. I don't let go of what I own, of my treasure. ...And she *is* mine."

Nothing had ever made him feel so strong, so determined. He wanted it all: a future with Alezya in the north, her mountains she could return to whenever she wanted, the child she needed back. He wanted it all with her. Facing the brother he feared the most was nothing compared to the prospect of losing that future.

Kassian stared at him for a while, silently, as if gauging his younger brother, reassessing him for the first time in a long time. Shenan and Sadara remained quiet, both holding their breaths.

"Kassian–" Sadara started, but Kassian interrupted her, raising his hand.

"...Take it," he muttered after a while, leaning back.

He'd spoken in such a low voice that his three younger siblings exchanged glances, equally confused.

"You'll let me have the north?" Kassein insisted, barely believing his own ears.

"Whatever you want to do with it," Kassian shrugged. "Be an emperor, a king, a tyrant... Whatever suits you. I don't care. ...Take the Shadelands and whatever lies beyond. I don't care anymore."

Kassein nodded and didn't comment.

Now that his facade had slipped, he could see his brother's actual state, and he didn't like what he saw. Kassian's eyes had already drifted back to one of the windows, watching the sky without seeing it, ignoring all three siblings who were staring in confusion. One could tell his thoughts were far beyond, toward someone or something out of his reach.

"...Kassian, you know if you ever need our help-"

"Go away, Kassein. All of you, leave."

It wasn't a tone that left any room for refusal, although Sadara looked like she wanted to say something.

Still, Kassein gave his older brother one last glance, and turned away, his siblings following him out of the throne room. Whatever monsters Kassian was battling, it was for his older brother to deal with. Right now, he had to focus on the north and this incredible new reality.

That was it. He owned the north. He'd expected his older brother's refusal, to have to fight maybe, not to walk away with an answer that would change the continent's history. Kassian had just agreed to fracture an empire that had stood centuries with its borders unchallenged, leaving Kassein a fraction of the Empire, giving it away like it was nothing.

Kassein had never dreamed of becoming a king or an emperor; he'd never envied his brother's throne for a second. But what he wanted was the power to own those mountains up north. To deal with the tribes, crush those who resisted, and own those who'd submit to him. He didn't care if he became the Dragon Tyrant they'd feared for decades; nothing would stop him from making the north safe for Alezya and her child.

For their children.

"That was unexpected," Shenan said with a light-hearted voice.

"You shouldn't have been eavesdropping," Sadara scolded him.

But their older brother shrugged.

"So?" he asked, turning to her. "Where *is* Kassian's little-"

"Kassein," Sadara ignored him, "I'm glad you came back, even if it's just for a short while... I'm guessing you don't want to stay for a bit? This is dreadful weather to fly in, and Tievin could see his family."

Kassein glanced at the Intendant, who raised an eyebrow, hopeful. He let out a faint sigh.

"We're leaving in an hour," he told the Intendant.

"Thank you, Your Highness," Tievin said, before running off.

Shenan scoffed.

"For someone who looks so much like his father, he sure is a mama's boy..."

"Isn't Evin retired yet?" Kassein frowned.

"As if he would ever retire." Shenan rolled his eyes, taking one of the cups from their sister. "No matter how much he may complain, that Imperial Intendant will work until his very last day, that's for sure."

"How are things in the north?" Sadara asked.

She glared at Shenan, who downed the drink in one gulp before stealing the other one to do the same.

"The usual," Kassein shrugged, "but it won't remain so for much longer."

"So you really plan to conquer those damn tribes?" Shenan asked before letting out a little burp that made their sister grimace. "They've been an eyesore for generations. Kassian may whine about it, but you'll be doing us a favor. No one but you gives a fuck about them."

"It is our birthland," Sadara frowned. "The north is... It is sad that our parents don't live there anymore, but it was still our home for a long time. Our older siblings grew up there even longer."

"I will take care of it," Kassein said, feeling the weight of his promise to his sister. "The Onyx Castle will always be our home."

"And if Kassein takes on the dirty job with the Northern tribes, Kassian will be able to focus on the damn west," Shenan scoffed.

"What's wrong with the west?" Kassein frowned.

Sadara slapped their brother's arm, making him grimace and rub his bicep.

"Nothing," she said. "All politics between here and there, but don't worry, Kassian is working on it."

"Should I tell Kiera to come back?" Kassein frowned.

"You've seen Kiera?" Both siblings looked surprised.

"She came to the north to help me," he nodded. "I had a few issues I needed her and Lorey's help with. As soon as I'm done with the north though, she will be free to leave."

"Oh, it's good to hear you've seen her," Sadara smiled. "Our parents were getting worried she hadn't stopped by in a while... although that's our same old Kiera. Mother will turn fifty this year though, and I'm sure she would love to see her for her birthday celebration. Darsan and Cessilia are making the journey."

"I'll tell her," Kassein nodded.

"That includes you too."

He didn't reply. The prospect of facing his entire family filled him with even more dread than confronting Kassian had. It made his throat dry, and for a second, he wished he'd downed those drinks before Shenan had. He could take Kassian being mad at him, but facing his disappointed parents was far worse, especially if all his siblings were going to be in attendance. His mother's birthday was still months away, but the mere idea of either letting her down or showing up already felt too stressful.

"...I'm going to go back to Kassian," Sadara announced. "He might not say it, but he could use the company right now. And you stay away from him, Shenan. Leave him alone; I'm serious."

She had punctuated her sentence with her index finger pointed at their brother, and Shenan held up his hands, although he had quite the arrogant smirk on.

"As you wish," he snorted.

"It was nice to catch a glimpse of you, Kassein," she smiled again at him.

Then, she turned around, shot another warning glare at Shenan, and walked back toward the throne room. The two brothers watched until she was out of sight, and Shenan rolled his eyes, looking down at the two empty cups.

"Better I drank those than him," he commented. "Kassian can't appreciate alcohol anyway."

"What's wrong with him?"

"What isn't?"

Shenan's scoff felt more factual than mocking, which made Kassein frown. He had rarely seen his older brother anything but calm, quiet, and composed. It felt like he had witnessed a completely different side of him in there, and it made Kassein genuinely curious about the Emperor's circumstances.

"How are things here?" he asked Shenan, hoping to get a straight answer from him, for once.

His brother let out a long, dramatic sigh.

"Lots and lots going on. With Father and Aunt Shareen gone, the politicians think they have a chance at pulling the Emperor's strings. They either kiss his ass or kill his mood, or a sweet balance of both for the smartest of them. There's a lot of unrest with the tribes in the west, as you may have heard... Kassian's trying to continue what our aunt started with the slavery abolishment, but it is not going according to plan."

"What's wrong with that?" Kassein frowned.

It had been their parents' dream to end slavery in the Empire. Their mother, a slave herself, had advocated for it as much as she could, and their aunt had already done a lot, forcing the hands of the nobles to agree to more and more regulations until they could eradicate it completely.

"What's wrong is that you cannot remove one of the pillars this Empire has been leaning on for centuries and not expect the economy to collapse," Shenan replied. "Cessilia's wedding in the east gave our economy the boost it needed to endure the first changes, but that was ten years ago. Trade has slowed, and a lot of people with very loud mouths are spreading the word that slavery would be a perfect solution to a lot of our problems, including the riots in the west."

"And how is Kassian dealing with that?"

"In the Kassian way... and unfortunately, he is nothing like Aunt Shareen."

"Aren't you here to help?"

Shenan gave him an amused look as if Kassein had said something unexpectedly funny. Then, he patted his brother's shoulder.

"Get back to the north, Kassein."

Just like that, he was dismissed, his brother leaving him alone in the corridor. Kassein let out a faint sigh. He had only spent minutes in the palace, yet none of his siblings had stayed to ask more than needed about his life in the north. Perhaps he had come on a bad day, perhaps it was because of the terrible weather, but he still felt the sting of disappointment.

Yet, after reflecting on it for a few seconds, he realized that he missed Alezya more. He loved his family; he loved all of his siblings and his parents, and they had grown up together with a bond that would be unbreakable. However, things were different now. They had all grown up, and after living with seven siblings, most of them had felt the need to find their own aspirations, their own people, their own goals.

This was the first time Kassein genuinely felt like his life had a clear direction, and Alezya was his north star.

Kassein decided to wait for Tievin by Kiki's side under the rain.

His sister's dark gray dragon didn't mind the downpour at all, and neither did he. The Capital was hot and humid, and it wasn't like he would fall sick or anything.

While he waited, he let his thoughts drift back to the memories he had of this place. The hours he had spent by the lake, with their mother or their older sister reading to them. This was his happy place when he was young. Not just the lake, but the imaginary lands his sister's stories would take them to. Things had never been the same after Cessilia's abduction, and that was when Kein had turned on him and when his father had begun to restrict his dragon so he wouldn't be able to attack Kassein. Either an older dragon was around to keep Kein from attacking him, or he would simply be bound by heavy chains.

He wondered where Kian, Kassian's dragon, was. Kian was a magnificent silver dragon, third in size after Kein and Dran, their second-oldest brother's dragon. But Darsan and Dran were both ridiculously oversized, even for their tall family. Kian had always been a long, tall, elegant, and majestic dragon. And it had hardly ever been seen anywhere but by its owner's side. Kassein had expected to see it in the throne room along with Kassian; that place had been designed ridiculously large for the sole purpose of letting the dragons in, but Kian wasn't there. Was their older brother in bigger turmoil than he had let on?

For the first time in a while, Kassein regretted that he no longer felt close enough to his older brother to lend him a helping hand. Perhaps his taking ownership of the north would do that.

It hit him then that he had gotten what he came here for: the north.

The north was now his, along with the Onyx Castle, and the chance to change things with all the Northern tribes none of his ancestors had ever managed to submit. Perhaps he would be able to kill two birds with one stone, taking that issue off his older brother's hands and revitalizing their childhood land.

"My lord!"

Tievin's arrival brought Kassein back to the present, and he frowned as the Grand Intendant came back with a sour expression, new fur coats on, and a bag that looked heavier than when they'd arrived; Kiki noticed too and welcomed him with a growl.

"Already?" Kassein frowned.

"Father was awake," Tievin snorted. "He interrupted my reunion with Mommy, who, by the way, was the only parent in the room delighted to see their child's face after so long without, and he most rudely told me to '*get back to my duties and not come back until I shall be done with it all*'—his words, exactly."

Kassein was hardly surprised. Tievin had been his mother's only child, very pampered and spoiled, and his relationship with his father had always been a strange combination of jealousy and egotism.

Still, he didn't question it, knowing Tievin could go on very, very long rants about his father, and they had a long journey ahead.

"Are we flying back straight away?" Tievin asked with a sigh.

"Yes."

Kassein didn't feel the need to stay here for the night, and he was eager to return to the north as fast as possible. The journey back would take several hours if the weather persisted, and he hated being that far from Alezya for too long. He was still holding on to the thought that she might have gone back to his tent for the night, Kein by her side, and he sure hoped he would find her there when they landed in the morning.

He patted Kiki's head apologetically, glad that the dragon was far more popular than he was and had clearly been fed while he'd been with his siblings. Thus, there was no protest about making the trip back already. They took off under the rain, which, luckily, had begun to slow down and stopped completely by the time they reached the halfway point of the journey.

Thanks to Kiki's pace and the fair weather, the journey back was far shorter, and they made it back to the North Camp just before sunrise.

Surprisingly, the North Camp wasn't quiet despite the early hours.

Kassein spotted many torches lit up, and the fire pits around the camp were lit up too, with many men outside of their tents and running in different directions. Picking a spot for Kiki to land, Kassein spotted his sister and Lorey amongst the ruckus, both women standing close. Not only them, but his dragon was there too, strangely flying low above them, and Kassein urged Kiki to land quickly.

The sight of his dragon brought a surge of hope to Kassein; there was no way his dragon would have turned away from Alezya. Perhaps Kein had followed wherever she'd gone.

But as he landed a few feet away from Kein and glanced around, his stomach sank; she wasn't on his dragon's back, under him, or anywhere nearby.

"Finally!" Kiera greeted him with an exasperated sigh. "It was high fucking time you came back. Your dragon has gone properly mad this time!"

"Where is Alezya?"

"We have no idea," Lorey shook her head with a sorry expression. "Kein just came back a while earlier and he's been acting... strange. He won't land; he keeps making those loops..."

"That bastard tried to attack Lorey!" Kiera barked, keeping a defensive stance between her partner and the orange dragon. "If that bastard brings its ugly head near her again—"

Kassein turned to his dragon, confused and angry. Kiki circled the two women and growled in warning, but strangely, that caused Kein to do another loop rather than land. Kassein was equally bewildered by his dragon's hectic behavior. It wasn't like Kein to retreat, ever.

He waited, his feet planted in the snow and his straight, stiff stance showing nothing of his inner turmoil as the orange dragon descended.

Kassein's eyes skimmed over his dragon's claws and then its back again, hoping for a silhouette or a curtain of black hair to appear along its silhouette. Yet, Kein eventually landed a few steps away from everyone, and there was no sign of their woman.

"Where is she?" he hissed to his dragon.

Kein retreated slowly and issued a low, warning growl, but this time, his owner's fury reached far beyond the dragon's. Kassein walked up to his dragon, his fingers grabbing the rust-colored skin as if he could hold on to it and tear the dragon's scales.

"WHERE IS SHE?!"

His outcry echoed throughout the mountains.

Then, a heavy silence fell on the plain. Behind him, Kiera and Lorey exchanged a pained look. All they could see was the tremble of Kassein's heavy shoulders, shaken by his heavy panting and fury, but they could feel his anger and despair. He heard Lorey approach him, perhaps to say something to comfort him, but he didn't care.

He had been holding on to the hope of seeing Alezya when he returned. Worse, he had thought that regardless of where she had gone, she would be safe under his dragon's protection.

But Kein was right here, and she wasn't. He glared at his dragon, hating the beast more than ever. There was only one thing that should have mattered to both of them and yet...

Then, slowly and unexpectedly, Kein lay down at his feet, burying its body into the snow as if the dragon could squash itself into the ground.

Kassein watched, still angry but perplexed. His dragon let out a low growl, and then suddenly, a muffled baby's cry broke the silence.

It was so unexpected that everyone around froze. Kiera and Lorey exchanged stunned looks, and Tievin was blinking excessively.

"Did Kein just... *wail?*"

While the rest of them were still utterly confused, Kassein slowly got down on his knees in front of the dragon. Just as he did, Kein slowly opened its large mouth. They watched, stunned, as the Commander retrieved something from Kein's jaws.

"No fucking way," Kiera gasped.

While the soldiers had kept their distance from Kein, both women and Tievin stepped forward, reaching the Prince just in time to see him extracting a bundle of saliva-covered gray fur. Gently, he pulled one of the corners, revealing a baby's face. They all stilled as the young, innocent, teary, and white eyes took them in. The baby's lips trembled before it broke into a proper cry.

With the resounding silence, the baby's cries echoed surprisingly loud around the camp, as if alerting everyone of its arrival. Lorey covered her mouth,

Kiera grimaced, and Tievin was simply frozen, his eyebrows nearly to his hairline. Kassein ignored them all; his attention was focused on the baby girl in his arms, all the tension in his body gone.

He slowly stood up, carrying her in the bundle of fur. He recognized that coat; he had given Alezya that coat.

If he hadn't been holding the baby tight, he might have realized his fingers were slightly trembling. His throat was tight, his heart drumming in his chest; Kassein let out a faint breath and slowly untangled the baby girl from the layers of fur, revealing more of her perfectly snow-white skin and, contrasting with it, the string of leather around her tiny neck, little fingers gripping a pendant at the other end of it.

More careful than he had ever been in his life so as not to drop her, Kassein slowly took her arm in his hand, his fingers brushing up her tiny, chubby forearm and lifting it up slightly. The child cooed at the feeling of his warm skin, her eyes going up to him.

Kassein didn't need to wrestle the pendant out of her tiny fist; he recognized Alezya's pendant and, even better, a whiff of her scent. His heart skipped a beat, and he leaned closer to the baby, who had calmed her crying down a bit to scrutinize him back.

That child smelled like Alezya. It was faint and mixed with many things, including his dragon's scent and the fur, but he would have recognized her smell anywhere, anytime. He was like a dog, so dedicated he'd pick up his owner's scent every time. It was her coat, it was her necklace, it was her scent. ...It was her baby.

Alezya's baby, so small, so fragile, and so white. Her hair, her skin, her tiny eyelashes, her misty irises, even the tiny fingers that grabbed his hand to inspect it. She was as white as the purest morning snow.

"...*Lumie*," he mumbled under his breath.

The baby whipped her striking white eyes back to him as if she recognized that word. It was definitely her name. Everything came back to him all at once, like he'd found the missing piece of a large puzzle to help make sense of it all.

"It was you," he whispered. "You're the one she wanted to go back for..."

Something like a strangled chuckle crossed his lips, dipped in sadness and relief. He was holding Alezya's last secret in his arms, and all of a sudden, everything made sense. Pieces of his heart fell back in place, just as his love for her instantly extended to include the part of her he was carrying in his arms.

It just all made sense. Her baby. He had seen all of the signs. The pregnancy markings. Lorey's intuition. Alezya's strength despite all odds, her desperation to go back there, her tears... They had all been for the baby she'd left behind.

How could he have thought it was because of a man? She was scared of men. She wouldn't have loved him so much if there had been another. No. Only a child made their mother's heart big enough for more.

Lumie is my family, she had told him.

And there she was. Alezya's family, the piece of her heart she couldn't bear to leave behind. Little Lumie was now staring directly into his soul with her big teary eyes, looking so much like her mother it was breathtaking. She had plump cheeks, thick, snow-white eyelashes, and little strands of white hair adorning her round head.

He hadn't thought his heart would ever have room to love someone else as much as he did Alezya, but he was proven wrong. It was as simple and powerful as that; Lumie had just lodged herself into his heart, with her mother, right where they both belonged.

When she began to whimper again, Kassein, who had never carried a child before, dropped the saliva-covered fur cloak in the snow and gently brought her against his torso, covering her with a side of his cloak.

The child immediately relaxed against his warm skin, and he could feel her tiny fingers wriggling against his chest. Slowly, he turned around, and Lorey moved first to come close to him, her amazed eyes on the little girl.

"...She's gorgeous," she whispered. "Hello, sweetie."

Lumie blushed and hid her face in Kassein's cloak, apparently already feeling quite comfortable with him.

"It's a... *child*," Tievin scoffed after a beat.

"Why the hell did Kein bring down a brat?" Kiera spat after a second. "And where the hell did your dumb dragon find the self-restraint not to chew her like a damn snack? She was in his actual- ...Also, what the fuck's with the arms? Are we going to talk about the fact that there are also two *arms* in his—no, no, don't eat them, you crazy dragon!"

Kassein ignored her, his eyes riveted on the toddler in his arms.

He ripped his cloak off his shoulders to fully wrap the little girl in it, holding her with one arm wrapped around her, his hand under her bum, the fingers of his other hand splayed against her back.

Lumie looked quite interested in her surroundings; her eyes opened wide as she glanced around. Kein, who had finished eating the arms, let out a slight burp, which made half the audience grimace, and let out a growl before it stood up again. The dragon's orange snout approached, sniffing in the child's direction. Far from being scared, the little girl giggled at the whiffs of hot air blown in her direction.

"She looks so much like Alezya," Lorey smiled. "Such a precious little girl..."

"She's her family," Kassein muttered, Alezya's words echoing in his mind on a loop.

Snow is my family. Lumie was her family, all of it in the shape of a tiny little snow-white body. He lifted the baby girl to get her a bit closer to his eye level to observe her some more, as if he couldn't get enough of discovering her features, of finding traces of her mom in her, or admiring how white her skin was, with dashes of pink and red on her cheeks and around her still teary eyes.

Lumie looked up at him before blushing again shyly when Kassein gave her a faint but genuine smile and she pressed her face against his neck to hide.

"That child is very... white," Tievin eventually said. "Is she, I mean, is this not slightly worrisome? ...Is she contagious?"

Kassein glanced to the side, noticing his Intendant was keeping a distance.

"We've seen a man like that before," Lorey told Kassein. "His hair, skin, and eyes were all white as snow. His clan called him the man of the moon, for he couldn't stand the daylight. He lived during the night and stayed indoors during the day."

Kassein frowned and glanced at the skies.

The first colors of dawn had appeared, but it would be a while before the sun properly rose up, and the child looked fine.

"So, are we sure she's Alezya's? Your woman had a brat?" Kiera asked.

"It seems so," Lorey replied in his stead, already smiling at the baby girl and offering her finger for Lumie to grab.

"Well," Kiera continued, "she's still gone, and now she's most likely back with her damn tribe. What are you going to do about it? Send Kein back? Is she just expecting you to take her kid and be done?"

Kassein's eyes went to his dragon.

The two of them missed Alezya terribly, and they didn't need to communicate for that; if Kein had returned without Alezya, it meant she wasn't in a place where his dragon could bring her back for now. Or else, he would have gone back the second they took Lumie.

At least, that was what he hoped. Kein had come back with Alezya's child but without Alezya. She'd learned to tame and order his dragon around, and now, he knew there had been a point to it. She wanted to save her child, at any cost. He was certain she would have never wanted to go back if it wasn't for Lumie. But she did go back. She had gone back, sacrificing herself and the protection Kassein had offered her to save her child. She had rescued her baby all by herself, and he'd done nothing to help.

The truth hit Kassein hard, although he was completely still.

Inside, however, it felt like his dragon had dragged his body over miles, crushing him under the weight of that guilt. He was powerless to help the one woman he wanted above everything. And now she was gone, most likely in danger again, or worse, already suffering.

Even if the horrible, worst possible reason why Kein had returned without her was eating him from the inside, opening like a void of anguish that was threatening to tip him over, Kassein tried to push it away.

He refused to even think about it. It couldn't be. No. He just needed to find her, bring her back, and it would all be fine. Alezya had to be alive somewhere, and he would bring her back.

Everything would be fine so long as he got her back in his arms.

His eyes slowly turned back to the line of mountains, gradually filling with cold rage. Those mountains. Those tribes. Those people who had hurt her, who were hurting her again at this very moment. He wasn't going to let them get away with it any longer. His dragon growled furiously, echoing his own thoughts.

They couldn't let it happen ever again.

They couldn't let her be hurt for a second longer.

"...Brother?" Kiera frowned, her eyes on the growling Kein. "What's going on in your head? Care to share?"

"I'm going to the mountains," he spat, turning around to carry Lumie away.

"What? Wait... No, what? Wait a minute!" Both women began running after him.

He was walking fast through the camp, and the soldiers scattered as quickly as terrified mice upon seeing Kein and Kiki following them.

"Kassein!" Kiera insisted. "What do you mean you're going to the mountains? You didn't mean *now*, did you? What about the plan?!"

"Alezya's up there. I need to find her. She could be hurt or in danger. I'll go and conquer them—every single one of them."

"There are people living in those mountains," Lorey reminded him with a nervous expression. "Children and women, like Alezya and her child."

"I won't harm any woman or child, ever," Kassein glared at her as if offended she would have even thought otherwise. "I will fight the men who deserve it. I'm starting with the ones that hurt Alezya, and they will regret it. I have to find her. Bring her back."

Kiera and Lorey exchanged a look behind him.

They had seen the tribes, and they knew women and children were never involved in the fights. If they had learned anything from being around Alezya, it was that women most likely had very little say at all in any matters, let alone battles.

They reached his tent, and gently, Kassein put the little girl down on his bed, although his thick cloak still surrounded her. He then glanced at Lorey, who understood and gave him a quick nod before going to the child. They switched places, Kassein tending to the fire while she kneeled to be at the baby girl's eye level.

"Hello, little moon," she whispered.

Then, she began to inspect the child gently, checking the toddler's body with her hands before picking her up.

"She's completely fine," she declared, her eyes going to Kassein's. "She's healthy, a bit petite, but based on her teeth and how she can sit fine on her own, I'd say she's probably nearing two years old. I'll give her a bath since she's traveled in a dragon's mouth..."

She grabbed a little basin in Kassein's tent and began setting everything up to clean the toddler. Meanwhile, Kiera's and Tievin's eyes were riveted on Kassein, both with similar confused expressions.

"What... What in the mighty dragon is going on?!" Tievin finally spouted.

"Alezya had a baby; she delivered it by dragon mail to Kassein," Kiera sighed. "Catch up, Tievin. Hey, you know what's actually funny? When I was still young and blessed with ignorance and asked Mom how babies were made, this is exactly what she told us: dragon delivery."

"That's adorable. Did you believe it?" Lorey asked with a chuckle.

"Sadly, I did," Kiera let out a long, dramatic sigh. "My eight-year-old dumb self spent an entire evening lecturing Krai about not bringing me any more baby brothers. You bet our grandmother had a *lot* of fun watching that..."

Lorey chuckled and, as if she'd understood the joke, Lumie also giggled. A stunned silence followed the cute, shimmery sound.

"Damn it," Kiera said. "Alezya's kid is cute, I'll give you that."

"Her name is Lumie," Kassein said.

He found it quite adorable how Lumie's head whipped around back to him every time he said her name. One could tell just by looking at her that she was a happy child; she let Lorey bathe her, giggling any time she was tickled, and let herself be clothed without complaint with one of the tunics and underwear meant for Alezya, which Lorey somewhat made fit with well-placed knots.

"I can sew her some proper clothes," Lorey announced.

"Watch her for me," Kassein muttered. "I'm going to the mountain."

"Not now," Kiera stopped him, placing herself between him and the tent's exit. "Kassein, you've already traveled to the Capital and back all night long. In fact, you didn't even tell us how that went, for one. Most importantly, you need to rest a bit. I know we have Dragon Blood and all, but even you need a couple of hours of rest before you get back out there and fight the tribes and whatnot."

But Kassein glared at his sister, unconvinced.

"Move, Kiera."

"No," his sister retorted, crossing her arms.

"Kassein," Lorey intervened before the siblings began a fight, "Kiera has a point. You need some sleep, and you won't be able to help Alezya if you're not in good condition. She's been gone for almost a day now, and whatever happened between the moment Kein took Lumie and when you came back, delaying finding her by a couple of hours won't change anything."

"We don't know that. She could be in danger," Kassein hissed. "She could be in pain, right this instant–"

"Wherever she is," Kiera interrupted him, "Kein clearly cannot get to her, or we both know your dragon would have taken off already. That means you'll have to search for her yourself, and we don't know how long that could take. Kiki needs to take a break too; she flew all night. Listen, I can take Kein and survey the mountains to try and locate her, but you need some sleep."

"Just a couple of hours," Lorey added, "and then I promise I'll look after Lumie while you search for her mom, and you can–"

"...*Ama?*"

All eyes turned to the little girl. Lumie was staring at them all with big, inquisitive eyes. She looked around as if looking for someone before her eyes went back to the adults present.

"*Ama?*" she asked again, her eyes getting teary.

Kassein let out a long, defeated sigh. The tears in the little girl's eyes broke his heart. Slowly, he went to her and picked her up in his arms before sitting on his bed with her.

Kiera took this as her cue to leave the tent.

"I promise I'll find your mama," he whispered to her. "I miss her too."

Lumie was staring at him, clearly confused, and she let out a hiccup. Lorey approached, patting the little girl's back.

"Get some sleep, Kassein," Lorey whispered. "Please. Kiera will look for her with Kein, and I promise I'll wake you up in a couple of hours. Then you can take the army up there as soon as you want."

"An hour," Kassein argued.

"Wherever Alezya is," she replied, "she managed to give Lumie to Kein. She sent her daughter to you, Kassein. Kein wouldn't land until you arrived. I'm sure she knew she could trust you with her, and I'm sure she will do everything she can to return to you both. You need to have some faith in her. Whatever happened to Alezya last night, I'm sure you'll be able to find her again–"

"We got a problem," Kiera announced, suddenly stepping back inside the tent.

"What?" Kassein frowned.

"Your dragon's gone. Again."

They all exchanged confused glances.

"Gone?" Kassein hissed, annoyed.

"Gone," Kiera shrugged. "He took off, and I have no idea where. The guard I grabbed said he went south, so I don't know what Kein's idea is because either he's making a weird big-ass detour looking for your woman, or your dragon's just officially gone mad."

Kassein was confused. Kein had always acted on its own whim, but to fly off now? Where to? If his dragon wasn't looking for Alezya, where could it have gone, and to do what? The only other idea he had was that Kein could have gone to rest, given his dragon had flown most of the night too, but why south?

"Well, at least that settles you resting," Lorey said. "Kiki's too tired to fly again so soon."

"Give yourself and my dragon a break, Brother," Kiera said. "As soon as she's up for it, I promise I'll go look for your dragon, but in the meantime, you need to get some shut-eye."

"I'll take Lumie to sleep in our tent," Lorey said, her hands going under Lumie's arms. "You can–"

"No."

Kassein's blunt refusal made Lorey blink and retract her hands.

"...She's staying with me," he muttered.

He refused to let the child out of his sight. Having already lost her mother twice, Kassein refused to let go of Lumie. He felt like they were both missing her mother, and he couldn't bear to have her away from him until he could resume his search for Alezya.

"...Alright," Lorey finally said. "You should all get some sleep; I'll make some better clothes for her in the meantime. I promise I'll wake you up then or as soon as there's a sign of Kein."

"Thank goodness," Tievin muttered, before stepping out of the tent first.

Kiera let out a long sigh too before stepping outside again. Lorey gave Kassein another sorry smile and followed her.

Although he had no will to sleep, Kassein laid down on his bed.

The only reason he agreed to this was because Lumie looked as tired as he was, both dragons were unavailable to fly in search of Alezya, and he wanted to be in peak condition to face the tribes who had hurt her and finally make them pay.

"You should sleep too," he said. "Sleep, Lumie."

Lumie, who was seated next to his torso, pouted her lips before climbing over him. He knew very little about children, except for the few times he'd seen his nieces and nephews in the Eastern Kingdom.

He could only believe Lorey that she was roughly two years old, but she seemed very small to him. Lumie babbled some unintelligible words before she spread herself on his torso, her cheek over his heart. She let out a cute sigh, and he covered her with a blanket, using his arm to secure her against him. He knew he wouldn't be able to really fall asleep, but he still closed his eyes, hoping she would do the same, and waited, an ear out for his dragon.

Kassein only realized he had indeed dozed off when the sounds of someone approaching instinctively woke him up. He first noted Lumie, who was deep asleep with a line of drool on his torso.

Securing her with a hand against her back, Kassein slowly sat up, only relaxing when he spotted Lorey quietly walking in.

"Kein?" he asked in a whisper.

"We found him," she announced. "He didn't come back, but Kiki and Kiera went to find him as soon as they woke up; they located him at the Onyx Castle. Tievin and Kiera are waiting for us there."

What was his dragon doing at the Onyx Castle?

Alezya could not have made the trip in a few hours without a dragon's help from the mountains. Careful not to wake up Lumie, Kassein gently put her down on the bed, and while Lorey quickly dressed her with the clothes she'd made, he got himself ready.

This time, he put on his armor and his scaled arm braces and selected his best blade. They had a long day ahead, and he needed both him and his dragon to get their heads into battle.

"Kiera sent Kiki back, she's waiting to take us."

Kassein climbed on his sister's dragon first before lending a hand to Lorey as she was holding a sleeping Lumie tightly bundled between them. Kiki took off quickly, having rested enough.

Kassein didn't know how long he had slept, but the sun had risen in the skies, and while they flew past the mountains, he couldn't help but check them from afar, hoping for a glimpse of raven hair somewhere.

His heart ached thinking about Alezya and what she could be enduring without him. She had made the choice to go back for her child, but at what cost? How had she managed to get Lumie to Kein? Had those men harmed her again?

The journey was quiet, Kiki quickly taking them to the Onyx Castle.

It didn't take long for Kassein to spot his dragon's bright orange scales amongst the black walls of the Onyx Castle, the snow blanket, and the green trees that surrounded the area.

His dragon was in their mother's garden, in a strange, cornered position and letting out warning growls that definitely cautioned others not to approach recklessly. Kiki landed at a good distance, wary of Kein's angry temper that morning.

Kassein got off the dark gray dragon first, and after taking Lumie from her to help Lorey dismount, he rushed into the garden, feeling something was off. He glanced ahead and noticed Kiera standing with her back to him, her arms crossed and her head tilted.

"Finally," Kiera greeted him with a scoff. "Did you get a good sleep? I hope you're wide awake for this part..."

"What do you mean?" Lorey asked, just as confused as he was.

Kassein clenched his jaw, frowning, but he willed himself to approach his dragon.

Right now, his mind was already saturated with chaotic, angry, and worried thoughts about Alezya, so he wasn't sure what else his dragon's fuss could be about. His sister was staring at something on the ground, tucked between the dragon and the wall of the garden, and next to her, Tievin was pacing in frantic circles.

"This is a problem," he was huffing when Kassein got near enough to hear. "This is a big, big problem. I should have prevented this. I knew this was coming; I told myself, '*Tievin, you put a stop to this,*' and I didn't! I should have said something, but–"

"My brother's sex life is hardly for you to comment on, Tiev, let alone make any executive decisions about," Keira scoffed. "Not that anyone could stop Kassein's di–"

"What the fuck is going on?" Kassein growled.

Despite his angry voice, the toddler in his arms, who was apparently awake, let out a giggle, and after a second, he reluctantly put her in Lorey's arms to walk up to his sister. That's when he finally saw what she was looking at. Two dragon eggs.

Kassein was so shocked that he froze, almost rearing back as if he'd been hit by an invisible punch. And he felt that punch to the gut too.

There was no mistaking which dragon those eggs belonged to, nor their significance. Kein was guarding them far too fiercely for there to be any doubt.

"...Alezya," he muttered, his throat tightening.

Pregnant. Alezya was pregnant with his child.

It felt so unreal that for the first time in all his eighteen years of existence, Kassein thought he might collapse. His heart skipped a beat before it drummed violently. He had just lost her again, and now, he had to swallow that he had lost the woman who was carrying his child.

"You fucked up bad," Kiera scoffed, as if it was funny. "You lose your woman for the second time, and she's carrying your kid? Two of them, apparently. Way to go, Brother."

"We need to inform the palace," Tievin mumbled, looking one shade too white and on the verge of passing out. "Two dragon eggs. The palace will freak out. And the mother is a tribeswoman, and we've lost her! This time, Father will have my head. Or expel me to another hellho–somewhere else. I can't. Why? Why me? There was already so much work with two of them, and now there are going to be two more! I'm not mentally equipped for this. This is a problem. A major problem. Maybe I can convince them I left before this. Right. Head south and maybe..."

"What are you going to do?" Kiera asked Kassein, ignoring Tievin's spiraling panic. "I mean, you got two baby dragons coming, but they're missing their mom and baby counterparts. Tievin's right on one thing: *this* is definitely going to be a problem. And yeah, Kassian's probably going to rip your head off."

For once, even Kassian's name wasn't enough to get a reaction out of Kassein. He was just staring at the two small eggs, so many emotions rushing through him that he couldn't settle on one.

Alezya was pregnant.

They had spent one night together, then she had left, and she was pregnant. With his... baby. He swallowed.

She had sent him Lumie and trusted him with her daughter's protection, but now, the moonlight of his dark life was gone, more vulnerable than she knew, and he needed her back immediately where he could protect her, shield her, and never let anyone or anything harm her again. Where they could be together. Alezya, him, Lumie, and the baby. Or babies. He looked at the two eggs, still absorbing the shock.

The eggs were small, but they couldn't have been more than a day old. One was snow white, and the other was as dark as obsidian. One looked slightly bigger than the other, but maybe that was an optical illusion of the color difference.

"...Isn't it strange?" Lorey muttered.

He turned back to her, but immediately, his eyes went down to Lumie. The little girl's eye met his under the fur blanket, and she immediately brightened up, extending her arms in an obvious request.

Kassein couldn't refuse her anymore than he could her mom, so he gently picked her up from Lorey's arms. The baby girl nestled her tiny bundled body against his warm chest, getting comfortable like they hadn't met just hours ago.

Kassein covered her with his cape, further protecting her frail body from the cold and sun.

"What is?" Kiera tilted her head.

"...There are *two* eggs," Lorey said, pointing a finger at the eggs.

"I guess my brother was *that* efficient," Kiera scoffed.

"Weren't Darsan's triplets' dragons all born from the same egg?" Lorey insisted. "His wife mentioned their egg was huge, and that's how they figured early on that she was expecting more than one..."

"Oh yeah," Kiera laughed. "Serves him right! That big dumb Dran probably had a great time popping that giant egg out of his-"

"We aren't actually sure how dragons lay eggs, my *lady*," Tievin interrupted her, rubbing his eyelids, "so I would hardly suggest we make assumptions about the... state of them after said eggs appear. What we do know is that they always have them in the place they consider safe, consider home, and away from human eyes. And Lady Lorey is right. There have hardly been any records of dragons having... multiple eggs at one time. Arguably, there haven't been any multiple births in a long time either. Lord Darsan's triplets are quite a unique record in the Empire's history."

"...It doesn't matter," Kassein finally said after a few seconds. "Alezya is with child, *my* child. She needs to come back here."

He turned his eyes back to Lumie, who had her cheek against his torso, her mouth in a cute little "o" while her pale eyes were riveted on the dragon eggs, full of curiosity. Even if it wasn't for her, Kassein would have been dead set on bringing Alezya back, but thanks to Lumie and the pregnancy, there was no doubt in his mind that this was where she needed to be.

Everything was finally making sense. Alezya had done it all to save her baby, this baby girl, and he loved her all the more for it. Perhaps he should have been hurt that she chose her child over him or that she'd left him again, but there wasn't any place for negative feelings in his heart.

Instead, looking at the precious little girl in his arms made him feel even more for her mother. He was going to be a father too, and he understood. There was nothing he wouldn't do for them. Alezya was a strong woman and a dedicated mother, and he adored her for it. Whatever was important to her would be important to him too, and he already knew Lumie now resided at the top of his priority list.

He loved that child. He didn't need time to get to know her or to come to terms with feelings. It was just a plain truth that had appeared as bright as day, and he didn't need to question it. He'd felt love for Alezya the second he'd met her, and Lumie had just barreled into his life the very same way.

Not only because she was Alezya's, he realized, but because she had made her mother the strong and beautifully resilient woman that she was today. The Alezya he knew had already given birth to Lumie and had been made braver and stronger by her identity as Lumie's mother.

And now, her mother was gone, and while she was under his protection, her future sibling wasn't. Kassein let out a heavy sigh and lifted the child higher against him, pressing his lips against her white curls of hair.

"I'll bring her back," he whispered his promise. "I'll bring her back."

There were a few seconds of silence, during which his sister rolled her eyes but didn't say anything. Tievin stepped closer to the pair of eggs, took out a notepad from somewhere under his layer of coats, and started frantically taking notes.

Lorey walked up next to Kassein and smiled at the glimpse of the toddler bundled in his arms.

"...How will you get her back?" she asked. "Kein would have brought her back already if it was possible, which means she's somewhere a dragon can't reach... I doubt she would have gone through all this hurt to be apart from her daughter again if she could avoid it. Wherever she is away from you two, she is there against her will. I don't know what she promised her people in exchange for sending Lumie to you, but it cannot be good, Kassein. Not when she is carrying your child or children."

"Doesn't matter," he replied. "I'll find her and bring her home."

And the Onyx Castle would be their home, he realized.

There was a reason Kein had chosen to lay its eggs here, and it meant this was the place that Kassein considered home.

In retrospect, that was the last physical place Kassein had actually truly felt happy in. He was in the North Camp out of necessity, and he had loathed every second back in the Capital. In contrast, the Onyx Castle retained many happy childhood memories, and he had liked seeing Alezya stand here too.

He made up his mind right there and then: he and Alezya would move here the second his war with the Northern tribes was over.

It wouldn't take long for this place to be ready for a family to live in, and it would make sense that as the ruler of the north, he would be more efficient at revitalizing the area from its stronghold.

Gently, he put Lumie back into Lorey's arms.

"Stay here with her," he said. "Watch the eggs."

Those eggs were all the hope Kassein needed. If Kein had eggs, that meant Alezya was pregnant, and most importantly, alive.

"I will," Lorey agreed immediately. "This place has everything needed for a child, and I can keep Kiki here to come to you if anything happens."

"What about us?" Kiera asked her brother, fists on her hips. "You never replied to my question earlier. Did Kassian give his blessing or whatever?"

"He did."

His sister raised an eyebrow, but after a beat, she nodded.

Although it was surprising that Kassein had gotten their older brother to concede the north to him, she knew he wouldn't be lying about such a matter. Therefore, she had to believe him, no matter how surprising.

"Well," she scoffed, "sounds like you guys finally agreed on something after all these years. That's good to hear. So now, what?"

"Now you and I take Kein to battle," he said. "We search for Alezya."

"About damn time," his sister sneered.

Despite his protests, they took Tievin back with them to the North Camp, flying on Kein's back and leaving Lorey with Kiki at the Onyx Castle to watch the eggs and Lumie.

Just like Kein had taken a while to leave its eggs, Kassein had been more than reluctant to leave Lumie behind, but he knew that was the most reasonable decision; he couldn't possibly take Alezya's child with him to battle, and he didn't like leaving her in the North Camp with only Lorey while he went to battle either.

It was best for the child that she remained in the Onyx Castle, which had been filled with plenty of things for children over the years. He was sure Lorey would find plenty of old toys, baby clothes, and other things his parents had left behind, and she could probably go and seek assistance from the women of the nearby villages too. Both of them would be safe there, and one less thing for him to worry about. Right now, he had to get his head into the battle ahead.

They landed back at the North Camp when the sun was high in the sky, but Kassein couldn't help but note Alezya had been gone for a full day and night now.

As soon as he got off his dragon, his eyes drifted to the mountains, once again searching for any hint of her presence. Similarly, Kein's eyes went to the mountains before the large dragon turned around, growling softly toward the south where its eggs were.

Suddenly, Kassein felt the need to do something he hadn't done in a very long time: he petted his dragon's head in a comforting gesture, feeling more in tune with Kein than he had in a long time.

"Let's get them back," he muttered to his dragon.

Kein replied with a heavy growl before it took off again, most likely to survey the mountains once more. It bothered Kassein that his dragon was incapable of locating Alezya, but at least he knew she had to be alive.

While his dragon left on another search for her, Kassein, Kiera, and Tievin summoned the generals again.

This time, all three of them had all the units under their command prepared for the upcoming battle, supplies ready, and every single soldier aware that they were waiting for Kassein to launch the attack.

They gathered around the large map Tievin had brought before, and Kassein leaned over it, analyzing the set of mountains that was displayed.

"My goal is to intimidate them first, to let them know what we're capable of," he said. "This tribe is the one I plan to destroy."

His index finger tapped on one of the mountains.

"Alezya's?" Kiera guessed.

"I think so," Kassein gave her a stern nod.

"This one isn't the easiest to access," Sazaran noted. "We have a couple of mountains that are the first ones we could access and launch an attack on. Considering all of our men are on foot, we could launch a first attack on those two mountains, make an example of them, announce to the tribes what we're capable of, and see how they respond."

"I agree," Herken nodded. "Since the Commander plans to negotiate with some of the tribes to establish peace, an initial display of brute force might show the tribes that they would be better off negotiating with us if given the opportunity. Those two mountains hide the tribes that have been attacking us the most, including the one who sent their sick men. I'm all for a punitive expedition."

"We will not be harming any woman or child," Kiera hissed with a warning tone, pinning all three men with her green-eyed glare, "and we will capture any man who surrenders rather than kill them. If we want to open negotiations with more tribes, it is important they see this as a fair battle, not a one-sided slaughter. Make sure every unit gets the word. I will personally crush the necks of anyone who harms a woman, child, or an innocent. Are we clear?"

The generals nodded in approval.

Kassein didn't doubt that none of the three experienced fighters were willing to harm a non-fighter, but in this case, it would be their duty to ensure that each soldier did the same. Considering that almost all of their units were criminals, some dangerous, it might not be easy.

Hopefully, the prospect of death at the hand of the Princess or one of their generals would work as enough incentive to keep them in line.

They resumed talking about the battle, assessing which entry points would be better to launch the attack.

"We should start at sunset," Sazaran said. "The night will be perfect for an infiltration mission and–"

"No," Kassein cut him off. "We will launch the attack as soon as possible."

"Commander, that–"

"That's not up for debate," Kassein retorted with a glare.

A few seconds of silence followed, the generals confused, and Kiera staring at her brother intensely.

After a while, she let out a sigh and turned to the generals.

"Looks like it's time for you to go and get our army ready," she said.

They understood they were dismissed and, without argument, all three of them left the tent quickly. Kiera sat down and propped her feet on the table, making Tievin grimace.

"You're itching to go get her, huh?" Kiera sneered.

"I can't waste any more time," Kassein nodded. "She could be hurt or suffering at this very moment..."

"Got it. I can guess it's even worse now that we know that she's with child."

Kassein had barely allowed himself to think about it.

He couldn't believe Alezya was pregnant from their one night together. It felt unreal, but it felt... amazing. There was a part of him that felt like he didn't even deserve it. He was the worst of his father's sons; how could he become a decent enough father himself? As much as he wanted to rejoice, and a part of him was truly thrilled at the thought that Alezya was carrying his child, he was absolutely terrified.

He already felt selfish and undeserving of Alezya's love. How could he be good enough for a child? For now, all Kassein could do was get the mother of his unborn children back.

"So we'll send the men to an up-front battle. What about you and me? We have Kein, and we could corner them from the back..."

"I need to find Alezya," Kassein said. "If Kein can't get to her, she must be inside that mountain with her tribe, or somewhere else he can't fit himself into."

"I'm not going to lie; those tunnels they've got going on are going to be complicated to work with, we have no fucking idea how far nor how deep they go between all the mountains. It's a battle on a scale and terrain we've never faced before. There's a reason none of the previous North Army leaders have managed to fully conquer these mountains or submit the tribes, I guess... We're on fully unknown territory, and they might be gone before we get there. They will definitely see us coming too. Ideally, we should find a way to dig them out of their holes and force them to come to the surface, but aside from going in ourselves, I can't think of anything good enough. We could always use fire to smoke them out, but that might harm innocents and–"

"No," Kassein cut her off with a warning glare.

His sister wasn't offended; she let out a long sigh and nodded.

"Got it. Let's just go the old-fashioned way then. You and I can use Kein to drop us off around the back, and hopefully, we'll get enough of them before they flee..."

Kassein hated the idea.

A mountain was no small battleground, and if Alezya was held captive, his enemies would have plenty of time to take her elsewhere.

He and Kiera were amongst the best fighters of the Empire, but even they couldn't split themselves to be everywhere all at once. He'd have to go in blind and locate Alezya quickly.

"We should find the best entry point and have Kein survey the area for us," Kiera said. "He loves chasing them as they crawl out of the holes, so that might be what we need. Maybe if he–"

She was interrupted by a familiar, high-pitched dragon growl.

She and Kassein exchanged a confused glance before they darted outside, alarmed. Sure enough, as soon as they stepped out, they recognized Kiki's familiar figure flying toward them. Why was Kiki back? Kassein felt worry pool in his stomach. Was something wrong with Lumie? With one of the eggs?

Before he could spiral too much, Kiki landed, and he noticed Lumie wasn't there.

"Lorey?" Kassein frowned. "Where's Lumie?"

"She's fine," Lorey said. "I left her with Lady Nebora; they're back at the Onyx Castle."

"Everything alright, honey?" Kiera helped her down from her dragon. "You look shaken up."

"I... I'm not sure," Lorey blurted. "Something... strange happened, I had to tell you. Uh... O-one of the eggs hatched."

The siblings glanced at each other, utterly confused.

"No way," Kiera scoffed. "Alezya shouldn't be due for at least another seven months. There's no way a baby dragon would have been born already. They usually wait pretty much for the due date-"

"It hatched, Kiera," Lorey insisted. "Not only that, but, I-... I mean, it's my fault; I should have stayed with it when I noticed something was wrong. Right after you left, I noticed the bigger of the two eggs was growing way faster than the other. I could see it grow with my own eyes! But I had to go and greet Lady Nebora; she'd just come to the castle after she'd noticed Kiki from afar, and... and when I told her the situation, we went back to check on the eggs, but the black egg was broken open, no baby dragon to be seen!"

"Wha-" Tievin choked. "What do you mean, Lorey, 'no baby dragon to be seen'? Y-y-y-you can't have *lost* a baby dragon!"

"I didn't even see it!" Lorey insisted. "The egg was just... broken open."

She directed her panicked eyes to Kiera.

"It can't mean something happened to the baby, right?" she asked nervously.

"I don't think so," Kiera grimaced. "Grandma told us that in cases when the... pregnancy stopped, the egg stopped growing and rotted from the inside. She saw it happen many times during our grandfather's reign. Are you sure the egg properly hatched?"

"Yes," Lorey nodded. "It looked like it. It was the normal size of a mature dragon egg too."

"There's no way the egg grew that quickly," Kiera frowned.

"Well, it did!" Lorey insisted, frustrated.

The two siblings exchanged looks, utterly confused. Kassein was just as shocked. They had never heard of an egg growing at an accelerated rate before. He had heard his brother's dragon, Kian, had been born hours early to save their mother, but it was most likely because her labor had started.

"What about the other egg?" he asked.

"The white one hasn't moved," Lorey said. "I asked Lady Nebora to keep an eye on it just in case, but this one didn't seem to be growing, at least not in a way we can see it grow second by second..."

"We lost a baby dragon," Tievin muttered. "Father's going to have my head. We lost a baby dragon!"

Kiera patted his shoulder with an amused smirk.

"Well, it's best to consider that this egg hatched super early for some reason. You know, maybe it wasn't even Kein's egg. Since Alezya can't have had a baby that fast, let's just assume it was another dragon's egg."

Kassein frowned. Kian hadn't been at the palace when he had visited. Had his brother gotten a woman pregnant as well?

"It doesn't explain why the egg grew so fast." Lorey crossed her arms. "Nothing explains how a dragon's egg could have grown and hatched so fast! I mean, you all saw it, Kein couldn't have laid those eggs more than a couple of hours after he brought Lumie, and... and..."

She stopped herself, her eyes opening wide, and then, suddenly, she turned to Kassein, opening her mouth and closing it.

"Lorey? You alright, honey?"

"Y-yes," she finally said. "I thought... but it was just a silly idea. It can't be."

"I'd love to discuss this fascinating phenomenon a bit more, but we seriously don't have time," Kiera sighed. "We have an attack to launch and an army waiting for us. That mountain is going to be no small feat to attack either. Look, we'll keep in mind that we could be looking for a lost baby dragon, but... Oh, my dragon!"

She clapped her hands together, her eyes opening wide in sudden excitement.

"Oh. My. Fucking. Dragon!" she exclaimed, turning to her brother. "Kassein, I'm a fucking genius!"

"What?" He frowned.

"Our tunnel problem! I just found the solution!"

"...How?"

Kiera grinned from ear to ear.

"It just came to me! Our issue is that *our* dragons are too big to get in those tunnels, right? Now, dear brother, what happens to be just a tad smaller than an *adult* dragon?"

"...A baby dragon," Kassein muttered.

"Exactly!! And who do we know happens to have a bunch of still-smallish dragons?"

"Oh, no," Tievin paled immediately. "No, no. No, no, no, no, Your Highness! Princess Kiera, please! No!"

While Tievin looked on the verge of collapse, sweating buckets with his panicked eyes frantically going from Kiera to Kassein, Lorey smiled.

"...Our nephews and nieces," Kassein muttered.

"Come on," Kiera squealed. "We are hours away from Darsan's place. I can fly Kiki, borrow a bunch of kids and baby dragons, and have them ready for the second assault!"

"My lady, PLEASE!" Tievin cried. *"Not the triplets!"*

Chapter 15

Alezya hadn't felt this cold in a long time.

Her body was sore, shivering, and heavy. She couldn't tell how long she had been stuck in this crevice. She missed the fur coats, the fire pit, and most of all, Kassein's arms.

Everything that had kept her warm, comfortable, and happy over the last couple of weeks was gone, and she felt empty. She had left Kassein, and now, Lumie was gone too, after she'd only had several hours with her. The mere memory of holding her child in her arms after so long and then having parted with her again so brutally made Alezya shed a tear.

She should have been happy she had accomplished her goal of sending her child to safety, or so she hoped.

Yet, Alezya couldn't find relief.

She missed them both. She wished for nothing more than to be with them, to hug Lumie, and for Kassein to hug her. She tried not to cry again, but another tear escaped, sliding down her cheek. Since when had she become so greedy, she wondered. A few weeks ago, she would have been happy and satisfied with knowing that Lumie was safe.

Now Alezya found herself dreaming of more, of a life with Kassein and her daughter, of a life where she was finally happy, safe, and cherished, where she could take long walks at the foot of the mountains with an amazing man by her side or fly far above them to foreign lands with his dragon. Where she would be by Lumie's side and watch her daughter grow into the beautiful young woman she was bound to become. Alezya had lost her own mother when she was a child, and now, at twenty years old, all she wanted was to be able to outlive her own mother and be by Lumie's side so her daughter wouldn't grow up motherless as she had.

She glanced around the tiny ice cave.

It was horrible to know that her mother had died in a place like this while trying to gain her freedom. How desperate must she have been to flee her father? To go back to the Lumiata Clan?

Her mother's clan hadn't attended the gathering, but Alezya still held some hope she would find them someday; she at least wanted to know about where her mother came from. She was curious about other clans now that she had gotten a glimpse of them.

It was clear as day that her father had lied about many things, and now, Alezya was curious about what else had been left out. She couldn't help but wonder how different things would have been for her if she had been born in a different clan. Would they have accepted Lumie? Were the other clans more open to their wives and daughters having more meaningful roles than childbearing?

She couldn't forget about the beautiful women she had seen at the gathering, nor how they carried themselves, unafraid of the men around them, like they were equals to their clan chiefs. Alezya was fascinated.

She had always thought Kassein's clan was the biggest mystery, because she had seen little of it, and now, she was far more curious about the clans she didn't know. When had they all become so divided?

They had far more in common than the Dragon Clan. The same language, the same territories... The same predator. When had the clans become so fractioned that they had different customs and values and only interacted once a month, if at all?

Alezya shivered again.

She was cold, freezing cold, but thankfully, morning had come, and it wouldn't be too unbearable for at least a few more hours...

She had little hope for the evening if her father didn't pull her out. The temperatures inevitably dropped low in the mountains, and there was no way someone would survive, especially not with so few clothes and nothing to warm themself.

Forcing herself to take a deep breath, Alezya fought against the pain to stand up, using the walls of her ice cage to survey her surroundings once more now that the sun was rising higher in the skies.

The opening was a long, narrow fissure, just wide enough for a human to squeeze through. In some places, it tightened unpredictably, which was why she had bruised her arms and legs during her fall, despite it having lasted mere seconds.

Now, the opening loomed about ten feet above her head, and the walls were impossible to climb, even with her talent. There was ice everywhere, making it too smooth and too fragile to climb. Even if she could hold on to some rock and climb, the angle would be hard to maneuver, and on such hard ground with most of the snow now melted, any fall could be deadly. No, any chance of getting out would come from someone out there throwing her a rope or something.

She didn't even need to look for another opening. The crevice was so small that she could see both ends, and it was barely big enough to hold seven or eight men squeezed together... It was a bit smaller than Kein's entire body, she thought.

She had thought briefly about calling for the dragon to help, but that was far too dangerous. If Kein landed anywhere wrong, the snow, rocks, and chunks of ice could collapse and bury her alive or crush her to death. Perhaps a leaner dragon, like Kiki, could have slithered its way in, but Alezya had even less hope of Kiki looking for her than she had for Kein.

While she was pacing, rubbing her arms to try to warm herself up some more, Alezya heard steps and voices nearby. She stood still and waited until, much to her disappointment, she recognized her father's men's voices.

"Food, you slut."

"Hey, watch it. She called the dragon for real..."

"Who cares? Where she is, the dragon can't help her out anyway. Just check that witch isn't dead."

Alezya glared at the hole above her, and sure enough, the sunlight was suddenly partially obscured by a man's head. Minutes later, something was thrown, and she pressed herself against the wall to avoid it.

She waited a few seconds until they were gone to get it. It was roughly packed, but she found some dried meat as well as some raw fruits and vegetables. There was more than she had expected, but she had no idea how often they would be checking on her, and they wanted to keep her alive.

Alezya ate some but kept the rest packed away for later in case they forgot about her or something; she wouldn't have put it past her father to starve her to try and make her more... malleable. She knew his ways all too well. If anything, she was certain he had no intention of simply letting her rot here. Having a daughter who could summon a dragon at will would be too tempting to pass up.

She wondered if he planned to get her out of there eventually or if this were a punishment she was supposed to endure until she was on the verge of death. With Lumie gone, that would be his only way to manipulate her...

There was no water, but with all the ice around, that wouldn't be an issue. Now that she wasn't expecting any more visitors for several hours at least, she decided to find a spot in the sun and try to warm up while saving her energy. She couldn't climb out, but she sure hoped to have enough strength left to put up a fight once she got out of there. She still had a chance to get away, and she would absolutely try.

Alezya wanted it. The future with Kassein, with Lumie, everything.

She didn't care about being greedy anymore; for once, she had her mind set to hold on to her chance at happiness until the end.

"Kriii."

She jumped awake with no idea how long she'd dozed off, looking up for the source of that strange sound.

It sounded like something creaking, and for a second, Alezya worried that the crevice was going to collapse by itself, and a couple of pounds of snow falling without warning seemed to confirm her suspicion.

But then, something leaped down, just a few feet away from her, and she jumped back, scared. The snow was sent flying left and right, and then, a dark mass of black scales appeared with undeniable wings, a tail, and two amber eyes. Alezya's jaw dropped. A miniature dragon?

She watched, astonished, as the small creature hopped around, surprisingly light and agile, coming toward her with a bounce in its step.

"No," she muttered. "Wait, wait."

She didn't know this dragon. It looked like a miniature Kein but with black scales and big orange eyes. It was so small, too. The little baskets she had seen in Kassein's childhood room flashed in her mind, and she knew how small young dragons could be, but seeing one in the flesh felt completely different.

Kein was impressively large, heavy, and imposing. This tiny dragon looked like she could carry it in her arms. It looked so young and... innocent, the way younger animals always looked way cuter than adults.

"Who are you?" she whispered, confused.

Was one of Kassein's siblings still a child? She remembered him mentioning some of his siblings had children with baby dragons. Was that one of them? But she had never met the children before.

And most importantly, what was a baby dragon doing by itself in the mountains? Where was the mom dragon?

Alezya looked up nervously, expecting some giant black beast to come and claim its spawn any second, but the sky was clear and bright above them, and things seemed... quiet.

That was until the little dragon let out another of its cute, high-pitched growls and tried to approach her again. It was fearless, but Alezya wasn't, and she retreated until her back hit the end of the cave.

The tiny black dragon followed her excitedly, its tail swishing and its baby dragon feet still hopping around like it was having fun.

Alezya watched, helpless and confused, as the little black-scaled creature was making tiny loops around her legs, lovingly rubbing its body against her ankles.

"Alright... Seems like we could be friends, then?" she muttered.

The dragon replied with another excited little growl that hardly sounded like a growl at all; it was far too adorable of a sound.

Alezya forced herself to take a deep breath, and then, slowly, she sank down to sit, not taking her eyes off the dragon to see what it would do.

Sure enough, as soon as she was down, it climbed onto her lap, curling itself on her legs despite already being almost too big. The dragon was heavier than it looked, but it was as warm as Kein, and immediately, Alezya felt grateful for its presence. Now, being too cold would hardly be an issue anymore if her new friend stayed by her side.

Feeling a bit curious, Alezya lifted a hand, and the black dragon eyed it, making her freeze.

"If you bite me, we're not going to be friends," she warned. "No biting."

She wished she had learned the word for "bite" in the Dragon Clan's language, but she had no choice but to be careful and trust the small dragon. If it had been a foreign adult dragon, she would have been much more freaked out and scared, but this one was so tiny and looked so much like a miniature Kein; there was a strange sense of familiarity to it. That and the fact that it had made itself at home immediately on her lap.

Inch by inch, Alezya lowered her hand toward the tiny dragon's back until she touched the hot scales and slowly caressed it. The dragon let out a tiny shiver of appreciation, closing its eyes and slightly lifting its wings before it put its head back down on her lap. Alezya smiled.

That baby dragon was cute, she had to admit. And it felt nice to have a companion down here.

"Are you a boy or a girl dragon? Oh, right, you dragons are neither... but you do have a mama, right?"

The little dragon remained silent, napping happily on her lap.

Alezya frowned.

"You probably have a name... What should I call you? Tiny? You're probably not going to stay tiny long... You're going to stay black-scaled and younger than Kein, I imagine. How about Niiru, then?"

It meant "small shadow" in her language, and somehow, it seemed to suit her new companion.

The little black dragon let out a yawn, stretching over her lap.

It was already so big that its hind legs and tail were on the ground next to Alezya. All the ice near its rear had melted too, leaving a little puddle of cold water seeping through the rocks.

Alezya glanced up at the sun shining on them again.

Had Kein managed to bring Lumie to Kassein? Had they figured out she shouldn't be out in the sun? Lorey seemed to be a natural caretaker, so she hoped her female friend would know what to do with a child...

She realized it was the first time she had thought of Lorey as a friend, but it was true. She had spent a lot of time with her in the past week.

With Kassein's sister too. That woman was a bit scary, and she had a lot of unwomanly attitude, but Alezya found her quite amazing. She was exactly the kind of woman Alezya would have never been allowed to be: loud, outspoken, unapologetic, charismatic.

And then there was Tievin, the most unmanly man she had ever met. That was the one man she hadn't felt threatened by, aside from Kassein, albeit for a very different reason. He was always pouting or whining, wrapped in a lot of fur coats, yet unable to hide how scrawny he was.

Alezya sighed and leaned her head against the wall, feeling slightly tired again.

She had no idea what was going to happen next. Her calling Kein had probably caused a commotion amongst the clans, and there was no doubt her father was going to try to leverage that first. He was probably making many threats, using both his daughter and the child he thought she carried. He ought to keep her alive at least, but Alezya knew he would make her pay for her treachery... and she wasn't sure he wouldn't actually kill her once he did figure out she wasn't pregnant.

"...Is she in there?"

Alezya frowned, looking up at the opening to try to see who the voices belonged to. They didn't sound familiar at all, and they were whispering. Her father's men didn't need to hide their presence.

On her lap, Niiru also glanced up, its tail swishing left and right with what Alezya guessed to be curiosity.

"Our spy said he saw her father push her down there," a second male voice spoke.

"He wouldn't have killed her, would he?" another voice asked nervously.

"Madman that Darak is, it wouldn't be surprising, but he needs her..."

"Who's there?" Alezya asked aloud.

There was a pause, and then, someone cleared their throat.

A vague shape appeared to be blocking some of the sun, and Niiru jumped on its feet next to Alezya, but she held the baby dragon by its neck before it flew and attacked or something.

"*Tawa,*" she whispered.

It let out a little growl of frustration but lay down next to her, its tail still furiously agitating, splashing water and snow around.

"W-we're from Munsa Clan. Are you Darak's daughter?"

"What do you want from me?"

"Our Clan Chief saw you at the gathering last night and, uh... Th-they think they want to negotiate with you rather than your father. It didn't seem like you two got along, so..."

"You think?" Alezya raised an eyebrow.

She was trapped alone in a crevice, and they knew her father had pushed her in there too.

"Sorry," one of the other voices said. "It's just... Everyone's a bit tense and confused after everything that happened. But, is it true you can command the dragon?"

"Sort of."

She guessed they weren't seeing Niiru from where they stood; they probably couldn't afford to lean too close to the opening without the risk of falling in themselves.

"And you can speak the Dragon Clan's tongue too?"

"I'm learning," Alezya said.

"A-and you're pregnant with one of their–"

"What do you want?" Alezya cut them off.

"Our clan wants to negotiate directly with you. They don't trust your father at all."

Alezya chuckled bitterly. *No one ever should*, she thought.

"What do they want to negotiate?" she asked.

"Th-the Dragon Clan. Could you... have them give us some immunity against the dragon? We're a small clan with few warriors, but we have a lot of resources. We're open to negotiating anything they would want."

"It's not just us," one of the other voices said. "After your Deklaan Clan and some of the bigger ones left, many of the smaller clans who are allied or neighbors discussed it, and they are afraid of what your father could do using the dragon."

"The dragon won't attack the clans unless I tell him to," Alezya said. "My father holds no power over the dragon. The orange dragon might listen to me, but it still belongs to the Dragon Clan."

"How did you make it listen to you?"

Alezya hesitated.

She glanced down at Niiru, who was still eyeing the opening, looking ready to fly and fight any second. For some reason, she had a feeling even a tiny dragon could do a lot of damage to some grown men.

"I befriended the Dragon Clan," she said. "I learned some of their language and their ways, and the dragon won't attack me."

She didn't need to tell them the details, only enough so they would know she was the one they should be dealing with, not her father.

Perhaps her chance to get out of here would come about in a completely different way than she had thought.

"So... If the dragon attacked, could you tell it to stay away from us?"

"I could," Alezya said, slowly getting up.

"A-alright. We will relay that to our Clan Chiefs. What would you want in exchange?"

Alezya scoffed.

"Getting me out of here and away from my father would be a nice start."

"...Oh."

She rolled her eyes. She couldn't believe they hadn't thought of that in the first place.

It felt strange to negotiate her freedom and her ability to keep Kein from murdering another clan from ten feet under them, her bum still chilled from the ice.

"We, uh... We should probably relay what you said to our Clan Chiefs before we free you. They have to decide what to do and how we will negotiate..."

Alezya frowned.

No, she couldn't let her chance to get away go so easily. She didn't want to risk spending the night down here and freezing until she got sick. Her father might think she had become somewhat invulnerable because she was pregnant, but she wasn't, and even if she had been, Alezya wouldn't have wanted to spend a single night in this crevice.

She had to get out, and she couldn't wait around for someone else to decide if she was worth saving or not.

"Do you think my father will leave me down here long?" Alezya hissed. "If he even gets a whiff of another clan trying to save me, he'll haul me to somewhere you won't be able to reach. He will be the one your clans have to negotiate with, and I will have no say. Is that what you want?"

"B-but you said he couldn't command the dragon!"

"He can't, but I can, and there are many things my father could do to force me to do his bidding. You saw how he treated me last night, how my whole clan treated me. Do you really want to risk me being thrown into a hole you can't get to next time? Leave your clan's fate in my father's hands? Or mine? Get me out now, or the Munsa Clan won't get any immunity from the dragon at all."

She heard them whisper in panicked voices, trying to decide what to do. Alezya glanced down at Niiru, who was also waiting but had turned its eyes to her as soon as it noticed her staring.

The little dragon immediately jumped to its feet, looking ready for action. It gave Alezya an idea.

"We really need to get out of here," she said.

"...We? Who's with you?"

"*Fly,*" she whispered to the small dragon.

Niiru let out a cheerful, high-pitched growl, and excitedly spread its wings, immediately flying high and out of the cave. She heard the panicked voices of the men, who had most likely not expected a baby dragon to jump out of there.

"*Come back.*"

Alezya would have never thought the training she had done with Kein would help her order around a baby dragon, but sure enough, Niiru flew back into the crevice, its tiny wings appearing to be just big enough to support its body weight.

Much to Alezya's surprise, instead of landing somewhere in the area, it dove right toward her, and she had nowhere to go, so in a last-second attempt to trust the young dragon, she opened her arms, and caught it as it landed all four paws on her. She almost lost her footing from how heavy the baby dragon was, but Niiru held on just fine, putting its front paws over her shoulder and nestling against her neck like it was the most natural thing in the world to cuddle against a human.

Alezya wrapped her arms around the young dragon to support it, but it was as heavy as Lumie, if not heavier, and she still had a hard time believing what it was doing. Its hind legs were pressed against her stomach, the claws digging into the leather, making her glad she wasn't naked, or this would have been painful for her.

"She has a dragon," someone whispered in disbelief. "She really has a dragon down there with her!"

"Get her out," another voice hissed. "Let's just get her out and bring her to the leaders. They can decide what to do with her then.”

Alezya let out a heavy sigh of relief.

Seconds later, a rope appeared, and she told Niiru to fly and get off of her so she could grab the bag of food and give it to the young black dragon to hold while it was flying next to her.

“*Fly,*” she said. “*Up.*”

Niiru let out one of its cute little growls, but instead of taking off, it flapped its wings just enough to remain at Alezya’s eye level, and while she held onto the rope and was slowly pulled up, it kept flying at her level as if checking on her ascent.

The lift was slow and scary, making Alezya hold on to that rope for dear life and mentally remind herself not to look down. She could climb the flank of a mountain very confidently, but being suspended by a single rope mere feet above rock-solid ice was one of the scariest experiences of her life. She would take a dragon ride any day over this.

She tried to have faith, but it felt insanely long. If anything happened, if her father’s men came or something and those men dropped her, she might fall to her death this time...

Finally, her head reached the surface, and two hands grabbed under her arms to drag her up to a safe position. Niiru, who was following close behind, growled as soon as the men’s hands touched Alezya, and they dropped their grip a second later.

“Niiru,” she scolded the young dragon.

It stopped, turning its big amber eyes to her with curiosity written all over its baby dragon face. Still wary of how unstable the ground around a crevice could be, Alezya crawled on all fours until she was in a safe-looking area, and let out a heavy sigh.

“A-are you alright?”

The men looked too scared to approach her now, with a fierce baby dragon guarding her. Alezya nodded, before she slowly stood. Her arms and shoulders were painful from holding on to the rope, but now that she was confirming for herself that there had been only three men to pull the rope, she couldn’t complain about the slow lift.

She immediately realized they were from the clan with the braids, as they all had some intricate hairstyles full of braids, as long as a woman’s hair.

“Munsa Clan, was it?” she said.

“Yes,” the oldest-looking of them nodded. “...Are you willing to meet our leaders? We can take you to them.”

“If we do, we should move quickly. If your father sees us...”

“I know,” Alezya nodded.

A clan intervening in the matters of another was never a good sign.

Her father could very easily use this as an excuse to start some war and launch an attack, and his allied clans would easily rally.

After the demonstration from last night, chances were that no clan would dare to come to the Munsa Clan's rescue either, far too scared that he'd call a dragon.

Quickly, the four of them moved away from the crevice, walking toward the first sharp turn they could find and walking down that path in search of a more concealed area.

Alezya kept glancing back to try and see if she could spot anyone from her clan, but she didn't know this area at all, and she had arrived when it was dark outside, making her even more confused.

Moreover, every time she looked back, she couldn't help but be distracted by the black dragon's little hops in the snow. It looked like Niiru was having a great time digging itself into the snow, making little snow tunnels for a while before suddenly emerging with a big jump, sending snow flying everywhere.

Alezya didn't dare tell the young dragon to stop its shenanigans; if anything, its black scales were far better concealed when it was burying itself under layers of fresh snow rather than walking on it. She only made sure it followed her while the Munsa Clan's men were leading her out of there. She had no idea where the little dragon had come from nor why it was staying close to her, but she felt like she owed it to Kassein to be responsible for it, although Niiru seemed to be doing a better job at looking after her than the other way around so far.

"Here," one of the men pointed at a tunnel that led into a foreign maze.

Alezya followed; she wasn't fond of the idea of following men she didn't know into enclosed spaces, but at least she had a dragon with her, and they couldn't be worse than her father. Or so she hoped.

"Do your leaders not like my father, then?" she asked, hoping chatting with them would help her understand how to negotiate her survival.

"Not many do," one of the men scoffed. "Most fear him more than they respect him. Many suspect Darak has been abusing his position as one of those facing the Dragon Clan to claim privileges and such. Things have gotten more tense ever since some clans stopped paying the tax, and it became clear it didn't affect how many times the dragon attacked at all."

Alezya frowned. What tax? Had her father made other clans pay for their safety? He couldn't guarantee anything. The few clans that fought with the Dragon Clan always ended up with dead men.

She knew information was power between the clans, but it seemed her father had manipulated a lot for his benefit...

They resumed walking, and Alezya found herself glad that Niiru was small enough to stroll by her side in the tunnel; she wouldn't have felt confident following the three men on her own, but no dragon Kein's size would have been able to follow them in there. Even Kiki's lean body might have been too big for most areas. There was plenty of room for Niiru though, and while the young dragon was small, Alezya had no doubt its sharp claws and fangs would be able to do a lot of damage if needed.

Right now, the little black creature was keeping up with them, staying near Alezya but wandering ahead or staying behind to sniff something, full of curiosity. At all times, it kept track of where she was, its amber eyes always glancing back to find a trace of her.

The tunnels were pretty dark, but the Munsa men had pulled out some torches and lit them as soon as possible, the fire glowing against the walls of the tunnels.

Alezya had grown up and lived in tunnels like these her whole life, but there was always something very intimidating about going into deep, narrow tunnels she didn't know. She missed the fresh air and the sense of freedom she had felt while wandering among the Dragon Clan.

Niiru was now sticking close to her heels as if it had sensed she was nervous or felt the need to stay right by her.

"...You're not quite like the rumors said," the youngest-looking of the three men said.

The other two immediately gave him annoyed looks, so Alezya guessed he'd spoken everyone's minds out loud.

"How so?" she asked, curious.

"That you're a witch," he said bluntly. "That you made a deal with some demon to have a cursed child. That you tried to kill the man you were betrothed to, but your father saved him–"

"My father *saved* my ex-husband from *me*?" Alezya scoffed.

The man grimaced. He had to have seen Vasilias' reaction to her the previous evening; while her ex-husband did seem infuriated to have seen her alive, he had definitely been the one to ask for her head.

"But is it true you have a cursed child? It looked... strange."

"She isn't cursed," Alezya hissed. "She's just different."

Niiru growled as if to back her up and warn them against insulting Lumie any further. Alezya didn't care about being called a witch, she had been called far worse plenty of times already. But she wouldn't allow another man to hurl yet another insult at her child. Lumie was an innocent child, and she wasn't responsible for her horrible father, her helpless mother, or how she looked. And she didn't look anything less than perfect in Alezya's eyes.

Truthfully, the only other person whose opinion mattered was Kassein's. Alezya would have given anything for him to accept Lumie, and she felt sick just thinking of the possibility that he might reject her like everyone else did. But Kassein wasn't everyone else, and she had to trust he'd remain the man she had known him to be.

"Alright," the man swallowed, glancing nervously at the tiny, angry dragon. "Anyhow... You don't really look like a witch either."

"Darak's words can never be trusted," one of the other two scoffed. "His daughters are supposedly always the most beautiful women amongst the clans, but he never showed them until the weddings. How many of the men who married into his clan were promised they'd be free to visit their families but never came back? And how many died 'honorably' in *his* wars against the

Dragon Clan? His warriors somehow always survive, but many of the men who marry into his clan are never to be seen again. No one wants to marry a Deklaan woman anymore."

Alezya hadn't been privy to any of the dealings of her clan ever since she had been cast aside because of Lumie's birth, but she had noticed that there had been fewer weddings.

She had always thought that her own failed marriage must have been the reason there had been so few afterward; her father had harassed her so many times about how much disgrace she'd brought upon their clan that she had hardly ever stopped to question it.

As it turned out, she might have been as blindsided as the other clans who didn't know what happened on the other side of the mountains.

"The way you stood up against him last night and the obvious... disagreement between you and him is what pushed our chiefs to send us after you," one of them explained. "A lot of clans have been unhappy with Darak for a while, but he has so many allies, and we have so little information... Your outburst against him and the Exkiu Clan last night was unexpected."

"And the dragon! The dragon, it... it really looked like it obeyed you."

Their eyes all drifted down to Niiru, who tilted its head.

This time, Alezya had nothing to do with it, but the young dragon was still very visibly stuck to her side. She didn't comment on it. Whatever reason the baby dragon had to remain stuck to her heels, it was helping her convince those men that she held far more power over the dragons than her father could, which was true.

For now, Alezya only cared about increasing her chances to return to Lumie and Kassein, and it seemed to be working that way, even if they were presently heading in the opposite direction. Each step took her farther from her father and farther from Kassein. If she could have spotted Kein, she would have absolutely rushed to the first cliff for the orange dragon to get to her, but there had been no sign of Kassein's dragon since it had taken Lumie away.

Moreover, she had already deserted Kassein twice; Alezya knew she had no right to expect Kassein or his dragon to come to rescue her again.

No, this time, she was determined to be the one to make the trip back, no matter how long it would take. It wasn't right for her to wait to be rescued again; a good man like Kassein deserved to be the one to be chased after.

She had no choice but to assume she would have to go back on foot, and there was no way she'd be able to cross the mountains between Kassein and her without help. Her father had far too much power over the area. The alliance she was offered from foreign clans was an unexpected development but very welcome.

She didn't only want to get back to Kassein; after what she had learned the previous night, Alezya was also determined to make her father pay.

The truth behind her mother's death had been the final blow to any filial piety she had left. The more she learned, the more she was convinced that he was trouble for all the clans.

They walked for a long time, and when they stopped to take a break, Alezya was surprised they offered her some food. There were also new foods she had never seen before, which they described as a mix of grain and fish wrapped in edible leaves, and she found it surprisingly good.

Niiru, on the other hand, ignored their food to focus on dried meat instead, and it did seem to like the little bits of fish the Munsa men threw its way.

Still, they remained at a reasonable distance from Alezya and her thirty-pound bodyguard. It was kind of fun for her to notice how three grown men were scared of a miniature dragon while she was comfortable with Kein, who was at least ten times Niiru's size.

They didn't stop for long, just enough to eat and share some water, before they resumed walking.

Alezya was impressed by the length of the tunnels they used. They were shockingly long and narrow, running deep within their mountain, and, from what they told her, they didn't belong to any clan but were mostly used as safe passageways from one mountain to another.

They had to step outside a few times, much to Alezya and Niiru's relief, but there was no other dragon in sight for the duration of each walk outside, and Alezya felt a bit more sad every time they re-entered tunnels without having seen Kein. Had the orange dragon given up on her? Or was there some other matter that kept it away? Did Kassein order his dragon to not go back for her? Or was Kein still with Lumie?

Alezya would have given a lot to have the answers to her questions, but right now, all she had was a tiny dragon, the prospect of an alliance with the Munsa Clan, and a silent promise to herself that she would do anything to go back.

"We're here."

Alezya was surprised when their tunnel suddenly took a sharp turn and emerged into a large cave with a large body of water.

She immediately noticed it smelled salty, and though she had only seen the sea from afar, she assumed that was probably what it was supposed to smell like.

The lake of that cave must be connected to the sea. How deep inside the mountains had she gone? She couldn't tell how many hours they had walked, but she was tired, and she could tell it was late.

The three men were welcomed back by many people of their clan, all with intricate braided hairstyles, and now that she stood closer to them, Alezya noticed they had shiny little pearls, stones, and little objects she'd never seen before woven into them.

While they greeted many people, they continued to escort Alezya past them, leading her through more corridors, more little caves with people and bodies of water of all sizes. Their lifestyle was probably organized around those bodies of water, as Alezya noticed many people were actively swimming in them, including children. There were nets hung nearby, little wooden boxes, and spears, and she wondered if they could actually fish with those.

"Those... lakes are connected to the sea?" she guessed out loud.

"They are," they nodded. "Our people are great swimmers. Children learn young how to swim fast and hold their breath long enough to get to the other side."

Alezya was stunned.

Their clan felt so different from hers; no wonder she hadn't recognized the food or some of the fabric of their clothes.

Their clothing was also much lighter than the Deklaan's, but she guessed they were also deeper in the mountains, not as high and exposed to the cold winds as her clan.

Even their bodies seemed leaner, with broad shoulders and long limbs too. Alezya wondered if their hairstyles helped them swim better, perhaps, or if it had another cultural significance that escaped her.

Eventually, they reached an opening that brought them outdoors again and into a cove that took Alezya's breath away.

It was a large dome carved into the mountain, but the ground was half rocks, half sand, and the sea was coming to lick the entrance with small waves.

All around the area were the Munsa people, gathered around little fire pits, walking with fishnets, or busy making wicker baskets. There were countless ropes, baskets, and fishnets hanging around the walls of the cove, some so high Alezya had no idea how they'd reached it in the first place.

There were children playing around in the inches of water, and as soon as it noticed them, Niiru let out a chirpy sound and jumped after them.

"Niiru!" Alezya stopped the dragon in its tracks. "No. You're going to scare them."

Niiru gave her a little disappointed growl and, instead of coming back to her, crouched down in the thin bed of water, its tail swishing little waves of water left and right. It reminded Alezya of how Kein could do exactly the same thing with snow and again, she wondered if Kein was related to Niiru somehow.

Leaving the small dragon within eyesight, she was led toward one of the gatherings.

It was one of the bigger circles of people, with some elders who didn't even glance up as they were braiding younger kids' hair, fishnets, or baskets, but she did recognize the man and woman with braided hair from the gathering. The man was frowning at her, his eyes going to his men who had brought her full of questions, but the woman didn't seem surprised. From up close, Alezya guessed that woman was slightly older than her, perhaps thirty years old.

"You brought her?" the man finally asked out loud, sounding annoyed.

"Darak had shoved her into a crevice," one of them admitted. "We kind of... had to strike a deal before he noticed us and took her elsewhere."

"What deal?" the woman asked.

"I would agree to meet you if they freed me," Alezya answered for them, "and I would consider making sure your clan was safe from the dragon."

Those words got a few more people at this gathering to raise their heads. The adults sent the kids off to play with their peers, and the atmosphere around grew tense.

The woman glanced around, silently checking in with the others, before she turned to Alezya.

"...Fine, let's talk," she said. "Sit down. You should have a meal since you have traveled all this way. And... is that dragon yours?"

Alezya glanced back.

In the few minutes she'd focused on the man and woman from the gathering, Niiru had begun chasing after the kids.

Far from being panicked, the children were howling with laughter and running in all directions with loud, excited screams. Niiru was having a blast making big jumps after them, splashing itself and the children with each landing. Alezya smiled.

"...He's a child," she said.

She was pretty sure Niiru had never tasted human flesh, and it didn't look tempted to try.

The young dragon looked the same as Kiki and Kein when they had been playing together in the snow, and although it could have easily bitten a limb or two off, it was just making a big show of running after the children, changing targets if it became too easy.

The multitude of kids running away from Niiru seemed to excite the young dragon far more than the prospect of a fresh meal.

"So long as he's fed something, he won't harm anyone," she added, just to be certain.

Dragons could be quite ill-tempered, so she didn't want to risk hunger becoming Niiru's priority before fun. She was almost certain she could reign the young dragon in if things escalated, but she'd rather not tempt fate.

"The dragon will be fed," the woman said, giving a nod to the men who had come with Alezya, who turned around, hopefully to go find a meal worthy of a young dragon.

Alezya finally sat down amongst them, facing a semi-circle of Munsa people while she had her back turned to Niiru and the kids playing in the bay. Thankfully, just the cute roars of laughter and high-pitched growls would be enough to keep her updated on that end.

"I am Ekata," the woman introduced herself. "This is my brother, Ekut. We are the Munsa Clan Chiefs."

"The two of you?" Alezya asked, surprised.

"Our clan has always had a pair of chiefs," Ekata explained. "A man and a woman. Sometimes a couple, sometimes a brother and sister pair. Ekut and I were born on the same full moon, and our previous clan chiefs saw it as a sign for us to become the next chiefs."

"But you didn't... speak up at the gathering," Alezya said, remembering how Ekata had stood back.

"Other clans aren't so... open-minded about female clan chiefs," she snorted. "We prefer to let them think Ekut is the only one in charge. A lot of clans already lost their place at the gathering for having female leaders."

Alezya immediately thought of her mother's birth clan, the Lumiata. She had faintly hoped to see them at the gathering the previous night, but just like Ekata, she wasn't blind; an all-female clan wouldn't have been welcomed.

"Since your father threw you in a crevice," Ekut scoffed, "I'm guessing we were right to think you and he have... different stances."

"They couldn't be more different," Alezya sighed, glancing back to check on Niiru. "Ever since my daughter was born, I have been treated as a pariah by my entire clan, except maybe for a couple of people. My child and I were shunned, merely kept alive so long as I remained remotely useful."

"I do not care about what happened between you and Darak," Ekata said, "but I believe you. He is a cunning, manipulative man. He certainly cannot be trusted, and his words even less. Which is why we figured talking directly with you might be our best course of action. Is what was said at the gathering true? That you can summon and control the dragon?"

"He obeys me to a certain extent," Alezya admitted, careful with her words. "If I call and he hears, he will come."

Or she hoped that was still the case.

She couldn't help but glance back at Niiru and, beyond him and the excited children, the sea.

How far had she gone from her home mountain? They had walked for hours, but they had been indoors so long that she had lost her notion of time. Judging by the sky, the sun would soon set, which meant she had sent Lumie away almost an entire day ago...

She was sore and tired, but most of all, she missed them dearly. She would have given a lot to spot Kein right then and have the dragon take her back to the Dragon Clan, to Kassein's arms.

"Let's... not do that right now," Ekut said, looking slightly nervous. "We wanted to talk to you first."

"What do you want from me?" Alezya asked.

"Is the part about you spending time with the Dragon Clan true?" Ekata tilted her head. "That you learned their language?"

"It is," Alezya said. "Their leader taught me some of their language, and I was with him most of the time."

"Why do they attack us?" Ekut asked. "Why do they launch the dragons after our people?"

"Because they see us as enemies," Alezya replied. "The clans that share a border with the Dragon Clan, like the Deklaan Clan, have been relentlessly attacking them. I saw it with my own eyes. A clan even sent people carrying a terrible disease to die in the Dragon Clan and infect them as well. But all the time I was there, the Dragon Clan never launched any attack themselves. The dragon even attacked some men from their own clan because they tried to assault me."

"The dragon defended *you* against their own warriors?" Ekata said with a fascinated expression.

"I had their leader's protection and his dragon's," Alezya replied with confidence. "They weren't allowed to touch me. The dragon killed them for harassing me, just like it would attack my father's spies or anyone who intended to harm their clan. But dragons don't hunt humans to feed themselves."

"But we never attacked the dragon," Ekut frowned. "We were still–"

"I don't think they know the difference between one clan and another," Alezya explained. "The dragon just sees humans in the mountains and assumes they are the same humans who attacked the Dragon Clan. My father's will to keep attacking is condemning all the clans to be eternally targeted by the dragon."

Ekut and Ekata exchanged a long look.

Alezya was aware that some of the elders that had their eyes riveted on their task or the kids were definitely listening in too.

She glanced back, and this time, Niiru was on the shore, playing a new game as the adults had brought little fish to feed the dragon, and the children were throwing them to Niiru, who was only too happy to go "hunt" its prey before eating it.

"I can't believe it," Ekut hissed. "We have been at war with the Dragon Clan for generations. All the clans always had to send men to the Deklaan Clan and the other border clans for the war, and it turns out... so many lives could have been spared?"

"Darak is a liar and a manipulative bastard," his sister hissed. "We should have known better than to ever believe his words again. It's good that most of the clans already started to doubt him after we lost so many men. It's not like any clan trusts him much after what happened with the Lumiata Clan."

"You know of the Lumiata Clan?" Alezya exclaimed, stunned to hear that name.

"Of course we do. Or we used to," Ekata corrected. "A decade ago, there wasn't a single clan who didn't know about the Lumiata, the matriarchal clan. They held such precious knowledge that no clan dared to harm them. Most even sought their help when diseases hit them or when their women were close to labor. ...All of the clans took a hit when the Lumiata suddenly disappeared years ago. We looked for them, as most clans did. Even a decade later, no one knows what happened to them... Many used to think they relocated, but none of the clans they used to trade with found signs of them anymore. There were some rumors the dragon had killed them, but many more of us suspect Darak did something."

"...My mother was of the Lumiata," Alezya admitted in a low voice, suddenly missing the necklace, her only physical memory of her mom.

The woman slowly nodded.

"We know who you are. Your mother... The Lumiata never married into another clan, and they never moved in with their partners. When your father took in a pregnant Lumiata woman, we all knew something was off. Your father claimed he was in love with your mother, and the Lumiata said an arrangement had been made... Everyone could tell something was going on. I'm sorry, but whatever bound your mother to Darak, it wasn't love."

"...I can imagine that," Alezya admitted with a tight throat.

She knew far too well the wretched depths her father was willing to go to get what he wanted, and she felt all the more sorry for her mother, who had more than likely been forced to carry his child.

"What do you think my father wanted with the Lumiata?" Alezya asked.

She knew her father's greed. As much as she had no doubt he was the type to take anything he wanted, including a woman, Alezya still knew him to be a cunning man. He wouldn't have risked making an enemy of so many clans only because of something like lust.

The woman exchanged a look with her brother before returning to Alezya.

"This is only a guess, but... we both know how obsessed the Deklaan Clan is with defeating the Dragon Clan. We knew the Lumiata were wise women who held incredible knowledge about medicine, the lands, life, and even the skies, warning other clans of snowstorms and thunderstorms long before they hit. According to our elders, the Lumiata weren't born in the mountains nor came from the sea like our clan; they had come from the rivers and settled in the mountains long after our ancestors. They came from the land, the same way the Dragon Clan had before they settled so close. Many rumors were going around that the Lumiata knew more about the dragons than any other clan, and we knew it had to be true to some extent; they were never attacked and never afraid to move locations when a dragon was roaming in the area. It was as if they knew something was... protecting them. I would bet anything that Darak, your father, thought he would be able to steal some of their secrets by marrying one of them."

"We think his plan was foiled when they refused to let him live with them," one of the elders left of Ekut suddenly spoke. "The Lumiata rarely allowed men to live with them, and it was far less likely for a Lumiata woman to go to the men's clan. Some of their women never even lived with the father of their child. And in all cases, if they had a daughter, the daughter was always sent to live with the Lumiata Clan, whereas if it was a son..."

"He lived with his father's clan," Alezya muttered. "But my father never sent me to the Lumiata Clan, did he?"

"Not just you," the older woman said. "Your mother wasn't able to return to her people either. Our clan was too far to know what happened at the time, but now, we know that there were many meetings between your father and the Lumiata. We think he wasn't letting your mother return, or your mother refused to return without–"

"Without me."

Alezya let out a heavy sigh. It was a huge blow, much worse than she would have thought. She had very few memories of her mom, but she knew she had been a kind, loving woman.

And now, she knew that her mom had fought as hard as she could to return to her home clan while refusing to abandon her child, precisely like Alezya had done with Lumie. Suddenly, she felt more kindred than ever with the mother that she hardly remembered anymore.

No wonder her father had hated her so much; she probably reminded him of the previous woman who had defied him...

"...My father killed my mother," Alezya suddenly spat.

Her words triggered a collective gasp around her, but she wasn't looking at them; she was glaring into the fire, remembering her father's taunting voice, the grin she could imagine on his face when he'd slapped her with that earth-shattering revelation.

"...I knew it," Ekata hissed. "That wretched bastard... I always knew Darak was the worst of them! The Deklaan clan chiefs have always been sick with arrogance, but that bastard... I'd bet you he did something to the Lumiata too!"

"We don't know that," her brother said. "I don't think he could have exterminated another clan on his own without anyone knowing."

"Oh, please," she rolled her eyes. "We know how Darak is, and he isn't the only one who hated the Lumiata as much as he envied them. I bet he convinced some other clans who thought the same that they had to get rid of the Lumiata. Look at last night! The Exkiu bastard was ready to slaughter the girl on the spot. The Exkiu Clan's previous leader hated the Lumiata just as much, and to whom did Darak marry his daughter, of all people? The son of that bastard!"

"Even if that's right, that has little to do with us," Ekut said, far calmer and resigned. "And even if it did, there is little we can do. We cannot avenge the Lumiata, even if he did what you think he did, that's... that's out of our hands. It's done now."

Alezya felt a strange mix of sorrow and annoyance toward that man.

She could understand he was trying to think with the best interests of his clan in mind, and it was no easy feat when they were talking about actual war with a clan that had most likely already annihilated another under their noses.

Still, Alezya didn't like this. She couldn't let her father go unscathed after what he had done to her mother and what he had very likely done to her clan. She needed to make him pay, and she wasn't going to be able to do anything if she couldn't find allies.

"It's done?" his sister scoffed. "We can't simply ignore what the Deklaan Clan did like cowards!"

"We're not sure what they did, Sister. Even if we had proof-"

"Even if we had proof, they would deny it," she hissed, "but no clan is blind nor deaf. We all know the same thing, and that is that the Deklaan Clan is dangerous. How many clans would believe us if we told them what they did to the girl's mother? Be real, Brother. We both know there are a lot of clans who would be happy if the Deklaan Clan got wiped out tomorrow. Even more so after what happened last night."

"My father deserves to die," Alezya said, drawing all the eyes back to herself. "Not only because of what he's done to me and my mother, but because of what he did to the Lumiata and all the other clans by perpetually antagonizing the Dragon Clan. He's blindsiding them all. Even the clans who are allied with him probably have no idea they will never win this war."

"What did you see, child?" one of the elders asked.

"The Dragon Clan is beyond anything we think we know," Alezya scoffed. "Far more. When I rode on the dragon, I saw land as far as my eyes could see. We're... We're so small compared to them. The men at the foot of the mountains are just a tiny piece of their clan. I saw more of their settlements, their black mountain. And there are far more dragons than what we know. The fact that we haven't seen them all means they're far from where we can see. If the Dragon Clan decided to, they could probably exterminate us all at dawn."

A heavy silence followed Alezya's words.

She wasn't sure they'd believe her or not, but she knew what she had seen; there were hardly any women in the Dragon Clan, but she had seen some in settlements near *Kalat Unshreik*. There had to be a lot more living beyond that. If Kassein had six more siblings with dragons as big as Kein, they had to be far away for her people to have never seen them.

Her father's dreams of victory were just blind delusions, and he was going to send many clans to their deaths with them.

The gathering the previous evening had been the eye-opener Alezya didn't know she needed. She had always been oblivious, but now, she couldn't remain passive.

"Alright," Ekata said, with an insistent look to her brother. "You know the Dragon Clan better than anyone in the mountains now. What can you help us do?"

"I... I need to get back to them," Alezya said, her throat tight with emotion. "Their Clan Chief, I could... I could tell him not all the clans want to fight him. That your clan has no intention of fighting."

Alezya wouldn't admit it to her newfound allies, but she was also dying to know if she could get back to Kassein and still be allowed by his side. With each minute she spent away from him, her anxiety got a bit worse that he wouldn't forgive her for another betrayal.

She was hopeful that Lorey wouldn't allow anything to happen to Lumie, and she knew Kassein wouldn't take his anger out on a child, but she wasn't confident she would also be spared.

As much as she never wanted to fear Kassein, and she firmly believed he was a good man, Alezya wasn't sure she'd be able to handle being rejected by a man she actually loved this time.

"It's not just us," Ekut said, now looking hopeful. "There are a few other clans who would want that... guarantee. Many of us haven't even dared to grow in size just so we wouldn't have to send men to the border to have them die at the hands of the Dragon Clan. If we could be sure, somehow, that we will be able to travel outside without the risk of being attacked by a dragon, it would be... incredible for our clan and others."

"I can't guarantee anything," Alezya admitted, "but I know their Clan Chief might listen to me if I explain things. I just need to get back to him—I mean, to the Dragon Clan, but my father will never allow me to cross the border."

Ekata frowned, exchanging another look around.

"Sadly, we're not familiar with the mountains you come from," she said, "but we can reach out to other clans who might; some of them we do trust."

"Thank you," Alezya said.

Ekata exchanged a long glance with her brother, who cleared his throat before he spoke.

"We... are also worried about the clans who will be unwilling to help us," he said. "After you were taken away from the gathering last night and the Deklaan Clan left, many clans argued for a long time. As my sister said, many clans like ours believe in peace with the Dragon Clan, or at least we hope to find a way for their beasts to leave us alone. But some other clans were less... optimistic. Many clans are too afraid or have lost too many to the Dragon Clan. They don't want peace, and worse, they believe your father does have the solution to end this war."

"This is madness," Alezya scoffed. "They don't even realize... Kein is—I mean, the orange dragon is just one of their dragons. They could wipe us all out in a blink if they wanted, or at least make it so we'd never be able to see the light of day again."

"We believe you," Ekata said, "but not all the clans do. Many of them would much rather believe your father's promises to end the Dragon Clan than think a woman can help them establish peace. Whether it's pride, fear, or anger, some clans won't listen to us, and certainly not to you. The Exkiu and Deklaan Clans hold far too much power. Your father sacrificed countless other clans' men for his war, and they won't be pacified so easily."

"...Is there a way we can convince them?" Alezya muttered, horrified. "They... They will just keep sending men to their deaths!"

"It sounded worse than that last night," Ekut groaned. "Some wanted to launch an all-out war against the Dragon Clan. There were... horrible ideas thrown around."

"What kind of ideas?" Alezya asked, alarmed by the fact that he wouldn't meet her gaze anymore.

Ekut looked nervously at his sister, so Ekata was the one to scoff.

"They... thought they might use you. Some wanted to use you as a hostage, others thought about using you as bait, and others wanted to kill you outright. Either way, I have to say it probably isn't safe for you to go out there right now. That's why we had our sentinels take a long but safe route home, to be sure you weren't followed nor seen by prying eyes. We might be able to find you a way back, but we'll need to reach out to other clans to see where they stand, decide if they can be trusted, and see how we can find a way back for you. Sadly, our clan has always been far from your home mountain, so we have no idea what it would look like to get you to the other side, but we can help you for part of the way."

"I appreciate your help," Alezya said.

She really did. If it wasn't for the Munsa Clan's men rescuing her, she might still be freezing in a crevice right now, or perhaps the target of other clans.

Her father was a fool to believe she was somewhat immune because she was pregnant, or perhaps he'd also hoped to keep her away from other clans by shoving her in a crevice while things went down.

It had certainly sounded like he expected to rally more clans to his mad plan in the upcoming days, using her as bait.

"If my father manages to convince other clans and launch some war, it will be a massacre," she muttered.

She had never given much thought about other clans before, but now, Alezya was forced to admit that she couldn't not care anymore, not when she had proof that she could potentially save other clans and hundreds of people in the process. Some of those clans might be wishing for war, but she was ready to bet a lot of them were misguided by fear, ignorance, and her father's empty promises.

She couldn't help but think of men like Suolk, good men who might be forced to partake in a meaningless war they'd lose their lives in. Many men might have been awful, like her father or Vasilias, but now, Alezya was willing to believe most men who would be coerced into battle did not deserve that fate.

"We will try to convince as many as we can and find you a safe path to the Dragon Clan. You're more than welcome to stay among us in the meantime," Ekata said. "You've had a long day traveling here. Share a meal with us, and then you can rest. I promise you'll be safe here while we figure things out."

Her brother didn't seem as willing to welcome Alezya, judging by his ongoing frown and contrite expression. Alezya could guess why: there was no guarantee another clan wouldn't try and fight them to get to her. Even if the Munsa Clan sentinels had been careful, they had been outside long enough that another clan's sentinel might have spotted them.

Alezya could hardly believe how things had escalated overnight; until then, she'd thought the clans got along well enough to make decisions together, but after the previous gathering, it was clear that things were much more unequal than she'd thought. A war could start between the clans at any given moment, let alone with the Dragon Clan.

It also baffled her how much power her father could wield simply because of all his lies and manipulations. They weren't the great clan they pretended to be; if anything, they seemed almost outdated compared to others. They didn't have the best weapons, clothing, tools, or craftsmanship.

Simply from watching the Munsa Clan, Alezya could see how their culture was different and more evolved than hers. They had nice traps for their food, well-designed outfits for their environment, countless fabrics on the floor and walls to protect their feet and skin, impressive nets and weaving techniques, accessories for the women, varied weapons for their men, and the children were running around freely, playing with nice toys and watched over by the whole community.

That would have never happened back home. The Deklaan Clan was stuck in its caves and rudimentary ways, its natural growth stunted by endless battles. Alezya remembered how her cousin had begged her to fetch herbs, how she struggled to find her food, how every resource was painfully sought for and hoarded.

Their clan wasn't doing as well as they wanted to make it seem, and she couldn't fathom how her father could stand proud amongst so many other clans who were more advanced and claimed he knew better.

His vile way of weaponizing their position and insight toward the Dragon Clan would have been almost admirable if it wasn't so despicable.

Alezya nearly felt regretful she'd given him so much more ammunition. She hadn't realized how much he could use her bond with the Dragon Clan to manipulate other clans even more.

Her father had brought most of his valid, adult men to the gathering, but from what she'd heard, he had recruited and sacrificed far more into helpless battles.

With all those thoughts in mind, Alezya gratefully accepted the meal she was given, which was rather welcome based on how hungry she was.

For a while, she chatted with Ekata, finding herself drawn to the female Clan Chief's outgoing and no-nonsense personality, which reminded her of Kiera but with a much more feminine and graceful energy. Ekut was pretty silent until they started to dive into how long Alezya had spent with the Dragon Clan and what she had experienced.

When she described how she'd learned their language, he stopped staring at his bowl to look up at her with a frown.

"How... You learned so much in just a few days?"

"Their language is rather simple," Alezya nodded, "and I am good at memorizing things."

"Still, it's... impressive," Ekut finally said.

Alezya smiled politely, unaccustomed to compliments. She couldn't remember the last time she had been sincerely praised for anything but her beauty. Lorey had been cheerful anytime she'd mastered new words, but it had felt more like she was praising a child. Being actually praised for something that had nothing to do with her appearance felt pretty good.

Another squeal of laughter erupted behind them, and Alezya turned around to see Niiru, still playing around with the children.

Now, some adults had apparently released fish, and the young dragon was chasing them around in the water, amusing the kids as he splashed them at each dive.

"...And that small dragon?" Ekata asked. "Did the Dragon Clan give it to you or something? Why is it small?"

"It's a baby dragon," Alezya said, "but I have no idea why it is staying with me. It should have a... mom dragon, but I haven't seen it. Maybe it got lost and smelled a bigger dragon on me. I genuinely don't know."

She had no clue why Niiru had come to her, but as she watched the young dragon happily eating little fish the children threw its way, Alezya knew she would watch over the young dragon just like Kein had watched over her. She owed it this much.

"We'll give you a space to sleep in," Ekata said. "You ought to be exhausted. Come with me."

As soon as Alezya got up to follow her, Niiru left the children and the body of water to run to her, following her into new tunnels. They were far better decorated than the bare walls of her own clan.

The Munsa Clan had hung countless decorations on the walls, covered most floors with layers of soft sand or a woven fabric she didn't recognize, and there were little shiny decorations hanging everywhere, mostly to reflect the light, she assumed.

Ekata took her to a little nook where someone had prepared a decent bed, a little washing basin with a bar of fragrant paste, and a neat pile of clean female clothing, and they had also brought her a new cloak.

While she was more than grateful for the piece of clothing, Alezya felt a pang of sadness, reminiscing about the warm fur coats Kassein always wrapped her in. She missed him and Lumie terribly, and she felt far from them.

Thankfully, she was far too tired to think about them for too long, and almost as soon as she had gotten rid of her dirty clothes and was done cleaning herself, she lay down; with Ekata's promise that she'd wake her up if anything happened, Alezya drifted off to sleep, Niiru nestled against her stomach.

Alezya was so deep asleep that it took her a while to realize someone was shaking her shoulder and trying to wake her up.

"Alezya, you need to wake up. The Dragon Clan is attacking."

"What?" She sat up immediately, wide awake.

Niiru rolled off her lap with a high-pitched growl, gnawing a part of her blanket as Alezya pushed it off her upper body. Ekata was crouched by her side with an urgent expression.

"Our sentinels just came back from the heights," she explained. "They're saying it's absolute mayhem down south. The Dragon Clan launched an attack against some of the clans near their own. We think they're attacking the Deklaan Clan, but we're not sure; we're too far away. We've sent people to check on the situation."

"Did they see K—the orange dragon?" Alezya asked as she quickly got up and began dressing.

"I think so," Ekata nodded, handing her the dress. "Do you want to come and see? It's too dangerous to take you outside, but we do have one spot from which you might be able to see the situation safely, if we can see anything."

"Definitely."

Quickly pulling her long hair into a bun and calling Niiru to stick by her heel, Alezya followed Ekata out of the little nook she'd slept in.

Judging by the ambient darkness, she'd slept well into the evening. This time, no children were playing in the cove when they walked by, only a few adults by the dancing fire pits.

Ekata didn't stop there, however, and instead guided her through new tunnels, narrower than the others, without any decorations anywhere. Some of the paths they took were going up so quickly that they even had to climb some of the nets the Munsa seemed to be constantly weaving, which had been hung there for safety.

Alezya wondered if their clan had made their weaving techniques a strength both underwater and vertically as she appreciated the strength of those nets while they climbed. So many of the dangerous climbs she'd undertaken before would have been made so much easier if she'd had access to such a thing...

Once again, Alezya couldn't help but think of how much each clan would benefit from exchanging more than raw resources and wedding promises with one another. It was just a thought at the back of her mind, but she still felt like there was a better future possible, one where the clans helped each other, traded more, and trusted one another.

"We're almost there," Ekata told her as they were climbing a particularly long and upright corner.

"I'm alright," Alezya nodded, glancing at Niiru, who was taking little jumps and flapping its wings to keep up with their ascent.

"You're a great climber," Ekata nodded.

Again, Alezya didn't know what to do with the compliment, but she sure appreciated it. Ekata reached the top first and held out a hand to help Alezya up.

Just like she had mentioned, it was a tight opening in the mountain, but one that had a narrow view straight toward the south. It was too dangerous to stay close to the long, vertical opening that was nothing but a visible crack in the flank of the mountain, which explained why their ascent had been so steep and narrow.

They were just a foot away from the edge, with a dangerous cliff that promised a certain death right below them and a tiny vertical nook in which a male sentinel of the Munsa Clan greeted them.

"Anything?" Ekata asked him as she and Alezya took his spot by the opening.

"It's already over," the man said. "It looks like they launched a lightning strike because it happened so fast. The dragon flew off just minutes before you arrived. We're not sure which clan was attacked yet, but it sure looked like the Deklaan's territory. The shouts echoed throughout the valley."

Alezya squinted at the opening, disappointed she had missed Kein and potentially Kassein.

Sure, they would have been too far away to see her, hidden behind the smallest crack in the mountain, but she sure would have liked to see them.

She still hadn't been able to confirm that Kein had delivered Lumie to Kassein. If not, what had it done with her? Did it keep her with it? Had it entrusted her to Lorey and Kiera? Or to Tievin, perhaps?

Alezya kept squinting toward her father's mountain, trying to see something, anything, but the Munsa territory was too far away.

It was already impressive how much distance she'd covered in a few hours, and it was nighttime too; she couldn't see anything, and her clan was probably hiding inside anyway.

She sighed and let Ekata take a look, grateful the Munsa Clan Chief had let her take a peek first.

"Why would they launch such a short attack?" Ekata frowned, squinting at the opening. "And using the dragon too?"

"...I'm not sure," Alezya confessed. "Maybe... I'm thinking he might have been looking for me."

She wasn't entirely sure, but it felt like the most likely explanation.

Kassein had definitely fought and sent men up the mountains to fight the clans before, but the timing was just too off. Why would he and Kein come back after she'd sent Lumie to them?

Alezya couldn't help but believe it was for her, and it made her all the more hopeful.

"You're sure it was the orange dragon?" she asked the sentinel.

"Certain," he nodded. "It's easy to recognize, even at night..."

Alezya let out a heavy sigh.

"You think they did some damage?" Ekata asked with a grin.

"Kein, I mean, the dragon is too big to get into the mountain, so they might have been sending him just to try and find me... but I can't say for sure."

"It had all the signs of some quick, punishing attack," the sentinel noted. "I didn't see the men, but I heard plenty of shouting, and the orange dragon was checking out anyone trying to leave the mountain from another way. It's hard to know what happened inside from where we are though. We're completely on the wrong side..."

They remained quiet for a few seconds, still glancing through the opening, but indeed, it looked like things were over.

Alezya let out a faint sigh. She really needed to get back to the Dragon Clan as quickly as possible. She was glad the Munsa Clan had rescued her because she was fairly certain she would have been dead by the time Kassein and Kein attacked her clan; they would have never found her in time.

At her feet, Niiru was also trying to peek through the opening, its tail swishing with curiosity before it turned its head toward her with a little growl.

"I know," she whispered. "I miss them too."

"We should go back down," Ekata suggested. "See if the other sentinels caught anything else."

Alezya agreed, and she followed her all the way back to the main cove, where, indeed, several adults of the Munsa Clan were standing and talking animatedly to Ekut.

They acknowledged their other leader with nods, but they had arrived right in the middle of what already seemed to be a very lively discussion. Alezya listened as several of the Munsa Clan sentinels repeated the same accounts from different points of view, although no one had seen much more.

Kein had attacked several flanks of the Deklaan Clan's mountain, even making some rocks collapse, and they were sure there had been some fighting. Ekut had sent men to inquire with the nearby clans, but their end of the mountains was so far from the other that they probably wouldn't get much more.

Ekata let her brother chat with their men, instead taking a step aside with Alezya. At their feet, Niiru let out a yawn, prompting her to lift the heavy dragon and carry it; the young dragon immediately nestled in her arms.

"If only that dragon had done some good damage to the Deklaan Clan," Ekata hissed. "We'd be better off without those leeches..."

Alezya could understand that woman's venom toward her clan, but she didn't entirely agree.

No matter how corrupted her father was, the Deklaan Clan wasn't just him. Even if many men followed his orders blindly, Alezya knew there were a few good people amongst them. She had seen very little of their goodness herself in the past, but still, she couldn't condone an outright massacre.

She was almost surprised to find herself worried about what had happened and how angry Kein and Kassein had possibly been. Had something happened? Had her father done something to prompt an attack?

She sighed, petting Niiru. Maybe they'd been looking for the baby dragon? Niiru was more than capable of flying back on its own, but the young dragon was clearly unwilling to fly away from her.

"The dragon," Ekata commented. "You called it by a different name before. Kain?"

"...Kein," Alezya corrected. "That's the orange dragon's name."

"Their dragons have names?" Ekata said, surprised. "Do you know many of them...?"

"No," Alezya replied, wary. "Only a couple. I don't even know this little one. He just appeared out of nowhere and is sticking to me."

"So... It's not your baby's dragon, then?"

Alezya opened her eyes wide in disbelief, but Ekata shook her head.

"I knew it was probably nonsense, but after what your father said last night, and seeing that you have a miniature dragon stuck to you... I didn't want to press the issue until you were ready to talk about it, but I can't help but be curious. If you can really get your own dragon, it could change many things..."

"No," Alezya replied, a bit too abruptly. "First, I'm not pregnant. I fooled my father into thinking I was. Even if I was, dragons aren't... born like that. Niiru probably belongs to a child from the Dragon Clan, and he won't grow into an adult size until much, much later. The orange dragon is so big because it belongs to a grown man, but not all adult dragons are the same either."

"How many dragons have you seen...?"

"Only a couple," Alezya confessed, "but I've learned enough."

Ekata gave a slow, thoughtful nod.

"No wonder your father was so... excited about you possibly controlling one of them. If we could have at least one of those dragons, like the Dragon Clan, we wouldn't lose any battles anymore. Any clan who can get their hands on one of those dragons would be able to force all the others to submit to them."

"Dragons aren't meant to be weapons," Alezya suddenly said.

Ekata blinked, staring at her with surprise, but Alezya was looking down at Niiru, who was quietly napping in her arms.

"Dragons aren't meant to win battles for humans," she said. "They aren't the brutal, man-killing monsters we thought them to be. I've seen it myself. They can be kind, caring creatures. Protective, even. They let humans sit on them to keep warm, Ekata. They can play around like young snow leopards, tease one another, and be silly. They will let a human they trust and care about order them around, and yes, they do not hesitate to kill, but never because of something like hunger or hatred. Every time I've seen the orange dragon attack, it was to protect someone else."

To protect me, Alezya thought.

Kein had killed several men of the Dragon Clan, men it had known for longer than her, simply because she had been in danger, and the dragon wouldn't tolerate that. She took a deep breath in.

"We should stop looking for ways to win against a dragon," she said, "or against the Dragon Clan. Our clans are capable of so much more, and we would be capable of wonders if we could learn to really work together, not merely coexist. The emergency of our survival has blinded us. I have no idea what has been attempted before, but if we actually tried to make peace with the Dragon Clan..."

"It's not like no one ever hoped for peace before. But we hoped for the Dragon Clan to be gone, not to... befriend them. You're the first person of our kind to speak some of their language in centuries, if not... ever," Ekata mentioned.

"I know, but after witnessing the gathering and spending time with the Dragon Clan, I cannot help but think there has to be a better future for all of us. My father is blinded by greed, and he is setting us all up for extinction when we should be aspiring to coexist with the Dragon Clan. If their dragons do not need to eat us, why would they keep fighting unless we push them to? I... I've lived with them. I've seen all that they have that we don't, and I don't think they envy us at all. If they have nothing to gain from fighting us, why should we keep pushing them to?"

"Is that what you've come to think? After spending time with them?"

"I've seen what I have seen. The Dragon Clan was attacked far more often by our people than they attacked us. It might be easy for the dragon, but the climb is hard and tenuous for their people. My clan has nothing they could want, Ekata, nothing. I was given far better treatment as a... guest in their clan than back when I was the Clan Chief's child. They eat meat and take hot baths every day; they have far more clothes than they need, and they fight covered in clothes of stone. The Deklaan Clan is of no interest to them, merely a bothersome piece of rubble under their feet. I don't know about the other clans that have been attacking them, but it is unfair that all of us live in fear and keep up this fight when we're being punished for a few men's decisions."

"...You speak like a true clan chief."

That took Alezya by surprise, and she glanced at Ekata, who was staring at her with a smile.

"I mean it," she continued. "I was raised my entire life to fit this role, but you, Alezya, are a natural-born leader."

"I don't think so," Alezya muttered, her eyes going back to Niiru.

"You were smart enough to learn a completely different language in a matter of days," Ekata said. "You can command a dragon. You survived on your own despite being your clan's pariah, and you managed to befriend the one clan everyone's scared of. I saw the way you stared at the Exkiu Clan bastard you were married to and at your father. You're no helpless woman, Alezya. You're strong and brave. And even when you're alone, miles away from anything and anyone you know, you still manage to care for a baby dragon and think about the future of all the clans. That's the kind of leader any clan needs."

Alezya didn't answer that.

She knew what a bad leader was: a man like her father, who was blinded by ambition and greed, dreams of victory and glory, so much so that he was dragging his own people to ruin. But for her to be a leader?

She had been her clan's daughter and then an outsider.

She was a mother and, certainly, a survivor.

At the moment, she also felt more feminine than she had in a long time because she was missing Kassein terribly. She hadn't allowed herself to feel vulnerable in a long time, but the mere thought of that man's embrace was enough to bring tears to her eyes.

"Let's get you in front of more clan chiefs," Ekata finally said. "If there's any chance of peace with the Dragon Clan, I believe you might be our best one yet."

Chapter 16

"Commander."

He didn't react to the General's voice.

Kassein was holding another man at the end of his sword, bleeding on the ground. He would have felt sorry if the man hadn't fought him with blatant hatred in his eyes, or if he hadn't pushed a woman out of his way to get to him earlier. Now, there was no mercy left.

Kassein wasn't sure what foolishness made those tribesmen more eager to fight him than to protect their women, but he would never understand. He finished the job and glanced around, furious.

The fight was over, and by all accounts, they should have won. The tribesmen who weren't dead or bleeding were fleeing.

And yet, it felt more like a defeat than a victory to him. How could it be otherwise when he hadn't found the one he'd come for?

"Commander," General Sazaran repeated, a bit louder.

"...She wasn't here."

His own words sounded choked up. Even from behind, one could see the tense muscles of his neck strained with fury.

Kassein angrily turned around and walked out of there, finding the first opening he could to set foot in the snow. The fresh, crisp, white coat immediately turned into a crimson puddle under him.

"I'm sorry we couldn't find the lady, Commander," General Sazaran said, "but the attack was a success. Our men are scouring the last tunnels we can find and have reported a handful leading toward more pathways. It sounds like your and the Princess' theory about them using countless tunnels to travel was right. The remnants of this tribe are fleeing to wherever they-"

"Let them go," Kassein interrupted him with a furious hiss, glaring at the General. "I was clear. Let them go and spread the word that I'm coming for the tribes."

I'm coming for her, was what he truly wanted to say.

Kassein hoped that, no matter how far away she was, Alezya would hear what had happened here. That she would know he was looking for her. Stubbornly. Desperately.

He returned his eyes to the skies, witnessing Kein helplessly circle again, flying over every mountain and clearing, his dragon's silver eyes scouring every crack, cave, and corner it could, looking for that pair of dark eyes they both missed.

Kassein watched, powerless, as his dragon let out furious growls in the skies, terrifying every tribesman back into their mountain but failing to make the one woman they were seeking appear.

Where was she? Every second that passed, Kassein felt like he'd rather be stabbed than worry. He hadn't experienced this level of agony since his sister's incident. He couldn't breathe every time he worried about how cold, hungry, or hurt she could be at this very moment.

He'd rather be the one to suffer, and he'd swap places in an instant, anything but the thought of Alezya going through torment.

"Commander," Sazaran said. "What do we do with the ones we captured? Shall we bring them back to the camp?"

"No," Kassein said. "Let them go. We need as many of them as possible to spread the word of what we're capable of."

"Annihilation?"

"...Or mercy." Kassein turned around, going back inside.

He'd picked this mountain, and one of the tribes they'd fought with the most, to make a point. He knew that was all part of the plan, and yet, while going in, he'd been helplessly hopeful. Maybe, just maybe, he'd find her there. Maybe Lumie would be able to sleep with her mom tonight.

Every time he thought of how little time the two of them must have had together, he felt even more sorry. The pull to frantically search every mountain was almost as strong as the one to fly back to the Onyx Castle and check on the little girl. It would be painful to face Lumie without her mother, but at least he would be able to check on one of them.

"I will give the orders, Commander," Sazaran said. "May I dare say, your command today..."

Kassein gave him a warning glance, but the General's expression didn't falter; the man only straightened more, standing tall with a respectful nod.

"It was a perfect demonstration, Commander in Chief," he said with a loud, solemn voice. "You may not enjoy it, but you do have the charisma a leader needs. Many men will remember the attack today."

Kassein didn't grant him a response.

He wasn't proud of this achievement, and he cared little for how much his men admired his strength. He needed to be even stronger, strong enough that Alezya wouldn't have to carry her burden alone and away from him. He only enjoyed the respite fighting gave him from being anxious about Alezya, even if it was only for a moment.

Kassein took one of the tunnels that would lead him back out of the mountain and toward their camp.

He was keeping an eye on their surroundings for any incoming attack, but given how much of a one-sided slaughter this had been, it was unlikely. Even if their opponents had seen them coming, they had been utterly unprepared for the attack. Why would they have been? Kassein had led so few excursions into the mountains, and they'd never wandered inside the tunnels, only taking on their scouts outside; they'd never led a raid like they had today.

Their enemies had stood no chance, and while most of their warriors had been foolish to fight until they had lost their lives, any non-fighters had fled the second they could. And Kassein's orders had been clear about letting them escape, so anyone who had stayed behind had basically chosen death... He had lost a few men, but his losses were a fraction of what that tribe had experienced. A lot of tribesmen had survived, but they had scattered in the mountains, and he doubted they'd dare to attack his camp again.

He did hope the survivors had noted that this hadn't been a full-on massacre. Kein hadn't even touched the ones who had stepped out, far too busy looking for Alezya.

"We're going back," he simply said after a while. "Leave them alone. Don't let the men grab any valuables either. We don't need any. We're leaving with what we brought, and if anyone disobeys, teach them a lesson. And I want a full report from each unit captain before sundown. As soon as my sister gets back, we're attacking again."

"Understood, Commander," Sazaran said, "but are you sure we don't want to keep any hostages...?"

Kassein pinned him with a furious glare.

"No. There's no point in negotiations; they don't have what we want."

Other tribes would get the message either way and without Alezya, they couldn't talk to her people.

His men behind him, he left the mountain tunnels and slowly started making his way back to the camp, but every so often, he couldn't help but glance southwest toward the Onyx Castle. He didn't know how long it would take for Kiera to convince his sister-in-law to part with the triplets' dragons to help him out, and come back from the Eastern Kingdom.

After a hesitation, he stopped in his tracks and watched as Kein made one last loop before heading toward him.

"Commander?" Sazaran gave him and Kein a couple of nervous glances.

"I'm going to the Onyx Castle for a bit."

"Don't you want to come back and celebrate this victory with the men?"

Kassein gave Sazaran an annoyed look; he'd never celebrated with his men and barely considered this a victory.

The General gave him a resolute nod.

"...I understand, Commander. I shall head back and make sure those reports are ready for you when you return."

Thus, Sazaran led the men down the mountain while Kassein went off-path to climb on his dragon's back.

He and Kein couldn't resist the urge to do one last survey of the mountains. Far too many hours had passed since Alezya's departure, and he knew that, even by foot, she could have reached the edge of the continent already.

There was hardly a human soul out on the mountains, and he wondered how fast the word would spread about today's battle. The tribes had probably seen Kein on the prowl and decided to hide in fear.

Alezya was the only one with nothing to fear from his dragon...

"Let's head home," he muttered as his dragon was already turning around.

Kassein realized he'd just called the Onyx Castle "home" for the first time in years. He didn't want to linger on the idea, but he could feel how it pulled on his heartstrings nonetheless.

Although they were tainted by melancholy and bitterness, one tragedy didn't erase all the good memories he had at the Onyx Castle or of his childhood.

When Kassein was still a warm and loving brother, and his siblings didn't think his dragon was mad... Even flying Kein, like he was at present, felt like a strange miracle.

Yet, for once, he and his dragon were of the same mind, aching to protect Lumie and find Alezya. Kassein still couldn't feel like he was anything but a fraud commanding the North Army, but for once, he felt like he had to step into those shoes and actually try to fill them the best he could. For Lumie and Alezya.

They landed minutes later, and while Kein immediately darted to the remaining egg, Kassein walked into the Onyx Castle.

It didn't take long to find them; he only had to follow the excited giggles of a little girl, which made his heart feel a bit lighter before he even pushed the door open.

"Come on, Lumie! You can do it, sweetheart!" Lorey was encouraging her.

To his surprise, Lumie was standing, albeit unstably, with her chubby little hands holding onto a stool.

Her butt kept wobbling a bit, and her head was turned to Lorey with a big, bright smile. On the other side of her, Lady Nebora was standing with her arms spread, ready to catch the little girl if she were to fall.

Nebora was an old friend of their mother's. She had always been a beautiful woman, and even now, she was aging very gracefully, with a few white streaks in her dark hair and crow's feet that emphasized her piercing dark eyes.

She had worked in the Onyx Castle for a long time, and was someone they had grown up around, closer than a servant but not as close as a sibling. She was like a strong-headed auntie who had always been around, helping out their mom when they needed it but having her own life down in the village with her husband and sons.

She was always close to their mom and kept a respectful and cordial relationship with their father, but she had never taken nonsense from Kassein and his siblings or their dragons.

"Look who is here," she gently told Lumie.

The little one swept her head to her, but as she did, her gaze spotted Kassein, and immediately, her pale eyes fixated on him and she broke into a big smile. Kassein's heart did a leap.

He couldn't remember the last time someone had shown this much genuine, unbridled happiness at the sight of him, and he couldn't help but respond with a smile of his own.

He hadn't smiled in such a long time that the muscles almost felt stiff in his cheeks, but Lumie giggled all the same.

The little girl dropped her hands off the stool to get on all fours and crawled to him at full speed. He crouched down and opened his arms, letting the baby girl close the distance by herself.

When she did, Lumie frowned and, after a hesitation, grabbed his hands to hold onto for support and, with a serious expression, lifted herself on two legs.

"She can walk?" Kassein asked, although his eyes were riveted on the baby girl.

"She should be able to if she's the age I think she is," Lorey said, "but it looks like she'll catch up quickly."

"Is that right?" Kassein whispered for Lumie to hear.

The little girl giggled at his voice and then began to inspect his hand, particularly a streak of orange scales that ran up his forearm from the earlier battle.

With a serious expression, she began to slap it, although her hand was far too small and soft for Kassein to even remotely feel any pain. It was more like her little hand was bouncing on his huge forearm.

"Are you having fun?" he asked.

As if in response, Lumie gave him a giggle.

He smiled back, letting her inspect his arms with that cute pout of hers while her other hand still tightly held onto him to keep herself standing. Even with him crouching down, she didn't quite reach his chin, so Kassein decided to sit down on the floor with her.

"She's so adorable," Lorey said.

"We were wondering where you would like us to prepare a room for her," Nebora said. "...And for yourself. Lorey filled me in on what you have been up to, Kassein. You didn't think to send a message that you would be moving back here? Do you know how long this castle has been abandoned?"

Kassein gave her an annoyed glance, but far from being intimidated like everyone else, including grown-ass warriors, Nebora raised an eyebrow.

"Don't give me that glare," she scoffed. "I'm not going to be intimidated by a boy whose diapers I washed, Kassein."

Lorey let out a giggle, but Kassein merely rolled his eyes, ignoring both women to look back down at Lumie, who was staring right back at him. Now, the toddler seemed curious about his face, which had come within her hands' reach, and she began to pat the beard on his cheek.

Kassein hadn't shaved since Alezya's departure, and the spiky texture seemed to entertain her plenty.

"So, which rooms do you want?" Nebora asked. "I'm happy to see this place inhabited again, but you need to give me time to hire some maids. This place is far too big for me to take care of by myself. Not that it would take long; plenty of youngsters are looking for work and would be happy to take that on. Should I put you in your parents' room?"

"No," Kassein immediately said.

Even if he took the Onyx Castle, he didn't want to touch his parents' room, at least not without their approval. That room felt somewhat sacred, and he wouldn't dare touch it or take ownership without asking them. He was even reluctant to touch any of his siblings' rooms in case any of them came back.

He meant what he'd told Kassian: this would always be their childhood home, and he would always welcome any of his siblings back.

But, realistically, their family of ten had outgrown the Onyx Castle a long time ago, and there would need to be some changes if he wanted his family to be able to stay while having his own here with Alezya, if she wanted it.

Suddenly, owning and taking care of their childhood home felt like a duty and an honor he was proud to take on. He took a deep breath just when Lumie pinched his chin with a giggle.

"...Prepare the nursery for Lumie," he said. "She can sleep in the cradle. I'll use Darsan's room for now. He's the most unlikely to come and stay here these days, and his room is near the nursery too."

He knew taking Darsan's messy room would give Nebora some work, but he didn't feel like using Kassian's room or his parents'.

Truthfully, his sisters' large bedroom was the one that would be the most fitting for him and Alezya to take over, but he needed all three of his sisters' approval for it. Once he did, he could always turn Kassian's and Darsan's rooms into guest rooms for his siblings, and this way, he wouldn't have to touch his parents' either. There were a few more rooms that had been abandoned or used for random storage and never touched by his parents that he could potentially look into as well.

Kassein realized how much he could imagine a new version of the Onyx Castle, one that would be *his* home but still be able to welcome his family at any time. He was nervous about touching anything, but the truth was, that castle had been abandoned for years and wouldn't come back to life without some profound changes.

It gave him comfort that Nebora nodded in approval of his plan.

"Alright," she said. "I'll get that started for you. I can get new bedding ready and Darsan's room decently cleaned in no time for tonight. I'll also get a couple of baby dragon beds ready later. From what I've heard, you might need them..."

Kassein nodded. He hoped Alezya would like what she'd find when she came back here, enough to agree to stay and live with him.

Lumie giving him big adorable smiles was helping with the aching pain of missing her mother, and he gently rubbed the little girl's back while she was still busy inspecting his beard and pinching his skin.

"But, Kassein," Nebora said, "are you truly going to own and rule the north? Lorey told me so, but I want to hear from you. Things have been hard for the folks up here. I hope you realize how big of a burden you're taking on. Many kids have moved south to find work. It won't be easy trying to revive the region."

"I am," he said, his eyes still riveted on Lumie. "I have a plan. We can open the route to the North Army and build demand for resources from there. The north also has the best woods that the rest of the Empire doesn't. We can use that to make the wood industry our primary source of income from the Empire. And the Eastern Kingdom too. I know Darsan established himself near the border to make their northwestern region flourish, and we can work with him. The north might have harsh living conditions, but we also have a unique climate, miles of untouched forest, and a workforce. And once I conquer the mountains and start trading with the tribes, we might even have new resources to trade with my siblings."

Nebora was speechless, staring at him with her jaw dropped.

After a second, she caught herself and glanced at Lorey in disbelief, but his sister's partner was smiling proudly.

"Since when have you been an expert on governing an actual kingdom, young man?" Nebora exclaimed, crossing her arms.

"...I grew up in the Imperial Family," Kassein said. "My siblings and I all had the same tutors, remember? Just because I never had any desire to rule doesn't mean I'm not capable."

That was probably why, albeit reluctantly, Kassian had let the north go. Perhaps he didn't care if Kassein succeeded or failed, but he wouldn't have given up a portion of his empire to a complete idiot.

Although Kassian had been the only one groomed to become the Emperor, Kassein and his siblings had grown up in the Imperial Palace. They'd seen their parents and aunts work. They'd all been taught by the best teachers, learned to understand commoners and nobles alike, and kept aware of the main matters of the Empire.

That was why Cessilia had become such a great queen in the east and why she could send Darsan to develop more of their territories. It was also why Kiera had always explored and tried to befriend new tribes in the west, and why Shenan and Sadara could work and support Kassian in the Capital. Sepheus' whereabouts were more mysterious, but last he'd heard, their youngest brother was now helping take care of their grandmother's domain.

Moreover, Kassein knew the north better than any of them now, and he could see its potential.

He had no greed to extend the borders, but he could find ways to make a small kingdom survive and thrive on its own. He knew best how many acres of woods full of prey they had, the potential of the tribes as allies, and how people in the north weren't afraid of hard work. Those who hadn't left for the south were those who could endure the harsh winter and would stay to help the north survive until it could prosper.

Even in the North Army, many men were sent there as criminals, sometimes the worst of the worst, but some were eager to turn their lives around and start anew. Killing tribesmen wouldn't bring them any glory, but making a new life in the north would be more than good enough for honest men.

Kassein could almost see it.

The villages expanding and thriving, becoming the beating heart of the north. The army in the north split between those who would guarantee the safety of the citizens and those who would be allowed back to that citizen's life once they'd paid their dues. If there was one man who believed in redemption, it was Kassein.

He would have no mercy for the wretched, but he'd allow a new life for those who were begging to leave their sins in the Empire and start anew.

Finally, there were the tribes. Once safe from the dragon and allowed to trade with his newborn Kingdom, they might become a vital part of this new country. While trying to survive, Alezya might have unknowingly set the first stone of a new era that would unite his world and hers. That was something he wanted to look forward to.

But first, he had to get her back by his side.

While Nebora talked to him about her plan for cleaning the Onyx Castle and rearranging the rooms, which included bringing a couple of maids and ordering new furniture from the village, Kassein's eyes were riveted on the little girl between his legs.

After a while of standing, it seemed Lumie had gotten tired and was now plopped down on his thigh, busy playing with his hand while the other one held her.

"Alright, I should go and start getting those rooms ready if you plan to sleep here tonight," Nebora said. "Lorey, darling, will you be alright?"

"I'll come to lend you a hand," Lorey said after glancing toward Kassein and Lumie. "Kiera and I can sleep in her old room, but I'll give you a hand with the nursery and their brother's room. Kassein, are you fine to stay with Lumie while we wait for Kiera to return?"

Although his eyes never left the little girl who was still busy inspecting his fingers, he gave her a stiff nod, aware of the stares of both women on him.

When they left, Lumie turned a curious eye toward them, frowning, before she whipped her head back to him with a question in her eyes.

"You'll sleep well here," he said softly. "I only wish your mom could sleep here tonight too."

"*Ama?*" Lumie's eyes immediately brightened.

"Yes, your mama," he smiled.

"Mama..."

Just then, Kein let out a growl from outside, and Lumie turned her head in that direction, her cute white eyebrows raised.

From the faint light still lingering beyond the mountains, Kassein guessed it would be safe for the little girl to step out. Gently, he prompted her to get on her feet, always holding her little hand, and stood up.

"Lorey said you should be able to walk already," he said. "Would you try walking there?"

Lumie frowned at his words, seemingly not too on board, but he gently took her little chubby hands in his and effortlessly lifted her to her feet. She glanced down as if impressed by that and let out a little giggle.

Then, with Kassein patiently guiding her, she took a step, and then another, although it was hardly an effort as Kassein's hands were lifting her all this time. Lumie kept giggling, giving little air kicks as if intrigued to be pretty much flying above the floors.

She was so absorbed with her air-walking that she barely realized they had stepped into the garden until she noticed the large mass of orange scales and stared at Kein, mesmerized.

The orange dragon was curled around its remaining egg, the white one, but its body was slowly crawling toward Lumie, belly flat on the ground and nose sniffing intently in her direction.

Kassein let go of Lumie, and she collapsed on all fours. Without a hint of fear, the little girl immediately barreled her way straight to the dragon, Kassein right behind her.

Most children would intuitively fear a beast the size of several adult humans, with a bright fire-orange color and strange silver eyes, but Lumie didn't hesitate for a second. Kassein watched carefully, but he knew all too well his dragon wouldn't hurt a hair on the little girl's head, just like it had immediately submitted to her mother.

Sure enough, when Lumie reached it and immediately undertook to climb its head, Kein didn't protest, instead enduring with unprecedented patience the little girl's kicks on its snout. Kassein came close, not worried about Kein but more about Lumie falling. He wasn't sure at what height it would be dangerous for her to fall from, but the little girl seemed determined to reach the peak of his dragon's back like it was the goal of a lifetime. With his hands hovering around her, he watched as she grunted, kicked, and grabbed his dragon's scales to make her way to the top.

"Tamed by a child," he muttered to his dragon. "Not so wild now, are we?"

Kein replied with a low-pitched growl, which prompted Lumie to stop in her climb and glance down at the orange scales, frowning at the sudden sound and vibration.

She then turned to Kassein as if looking for an explanation. He leaned over her, putting a hand on her back, and tapped his dragon's back.

"Kein," he said gently. "This is Kein, Lumie. Kein."

"Kein," she repeated.

"That's right," he said, his index finger pointing at the orange scales again. "Kein."

Lumie glanced down at the orange scales. Kassein gently grabbed her, lifting her so she sat as if she was riding the dragon, at the top position she'd been trying to reach. Kein then lifted its head, twisting its neck so its silver eyes could see the little girl.

Lumie giggled excitedly.

"Kein! Kein!" she chanted.

In response, Kein let out a growl and a whiff of hot air in her direction, which made Lumie giggle some more and slap her hands down on the orange scales excitedly.

Kassein watched the little girl play with the current largest dragon in the Empire, a man-eating beast, as if it was her new favorite toy. The young girl was so full of wonder and energy that he couldn't look away.

She looked a lot like her mom, a younger, chubbier version of Alezya, except for her extraordinary eye and hair color. Kassein had often seen people from other tribes, like his mother, stand out in a crowd due to their lighter skin, hair, and eye colors, but never had he seen a human as pale as Lumie.

As the sun had set and the night was darkening, he could see her skin almost ready to glow under the moonlight.

It was no wonder Lorey had heard someone call this a "moon child." It made him smile, remembering how he had called Alezya his "moonlight" while he still had no idea that she had a white-skinned child.

While watching Lumie play on his dragon's back, he couldn't help but let his thoughts wander back to her mother, equally worried and hopeful.

Would she agree to live in the Onyx Castle with him? Would she trust him to protect them after he'd failed twice already?

Kassein was dying to get back on Kein and fly above the mountains again, but Lumie was the only one grounding them both there. He knew he had to think rationally and listen to Lorey and his sister before he made another mistake. It was frustrating, but he had no choice.

They had to tread carefully with the tribes if they wanted to get a chance at that future they'd dreamed about.

He was the new King of the area, the owner of an abandoned castle, a wild land, and hostile communities. Even the nearby village might not take too well to being discarded by the Emperor and entrusted to the "Wild Prince" instead.

Still, if he hoped to be even remotely worthy of Alezya's trust, he had to do what he could with all of that. He hadn't allowed himself to hope for a long time, but all of a sudden, the possibility of a happy future was too blinding to ignore.

Just like that, he remained with Lumie, letting the child play freely in the Onyx Castle's garden and distract him with her exploration.

He was behind her for everything, telling her about his mother's plants, letting her dirty her hands and knees in the soil, and keeping her from trying to chew random things she picked up.

Kein had lost patience before him and taken off almost as soon as Lumie had gotten bored of him, but for once, it made Kassein feel better that his dragon was scouring the skies above the mountains. If the dragon caught sight of Alezya, Kassein would know.

Kassein heard the dragon's cries shortly before dawn.

He woke up immediately after having spent only a few hours sleeping and most of the night with his eyes on the window. On his chest, Lumie, who hadn't slept in the cradle but in his arms again, whined in her sleep before she stirred too, upset by the sounds. Kassein quickly wrapped her up in the small fur blanket he'd grabbed for her and readjusted his arms for the little girl to stay asleep and comfortable while he rose.

He'd been half-asleep when he'd heard it, but the dragon's cry didn't sound like Kein or Kiki's, which made him hurry outside to see who had come. Baby dragons couldn't make such loud sounds either, and he didn't think his nieces' and nephews' dragons had reached their adult forms yet, so it had to be someone unexpected.

Once he stepped outside into the entrance courtyard of the Onyx Castle, he found Kein already waiting, his dragon eyeing the sky with its tail nervously swishing.

Although all the living dragons belonged to their family, Kein and Kassein couldn't say they had a good relationship with all of them, like their older brother Kassian's dragon, Kian, who'd fought Kein the last time they'd crossed paths.

For a second, Kassein worried that it was indeed Kian flying toward them: the incoming dragon had a long, silver-like body and was much bigger than Kiki and the tiny dots flying next to them that had to be the triplets' dragons.

But, as the visitors came closer, Kassein was shocked to realize the bigger dragon of the bunch wasn't silver but the color of ice, a shimmery opal color, and that it wasn't Kian but Cece.

Cece was their older sister Cessilia's dragon, the one who'd mysteriously returned as an Ice Dragon after being trapped in the mythical lake of the Imperial Palace after its apparent death years ago during *that* incident. Cece was also one of the largest dragons in size since Cessilia had become Queen and gotten married, and it had produced three younger dragons just as Cessilia had three children with her partner, the Eastern King, Ashen.

Kassein relaxed a little upon realizing who the visitor was, but not completely. He hadn't seen his older sister in years, and he had ignored many of her letters over the years too.

Moreover, Cessilia had always been different from his other siblings.

She was like a second mother figure to them and far too good at reading people. She was incredibly kind and so good toward others that despite being a foreign queen, she had quickly become an incredibly popular queen in the Eastern Kingdom.

This was precisely what scared Kassein: Cessilia was far too kind.

"Good morning. Is that Her Highness?" Lorey said, stepping out of the castle behind him.

Kassein only gave her a stiff nod while he mindlessly rubbed Lumie's back to calm himself down. The baby girl was still fast asleep under the cover, her body completely limp against his bare torso, and for some reason, her presence was grounding him and allowing him to stay somewhat calm.

Kein, on the other hand, was growling. Kassein knew his dragon was growling at him, just like he knew that as angry as Kein was, it would never attack while he was holding Lumie.

Graceful as ever, Cessilia's dragon Cece landed elegantly outside of the castle courtyard, and his older sister jumped down with a bright smile lighting up her face as soon as their eyes met.

Kassein's heart ached, and he could only reply with the shadow of a smile himself, and a faint nod.

Behind her, Kiki, who was half Cece's size, landed next. And then, the tiny dragons each landed, although it looked more like the triplets had decided to dive-bomb into the snow rather than land properly.

Each baby dragon landed with a little high-pitched growl of excitement. Bora, the peach-colored dragon, and Leni, the brown one, both found piles of snow to barrel in and play with as soon as they landed. Meanwhile, Vele, which was yellow, and a Water Dragon like Kiki and Cece, began running around immediately, tunneling through the foot-high snow.

In a matter of seconds, the triplet dragons managed to turn all of the snow in the area into a mini-snowstorm, ignoring Kiki's annoyed growls.

As their owners were ten years old, the young dragons were still relatively small, as most dragons grew exponentially once their owners reached teenagehood. Bora and Leni were Earth Dragons like Kein and, therefore, bigger than their sibling, but they were still only the size of a large dog. Given that their genitor, Darsan's dragon Dran, had been one of the largest dragons in existence, they were probably going to grow in size very quickly at some point.

"Do you three ever calm down?" Kiera protested after receiving another wave of snow in the face. "Stop it!"

Cessilia rolled her eyes with an amused smile, ignoring the little mayhem to walk directly toward her brother.

She ignored Kein's growls and went straight to Kassein, wrapping him in a hug. She had always been the tallest of the sisters, and that was perhaps the only thing she didn't take after their mother; for everything else, Cessilia looked a lot like their mother.

From her gentle green eyes to her long chestnut-colored hair, her thin limbs, and her thin, rosy lips. She also had the palest skin of the three sisters, slightly more tan than their white-skinned mother, but it was glowing from her days on the coast.

Now that she was a mother of three and approaching thirty, Kassein couldn't help but notice the few white hairs while he hugged her and how her body felt softer than he remembered too.

"It's so good to see you," she whispered in his ear with that soft voice of hers.

Kassein couldn't say what he'd been expecting, but his body relaxed instantly at her words, warmth spreading throughout his body gently.

Cessilia stepped back, giving him one of her kind, genuine smiles full of sisterly love, and his throat tightened a bit. All he could do was nod, feeling sorry for not being able to return his sister's affection properly, but Cessilia didn't say anything. Instead, she kept smiling, and her eyes drifted to the little girl in his arms.

As the sun was starting to come out, Kassein had been careful to keep Lumie hidden in the fur blanket, but standing so close, Cessilia could easily catch a glimpse of the little girl through an opening, and her smile brightened up some more before she redirected her eyes at Kassein.

She pressed a hand against his cheek, her thumb rubbing his beard.

"It's a good sight to witness you like this," she whispered.

"Half-asleep?" he managed to groan.

"Almost happy," she said, pointing her chin at the little girl in his arms.

Kassein frowned in confusion.

He hadn't felt happy in a long time, but... after thinking about his sister's words for a second, he knew there was some truth to it.

He cleared his throat, and adjusted Lumie in his arms a bit, trying not to look his older sister in the eye.

"I'm sorry I never... replied," he muttered.

"I know," Cessilia shrugged. "I hoped you still read the letters, that's why I kept writing to you anyway. You should come see your nieces and nephew when things are calmer here. They'd love to see an uncle other than Darsan sometimes."

Kassein didn't think any of them were a better uncle than Darsan, but he still nodded.

He knew he had been avoiding his sister and her family for a long while, and he wasn't too proud of it. It was just far too painful for him.

He had read some of the letters, but he was ashamed to say he'd ignored more. Somewhere behind him, Kein's growls intensified, and Cessilia immediately pinned his dragon with a glare.

"Kein, enough."

Her voice was cold and imperious, and Kein obeyed, finally lowering its volume and lying down.

Immediately, the dragon's apparent calmness got the triplets' attention, and the next second, Kein was the new playground for three dragons a fraction of its size.

Cessilia let out a faint sigh, turning her attention back to Kassein.

"Kiera filled me in on what's going on. What does it take for you to ask for help, Kassein?"

"It's just... The triplets' dragons are the size we need. I wouldn't want to bother anyone else."

Cessilia shook her head slowly.

"You're not a bother to anyone," she said, patting his cheek again. "Certainly not to me, Kassein. And you do know I also have three children with three small-sized dragons, right? Don't lie to me, Kassein. I know sending Kiera to ask Darsan was the easy option for you. I'm lucky I happened to be visiting him when our sister came, or else I would have never known about what you're trying to accomplish here, would I?"

He lowered his head. As always, Cessilia was right, and he didn't have anything to answer to that. His sister let out another faint sigh.

"...Will you take a walk with me?" she asked gently. "We haven't talked in a while, just the two of us, and I feel like it's a conversation that's much overdue. If ever, I think there are some things you need to hear now."

After a hesitation, Kassein gave her a stiff nod.

Gently and reluctantly, he transferred Lumie over to Lorey's arms and followed his sister outside of the Onyx Castle.

For some reason, Cessilia wanted to walk outside, and they quietly took the pathway to the village, past the mess the young dragons had made and back to where the snow was a thick, fresh layer over the wild grass and bushes.

Cessilia was walking comfortably, despite only wearing a thin coat and leather shoes. Just like everyone in their family, she was rather resistant to the cold, but living in a coastal city and having an Ice Dragon might have made her even more immune, for she walked as if it was a nice spring day, not a skin-biting windy and cold morning.

"I missed the north," she admitted after a couple of minutes of silence. "I love the Eastern Kingdom and I love the sea, but sometimes, I get nostalgic about this place. We don't get snow in the Eastern Kingdom, and my children have never seen snow yet."

"...You should bring them here someday," Kassein said.

"I would love to," Cessilia smiled. "It would be nice to show them where their mom grew up... and see their uncle too. Mom and Dad visit us often, but everyone else is so busy. I would love for you to settle in the Onyx Castle, Kassein. Truly."

He stopped in his tracks, thinking about his sister's words, and an aching knot formed in his throat. He glared at a bush on the side, and somewhere far behind, they heard Kein growl furiously and take off.

"...You really think I deserve to?" he said. "I... I asked Kassian and he agreed, but..."

"If not you, who else?" Cessilia asked. "Kassein, look at the Onyx Castle. It's still our home, but it doesn't belong to anyone anymore. Father and Mother understandably grew tired of this place once we all left the nest. All of us siblings are either busy with matters of the state, traveling the world, or settling elsewhere with our families. We would all love to see the Onyx Castle inhabited again, but it needs a new, young family in it."

Kassein's heart ached as his thoughts inevitably drifted back to Lumie and Alezya. He looked around, feeling lost. He didn't want to walk to the village or even back to the Onyx Castle.

He just wanted to be wherever Alezya was, bring her back to Lumie, and protect them—make sure they were safe, healthy, and happy. Even if he yearned for their love, he wouldn't ask for anything in return.

For the first time, he simply wanted to dedicate himself to someone else's well-being, and he knew he would be perfectly content with that.

He tightened his fist, his shoulders squaring just as the thoughts swirling dangerously in his head echoed his dragon's furious growls in the distance. He could feel his dragon roaming above the mountains, once again doing what they were both aching to do and searching desperately for a trace of Alezya.

Yet he was grounded there, his feet unwilling to move, feeling like he was lacking and terrified by the mere thought of failing.

"...What if I mess up again?" he muttered. "If they get... hurt... because of me, I..."

Cessilia turned around, giving him a sorry expression. She looked about to say something, but she just licked her lips and glanced around, until her eyes settled on a tree trunk lying a few steps off the road.

"...Come sit with me," she said.

Before he could answer, she was sitting on that trunk like it was a bench, and she closed her eyes, letting the cold wind caress her face.

It took Kassein a couple more seconds before he willed his feet to move and follow her steps. He sat next to her, and for a couple of minutes, they remained silent, Cessilia with her face toward the sunrise and Kassein staring down at his feet, his head low between his shoulders.

After a little while of the two of them listening to the gentle sounds of nature around them, Cessilia let out a long breath, and put a hand on his shoulder.

"You can't undo what happened, Kassein. But you have to learn to live with it and move on."

"It was my fault." He closed his eyes. "If I had controlled Kein better, if I had only done something about my dragon sooner..."

"We both know this isn't about controlling Kein," Cessilia whispered gently, now rubbing his arm.

"I... I don't know what to do," he whispered. "I'll never repair what I've done, Cessi. I can't. There's no way for me to ever repay that man's family. It is my fault, I know that. I... I should have known that was bound to happen.

Kein and I destroyed countless buildings during our fights, but that day... That man... It's all my fault. I didn't even realize someone was dead until after... The building collapsed, and someone screamed, and I... Kein wasn't stopping... If Kian hadn't attacked, it could have been even worse..."

"Kassein, stop. You can't keep doing this to yourself. Yes, we know what happened was a tragedy. But, as much as you regret it, something like that is bound to happen again until you make it stop. You're the only one who can stop Kein, and you haven't found the way yet. You need to do that, Kassein. If not for yourself, for *them*."

"I want to," he whispered. "I just... I don't know. I don't know how."

His sister moved her hand from his arm to his shoulder, pressing gently. Kassein still couldn't bear to look at her, but he heard his older sister take a deep breath in, as if this was as hard for her as it was for him.

"Dragons are... a part of us," she said. "Maybe the most raw, genuine, and untamed part of our soul. Mom always said our dragons reflect our deepest and strongest emotions. When I lost Ashen and my voice, I was lost for many years, Kassein. I didn't... It was hard for me. Our parents were there, you and the rest of our siblings were there, but I... A part of me broke that evening, and I lost a part of myself. I lost Cece, and I was so... I couldn't deal with the sadness that was suffocating my heart. I was there, and I was alive, but... I wasn't living. I think Cece came back precisely the moment I found myself again. When I let myself truly feel, and be emotional, and be real again."

She moved closer to him on the tree trunk, her hip touching his, and gently caressed his nape with her fingers.

"Kassein, you were the most caring boy I knew," she whispered. "You were one of the youngest, and yet you were always looking out for everyone, even for Sadara and Shenan, who were years older. You're so kind. Too kind, even. What happened that night... I know I should have talked to you before about it."

"No," Kassein groaned. "Cessilia, don't—"

"I didn't because I couldn't," Cessilia ignored him. "And then, when I could, I was so far away, and it had been so long, I thought you were over it. I never realized that you... you still carried that burden with you so many years later. And I am sorry, Kassein. I am so, so sorry that I left you and Kein with that wound and never realized. I should have told you a long time ago it wasn't your fault, Kassein."

He closed his fists tight, glaring at a patch of snow ahead, but his sister covered his fist with her other hand, gently rubbing his skin with her thumb.

"Kassein, none of what happened that night was your fault. You were just a boy, and I was ten years older. I don't blame anyone but myself for what happened; I made my mistakes, and I learned to live with them. But you should not be forced to live with that pain too. None of what happened to me was your fault, Kassein. Absolutely none of it. Do you hear me?"

"You don't understand," he hissed through gritted teeth. "If I hadn't listened to you, if I had stopped you, or if I had told Dad or Kassian—"

"It would have ended the same way, either way, Kassein. Do you think my baby brother could have stopped me? Do you think I would have let you get to them if I'd had any doubt you wouldn't listen to me? All you did was do exactly what your older sister told you to, Kassein. I am, and I was, ten years older than you. I carry the weight of my own decisions, but I will not let you carry that too."

She moved to kneel in front of him, her hands moving to his cheeks to force him to look her in the eye. His eyes were misty, his jaw trembling, and his fists shaking; Cessilia gave him a sad, sorry smile.

"Kassein, you might be a grown man now, but you're still and will always be my baby brother, and I love you. ...And I am so, so sorry about what happened and that you felt any guilt for it."

"But Kassian—"

"Kassian said a lot of things he never should have because he was a lot madder at himself than he was at you," Cessilia cut him off. "Our older brother always has too much on his plate, and when it overflows, rather than ask for the help he needs, he turns to anger and lashes out at others. Whatever he said to you, Kassein, isn't what he truly thinks. He loves us. He's terrible at being honest, but he does. And you let me worry about him. Right now, I want you to do something you should have done a long time ago, Kassein."

He swallowed, trying hard not to cry. He hadn't cried in a very long time, but his older sister was opening up old, deep, and raw wounds in a way he hadn't been prepared for. His chest was painful, his heart was heavy in his ribcage, his throat tight, and his eyes burning.

Cessilia let out a heavy sigh, her thumbs caressing his cheeks.

"You need to forgive yourself, Kassein," she whispered. "None of what happened was your fault. You were just a boy. All you did was listen to your big sister, who was madly in love. Stupidly in love, I should say. You shouldn't have been there. It was my decision. I disobeyed Dad and left. I know everyone blamed themselves one way or another for what happened to me, but you, most of all, did not deserve it, Kassein."

"It was my fault," he hissed. "I could have stopped it all. I—"

"Kassein."

His sister's gaze hardened, and she looked into his eyes with the most determined expression he'd seen her with in a long time.

"It's over," she said. "It happened, and we cannot take it back. But I do not blame you. If I ever did, I forgive you. Mom and Dad never blamed you. Kassian was no madder at you than he was at himself, but this is all long over. It's been fifteen years, Kassein. I am fine. I am healed, and I am happy. I found Ashen again when we were both in a much better place, and now, I am the mother to three of your wonderful nieces and nephews, and I am happier than anyone could hope to be. And you deserve to be happy too. You, of all people, deserve to move on."

"I... I don't..."

As she witnessed the first treacherous tear escaping his eyes and crossing his cheek, his sister took a deep breath, her expression softening.

"Kassein. I know better than most people what it is like to hate yourself, to let yourself be eaten up by regrets. But it does absolutely nothing for you or others. Nothing can change what happened, no matter how much you resent yourself for it. It's over, baby brother. You need to move on and let your regrets go. You need to forgive yourself once and for all. Make Kein stop."

"I.. I don't know... He..."

"Don't lie to me, Kassein," she whispered. "We both know exactly why your dragon wants to harm and kill you. He's not the one who truly wants that; he's just echoing the pain. Our dragons reflect our deepest and strongest emotions, remember?"

Another tear escaped his eyes, and he kept his eyes riveted on his big sister's teary eyes.

He'd never said it. A part of him had always known, but he had never let himself face that shameful truth.

How much it hurt. How much he loathed himself and how much he couldn't make his dragon stop. Because he couldn't stop hating himself; the pain, the guilt, the self-hatred was too much.

Cessilia was right; Kein was just a tool. A tool he had been using, subconsciously or not, to harm himself. To punish himself. Because he resented himself so much that he had wanted to...

"I'm sorry," he broke down, tears streaming down his cheeks for good this time, even as he covered his face with his hands, his shoulders shaking.

"Kassein," Cessilia whispered again, her voice breaking as she moved to hug him. "I'm the one who should be sorry. I didn't realize where your pain had stemmed from. Let it go, baby brother. You're fine. You're good. You are a kind man. You're only as wild as the pain you allowed to hurt you, and it ends now. Now, you have a woman who loves you, who trusts you so much that she left her baby with you. You're a protector, Kassein. Gods, you're so much like Dad. You deserve to forgive yourself and be happy, baby brother. If not for you, then for that young woman and her baby girl. They need you, and you deserve to let them see the best of you."

She kept gently rubbing his back as he sobbed and until he calmed down, whispering words of comfort like only his older sister, who had been through equal pain, could.

After he had calmed down a bit, they stayed in a quiet, tired silence for a little while.

It took Kassein a few seconds to realize Kein had stopped his angry growls. Instead, if he focused, he could sense his dragon flying calmly above the mountains, no longer a threat.

He forced himself to take a deep breath in and exhaled it. He opened his eyes again and caught his sister smiling at him.

"What changed for you?" he asked.

"...Same thing as you," she whispered. "I found someone I loved more than I hated myself. That was all I needed."

Kassein gave her a slight nod because, again, his older sister was right. He felt like that statement perfectly summed up his relationship with Alezya.

He didn't know how or why, but that woman had just lit up an entire world for him. He felt like he could break the chains of the "Wild Prince" title and be whatever she needed of him.

A friend, a protector. A devoted lover, if she'd allow him.

By the gods, he was ready to worship that woman to the end of his days if she let him.

"I wish you could meet her," he finally told his sister, clearing his sore throat. "Alezya."

"I will, I'm sure. One day. When you two finally come to visit."

"Or you could come back. I'll make sure the Onyx Castle can welcome you anytime. Anyone."

"...That would be nice," she said. "That old castle needs a fresh start, like you. This whole area does, actually. You did good, Kassein."

"Not yet," he shook his head, getting up and offering a hand for his sister to do so as well, "but I promise I'll try my best."

"I know you will."

Just like that, they slowly walked back together, enjoying the companionable silence until the Onyx Castle was back in sight, and Cessilia switched the subject to ask what he'd planned to do with it and gave her approval for Kassein to do as he saw fit.

"I have good and bad memories there, but I'll be happy if you make happier ones. My heart had already taken residence far away in the east a while ago. I doubt Kiera will care, either... How about Sadara?"

"I'll write to her later."

"Or you could visit her more often," Cessilia said with a pointed look. "She writes often, but I get the sense that she isn't very happy in the Capital. You know how reserved she is, she'll never admit something's wrong if she can help it."

"I don't think any of them are," Kassein admitted, thinking about their siblings in the Capital.

"I guess I know where I should stop next, then. After visiting our parents, of course. Please, you have to come to Mother's birthday celebration."

"I will."

"Bring your lady then," his sister winked, "and her child too. Mom will be delighted."

Kassein gave a noncommittal nod.

That was months away, but he sure hoped he and Alezya would be together then. And visiting his parents together suddenly seemed like a much more enticing idea for the future.

He and his sister returned to the Onyx Castle, and they found Kiera waiting outside, arms crossed with a disgusted expression directed toward the castle.

"Why the long face?" Cessilia asked.

"Dran's evil spawn is absolutely wreaking havoc inside," Kiera grunted. "Lorey might be more patient than I am, but I am not going anywhere near those little monsters. No wonder their mother was so happy to lend them."

"She sure was quick to say you could keep them as long as you'd like," Cessilia chuckled toward Kassein.

"Lumie?" he asked.

"She's inside too, with Lorey. I think Nebora is doing the laundry or something... What's with your eyes?"

"Nothing," Kassein said, walking past her and inside the Onyx Castle. "Get ready to leave; we're launching the second attack on the mountains."

"Finally," Kiera rolled her eyes. "Might as well unleash that miniature mayhem onto our enemies... Hey, pipsqueaks! Get out of there! Time to go to war, all of you rascals! You'll get to chew something other than the furniture..."

One by one, the small dragons raised their heads from whatever they were doing, which was indeed biting chairs for two of them, while the last one was on the floor playing with Lumie under Lorey's surveillance.

Ignoring the young dragons' high-pitched grunts, Kassein scooped Lumie into his arms, and the little girl squealed happily.

"I have to go find your mama, Lumie," he whispered to her.

"*Ama?*" Lumie immediately said.

"Yes. I'll find her, Lumie. I promise."

Just like that, Kassein pressed a little kiss on the young girl's forehead, making her squeal in delight, before he handed her back to Lorey.

He couldn't help but note that Lumie seemed disappointed to not be in his arms any longer, her disappointed eyes following him, and that made Kassein a bit happy. To not make the heartbreak any worse than necessary, he quickly turned to Lorey.

"Watch her for me," he asked with a tight throat.

"Of course. You guys stay safe. I hope you find Alezya soon."

He nodded and turned around before Lumie's sad eyes broke any more of his heart. He would never forgive himself if he couldn't bring that little girl and her mother back together.

Luckily, it didn't take too long to herd the young dragons outside, as they were all too excited to chase after Kiki and Cece and watch as Kein was coming back.

Cessilia, who had been waiting outside, wrapped her younger brother in a hug before he could protest.

"I have to go home," she said. "Ashen and the kids will be worried. But I insist you visit me soon, once things calm down here. I'm sure you'll be alright, Kassein. And remember, we're always here to help. Alright? We're your family."

Kassein could only give her a choked-up nod, but that was enough.

Cessilia patted his cheek once more and then turned to say goodbye to Kiera and Lorey before they parted ways to go to their dragons. While he walked up to Kein, they watched as Cessilia took flight on her dragon.

"Leni, Bora, Vele!" Kiera called the small dragons. "Come on, you little twerps, time to break shit, run wild, and scare grown men; you're going to love that!"

Whether they understood or not, all three of the smaller dragons took off after Kiki, happily chasing the older dragon, though they seemed just afraid enough of Kein to keep a distance. Given that the orange dragon was considerably bigger than them, while Kiki was about twice the size of the three of them combined, it was understandable.

Still, the triplets seemed happy to give chase to their older peers, climbing up the skies while Cece was flying back toward their homeland in the east. As dragons had no predators, it was likely that the triplets were allowed to roam on their own because all three seemed very comfortable exploring a new area, happily teasing each other mid-flight and letting out high-pitched little growls as they played around.

Unlike them, Kiki and Kein were in no mood to play.

When their group landed in the North Camp, they were immediately greeted by rows of soldiers in full attire for combat, all three generals lined up with Tievin at one end, waiting for them.

"Welcome back, Commander in Chief," Sazaran said first. "Our recruits spotted you and the Princess, so we got everyone ready for battle."

"Are those young dragons really a part of your plan, Commander...?"

As soon as the triplets landed, they immediately pounced on Kein's back, chased one another at full speed between the ranks, disrupting the tight lines of men and prompting horrified shouts here and there, and did their new favorite game of dive-bombing into piles of snow until there was nothing but puddles under them and everyone around was drenched.

Tievin was on the receiving end of one of the last waves, and the poor Intendant let out a long, tired sigh before wiping his face with his sleeve.

"...And they're not even teens yet," he groaned.

"Enough!" Kassein barked.

Immediately, all three of the young dragons froze where they were, and just as Kein let out a loud growl of warning, they all scampered in a line behind Kiki, heads and bellies flat on the ground.

"Gods save the Eastern Kingdom," Kiera sighed. "Anyhow, yes, those three terrors are the core of our plan. We unleash the brats inside the tunnels, let them force the tribespeople to flee, hopefully out of the mountains and into the open, and our army will be out there to greet them while we look for Kassein's lady and do some cleaning."

"We will split the army here," Kassein said, pinning all three generals with a stare. "Herken, I'll entrust you with the defense of the North Camp. There's a high chance that some tribe might attack down here once they realize two-thirds of our army have been gone for a while. I'm counting on you to stand your ground here and ensure everything keeps running smoothly."

Herken gave a solemn nod to his Commander in Chief.

Many army leaders might have been offended that they were picked to stay behind, but it took a man with the unwavering loyalty and resilience of Herken to defend a stronghold two-thirds emptied of its forces. The oldest General knew it was a big testament of trust for Kassein to ask him to stay and take care of the camp in his absence when he'd most likely be gone for several days.

Next, Kassein turned to the other two generals, Sazaran and Kauser.

"We will attack the mountains one by one until we find what I came for," Kassein said. "We might have to camp up there for several days or send men back to the camp for supplies. We will alternate men who attack and those who rest to maximize each battle and secure a retreat route as we go. Defeat is not an option, but I want every soldier we bring to follow the rules, the same as before. No killing a man who surrenders, no killing those who choose to flee, and no harming any woman or child."

"We are not thieves," Kiera added with a warning glare, playing with one of her swords. "We're not ransacking those mountains, merely showing those tribesmen what we're capable of and why they'd be better off negotiating once we find the woman."

"Commander," Kauser cleared his throat, "are you sure the tribeswoman will be willing to... translate for us?"

Kassein immediately pinned him with a furious look.

He knew his men were aware that Alezya had left again and that they were looking for her. What he didn't like was them questioning his motives or hers. But before he could speak, on his right, Tievin interrupted the heavy silence with an artificial cough.

"If I may, General Kauser, given her circumstances, Lady Alezya has proven incredible righteousness of character since the Commander in Chief met her," he said. "I personally observed a lot of the lady's actions in the camp, and nothing she has ever done should lead us to doubt her. She spent considerable amounts of time alone with Lady Lorey and never once did anything to harm her. That woman can also order the Commander's dragon around, which, as you know, is a considerable feat. Yet she's never once used Kein to attack, not even when she was harassed; according to every report we got, the dragon intervened of its own volition. Finally, even if we did choose not to trust her, there is no one here nor in those mountains that we know of that has managed the incredible endeavor of being able to speak both languages. It is most impressive that Lady Alezya has managed to learn so much of our language in such a short length of time. As far as the Commander in Chief is concerned, that woman currently represents his best chance at finally pacifying the Northern territories, which, as all of you gentlemen might need to remember, was our primary mission in moving to this land of despair and ice and everything wet and cold."

A long, stunned silence followed his tirade.

Even Kassein was staring at the Intendant with a surprised look; Tievin was the last person he would have expected to speak up for Alezya.

After a while, Kiera broke into a big grin.

"Well said, Tiev. ...Now, why are you hiding behind the General?"

"Just in case," Tievin grumbled from somewhere under General Sazaran's shoulder, his glare hopping from one of the small dragons to another. "When are you leaving, Commander?"

"As soon as everyone's ready," Kassein replied.

"We will have the preparations finished within the hour, Commander in Chief," Kauser said. "I'll send a couple of units ahead to clear the way and ensure we don't run into an ambush until our destination. Will you lead the attack from the ground?"

"Kiera and our dragons will lead the attack," Kassein said. "Kein and I will keep looking from above while the triplets and Kiki will launch the attack when we give them the signal to."

His sister grinned in approval; she probably didn't get nearly as much fighting done while she explored the west, and his sister seemed excited to be on the frontline, already playing with the swords she rarely parted from.

"And I'll decide what to do with my own dragon and start brawling when I damn well feel like it," Kiera snorted. "I can't let my brother have all the fun, can I?"

The generals replied in solemn nods, and Kiera scoffed.

"I'll lead the first charge with the kids, then," she said, whistling to get the dragons' attention. "Just make sure whoever is supposed to come with me doesn't get their shins bitten or something."

"Yes, Your Highness," General Sazaran said. "Captain Dajan, Captain Leslo, your men are up for the scouting! Follow Princess Kiera's lead! And... well, watch out for the younger dragons."

Kiera left first, riding Kiki while she ran on the ground, the excited triplets on their heels and the men a careful distance behind. Meanwhile, Kassein turned back to his generals.

"Get to work," he said. "Follow Kiera as soon as you're ready. I'll meet you up there."

He didn't wait for their nods to turn around and head for his tent.

The place had become cold in his absence as no fire had been lit in a while, and it made him miss Alezya's presence all the more. Kassein didn't waste time getting ready. He quickly got changed, selected the best weapons for the fights ahead, and, after a hesitation, grabbed one of Alezya's new coats to take with him.

No matter how thin his hope was, he couldn't let go of it, and if he found her, he wanted to take care of her the best he could.

Kassein stepped out of his tent and found Kein waiting for him.

He only took a second to pat his dragon's neck before he climbed onto Kein's back and took off. If it had been entirely up to him, Kassein would have been scouring the skies all night. Yet, Lumie needed him too, and he was glad he had spent the night at the Onyx Castle with the little girl, no matter how restless he was about Alezya; she had sent her daughter to him, for him to care for. Even if he would have given everything to look for her, he had to honor her wish.

Moreover, Cessilia's words from that morning were carved in his mind, and he kept thinking about them on a loop while taming his anxiety and anger the best he could, for now. But, for Alezya, he was trying his best to be a better man than he had been. He couldn't put her or Lumie at any kind of risk, and that involved fighting with his dragon.

That one reason was good enough for both of them, it seemed. It was already a strange sensation to no longer feel the anger radiating off his dragon whenever he was near Kein.

There was nothing that would fully end the frustration, guilt, and self-resentment he'd carried all these years, but Cessilia's forgiveness had allowed him to let go of a lot of it.

Now, he didn't have to fear fighting with his dragon again, and for the best reason: even if they hated each other, they needed to be better, for Alezya's and Lumie's sakes. His older sister was right: they deserved the best of him, and the worst of him had led him to fight his dragon in the Capital, destroy countless buildings, and kill a man.

Even if his sister insisted he wasn't to blame, Kassein knew he would never be able to fully atone or forgive himself for what had happened, and he didn't want to.

Instead, he intended to carry that guilt all his life so he would never forget what he'd done and never do it again.

He and Kein took off high in the skies, but their eyes were already analyzing what was going on below, and it didn't take long to spot Kiera and the men ahead, quickly making their way up the mountains.

From where they flew, he could see the triplets were happily running ahead, probably thinking this was some fun walk they were on. Kassein knew his sister didn't need him to launch an attack and could well have led this entire operation by herself, but he wanted to be there in case they found the smallest trace of Alezya.

He hadn't seen her in far too long, and he hated it.

He had never missed someone so much in his life, and the pain was becoming so much that it almost felt physical. He was dying to grab ahold of her black hair again, caress her skin, look into those deep black eyes, smell her scent, and bask in her warmth. Every memory of the two of them in his tent, touching, caressing, kissing, was becoming almost too painful to remember.

Underneath him, Kein echoed his distress with a long, high-pitched growl.

"We will find her," he whispered to his dragon, his eyes riveted on the mountain paths below. "We'll find her, Kein."

The mountains had never seemed so vast, daunting, and mysterious, but that was an enemy Kassein wasn't afraid to take on.

He would search every single one of those mountains, battle every tribe he came across, and inspect every nook and cranny until he found Alezya. His men had been aching for a fight, and now, so was he, and it wasn't against himself nor his dragon anymore.

The tribes were about to taste what he'd been too lazy to hit them with all this time.

He circled the mountains several times, Kein flying lower each time, ensuring their presence was known.

The sun was steadily rising, and it was a clear, bright day, one where the tribes would definitely see his dragon coming and hurry to hide inside.

What they didn't know yet was that now, his sister was coming from the ground too, and their hiding inside wouldn't stop his army anymore.

For the longest time, Kassein hadn't cared about those tribes. So long as he didn't fulfill Kassian's order, he could stay here, in his relative exile, fight when he felt like it, and let the world forget about him, but things couldn't have been more different now.

Now, he was desperate to inspect every mountain, search every tribe for a woman, and make this area safe. To establish peace just so that a woman and her child could live happily in it, now that was a cause worth living and fighting for.

Kiera reached the entrance of the first mountain, a different one from the one they'd attacked the previous day, and Kein dove to the other side, ready to look for escapees.

For the first attack, he wanted to observe how the tribes would react. Since Tievin had established that there were several tribes and that they might not be as harmonious as they'd previously thought, Kassein was more curious to notice the differences and the dynamics between them.

Would the nearby tribes come to the rescue? Or would they simply be left alone to their fate?

Kiera had picked one of the mountains that definitely wasn't Alezya's, so he could be at ease knowing she had a low chance of being brought into the scuffle, even if it was also disappointing.

Kein flew lower, and soon enough, they heard shouts, screams, and the familiar sound of fighting going on. Kassein listened as the triplet dragons' excited, high-pitched growls echoed from all sides of the mountains, spreading absolute chaos inside.

Much to his relief, he witnessed first-hand as his sister's plan worked perfectly; within minutes, there were tribespeople who ran out of openings from the mountain, rushing down pathways or climbing to safety.

He kept Kein hovering above, high enough in the hopes that it wouldn't scare any tribespeople and make them slip and fall to their death or something like that. Still, the mere sight of his dragon was enough to have some of them scream and run back inside through the nearest entry point possible.

For a while, it was a strange sight to see people appearing out of an unsuspected hole, running down a flank of their mountain, and disappearing through another, but Kassein kept observing, trying to gather every morsel of useful information while maintaining a distance.

He spotted women running with children, elderly, and younger men carrying supplies, but this time, it didn't seem like any warrior was running from the fight.

He observed, letting his sister have her fun, not worried at all about her; with Kiki probably waiting on the other side of the mountains, a few men with her, and three young dragons running amok, Kiera was most likely having a great time.

Moreover, from what they'd seen previously, the tribes' caves were too narrow for them to be ganged up on, and the tunnels too loud for anyone to come and take them by surprise. While they made for great hideouts from sky-bound threats, grounded armies, and adult dragons, those mountains were nearly impossible to defend once they were invaded. If Kassein had desired to do so, he would have probably been able to conquer the entire area in a matter of weeks. But he had no desire to exterminate the tribes and no reason to.

The Dragon Empire had always thrived without taking an interest in what the mountains had to offer aside from hostile inhabitants and miles of unexplored caves and tunnels.

Kassein's father, the previous ruler of the land below them, had never cared more about those than making sure they didn't make a scratch on the North Army and his children could safely use the forest beneath as a playground. There had been no chance to open communication and, therefore, no previous known attempt at peace aside from a mutual disinterest.

Funny how everything had changed because Kassein, the least interested of all, had found one good reason to force contact.

He waited while his sister took her time clearing every tunnel and cave, making circles around the mountain with Kein, and watching the rest of his army ascend.

It didn't seem like the tribe had a proper evacuation strategy, a predetermined escape route, or a fallback place, for everyone had fled in all directions.

Most surprisingly, they didn't seem keen on fleeing to seek help from nearby tribes either, as he didn't see anyone try to climb into the entrance of a nearby mountain.

Instead, the fleeing tribe was taking cover under small gatherings of trees, in small crevices or natural caves, or climbing up or down their mountains, but never fleeing laterally. Sure, it would have taken them a while longer to get to the next mountain, and as soon as they realized Kein wasn't diving, they could have fled to any other nearby peak.

But that didn't seem to be the case, which made Tievin's theory stronger: the tribes weren't as tight-knit as they'd thought. Kassein ground his teeth, annoyed; that probably meant that not only did Alezya not have a tribe she could have escaped to when her own harmed her, but if she wasn't back with her tribe, she could be anywhere in the mountains.

Did she truly have no place to fall back on, no one else to turn to, when her own people had let her be beaten and bruised?

He tightened his fists just as Kein let out equally furious growls. That was why she'd risked everything to go back and save Lumie and why she had sent her little girl to him; Alezya had no one else.

"Let's go," he hissed.

Kein dove down to the mountain and landed brutally, the rocks breaking and falling under its claws while its furious growls echoed throughout the range. Kassein hoped that Alezya could hear that and that she would know he was coming for her.

He jumped off Kein's back, falling until his feet landed on some natural plateau, and began climbing up toward the nearest entrance he could find.

Once he stepped inside the narrow tunnel, it was easy to find his sister: all he had to do was follow the panicked screams and the tiny dragon grunts and screeches.

A man carrying a spear but without any injury on him appeared at one end of the tunnel, spotted him, and turned around with a panicked expression. Kassein frowned, confused. What kind of warrior turned around at the mere sight of an opponent?

He wasn't surprised when he crossed paths with a few defeated men, although, as agreed, his sister and their men hadn't killed any, instead leaving them unconscious and battered.

He kept walking down the tunnel and first came across Vele; the young dragon was digging through baskets and ransacking something that smelled like dry meat.

"Leave it," Kassein hissed.

The little dragon replied with a high-pitched growl, but under Kassein's stare, it stopped immediately, tucked its tail, and scurried off.

Kassein followed its yellow scales down the tunnels and found Bora next, the one with a coral hue, which was grunting and trying to pull a thick piece of fabric out of an elderly woman's hands. The younger dragon seemed to be having fun playing tug-of-war, but the woman was absolutely terrified, with tears in her eyes, and doing her best to hold on to the fabric while staying as far from the dragon as possible.

"Bora," Kassein called the dragon. "Leave it."

Bora immediately let go, turning its innocent-looking big black eyes to him instead, and the woman fell back, her piece of fabric still held in her hands. Kassein didn't know why that woman was so desperate to keep it, but he could guess Bora was merely playing because the young dragon seemed to lose all interest as soon as Vele appeared to play, and they chased each other down another tunnel.

Kassein turned toward the woman and noticed she looked even more terrified of him than she was of the young dragon.

He switched hands so his blade would be farther away from her, and seeing as she seemed paralyzed by fear, he extended a hand. The elderly woman's first reaction was to jerk back, but Kassein didn't move.

Instead, he waited calmly until the older woman relaxed enough to recover her ability to move. She didn't take his hand, but her eyes were riveted on him with a mix of confusion and fear while she slowly got up, her entire body shaking. She didn't seem harmed, and Kassein wondered why she hadn't run away with the others. Maybe she wasn't confident in her running abilities because even once she stood, she only retreated until her back hit a wall, still transfixed on him.

Kassein couldn't waste any more time here; only the gods knew what more mayhem the young dragons were up to, and he had to reunite with Kiera to finish this raid. So, he simply turned his back and left the older woman alone there, hoping someone from her tribe would get her out of there or something.

He hurried down the tunnels, inspecting cave after cave, instinctively trying to catch a whiff of Alezya's scent while he analyzed the aftermath of the first attack; despite the time it must have taken them to scale this first mountain, their army had just arrived and was catching up, and he crossed paths with some of his men before he found his sister, all of them giving him respectful nods.

Kassein was relieved to confirm that they were respecting the orders to let the tribespeople live, as he didn't see any bodies, only injured people who hadn't been able to flee and some warriors bound by ropes or knocked out.

While the warriors would behave unless they wanted to lose their heads, he had been more worried about the young dragons who weren't as keen to follow orders. Thankfully, it seemed like the triplets didn't have any interest in biting human flesh and, instead, had been far more interested in playing chase and ransacking everything they found for food.

They ran past Kassein several times, racing through the tunnels in loops and proving to be a nightmare to herd, as even his men were wary of the miniature dragons and regularly had to jump out of the way when one to three of them barreled by.

In fact, he located Kiera simply by following his sister's furious voice.

"Get back here! I said no stealing, you little shits!" She was shouting after them when he finally found her, standing before a group of their men and a pile of knocked-out opponents.

"We're done here?" Kassein asked as soon as their eyes met.

"We are," Kiera said. "There wasn't much of a fight; many of them freaked out the second they saw the dragons inside... Not that those brats did more than break stuff and run around. Most of Sazaran's and Kauser's men have arrived too. They're blocking the path to the camp, checking the last corners, and knocking out those who wouldn't back down."

"Casualties?"

"A few," Kiera shrugged. "Some of their men wouldn't stand down and fought until I killed them. A couple more fell to their deaths on the east flank. The captains are going around compiling reports, but basically, we're good to go. We might catch some more on our way to the next mountain. At this pace, we could have three or four done before night falls."

"They're not going to the next mountain," Kassein informed his sister. "All of those I saw were fleeing in all directions, but they didn't have any proper exit strategy."

"They didn't get any reinforcement either," Kiera said, raising an eyebrow. "It sounds like Tiev was right; they're not as tight as we thought. That's good news for us though, isn't it?"

Kassein nodded, although he didn't care too much for this kind of good news; he was still annoyed that they would have to search each mountain individually to find Alezya.

He had a general idea of where her home was, but with all the tunnels and entrances, it wasn't exact.

"Your woman's tough," Kiera said, reading his mind. "I'm sure she's fine."

"I need to get to the mountain she came from," he said. "If they still have her, she might be injured or worse..."

"Shall we attack one of those which were most likely to be her home next? The next mountain over is the one she was always staring at, according to Lorey. It means she was quite far away when you first found her, but it's not that unlikely."

"Let's do that."

Kiera and Kassein worked together to lead the army to the next mountain they wanted to target, while the generals were tasked with making sure no man was left behind; as much as the generals and captains were reliable, they couldn't forget that a large portion of the army was former criminals, and Kassein didn't want to risk a single one of them harming a woman or attacking an innocent while he wasn't watching.

Thankfully, most of the men were excited at the prospect of another battle and followed without protest, and because they were all mixed in larger groups, no man could be left alone without someone noticing they were missing.

They were halfway to the next mountain when they confirmed all the men had followed, minus those who had been killed in the first battle.

"I'm still impressed by this army of ruffians," Kiera said. "I expected a lot more to rebel or try some shit."

"Those who disobey know what awaits them," Kassein simply commented.

"The Commander made a great example of the consequences of such actions," Sazaran nodded. "Many of our captains commended his strong hand in leading the camp. Between you and me, there are also many fights between the men, and those who have committed the worst crimes are often killed during the training duels by their opponents. After the Commander in Chief personally annihilated one of our worst units, we haven't had any issue with someone stepping out of line. Although, not all of our men are downright monsters. Many are actually hoping to redeem themselves and turn over a new leaf!"

Kassein let his sister talk to the generals, but he was surprised by how much they praised him.

He had never been very vocal in leading his camp. While he had never cared about being too hard on his men, never letting the slightest offense slide, and never backed down from drawing blood, he hadn't expected his unforgivingness to be seen as strong and dependable leadership.

The more he listened to the General, the more Kassein realized his regular need for violence had made his command even more respected, if not feared, which might have been an unexpectedly valid way to force former criminals to stay in line.

And while he and Kein wouldn't fight anymore, he certainly had no intention to let any man who disobeyed orders or tried to do vile acts under his watch get off easy; Kassein might not enjoy the position of Commander in Chief per se, but he had a strong sense of justice, respect from his generals, and the strength to make any man surrender.

"Kassein?" His sister dragged him out of his thoughts. "We're almost there. What's got you daydreaming? Your woman?"

He glanced ahead at the mountain they were indeed about to reach and the generals who had left their side to go and give orders to the men, tightening the ranks, splitting them to various entry points, and securing the route back.

Now it was just him and Kiera leading, and with the young dragons running around their legs, most of their soldiers remained at a reasonable pace behind.

"I just... I never wanted to lead this army, but the generals are praising me like I did something more than fight my dragon and kill murderers."

His sister chuckled.

"Sometimes a leader with a lot of charisma is more than enough. It's not like you were a complete slob either, from what I heard. You showed up, attended meetings, solved conflicts, and exercised authority when they needed you to. Tievin did the paperwork, but you were the one who kept the men doing their tasks rather than fighting or pulling some bullshit. We were born and raised to be leaders, Kassein. Don't think you failed just because you didn't rule an entire empire. And I'm sure you'll do great leading the north too. Not every leader needs to be involved in every aspect of their territory; sometimes, trusting others to know what to do has its perks. In a tense area with lots of fighting and an army of criminals, a stronger guy to show who is in charge might have been just what was needed. Isn't that the whole plan? Show the tribes who is the strongest and have them realize cooperation is in *their* interest. Sometimes diplomacy requires a bit of ass-kicking first, Kassein. Don't worry; you've got things right."

She patted his shoulder, and he nodded.

Either way, he couldn't turn back now, and for Alezya's sake, he wouldn't back down. He didn't care how many men he had to beat up to get to her, but she was his best reason to keep going.

If his strength could be used to protect and defend rather than intimidate and kill, that would already be more than enough for him.

They finally reached the next mountain, and this time, Kassein didn't let his sister lead the battle on her own; they split up in one of the tunnels, and as soon as he encountered people from that tribe, the fighting began.

Not only was Kassein attacked merely a few steps after walking inside, but he heard the echoes of his men encountering various opponents all around too.

This time, the tribe had probably seen them coming and decided to put up more of a fight, but they were no match for him.

Moreover, the three dragons were already doing what they had been brought here for, dashing through the tunnels, causing panic amongst the enemy rank, and spreading chaos in every corner of the mountain; their favorite game seemed to be running as fast as they could through the loops of tunnels with excited growls, but to the tribespeople, it seemed to be the most terrifying occurrence ever.

After another corner, Kassein emerged in a larger cave, half a dozen of his men on his heels, and found an equal group of warriors waiting for them, looking prepared to fight.

Just then, Bora happened to be dashing from one tunnel again, and one of the tribesmen tried to take a swing at the young dragon. While Bora froze at the sudden attack, Kassein stepped in, blocking the weapon with a furious glare; he had brought the young dragons to help, but he wouldn't let any harm come to them. Seeing it was safe, his niece's pink dragon growled furiously and attacked the man's leg in retribution.

Blood flew, and the battle started with Kassein's men spreading to take on their opponents.

Perhaps alarmed by Bora's growls, Vele and Leni also stopped racing to join the fight, and soon enough, their opponents were trying to run away before they lost limbs to their fangs. Kassein killed two men, and stopped, letting his men finish the fight there.

Just as he was looking around to assess the fight, something caught his attention. He froze, and turned his head, his heartbeat picking up a frantic rhythm.

"Alezya," he muttered under his breath.

It was faint, but he recognized her smell.

He would have recognized her smell anywhere. Leaving his men to finish that fight, Kassein rushed down one of the tunnels, pushing or punching people out of his way, following the scent with growing hope.

She was near. He could smell Alezya's faint scent, and the more he walked, the stronger it got.

Kassein was vaguely aware that he walked past ongoing battles, fleeing tribesmen, and had young dragons on his heels, but he couldn't stop nor care about anything else.

He kept rushing through the tunnels, turning back when he got to dead ends, re-entering when he unexpectedly stumbled upon openings and cliffs.

Alezya's smell was like a siren call he was desperate to find the source of, even if the stronger it got, the harder it was for him to find it.

Eventually, he reached a corridor that seemed narrower than the others, and he could almost physically feel the pull to its end. He had to bend so as not to hit his head, but he kept going, confused about this smaller area.

Finally, he reached its end, which forced him to crawl to the little cave that was waiting for him there. His heart dropped with disappointment upon finding it empty.

Leni, who was the last baby dragon following him, dashed inside, sniffing around curiously. Kassein looked around the tiny space with a heavy heart and growing anger.

He hadn't found Alezya, but he had found where she once lived.

It was evident by how her smell filled the space. He forced his large frame inside and sat in the narrow space, inspecting every inch of it, trying to find the faintest traces of Alezya's presence.

A little basket that smelled like berries was knocked over in a corner. A pile of ragged fur blankets that smelled like Lumie, carefully arranged. A small toy made of carved wood and rags. The large cover blocked an impressive opening, which was a window on the outside of the mountain.

Upon lifting it, Kassein spotted a little spot of dried blood on the outside, and his anger rose another notch; Alezya had fled through this impossible, almost vertical exit.

He glanced around the cave, which wasn't even tall enough for her to stand up in, and it was so narrow he could touch both ends with his extended arms. While Leni climbed into the pile of fur blankets that would have once been Lumie's bed, Kassein took the little toy.

He glanced around and decided to take the two best-looking fur blankets too.

"Leni, let's go."

The young dragon followed after him as Kassein left the cave, again having to crawl and contort his massive frame to get out.

When he emerged, Bora and Vele appeared, following his sister.

Kiera grimaced.

"What kind of dusty hole did you crawl into and why?"

"I found where Alezya lived," he said.

He presented her with the toy, and Kiera's expression fell, turning into genuine surprise.

"Damn," she muttered. "So this was indeed her home... Her tribe sucks, by the way. Half their warriors fled along with their women, kids, and old people. I know we're supposed to let them go, but really, they could have put up more of a fight. It seems like they just left some men here to die to slow us down. ...Well, what do you want us to do? Now that we know she isn't here..."

"The plan stays the same," Kassein said, more determined than ever. "We battle every tribe until we find her. Make sure the men don't leave any cave or crevice unchecked either. If Kein couldn't find her and she couldn't come back, she might be imprisoned somewhere he can't get to."

"Let's hope she hears you coming and decides to show up," Kiera sighed. "This could take a while..."

"We'll camp in the mountains," Kassein said. "Our men knew this one was going to be a long campaign."

"Yeah, yeah, I know. I'm used to sleeping in weird places, don't worry. And Sazaran and Kauser are already making sure we have a secure route back, not for retreat but to be sure we can send injured men and bring whatever we need from the camp. Not that we've had many casualties or injuries; it looks like the dragons are scaring the tribespeople out faster than we can get to them, and I guess the word might be spreading fast that we're invading their neighbors. We might have to move fast if we don't want the next couple of mountains to be empty by the time we get there."

Kassein nodded, and just like that, they gathered their men, and while some were left behind to finish searching the mountain and deal with the aftermath of the battle, most followed them to their next battlefield.

While he was disappointed that he hadn't found Alezya, Kassein was even more convinced he had to bring her back.

Knowing she had been forced to live confined in a small cave infuriated him; by then, they had seen and explored enough of those caves to know the tribes actually had decent living spaces, carved the stone around them to create furniture, and had large caves to share.

The fact that Alezya's scent had been confined to such a small space and faint everywhere else in her tribe's stronghold told him all he needed to know, and it had Kassein grinding his teeth and tightening his fists just thinking about it.

That woman deserved a lot more; she deserved the world.

Kassein didn't think he deserved her, but he was surely going to try to do what he could to make her believe he did. He was going to start by offering her to live in the Onyx Castle, where she would never have to run or worry about food or the cold ever again. He wanted to cover her in the best fur clothes, hunt that meat she loved so much every day and feed it to her, and even make new toys for Lumie to play with. He wanted to make a place where she would feel safe, be able to explore and take dragon rides on Kein's back if she wanted, and for her skin to never show a bruise or a cut ever again.

Kassein didn't need to put much thought into the battle; the tribesmen were far more terrified of him than they were of his men or the young dragons, and most didn't even seek to fight with him, and he didn't pursue them.

Instead, he was more interested in exploring their habitat, getting a sense of who those people were and how they lived. It was strange to him how the inside of each mountain could be so different.

The one he had found Alezya's cave in had felt bare and raw, with the minimal amount of resources, while the one they stood in now had not only plenty of fabrics and food but also many manufactured items and tools with complex designs, colorful paintings covering their walls, strange little objects gathered in corners which he guessed might be some sort of shrine, and outside, little patches of vegetables and fungi they grew.

That tribe was also the one who had left almost no man behind and fled immediately upon seeing his army coming.

Thus, he and his men would actually be leaving their mountain as they had found it and immediately moved on to the next one.

Again, the fourth mountain, the last one they would conquer for the day as the sun was setting, showed yet another different lifestyle; instead of paintings, those people seemed to be hanging lots of dried herbs in their tunnels, had countless hand-drawn maps of the area lined on the walls, and communal spaces with large beds probably meant for larger families to share. Their diet also seemed to revolve more around fishing in a lake they probably had access to, as he found countless fish skins hanging around and plenty of fishing tools too.

Kassein couldn't remember having seen food other than a few baskets of fruits in Alezya's home, and the lingering scent of meat. He remembered how much she had loved the meat soup; that was the first thing he'd feed her once he brought her back.

"Kassein," his sister drawled, not for the first time. "Come on, you can't keep daydreaming while your men do the grunt work. Not that there's much need for assistance, but... are you going to keep carrying that?"

The fur blankets he'd taken from Alezya's cave were on his shoulder, and he had kept Lumie's toy in his free hand all this time without realizing.

Upon noticing that fact, he looked back up at his sister.

"...Can you handle the camp here tonight?"

"The men are already setting up in a clearing," she shrugged. "We might have to schedule some serious rounds to ensure we're not attacked in our sleep, but Sazaran's on it. ...Why? Where are you going?"

"Back to the Onyx Castle. I'm taking Kiki, and I'll be back before dawn for the next battle."

"What?" his sister barked. "Hey! You can't leave me to babysit your dragon, Dran's evil spawn, and your entire army! I'm not a bloody babysitter, Kassein!"

"You said it yourself," he said over his shoulder as he was already walking out. "We're born leaders. It's just for a night, you'll be fine."

"You selfish ass!"

Kassein ignored her protests, and as soon as he located the dark gray dragon, he climbed on and had his sister's dragon take off in the direction of the Onyx Castle.

He knew Kiera wasn't that reluctant, or else Kiki would have never taken off.

Although it was indeed selfish of him to abandon his army in the mountains and spend the night at the Onyx Castle, he was desperate to check on Lumie.

Moreover, he knew his army didn't need him for the night; even though they had hiked in the mountains all day, the battles hadn't been nearly as exhausting as they had anticipated, and they would have no problem guarding a camp in the hills from attacks for the night.

Kassein was far more anxious about Lumie spending another night without her mom, and he urged Kiki to fly south as fast as possible.

He made it long after night had fallen, but to his surprise, he found Lorey and Lumie out in the gardens of the Onyx Castle.

Both raised their heads as soon as they noticed Kiki's silhouette and as soon as Lumie broke into a huge smile upon seeing him, Kassein couldn't help but smile back and jump down from the dragon to get to her.

This time, the little girl had been changed into proper clothes, a tiny outfit made of comfortable wool and gray fur, which covered her hands and feet too, only leaving her face visible under a cute hood.

"Hello, little moon," he whispered as he hugged the little girl.

"Welcome back," Lorey smiled. "Did everything go well up there?"

"We didn't find Alezya," he said, "but the fights were easy; most fled before our arrival."

"I'm sorry to hear that. Maybe you'll have better luck tomorrow. Hello, Kiki."

Understandably, his sister's dragon went to Lorey's side while he was all focused on Lumie. The baby girl was looking up at him while chewing her mitten, her cheeks rosy.

Kassein smiled and handed her the little toy he had found.

"Is this yours?" he whispered.

After a second, the little girl's eyes opened wide with recognition, and she took the toy with a squeal of delight.

"Your room and the nursery are ready," Lorey informed him. "Are you spending the night?”

“Lumie is sleeping with me,” he decided, “but I left Kiera in charge; I’ll leave before sunrise.”

“Understood,” Lorey said with an approving nod, following him inside. “I’ll be sure to wake up to take care of her and see you off, then. Now, will you tell me how much mischief the triplets got up to?”

Chapter 17

Alezya tightened her fur coat around her, her eyes riveted on her little window of the sky. The sun was starting to set, but she could still feel the tension growing in the mountains. It was the second day since she had arrived in the Munsa Clan, and while they were far away, all eyes had been fixated on the other end of the mountains, to the far south, to watch the absolute mayhem that was going on. For clans who rarely communicated, she felt like the panicked rumors about the Dragon Clan's attacks were spreading incredibly fast. It was impossible to miss Kein's large figure, as the orange dragon had been hovering above the mountains restlessly.

If she could, Alezya would have found the nearest cliff and shouted for the orange dragon to see her. Unfortunately, she wasn't sure Kein would have made it to her before she was killed.

While the Munsa Clan had been hiding her for almost three days now, many of the other clans were searching for her.

Ekata and Ekut's worries had been quickly confirmed: her father, Darak, had not only put a price on her head but had also convinced the other clans that the Dragon Clan's attacks were somehow her doing. According to him, the only way to stop the destruction was to kill Alezya.

She was grateful that the Munsa Clan was among those who distrusted him, but the word was spreading fast. Ekut and Ekata were carefully reaching out to select clan leaders, trying to determine who might be willing to hear her out and who would betray her the moment they learned she was in the Munsa Clan's care.

Confined to their mountain, she remained hidden from prying eyes yet desperate for information. She was grateful for the meals, the warm clothes, and even the way her hair had been braided in the Munsa style, but she knew this was only the calm before the storm. From what she had gathered, the Dragon

Clan's attacks were unlike anything before. These were not brief, scattered skirmishes where warriors clashed and quickly withdrew. Entire mountains were being raided, and clans were driven from their homes. Worse, the Dragon Clan was no longer retreating after their attacks; they were staying.

All Alezya could see were glimpses of Kein from time to time, and she was desperate for every bit of information the Munsa Clan scouts brought back. Panic was rising, and displaced clans were seeking refuge elsewhere. As fear spread, more and more clans leaned toward her father's plan, believing they had to fight back before it was their turn.

Some, however, were unsettled by something unexpected. While the first accounts described savagery and chaos, the more survivors gathered, the more confusing the truth became. Many of them, expecting to be slaughtered, had instead been allowed to leave, walking past their attackers without a fight. That knowledge gave Alezya a flicker of pride, knowing it had to be Kassein's doing. He was leading the charge, yet sparing as many as he could. More importantly, it was causing fractures in her father's plan. The more clans questioned the true purpose of these raids, the less unified they became.

When the Deklaan Clan was attacked more violently than the others, or so they claimed, they were the first to declare that the clans had to retaliate immediately. But few were willing to take the fight to the Dragon Clan head-on. Many still clung to the hope that if they stayed out of it, they would be spared. According to Ekata's latest reports from clan gatherings, leaders were divided; some prayed the dragon would pass them by, others debated fleeing before they arrived, and still others weighed their chances of survival if they followed Darak into war.

Meanwhile, Ekut and Ekata continued their delicate work.

They met with other leaders in secret, sorting out allies from enemies and searching for those they could trust with the truth. But time was running out, and Alezya was growing frustrated. It wasn't just about being trapped indoors, confined to a handful of caves so she and Niiru wouldn't risk encountering someone who might inadvertently spread the word. After all, she had been in tighter spaces before. What unnerved her was how little she knew about what was happening and how powerless she felt because of it.

The Munsa Clan's mountain was low, offering little view of the south, and each day spent waiting only made her more anxious. If not for the very real risk of being struck down by an arrow the moment she stepped outside, she would have left long ago or attended the gatherings herself. She only held back because one wrong move wouldn't just endanger her and Niiru, but the entire Munsa Clan as well. These people had been good to her, and she knew they were working tirelessly to secure meetings with clan leaders she could trust, but it wasn't enough. How many more clans would be forced from their homes in the meantime?

The Dragon Clan was advancing at an alarming pace, and some clans were fleeing before they even arrived. The pressure was mounting, Alezya could feel the situation spiraling further out of control every day, and being confined to a cave did not sit well with her.

"Let's go, Niiru," she called to the young dragon.

Their little duo had been assigned to a tiny cave, either to give her some privacy or to keep her away from curious eyes. Either way, Alezya appreciated the gesture, but quiet was the last thing she needed at that moment. She quickly climbed down to reach the lower caves, Niiru sticking to her side as the young dragon had for the last couple of days. Whenever given the occasion, Niiru would play with the Munsa Clan children, but it never let Alezya out of its sight; if she was going somewhere, Niiru would follow like a little shadow. Thus, many children were delighted with Alezya's arrival into the main cave, and Niiru ran off to play in the water right away while she walked toward the gathering of elders.

"Ekata," she greeted the female Clan Chief upon seeing her there. "Any news?"

"Good and bad," Ekata said, standing up from the circle. "I was about to come and get you. The Dragon Clan attacked its ninth mountain today. Two of those they raided were empty, but they seem to stop at sundown, like before. I think you were right; they're searching for you. There are too few clans reporting deaths, except for the Deklaan Clan, which claims half their warriors were brutally massacred, but it doesn't match the others, and I wouldn't trust a single word that comes out of your father's mouth."

"Neither would I," Alezya nodded. "So? What's the word out there? What are the clans doing?"

"Fighting over what to do, as usual," Ekata grimaced. "Your father seemed to be really raising an army, with an 'If you're not with us, you're against us' mindset that is seriously irking some and making other clans feel intimidated. I wish I could say many are ignoring him, but there's too much unrest. Even if there are many survivors, no one wants to wait for the Dragon Clan to get to them. Since the dragon isn't attacking, many think we stand a chance."

"We don't," Alezya said. "Kein would take seconds to annihilate them all!"

"That's not all," Ekata sighed. "There are accounts of... small dragons attacking with them. People disagreed on how many small dragons there were, so the information was confusing, but they all agreed small dragons were charging in with the Dragon Clan. Some said a dozen, others three or four... Either way, the Dragon Clan is unleashing them in the mountains and causing chaos. Do you know anything about that?"

Alezya's jaw dropped, and her eyes drifted toward Niiru, who was playing in the water with the children again. She remembered a conversation she'd had with Kassein, or at least some sentences she'd tried to understand. His siblings had dragons, and his siblings' children had dragons... Were they using baby dragons, like Niiru? Why? Because Kein and Kiki were too big to attack inside the mountains? Why would they finally decide to send dragons inside? Had

Kassein lost patience and summoned smaller dragons to attack the clans?

"I-I'm not sure," she admitted. "I knew small dragons existed, young dragons like Niiru, but... I-I don't know."

"Well, the fact that you were right and there are more dragons than we know is also scaring the other clans," Ekata explained, "and your father keeps trying to convince everyone that everything will stop if you die."

"I can make it stop," Alezya declared confidently, "but not with my death. I can tell Kassein, I mean, their Clan Chief, to stop the attacks. I promise. He listens to me."

Or at least she hoped he still would, and she hoped they were right in thinking the attacks were mainly to find her.

"I trust you, Alezya. Trust me, we believe you; we've seen how the small dragon is with you and what happened at the gathering. The problem is, it is tough to convince the other clans when we can't outright tell them that we've got you. We don't even have enough time to meet those we can convince; the situation is evolving minute by minute. As soon as the daylight comes, the Dragon Clan starts attacking, and every clan starts freaking out, thinking that they're next. At this rate, the Dragon Clan might even reach us in three or four days."

"Let me help," Alezya insisted. "Please, just let me talk to the clan chiefs who might listen. If I just tell them-"

"I know," Ekata said, raising a hand to interrupt her. "That's our plan, and I was about to come get you for that purpose. We don't have much time, and Ekut is talking to some clan chiefs we think we can trust. We're having a gathering in a clearing a couple of hours from here. We picked a place not too far from the Dragon Clan to show them we're not afraid, and we believe our claim."

"What did you tell them?"

"That we know how to prevent attacks from the Dragon Clan and that Darak's word is goat shit. Trust me, they are very much inclined to believe the latter. But I need to bring you there this time."

"That's what I want," Alezya gave her a firm nod. "I'll convince them."

"I hope so," Ekata sighed. "This is a big risk we're all taking, Alezya. If we are attacked..."

"I know," she muttered.

Alezya had spent enough time with the Munsa Clan to know they weren't fighters. They did have some men who could be decent fighters, but compared to other clans, they wouldn't stand a chance. Unlike clans like hers, they had never been bothered much by the dragon, and they relied more on how unremarkable their mountain was to avoid fighting with their neighbors. With much of the Munsa Clan's strategy being about remaining unnoticed, it was already remarkable that they were going to such lengths to stop the war with the Dragon Clan and her father's plans.

"You should bring the small dragon," Ekata said after a beat. "We'll give you a bag to carry it."

Thankfully, Niiru was small enough that the young dragon would fit into a large leather bag that Alezya could put on her shoulder.

She wasn't sure how long the young dragon would endure being stuck in there, but at least it got in and out of the bag when she asked it to without a fuss. She packed a few dried fish for the road, and just like that, she, Ekata, and a handful of the Munsa Clan's fighters left the caves of their clan to meet the others.

While in the tunnels, they let Niiru roam around them, sometimes rushing ahead but always coming back to keep Alezya in sight or when she whistled for the small dragon. She felt strangely pleased with how obedient the young dragon was and with the admirative looks of the Munsa Clan people whenever Niiru came back to rub its warm scales against her ankles, its big eyes looking up at her.

For whatever reason, the young dragon seemed to obey and adore her the same way Kein did, sticking to her side unprompted even when she could tell it was dying to run off and explore. It was for the best, however, given that they had now left the Munsa Clan territory and were navigating through unclaimed, neutral tunnels.

She kept calling Niiru back until the small black dragon understood that it had to stay with her, and Niiru did, making little hops around her and burning its extra energy by dashing between the Munsa Clan people that surrounded them. By now, they had all stopped jumping every time Niiru ran past without warning and were instead looking out for external threats; two men were walking ahead of them, Ekata was by Alezya's side, and three more people were at the tail of their group.

They held fire torches, spears and tiny daggers as weapons, and all of the Munsa Clan carried fishnets at their belt too. Alezya had only been given a small dagger, but she hoped that Niiru's fangs would be enough if things went south. She had tried a couple of times while she was alone, and although it looked much younger, Niiru seemed to understand the same commands in the Dragon Clan's language as Kein did.

Alezya hoped she wouldn't have to unleash the small dragon on anyone though. The fact that Ekata looked nervous about the clandestine meeting couldn't be a good sign. They barely talked during the trip, instead everyone keeping an ear out for any incoming enemies or whatever was going on outside. Some of the tunnels were so deep and narrow that they had to bend, walk in a line, or jump over a couple of crevices, and Alezya guessed they were deep under the ground, which, compared to the heights of her home, was unsettling. It took a while before she felt like they were finally going up, and the first rays of natural light reappeared, with a faint breeze of fresh air.

"...How small were the new dragons?" she asked Ekata in a whisper, her eyes always on Niiru and the path ahead.

"Depends who we asked," Ekata groaned. "According to your father, they were the size of three men, which is strange, given that you told us your caves aren't any bigger than ours. According to most, they were barely bigger than a snow leopard but definitely bigger than this one. We wish we knew the actual number, but many people said everything happened too fast, and the smaller dragons were running wild everywhere... much like this one, I guess."

Niiru was indeed full of energy and kept running back and forth to inspect the tiniest holes, hunt something invisible, or dash past their position and back. The dragon could move with ease in the narrow tunnels, given its small size. Kiki was definitely too big to get into any of the tunnels, so Alezya guessed Kassein must have brought new dragons.

Why? Was he really looking for her? Her heart ached just thinking about it, about him searching for her.

What of Lumie? He had let many people survive; it had to be a good sign, right? She had seen him kill men without remorse for harming her, or at least let his dragon do it for him.

A scarier, more insidious worry nagged at her that he was looking for her, but not for the right reasons. What if he was mad she had left him again? What if Kein hadn't brought Lumie to him? What if he didn't have her baby girl? What if her crazy bet hadn't worked, and everything was going wrong?

Niiru's high-pitched growl pulled Alezya from her spiraling thoughts. The young dragon, which had been quiet for a long time, was still by her side, its eyes riveted ahead.

"We're almost there," Ekata explained.

Alezya nodded stiffly, remaining quiet. She crouched and made a small gesture for Niiru to get into the bag hanging at her hip, although its black head and tail stuck out, visibly too curious to miss the action. Alezya let the young dragon see and sniff around until they reached an opening, then, she gently tucked its tail and head inside the bag, and much to her relief, she only got a little protest growl in return, but Niiru curled up obediently.

They emerged directly onto a little hill of cold grass covered by thick pine trees. After so long following torturous corridors, Alezya had lost track of their location, but it only took her a moment to spot the mountain hills between the high trees and realize they had indeed headed far to the south, closer to Kein and Kassein than she had been in days.

She couldn't see the orange dragon roaming the skies anymore, but it was past nightfall, and after a few seconds, she realized the mountains weren't quiet; the wind was carrying a low chorus of voices and human activity, as well as the familiar smell of a campfire. Either another gathering was happening a couple of mountains over, or it was the settlement of the Dragon Clan's camp. Alezya's heartbeat couldn't help but accelerate at the prospect that they had gotten much closer that day. The Munsa Clan people probably had the same realization because their heads were all turned in the same direction with nervous expressions.

"We have to move quickly," Ekata whispered.

She took the lead to guide their group down the hill, between the trees, toward a rocky path.

It wasn't a large area, but it had a little river zigzagging down, enough trees to hide them from prying eyes, and barely enough space for their group to get down in single file. It was so narrow and steep that, several times, they had to help each other climb down rather than walk, and the river would curve into little waterfalls next to them. They could hang on to some tree branches nearby, but a couple of times, someone would slip on the wet rocks and almost twist their ankle, making everyone else gasp and hold their breath until they confirmed they were fine in a whisper.

It was a strange, slow procession, especially as they were careful to be as quiet as possible, though the river and ambient noise around probably covered any sounds they made. Alezya was used to climbing steep, ice-cold heights and standing on sharp cliffs, not torturous and slimy paths, where they could tumble down any second. While living in caves had gotten them all accustomed to the dark, it was still tricky to spot the slippery areas on dark rocks, muddy snow, and wet moss, and everyone walked with their eyes riveted on their feet, progressing slowly and carefully.

Thankfully, it was only a matter of minutes before they reached the gathering. Seconds before they sighted them, Ekata gestured for Alezya to hide under the hood of her coat and check that Niiru was still tucked in the leather bag; to her surprise, the young dragon was still curled into a ball of dark scales and dozing off.

Alezya was positioned at the back of their group when they reached another group waiting for them, although there wasn't much space to stand on anyway; Ekut and two of their men were standing on one side of the river, and a little group of eight men were waiting on the other side.

It was dark, but no one had bothered to light a fire, most likely too scared to be spotted. Their only source of light was the moonlight peeking through the thickness of the pine trees above them. Ekata took position a step behind her brother, who simply gave them a nod; it looked like they had arrived mid-argument.

Alezya peeked from under her hood to identify the others; given their attires, hairstyles, markings, and stances, she guessed they were facing the representatives of three or four clans. They were exclusively male, which made Alezya feel unsettled right away, and she put a hand in the bag, gently petting Niiru's warm body to soothe herself.

"Your claims are as empty as Darak's," one of the clan chiefs was saying in a hushed voice, and Alezya couldn't remember seeing him at the gathering. "We came here because you claimed you could stop the dragon, but if this is all just a fallacy to go against the Deklaan Clan..."

"The Deklaan Clan will do nothing but sacrifice others," Ekut insisted. "Whatever army they're trying to rally will inevitably die. There's no way we can win against the Dragon Clan."

"We don't have a choice!" they hissed back. "The Dragon Clan's attacks are relentless! They're coming for all of us, and if we don't stand, we will be wiped out next!"

"No clan has been wiped out," Ekata said. "You all heard the other clan chiefs. Most of them survived and were allowed to flee. Those who didn't fight were let go!"

"Silence, woman!" one of the clan chiefs barked.

He was immediately greeted with not only Ekata's furious glare, but also some from a few of the other men, and not just the ones from the Munsa Clan. Ekut gave his sister a sorry look before he spoke up again, careful to keep his voice low.

"Darak claims half of his clan's warriors got wiped out," he said, "but he claims so every other month, and you all know we can't trust his words. Every clan keeps sending men to fight the Dragon Clan, and they're the ones who die, but Darak brings the same men completely uninjured to every gathering!"

"We have no way to know what's going on in the south," one of the men insisted. "Even if Darak is lying, how would we know? The facts are that the Dragon Clan keeps attacking, and he's the only one who knows-"

"My father is a liar," Alezya said, suddenly stepping forward.

She exchanged a resigned glance with Ekata before she pulled back her hood with one hand, revealing her face. The foreign clans let out a collective gasp, and some stepped back in shock. She hadn't expected such a reaction, but she didn't give them time to recover.

"My father keeps sending men to their deaths," she said. "He lies to you all. We have no chance against the Dragon Clan, and the Deklaan Clan has survived all this time by feeding lies to the other clans to maintain the illusion of supremacy they do not have. The men he takes to the gathering aren't a fraction of his warriors like he claims; it's almost all of them. I only know a handful of men who married into our clan and weren't sent to their deaths."

She thought of Suolk, who had probably only survived so long for him to give children to her cousin. He was also likely to be sent off once they had enough.

She couldn't believe she hadn't realized the ramifications of her father's evil doings before.

Alezya knew she had been kept oblivious and away from the affairs of her clan, but now that she had a glimpse of the bigger picture, the facts were piling up and showing things were worse than she could have imagined, and her father was a cruel man. The men sent from other clans most likely didn't survive long enough to even notice what was going on or report back, and living at the edge of the Deklaan Clan, she hadn't been involved enough to notice foreign clansmen coming and disappearing either. It was no wonder her father didn't allow women at the gatherings; many would have probably spoken about losing their husbands and partners.

The men standing on the other side of the river all stared at her in disbelief, some more shocked than others.

"I-it's that witch!" one of them shrieked. "The one they sent off to the Dragon Clan!"

"That witch is trying to save you all right now," Ekata hissed. "How about you stop hiding and actually listen to someone who knows what they're talking about? She's the only one who's spent time with the Dragon Clan and survived!"

"That witch commands the dragon," a man with long white hair hissed, glaring at Alezya like she was evil personified. "Who knows if she isn't just trying to trick us all to feed us to that beast?!"

"Why would you help us?" another chimed. "Half the clans want you dead right now!"

"Frankly, I'm doing this for those who don't," Alezya retorted. "I am no murderer or coward like my father. I have nothing to gain by watching men die. I know the mountains, and I know that behind the warriors, dozens of families, wives, children, and elderly do not deserve to die. There are people like me, those who don't get a say and are sacrificed to a meaningless cause anyway. And I don't want to stay mute or passive anymore. I can't. Not when so many lives are at stake, and I can do something to save them. My cousin and her husband risked their lives to take care of my baby while I was with the Dragon Clan. Ekata and Ekut of the Munsa Clan risked a lot by hiding me for a couple of days. Many of you might want me dead, but you're making foolish decisions out of fear on behalf of people who do not deserve to die pointlessly. You all can feel free to join my father's army and die if you please. I do not care for powerful men who want to run to their deaths out of greed or pride. Go for it. That's your choice to make, no matter how foolish it is. But I am standing here because there is a chance I can save many innocent lives by speaking up, and I refuse to be silenced or passive any longer."

The others seemed a bit torn over her words; Alezya thought she recognized a light of hope in the eyes of half of them, who were staring at her, but the others were exchanging looks, and she could tell they didn't trust her.

"What do they want?" the younger man asked. "The Dragon Clan. Why are they attacking now?"

Alezya hesitated, exchanging a look with the twins before clearing her throat.

"I'm not sure," she confessed. "They might be looking for me."

The white-haired man's eyes narrowed.

"It's settled then," he hissed. "We can just give them your head!"

Immediately, the Munsa Clan pulled Alezya to the rear of their group and drew their weapons, but on the other side, only half of the foreign clans had moved. The two men who seemed to be escorting the white-haired man had drawn out weapons, but the others were exchanging nervous glances and looking between the white-haired man and Alezya, clearly unsure.

"What if we kill her and they attack us back?" one of the men whispered. "I have wives and children waiting for me back home. If we have a chance that the Dragon Clan might spare us..."

"You know our clan never fights if we can help it," Ekut insisted. "What would we gain by lying to you?"

"Who is to say you haven't already made an alliance with the Dragon Clan to sell us all out?" the old man hissed. "Let them conquer the mountains, feed us to their dragon in exchange for your own lives!"

"You heard the first accounts of the survivors, you stubborn old bat," Ekata retorted. "The Dragon Clan can send dragons inside the caves; they wouldn't miss if they were trying to wipe us all out, and they certainly wouldn't bother to ally with our clan! This woman might be our best chance of survival, can't you understand that? She's the only one who's been with the Dragon Clan, survived, and even learned their language!"

"...Do you really think we can be spared?" another man asked Alezya before the old man could speak again.

"I'm certain of it," Alezya said firmly, taking a step forward despite the Munsa's attempts to keep her at the back. "The Dragon Clan aren't as bloodthirsty nor savage as we've been led to believe. Even dragons are kind, smart creatures."

"They're gods," another man whispered. "How can we understand a man-eating god...?"

"They don't eat humans to survive," Alezya exclaimed, exasperated. "The dragons don't need to eat or attack us at all. We have nothing they would want! Their clan is far bigger, richer, and stronger than any of our clans, or even all of us combined! I ate meat at every meal when I was with them. I was given new clothes every day, and their leader let me take whatever I wanted because, no matter what it was, he had dozens of them."

"You're their whore," the white-haired man hissed again. "You opened your legs for their leader in exchange for—"

"Look at their attacks!" Alezya insisted, pointing a finger toward the south. "Their dragons could destroy the mountain if they wanted, collapse our caves, and murder dozens! Why are so many people allowed to survive if not because what they want isn't there? They're not trying to conquer, they never meant to!"

"Darak said it was because they managed to flee..."

"My father has been lying through his teeth for years," Alezya retorted. "He's the one who's been launching attacks and forcing them to respond in return! I wasn't sent to the Dragon Clan on some master plan; my own father chased me from my home once I wasn't of any use to him anymore! I was left for dead in the mountains when the Dragon Clan Chief found me and saved me. The only reason I returned was for my child whom my father kept captive!"

"...The cursed child," someone muttered, immediately getting a glare from Alezya. "But... someone saw you feed it to the dragon."

"My child is alive," Alezya hissed, her eyes blurring with tears of frustration. "She is alive and safe with the Dragon Clan. And as soon as I get back to their Chief, I'll see my baby again."

Those last words weren't to convince anyone but herself. If she had even dared to think that things might not have gone as she hoped, if she had lost faith in Kein and Kassein, she might as well have abandoned any hope she had now. She had done everything for Lumie's sake. If her child wasn't alive and well, there was absolutely no point to all of this.

Alezya was pulled from her thoughts by Ekata's gentle but firm hand on her shoulder. The two women exchanged a silent understanding nod before she turned back to the other clan representatives.

"...We've chosen to believe Alezya," Ekata said. "Our clan has never been willing to believe in the Deklaan's claims, and we won't start now because we're guided by fear."

"That's easy to say when you live on the other side of the mountains," someone muttered. "You guys will be the last ones killed!"

"And we have nowhere to run," Ekut retorted. "But even if we're the farthest, so what? You've all heard how fast the Dragon Clan is progressing. Entire clans are fleeing this very second, and it's only a matter of days before they reach us. Trusting this woman who already survived them once is the only way to go forward. Fighting will only precipitate our end."

"Who's to say she isn't a spy for her father? What if Darak is merely testing us all before he raises an army?!"

"My father is a cunning man, but even he can't anticipate the Dragon Clan's attacks," Alezya said, "and I have nothing to gain whether you believe me or not. The only thing I know is that I will most likely be safe from their attacks, but I can't say the same for everyone else."

"Don't be stubborn and get yourselves killed," Ekata insisted. "Come on. We reached out because we know we can survive and we want as many clans as possible to survive too. Many of us didn't trust Darak before, why should we trust him now? That plan of his is madness! Do you guys seriously believe we have a chance against the Dragon Clan? Darak is the one who's been claiming they're invincible all these years, and we've lost countless men to his battles!"

"...How can you guarantee we will be safe?" someone asked Ekata, although their eyes drifted to Alezya.

"I can talk to the Dragon Clan Chief," Alezya insisted, stepping forward. "He listens to me—"

"Why would the leader of the most powerful clan in the world listen to a woman?!" the old man grunted again. "This is nonsense! That witch is doing that tyrant's bidding, that's what this is! She will sell us all out after she sold herself!"

"Watch it, old man," Ekata hissed, drawing her blade out.

"I knew it! Traitors! You summoned us here to sell us out!"

Things were escalating too quickly, and Alezya realized this meeting had been a mistake.

No one was concealing their voices anymore, instead shouting at each other, meaning they could be heard down the valley at any moment now, and depending on who heard it, things could potentially get much worse. Alezya looked up again nervously, silently hoping Kein's orange scales would cover the skies right this instant, but all she got was the cloudless night and wind shuddering the trees.

"The Deklaan Clan are liars!"

"We can't trust the Munsa! They hid that witch while we were all running from our homes!"

"She's our only way to survive, you fools!"

"These negotiations are a trap," the white-haired man hissed to the others. "We should just capture that woman and use her as a hostage! The Deklaan Clan will know what to do with her!"

"Touch me, and that will be the last thing you do, old man," Alezya hissed, her eyes darting back to him.

"W-wait," a man from a different clan exclaimed. "You can't decide for all of us! What if she's telling the truth? If you harm her, you might condemn us all! No, our clan will go to our elders and explain—"

"Nonsense! There isn't a minute to lose! Capture that woman, now!"

The man took a step toward Alezya, ready to cross the thin stream, and all hell broke loose at once: she pulled out her blade and slashed his wrist in one movement, but at the exact same moment, someone grabbed and brutally pulled her back.

Alezya felt the pull, her feet slipping on the wet ground and her body inevitably losing balance.

She didn't have time to lower her arms, only to see the men on the other side either draw weapons and launch themselves toward them or run away, and then, her vision toppled. Ekata shouted something, and right after, Alezya's body hit the ground, not in a singular, violent shock, but instead she felt different parts of her body hit the uneven ground, causing more pain in certain areas than others.

Shouts echoed just as her head rang, and someone screamed in pain, a voice that sounded like hers, as deafening as the violent pain that hit her limbs.

The fight got louder above her, and it took her a second to recover, find the ground she'd brutally hit, and feel the tears welling in her eyes.

She barely managed to roll onto her stomach, various areas of her body protesting in atrocious pain.

When she blinked the tears away and glanced up, all she could see were limbs moving fast, weapons crashing together, and a chaos of shadows. Someone stepped on her, and she cried out, curling up on her flank.

As she tried to pull herself up, her body slid down, and pain radiated through her hand and wrist, making her wince. Alezya let out a frustrated grunt, but her survival instincts were fighting to take over; she had to move or she would be killed. It was too dark, but she knew everyone was either trying to kill her or protect her, or they were part of the silhouettes she could see darting through the trees, running away from the fight.

"There! She's there! Grab her!"

Alezya managed to get on her elbows and drag her body up, but something was wrong, and she couldn't pull her own body far. She couldn't pinpoint where the pain came from, but it was too much to move, and waves of pain kept crashing, making her cry and her head spin. When someone grabbed her wrist, she let out another scream of pain.

"Here! I got—"

The pressure on her wrist disappeared, and another high-pitched scream echoed, one that wasn't hers this time. Alezya glanced up, and much to her shock, Niiru must have jumped out of the bag at some point, because the small dragon was fangs deep into the forearm of the man who had grabbed her, and growling furiously. She didn't have time to feel an ounce of relief: the wounded man started trying to punch the young dragon's head, and after a couple of hits, Niiru let go with an angry growl, jumping down to Alezya's side.

"Niiru!" she shouted. *Go away! Fly! Go to Kein! Niiru, fly to Kein!*

But the young dragon either didn't understand or didn't want to. It remained stuck on the ground, its tail furiously swishing left and right, its body arched like an angry feline, standing all of its two feet tall between her and the man.

"Niiru, go!" she begged the dragon through her tears.

She wouldn't forgive herself if the young dragon got any more hurt here. Somewhere past her feet, she could hear the fight going on, grunts, shouts, and the furious clashing of weapons, but Alezya was in a position where she could only see upward of the valley, not toward the fight. It didn't matter; all she could focus on was the baby dragon defending her with all its tiny might.

"Niiru, please!" she cried.

"Alezya!"

She heard Ekata's voice, and the next second, someone was jumping over her and swinging a long fishing spear at the man, forcing him to step back. It took her a second to recognize Ekut's back just as his twin sister appeared at her side.

"Alezya! Oh, thank the gods, you're alive. Are you alright?"

"No," Alezya groaned. "I can't... I can't get up."

"Let me help you— Easy, baby dragon, I'm helping her!"

Niiru stopped growling at Ekata, instead turning back to Ekut, who was fighting the man, to growl in support. It gave Ekata a second to help Alezya sit up, despite the atrocious pain. The fighting was nearing its end already; the men who hadn't fled were dead or bleeding, and much to her dismay, Ekata's arm was covered in blood too, and two of the Munsa Clan's men were lying lifeless. Alezya gasped in shock.

"I'm so sorry," she cried. "This is my—"

"Oh, no," Ekata grunted. "If anyone, it's my dumb brother's fault for inviting that old stubborn fuck!"

"I told you the others insisted he come too!" Ekut groaned between two jabs of his spear. "And can we please have this fight later?! Seriously!"

"What are we going to do," Alezya muttered, her eyes still riveted on the dead men lying by the river.

"We got our message across," Ekata muttered. "Now we can only hope some of the men who fled understood and-"

She didn't get to finish her sentence; a deafening growl shook the skies.

All their heads whipped toward the skies just as a large shadow covered them. The others gasped, but a wave of hope and relief submerged Alezya, her heart making a violent leap in her chest. Orange scales flew and disappeared, another growl echoing loudly somewhere above. A few steps away from her, Niiru sat and tilted its head toward the sky, its tail swishing again curiously before it took off.

"No!" Ekata said, trying to reach the baby dragon before it flew out of hand.

But Alezya grabbed her coat, shaking her head.

"No! No, let... let Niiru go."

She wasn't sure about the connection between Niiru and Kein, but she wasn't worried. Instead, she was more frustrated by the configuration of the land they were on, which made it impossible for Kein to land. It was too steep, too narrow, and too full of trees. She knew the Munsa Clan and their allies had probably picked this spot for this very reason, and sadly, it was working; Kein couldn't land.

The relief of seeing the dragon had been so high she felt all the more disappointed, her hopes shattered after existing for a second. The dragon couldn't land and save her this time.

Ekata came back by her side, although she kept sending panicked glances toward the sky.

"Let's get out of here," she muttered, a bit late. "Before those bastards bring reinforcements..."

Something cracked loudly nearby.

On the other side of the river, a couple of fights were still going on besides Ekut's, but everyone stopped and froze at the strange sounds coming their way, an ominous feeling filling the air. There were more noises of wood brutally creaking, a heavy thud, and then crisp steps on the rocks. Something large and heavy was coming toward them, and their steps were far too steady on the treacherous ground.

To her credit, Ekata extended a shaking hand before Alezya, and everyone turned their weapons south. The steps got closer, and everyone held their breaths as a large silhouette busted through the trees.

"Kassein?" Alezya gasped, unable to believe her eyes.

The man himself stood on the other side of the river, his eyes darker than ever before. In a split second, those dark irises met Alezya's teary, shocked ones, and she saw him slowly take in her state, lying on the river bed, probably not looking good at all.

His eyes went from dark to hellish, and the nearest man hadn't had a chance to move yet when Kassein kicked him brutally in the torso, sending him crashing down the rocks. Somewhere above their heads, Kein echoed his master's fury with another deafening growl.

Kassein had just turned around when several men suddenly stepped out of the trees, long blades drawn, and Alezya couldn't guess if they'd been waiting to ambush or if the foreign clans' reinforcements had arrived at the worst possible moment. Either way, their timing was most unfortunate, as they ran right in Kassein's path.

They hesitated for a second, before one of them launched themselves at him; he didn't even get to finish his attack when Kassein's large sword swung, and a limb flew.

"Oh, gods..." Ekata muttered.

Alezya was thinking the same. As much as she was relieved to see him, she had never seen Kassein look so furious or so terrifying.

He moved slowly, like a predator amongst prey, dominating the whole area effortlessly with his sole presence. He was simply walking, taking a couple of steps to place himself between Alezya and the incoming men, and yet no one dared to move an inch. Their eyes were riveted on him with a mix of raw fear and sheer terror, almost too scared to even blink.

Alezya swallowed slowly. The scene had gone so eerily quiet that she could hear her own frantic heartbeat and Ekata's panted breaths.

The realization hit her: those men were all going to die. They had come as reinforcements to save men who were already dead or dying, and they were all going to die. And judging by the ice-cold tension and the seconds that passed with everyone perfectly still, none of them were too eager to meet this god of death.

"K-Kassein," she muttered, her voice breaking a little.

He slowly pivoted his head just enough that his eye met hers over his shoulder. It was the first time Alezya felt so much apprehension toward this man, and yet, she didn't flinch.

"*D-don't,*" she muttered. "*Don't hunt them.*"

She didn't have the exact word for "kill," but she knew he would understand. She waited a couple more seconds before she redirected her eyes to the men who'd emerged from the trees, the ones who had survived the previous fight, and the ones who were stepping away from Ekut, crossing the river to join the others. Ekata supported her as she fought the pain to sit up.

"I'll let you go," she hissed, glaring at all of them with tears in her eyes. "I'll prove what your clan leaders don't want to believe. The Dragon Clan doesn't want to kill you. This man could kill you all, but he won't because I can ask him not to. Tell your clan leaders that if they follow my father and choose to fight, you won't survive. Tell them to choose whether you all die or live."

A few seconds of silence followed her words, before Ekata scoffed.

"Didn't you hear her? Fuck off!"

Her voice seemed to jerk a couple of men into moving, and then, progressively, they all stepped away toward the trees, disappearing one after another. Alezya watched until all of them were gone, and Kassein glared at the tree line for a few seconds longer.

Then, he spun around and ran to her.

"Kassein," she whispered.

"Alezya."

He dropped to his knees next to her, immediately brushing Ekata's hands aside to take her in his arms. One arm wrapped around her back to support her, while the other began checking her body for injuries, his eyes scanning every inch of her.

But Alezya had momentarily forgotten about the pain, too relieved to see him to care. She lifted her hands to his face, an overwhelming wave of relief filling her like never before. Only once she touched his face did she confirm that he was truly there, tears of happiness filling her eyes.

He pressed a long kiss to her forehead, and she closed her eyes, taking in his scent, her limbs relaxing as his familiar smell surrounded her. He was sweaty, and he looked like hell, but he was there for her, not an ounce of resentment to be seen, and that was all she needed.

Suddenly, while Kassein held her, something flashed to the top of her mind, and Alezya urgently patted his arm.

"*Kassein, my baby,*" she said, trying to remember his language as fast as she needed to ask. "*Lumie, my baby. Did you—*"

But his hand interrupted her, cupping her cheek and jawline, and before she could get another word out, Kassein pressed his lips against hers urgently, desperately, kissing her like he needed it to survive.

Alezya's body immediately reacted, her heart jumping in her chest, her stomach twirling excitedly. She felt the heat of his strong, firm hold warm up her entire body in a matter of seconds, like hot lava pouring over her. She was exhausted, she had been cold every day she'd been away from him, and Kassein's embrace was washing all the hardships and discomfort away. Alezya barely found room to breathe, let alone speak a word. Kassein's thick lips were relentlessly tasting hers as if they'd been apart for months, not days.

When she finally found the strength and willpower to gently push his chest away, not making a dent in his position but clearly indicating she needed a break, he reluctantly pulled back, breaking their kiss with a lingering pout.

"Kassein," she breathed. "*My baby. Lumie.*"

"*With Lorey,*" he pressed his large hands against her cheeks, cupping her face again. "*Lumie is with Lorey. She's fine.*"

He gave her a strong, determined nod, and after an extra second of looking into his dark green eyes, Alezya let out a long sigh of relief, the last ounce of pressure vanishing off her shoulders. She allowed herself to go limp in his embrace, some final tears escaping her eyes.

Her baby was fine and safe with Lorey. Kein had saved her.

She had tried to believe it until now, but it was nothing compared to the relief of knowing, for sure, that her baby girl was fine somewhere. Kassein's hand moved to hold her neck, his thumbs gently caressing her hair as he kissed her temple.

"*She is like snow,*" he whispered into her ear, "*and she is like you.*"

"*It's my baby,*" she let out a broken laugh between her tears, wishing they had more vocabulary to say everything that needed to be said about her baby.

She looked up at Kassein, and he was smiling down at her, a smile so rare and gentle she couldn't help but mimic it back.

"*She is yours,*" he whispered. "*So small. So white. She is hassna.*"

"*What is hassna?*" Alezya frowned.

"*Like you,*" he whispered. "*You're hassna.*"

The way he looked at her, his thumb caressing her cheek and his eyes filled with something dangerously akin to admiration, made her blush. Whatever *hassna* was, it seemed like a very good thing. Alezya let out a long sigh of relief, and let Kassein hug her again, more tenderly, pressing the side of her face against his strong torso. This position had to be uncomfortable for him, but she didn't care at that moment.

She had almost forgotten how warm his skin was, but she never wanted to part ways with him again. Then, he put his arms under her back and knees, and lifted her effortlessly.

A sudden loud growl made her jump against his torso, and Alezya turned her head to see Ekut, who had walked up to them at some point, had just fallen backward, bum in the water, while Kein was growling somewhere above their heads.

She couldn't see it, but Alezya could feel the dragon's silver eyes on them from above, and she guessed it had landed on some cliff nearby. Kein growled some more, and the orange dragon sounded upset.

"I-I didn't—" Ekut fumbled, his terrified eyes looking for the source of the sound.

"*Kein, tawa.*" Alezya said to the air above them.

Kein let out another angry growl, but a second later, there was a loud, sharp flap of wings. Alezya guessed he had simply repositioned himself, perhaps onto a higher cliff to better watch over them. She felt a stab of regret she couldn't hug Kein's warm scales too, but there was no space for a dragon to land here.

Still, she could hear Niiru's chirpy growls in the distance and guessed the younger dragon was zipping around Kein, playing in the air.

"*Kassein,*" she said. "*You...*"

Her words died in her throat as she noticed his state and, more worryingly, a thin trail of dried blood on his skin. Her blood went cold, panicking. She tried to pull back a bit to take him all in, and realized his hands were covered in dried blood, and he had some on his face too.

"*Kassein*," she said, her panic rising again. "*You... hunt? Who?*"

His expression suddenly went serious, his anger palpable.

"*Men*," he hissed. "*Men who hurt you.*"

He took her forearm and lifted it, showing the cuts and bruises she'd gotten from her fall. Upon spotting some dried blood on her wrist, Kassein frowned and immediately brought it to his lips, licking the dried blood off her. Alezya blushed; his intimate demonstration suddenly reminded her of where they stood, and the two pairs of eyes witnessing this interaction. She pulled her wrist away, leaving Kassein to lick his lips in a movement that did something to her lower belly.

Ekut was still ass-deep in the water, but Ekata was staring at Kassein with an amused expression and suggestively biting her lower lip.

"Damn, now I know how you learned their language that fast," she teased, her eyes riveted on Kassein's torso. "I would have tried hard to ride *that* dragon too."

Alezya tried to ignore the violent pang of jealousy that hit her.

After all, she was the one carried in Kassein's possessive arms, and Kein, still looming above, wasn't allowing Ekut to move an inch closer to her either; His fierce glares made that perfectly clear.

Therefore, she grabbed Kassein's hand, exchanging a glance with him, before she addressed Ekata and Ekut.

"This is the Dragon Clan Chief," she explained, wiping her tears with her free hand. "Their *Aqayir.* His name is Kassein."

"Alezya."

She turned her eyes back to Kassein, who was staring at her intently, his eyes full of questions. She wished she had learned his word for "sorry," but right now, that was all she could do.

Kassein stared at her some more, and she took a deep breath, trying to sort her thoughts quickly. Alezya had been so determined to get back to Kassein first that she hadn't had much time to think about what would come after that. Then, his eyes drifted to the Munsa men who'd survived the fight and were trying to step closer, turning into something much fiercer, much more dangerous.

Immediately sensing the danger, Alezya put a hand on his cheek.

"*No*," she said. "*No. They are friends.*"

She could almost feel the tension drop as Kassein's gaze softened and drifted back to her. She smiled to let him know she was alright.

"*Where is Kiera? And Lorey?*"

"*Lorey with Lumie. At Kalat Unshreik,*" he said. "*Kiera in the mountains. With the men.*"

Alezya was shocked Lumie was there and not with his clan.

Was it because he didn't want to take her baby in the mountains with them? Or to be sure she would be safe and comfortable with Lorey? Either way, she was more grateful than ever.

"With Kiki?" Alezya asked. *"And dragons?"*

Kassein gave her an affirmative nod. So his sister had been with him attacking the clans... Now that he was finally there, Alezya didn't even know where to begin. They had only been separated for days, but it felt like so much had happened since she'd left him again.

She took a deep breath and turned to Ekata, Ekut, and the rest of the Munsa Clan, who had their eyes riveted on them.

"Can you ask their clan leader?" Ekut asked. "To... leave us alone?"

"Kein won't attack you now," Alezya said.

She turned back to Kassein.

"Kassein, this is Munsa Clan," she said before pointing at the pair of siblings. *"The Aqayir of the Munsa Clan. The man is Ekut, and the woman is Ekata."*

He barely took a second to glance at them before returning his focus to her.

Truthfully, Alezya didn't need the Munsa Clan's help anymore, now that Kassein had found her. She could have just flown away with them, back to the Dragon Clan, and this would all be over. She would be safe, free to leave the clans to their infighting.

And yet, the very second the relief hit her with that thought, she knew she couldn't do that. Not after they had rescued her from the crevice, fed and sheltered her, and after all that time she had spent with those people hiding her from the other clans at their own expense. Not after they had shared concerns about what her father could do, what he had done to the Lumiata, and how he threatened a lot more clans.

She couldn't just fly away and abandon everything here. Softly, Alezya let out a resigned sigh and tapped Kassein's shoulder, gesturing for him to let her down. At first, he didn't want to, giving her a frown, but after a second, he gently let her down, although his arms were still firmly locked to support her. Strangely, standing up didn't come with the waves of pain that she had expected. She was still in pain, but compared to minutes ago, the pain had strangely subsided.

"Alezya?" Ekata called her with a bewildered expression. "You're aware you have... some... I mean, what looks like dragon scales appearing on your skin?"

Alezya blinked at her, confused by Ekata's words for a few seconds.

Then, her eyes followed the woman's confused gaze, and much to her shock, she indeed found a trail of white scales growing on her wrist, right where she was certain she'd had a large cut just minutes ago.

Her jaw dropped, and she couldn't suppress the need to touch it with her fingers. It felt like scabs, and she was tempted to scratch to see if they came off, but instead, she was mesmerized as she saw more of her wound turn into snow-white scales. Alezya gasped, and immediately, clocked other parts of her body; a lot was covered by her clothes, which were now dirty, but upon inspecting her other hand and wrist, she found more white scales. She turned to Kassein for an answer, and he didn't seem surprised at all when she lifted the former wound for him to see; he only grabbed her hand softly.

"This?" she gasped. "*Kassein, what is this?*"

"*Dragon,*" he said. "*Dragon Blood.*"

"*I'm not a dragon!*"

"*No. Baby.*"

She didn't understand what nonsense he meant, and for a second, she even thought she'd understood the wrong word. But then, Kassein did the last movement she expected; he spread his hand wide on her stomach.

Alezya frowned, but he stared at her earnestly.

"*Baby,*" he said. "*You, Alezya. You have my baby.*"

She let out a nervous, confused chuckle.

"*No,*" she said. "*No, Kassein. I can't. I'm not with baby.*"

"*You are. My child and Alezya's child.*"

"*No,*" she insisted, although her confidence was slowly decomposing. "I... No. No way, Kassein. You couldn't already know even if I was truly pregnant!"

Even if she had reverted to her own language out of frustration, Kassein patiently caressed her scales with his index finger, his calm green eyes riveted on her, his other hand cupping her cheek.

"*Yes,*" he said. "*You're with child. The baby gives Alezya dragon skin. And Kein has an egg too.*"

"*Kein has an egg?*" she repeated, shocked. "*A... baby dragon's egg?*"

Kassein gave her a nod, the hint of a smile on his lips.

"*Alezya's baby dragon,*" he whispered, stepping closer. "*Our baby.*"

Alezya felt like the ground was falling underneath her. Was she pregnant? She had only had sex with Kassein once! Granted, it had been one very nice time, but what were the odds of her falling pregnant? She was so shocked it took her a second to remember the herbs.

"*No, no,*" she shook her head. "*Kassein, I ate medicinal herbs. I can't have a baby.*"

"*Medicinal herb?*" He frowned.

"*Yes. With Lorey. The medicinal herbs, I ate herbs to not have a baby!*"

"...Is everything alright?" Ekata asked, sounding worried.

"No," Alezya sighed. "I mean... I-I don't know."

She was utterly confused. If Kassein was right and she was pregnant, how much worse would that make things? They were pretty much at war, her clan had banished her, and most of the other clans wanted her dead!

Alezya closed her eyes for a second, and focused on Kassein's warm hands on her. She knew things were different from the last time she'd gotten pregnant. Kassein was by her side, and he wouldn't reject her. She wasn't at the mercy of her clan anymore, and Lumie was safe. Even if she was pregnant, the baby had just proven it could survive a brutal fall and even heal her wounds... As incredible as it sounded.

Alezya slowly reopened her eyes, gazing at the wounds, or what they now looked like. White dragon scales... and they were too real. Could an unborn child truly do such a thing?

She dared to glance up at Kassein. There was now a slight line between his eyebrows, and she knew he was worried about her reaction. She was sorry, but how could she not have been shocked, and underprepared for such news?

Still, Alezya forced herself to calm down. Even if she was pregnant, the child was very small, and she had months before it would be born unless the Dragon Clan's babies had more surprises in tow. And Kassein was there, by her side, and she knew she could trust him.

After another few seconds, she schooled her expression and tilted her head to press a soft kiss on his lips. Kassein relaxed a little, although his green eyes were still scrutinizing her.

She was trying to think of what to tell him and how when, in the distance, they heard shouts and male voices. As they were not speaking the Dragon Clan language, Alezya guessed the foreign clans were coming in this direction. Either someone else had spotted the gathering, or the men from before were bringing reinforcements. Either way, she didn't want to stay and find out.

"We have to go," Ekata said, echoing her thoughts.

"Let's go back," Alezya said, just when Kassein was pulling her in a different direction.

It hit her then that he wanted to take her where Kein would reach them, to bring her back to his clan.

For a second, Alezya was very tempted to follow him. But, first, would they have the time? Their assailants could be heard approaching fast, and even if Alezya didn't lack faith in Kassein's fighting skills, the Munsa Clan's men were exhausted. If there was another battle, they could lose more, and they might not even make it back to their tunnels, and that would be on her conscience.

Moreover, their plan was now known. They'd told other clan members who had fled, and they had been seen with her. If Alezya left them now, the Munsa Clan would still be known as the clan that had allied with the Dragon Clan. Now that others had seen Kassein with them and how they had defended her, they couldn't go back to how things were before, to them being just some neutral clan...

"Alezya, we have to move," Ekata insisted.

Alezya made her decision in a split second. She turned to Kassein, grabbed his face, and kissed him. It wasn't one of their soft kisses. It was a strong, determined kiss, one of the few where she was the one leading.

She didn't even give him the time to respond. Alezya pulled away, she intertwined her fingers with Kassein, and she pulled him toward the Munsa twins. Her clutch wasn't so strong that he couldn't get away, and she marked a clear stop, turning back to him with pleading eyes.

"...*With me?*" she asked, at a lack for better words.

Thankfully, Kassein only took a glance at her, at the Munsa, and he nodded. Alezya felt a wave of relief, but she didn't have time to linger. Pulling

Kassein with her, she walked up to Ekata.

"Let's go," she urged her.

"Really? We're taking... the Dragon Clan Chief to our clan?" Ekata asked, although they were all already moving.

"They know," Alezya said, trying to breathe as they quickly trekked their way back. "The other clans know you have me, and they've seen him. Your clan might be attacked in the next hours, Ekata. We need to get back to your people right now."

Realization seemed to dawn on the twins, who exchanged a nervous glance, before everyone accelerated.

"Alright, but what are we trying to accomplish by bringing him?" Ekut asked.

"I need to explain to him," Alezya said. "I need to tell him there are clans who do not want to fight the Dragon Clan, and then he can— Oh, no, I forgot Niiru. Niiru!"

She called after the young dragon, somewhat unwilling to let it wander on its own. She didn't doubt Kein, but Niiru was a small dragon and the mountains were vast, and somehow, she felt responsible for it.

Thankfully, she only had to call the young dragon twice before a little dark arrow landed ahead, jumping excitedly on the rocks ahead of them.

"...Niiru?" Kassein asked behind her, a light teasing tone in his voice.

Alezya turned back to see a rare grin on his lips, and she blushed.

"*I don't know the baby dragon's name,*" she said.

"*The name is Niiru,*" he said matter of factly.

He was going along with her choice then, and Alezya found herself pleased but also confused. Didn't that young dragon have a name already? Wasn't it one of his nephew's dragons or something?

She didn't have time to ask more, unfortunately. They were rushing to get back inside the tunnels, too aware of the enemies somewhere behind them and trying to catch up before they made it to the tunnels. How secret was the entrance the Munsa had used? What were the chances they would be followed inside and tracked all the way back to their homes?

They didn't have time to wonder, and they had to rush either way. Alezya heard Kein growl angrily above them, and she sure hoped that would deter their enemies from rushing to their deaths. With Kassein right behind her, supporting her waist every time she showed the first sign of slipping on the rocks, she managed to follow the Munsa twins and their incredible pace back to the tunnels.

The pain was gradually leaving her body, and she was aware of the white scales that felt like dry skin, but she didn't have time to think about it. Alezya was blindly climbing and rushing behind Ekata, feeling like the journey back took twice as long than it did on their way down, until finally, they reached a cave. The twins ran inside first, and with Kassein still behind her, Alezya followed them, the surviving Munsa Clan men closing their reduced group.

This time, they were in the dark, but the twins didn't seem to have much trouble navigating the tunnels, and after Alezya stumbled for the second time, nearly hitting a wall, Ekata grabbed her hand to guide her. She could feel Kassein behind her, and strangely, his large frame didn't seem to slow him at all.

When she felt his hand block her head from hitting a rock above, she realized he could somehow see in the dark, another thing to add to his strange half-dragon self.

"Alezya."

Kassein gently pulled on her hand, making her stop, and their entire group came to a halt. She turned around, her free hand finding his bicep under his cloak, effortlessly finding the heat of his body.

"Alezya?" Ekata asked. "What's going on?"

They got the beginning of an answer seconds later. A heavy, loud sound echoed above their heads and throughout the mountain.

Alezya instinctively stepped into Kassein's embrace, and he locked an arm around her, but she didn't find him tense at all. Then, she heard Kein's loud growl, followed by loud thuds, like several heavy things were hitting the ground, and somewhere in the distance, the very faint sound of screams. Male voices screaming. It took her just a moment to recognize the sound of rocks breaking and piece everything together.

"A landslide!" she gasped. "Kein broke some rocks above the opening; I think he provoked a landslide to seal the entrance to this tunnel!"

"The dragon?" Ekata muttered, fear in her voice. "It's... aware we're inside, right?"

"We're far enough, now," Alezya noted, trying to glance back into the darkness. "Even if some men got in, at least more can't follow us..."

"I hope you're right," Ekut said, "but there are way more tunnels leading home; we have to hurry up."

Their group resumed their journey back to the Munsa Clan, progressing quickly and keeping an ear out for men who had followed them into the tunnels; fortunately, if any men had, they didn't manage to catch up, or they were lost in the maze of tunnels. Alezya was following the twins, but she would have been completely lost on her own.

After a while, they finally found an opening and some fresh air, and the Munsa Clan managed to light up torches to illuminate the last portion of their journey. Now that they had light and could walk faster, it didn't take them long to finally return to the Munsa Clan's cave, and Niiru darted ahead as soon as the young dragon recognized the area.

The relief of being back only lasted seconds, as Ekut tensed as soon as they stepped into the large cave their clan used as a main area, the one with the bay.

"...Strangers," he muttered.

Alezya turned her head, and indeed, there was a large crowd gathered near the elders and some fighters of the Munsa Clan. Alezya guessed the large group was composed of representatives of at least half a dozen different clans, probably more. It was hard to tell in the sea of foreign faces. Ekata let out a faint sigh of relief after a few seconds.

"Those are our allies," she explained to Alezya. "Those we trust unconditionally. We had sent messengers to explain the situation to them. I guess they decided to move at night. There's no risk that *those men* will turn on us."

"I told you I did not invite the Habash Clan!" Ekut protested. "They invited themselves with another–"

"I don't care," his sister retorted. "You're in charge of telling the families of the men we lost, Ekut."

He grimaced, shaking his head with annoyance.

Alezya was a bit surprised he didn't fight his sister harder, but she was starting to wrap her head around their strange co-chiefs position. Ekata truly acted as his equal, and Ekut was letting her take charge in some matters. Thus, he stepped aside, most likely to find someone to send word of the deceased, while Ekata walked up to the group of their elders. Rather than follow her, Alezya turned around to Kassein. He already had his eyes on her, showing very little interest in everything else that was going on around them. She took a deep breath and tried to explain, pointing a finger toward the twins and the rest of their clan.

"Munsa Clan," she said. *"They're my friends. They gave me food."*

Kassein nodded slowly and glanced around the cave before his eyes returned to her. Alezya licked her lower lip, trying to think of a way to quickly explain things with her limited vocabulary.

"My home mountain," she said. *"They... hunt me. Again."*

He frowned, and she could almost feel the anger rising in waves from him, so she gently put her hands on his biceps to ground him with her. She noticed again that he was completely shirtless under his cloak, and she wondered why he wasn't wearing his protective gear. Had he taken it off before he and Kein had come to her rescue? Did he not even need it to fight the clans? Alezya shook her head, forcing herself to focus.

"My home mountain, they are the Deklaan Clan."

"Deklaan Clan?"

"Yes. My clan. *Their name is* Deklaan Clan. *You hunted them. Before."*

"Your home," he said, frowning again. *"I saw it. Lumie and Alezya's home. Small."*

Her throat tightened. Had he found the small cave she had lived in with Lumie? She felt strange, thinking about that place. It was a small and uncomfortable cave she had found, but she had tried to make it as hospitable as possible for her and her baby. To think that Kassein had seen it was more than a strange feeling. She couldn't even imagine his body going through the small tunnel she'd had to crawl in to get in there every time... She gave him a little nod, but looked down, embarrassed.

"*Yes. Lumie and mine.*"

Kassein didn't let her get away with hiding and gently cupped her cheek, pulling her to look up again, and pressed another long kiss on her forehead. His warmth spread throughout her whole body. Alezya knew they didn't have the luxury of spending time thoroughly enjoying their reunion, but she still leaned a bit more into him before she cleared her throat and looked up to talk to him again.

"*The* Deklaan Clan, *they hunt me,*" she said. "*They hunt the Dragon* Clan *too, and they hunt the* Munsa Clan. *My friends.*"

Kassein barely glanced at the people behind her, but Alezya knew he understood.

"*They are friends,*" she said. "*The* Munsa Clan *are friends. Kein can't hunt them.*"

"*Yes,*" Kassein nodded. "*Kein obeys you.*"

Alezya smiled. She had truly needed this kind of affirmation lately. After all the hardships of the past few days, knowing that the biggest dragon in the area still obeyed her will was the kind of good news she needed to hear.

"*...Come,*" she said, gently pulling his hand.

Kassein didn't resist at all, letting her pull him along toward the gathering that was happening.

Alezya was well aware of all the pairs of intrigued, scared, or confused eyes on them, but she had to keep the end goal in mind: save the clans, go back to Lumie, and end her father's madness. It felt like a daunting task, but with Kassein by her side and his Dragon Clan as their allies, it was far from impossible. She reached the group, who now all had eyes on her and her companion; the Munsa Clan elders seemed utterly stunned, and the representatives of the other clans even more so, not hiding the fear and uneasiness in their expressions.

Alezya wasn't sure where to start, but luckily for her, Ekata spoke first.

"Everyone," she said, "this is Alezya. She is Darak's daughter and one of the Lumiata. We rescued her after that bastard threw her in a crevice after the last gathering, and we have been hiding her ever since. As you already know, we are trying to rally as many clans as possible against Darak's madness. We never wanted to fight the Dragon Clan in the first place, but now, thanks to Alezya, we also know that they never had any intention to fight us either."

"...So she really speaks their language?" a young clan leader Alezya had never seen before asked.

"She does," Alezya replied with a stern expression, annoyed he spoke like she wasn't there.

He blushed, shocked about her tone, and gave her a nervous glance before his eyes darted to Kassein, and he returned to avoiding their general direction entirely. Kassein, standing behind her, half a head taller than anybody else, definitely intimidated everyone present, and maybe Alezya wouldn't have been so bold without him standing like her shadow.

There were clan leaders twice his age and at least thirty male fighters standing, but everyone seemed equally scared to even look their way. That put a faint smile on Alezya's lips, and she leaned until her back was against his torso, his large hand on her hip.

"She truly does," Ekut added as he arrived at his sister's side. "Hence their leader, the Dragon Tyr—I mean, their Clan Chief, agreed to follow us back. We can negotiate with them. We have a chance to stop all the fighting."

"But Darak won't stop," said another clan leader. "I was at a gathering he held just hours ago. This man and several other clans believe they can trap the Dragon Clan in the mountain and kill them if they raise a big enough army. I've heard a dozen clans pledge allegiance to him!"

"It's true," another man said. "I've heard the Exkiu, Farghi, Upatkyaa, Huvo, Hamirri, and Taisja Clans already agreed to join him."

"The Tuul, Huippi, and Havitja too," someone else added.

Alezya paled; even if she didn't know half of those, she knew that was a lot of clans. She had been confident knowing that Kassein's army was slowly kicking clans out of their mountains and showing effortless dominance, but could they win against so many clans? And that was just those who had joined her father! She knew there were more that might have agreed to his plan since or might still be on the fence.

There were many mountains and probably almost as many clans. What if hundreds of people joined the fight? Kassein's men were in foreign territory, and he couldn't have brought his entire clan up there. What if, actually, her father's madness did stand a chance? What was she getting all of these clans into? Kassein had begun fighting because of her, and now, every clan in the mountains was picking sides. This was going to turn into an all-out war between the clans, with dragons added in the midst!

If it wasn't for Kassein firmly holding her waist and his reassuring heat against her back, Alezya might have seriously panicked. But instead, she tried to swallow her increasing anxiety and listened.

"That's not good, and more people than we expected..." Ekata frowned, echoing her thoughts. "What about those who didn't pledge allegiance to him?"

One of the younger clan leaders grimaced.

"I... I told him I needed time to think," he admitted. "His speech was enticing, Ekata. It wasn't just about slaying the dragon and getting rid of the Dragon Clan, but being one big, united clan like we've all dreamed of. He talked about trades between the clans, the safety of traveling from one area to another, sharing passageways... He even told us about taking over the wealth of the Dragon Clan, that winning this war would make us richer than ever before once we conquered the lower lands."

Alezya snorted.

"Let me guess," she said. "My father would be the one leading this new grand clan?"

"He... did imply something like that," the man sheepishly admitted. "We thought all of it kind of sounded too... idealistic, especially coming from a man like Darak. He gave us until dawn to think about it and send a response, hence we hurried to meet you in person rather than sending scouts. If we don't give him a response quickly, who knows how he will react..."

"Ugh," Ekata rolled her eyes. "Men."

She exchanged a look with another older woman in the group, who nodded. Her twin brother sighed, turning back to Alezya.

"...Truthfully, we never planned to be involved in a battle of this scale either. We only saved you in the hopes you could ask the Dragon Clan to spare us, but obviously, things are evolving beyond our control. Now the other clans will know we have you, and the word will spread quickly that we... I mean, I guess we're sort of allies with the Dragon Clan. At least, that's probably what they will think, meaning that we cannot back away."

"And we won't," his sister frowned.

"We won't," Ekut nodded. "...But can we trust them? Trust him?"

Several glances shifted above her head to Kassein, and Alezya felt him tense behind her. She turned to him, holding his hand tight.

"*These are friends,*" she said in his language, triggering some surprised gasps behind her. "*They are the* Munsa Clan, *and other* clans, *from other mountains. The* Deklaan Clan, *my home* clan, *they hunt them. They can be friends with Dragon* Clan?*"

Alezya knew her grammar was probably disastrous, but it mattered little as long as she got the message across. Kassein observed her for a long time, not giving a glance at the dozens of pairs of eyes on him.

"*...Friends with Alezya?*"

"*Yes,*" she replied instinctively. "*The* Munsa Clan, *they are my friends. Their friends are my friends too. They want to be friends with your Dragon* Clan.*"

Kassein's eyes lifted from hers to look behind her, and Alezya stepped aside to see how the clans' representatives would react.

To her surprise, after a couple of awkward seconds, several of them lowered their heads in an unequivocal, universal sign of submission.

It made Alezya choke up a little, for some reason. Her people, all the clans, had been terrified of the Dragon Clan for generations. They called Kassein and his relatives dragon tyrants; they'd been terrified of his family and their dragons their entire lives, and yet, right now, they were standing within inches of him and willingly putting their lives in his hands.

She knew it wasn't much of a choice for them, and yet, she found herself a bit happy that they were choosing to trust this stranger over her father. All because of her, one woman who had been the first to approach the Dragon Clan, learn their language, and... trust Kassein.

Alezya hadn't had a choice in many of those things, with how events had unfolded, and a lot of it had merely been for the sake of her and Lumie's survival, but it didn't change the outcome.

"Are we good?" Ekata asked after a beat. "I mean, I'm glad he's... here and willing to listen, but I think we need to get moving quickly. The word is going to spread fast, and we have a lot to do. Find more allies, move our people to a safer area, and decide what to do against Darak... We can't stay here."

"I agree," Ekut nodded. "Darak is going to hear what happened and understand we're allying with the Dragon Clan; there's no turning back now. We have to move to the Dragon Clan's position before they get to us."

"Wait! There are more clans who will be willing to listen," one of the younger clan leaders suddenly stepped forward. "If we can spread the word, we might rally more. Many don't believe much in the Deklaan Clan but feel like there's no other alternative. If we let them know..."

"It's going to be complicated," Ekata muttered. "We're running out of time already. If we wait for everyone to make up their minds..."

"No, but we don't have to wait," Alezya stepped forward. "Look, even if the men we fought go to my father's or his allies tonight, they won't attack us right away. He was expecting an answer from the clans by dawn, right? Let's do the same. We don't need to wait for each clan; just send scouts and spread the word that your clans have allied with the Dragon Clan and that there is an alternative to rallying with the Deklaan. If they know there's an alternative, they might rally around us. We don't even need them to fight Darak with us, only not to fight against the Dragon Clan. I refuse to cause more casualties than necessary. Let them flee or hide if they want; I'd rather them hide and survive than be forced into a meaningless battle they never wanted to risk their people with. My father was always willing to risk other people's lives rather than his own; I refuse to do the same. People should be allowed to step away from a war they didn't choose."

There were a few seconds of stunned silence after her words, and Ekata gave her a proud smile.

"Spoken like a true survivor and fighter," she smiled before turning to the men. "You heard her. Let all the clans know what we're doing since there's no hiding it from our enemies. Darak might convince a lot of clans, but many will be tempted to step away if they can. Those who want to fight with us are welcome too. Let it be known to all the clans, not just the big ones. Send scouts to every corner of the mountains, no matter how long it takes, and be sure the word is spread. If we're fighting for the future of all clans, they should know."

"We will spread the word," one of the clan leaders said, and many nodded in agreement. "Give us time to move our people away from Darak, warn our allies, and I promise my warriors and I will join the fight against this madman. We've wanted peace with the Dragon Clan for generations, one way or another. If it is as simple as this, if we can finally get it, this is worth one last battle."

"I agree," another clan leader said, crossing his arms. "Enough of this nonsense and enough of sending our men to die! Enough of Darak! If the Dragon Clan leader is reasonable enough to listen to a woman, what have we lost our sons for?"

"None of us want to fight alongside Darak," one chimed in. "I'm sure some clans will refuse to fight at all if they can."

"...Are you sure the Dragon Clan won't attack us?" someone else asked, eyes drifting between Alezya and Kassein. "Are you certain you understand this man?"

Alezya hesitated for a second, and then she glanced toward the lake, the one with the large entrance toward the sea. Then, she turned back to Kassein. He gave her a slight nod. She wasn't sure if he understood what she wanted to do or if he was just saying yes to anything she would ask, but anyway, she turned to the lake, holding his hand.

"Kein!" she shouted into the cave.

Her call echoed through the rocky walls, and for a few seconds, a stunned silence befell the large area.

Niiru was the first to move. The young dragon, which had been playing around in the water and primarily unnoticed until then, stood on all fours, head perked up, its tail swishing excitedly. Some men who hadn't noticed the small, dark dragon until then let out surprised gasps and shocked whispers, but they hadn't seen anything yet. Alezya couldn't suppress a smile when a loud, menacing growl shook the entire cave, making the whole group of men jump and take several steps away for some. Behind her, she felt Kassein's torso press against her back again, his fingers tightening around hers.

Then, at the low entrance of their cave, Kein appeared.

The bronze dragon's head peeked in first, and then, as it spotted Alezya, the dragon slowly crawled its way inside, triggering some panic among the crowd. Thankfully, all children were long in bed by now, hence Niiru had found no playmates in the water, but there were plenty of adults present, the Munsa and their visitors, who all let out a concert of shouts, screams, and for some, freaked out enough to run into the nearest tunnel. Kassein's hands didn't move, but after a beat, Alezya gave him a little smile over her shoulder before she stepped out of his embrace and toward the water.

Kein was slowly crawling its way inside, belly-deep in the water, its silver eyes scouring the area with interest. It was no wonder the dragon couldn't have spotted this cave before; it was facing the sea at the northeastern end of the continent, the farthest away from its home, and its humongous body could barely fit through the opening. The cave wasn't even large enough for its wingspan. Did the dragon find it now because Kassein was there, and it could sense its owner? Had it just found the entrance following her voice since it had been in the area post-battle? Alezya didn't know, but she was grateful to see her scaled friend there.

While everyone else but Kassein was still frozen in fear, Alezya alone marched toward the dragon, not fearless but feeling braver than ever.

She hadn't seen Kein in a while, and although she had missed the dragon, she was still aware it was a giant beast that didn't think like humans. It might have forgotten her, or it might be more resentful than Kassein for how they'd parted ways. She had simply entrusted the dragon with her child and barked at it to fly away... It wouldn't be outlandish for Kein to be mad at her.

And yet, when she took her first steps in the water, the orange dragon let out a soft, long, gentle growl that made her smile. Alezya only had to extend her hand, and seconds later, Kein approached, pressing its hot snout against it.

"Hello, my friend," she smiled. "I missed you."

The dragon let out another growl and approached even closer, letting Alezya pet its neck as it curled its large body around her.

In the meantime, Niiru had already made its way to the giant dragon and was now fiercely trying to climb the mountain of scales. It made Alezya chuckle at the sight of the tiny black dragon trying to climb Kein, who was eyeing it curiously. When Niiru lost balance and rolled down the orange scales, only to land in a splash of water, Kein put its snout in the water and suddenly sneezed a wave at the young dragon. Niiru let out an amused growl, rolling and jumping in the water, before it ran back toward Kein, unafraid, only to be grabbed in its maw and sent flying into the water with another splash. Niiru jumped out of the water and ran back toward Kein for another round.

Meanwhile, Alezya smiled, petting her dragon friend.

"Thank you," she whispered, pressing herself against its warm body.

Then, she turned toward the crowd gathered on the bank of the body of water while she pressed her body against Kein's, its scales warming her back. Everyone was watching her like she was absolutely mad, their eyes wide in disbelief.

"This is Kein," she said, the cave echoing her voice. "One of the dragons we've learned to fear our entire lives. And yet, when it could have killed me many times, this dragon saved my life, saved my baby's life. He's never hurt me either, and he is my friend now."

She could see all of their stunned expressions, watching her stand fearlessly next to the incredible beast. Kein was still busy entertaining Niiru's shenanigans, its snout pushing the young dragon around in the water. Now that she could witness it entertaining a young dragon a fraction of its size, Alezya could barely remember how much she had once been terrified of Kein. It was like the day its silver eyes had pinned her against the mountain, so sure she was about to die, was forever ago, but the truth was, it had merely been a few weeks.

Now, she trusted Kein far more than she trusted most men.

"He doesn't eat humans," she said. "Well, not to feed himself. The only time I've seen him do so was when some men assaulted me. Men from the Dragon Clan, and I'm sure it attacked men from the Deklaan Clan who hurt me too. If I asked, it would attack you too."

There were a few shocked reactions, and some now seemed to back away from her as much as they were scared of the dragon. Only the Munsa Clan seemed unafraid. Kassein was standing with his arms crossed, his toes inches from the water, his eyes riveted on her at all times.

She gave him a little smile, thankful for his endless patience.

"Why does it... obey you?" a man asked. "C-could it obey someone else?"

Alezya knew there was probably a longer, more complex explanation that lay in her relationship with Kassein. She glanced at him again and slowly detached herself from the dragon to close the distance to its owner. Kassein's hand was extended several seconds before she reached it, and he closed his fingers around hers, immediately pulling Alezya closer to him. His skin was as warm as his dragon. She turned toward the small crowd.

"The short answer is because it wants to," she said. "I spent time with them, and I befriended the dragon. I learned their language enough to know a few commands too."

Then, she turned to the dragons.

"*Niiru, Kein? Growl,*" she ordered in Kassein's language.

Immediately, Kein turned its silver eyes to the crowd and let out one long, furious, and menacing growl that had most of them panic again.

A few ran toward the nearest tunnels, hid behind others, or ran to the wall like Kein wouldn't be able to reach them. Secretly, Alezya found it a little bit funny, and she had to bite her lower lip. Even better, Niiru made a little jump to climb on Kein's back and, like a miniature version, imitated Kein's growl, letting out a sound that was far cuter than fierce.

"...It's fine," Alezya told the group of terrified adults. "I was just trying to show you what I can ask them to do, like growl."

Not looking annoyed in the slightest, Kein moved into the water, walking up to Alezya until it could press its snout against her core. She smiled before remembering she was pregnant, according to Kassein. Could the dragon feel that she had a baby in there? Was she genuinely pregnant? It still felt too crazy to believe, and right now, she couldn't focus on that. With a hand petting Kein's head and Kassein's arm around her waist, she turned to the clans again.

"See? I promise the Dragon Clan will be on our side. You may stay out of it, but my father is set on fighting them, and he will take many clans down with him, but he won't win. I don't think so."

Not with Kassein and Kein fighting. She had seen both of them in action many times. No matter how many men her father threw at the Dragon Clan, and though she was still scared to find out the actual number, Alezya still believed Kassein would come out victorious.

There were a few seconds of silence, but after a lull, several of the clan chiefs exchanged glances and determined nods before turning to her.

"Fine, Alezya of the Lumiata Clan," said one of the clan chiefs, stepping forward. "The Samial Clan shall ally with the Dragon Clan. So long as they uphold the promise to let us live and have the dragon leave our mountains alone, we will fight with them. The Deklaan Clan has abused our trust for too long for their gain, and we refuse to stand aside while the future of our mountains is decided in this battle. It won't be said that my clan hid like cowards while the Dragon Clan won that war for us."

"Nor mine!"

"Neither will we!"

Just like that, several clans reconfirmed their desire to fight, giving her determined nods and fierce gazes. Alezya tried to take it all in calmly, but she felt strangely empowered to see so many clan leaders addressing her like they would a peer. She had been the pariah of the Deklaan Clan for the longest time, and now, she was hailed as a leader.

"Alright," Ekut said, gesturing for the attention to get back to him. "Alezya will explain to the Dragon Clan who the enemy is, but we need to be sure who our allies are. Reach out to any clan you know that might still be on the fence. From what we've heard, Deklaan has rallied at least eight or nine clans to their cause, and their numbers might still be growing. The Dragon Clan might be mighty warriors, but like you said, they won't fight this whole battle for us. We need to properly rally with them and get ready for the biggest war our clans have faced in decades."

Alezya listened while leaning into Kassein as the twins took over the war plan. The first part was all about leading their new allies to the Dragon Clan; the Munsa Clan couldn't stay here after the word was most likely already out that they were now allied with her and Kassein, and their warriors had to gather somewhere to prepare for the battle. When she turned around and tried to explain, using as much of his vocabulary as she could and with many hand gestures and pointing at the men, Kassein focused on her, his eyes drifting to the clans every now and then and nodding along.

"*We hunt those who hurt you,*" he finally hissed.

"*Yes,*" Alezya nodded, cupping his cheek. "*The other* clans, *my friends, want to be friends with the Dragon* Clan *too, and hunt together.*"

"*Together,*" Kassein nodded.

"Alezya?" Ekata called her in a whisper, approaching them while her brother was still talking to the other clans. "Let him know our Munsa Clan will be fighting by the Dragon Clan's side. But the truth is, we cannot guarantee who will be on our side or not. So, what we will do is ask the other clans to attack the Deklaan Clan from different angles. Since we cannot be sure who will switch sides, we will send them out of our way. Either they fight the Deklaan Clan as promised, and we can corner them, or we will have a more significant battle ahead, but at least we won't be in an ambush. We know which ones we can trust for sure and those we will bring with us to meet the Dragon Clan. Now that we've got everything we need, you two should leave, Alezya. We will find the Dragon Clan, but you should go with him and explain to his clan. You've done more than your share already; let us handle things from here. We will meet you tomorrow at dawn."

Chapter 18

Kassein's eyes were riveted on Alezya, unable to look away.

He feared that if he blinked, he might just lose sight of her again. Did she realize how beautiful she was, with the white scales of their unborn baby covering her skin and that fierce gaze of hers, those dark eyes captivating all the people present?

He didn't enjoy seeing this crowd staring at her, but even without understanding their language, he could read the respect they had for her. When she spoke, they listened. They were all afraid of him; it was all too obvious, but they listened to Alezya, and whatever she said, those men agreed with it, their expressions changing.

Kassein had understood some of it. Unexpectedly, his moonlight had been far from helpless while he was desperately looking for her.

Somehow, she had found allies, this Munsa Tribe, and now, they were gathering people to fight alongside them. What Alezya had told them to convince them to fight alongside his army rather than against them, he had no idea. She had talked to them about Kein and made his dragon growl like it was her pet. He could tell many had been impressed, and so was he. She'd used his dragon for a demonstration of force or perhaps to earn their trust.

Either way, he didn't care; she already had his heart, so it wasn't surprising that she owned his dragon too. It had almost been sheer luck that he and Kein had heard her screams. His dragon had been restless since the minute they'd lost her, but even more so that day, and before heading back to the Onyx Castle, he had decided to ride Kein above the mountain once again with little hope.

Now, he was endlessly glad he had. If he had been minutes later, Alezya might not have made it, and he would have never forgiven himself.

Seeing her on the ground, covered in mud and blood, had already been enough to send him into a murderous trance. Now, with the Dragon Blood healing her from inside and the mud drying on her limbs and clothes, she looked as beautiful as ever. She was talking to that other woman, the one who kept glancing in Alezya's direction while talking to the men.

After a little bit, the two women nodded, but one of those solemn nods had a lot of underlying meaning. Alezya turned to him, and he was curious to know what she was expecting from him next.

"We must go," she said.

"Go?"

"To Kiera," she explained, making that adorable pout she made when she was focusing. "With Kein. We go to your men. We wait for the Munsa and our friends."

"Why?" he asked, wrapping his arms around her waist.

"Danger here," she said, glancing toward some of the tunnels. "The men who hurt me... They come."

Kassein nodded. This much, he could understand. Alezya pulled him along toward Kein, clearly making the executive decision for the two of them, and he didn't resist, pleasantly surprised. There was something irresistible about watching her take charge; weeks ago, she was trembling and shivering in front of him, and now, she merely needed him to help her climb his dragon. As soon as she sat down, she shouted something at the Munsa Tribe before calling Niiru to follow them. Even his dragon was entirely at her beck and call, but it had been so for a while now. The dragon was too big to turn around, but as soon as it understood Alezya meant for them to leave, it slowly retreated until its body was out of the cave, half-floating in the sea, until it had room to take off.

"Do you want to go see Lumie?" he asked.

Alezya tried to whip her upper body around so fast to look at him that she almost fell off the dragon's back, and he had to support her with a hand. He loved how her eyes became misty every time he mentioned her child.

"...Lumie?" she whispered.

"She's at the Onyx Castle. With Lorey."

"But... The others..."

She pointed at the mountains, her eyes torn with worry, but he gently wrapped her hand in his.

"We can come back in the morning. Before the sun rises," he emphasized, accentuating his sentence with a finger toward where the sun had set.

He was becoming more and more impressed with how much of his language Alezya could understand and how much Lorey had taught her in such a short time. Yet, to his surprise, Alezya hesitated a few seconds before she nodded. He immediately wrapped his arms tighter around her, holding her in his embrace, and her head leaned into the crook of his neck.

He had missed how perfectly she fit in his embrace. He pressed another kiss to her temple, annoyed that so much of her body was covered in dirty and too-thin clothing; he couldn't wait to get rid of it all.

They didn't talk on the flight, and after a while, he realized Alezya had fallen asleep against him. He had noticed she looked exhausted, but he had no idea what had happened to her. So, he had Kein make an extra round above the mountain, trying to see if he could find any helpful information. There seemed to be tribespeople here and there, appearing on small cliffs or briefly traveling outside, and a couple of them running through the darkness, probably thinking they wouldn't be seen under the cover of night. It was irritating that he couldn't tell who was friend or foe to Alezya and slay the latter immediately. Instead, he noted the locations before he finally had Kein fly south toward the Onyx Castle.

When they landed, he gently lifted Alezya off his dragon, carrying her against his torso. While he had tried to do so as gently as possible, she still felt the change in position and woke up, slowly opening her eyes and letting out a yawn.

"Kassein?" she mumbled.

"We're here. The Onyx Castle. You'll see Lumie."

That was enough to wake Alezya up completely, and he let her stand up, although he kept a hold of her hand. He had intended to take her straight to see the egg after landing in the gardens, but they were both caught off guard as they found Lorey seated gracefully on a stone bench with Kiera standing next to her, engaged in what appeared to be an intense discussion. Lumie was playing with a toy at Lorey's feet, a tiny dragon plushie that looked familiar to Kassein.

"Lumie!"

As soon as she saw Lumie, Alezya ran ahead of him to her child. Lumie barely had time to look up before she was scooped into her mother's arms. As soon as she realized who was holding her, the toddler let out excited giggles.

"*Ama! Ama!*" she kept chanting, patting her mother's face.

Alezya was in tears, and it definitely pulled some strings in Kassein's heart. He walked up to them, putting an arm around Alezya's waist and pulling her into him while he pressed a kiss on Lumie's white curls. She was whispering something to her daughter, rubbing her wet cheeks against Lumie's and smiling, looking happier than he had ever seen her. He felt her lean into him while she hugged her baby, and that faint movement made him happier than anything she could have said; Alezya quietly acknowledging his presence while she celebrated her reunion with her baby was a feeling beyond compare. He rubbed her back for a few more seconds before he looked up at his sister and Lorey.

"What are you doing here?"

"Nice to see you too," Kiera scoffed.

"The camp," he growled.

"The camp is fine," his sister rolled her eyes. "As incredible as it sounds, grown men can take care of themselves without any female supervision for a couple of hours, Kassein. I left the generals in charge. I also visited Tievin, by the way, and he said Herken's doing just fine."

"And the dragons?"

"Kiki took the kids to hunt far away," Lorey explained. "They should be back shortly. Speaking of baby dragons..."

While Kein had naturally gone to check on the remaining egg, Niiru had followed in its shadow and was now taking curious sniffs at the remains of the broken egg.

"You found that missing brat," Kiera noted.

"It was with Alezya?" Lorey guessed. "...Did you tell her, Kassein? That she is very likely pregnant?"

"I did," he said, "but I'm not sure she believed me. She said something about medicinal herbs and you."

Lorey frowned, her eyes going to Alezya.

"Oh, gods. She was taking this herb," Lorey said after a hesitation, her eyes opening wide. "The one to stop bleeding? When I took her to your mother's greenhouse at the camp, I saw Alezya sneak some in her bandages. I don't think she even knew I noticed, but I thought she was taking it for her injuries, so I didn't say anything. Now I think she might have been using it for a different purpose..."

"To stop her menstruation? Why would she do that? She was only with Kassein," Kiera frowned.

"Exactly. Maybe she wasn't willing to have a child. I can't fault her, given her circumstances..."

Kassein felt like he had gotten punched in the gut. Alezya didn't want the child?

He looked down at her, and she had calmed a little, although she was still holding Lumie tightly in her arms. Now, the baby girl was looking far more curious about Niiru, who was playing around in the garden, dashing through the grass, gnawing on Kein's tail, or making loops around their legs. While he was still lost in his thoughts, feeling somewhat upset, Kiera suddenly burst out into loud laughter. He could already guess what his sister was going to say, so he closed his eyes with a sigh, their reactions leaving Lorey utterly confused.

"What is so funny?"

"She took this herb to try and prevent herself from having a baby with Kassein?" Kiera kept laughing.

"Yes, or at least that's what I think, but— Will you stop laughing? That is *not* funny, Kiera."

"Lorey, honey. Who's the most knowledgeable person we know about herbs?"

"...Your mother?" Lorey frowned.

"Exactly. The same mother who had eight of our dad's children. *Eight*, Lorey. Eight of our dad's massive babies. Do you really think our mother wanted to have another child the same year she gave birth to Darsan? *Darsan*? Darsan and his big head?"

"...Those herbs don't work?" Lorey realized, baffled.

"Oh, they probably work fine for regular humans, but they don't work on this kind of specimen," Kiera pointed a thumb at her brother. "Our kind's *seed* is apparently far too strong for that. I mean, Mom never complained about having any of us, but she probably would have loved to be able to space some of us out a bit more. Putting some physical distance between herself and our dad helped, at least for a little while. Remember how our father stayed in the north while Mom often traveled to the palace? I mean, she also had to do so for duty's sake, but you know, it probably made it easier for them to physically stay away from each other. And just as Kassein here apparently demonstrated, dragons are scarily efficient. Not that I'm going to ask how many tries that one took; I don't want to know."

Just once, Kassein thought. He wouldn't admit it to his sister, but one time was all it had taken to make Alezya pregnant. Still, the fact that she had tried not to get pregnant unsettled him. What if she didn't want the baby? He hadn't thought much at the time, but he hadn't been thinking much at all because it was his first time, and all he could focus on then was Alezya. Gently, he pressed another kiss to her temple.

"Alezya," he called her.

She finally tore her eyes away from Lumie to look up at him.

"The baby," he said.

She smiled, and her eyes returned to Lumie with a big smile.

"No," he said, taking a breath in. "The other baby."

To make his point, he splayed a hand on her stomach under Lumie's bum. Alezya's expression fell a bit, and she frowned slightly, but not in a disappointed or disgusted way. It seemed more like she was still confused.

"Do you not want the baby? Do you not like it?" he asked, his heart beating with unprecedented unease.

She didn't respond. Her lips parted, but no sound came out, and after a second, she closed them again. Kassein felt his heart drop to the pit of his stomach, but he steeled his nerves. It was her decision. As much as it would tear him apart, he wanted Alezya to want the child, and if she didn't, he refused to force the hardships of pregnancy on her.

"You took medicinal herbs," he said, "to stop bleeding. Because you don't want the baby?"

After a second, Alezya glanced briefly at him, tears in her eyes, before glancing down at Lumie. She must have seen some of the dread in his eyes because she softened her expression a bit and moved Lumie to her hip to free a hand to cup his cheek. She took him by surprise by getting on her toes and pressing a quick kiss on his lips.

"It's your baby," she whispered after a while, a tender look in her eyes. "I like the baby, Kassein. I'm..."

She bit her lip, visibly struggling to find the right word. After a few seconds of frowning, she glanced toward Lorey, then Kiera, then the dragons before she pulled her gaze back to him.

"Danger," she said in a hoarse voice. "So much danger for the baby and Lumie. My home hunts me. Men hunt me."

"...You're scared," Kassein finally understood.

Alezya gave him a faint, trembling nod.

"It's Kassein's baby," she let out a tear. "I like Kassein's baby. But... Lumie is..."

A wave of relief hit Kassein.

Although it wasn't what she had anticipated, Alezya didn't *not* want the child. But it was true that things would have been a lot easier if she wasn't pregnant, and he could understand that. They'd had sex before she had reunited with Lumie. Of course, she would have wanted to save her child and ensure their safety before she even considered another. Alezya was a mother and a good one too, despite the circumstances and everything against her.

It made sense that she would have been terrified to bring another child into the world when she couldn't even secure Lumie's safety. He had witnessed firsthand how worried and heartbroken she had been when she was separated from her baby girl. It wasn't that she absolutely didn't want that baby with him, but that woman was too wise and caring, and she had considered their situation and knew the timing for this new pregnancy was far from ideal. He couldn't resent her for that, not one bit.

Their baby was a happy, unexpected accident, and just then, Kassein knew that Alezya would love them too. She was too good of a mother not to. He could understand that she was scared, but he wasn't; he was ready to protect them all.

While Alezya was still looking at him with sorry, tearful eyes, he gave her a gentle smile and pressed his lips against her forehead. Her body relaxed a little, and as Lumie let out a giggle, he turned to the baby girl, doing the same to her and triggering more giggles.

"Don't cry," he whispered to Alezya. "Don't worry. I'll protect you, and Lumie, and the baby. I won't let anyone hurt you anymore. You're safe."

Alezya nodded and leaned into him, her face again fitting perfectly into the crook of his neck while he caressed her long, silk-like hair.

Meanwhile, Niiru came to their feet, and Lumie cheered excitedly, trying to tear herself from her mother's arms by leaning over toward the baby dragon.

"While we're addressing some matters..." Kiera said. "That is our runaway baby dragon, isn't it? Because that's not the regular size of a newborn dragon. Even Dran wasn't that big!"

"She named it Niiru," Kassein nodded.

"Niiru," Lorey repeated with a smile. "That's adorable... and he looks like your father's dragon, doesn't he? He's even darker than Krai! He's as black as ink, like Shan."

Niiru heard its name and scurried to Lorey, making a loop around her legs, before it ran to Kein, playing with the older dragon again, this time by gnawing its maw while Kein tried to bury the unruly child under its chin.

"It doesn't make sense," Kiera scoffed. "Why would the tiny black dragon be stuck to Alezya? Dragons aren't born until the children are, and Alezya's baby was conceived just days ago. Even if Alezya is pregnant and that is her child's dragon, it makes no sense that it hatched so soon! Nor that it's that big!"

"...Unless that dragon's baby is already born," Lorey muttered.

Kiera frowned at Lorey, and Kassein gave her a confused glance.

"What do you mean?"

The young woman took a deep breath, glancing toward the egg Kein was guarding next to the broken one then back to Niiru. The young black dragon had now been flipped on its back while Kein's head rested on it, and the new game was to escape by pushing its tiny paws against the massive head with little growls of protest.

"It's... I know it's a bit of a far-fetched theory, but I've had it since we talked about it last time, and if we consider the facts that we do have, I think I'm right. Niiru is very likely one of Kein's babies, which means that Niiru would be attached to Kassein's child. But Kassein has no blood-related child so far, and of all the humans it could have fled to, Niiru went far to find Alezya. He found her when Kein couldn't. Baby dragons usually stick to their human moms, like how your dragons were always with Lady Cassandra while you were growing up, and your grandmother always said your father's and his siblings' dragons did the same. We can also all see for ourselves that Niiru grew at a very fast rate as if it was catching up to his human. And we don't know exactly whether Kein laid either egg or if he had both eggs at the same time, but when did he *last* fly off before that happened? Right after Kassein met Lumie, Alezya's already born child."

"...Are you trying to tell us you think Niiru is... Lumie's dragon?" Kiera blinked. "Honey, that makes no sense. That child doesn't have the blood of a dragon! She isn't Kassein's biological–"

"She might not be his *biological* child nor have the right bloodline," Lorey interrupted her, "but look at the three of them! Kassein adopted her the minute he met her. He cares about her as much as his unborn child. She's the baby of the woman he loves, and Niiru is exactly the right size to be the dragon of a child her age, isn't he? *And* he acts with Alezya the way your dragons act around your mom! What if Kein decided Lumie *was* Kassein's, regardless of blood? She won't have your unique Dragon Blood characteristics, but she could still very much have a dragon! All it takes is for Kein to give her one! She won't have your scales to heal, and she might not have your strength nor all of what makes your bloodline special, but she could have a dragon."

"This... This is insane," Kiera scoffed. "What's more insane is that I am actually starting to believe this. You're saying Kein would have... sensed Kassein basically *adopting* her and decided, yep, that kid gets her own dragon?!"

"Listen," Lorey said calmly. "We have never fully... understood everything there is to know about dragons. No one has ever seen them lay an egg, nor do we know how they sense when their owner fathers a child that's not even in their body as soon as the child is conceived. We don't know how they can even reproduce while being genderless and incapable of mating. We don't know how your oldest brother's dragon knew it had to hatch early to save your mother. We don't know how your father's dragon *sensed* your mother was related to the original tribe of the Water Dragon, either. Your sister Cessilia told us about another dragon that survived his owner's death for years to protect his sister, and you know her own dragon came back to life years after we all thought she died. Your grandmother told us countless incredible stories, Kiera, like how your grandfather's dragon scales changed color to turn gold when he became the Emperor or how a centuries-old dragon gave its life to resuscitate one human. We know for sure that stranger miracles have happened. Why is it so hard to believe that Kein could sense that Lumie would be Kassein's adoptive child and decide to give her a baby dragon as well?"

A heavy silence fell, and eventually, Kiera was the first to move and throw her hands up in a defeated movement.

"A headache," she finally mumbled. "This is going to be such a headache... Gods, Tievin's going to go crazy with that one. Nobody tells him without me there; I want to see that."

"You may think it's crazy," Lorey chuckled, "but my theory is the only one that holds up, love. There's no better explanation as to why Niiru hatched so fast while being Kein's and is now stuck to Alezya. Kassein adopting Lumie is the only explanation that works. Look at it!"

They did, and Niiru had gone from playing around with Kein to rubbing its back against Alezya's legs like an overgrown cat. Kassein and Kiera exchanged a long look, having a silent conversation with their eyes. Although Lorey's theory was indeed crazy, it still made a whole lot of sense. They had grown up in a family of eight siblings, and they knew Niiru was the size of a toddler's dragon. Plus, there was no denying how obsessed that young dragon was with Alezya.

"Alezya has scales," Kassein noted, gently raising her wrist to show them.

"*White* scales," Lorey noted, "from the baby she's carrying, the one with its dragon in the white egg. So, Niiru..."

"Niiru came from that hatched black egg and has to be Lumie's," Kiera scoffed. "Alright, got it. This is insane, but let's just... run with that one because I'm out of ideas. And I have to admit that little shit does look like Kein."

It was unmistakable whenever Niiru was near Kein; the young dragon was indeed a copy of Kein, except for its colors: all black scales and amber eyes.

After a beat, Kassein gently took Lumie out of Alezya's arms and, under her confused eyes, put her toddler down on the ground.

Immediately, Niiru came near, and instead of sniffing her like it did the other humans present, it immediately jumped over the little girl's legs, and swirled around her grabby hands, making Lumie squeal.

Alezya seemed a bit nervous at first to see the dragon so close to her child, but after a few seconds of observing the two of them playing around, she relaxed. Soon enough, they were chasing after each other in the garden, both of them on all fours, and though the young dragon was obviously faster, it made loops around Lumie, delighting the little girl.

"Are you spending the night here?" Lorey asked Kassein.

He nodded.

"Alright," she smiled. "I'll go and prepare a bath for you. You could both use one, no offense... Kiera?"

"Yes, yes, I'm leaving," Kiera grimaced. "I'm going to sleep in the mountains, on the floor of some cave, with a bunch of stinky men, while my brother gets to sleep all comfy in his bed in the Onyx Castle while I watch *his* army prepare for the battle that *he* decided to launch for *his* girlfriend. No big deal!"

Just then, her dragon, Kiki, appeared above them in a swift flap of wings, and while the dark gray dragon elegantly landed, three balls of bright colors hit the ground. Alezya gasped and immediately went to grab Lumie, visibly rendered nervous by the triplets. It was a fair reaction, given that the three of them immediately began fighting on the ground, with loud growls and rowdy movements, and twice, one of them bumped into Niiru before jumping to attack a sibling again. The triplets were about two or three times its size, and after being knocked over twice, the tiny dragon quickly darted to stay next to Kein, hiding under its wing, intimidated. When the triplets finally noticed the smaller dragon, a growl from Kein prevented them from picking on Niiru.

"Those little-" Kiera hissed. "You've hunted and ran all day already, will you calm down? Do you know how many times I had to stop them from biting people's toes today? What's with their obsession with toes? Those can't possibly be any good to eat!"

"...Baby dragons?" Alezya asked with a nervous voice, her eyes riveted on the rowdy bunch.

"Those are children dragons," Lorey chuckled. "They're small but not babies anymore. Ten years old."

Alezya nodded at her ten raised fingers, but she was still giving a defiant look to the three little terrors, who were now off on a race around the Onyx Castle, it seemed.

"I am *not* taking those three shitstains for the night," Kiera hissed. "You're in charge of those little assholes. As if it wasn't already enough that you left without a word earlier and left me behind with them..."

"Yes, yes," Lorey smiled, walking up to her to press a kiss on her cheek. "Don't worry, we've got them. Kassein will bring them back in the morning."

Kiera's frown lessened a bit after a look from Lorey, and she let out a sigh. As her partner seemed pacified, Lorey walked back inside, and for some reason, the triplets followed behind her, perhaps excited to explore the Onyx Castle or maybe hoping she'd feed them. Once they were gone, Niiru popped its head from under Kein's wing and made its way back to Alezya's feet.

"Speaking of the morning... Now that you've got your girl back, what's the plan?" Kiera asked, turning her eyes back to her brother. "We were looking for her, but now that we've got her, do we keep attacking the tribes? Not that I mind, but-"

"Alezya has a plan," he said.

Kiera's jaw dropped.

"Excuse me?" she scoffed. "*She* has a plan? What do you–"

"She has allied with tribes that do not want to fight us," Kassein said, his eyes on Alezya, who was returning his gaze with a little frown, Lumie pressed against her chest. "They will be joining our army to fight those who attacked her. Her home tribe wants to attack us."

"...Alright," Kiera muttered. "I don't really care whose butts we kick, to be honest. But how do you know that...?"

"She told me. She had me meet them too," he said, pride coating his words. "Alezya managed to save herself, and she met with other tribes. When I found her, there was some sort of meeting going on, but they were fighting. Those who were on Alezya's side called themselves the Munsa. They took me back to their home, and there were more people there, probably other tribes. The tribespeople she showed me respected and listened to her."

After a beat, Kiera sighed and gave him a nod.

"Fine. I mean, that woman has proven time and time again that she's smart... but are we sure they want us to keep fighting? They don't want us to just fuck off?"

"No. Alezya said some tribes were still hunting... attacking the others, and she wants us to fight alongside them."

He glanced down, and Alezya was intently staring at him, probably trying to decipher each word. He gave her a gentle smile and petted her hair, trying to comfort her while she hugged Lumie against her chest.

"I see," Kiera nodded. "Well, not that I mind a good brawl, and your men might enjoy an actual fight too. All the tribes we've come across so far were busier running away than actually defending their homes, for some reason."

That was mostly due to the trio of young dragons running absolutely berserk inside the tunnels; Kassein hadn't anticipated the triplets being so efficient, but the three of them were terrorizing the tribes before any of his men could even launch attacks. While it was a lot of fun for the young dragons, he had no intention of putting them in any more danger.

It had been fine for them to run amok, and truthfully, the three of them were too small and too fast for the tribespeople to land a blow, but in a real battle, he couldn't guarantee one of them wouldn't be hurt.

"Let's bring Tievin to the camp tomorrow," Kassein said.

"Tievin?" Kiera raised an eyebrow with a sneer. "You want to bring your paperwork guy to a battlefield? He's already two seconds from shitting himself on a normal day in the camp, Kassein!"

"If we're going to negotiate with the tribes and convince them we can be their allies, we can't only have fighters present. Tievin can stay at the back with the young dragons."

"...You want Tievin to babysit the triplets?" Kiera chuckled. "Kassein, they're going to eat him alive!"

"He'll be fine."

Tievin ranted a lot, but Kassein knew there was no chance the young dragons would actually harm him; they had been raised not to harm humans, despite the impression they gave their enemies. While painful, their bites were just their way of playing and never meant to actually maim, more of a nibble.

Moreover, he knew he was going to need to move the entire army north. From what he'd seen in that cave, the battle was going to be far more significant than he'd anticipated. It wouldn't be about chasing one tribe after another from their mountains anymore; he could sense a real fight looming, and the movements he had spotted from the skies seemed to confirm so too.

His sister's wish would be fulfilled soon.

"We need to catch some sleep," he said, wrapping an arm around Alezya's shoulders. "Tomorrow might bring the biggest battle of all."

"One can dream," Kiera snickered. "Fine, I'll pick up Tiev, but I'll expect you guys before dawn tomorrow. This is your army, Brother, not mine."

"I know."

For once, Kassein felt more attached to his role than ever; having a purpose had changed everything. His sister let out a long sigh, and then turned around just as her dragon came close, preparing to depart.

"See you, Brother. Good luck explaining it all to Tiev tomorrow!"

Kassein grimaced as his sister took off; he definitely didn't want to be the one to deliver the news to his Intendant, but he'd have no choice. Tievin's extensive knowledge would more than likely be crucial in the upcoming battles...

"Let's go," he whispered to Alezya as his sister's dragon flew away. "Let's go sleep."

Alezya glanced toward Kein and Niiru, still hiding under its wing, but as both dragons looked peaceful and sleepy, she followed him inside. As promised, Lorey had prepared a hot bath for them, and when he led Alezya there, her lips parted slightly, and the envious look in her eyes made him smile.

This bathing room was one of the most captivating spaces in the Onyx Castle. A single arched stained-glass window pierced the darkness, casting pale moonlight that shimmered faintly against the shadowy surfaces. At the center of the room, a round bath was hewn directly into the stone floor, about thirty inches deep and spacious enough to fit half a dozen people, brimmed with steaming water that carried a faint, earthy aroma of herbs. A handful of delicate flowers floated lazily on the surface, their pale hues illuminated by the dim light. Along one wall, simple baskets held bars of soap of various colors, while neatly folded towels rested beside them.

Lorey smiled and gently took Lumie from her mom's hands while Alezya was still in silent awe.

"I'll watch her while you two bathe," she told her.

Her wink and little head movement toward the bath were probably enough for Alezya to understand, and though she stared longingly at Lumie, she let Lorey take her.

Alezya stared at the empty doorway after Lorey was gone, and although she knew Lumie was safe, Kassein could understand how hard it was to let her go minutes after they'd finally reunited.

"She's with Lorey," he whispered against her hair, gently taking off her first layer of clothes. "Lumie is fine, my moonlight."

Alezya only gave him a little nod, a bittersweet mixture of relief and sadness in her eyes. Kassein was longing to see her smile again; the smile she'd given her child had been the most beautiful of all, and he couldn't wait to see her smile like that again.

But for now, Alezya deserved some time for herself; he wasn't sure what she'd gone through in the time they'd been apart, but he wanted her fed, warm, and happy by any means. The clothes had to go first; all of it was too wet and dirty, and Alezya deserved nothing but the finest. He knew he could count on Lorey and probably Nebora to have some clothes ready for her when they got out of the bath.

Gently, he finished undressing her, quite happy with how she blushed but didn't shy away from his touch. His fingers lingered everywhere they could on her skin, delighted to caress the tawny beige shade, angry at each cut and bruise he found, even as snow-white scales covered each injury. Alezya shivered as she finally shed her last piece of clothing, red with shyness, and he delicately held her hand while she stepped into the bath. He trusted Lorey to have made it warm but not too hot for her, and Alezya did seem to find it to her taste as she sat in the large bath.

Kassein didn't hesitate for a second before he quickly undressed and stepped into the water with her, watching Alezya's reaction before deciding to sit behind her, and to his pleasure, she leaned back to rest against his torso with a contented exhale.

"I missed you," he whispered against her shoulder.

She hummed softly, and his hands caressed her body gently, pouring water over her shoulders, washing every speck of dirt off her skin.

After a few seconds, he felt Alezya relax, and she put her hand on his forearm, pulling him to wrap his arm around her stomach. She wanted to be held, and it made him happy. Kassein smiled and brought her other hand to his lips, kissing the back of it. He witnessed the tip of Alezya's ears flushing a bit. After a second, he moved the hand that was around her stomach, gently caressing her belly.

Thinking she was growing a child they'd conceived together was an indescribable feeling, a tangle of too many emotions to label. It had to be very small, yet knowing it was there, he couldn't stop touching her belly, thinking about how it would soon grow full. His hand moved gently, but as Alezya released a faint exhale, the air subtly changed around them. A heated tension was slowly rising, and after a hesitation, she pressed on his wrist, and guided his hand down. Sure enough, her legs slowly parted, and he kept going until his fingers reached the hairy mound.

"You're so beautiful," he whispered in her hair, and he felt Alezya relax a bit more.

Her hands moved, one covering his and the other rising to hook his nape, caressing the tiny hairs on his neck.

"Kassein," she said in an exhale, her voice raspier than usual.

"I want you," he breathed in her ear.

She nodded and kept guiding his hand down, allowing him to caress her slit, letting out a little satisfied gasp when his fingertips finally parted the lips.

"Kassein," she whimpered.

"I know," he smiled. "I got you. I'm right here. Show me. Show me how you want me. Anything you want, I'll do it. Show me."

Whether she understood some of his words or the heat in his voice, Alezya blushed and breathed louder, arching her back a bit and tightening her grip around his nape. He loved how she could be honest about her desire now that they could catch a break, away from all that could have worried her. It was like he'd only gotten glimpses of her before, and now, he was getting to see the woman who had been pushing her desires coming to him, all her needs and wants unleashed.

Her hand was firm on his, guiding him into what she liked, her breathing growing louder as he breached her, and she began grinding her hips against his fingers, egging him on. Kassein bit her shoulder, finding her painfully beautiful with dim moonlight on her skin, the melody her voice let out, and the shy yet needy movements of her body. It was like playing a unique instrument that only responded to his touch, and the sounds she made were the most beautiful. Her back arched some more, and Kassein pressed his fingers deeper in, his thumb roughing up her button and making Alezya's gasps and moans echo in the room.

Her wriggling body was making small waves in the water, but Alezya didn't care; her desire had taken hold of her movements, and right then, she was focused on her burgeoning pleasure. Her grip was getting tighter on his skin, and Kassein loved that; he swallowed hard, pressing firmer into her, noting how she loved his rough movements, closing her eyes as tiny erratic moans escaped her lips. He moved his other hand to her chest, and just as he started playing with the soft, supple breast, Alezya let out a louder cry, her back arching some more.

"I love the way you shiver when I touch you," he whispered in her hair, loving how she quivered even more at his hot breath against her ear. "Your body is so beautiful, my moonlight. I want to know what you love, I want to make you feel good. You need to teach me. I want to know everything. I want to know what feels good to you, what makes you moan, what makes you ache for more. I need to know, Alezya. Please. You have no idea how much I want you. I desire you more than I've ever wanted anything in my life. I want to touch you all night, my moonlight. I want to hear your voice and make you moan with pleasure until dawn comes. I want to do so many things to you... You might be scared if you knew how much I desire you, Alezya. I want to mark you everywhere as mine, even if you already carry my child. I want my seed deep inside you again."

She moaned, and Kassein smiled, feeling almost guilty for spilling his darkest secret to her unsuspecting ears.

And yet, as if she'd caught some of that, Alezya's hand moved from covering his between her legs to slither behind her back, suddenly looking for something between his lower body and hers, and when she touched his length, Kassein let out a groan.

"Kassein," she whined. "You. I want you."

"No," he groaned, increasing the movement of his fingers on her clit, ignoring how his self-control was reaching its breaking point.

"You," Alezya insisted, squirming in his arms. "Kassein. Kassein."

She fought his embrace enough to turn herself around and suddenly assaulted his lips, taking him by surprise.

Kassein groaned, but there was no fighting her fierce attack; Alezya was using her tongue and pressing her whole body against his, rubbing her slit against his girth without mercy, and there was no self-control that he could muster up to resist that. He could barely believe that she was the one attacking him, initiating this, and he loved her fearless ambush.

He tangled his fingers through her hair, gripping it and pressing her closer against his body, answering her kiss with the same heat. Even with Dragon Blood, he'd never felt so animalistic as he did at that moment, rough need and unbridled lust guiding his every move. He was so hard it was almost painful, and when Alezya looked at him with those irises of liquid darkness glowing with desire, her swollen lips breathing hard, he felt his last restraint snap.

He moved from under her, circled her in a movement, pressed her hands against the stone, and before she could react, he was behind her, his length against her ass, his knees pushing hers wide, his large torso covering her back.

"Kassein," she whimpered, and he slithered his arm under her chest until his hand could hold her throat, pulling her up to kiss him.

"Can I...?" he asked, his tone carrying the desperation more than his words.

"Kassein," she kept whimpering, her voice saturated with desire. "Yes. Yes, Kassein. Yes."

He pressed another kiss to her lips before he let her go on all fours, bracing herself with her hands splayed on the wet stone while he lined himself up, pressing the tip in.

Without warning, Kassein filled her all at once, and Alezya let out a shocked cry. He waited a few seconds, letting her adjust and delighting in the tight sensation of her clenching on his length. He knew he had been rough, but before he could even worry he'd hurt her, Alezya's shaking hand touched his hip, her fingers gripping his ass, and she arched her waist suggestively under him. He smiled.

Kassein pulled back out and then sunk back in, listening to her throaty moan. Slowly at first, then at a more steady pace, he filled her, again and again, listening to her strained voice. There was no holding back, nothing that could stop their love-making. All they both wanted was primal, fulfilling sex and wild kisses.

Kassein held her hip with one hand and covered Alezya's fist on the ground with the other. She was on her knees, legs in the water up to her thighs, her hands braced on the stone while his rough thrusts shook her, and he pressed hungry kisses on her nape, shoulder, and back, everywhere his lips reached, each thrust punctuated with a beastly grunt against her skin. She kept crying his name, again and again, until her voice sounded hoarse, and her words turned into erratic moans.

"My Alezya," he whispered. "My moonlight."

"Kassein. Yes, yes..."

He moved his hand to her clit again, and he had barely touched her when Alezya let out a shocked cry, her entire body bursting into a violent shake. He kept his hungry pace, giving her deep, fierce thrusts as her orgasm ripped through her. She spasmed violently under him with chaotic moans until her voice broke and her upper body gave up. She slowly fell on her elbows, her cheek against the wet stone. Kassein gently put his arm under her and placed his hand between her cheek and the cold stone before he resumed his thrusts, tearing some hoarse moans out of her.

"Kassein," she cried, exhausted. "No... No more... Ah... Yes... hm, yes..."

"I'm almost there," he hissed between his accelerating thrusts, picking up a fast pace again with loud grunts. "I'm almost there. Again. Just a bit more. Um. Please, please. Fuck. Ugh... Please. Please, Alezya. Take me. Please... Yes. Yes. Ugh, so good. So fucking good. Take me. Fuck, yes. Yes..."

"Yes," she cried. "Yes... Yes..."

He kept going tirelessly, accelerating when he felt his own release coming, dragging more broken cries from her. Finally, he burst in one last deep, fierce thrust, pinning her against the stone as he released himself inside her, a guttural groan of satisfaction escaping him. It seemed to last forever. Every inch of his body burst in an explosion of ecstasy, leaving his limbs awash with relief. No words were exchanged as they both caught their breath, exhausted and still shaken by the unprecedented violence of their climax.

Kassein recovered first, letting out a long, satisfied exhale before he slowly pulled out, triggering another shiver from Alezya. He leaned over her and gently combed her hair back, peppering kisses on her red skin.

"Alezya? Are you alright...?" he whispered. "I'm sorry. I was too rough."

But she let out a gentle hum and finally willed herself to move, lifting her hand above her head to caress his cheek. She was still lying on the stone with her eyes closed, but she looked content, caressing his spiky cheek and breathing slowly, a smile on her lips.

Kassein finally allowed himself to smile too, and pressed another kiss on her neck before he gently dragged her limp body back into the water, letting her lean against his torso while he hugged her from behind. She looked tired, and he would have thought she was asleep if it wasn't for her fingers mindlessly caressing his forearms. He grabbed one of the soaps, proceeding to quietly, gently clean her skin while they both lingered in this daze.

Kassein took his time to clean every inch of her skin, glaring at every patch of white scales he came across, knowing it betrayed a cut or a scrape. The scales mostly healed surface injuries, so he glared even more at the visible bruises on her legs and ribs, when Alezya flinched slightly at his touch.

"You're hurt," he whispered, pressing his lips to her temple.

"I have you," she said.

She might have chosen them out of a limited vocabulary, yet Kassein felt her words held so much unspoken meaning. She had him. She was safe with him, and Lumie was safe too.

Kassein put down the soap, and tightened his arms around her.

"You have me," he whispered back, intertwining his fingers with hers.

A few seconds passed, and he could still feel her relaxing, but neither of them felt ready to get out of the bath, or this little room where it was just the two of them. As the water cooled to lukewarm, Kassein put another kiss on her shoulder.

"I like it," Alezya whispered.

"My lips?"

"Your lips," she nodded. "On me. And... your hands."

She grabbed his hands, pressing them against her belly and thigh.

"I like it," she said. "And... I like your meat."

Kassein froze, confused, before slightly moving to face her.

To his surprise, he found Alezya with a mischievous look in her eyes, biting her lower lip. With that blush on her cheeks, she looked younger than she'd ever looked before, and he raised a confused eyebrow.

"My meat?" he repeated.

After a hesitation, Alezya's eyes unmistakably lowered, following the line from his torso to his submerged region. Kassein's jaw dropped.

"My *meat*?" he repeated, this time with a smirk on.

Alezya blushed even more and looked away, finally acting a bit ashamed of her joke. He knew she had picked the word on purpose, and he laughed at her bashfulness, pulling her tightly back into his embrace.

"You like my meat," he chuckled.

"Hush," she tried to push him away. "I'm cold. No more."

"No more meat?" he laughed, watching her step out of the bath.

"Kassein! No more!"

But he was still grinning when he left the bath, and they both wrapped themselves in bath towels. He didn't let her run away when they left the bathroom, and instead circled an arm around her and gently guided her out and back to his room.

There, they found Nebora just stepping out, causing her to stop in her tracks, her eyes meeting Kassein's. Again, he felt Alezya slightly stiffen against him, like she did in the presence of strangers, and he rubbed his thumb against her skin.

"Well," Nebora said, putting a fist on her hip, "there's one smile I haven't seen in a long time."

"Thank you for preparing the bed," Kassein muttered, although his ears were burning.

"You're very welcome, young man. Looks like that lady's taking care of you, alright..."

She directed her smile at Alezya, and Kassein felt his lover take a slight step back, pushing herself a bit in his arms, but she recovered fast.

"Lumie?" she asked.

"Lorey's bringing her soon, don't worry. I'll tell her. Unless you two need some more privacy?"

"No," Kassein immediately replied. "Bring her."

"Got it. Good night!"

Nebora left, and Kassein pressed a kiss on Alezya's head before grabbing the fresh clothes. He had no doubt Alezya would want to spend the night with her child and get as much time as she could with her, and he was completely fine with it. He embraced it completely, and in fact, he was almost looking forward to their first night together, the three of them. Or four.

Once they were dressed, they sat on the bed. Not long after, Lorey walked in, carrying Lumie in her arms. She passed the little girl to a relieved Alezya before stepping out. As soon as she was with her mom, Lumie brightened up, climbing onto her mom's lap and letting Alezya play around with her, tickle her, and leave loud kisses on her chubby cheeks.

Kassein watched them in silent awe, feeling his heart warm up at the sight of those two and their dazzling smiles. This was exactly what he'd envisioned when he'd dreamt of reuniting daughter and mother, and he felt privileged to get to witness this adorable scene.

Moments later, Lorey returned with a tray piled high with food, and he stood to take it from her. She gave him a little smile, and quietly bid them good night before stepping out, closing the bedroom door behind her.

"*Ama! Ama!*" Lumie kept chanting in her mom's arms, too excited to go back to sleep.

Alezya kept chatting with her child in their language while eating, and Kassein couldn't stop listening and staring. He prepared them plates of food and brought them to the bed, letting Alezya settle Lumie on her lap and feed her daughter patiently. He ate his own quietly, unable to stop watching the duo interact.

Every now and then, Alezya would gaze at him, smile shyly, and then go back to her daughter. Lumie also smiled at him, like everything in this room could make her sparkle with joy.

Kassein ended up wolfing down his own meal in minutes, and then, he positioned himself next to Alezya and started drying and combing her half-wet curls, enjoying his front row seat to the most adorable scene.

Alezya was sitting cross-legged next to him and leaning over her baby, giving her bits of her soup and exchanging in their language with delighted smiles and excited sounds. He wasn't sure if Lumie could understand or speak more than a few words, but Alezya was having a full-on conversation with her child, it seemed, and seeing her smile so brightly was all he wanted. Lumie seemed to be having the time of her life too. The baby girl was seated facing her mother, and she kept bouncing and clapping her hands with the force of excited giggles between each spoonful.

After a while, Niiru also popped into the room and climbed on the bed, making little circles around the humans present. It didn't take long before they finished everything on the tray and laid down, their voices going from excited to gentle whispers, and the bedroom went quiet. Lumie was curled up in a small but thick blanket between her mom and the wall.

Alezya was on her flank, her head resting on Kassein's bicep and his arm around her waist, her hand gently petting Lumie's tummy. The little girl had exhausted herself after a good meal and so much excitement, and she was already dozing off. Niiru had made its way next to Lumie too, and had its body curled around her.

The trio made for an adorable sight, the little girl holding the dragon's tail in one fist and a strand of her mother's hair in the other. Lying behind Alezya, Kassein had a perfect view of this little family when he glanced down, and he could see Lumie's long white eyelashes, her mouth in a cute O, her breathing slow. Next to her, Niiru let out a little grunt, rolled onto its back, and then started snoring faintly. Alezya chuckled against him, and he couldn't resist pressing yet another kiss against her hair, perhaps the hundredth since they'd been reunited. He loved her hair, and now, her curls were smooth and smelled heavenly.

When he felt her let out a little sigh, he worried, rubbing his thumb against her belly.

"Alezya?"

She remained silent for a few seconds, but then, she turned around in his arms until he could see her eyes and the unshed tears in them.

He frowned, but she smiled and pressed a hand to his cheek, followed by a long kiss. This time, it was a chaste kiss, but strangely, it felt more meaningful than most.

"...You're happy?" he whispered, a guess and a hope.

"*Kiitso,*" she replied quietly.

It took him a few seconds to remember what that word meant, but when he did, he relaxed and leaned over to kiss her deeply.

After a while, Alezya pressed a hand against his chest, pushing him away. Kassein groaned, but he finally leaned back, making her chuckle.

"No more?" he whispered.

"No more," she smiled. "Sleep?"

"Really? No more meat?" he whispered against her ear.

"Kassein!" She slapped his bicep, making him chuckle in her neck. "No.

Sleep."

"Alright," he smiled, relaxing against her and holding her closer. "Alright, my moonlight. Good night."

The next morning, Kassein woke before sunrise to an irritating sensation on his toes. He wiggled them in protest, earning a gruff grunt. Lifting his head groggily, he squinted at the foot of the bed, where his long legs hung over the frame. A small, brown dragon was happily gnawing on his toes.

"Leni," he groaned, voice heavy with sleep. "Off."

The young dragon snorted and resumed chewing, undeterred. Kassein sighed, grimacing at how his feet were already slick with saliva and dusted with faint bronze where his dragon blood had started healing the skin. Leni had been at this for a while. With a firm shake of his foot, he dislodged the persistent dragon and sat up, rubbing his face. Niiru was gone, but Lumie and Alezya were still deep asleep next to him. Smiling, Kassein leaned over and kissed Alezya's cheek, soft and deliberate, until she stirred. Her eyelids fluttered open, and she let out a contented sigh, her hand reaching up to touch his face.

"Good morning, my moonlight," he whispered.

She stretched languidly, sitting up just as Kassein shifted to rub Lumie's belly. The little girl frowned adorably in her sleep, squirming under his touch. Alezya's brows knitted as she leaned toward the curtains, pulling them shut to shield Lumie from the faint light of dawn.

"Kassein..." Her voice was quiet, tinged with unease. "The sky..."

"I know," he murmured, gently lifting Lumie.

Bundled in her blanket, the little girl clung to him without fully waking, her tiny fist gripping the fabric. Getting up too, Alezya glanced up at him, her expression conflicted. Kassein leaned down and pressed a reassuring kiss to her lips.

"I've got her," he said gently. "Let's eat."

He guided her through the Onyx Castle, first stopping by his siblings' rooms to gather extra layers of clothing for Alezya. Then, they raided the kitchen for fruits and worked together to coax Lumie awake and make sure she ate something. Neither of them spoke much, as it felt too early for this, but Kassein noted how Alezya stood close enough that their bodies were constantly touching in some capacity. She would keep her arm against his, let their fingers brush, and keep her body attuned continuously to his, like a flower around the sun, always naturally seeking his warmth and presence. There were tender looks, faint smiles, and a light kiss now and then. It felt natural, like a family life they could easily grow accustomed to, and he loved that between them. Kassein savored this fleeting sense of domesticity. He wanted that for them, for Lumie. But he knew the days ahead wouldn't allow it yet.

The skies outside remained unnervingly dark as they left the kitchen and roamed through the castle, heading outside. Though dawn had broken, the heavy clouds cloaked the sky in an ominous shade, blurring the line between night and day. Thanks to being tightly wrapped in the blanket, Lumie was safe from the chill when Kassein stepped out, cradled securely in his arms. Given how dark it was, she might even have been safe from the sunlight. Alezya followed close behind, and he was sure she shared the ominous feeling as she also kept glancing at the dark clouds ahead with a frown.

Lorey was already awake, wrapped in a similar thick cloak and tossing chickens across the yard. The triplet dragons, unbothered by the weather, were pouncing on the prey, squabbling as they scrambled to claim their share. Niiru had learned better than to compete with the rowdy bunch and was careful to stay away from the rabble, dragging its meal closer to Kein for safekeeping. The scene might have been amusing if not for the oppressive weight in the air.

"Morning," Lorey greeted them politely. "I hope you're ready for a busy morning. Did that little sweetheart sleep well?"

She had been kind enough to direct her question to Alezya, who shyly smiled back as Lorey gently rubbed Lumie's back, peeking at the little girl under the cover.

"We go?" Alezya asked Kassein. "To the mountain?"

He gave her a nod.

"Kiera is waiting for us, with our people. Hopefully, the Munsa Tribe will be too. They should have found our army by now."

Alezya reacted to the mention of the Munsa Tribe and gave him a little nod, but her eyes were filled with sadness when she redirected them to Lumie. Kassein's heart sank when he saw her immediately tear up a bit, and she leaned over to press a long kiss on her little girl's forehead.

She whispered some words in their language, and right there and then, he decided that he was definitely going to learn their tongue. No matter how long it took, even if it took him years, he would understand them. He let Alezya take Lumie from him to hug her little girl, wrapping an arm around her waist and pressing his lips to the crown of her head.

When she handed Lumie to Lorey with a tearful smile, he tightened his hold on her, letting her lean into him a bit more.

"Kiera will have already collected Tievin," Lorey gently said. "You guys should get going before the storm comes."

Kassein agreed with a quiet nod. He wished he could have given Alezya more time with her child, but if they were to reunite with his army, they had to get going. He was fairly certain his sister would already be getting impatient.

"Alezya," he gently whispered her name, steering her toward his dragon.

She swallowed and turned her head toward him, giving him a nod and a brave smile that made his heart ache. Kassein let out a faint sigh, and just as she was about to get in step with him, he stopped himself and took a second to press his forehead to hers.

"I promise I'll bring you back to her soon," he whispered.

Whether she understood or not, Alezya nodded and pressed a quick, shy kiss to his lips. Then, she was the first one to turn away from Lumie and take the first determined step toward Kein.

The orange dragon slowly stood, immediately gathering the attention of the younger dragons. Kassein helped Alezya up, and soon enough, they were in the skies, the Onyx Castle reduced to a dark spot in the white background, flying against the wind toward the mountains.

He was glad they'd taken the time to grab thicker clothes for Alezya because the air was biting, and though she didn't seem cold on the inside, her skin was still turning red wherever it was exposed. He moved to shield her body with his as much as he could, but they couldn't get to the mountains soon enough. Kein flew as fast as it could, with all four younger dragons in its wake, flying where its larger body would shield them from the strong winds. The triplets were big enough to endure, but Niiru was exhausted by the time they arrived, and the young dragon darted under Kein as soon as it landed.

Alezya was obviously glad they had made it too because she didn't wait for Kassein to venture inside the mountain, the triplets right behind her while Niiru stuck closer to Kassein. Inside the cave, they first walked past some of their scouting units, who politely greeted Alezya with nods and bowed even lower to Kassein. He slowed down, quietly inspecting his troops as they walked past.

At first glance, there were a few injuries, but nothing too notable; it seemed his men were having a more challenging time with the rough environment than fighting the tribespeople. Many had ice burns and cuts on their hands or were trying to repair their shoes and boots. Overall, it seemed like the morale was still decent, and he suspected his sister had sent some for supplies or to hunt because many men were sitting down and having a meal around little campfires as they walked past them looking for his sister.

"Finally!" Kiera welcomed them with an exasperated groan. "I'm sure I had told you to get your ass here before dawn! I was wondering if you would even get here by midday!"

She stood with her fists on her hips, looking fresh and ready for a new day. She was wearing a new outfit and heavier armor than usual. Her hair was also now swept into a sleek, high braid adorned with intricate silver accessories, a fitting updo for the windy area and upcoming battles. It was clear that her short trip back to the camp had been well-spent.

"Tievin," Alezya blinked, visibly surprised to see the Intendant standing there.

Tievin gave them a polite nod, but based on his messy hair, Kassein could guess his sister had dragged the poor man out of bed early. Either that or Tievin's hair hadn't endured the flight well. Either way, his Intendant looked more sullen than usual, and he was holding on to his notepad for dear life as the triplets immediately darted to him.

"Oh, gods!" He squirmed. "No! Don't you dare! Stop it! No, no! Enough! Gods, would you calm down, you toe-chomping pests!"

The triplets didn't stop, and his hysterical screams didn't even slow them down; they trampled over one another to get to their prey. The poor man began jumping from one foot to another, trying to stay out of their little fangs' reach. Despite the triplets being as large as dogs, the three of them were all trying to get a bite of Tievin's toes for some reason, even as they tripped over one another and squabbled under his feet.

Suddenly, Vele managed to tear off a piece of leather with a loud rip, and Tievin screamed.

Without warning, Alezya suddenly walked ahead of Kassein.

"Down!" she suddenly barked.

All three young dragons froze and immediately laid belly-flat on the ground.

After a second of being completely still, they slowly turned their big eyes to her with a shocked, almost scared look in her eyes, while Tievin carefully stepped away from them.

"Ah!" Kiera scoffed. "...I'll be damned. Well, she definitely has the dragon mama thing down!"

Kassein silently agreed, smiling proudly. It was pretty funny to see the rowdy triplets lying down, quiet and scared of Alezya's scowl.

After a second, two of them sat up, while the other remained lying down, rolling onto its back, and all three of them kept their eyes on Alezya, their tails swishing left and right with interest.

"Thank you, my lady," Tievin said, with a nervous look toward the triplets. "That was quite... Wha–Whose dragon is this?"

Niiru had come into the cave and popped its head out from behind Alezya's legs, watching the tamed triplets with a curious expression, as if trying to figure out what it had missed. As if feeling bolder now that those three were acting calm, the little black dragon began strolling around the cave. It stopped to sniff a dumbfounded Tievin and then glanced around the tiny cave before walking away to venture between the legs of the nearest men.

"Oh, I've been waiting for this," Kiera smirked.

"W-w-what is going on?" Tievin insisted, blinking at the young dragon. "Whose dragon is this, Your Highnesses? Lady Alezya?"

As Tievin was pointing toward the small dragon, Niiru came around, sitting before him.

"It's Niiru," Alezya said.

"Niiru?" Tievin repeated. "That's... What kind of name is that? Whose dragon is this?!"

Kiera was biting her finger with a large grin, her eyes darting between Kassein and Tievin with excitement. After a second, Kassein let out a sigh, and stepped forward, wrapping an arm around Alezya and splaying his hand on her stomach.

"It's Alezya's daughter's," he said. "The egg that hatched, the young dragon we were missing. That dragon is Lumie's."

Tievin scoffed.

"No," he spat after a second.

"No?" Kassein repeated.

"N-no, Your Highness. Miss Lumie is not your child. She doesn't have the Dragon's Blood, nor was she fathered by one of... of your relatives, that we know of. It can't. It cannot be."

"Kein spawned Niiru's egg," Kassein said.

"B-but!" Tievin squawked. "I-it would need to be *your* baby's dragon to be Kein's!"

"There's an egg for my biological child too."

"Your... Y-your... But-W-...Wha-... B-but the two eggs-"

"Both eggs are Kein's," Kassein explained with patience. "The one that hatched fast was Niiru's, Lumie's dragon. The one we were looking for. The other one is for my baby that Alezya is carrying."

Tievin opened his mouth, but no sound came. Kiera let out a sigh.

"Nevermind, this is boring. Anyhow, we found the missing dragon and Alezya's for sure pregnant, Tiev."

"Really? For sure?" he exclaimed. "B-but this dragon-"

"Is her first child's. Lumie's," Kiera sighed. "Kein decided to give her a dragon. Crazy, we know, but that's the theory Lorey came up with, and so far, there's been nothing to prove her wrong. Niiru is Lumie's dragon, the one that hatched ridiculously early, and the second one is for the unborn babe Alezya's carrying. The egg is still growing in the Onyx Castle's garden. And look at the scales she's got. White scales. Like the other egg. And Niiru? Black as his egg."

There was a long silence. Alezya frowned, probably from hearing her name several times, while Tievin had stopped reacting entirely. He was properly stunned, silent, and immobile. Kiera tilted her head.

"Do you think he passed out? Standing up? ...Tiev?"

"It can't be!" Tievin suddenly jerked. "It's impossible! There is no way Kein decided to make a dragon for a-"

"Enough," Kassein suddenly seethed.

His angry tone calmed Tievin's protest immediately, and the Intendant went a bit pale under his glare. Even Kiera pressed her lips together.

"Niiru is Lumie's dragon and Kein's child," Kassein growled. "There is nothing to argue."

"I... I understand," Tievin finally muttered. "And Lady Alezya is indeed... with child?"

"Yes."

He lifted Alezya's hand, showing off the white scales that peppered her skin to Tievin, who observed them with a frown. After a while, the Intendant let out a long sigh, leaned his head back, and massaged his eyelids. Then, he straightened up, and bowed.

"Congratulations, Your Highness," he said, "and congratulations to Lady Alezya on the pregnancy."

Alezya was now looking down at Tievin with a frown, obviously confused. Kassein nodded, dismissing the situation entirely, and turned to his sister.

"So?"

"So?" his sister scoffed. "You leave me in charge all night, and all you have to ask is 'so'? Seriously... Well, nothing much happened, alright? The scouts we sent spotted a lot of movement everywhere in the mountains. Little groups going in all directions but ours. There's definitely something going on out there. All the tribes are agitated."

"They're rallying allies," Kassein explained.

"Allies?" Tievin raised his eyebrows.

Quickly, he explained everything that had transpired with the Munsa Tribe and the other tribes Alezya had spoken to. He had already explained some of it to his sister the previous night, but he took the time to give a more detailed account for Tievin to hear. Kiera listened with a frown while Tievin was already furiously writing in his notepad, frowning. Alezya, who seemed to understand some of what he said, nodded along, her eyes alternating between the three of them to gauge Tievin and Kiera's reactions. When he was done, his sister blinked.

"...This is such an unforeseen development," Tievin whispered. "Those people... Those tribes are really splitting over whether or not to fight us?"

"It's crazy," Kiera nodded. "We've been hunting them without distinction, they shouldn't hesitate!"

"They seem to have noticed we're only after some of them. Alezya seemed to say her birth tribe was hell-bent on attacking us, but the ones she had me meet were of a different mind. She showed them Kein listened to her too. I think they're scared of us, and most of them have no intention to fight. They're terrified of Kein, but they live too far to care what happens on our side of the mountain. I think there's more going on between the tribes than we know."

"So they would have their own reasons," Kiera shrugged, "but are we sure that we do want to keep fighting? You got your girl and her kid, Kassein. If you wanted, we could stop things here and go back to the camp."

Tievin raised his eyebrows in question, probably in favor of that option as well. Kassein hesitated, before he gently pulled Alezya to face him.

"Do you want us to keep hunting?" he asked her. "The tribes, the mountains. Your people, the... Deklaan, was it?"

Alezya nodded.

"Your friends. Do they want to hunt too? ...Why?"

She licked her lips, glancing around, before she suddenly grabbed Tievin's notepad, snatching it and his pen out of his hand and getting on her knees to start scribbling something. All three of them gathered around her after a moment.. Alezya wasn't a great artist by any means, but it didn't take long to realize the triangles she made were meant to be those mountains. She made a circle at the bottom, and lower down, a black dot. She began by pointing to the dot.

"Onyx Castle, yes?" she asked them.

They all nodded, and she moved to the big circle.

"Kassein's home," she said. "Kassein's men, with the medicinal herbs and the fire. And the forest."

She moved up, showing the triangles, and Kassein nodded.

"The mountains."

"My home," Alezya nodded, pointing at one of the triangles nearest to the camp. "Deklaan *Kulani*. This mountain, we attack Kassein's home. Those *kulani*, they hunt Kassein's *kulani*. Munsa *Kulani*, here. They don't hunt Kassein's *kulani*. They don't want to. But my home *kulani*, my father, they want men. More men to hunt Kassein's men."

"Your father?" Kassein frowned.

Alezya paled subtly, and immediately, he knew he would despise the man. Was she scared of her own father? Alezya seemed to hesitate, glancing at them before she ran her hand through her hair.

"My father is a bad commander," she explained. "My Deklaan *Kulani*, they hunt Kassein because of my father. The other *kulani* too. They give men to my father to hunt Kassein and Kassein's men. And to hunt Kein. A lot of men. But the other *kulani*, they don't want to hunt Kassein. They are scared. Their commanders don't like my father. They don't want to hunt Kassein. They are scared of Kein. If Kein stops hunting, they stop hunting too."

"...Well, now that makes things a bit clearer."

"The lady's understanding of our language is impressive," Tievin blinked, clearly stunned. "Archaic for sure, but certainly impressive for a few weeks..."

"Aside from Alezya having the speech of a six year old, can we talk about what she said?" Kiera said. "They would stop fighting us if we tell Kein to stop? That's it? They've been the ones sending men down to fight us!"

"Not their men," Kassein said. "Alezya's father's been sending other tribes' men to attack us."

"With their position, it makes sense," Tievin said, clearing his throat. "Based on Lady Alezya's rudimentary but explicit design, it is most clear that her tribe has enjoyed a privileged position to attack our camp. If my theory that each tribe has been behaving independently is right, and based on what I have seen of the mountains so far, it appears I was, then it is most understandable that the tribes have been suffering from a cruel lack of information that has led them to rely solely on the misinformation provided by individuals like Alezya's father. Crucial information that could have very likely been weaponized to assert dominance in negotiations regarding resources by threatening their safety. Thus, all of this indicates that those tribes have been subjected to Lady Alezya's father's intentions regardless of their own."

"...Meaning?" Kiera grimaced.

"Some tribes had no choice but to fight us," Tievin shrugged. "The Commander's dragon, along with the others of your relatives, have been a constant threat to the tribes. I might add that the previous generations were even less kind to the people of these mountains. Since your father, I am inclined to believe that there have been far fewer killings."

"I get that part, but why would Alezya's father and his tribe be hell-bent on sending men to fight us? They always lose! What's the point? Why would he want to keep going? And worse, based on what Kassein heard from that Munsa Tribe, the guy's rallying even more people to his lost cause too."

"Well, it is hard to determine for sure with the limited information at my disposal, but I would be inclined to believe that their socioeconomic situation is to blame for this ongoing war. More precisely, if he could convince other tribes that sending fresh troops to lead the fight was vital, Lady Alezya's father might have also enjoyed the unique advantages that came with his position. He might have coerced the other tribes into thinking he needed more supplies, for example, or enjoyed trading agreements or perhaps favors from other tribes. Everything points to this man leveraging their unique insight into the situation with our army to scare the other tribes into providing him with whatever he needed to keep us, the enemy, away from the other tribes. Mind you, our recent progress toward those mountains since His Highness became the Commander of this army might have been a tipping point in the situation between those tribes, cementing Lady Alezya's father's power unknowingly."

"In other words, that asshole is using other tribes' fear of us to get free things and sacrificing men to fight us?" Kiera grimaced. "They're the ones who have been sending people to die attacking us!"

"Well, I would say there are probably more nuanced parameters and that those are mere conjectures based on what we could decipher from Lady Alezya's explanations and our own observations, but... yes."

A stunned silence followed, and Kiera let out a whistle.

"By the dragon ancestors," she said. "Well, that explains why she left her tribe, then. I would have flown off too if my father was that much of a manipulative bastard!"

That reminded Kassein of a question he had wondered a long time ago, and hadn't thought about for a while. He frowned and slowly turned to Alezya, trying to find a way to voice this properly.

"Alezya, you said your home tribe hunted you. The Deklaan Tribe. The one who hunted you... Was it your father?"

He regretted his question almost as soon as he'd uttered it. Alezya's face turned pale, and angry tears appeared in her eyes. She clenched her fists so much that Tievin's pen snapped.

"...Yes," she hissed angrily. "My father hunted me."

"...Why?" Kiera asked.

"Because Lumie," Alezya confessed, a tear escaping her eye.

Kassein immediately used his thumb to wipe it away, then put his other hand under her elbow and pulled her to stand.

"Lumie?" he asked.

"My baby," Alezya said. "She is... like snow. She is not..."

"She's all white," Kassein patiently translated for her.

Alezya nodded.

"Father is... He doesn't like Lumie. Because she is white like snow, he hunted Lumie. He hunted Lumie to give Lumie to Kein. He wanted Lumie to be dragon food."

"He wanted to feed your baby to Kein?" Kiera sneered. "What the...?"

"I said no," Alezya kept going. "I took Lumie to the mountains. To leave. To other *kulani*. But... Father's men hunted us. Hunt Lumie. So I..."

"You ran away," Kassein said. "You saved her, Alezya. Lumie is fine."

As tears had begun streaming down her cheeks, he pressed a long kiss on her forehead, rubbing her back to help her calm down. This was the first time she'd told him the entire truth about how she'd come to be with him, about why he'd found her beaten and bruised. By her own father's men, no less...

"That man has to die," Kiera declared, echoing his thoughts. "I've decided. He's dead. What a bastard!"

"I concur," Tievin said with a sour expression and a nod. "What a horrible character! To sacrifice a poor child! His own blood, no less! By the almighty dragon, he's despicable!"

"And Lumie's father?" Kassein asked.

Alezya's eyes opened wide, visibly surprised to hear him ask. She avoided his gaze for a second, causing his heart to skip a beat with worry, but when she returned to Kassein, her eyes were filled with fury and disgust, nothing else.

"He said... he called Lumie *rakshnia*," she muttered.

"I'll take it that's bad?" Kiera tilted her head.

Alezya nodded with an angry expression.

"Really bad," she seethed. "He said Lumie isn't his baby. That I made Lumie with *rakshnia*. Bad blood. But I did not. Lumie is not *rakshnia*, Lumie is just white. Snow child."

"...He didn't want her?" Kassein hissed, furious and dumbfounded.

How could a man refuse his own child? Lumie was an adorable little girl, as beautiful as her mother. He had seen men agonize over their wives not being able to have a child, and that man had refused his simply because she had been born a different color? He clenched his fists, while Alezya's eyes grew angrier.

"He didn't want Lumie," she muttered. "He said... he wanted to hunt Lumie. I said no. He said I couldn't have Lumie, but I wanted Lumie. So I go back to Deklaan. To my father."

A jealous, ugly part of him was relieved that this man had rejected his child; if he had been a half-decent man, Kassein would have never met Alezya nor been given the chance to adopt Lumie as his own. Thinking this, he took a deep breath in, and pulled Alezya in for a gentle hug, putting his lips close to her ears.

"Lumie is perfect," he whispered. "Your baby is as beautiful as you, my moonlight. Your little snow girl is beautiful. I'll love you both. I'll protect you both. I've got you two."

He let her relax against him, rubbing her back while emotions she'd kept suppressed for a while emerged in the form of quiet tears against his torso.

"Alright, I'm adding him to my list," Kiera grunted. "Lumie's bastard father is a dead man too."

"...He's mine," Kassein suddenly hissed.

His sister raised an eyebrow, but Kassein pinned her with a glare that allowed no refusal.

"He's mine," he repeated.

"...Gods, eighteen years old, and you still can't share with others," Kiera rolled her eyes. "Alright, fine. I'll probably have more than my fill of her tribe's bastards to kill, anyway. Bonus points to whoever gets their hands on her wretched father first."

Kassein didn't care which one of them would get to him first, but he certainly wanted to make Alezya's father's death as slow and as painful as possible. He couldn't understand why a man would have thrown out and hunted his own daughter and grandchild. The truth was, Kassein had cared very little about which tribes he would have to defeat until then, but now, he had one he planned to destroy above all else. He hadn't felt such a desire to fight in a long while, but now, his blood was boiling, and outside, Kein's furious growl echoed through the valley too. His sister grinned sinisterly.

"...You and me both, Brother," she smirked. "We do need a proper plan, though. We might have a dragon, but this is foreign territory for us, and if we've learned anything, it's that they are gearing up for this fight. So what's it going to be?"

Kassein turned his eyes back to Alezya, and cupped her face in his hands, gently wiping her tears with his thumbs. Even with her eyes red and her lips in a pout, she was adorable. He gave her a confident smile.

"...We need to meet with the *kulani* that will be our allies. The Munsa, and the others. Alezya can translate a plan for us."

"Sounds fine to me," Kiera shrugged, "but where do we meet them?"

"We'll find them. Alezya probably knows how to find them."

At the mention of her name, Alezya frowned slightly.

"The Munsa *Kulani*," Kassein said. "Your friends. Where are they?"

"They find us," Alezya said. "They say they come to Dragon *Kulani*."

"They might take a while," Kiera frowned. "We've made our position a bit clear with how much ruckus we made, but it might take them all day to come to us."

"It might be worth using Lady Alezya's knowledge to meet those people halfway," Tievin noted. "You might save some hours by walking through the mountains to meet them before they get here, since the Commander and Lady Kiera quite effectively emptied the previous mountains..."

"Let's move the army along," Kiera nodded. "No point in staying here either. And Herken mentioned things have been quiet on his side, I think the tribes won't dare touch the camp with us here. We should consider having him send some of his men to secure the route back..."

"Let's have the whole army come up here," Kassein suddenly decided.

"What?" Tievin squeaked. "But, sir, the camp-"

"The camp is nothing but a bunch of tents and supplies in the middle of nowhere," Kassein hissed. "If we empty it and bring it all up here with us, it doesn't matter. I'd rather ensure we have enough men up here to win whatever war is coming than have a third of my men guarding a piece of land."

"...It's a good point," Kiera said. "If anything happens to the camp, so what? As you said, it's in the middle of nowhere; it's not like there's a village nearby for them to raid or something. Even if they did try to reach the village, it would take them days by foot, and Nebora and Lorey would know what to do."

"Well," Tievin nodded, "it does sound like a sound decision, sir. I shall organize the General's arrival and coordinate with all three generals to move the army to follow you with minimal risks and optimal supplies."

"I'll fly Kiki back to the camp to tell Herken," Kiera said, "and then I'll tour the mountains and see if I can gather any intel. Do you want me to fly Kein too, just so the enemy doesn't know our position? Not that I trust his crazy ass not to throw me off, but..."

"Kein will fly off," Kassein said. "I'll have him roam the mountains, be sure the tribes feel that we're coming for them, friend or foe."

"You're keeping the three terrors," Kiera said.

"I think Alezya can handle them," Kassein said with a smug smirk.

His sister rolled her eyes.

"Alright, whatever. See you all later!"

Just like that, she left to find Kiki outside, and soon after, they heard Kein take off with a growl too.

"We are going to find the Munsa and your *kulani* friends," Kassein told Alezya. "We're taking the baby dragons with us. Tievin will follow us with the army."

"May I suggest you take a unit with you?" Tievin said. "I think I remember that the young Captain Dajan had some positive interactions with Lady Alezya, sir. Keeping some men with you might be helpful if you are to walk ahead."

"Fine," Kassein nodded.

It didn't take long to find the young and eager Captain Dajan and his men, and within the hour, their little scouting unit was ready to depart, Alezya and a tiny herd of young dragons leading them.

While Niiru was sticking by her side, the triplets were happy to run ahead in the tunnels, even if they got lost a couple of times and had to turn back, enough that Alezya quickly learned all three of their names from Kassein and that they were his ten-year-old nephews' and niece's dragons.

The dragons were quite efficient in clearing the path ahead, as their sense of smell easily led them to formerly occupied areas, toward random animals' lairs even, and emptied the tunnels rather quickly. A couple of times, they heard scared human voices running away, but Alezya ignored them, focusing on the direction she was headed. They didn't stay in the tunnels long and, instead, resurfaced on one of the mountains, switching to traveling outside, which was better for keeping an eye on the dragons and the movements ahead.

As planned, Kein was roaming above their heads, guaranteeing that their enemies wouldn't dare show, so they could make good progress by avoiding the indoor mazes of tunnels and cramped caves and taking a main road instead. Still, they walked for a long time, only stopping for a quick lunch break, and Kassein was impressed with Alezya's endurance. He had already noticed she had a great physique under her injuries, but it was his first time seeing her thrive in her environment, and he could easily see how she had survived so long in the mountains while being poorly treated by her tribe. Twice, she designated bushes or herbs with edible food for his men to stock up on, and she once prevented them from falling into a crevice nearly invisible to the naked eye.

Every time they had to climb, she made it look like she was as light as a feather and as nimble as a young dragon. Although he positioned himself to secure her position at all times and only let her hand go when he had to, Kassein felt a bit of pride seeing Alezya move around like this was a casual walk.

Meanwhile, Dajan and his men were beginning to tire from the relentless challenges of the trek; shoes trudging through thick snow, the uneven footing, and the constant shifts between steep ascents, swift descents, and sudden climbs were taking a toll on the men. None of them complained when a woman was leading them without showing a hint of fatigue herself, but it was clear they were exhausted.

It wasn't until later in the day, close to the late afternoon, that Alezya suddenly froze and recalled the adventurous young dragons with a gentle whistle.

When Bora, the most stubborn of the trio, failed to return, Kassein clicked his tongue angrily, prompting the young dragon's immediate sheepish return and a curious glance from Alezya.

He raised his eyebrows, but before he could say something, someone appeared ahead of them. Immediately, many of his men put their hands on their weapons, but Kassein raised his hand to stop them.

He was watching Alezya's demeanor, and she didn't seem nervous about whoever they'd run into. As soon as the person was within range, Alezya spoke to them, and they exchanged words for a couple of seconds before Kassein saw her shoulders relax.

"It's friends," she said.

"The Munsa?"

She gave him a nod, and walked up to the stranger. Even if they'd doubted the newcomer, that person was far too intimidated by the little herd surrounding Alezya to approach her, and instead, they turned around to walk back, guiding them to wherever their tribe was stationed.

Their group was led back inside the tunnels, and it didn't take more than a few minutes before they ran into an impressively large gathering.

"Bora?" Kassein called the dawn-colored dragon. "Go get Kiera and Kiki. Bring them here."

He then sent Leni back the same way to guide Tievin, knowing the Intendant would know to follow the younger dragon with his troops all the way here. The triplets may have been a lively and mischievous trio, but as ten-year-old dragons, they understood a lot more than they let on when they weren't playing or bickering.

Kassein stood silently, his presence as constant and close as a shadow to Alezya. His hand rested lightly on her waist while she engaged with the gathered tribespeople, his watchful eyes alternating between her reactions and the crowd.

To his relief, Alezya appeared comfortable among them—he recognized familiar faces from the Munsa Tribe mingled with a handful of others from the previous gathering.

Many, however, were seeing him for the first time, their expressions marked by a mix of curiosity, apprehension, and respect. He could feel the weight of their glances even more when he looked elsewhere, their eyes continually shifting between Alezya and himself.

Choosing to ignore the attention, Kassein kept his focus on Alezya as she was talking to the crowd. The gathering was a strikingly eclectic mix, and from their diverse clothing, distinctive markings, elaborate jewelry, and varied hairstyles, Kassein estimated there were representatives from at least six or seven tribes, clustered together in small groups. He couldn't understand Alezya's speech, but he heard the word she used for dragons and his own name a couple of times, as well as the name of her tribe. It was likely that she was explaining to the newcomers what she had already explained to the Munsa before and catching them all up to speed.

Then, it was their turn to talk, and there were definitely some questions, Alezya answering and explaining things patiently, pointing at the two young dragons by her side, at Kassein, and so on. But mostly, he realized those people were introducing themselves to her, with hands lightly directed toward their leaders or what he guessed were their seconds or heirs. Then, there was some more talking, some outrage that, luckily for them, wasn't directed at Alezya, but the name of the Deklaan Tribe came up a couple of times. It took a little while, during which he was happy to stand back and let Alezya take the lead.

She might not realize it herself, but Kassein could witness that she had the traits of a leader: she was speaking unafraid, not intimidated by those tribe chiefs who spoke back to her, some of them twice her age, and he could tell when she was fervently defending a point. The Munsa brother and sister, were eagerly talking along with Alezya too, no doubt supporting her based on their corporal cues.

Again, Kassein felt frustrated at his lack of understanding of their language, something he was going to remedy as soon as he could. He didn't mind letting Alezya lead, but he wished he could have been able to support her better.

Luckily, it didn't seem like he needed to intervene; it was clear Alezya was the one leading the discussion, and one by one, the tribe chiefs' questions lessened, leaving them to stare at her with focused frowns or nod along.

Just as most of them looked to be done talking, Kiki's familiar high-pitched growl echoed from outside, frightening the assembly. Seconds later, Kiera waltzed in, attracting many curious stares.

"You found them," she beamed at Kassein. "How are things going?"

"Alezya is handling it," Kassein shrugged.

"Ugh, you don't have to look that smug when you say that. Alezya? Everything going well?"

Alezya turned to them and gave them an assertive nod.

"The Munsa *Kulani* found a lot of friends," she said. "This is other *kulanis* that want to hunt the Deklaan *Kulani*. But Deklaan *Kulani* has found lots of friends too. It's... big hunt."

"A big battle," Kassein rectified for her.

"Big battle," Alezya nodded.

"Promises, promises," Kiera grinned. "So? They've got a battle plan, something?"

"Alezya? Where do we battle?" Kassein asked.

Alezya turned to the others, likely translating, but the Munsa looked at a loss. The siblings exchanged a sour expression before talking to Alezya. Kassein couldn't understand, but he could spot the tension in her shoulders, the frown between her eyes, and the tone with which she spoke to the Munsa.

After a while, she shook her head and turned back to Kassein.

"The *kulani*, they all want to battle or leave battle. They go to Munsa and us or to Deklaan to do battle. All the *kulani*. Munsa *Kulani* said where to find our friends. But battle... after a night and a day. At night. But Deklaan and Munsa are talking to know where to battle. We... We wait for Deklaan to go."

"Tomorrow night, then," Kiera nodded. "That's fine by us. Gives us just enough time for the army to get here if they hurry a bit. Good thing we sent for Herken already."

"It sounds like the Deklaan Tribe wants to decide where the battle will occur," Kassein frowned.

"So what? I doubt there's a place they can find that could increase their chances," Kiera hissed.

"Well, actually," Tievin's voice suddenly rose from behind, "they are likely to try to find a setting where your dragons cannot intervene, Lady Kiera."

They turned around to see an exhausted-looking Tievin stumbling inside, with the young dragon pulling on his cloak. General Kauser was right behind him and gauged the audience with a surprised expression.

"Quite a crowd you've got assembled here, Commander!" he exclaimed, putting his fists on his hips.

"These are all the tribes willing to fight alongside us," Kassein explained. "It sounds like all the tribes are picking a side at the moment, and the Deklaan is trying to get the last word as to where the fight will happen. "

"Ha!" Kauser exclaimed. "Let them pick! Who cares? We can wipe out those people in a blink!"

"The goal isn't to wipe them out," Kiera hissed. "As much as I like a good rumble, we're still officially trying to pacify the north. We will fight so long as they want to fight us, but no need for extra bloodshed."

"As you wish, Princess," Kauser grunted.

"Kiera is right," Kassein said, "and we can't underestimate their knowledge of the terrain. We might walk into a trap or something. We will send scouts as soon as we know the location, but in the meantime, prepare for an all-out battle and coordinate Herken's arrival with the rest of our troops."

"Understood," Kauser said.

The man left the cave, and Tievin let out a little sigh, tightening his cloak around him.

"Well, Commander, I shall make sure the troops are ready in time," he nodded. "Thanks to General Herken's arrival and the short delay until the battle, I am not too worried about resources. I wish there had been more time to map out the area properly, but I guess it would have been a challenge either way if our opponent had insisted on picking the battle place."

"The Munsa," Alezya said. "They tell friends where to go, where to battle. Kassein and Kiera and Kein... Strongest. They battle Deklaan first. Deklaan will want to battle Kassein. But Munsa and friends know where to battle best."

Based on Alezya's gestures, they could deduce that their allies would corner the enemy and attack from side positions while they took them head-on. Kassein nodded; that was fine with him. They had never intended to let the tribes do more than help, and this had always been his war.

"In other words, we're to be the decoy," Kiera grinned. "Fine by me. I like a challenge, and your men have been eager for a proper fight too."

"We should keep Herken's portion of the army at the back for support," Kassein nodded. "If the Deklaan Tribe and their allies want to focus on our forces, they might as well be confused about how many of us there are. We can set up a camp near enough to the battle that they won't be able to corner us and where our allies can retreat if things go wrong. Alezya will be able to show us where to go."

Kiera and Tievin nodded, and Kassein turned to Alezya.

"We will wait to see where the Deklaan *Kulani* wants to fight," he said. "We will listen to you and the Munsa. When the battle starts, you can fly to the Onyx Castle with the baby dragons. We will–"

"No!"

Alezya's blunt refusal took him by surprise. He was confused about what she was suddenly upset about, but before he could react, she went ahead and took his small dagger out of the sheath at his thigh and showed it to him.

"I battle too!" she insisted. "I don't go to Onyx Castle! I battle the Deklaan *Kulani* with Kassein and the Munsa!"

Kassein immediately stiffened.

"No," he grunted, gently taking the dagger out of her hand. "You're not coming. Kein will take you back to Lorey before the battle."

"What?" Alezya frowned. "Kassein!"

"Ooooh, I was wondering when the honeymoon period was going to end," Kiera grinned, crossing her arms. "I guess this is it."

Her brother sent her a furious glare, but there was no wiping that smirk off Kiera's face, and more importantly, Alezya was stepping forward, trying to take that dagger back.

"Kassein!" she protested, more anger in her voice.

"No," he said. "You're not fighting, Alezya. I am not putting you in danger."

"This is my home!" she argued.

"The home that hurt you," he said. "They hurt you before; I'm not letting that Deklaan *Kulani* do it again. I am not letting you in the middle of danger, in the middle of a battle-"

"Not my home, men!" She rolled her eyes. "My home here! The mountains! The friends! The Munsa! All the *kulani*! My home, my friends! My battle, Kassein! I battle too!"

"No."

"I come and battle too!" Alezya shouted angrily.

And now, Kein was growling furiously outside, as if to echo her protests. Kassein rolled his eyes, while his sister grinned some more.

"Having mixed feelings, are we, Little Brother?"

"Stay the fuck out of it."

"Oh, I'm enjoying my front row seat just fine, thanks."

"Kassein!"

"She isn't coming."

"Well," Tievin suddenly cleared his throat, "it definitely sounds like Lady Alezya wants to come, and if I may, I think she should."

This time, his glare landed on Tievin. Alezya stopped shouting, her eyes darting to Tievin with a hesitant expression as if she were trying to decipher what was going on.

"What?" he hissed. "She is no fighter, Tievin."

"Yes, I do understand that, Your Highness. However, I do have to point out that Lady Alezya is right; this is her home, while our army is in foreign territory. Moreover, I would like to point out that, despite my very best efforts, it is still quite an arduous task to tell these tribes apart and, therefore, determine who is friend or foe. We might have walked into this gathering completely unaware of those people's allegiance if not for Lady Alezya. However, Lady Alezya certainly can, and she's the only one to speak our language, or well, the basics of it... It might be worth considering including her in the battle, sir."

"...Tievin's right," Kiera shrugged. "How do you expect to fight if you don't know which ones to slay? Are you going to explain to those people after the fight that you killed some of our allies too? Your woman went through all this trouble to get us allies and a proper battle, Kassein. I think she's a fighter in her own right."

"She's pregnant, Kiera, with my child. I am not risking her anywhere near the battle. She could get injured or killed, and I cannot protect her while I-"

"Kassein, I know!" his sister exclaimed. "And I didn't say she had to be on the ground with us. But what about letting her ride her bestie?"

"...Kein?" He frowned.

"You know another giant dragon obsessed with her?" Kiera raised an eyebrow. "Think about it. She would get a bird—I mean, a dragon's eye view of the battlefield, be protected by Kein's big ass, and be able to direct men and shout orders from above. And if anything happens, your dragon would be there to protect her, and you'd know instantly if something's wrong. She'll be safer in the skies than anywhere else; the enemy doesn't have a dragon, do they?"

Kassein was thinking about it. He still didn't like Alezya being anywhere near the battle, but his sister's idea might have been a decent compromise. Alezya, who was looking between them with a frown, seemed confused. Tievin cleared his throat.

"Lady Alezya, how would you feel about flying Kein during the battle?" he asked with exaggerated gestures. "Kassein and Kiera battle, and you, on Kein?"

Alezya seemed to hesitate, glancing at Kassein.

"Not to the Onyx Castle?" she insisted with a frown.

"...No," he sighed. "Kiera and Tievin think you should fight. But you would be safe with Kein. Flying above the battle."

He waited while Alezya seemed to be hesitating, glancing at Tievin, then Kiera, then back to him.

"...I fly with Kein," she finally said, sounding doubtful. "To battle?"

Kassein nodded. He didn't want Alezya anywhere near danger, but from her spark of fury, he could tell she wouldn't have backed down without a compromise, and Kein was likely to be the safest bodyguard he could find her. His dragon wouldn't allow anything to happen to her, and if things were to take a wrong turn, it would fly out of there and take Alezya back to safety.

From her expression, he could tell she wasn't fully convinced, but it didn't matter; her safety came first, and she had already agreed to that compromise.

"I don't want you in the battle," he said, "but you would be safe flying Kein."

She was still hesitant, but Kassein stepped forward, gently pressing his hand against her stomach.

"For the baby," he whispered. "I want you safe. Not hurt or in danger. You will be alright with Kein. My dragon can protect you. Yes?"

After a second, Alezya finally gave him a little nod.

"Yes," she muttered, putting her hand on his.

Chapter 19

Alezya wasn't fond of Kassein trying to keep her away from the battle, but she understood the baby was on his mind, and she could accept that. However, she refused to be completely helpless. Knowing she would be riding Kein alone, she was a bit nervous, but she liked that compromise, mostly because she knew the orange dragon would listen to what she wanted to do. In fact, she was almost certain that between her and Kassein, Kein might be slightly more likely to listen to her; she wasn't completely sure, but hopefully, she wouldn't have to test it out.

"The children dragons?" she asked. *"They fly to Kalat Unshreik?"*

"Yes," he said. *"Too small."*

Alezya nodded. They could agree on that; she didn't want Niiru or any of the younger dragons near the battle. She'd come to really like Leni, Vele, and Bora, although their favorite pastime seemed to be terrorizing the humans around them. She was curious about what kind of children had such turbulent dragons.

"Alezya?" Ekata called her. "Is everything alright?"

"Yes," she nodded. "I was just talking to them about the upcoming battle... I don't think they mind us not picking the battle location."

"As if we had a choice," Ekut grunted, his fists on his hips. "Those bastards are trying to corner us in an area that will favor them. We will know by dawn though. Our scouts that have gone to negotiate should return by then."

"If they aren't slaughtered before they make their way back..." Ekata muttered. "Anyhow, are you sure they're fine with our plan? They agreed?"

"They did," she nodded. "I explained it to them, but I think Kassein and his sister here, Kiera, are confident enough that they will win. Kassein mentioned he wants me to ride his dragon, so..."

"You will ride his dragon?" Ekata muttered, sounding impressed. "Really?"

Alezya blushed, a bit embarrassed but proud.

"Yes," she said. "I've only flown Kein alone once before, but... it should be fine."

The two young women turned to Kiera and Kassein, who were in similar stances with their arms crossed. They were visibly waiting for them with the same calm posture, both radiating silent power.

"I'm not too worried," Ekata scoffed. "Honestly, I'm not convinced just their clan leader and his sister wouldn't be able to win this war by themselves."

Indeed, if Kassein was impressive in terms of size, Kiera wasn't far behind him. She was imposingly tall and muscular for a woman, with a lean body and toned muscles that left no doubt about her fighting skills. Not only that, but she was carrying a pair of long swords hanging at her sides, a smaller blade attached to her hip, and something like a bow attached to her back.

"I've seen them fight," Alezya nodded. "They really are good. They are not just strong but incredible fighters as well. But we will need more to win this battle if what we've heard so far is true..."

All the accounts they had gotten so far from nearby clans and bold spies hinted at a large-scale battle coming. Many clans that Alezya had never heard of before had left their mountains to partake in the fight; they had joined either her side or her father's. If it weren't for the Dragon Clan being on their side, they would have been a lost cause. From what they had heard, her father had already rallied over a dozen clans for sure, and the numbers were growing. Alezya's message had spread, begging people to trust the Dragon Clan to spare them, but from what they'd heard back, too many feared Kassein and his men too much to trust them. She knew Ekata wasn't saying it, but too few clans had decided to rally with them, while some had shamelessly announced they wouldn't partake in the fight at all, coming up with excuses like they were too far to be concerned or they had too few fighters. Alezya could understand their fears, but she wasn't sure she would be willing to forgive cowardice once this was over. There were too many lives at stake, and she had a feeling that those who had chosen to stay away from the fight had done so knowing that either way, they would win. Either the Dragon Clan was gotten rid of, they would win and uphold their promises to stop hunting the survivors, or it had all been a trap and the Dragon Clan would keep hunting them anyway.

"We can definitely win," Ekata nodded, "but what we need is to be sure we can coordinate the attacks with the Dragon Clan. They won't know who to attack if we don't tell them, and we can't afford to have any of our fighters decimated by them."

"I like the idea of Alezya flying above the battle," Ekut nodded. "Since you're the only one who speaks their language, you should be able to direct them where we need them."

"...We should all know it," Alezya frowned.

"What?" Ekata asked, confused.

"We should all learn their language," Alezya insisted. "I can't direct everyone, even from a dragon. What if something happens to me? No, I need all our clan chiefs to know the basics of the Dragon Clan's language."

"But how? I mean, we do have most of our allies gathered here or in the caves nearby, but–"

"Gather them now," Alezya said.

Then, she turned around and, out of the blue, walked to the trio. She passed Kassein and Kiera, who were watching her with the same curious expression, and grabbed Tievin's sleeve. The poor man had been busy trying to get Leni and Vele to stop chewing on his coat, but it only took one glance from Alezya for both young dragons to stop. Then, she pulled on his cloak and dragged him over to the little gathering of clan chiefs.

"This is Tievin," she said. "He's their Clan Chief's assistant or something, and most importantly, he's an educated man. He does all their writing and reading, I think. He can teach us all."

While the rest of the clan chiefs arrived, she turned to Tievin, who blinked, utterly confused. Alezya granted him a smile, but that only made him grimace nervously and step back.

"*Tievin, you teach us words,*" she said.

"*M-mi-mi dyiati?*" he mumbled. "*What are you–*"

"*Us,*" she insisted, pointing at the clan chiefs and herself. "*You, Tievin. You teach us the Dragon* Kulani *words.*"

"*An lestu taqin fahamu–*"

"*No,*" Alezya stopped him. "*Tievin speak the dragon words. Tell us words.* Dragon *is dryagaan.* More *is inkir.* Meat *is taam.*"

After a bit, Tievin turned to Kiera and Kassein, exchanging some words, but Kiera shrugged, while Kassein remained with his arms crossed and an implacable expression. Then, Tievin let out a heavy sigh, combed his long hair back, and, to Alezya's surprise, quietly arranged his layers of fur coats, which turned out to be three of them, to be able to sit down on the floor. The young dragons immediately darted to try and bite his pen, his notepad, and whatever else they could, but a word from Alezya had them lying down and pouting around Tievin.

"*Thank you, Dyiati Alezya,*" Tievin said. "*This. This is mountain, yes?*"

Alezya gestured for all the clan chiefs to sit down with her, and suddenly, the cave transformed into an impromptu classroom for a crash course in the language of the Dragon Clan.

Though reluctant at first, Tievin proved to be a surprisingly effective teacher. He filled every inch of his notepad with sketches, accompanied by exaggerated gestures and deliberate repetition of each word until the group grasped its meaning.

Even when his antics bordered on the ridiculous, he pressed on, his determination eclipsing any embarrassment. The leaders sat around him, echoing each word and phrase, ensuring they could navigate basic conversations, issue simple directions, and piece together rudimentary sentences in the foreign tongue. After a while, Alezya felt a warm presence behind her and leaned back against Kassein's solid torso.

Where Lorey was patient and understanding, Tievin was an uncompromising instructor. As he made the Samial Clan Chief repeat the same word over and over, Alezya began to wonder if they'd have to intervene to save the man from being strangled out of sheer frustration.

Still, despite his relentless methods, Tievin's efforts paid off. By the end of the session, they had all mastered enough of the language for the battle ahead. Alezya herself had learned how to give clear directions, indicate locations, and use critical commands like "retreat," "forward," "turn around," and "attack."

She had to admit, choosing Tievin had been a far better decision than she anticipated. Not only did he teach them the essentials, but he also provided invaluable insights into the structure of the Dragon Clan.

He introduced them to Kassein's three senior fighters, explained their roles, and detailed how they could be most effective with their unique weaponry. Then, to everyone's surprise, it was his turn to ask questions.

Alezya hadn't expected it, but right when they'd thought they were done with his lesson, Tievin suddenly seized the opportunity and kept talking with his own barrage of questions. One by one, he interrogated the clan chiefs about their fighters—their strategies, weaponry, and techniques—and even asked to see their weapons.

Though Tievin declined to handle the weapons himself, Kiera jumped in eagerly, her excitement growing with each new tool she inspected. Before long, her enthusiasm escalated into challenging several men to duels outside, clearly reveling in the chance to test the strength and skills of other fighters.

Unlike his sister, Kassein appeared relatively indifferent to the proceedings, quietly observing everything as it unfolded.

Occasionally, one of his men would approach, exchange a few words, and leave with nothing more than a nod or, at most, a blunt three-word reply from him. For a clan chief, Kassein seemed unusually relaxed, though Alezya could sense his sharp vigilance. His gaze roamed constantly, silently tracking everyone and everything in the area.

When Tievin finally finished his interrogation of the others, he turned to Kassein, initiating a lengthy discussion.

The two spoke in low voices, with Tievin jotting notes in his ever-present notepad, their conversation marked by an intensity that suggested deeper strategies were being laid out. She hoped their warriors were ready for the battle ahead because from what they had heard, the fighters that the Munsa had rallied would be in severe danger otherwise.

She understood Ekata's plan of spreading out their fighters to avoid being cornered regardless of the determined battlefield, but Alezya couldn't help but think many of the clanspeople were going to die in this war. It felt like everything had been blown out of proportion in a matter of days, and now, from every corner of the mountains, the clans were taking sides or hiding in fear of the outcome. The entire future of the clans was going to depend on whoever won this battle.

When she gave herself time to think, Alezya was overwhelmed by doubt. What if her father had rallied even more clans or found a horrible plan to trap them and the Dragon Clan lost? What if Kassein was injured or killed? Or Kiera? What if they lost so many people that the clans held her responsible?

"Alezya."

Kassein's gentle voice took her out of her spiraling thoughts as if he'd sensed her inner turmoil. Gently, he brushed her hair back, pressed a swift kiss to her temple, and then got up, offering a hand to help her up.

She hadn't realized they'd been sitting for so long that her legs had gotten a bit sore, and she stretched, looking around. Tievin was now chatting with two of the three men who were Kassein's senior fighters, and they could still hear Kiera fiercely dueling outside. At another end of the cave, the clan chiefs were having an animated discussion about how to combine their forces best. It made Alezya realize she was the only one without a clan there, despite being a central piece to the upcoming battle.

Strangely, she felt far closer to the Dragon Clan than any of the others, and she kind of liked that. Kassein's men also interacted with her with extreme politeness, as if she was just as important as Kiera or Tievin. It was a bit overwhelming.

Just then, the voices outside changed tones, and some men came rushing into the cave. Kassein reacted first, pulling Alezya behind him, but after a second, it was clear there was no danger: the pair of exhausted men who had just walked in wore the attire of allied clans.

"Finally!" Ekut exclaimed, walking up to them.

"How did it go?" Ekata asked with a concerned frown. "Did everyone make it back?"

"Yeah," their man nodded. "The others are behind us. That Deklaan Clan bastard made a big show of sending us back unharmed out of 'fairness,' he said. He is confident he will win this war, Munsa Clan Chief. That man's arrogance was oozing from all his pores."

"He's rallied over a dozen clans," the other man shook his head. "Some of them looked like they didn't want to be there; I think he threatened them, to be honest."

"Damn it!" the Samial Clan Chief hissed.

"What else was said?" Alezya asked.

The two men exchanged a nervous glance.

"Well, he made a point of telling all the representatives who attended that this was their last chance to rally to him before the battle tomorrow at dusk. That those who didn't help him were basically deserters, and he wouldn't forgive traitors."

"What?" Alezya scoffed. "He can't force clans to fight for him!"

"Oh, he is trying," the scout grunted.

Alezya felt Kassein's hand on her shoulder, and it helped her calm down a bit. He could probably feel her tension, but she would have to wait to explain to him.

"Fine," Ekata sighed. "We can send a similar message, minus the threats. That clans are welcome to stay aside, but if they fight alongside Darak, they're enemies."

"This might scare some into rallying to him," Ekut noted.

"And it could convince others to stay out of it," Alezya insisted. "I'm for it."

They nodded and turned their gazes back to the scouts, who had taken this opportunity to drink some water. Then, one of them wiped their mouth.

"...There's more," he admitted with a serious expression. "They've picked a location. ...It's the Wailing Rift."

A silence followed his words.

"The Wailing Rift?" Ekata repeated.

Alezya let out a scoff.

"Is that a joke?" she said. "The Wailing Rift doesn't exist. It's just a legend to scare children. ...Right?"

The twins' expressions looked far too somber for her taste. They exchanged a look, and Ekata shook her head.

"No, it does exist," she muttered after a bit. "It's located in the west, about... twenty-five miles away. With our load, the terrain, and the size of our group, it's a fifteen-or-so-hour trek from here. We've never been there ourselves, but we've heard from other clans that it does exist, and it sounded as treacherous as the legends say too. By all accounts, it has to be one of the worst possible locations for a battle of this scale..."

"Darak has made allies with the clans located near the rift," Ekut groaned. "That's the only possible explanation for them picking that area. They'll take full advantage of the terrain while we are in the dark unless we find another clan that knows something useful. But it might be too late for that. If they want us to arrive by dusk, we'll barely have enough time to make the journey..."

"We can ask around," Ekata shrugged, "but I'm betting they already know we won't find anyone. As you said, they probably picked a terrain that gave them the upper hand. I bet it's too deep and too narrow for the dragon as well. According to what we know, it has large rock towers that are pointed at the sky, high and sharp. Our people who have seen it describe it like a giant crevice with fangs... Darak's so shit scared of the dragon he will have picked a narrow rift to minimize the dragon's attacks."

"He picked somewhere that's far enough that our men will be tired by the time we get there too," Alezya muttered.

"That bastard!" the Samial Clan Chief hissed. "He is acting confident of his victory in front of the clans while setting this battle like a spineless coward! I'd like his nasty tongue ripped out of his throat!"

Alezya was just as frustrated. She hadn't anticipated this while letting her father pick the terrain, even if she was sure he wouldn't have gone with anything they suggested anyway. But his decision was a significant blow. A twenty-five-mile trail through the mountains was no promenade. Kassein's men and the clans would have weapons, equipment, shields, and camp supplies to carry. Alezya clenched her fist, frustrated. It was just like her father to use every single tool at his disposal to weaken his enemy rather than risk facing them on equal footing.

"Let him pick whatever terrain he wants," she hissed. "My father will always play dirty either way. We shouldn't think this will be his only trick."

"Understood," Ekata nodded, "and it's not like we have much of a choice anyway. We should focus on how to keep our forces strong enough for battle after a fifteen-hour journey!"

"We'll find a way," Alezya muttered. "We can make them wait. Even if we do take fifteen or sixteen hours, we don't have to arrive right away to fight. Let's make him wait for us instead. Not long enough for him to set traps, but just enough to unsettle him. My father is forced to wait for us anyway. He might have picked the battle location, but we should use that to set the pace. He might have decided on dusk, but he won't have anyone to fight until we arrive; let him wait and simmer in the fear he's trying so hard to hide. I know my father enough to know it's all an act. He's always acted more confident than he is to hide how much of a coward he is. Tell the other clans and our men. We might have to get up at dawn and get moving right away. We need to gather as many supplies as we can and be ready for an early departure."

"Sounds like a fine plan to me," Ekata nodded, her brother agreeing quietly.

"I'll explain to the Dragon Clan meanwhile," Alezya said.

While the twins left, she turned to Kassein; Kiera and Tievin gathered too, having visibly understood some big discussion had taken place. Alezya took her time to explain, to be sure they had understood most of it.

The fifteen-hour hike, the treacherous battleground, and the plan to have their allies surround their enemies. She was certain Ekata and the clan chiefs had already sent scouts, and she knew some of them would use birds to have messages cross long distances shortly, so she knew their other allies would be moving too.

"*Fifteen?*" Kiera tilted her head, not looking all that troubled about the long journey.

"*A day,*" Alezya emphasized with a nod, worried they didn't understand. "*Long day.*"

Kassein and his sister exchanged a few words, out of which Alezya only briefly caught the words "dragon," "Kein," and "flight."

"Kassein?" Alezya asked, perplexed.

Without explaining, he suddenly began grabbing the different bags of supplies he could find around the cave, Tievin talked to their senior fighters quickly, and Keira stepped away, leaving Alezya utterly confused.

In fact, it took several minutes for her and the other people around to understand what the Dragon Clan was doing. Bit by bit, they were gathering all the supplies outside, and wrapping it all up with tight ropes.

The powerless clanspeople were left to watch as slowly, a little mountain of supplies was assembled, almost everything but their weapons and coats. Then, when Alezya was left standing outside staring at all their stuff, the twins came back to her side, looking just as confused.

"What's going on?" Ekut exclaimed. "They walked in, and their men started gathering our food and everything! Our men are nervous!"

"They know we need that stuff, right?" Ekata frowned.

"I-I'm not sure yet," Alezya admitted.

Out of nowhere, Kein arrived, along with Kiki, and all of a sudden, it became clear to Alezya.

"The dragons," she said. "They're going to make the dragons carry our supplies!"

"What? Really?"

"I just explained to them about the journey and all. I was nervous they hadn't understood, but I think they plan to make the dragons carry all of our stuff!"

"Oh, that makes sense," Ekut blinked. "They left everyone their weapons and cloaks."

"It's going to save everyone a lot of time and energy if the dragons can carry all this around," Alezya gasped.

She walked up to Kassein, who took her hands.

"*Kein take it and fly?*" she asked to confirm.

"*Kiki too,*" Kassein nodded.

Did that mean dragons could carry this much weight? She'd had doubts upon seeing the mountain of supplies, but divided between Kein and Kiki and knowing the distance would be short for them, it didn't seem impossible. She was certain they were smart enough to make multiple trips if needed.

She smiled at Kassein, already feeling better. This was going to be helpful in keeping everyone's spirits up if they didn't have to worry about hauling heavy loads.

"I guess that means we're all ready for tomorrow, then," Ekata shrugged. "I'll inform everyone to sort out what they want to carry and what they want to leave to the dragons, and we should have a nice dinner; we'll need the energy and all the extra sleep we can get tonight."

"I'll organize the night watch with one of their senior warriors," Ekut said. "We should start working with them and get ready."

"Can I help?" Alezya asked.

"You can rest," Ekata winked. "Let the men do the work for once."

Alezya didn't feel like resting much though, so while everyone got busy inside, she took Kassein along with her to go hunting and pick herbs for dinner. She showed him the kind of traps she usually built to catch small prey, herbs she picked, and which were poisonous. She didn't have time to wait for prey to fall into her trap, but luckily and to everyone's delight, the dragons showed up with freshly killed prey for the humans to share, and kept going out to hunt, again and again, as if they'd decided to feed the entire group of humans, until they eventually stayed and ate their own share.

"There's enough meat for everyone," Ekata remarked with a shocked expression.

"That's life with the Dragon Clan," Alezya beamed, petting Kein for its good job.

Thus, they had to find a large clearing to make a fire big enough to cook it all, and there was a continuous stream of meat-filled plates being delivered from there to inside the caves they were occupying.

Alezya and Kassein isolated themselves in a corner to eat, but soon enough, everyone had to gather and crowd the caves as a heavy downpour started outside, ending the cooking session and forcing everyone to run back inside with the last plates.

Despite the terrible weather and the prospect of the battle, Alezya noticed the morale was good; men were delighted to have meat for dinner, and since the word had spread they wouldn't have a heavy load to carry, their confidence had climbed too.

Even more shocking, the Dragon Clan's fighters seemed to be making a conscious effort to try and mix with the other clans. She spotted Dajan nearby, laughing with a bunch of men and women from the Munsa Clan as they all made wide gestures to understand each other. The Samial Clan Chief and Ekut were also seated with one of the Dragon Clan's senior warriors, and she was fairly certain they were talking strategy. Kiera was apparently having a blast defeating some of the fighters in arm wrestling, and Tievin was talking to other people from the Northern clans, visibly teaching them more words and learning some of theirs.

It moved Alezya, how easily they were all chatting and finding ways to communicate and laugh together. She knew most of them were fighters, as the Samial and Munsa Clans had hidden their elders, women, and children in caves nearby, and apparently, it was enough for all those men to bond. It wasn't completely seamless; arguments erupted a couple of times, but they were quickly defused by other people separating the fighters. Once, Kiera even grabbed one of their men by the collar, and dragged him outside in the rain like a child. Alezya wasn't sure what happened, but when the man returned a while later, he was drenched, had a massive bruise on his cheek, and sat in a corner with a sour expression.

Alezya noticed that although he didn't say a word all this time, Kassein's presence was enough to tame some of his men; when some discussions became heated, a single glance in their direction was enough for the Dragon Clan warrior to pale and calm down.

Alezya couldn't help but love his quiet strength. All her life, she had known men to raise their voices and act violently the second she uttered one wrong word.

Kassein was different; he was the most powerful man she'd known, and yet, he managed to make his aura alone enough to tame other fighters and coerce them into behaving. He spoke softly and never raised his voice; he was only violent toward his enemies and if provoked first. He didn't even seem to speak much to his own men; everyone seemed to go to Tievin or one of those senior fighters when they had questions, and yet, it was clear he was their leader. Alezya's father would have never allowed another fighter to give orders in his stead, and most clan chiefs wouldn't even allow a woman to speak up at all.

Yet, Kassein had trusted her blindly to coordinate their efforts with the Munsa and the other clans and relay the information despite her limited vocabulary. Tomorrow, he was going to take all of his fighters to war because she needed him to.

Alezya let out a faint but content sigh, relaxing against his torso with her belly full and her body warm, thanks to her fancy coat and the hot-skinned man surrounding her with his long and thick limbs.

"Sleep?" Kassein suggested, and she nodded.

It was as if his whisper carried the weight of a shouted command; all around them, the Dragon Clan fighters fell silent or reduced their voices to hushed murmurs. They moved with purpose, swiftly gathering the remnants of their dinner for cleanup, unpacking their bedding, and lining up along the walls to settle in for the night. They even took out large blankets to share, covering up to three men with some, including fellow fighters from the other clans as they joined them without distinction.

It was like a ripple effect, everyone preparing for sleep simply because Kassein was. The sight brought a smile to Alezya's lips as she curled up beside him. For once, she didn't feel the cold floor; Kassein's arm was her pillow, his breath was warming up her neck, and she was basking in his heat, so relaxing that the rhythmic drumming of rain and the rumble of thunder outside became a soothing backdrop, lulling her into a peaceful sleep before long.

The night felt like it had lasted seconds.

Alezya was stirred awake by the subtle activity around her; after years of either sleeping with one eye open or alone with Kassein, she had grown attuned to even the slightest movements. The quiet rustling of dozens of men preparing for a long journey was more than enough to rouse her.

She could tell Kassein was still asleep behind her, even slightly snoring and unbothered by the ruckus around them. Kiera was the first to notice Alezya's open eyes and approached, nudging her brother's feet with a firm kick.

"Kassein," she barked. *"Up."*

He answered with a growl, and Kiera rolled her eyes before turning around, fists on her hips, and suddenly yelling orders without the need for any translation. All the men who weren't already up jerked awake or sat up with visible panic. Alezya smiled and spun around. Kassein was still very much asleep and remarkably unbothered.

"Kassein," she whispered, before putting a peck on his lips. "Wake up, my love."

He blinked awake and groaned before hiding his face in the crook of her neck, making Alezya smile. She patted his torso.

"Come on," she said, not bothering to use his language. "We have to get up and go."

She had to use some more pushes and kisses to nudge him awake as if they were alone in the cave and not surrounded by dozens of men preparing for war. By the time he finally sat up and stretched, almost everyone around was gone or carrying their stuff outside.

Ekata came to find Alezya with a yawn.

"Slept well?" Ekata asked.

"Great, actually," Alezya confessed while standing up, leaving Kassein to get up at his own pace. "How is everyone?"

"Better than I would have expected, actually," Ekata blinked. "I think having a really nice meal with meat and getting to know our allies boosted everyone's morale. The downpour also helped get rid of some of the snow outside, so our journey will be easier than anticipated, thanks to that and the dragons carrying a lot of the supplies. I don't want to be too optimistic, but I'd say our odds aren't looking too bad for now."

"Yeah, I think it's going to be helpful. Is everyone ready to go soon?"

"The sun's starting to rise, so yeah, they should be. Look, we discussed with their people and our clan chiefs, but we think it's better if we, the Munsa and Samial, lead the way. Their men are obviously in great shape, but they don't know how treacherous the terrain can be up here. Some of them were showing us their scrapes from yesterday. We already sent our best scouts to clear paths ahead, and we were thinking of leading their fighters in small groups to be sure we keep a good pace while we're in a flat area and can lead them out of the tricky trails. We can't afford to lose anyone due to a stupid fall or something. Is that alright with them?"

She asked while glancing at Kassein, but from what Alezya could tell, he was still half asleep and slowly putting on his protective coverings with a grumpy expression.

"I'm sure it will be, but you should tell Tievin and Kiera, or better yet, those senior fighters we met yesterday, Sazaran and Kauser. Kassein's more hands-off... Don't worry, they'll listen."

"Got it. That Tievin guy is getting really good at understanding us, actually. It saves time."

"He's great," Alezya smiled.

Ekata walked away, and Alezya quickly made sure she and Kassein were ready to join everyone outside. The rain had reduced to a faint drizzle, which actually worked to their advantage, and the day wasn't cold enough for it to accumulate again.

Outside, an impressive procession had formed.

The men stood in neat lines, and Ekata's plan seemed to have been carried out to the letter, as for each gathering of men, there were scouts of each clan leading them. Not only from the Northerners, but it seemed the Dragon Clan had assigned some of their people to partner up with them and share the scouting and unit-leading tasks. It was probably a good idea, given how temperamental Kassein's men could be and the limited communication... The bulk of the fighters were tightly assembled along the trail, but it wasn't until they were all outside that Alezya grasped the sheer size of their force.

She couldn't help but wonder if Kassein's men had spent the previous night in nearby caves and she simply hadn't seen them, or if more had arrived throughout the night. It now looked like there were hundreds of them, filling every available inch of the nearby trails, with some stretching far down the mountain path. More piles of supplies were gathered for the dragons to carry, though it was clear it would take multiple trips for Kiki and Kein to transport it all.

Neither Kiera nor Kassein seemed the least bit concerned. The siblings were in full gear, wearing it as if it weighed nothing. They hadn't bothered with cloaks, unlike the others. While Kiera was already off chatting with Tievin up the route, Kassein didn't even look at his men before he turned back to Alezya, his expression softening as he carefully adjusted her cloak, his concern evident in the gesture.

"Sleep? Cold?" he asked.

Alezya shook her head. She was fine and, for the first time, starting to feel optimistic too. She had underestimated how formidable his clan was and how many of his men he would mobilize for this, but now, it was evident Kassein didn't have any thought of losing.

He pressed her cheeks between his hands and leaned down for a kiss as if there weren't dozens of men in the vicinity. As expected, no one dared to say a word or even glance twice in their direction. Instead, the crowd parted ways with respectful bows and ready stances when he guided Alezya ahead, and she was glad he wasn't putting her at the back.

If there was one thing Alezya was confident about, it was her endurance, and she refused to not make the same journey as everyone else; she knew the mountains well, and she could have easily been as efficient as any of the scouts out there.

Even better, Kassein let her take the lead as they passed by lines and lines of men, some from various clans even greeting her as she walked past. Once again, Alezya felt both burdened and proud about her sudden status among all the clans. Ekata took the time to inform her of everything, and she was made aware of most decisions from either side; Kassein even let her make some for the Dragon Clan, at times.

From running away to save her child to the woman who was now leading a gathering of warriors larger than she'd ever seen was just an eerie experience for her.

"Let's get going," Ekut said as they met him at the head of the procession. "Our first scouts came back and cleared the way. They're going to continue ahead, making sure we don't run into any problematic grounds or an ambush."

"Yes, Ekata told me," Alezya nodded to him and the Samial Clan Chief. "Let's go."

Just like that, with a few words from her, hundreds of men began to march toward the battle ahead.

It took a few minutes, but before long, columns of men were venturing on the endless trails of the mountains, some chatting, some quiet, but at a steady pace led by Alezya and the clan chiefs.

The few groups of men marching ahead to clear the route were doing a great job, coming back regularly and filling them in on the terrain and best routes, the decision usually made quickly between the clan chiefs.

It didn't take long for Kiera to be bored with the trail, however, and she whistled for Kiki to come get her before she joined the scouting efforts, mapping their road from the skies. She and Ekut seemed to get along well, even teasing each other at times like siblings would. Tievin was the first one to be panting, and by the end of the first hour, he'd shed one of his cloaks and tied his long hair in a bun. Alezya was fairly certain she heard him complain and grumble in a low voice in their language, but he didn't ask for a break. No one asked to stop, and whenever she glanced back, almost fearing they'd lost some of the group somehow, she could always find the long columns of men still keeping up, as far as her eye could see through the sinuous route. The lessened load, the weather that seemed almost perfect for their journey, not too cold nor too warm, and the filling dinner really did seem to have brought the spirits up.

It was a couple of hours later that they all agreed to take a break to check that all the fighters were keeping up and have a short breakfast. Kassein took Alezya to sit on a rock, and to her surprise, he somehow managed to produce dried meat and fruits from the satchel she hadn't even noticed attached to his belt.

"You have food?" she asked.

"For you and baby," he nodded.

So he'd taken the time to find a satchel he definitely didn't have before just to carry their food.

Alezya smiled, feeling touched. Kassein made sure she ate and drank well, and while they rested and waited for everyone to finish their meals, he even sat on the ground and massaged her legs. She would have refused out of embarrassment if the sensation hadn't felt so good.

Instead, she acted as if this was a completely normal situation and took a look around. All the men within her eyesight were eating, taking supplies out of the few bags that had been carried, sending one or two to replenish water in a nearby stream the scouts had identified, and even trying to discuss the difference in diets between the clans, from what she caught.

The Northerners seemed utterly confused about the Dragon Clan boiling their water to warm it up without adding at least some herbs to it, and when they forced them to try some, the Dragon Clan laughed, pleased but not shocked at their tea. Why were they drinking unflavored hot water, then? She was a bit confused, but it seemed the men were happy to laugh about it. The pleasantries didn't last long, though; they couldn't afford to rest, and despite a few protests, soon, everyone resumed walking again.

It was good they'd stopped because the harshest part of the journey was still to come; crossing more than twenty miles across mountains made for some grueling physical exercise, some tortuous paths, and a couple of uphill climbs that made everyone shut up and let out collective groans.

Alezya noticed Kassein's hands were always nearby to catch her at the tiniest hint of her slipping as if he was the one who'd grown up climbing icy rocks and not her, and it was slightly infuriating to see how his colossal frame didn't seem bothered at all by the extra physical exercise; despite his large shoulders, he moved like a snow leopard, unbothered by the elements. Behind them, she definitely heard a few men letting out swears as they slipped, and a couple of times, there was a commotion, with a man caught by his teammates before he fell into a crevice no one else seemed to have noticed, and another who twisted his ankle.

This was how Alezya realized that some men in Kassein's clan were actually trained as some sort of healers because in record time, the man's ankle was covered with some unguent, bandaged, held between wood pieces, and he was carried to the back of the procession.

Thankfully, there were no more accidents as they reached midday, when they finally agreed on a break, to everyone's relief, and again, all the clans had no trouble coordinating lunch, some even running off to hunt nearby. The leaders gathered to eat together, and Kiera landed, coming up to them while Kiki flew off again, probably to help Kein carry the supplies over.

"We're making good progress," Ekata said. "I didn't think we'd reach this clearing until later."

"Alezya!" Kiera called.

She looked up, and Kiera marched over, snatching Tievin's notepad out of his hands on her way, before she slammed it on the ground at their feet, and began drawing something.

Alarmed, Alezya approached, wondering what had Kiera all riled up, but quickly, she recognized a landscape, a strange landscape with what looked like giant stalagmites and a narrow rift.

"The Wailing Rift," Ekata muttered.

"*This*?" Kiera tapped the drawing. "*Battle, yes?*"

"*Yes*," Alezya nodded.

"*It's too small for dragons*," Kiera said, mainly to her brother.

Kassein nodded, but they weren't as surprised as Alezya had feared; she'd managed to warn them of that ahead of time.

So, she turned to Kiera, trying to understand.

"I told you," she said. *"Last night."*

"Too small for Kein," Kiera scoffed, *"but too small for Kiki too!"*

"I know," Alezya bit her lip, "but I think we still can fight. *Battle with a lot of Dragon* Kulani *men. Kiera and Kassein battle too."*

Kiera groaned.

"But Kiki loves to fight!"

Alezya's jaw dropped. Was that what she was annoyed about? That her dragon wouldn't get to fight?

Alezya slapped her forehead. Of course. She had never seen Kiera actually look intimidated by anything. She should have known better than to think a battle location was going to be an issue.

"More for you and me," Kassein shrugged. *"And Kiki can fight a bit."*

Kiera grimaced, but he was right. Kiki was much smaller than Kein, and the dark gray dragon's body was considerably leaner too. Alezya would agree that Kiera's dragon could probably find ways to cause a lot of damage to the enemy even without being able to get everywhere.

Moreover, the stalagmites, or whatever those spikes were, wouldn't move, so it's not like Kiki could be hurt unless the dragon impaled itself... It was more of a solid anti-dragon defense for the area, as they had probably tried to pick the one area that would be bothersome to dragons. Seeing the others were worried, Alezya quickly explained why Kiera was upset, and they relaxed.

"How much farther is it?" Ekata asked. "This is unknown territory for us beyond this point; we're going off what we learned from our allied clans..."

Alezya relayed the question to Kiera the best she could, who shrugged before drawing a line and marking points.

"...We're almost two-thirds of the way?" Ekata gasped. "Did we make it that fast already?"

"We had a heavy load taken off our shoulders and good weather conditions," Alezya said, "and the Dragon Clan is doing much better than we expected too."

"That's good," the Samial Clan Chief nodded. "We could have time to rest before the battle and take them by surprise!"

"I doubt they expect us anytime before dusk," Ekut agreed, "but we might make it, and with some energy to spare!"

"Kiera?" Alezya called out to her. *"Take Kein and Kiki and fly the mountains. Fly this. The* Wailing Rift.*"*

She pointed at the drawing with intent, teaching her their name for it, and Kiera nodded with a shrug.

"Why?" Ekata asked.

"If Kiera keeps flying over it, they'll see the dragons," Alezya said. "Even if they don't expect us, they have to be watching the area since we're bringing the battle to them, but they don't know when. It's better if we keep them on their toes. Either they'll be on edge the whole time, or they'll relax and think the dragons being sighted before dusk doesn't mean anything. Like you said, they don't expect us until then; let's ensure they might not expect our fighters when we do arrive."

"Brilliant," Ekata smiled. "Brilliant idea, let's do that."

Just like that, Kiera took off, and Kein and Kiki left the supplies in the clearing for them to take the rest of the way later while the humans covered the trip by foot.

Their lunch break had been long enough, and no one complained when they resumed their march. Alezya was most surprised by Kassein's men; no one dared to voice a complaint no matter how harsh the trip was getting, and in terms of speed, no one was slacking either. She had seen how much all of those men trained, so she couldn't say she was completely shocked, but she certainly felt appreciative.

The last part of their journey seemed to be the longest, though; this time, the trail was more tortuous, even forcing their forces to stand in one or two lines at times and slowing them down as they had to double-check slippery paths and treacherous gaps.

Again, she was impressed at how organized Kassein's men were, some of them taking the lead to secure paths or rearranging the ranks, others relieving each other from scouting missions, and some even running back and forth to check that everyone followed and could keep going. At some point, she wondered if this wasn't also about pride: no one from the Dragon Clan wanted to lose to the Northerners' quick pace or slow down their group. Most of the men seemed incredibly determined, and as they got closer to the Wailing Rift, Alezya noticed the atmosphere was getting tense, a foreboding tension gradually rising. The skies above them were getting darker too, adding to this ominous feeling; the rain that had been a drizzle until then seemed to be menacing, and about to take a turn for the worse at any second.

They had reached one of the rare areas with trees, nestled between two mountains along a winding trail. It was lower than the cliffs above, offering shelter from the wind and making the air less biting. However, the terrain was steeper and more unpredictable, demanding careful navigation and for them to tighten their ranks.

Suddenly, a pair of scouts ran back, making large gestures and clearly making them all stop. Kiera arrived too, but Alezya hadn't seen Kiki land anywhere nearby.

"We're almost there," the scout said, out of breath. "Our scouts ahead confirmed it. We're now about five miles away from the Wailing Rift! If we don't stop here, it will be hard to conceal our arrival."

Next to him, his partner from the Dragon Clan was probably saying the same thing to Kassein, based on his animated gestures, and Kiera seemed to confirm his words. She went on to make some gestures that had Alezya guess she was explaining what the Wailing Rift looked like from above to her brother, so Alezya focused on the clan chiefs instead, and they all looked shocked.

"Already?" Ekata gasped. "We're more than two hours ahead!"

"That's good," Ekut nodded, checking the dark skies above. "Dusk isn't going to be soon; that means we have plenty of time to get ready and rest before the battle."

"Did you see the enemy?" the Samial Clan Chief asked.

"Some of them," he nodded. "It looks like some clans are positioned already, and we're trying to inform our allies that we've arrived so they can join us here without being noticed, but it might take a little while."

"Hopefully, we can meet some of their representatives without Darak knowing we've arrived already..." Ekata muttered.

"The Dragon Clan's helping us out," the scout nodded, pointing at his partner. "I admit they're... they're outstanding fighters. We were spotted twice, but they killed the enemy scouts before they could report back."

"That's good," Ekut nodded. "Keep moving with them then; just be sure they don't kill allies. We can't afford a rift with our allies."

"We're good at communicating now," the scout nodded confidently.

"Alright," Ekata sighed. "We all should have stopped walking by now; let's inform everyone we're taking our last break before the battle. I'm guessing the dragons will bring our supplies, so we should have the men use the extra time to eat and rest, and wait for our signal to get ready."

"Even if they spot us, Darak won't come here," Alezya said. "He's too afraid of the dragons. It would be better if we kept the element of surprise though, so let's keep scouting the area. And I'll ask Kassein to have more men ensure that we're not noticed until the right time."

"Sounds good to me," Ekut nodded along.

So, Alezya was in charge of explaining the situation and their current plan to Kassein, Kiera, and Tievin, while the twins and the Samial Clan Chief did the same with their men.

It took a while for her to explain with her limited vocabulary, but once they did understand, no one argued; instead, Kassein called over his senior warriors, they discussed for a couple of minutes, and then, everyone parted ways. The dragons flew away for their last trips to bring the belongings before they rested along with the humans; it would have been suspicious if they made too many flights above the Wailing Rift now that they were near. While scouts from each of the three clans scattered, everyone else prepared for a long, deserved break that was utterly different from the previous ones, Alezya realized.

First, as soon as Kein and Kiki had brought their things over, she saw all the men work together to distribute their gear and the extra weapons, allocate food, and carefully pack up the rest of the supplies. Some established tents, and she realized those were for their healers, as some who had suffered injuries during the trip were brought in to be cared for. When the food was all distributed, they all ate quickly, no longer in a cheerful mood like before but instead in understandable silence, mindful to not attract attention to their location.

Then, as instructed, all the men decided to rest, some sitting, some lying down. Still, Alezya noted everyone had been allocated their equipment and kept it close in case they were suddenly under attack.

She went to sit down against one of the trees, unwilling to lie down on the cold ground. As soon as she did, Kassein came to her and, without a care in the world, lay down to rest his head on her lap and closed his eyes, ready to sleep in full gear. It didn't take long until Alezya heard him snoring, and she wasn't even really surprised. Combing his hair with her fingers, she glanced around as everyone seemed to have spread out on every nearby piece of ground to rest.

While most of the fighters found positions and spots to nap, a handful remained alert and in full gear, and Alezya guessed those were the elected sentinels. She couldn't help but feel her heart tighten at the sight of those hundreds of men, peacefully napping in an icy forest in the middle of nowhere between mountains... and in a few hours, they would be in the middle of an all-out war. Alezya's heart tightened at the idea; she had seen battles before, but the one that was coming was going to be bigger, and far worse.

As if he felt her nervousness, Kassein's hand suddenly came up to grab hers, and intertwined their fingers gently; she hadn't even realized he'd stopped snoring.

She pressed her palm against his, finding comfort in his warmth while she tried to relax. She had the strongest fighter of all by her side. No matter what happened, victory was theirs; she was sure of it.

"Nervous?"

Ekata's voice took her by surprise. She sat down next to Alezya, and she looked tense too.

"How could I not be?" Alezya whispered, rubbing her thumb against Kassein's skin. "It feels... unreal. The calm before the storm."

"Quite literally," Ekata muttered, glancing up at the dark skies above them. "I'm nervous too. A lot of my men are here... but at least, this is the best chance we'll ever get at changing the future. This battle will shape the next generations. That's what I'm telling myself, I guess."

"It feels strange to battle other clans for... all the clans' sakes."

"Some of the old ways have to go, Alezya," Ekata muttered. "Some of those clans are too set in their ways; they'd never negotiate with the Dragon Clan. If we show clans that we can get along enough for this, we might create a future that leads to our survival. How many of us haven't evolved in generations? How many young women like me and you are sold and sacrificed by men who can't do better? This isn't just about the Dragon Clan; this is about all those who had too much pride to believe in a woman talking about peace. They chose war, Alezya, and you and I chose survival. If we didn't, I bet you one day my clan would have been erased like the Lumiata was, simply because we do not want to follow men like Darak and submit. Or another young woman would have died in the snow after being repudiated for something she didn't do."

"...I know," Alezya muttered, thinking of Lumie.

"Men can fight, but women endure pain better," Ekata said with a dark expression. "We are survivors. We endure pain, and we protect others. Your man's hands might have been made to fight, but yours were meant to nurture. And I guarantee you that when this fight is over, whatever future you create next will be infinitely better than the one Darak devised. He places pride in his wealth, but you? Your child is your pride, and that makes you more powerful than a greedy man like him. All he cares about is the present, but us? You and I, we think about the future. And this is the future we fight for."

Alezya let out a nervous chuckle.

"...I started a war for my daughter," she smiled. "Isn't that what being a mom is all about?"

"Damn right," Ekata grinned.

She glanced around, and the clearing was incredibly peaceful and almost quiet. The drizzle had slowly turned to rain, forcing the men to cover their faces with their shields or cloaks.

"...What do you think will happen when this is over?" Alezya whispered.

"Things will change," Ekata shrugged. "No more of each clan keeping to themselves. I want to do what Darak claimed: let everyone roam free and create a nation out of all the clans. To each their culture, but why weren't we ever able to mix at all? I want to see the south and tour every mountain. I want a glimpse of the Dragon Clan too, to know where those strange people come from and why they're not like any of us. I want my kids to be able to go wherever they want to go, meet dozens of clans, and learn everything. I never want my people to be confined to caves ever again."

"...I used to dream of flying away so much," Alezya confessed. "I love climbing because it was the only taste of freedom I ever got, perched as high as I could get. On the dark days, I thought about falling... but on the good ones, I dreamt that I could take flight like one of their dragons to wherever the wind would take me."

"And now you fly a dragon," Ekata winked.

"And now I fly a dragon," Alezya agreed, glancing toward Kein's large figure.

The dragon had somehow managed to find itself a spot nearby, once its deliveries were done, and had stretched itself belly-flat on the ground, napping like its owner without a care in the world.

Alezya let out a heavy sigh, and closed her eyes to rest, leaning her head against the tree and thinking about the old days, full of fear, of crawling through tiny holes, climbing skin-cutting cliffs, and being pinned to the mountain by a giant dragon with silver eyes...

"Alezya."

She jolted awake, disoriented, unsure when she had even fallen asleep.

Kassein's piercing green eyes locked onto hers with an intensity she had never seen before. He was no longer resting on her lap but kneeling in front of her, his expression more serious than ever.

"*Battle,*" he said simply.

That one word was all it took to shake off the last remnants of sleep. Alezya nodded and took his hand as he pulled her to her feet.

The camp was in chaos. Warriors scrambled to get ready, some snatching a final bite to eat while others rushed to take their places in perfect formation.

"Darak's men spotted us," Ekut appeared beside her, his face dark with fury. "One of their scouts slipped past ours and spread the word. We have to strike now, or we risk walking into a trap."

"The men are rested enough," the Samial Clan Chief declared with a firm nod. "We've got this. Let's end it before the sun rises!"

Alezya glanced up, but thick storm clouds loomed overhead, making it impossible to tell if dusk had already passed. It didn't matter. Around her, everything was moving at breakneck speed—warriors colliding, orders being shouted, weapons being secured. The sheer urgency of it all made her pulse race.

This was it.

The war was beginning.

Before she could fully process the gravity of this moment, a large, warm hand took hers. She barely had time to react before Kassein pulled her through the chaos, weaving between warriors until they reached Kein. Without hesitation, he lifted her onto the dragon's back, settling her into position as if she weighed nothing.

Her heart pounded wildly in her chest. She squeezed his hand, unwilling to let go.

"*You stay with Kein,*" he said. "*Safe. Fly above battle.*"

"Kassein," she whimpered, feeling on the verge of tears.

She didn't want to let go. She didn't want to take off while Kassein, Kiera, Ekata, and hundreds of men were going to rush into this battle. This was one of the most terrifying moments of her life, and she didn't know how to deal with it; all she knew was that she didn't want to let go of Kassein's hand. It was like she was reliving the moment she had left Lumie in that tree trunk all over again; she felt like her heart was being ripped out of her chest, her stomach a block of ice.

Only Kassein didn't seem worried at all.

For some unspeakable reason, that man seemed impossibly serene. He lifted her hand to his lips, pressing a long kiss while his eyes were riveted on her. Alezya could ignore the rain, the chaos of men running and shouting, the howling wind, but she couldn't stop looking into his eyes. She couldn't shake the horrible feeling that she might lose him.

"Kassein," she whimpered again between her tears.

But then, he let go of her hand, barked a command, and Kein took off. Alezya barely had a second to brace herself before they shot into the sky. The force of the ascent pressed her back, the wind howling in her ears as rain lashed against her skin. Below, Kassein and the warriors shrank into a blur of frantic movement beneath the cover of the trees. She sucked in a deep breath, her chest tight. This was what she had wanted—to be part of this battle, to fight alongside them. Now wasn't the time to panic. Especially not when she was riding a dragon.

Alezya willed the hysteria away, forced herself into taking a deep breath, and angrily wiped her tears and rain-saturated cheeks.

"Let's go see that Wailing Rift," she muttered.

Perhaps Kein heard her, because the dragon replied with a deafening growl that shook the area awake. She saw birds take off in fright ahead of them now that the largest predator of all was roaming the skies. Those weren't her prey, though.

Focusing on shifting her hips to navigate Kein and keep a tight hold on those spines or whatever it was that she could grab on the dragon's neck, Alezya only took seconds to get used to riding alone. It wasn't as smooth as Kassein's riding, and she missed his warm and reassuring presence behind her, but she was pretty confident she could direct Kein by shifting her weight or shouting what she wanted the dragon to do.

It didn't take long until she saw the Wailing Rift, and to Alezya's horror, the scary tales she'd heard as a child were shockingly accurate.

This place was unlike any landscape she had seen in the mountains, and she thought she'd seen it all. But the Wailing Rift wasn't a valley nor a pass. It looked like the giant maw of a starving beast carved in black rocks and ice. The mere sight of it sent a chill down her spine.

It looked like a twisted, fractured gorge, a jagged crevice of blackened rock and treacherous snow stretching for miles. Knife-sharp cliffs extended like broken teeth at unpredictable angles, and she could guess just as many thin and treacherous crevices were waiting to lure men into the darkness of its depths under the thin, unreliable coating of ice and snow. She couldn't believe this was the place her father had picked.

One had to be a madman to go in there willingly, let alone elect it as a battlefield! How deep was this place? She couldn't even see the end of it; its depth was too dark, the shadows and angles too hard to figure out.

There was a howling wind haunting this rift along with an unexplainable, eerie mist, and suddenly, the tales she'd heard as a child of deceased gods haunting this place didn't seem so far-fetched. This place looked like a centuries-old graveyard in the making, a death trap of danger waiting to lure the living. And they were about to send hundreds of men into this hellhole. Her father had chosen the worst battlefield, not just for them but for everyone.

Alezya was horrified; many men from both sides would die not in battle but impaled on those jagged rocks or swallowed by those crevices. There was definitely no place for Kein to land or even get close to. With its humongous size, Kassein's dragon would clip its wings or impale itself before it got close to any human down there.

Alezya was horrified by this nightmare of a battlefield before her, but it was gradually replaced with fury when she recalled this had been her father's choice and the choice of the madmen who had followed on his warpath. Those men were so blinded by their fear of a dragon that they would willingly march to their own deaths in this antechamber of hell.

They were so obsessed with winning that they never once considered peace. They wanted this war, and they were ready to let this land, and the gods that haunted it, reap their lives and those of their brothers for it.

She considered turning around, warning Kassein that this was madness and too many people were going to die here, but it was too late; on both ends of this gorge, she could see men descending at impressive speed through the cracks and tortuous paths, converging toward its depth.

It took her a few seconds to realize that it wasn't just the wind that reached her ears; it was now combined with the voices of hundreds of men, long battle cries echoing through the rocks as they all ran toward their enemy.

It wasn't just down the gorge either; as Kein did another loop around the Wailing Rift, Alezya realized men were descending from all sides, some emerging out of secret caves and others negotiating their descent as fast as they could while trying not to break their necks before they made it to the battlefield. When she saw the first man trip, fall, and break his body like a twig on the rocks, she grimaced, her heart sinking.

This was merely a glimpse of how dozens of men were going to lose their lives today because of her father's madness.

"We need to stop them," she hissed.

The dragon roared with her, momentarily startling some of the clans. She saw some nearby groups freeze and glance up, wary of the predator flying above their heads. One group that had to be their allies barely seemed to flinch, while the others were either running to hide or directing their weapons toward Kein, bows and other throwing devices emerging and being aimed at the dragon.

That was precisely what Alezya needed; she prompted Kein in the direction of a mountain in which a disorganized clan was freaking out and trying to run inside, and as if it had read her mind, the dragon roared and furiously ripped the mountain's flank with its claws, making dozens of rocks break and fall, creating a landslide and an avalanche all at the same time before it took off again.

Alezya felt proud; she wouldn't be so useless if she could block some of her father's allies. She knew Ekata's plan to try and use their allies to surround their enemies, but clans were converging from all sides to join the battle, and now, it was up to her to prevent their enemies from advancing and let their allies through.

Again, Alezya had Kein speed up, doing a quick tour of the area while she tried to identify friend from foe; she had limited knowledge of the foreign clans, but their reaction to Kein's arrival was all she needed. The difference was so evident between their allies, who trusted the dragon wouldn't harm them, and her father's allies, who systematically panicked anytime they were near. Even Kein seemed to pick up on their fear, as the dragon attacked any clan that showed weakness without needing Alezya to prompt it.

Their duo was becoming almost symbiotic, as if Kein could read her mind and understood perfectly the slightest shift in her movements.

Alezya did try to shout commands, but by now, they were riding through a thunderstorm, and most of her voice was carried away by the strong winds, the thunder, and the heavy rain. It was bad enough riding in that cataclysmic weather; she could barely think about what it had to be like down below. After they'd wrecked yet another ridge, she decided it was time to check on the battlefield, and she and Kein turned around, risking their lowest ride yet.

Alezya was nervous about accidentally clipping one of Kein's wings on the mountains or the dragon impaling itself on an unseen cliff. She tried to prevent the dragon from going too low, but she had to check how the battle was going, and the weather made it harder to see what was going on down there. It took her a lot to convince Kein not to approach too close as Kassein's dragon was far bolder, while she looked for its owner.

It was absolute chaos down there.

She was glad she hadn't seen when both sides had collided because now, it looked like a sea of men, and she could hardly believe it wasn't a bloodbath already. There were a lot of people lying still, injured, dead, or dying, and she tried not to think about it while she focused on the people she wanted to see alive and standing.

Thankfully, it didn't take her long to spot Kassein; his bronze coverings were shining, his stature amongst the largest of all, and from what she could see, he was effortlessly dominating his surroundings.

There was a large area of defeated men around him, and he stood at the epicenter like a god of war, leaving a trail of death and destruction in his wake. Alezya had Kein hover in place while she eyed her lover as if she needed to see for herself that he was holding his own.

After a few seconds of observing Kassein, it hit her that she had never seen him fight so hard, so... furiously. He looked wild, enraged, and unstoppable. It was like watching a wild beast unleashed on the battlefield, a human-sized dragon sowing fear in his wake. His attacks weren't reckless, but he fought with all his furious might. She noticed how the men around him desperately avoided engaging him, forcing him to seek out opponents, hunting them down with merciless efficiency.

He didn't seem set on finishing them off, either; he didn't chase those who fled, nor did he linger to end the fallen. Instead, he simply moved on to the next target, leaving them in the aftermath. She wasn't sure if it was out of mercy or pragmatism, but she liked it all the same; many of those men had marched into war without truly understanding what they had signed up for. Alezya tried to look for Kiera, but before she could locate anyone else, something suddenly grazed her, and seconds later, she felt the searing pain and screamed.

Kein growled in echo to her pain, and the dragon got them out of there just as Alezya realized an arrow had nicked her. She let out a wail of pain, taking in her ripped sleeve and the large bleeding stain that was already spreading. It had to be sheer, impossible luck that someone had managed to hit her amidst this chaos and the thunderstorm, but they had been relatively still for too long.

Alezya held onto Kein, biting her lip to ignore the pain while the dragon flew away from danger. She realized it could have been Kein that had been hit, all because she'd worried too much about Kassein.

She couldn't make that mistake again.

"We need to stop this war," she hissed.

Kein growled again as if in agreement, and soon, the dragon found another mountain's flank to attack. Alezya let it scratch the rocks and ice, inspecting her wound again. Thankfully, whatever magic this pregnancy had unlocked was working because white scales were appearing under the ripped coat to cover her wound, patching her flesh and numbing the pain.

"Thanks, baby," she whispered to herself.

Feeling a bit better, she looked around; most of the mountains were now empty, she guessed, as most of the enemy and allied forces had descended into the Wailing Rift to join the battle. They weren't going to stop or get out of there until the war was over, and that meant a lot of dead people. Alezya's anger rose again. She had to put a stop to this madness, no matter what.

"I need to find my father," she hissed.

Ultimately, if there was one thing she'd learned, it was that clans followed their leaders, and if their leaders stopped fighting, so would the clans. She hoped they would be able to see that they had to stop fighting, that their survival mattered more than her father's empty promises.

But she knew no truce would be possible while her father filled their heads with his poisonous lies. He was the one they were all following into the abyss, and she had to stop him before he sacrificed hundreds for his greed.

She rode Kein to survey the battlefield again, noting how many men lay dead already and the awful amount of bodies wrecked on the jagged cliffs; one man was even impaled through his torso, his lifeless limbs blown by the wind in a sorrowful sight.

Alezya even spotted some men who were hiding from the battle, hidden in gaps or shivering behind rocks, and she couldn't blame them; it was a massacre down there. She tried to be careful as she swept Kein above the battlefield, watching out for treacherous knife-sharp cliffs and anyone who would target them.

They made several passes, Kein sometimes crushing a man who had the audacity to stand out there between its fangs or claws while Alezya leaned to survey the area. It was almost impossible to recognize anyone with the rain battering them, the darkness that had overtaken the scene, and the distance.

The only good thing was that the mist was gone, and occasionally, a bolt of lightning from afar would suddenly illuminate the scene. Alezya glanced up, growing nervous as it felt like the thunderstorm was coming closer; she was fairly certain even a dragon wouldn't take a lightning bolt too well, and she didn't want them to end up burned to a crisp mid-air.

They had to find her father fast.

"Where are you, Darak?" she hissed as they did another pass of the battlefield.

Where would her father have chosen to stand? He was arrogant, and a manipulative leader. He would have wanted to make sure they knew who was in charge. But he was a coward. She had never seen him go to war himself, and he never risked his most trusted men either...

"He isn't down there," she realized.

Her father was a coward.

He had a big, smart mouth, but if there was one thing she knew, it was that he never joined a fight he wasn't sure he could win; he was far too spineless for that.

He had sent hundreds of men to their deaths, never once risking his own life. Alezya was red with fury. The manipulative bastard had dragged more than a dozen clans into his war, but he wasn't even there. Of course, he wasn't. He would trigger a war, send hundreds to die, and then wait to collect all the glory. Perhaps he even prayed some other clan chiefs would lose their lives, giving him less competition.

It was possible the Deklaan Clan wasn't down there at all; she wouldn't have been shocked if he had come up with some mastermind plan that justified him staying behind or lied about what his clan would do.

"You're going to pay for this, Father," she hissed.

She took Kein for a larger tour of the rift, trying to locate her father.

He had to have chosen a safe place from which he would be able to see the battle. She couldn't imagine him not wanting to rush to the forefront if the victory was theirs so he could take all of the credit.

He wouldn't have positioned himself at the rear, but more like right above where the main battle was, close enough that it would take him minutes to descend and reap the benefits of other men's sweat and blood.

Alezya focused on the mountains close to where Kassein fought, scouring the area with hawk-like eyes to try and find a familiar face.

It took her several minutes, but finally, she spotted one.

It wasn't her father, but she noticed a man who was standing guard outside, a bow in his hand, and she recognized him as one of her father's warriors; it was one of the bastards who had grabbed her and shoved her during the gathering.

"Get him," she hissed to the dragon.

Kein roared and surged like a fury.

The man, who had probably relaxed upon noticing the dragon had only been making lazy loops until then, barely had time to panic, let alone flee. For its humongous size, the orange dragon could be deadly fast. Kein's angry fangs ripped him apart mid-scream, and the dragon threw the bloody remains down the rocks with disdain.

Then, it climbed on the flank of the mountain, looking for any other humans to devour, its claws ripping at the mountain's flanks, triggering slow avalanches and landslides. Alezya let the dragon furiously scratch all it wanted; if she wanted to get to her father, Kein might have to dig the Deklaan Clan out.

The dragon was latched onto the cliff and almost vertical to the ground, so Alezya had to focus all she could on holding on, but she kept a watchful eye on their surroundings, knowing they were more vulnerable when they weren't up in the air. And, sure enough, she saw a man appear in a dangerously close opening; she didn't hesitate, and with the fluidity and assurance only a seasoned climber could have, she leaped to the mountainside and hurried to reach him.

Whether by luck or his own distraction, the man failed to notice her in time, too fixated on aiming for the dragon. Alezya reached him right before he saw her and pushed him off the edge.

His scream tore through the air, echoing off the cliffs until it was silenced by a brutal end.

She didn't have time to look down; she glanced into the opening and seized her only weapon, the dagger she'd gotten from Kassein. It was a small blade, but it was sharp, and it felt right in her grip as she ventured inside while Kein continued to cause chaos outside. She had to find her father, kill him, and put an end to this.

Storming into those tunnels alone was probably reckless, but she had no choice; each second her father lived, more lives were sacrificed.

At the very least, she was in her element, infiltrating dark tunnels and making herself as silent and invisible as she could. Alezya was no fighter, no warrior, but she had spent years mastering the art of moving unseen. She knew how to make herself silent and invisible in the darkness, and Kein was providing a remarkable distraction too.

She could feel the ground shaking under her feet and hear the chaos of panicked men weighing their chances to get out of there before they were buried alive. From the frantic shouts echoing through the tunnels, it was clear her father had kept only his most trusted guards by his side, maybe half a dozen men or so.

Before long, she heard his voice barking sharp, commanding orders like he always did, trying to prompt his men to get out and fight the dragon while he would no doubt flee somewhere like the coward he was. Alezya sneered and crept deeper into the tunnels. She was about to round a corner when a man appeared, a flash of surprise in his eyes, and she moved out of pure reflex. Her wrist snapped up, the blade slicing across his throat in a single practiced motion. Kiera had drilled this move into her, and now, without a thought, it had come to her from muscle memory.

The man's breath hitched, his eyes wide with shock as he crumpled to the ground, blood pooling at her feet. He was dead before Alezya even registered what she had done, but when she did, she had to cover her mouth to suppress a yelp of fright.

She had never killed a man in cold blood before.

Sure, she'd reacted instinctively, and she would likely be the one dead if she hadn't, but it wasn't easy to get over.

She squeezed her eyes shut for just a second, then forced herself to step over the body and keep moving, listening to Kein's roars for comfort. She had wanted this war; her hands couldn't remain blood-free when everyone else was risking their lives killing their opponents. With this thought in mind and a slightly shaking hand, she kept going in, cautious.

This time, she didn't have time to silence the man before he spotted her at the end of the tunnel; Alezya knew he had seen her, and she tried to hurry, but she couldn't get to him in time before he shouted.

"She's here! That damn bitch is here!"

Alezya threw herself at the man, dagger first, with the fury of a hungry dragon. This time, it wasn't anything that Kiera had taught her; this was about sheer survival and doing as much damage as possible to silence this man before more came.

Blood flew, and she didn't know who it belonged to, but she didn't stop. She swung her dagger like a mad woman, so focused on defending herself she barely registered what the man's blade was doing. Some of her movements felt familiar, echoes of lessons drilled into her by Kiera, but mostly, she was doing what she knew: she fought for survival.

She fought like a wild animal backed into a corner; she struck anywhere and everywhere she could in a frenzy. She felt pain flaring across random parts of her body, but she didn't stop.

Finally, she felt her blade sink deep, and she froze, slowly taking in the scene.

It was a gruesome sight.

She had cut the man on every visible patch of skin, and bleeding gashes disfigured his face, torso, and arms. Now, her dagger was sticking out of the side of his skull, and he crumbled backward.

It took Alezya everything she had to crouch down, ignore the pain that was searing all over her body, how much she trembled and hurt, and pull her dagger out with her bloodied hands.

She knew she was found. She knew more men were coming, but she stood, taking a second to face the raw emotions that shook her. There was blood everywhere, some of it hers, and the madness of what had just happened was a lot to take in.

Still, she ignored the blood dripping from her hands, her pounding heart, her ragged breath, and the pain that was already subsiding, and willed herself to move.

Footsteps were rushing her way, and she decided to shed her tattered cloak, which was soaked with rain and blood, heavy, torn, and impairing her movements. That's when she noticed the streaks of white shimmering along her skin.

The wounds slashed across her body were closing; under the patches of blood, the raw flesh was gradually being covered by smooth, reptilian scales. Alezya let out a faint exhale of relief as the pain faded, and she realized she wouldn't bleed out in this mountain, not with Kassein's baby somehow protecting her. She wasn't sure how good this healing magic was, but it was good enough for now.

When two more men arrived, her chances of survival had already risen dramatically thanks to it. Not only was her baby shielding her, but the narrow tunnel also worked for her. The men were forced to line up to face her, and Alezya had somehow gathered her composure enough to get into the fighting position Kiera had taught her, and got ready for their attacks. The first man glared at her with the most disgusted look she'd seen in a while.

"You damned witch," he spat at her. "This is all your doing! You dragon slut!"

"This dragon slut is about to kill you," Alezya hissed back with a fire she didn't know she had.

He launched himself at her, but this time, she was ready, and she side-stepped at the right moment to avoid his blade and swung her dagger, stabbing his arm and forcing a scream out of him.

Kiera had taught her better than to stop moving mid-fight, so she ripped the dagger out and planted it again in the next available piece of flesh, his flank. Alezya had never been much of a fighter, and apparently, they had thought so too, because both men looked utterly confused.

She didn't give them time to recoup and stabbed a third, a fourth, and a fifth time, not stopping until the man collapsed off to the side with a groan, his partner looking horrified.

"You're going to pay for this!" he roared.

Alezya wasn't confident nor foolish enough to answer his taunt, so she focused on his incoming attack, bracing herself for it.

She was grateful the narrow space didn't allow for large weapons because he swung his sword fast, and she barely had room to avoid it.

The blade grazed her arm, but most of it fell on her white scales, and she barely felt the flicker of pain. Instead, she lowered herself and just about managed to stab his leg twice before she was brutally hurled against the wall.

Her head hit the rock painfully, and for a dizzying moment, the world blurred. Agony spread through her body, her left side crushed before she was wrenched away and slammed onto the ground.

A brutal kick landed against her ribs.

Then another. And another.

The sharp snap of bone stole her breath, and she barely managed to suck in enough air to let out a strangled cry.

As soon as she could, Alezya fought through the pain to curl inward, arms tightening around her belly. She took the brunt of the next hit on her shoulder, her ribs aching, but her baby was safe. They had to be safe. It felt all too familiar, that overwhelming, desperate need to protect her child at all costs, just like when she'd hidden Lumie away. Just like before, she would endure whatever it took to make sure her child lived.

She thought she might have heard Kein growl in fury, but her ears were ringing too much, and she felt too dizzy to process any other sound.

Her attacker was enjoying this, she realized. Stomping her on the ground, kicking her, beating her to death.

Panic clawed at her mind as she tried to move, to crawl, to do anything, desperate to get away. The pain was insufferable, and fear rose as she thought about her child. She knew the baby had to be strong, but neither of them could take much more of this.

Alezya let out another yelp, desperate. She was drowning in a sea of agony, and it wasn't stopping. She couldn't even tell if the hits were still raining down on her or if she was just enduring the ripples of pain.

The man shouted something, and she tried to regain her senses, but she couldn't. Then she saw it. The blade. Swinging down toward her.

Alezya had no time to think, no strength to fight back. She closed her eyes.

A scream echoed, but the pain didn't come.

Instead, Alezya somehow caught her breath and forced one eye open. To her surprise, the man was the one with his mouth wide open in horror, stumbling back, a furious black shadow hooked to his throat, blood gushing everywhere.

It took her several seconds to align her senses enough to recognize the black lump of scales ripping his windpipe out.

"Nii-... Niiru?" she gasped.

The man fell, choking on his own blood, and the little black dragon finally let go with an enraged growl, its tail furiously whipping the air and its body on alert.

"Niiru," Alezya muttered, forcing herself to sit up through the pain.

Again, she could feel the magic helping her pain recede, and she allowed herself a few seconds to catch her breath and let the young dragon's presence sink in. What was Niiru doing here? It was supposed to be back at *Kalat Unshreik*, safe. Had it flown all the way here on its own? Once the man had stopped moving, the young dragon turned its big wide eyes to her and hopped over to her side, with a little high-pitched growl that almost sounded concerned.

"I'm alright," she muttered.

At least she was still alive, which she wouldn't have been so sure of just moments ago.

Gritting her teeth through the pain, Alezya managed to get up, well aware she owed her survival to a baby dragon and her unborn child. Or perhaps the gods that had shunned her for so long were finally making it up to her.

"Let's finish this," she whispered to the young dragon.

Niiru let out a grunt and charged ahead, nearly invisible in the darkness. Alezya's breathing was slow and uneven, but she'd never be grateful enough for how the pain slowly subsided, and a dull ache replaced the pain. She couldn't believe she'd been nervous about this pregnancy; half-dragon babies were amazing.

She had been surprised that more of her father's men hadn't arrived to finish her off, but the tunnel now seemed empty, and she realized that while she fought, Kein had calmed down or flown off.

The mountain had stopped shaking like a localized earthquake, and things were much quieter. She and Niiru progressed quietly, wary of any incoming sound. The young dragon was ready to attack at any second but stuck close to her, suspiciously inspecting every corner before Alezya reached it. Had they left? Or had her father lost men to Kein? Had Kein killed him? Still, Alezya proceeded cautiously, with a feeling this wasn't over yet.

Suddenly, Niiru started growling, and right after that, her father stepped out of the shadows, an arrow pointed right at her.

They had arrived at the end of a tunnel, and she could see the wind and rain battering the opening right behind him. She guessed he had sent his men to distract Kein, because she could hear the dragon's growls coming from somewhere else on the mountains, conveniently away from that one opening.

"There you are," he hissed. "My traitor of a daughter."

"And child of a coward," Alezya hissed. "Hiding while others do your dirty work has always been your strong suit, Father."

"I am no coward!" he barked. "I am a leader. And leaders don't fight in the front like expendable pawns."

"Is that what you told the men you sent to die?" she shot back. "Is that what you told the other clan chiefs you manipulated? Tell me, Father, where are those clan chiefs now? Hiding like cowards, like you? Or down there, on the battlefield, bleeding for a war *you* started? A war *you* wanted! How many more will you sacrifice to feed your greed? How many lives will you destroy while you cower in the shadows like the vain, spineless coward you are?"

His expression turned ice-cold, deadly, and filled with rage. At her feet, Niiru growled furiously in warning, and Darak's eyes darted to the young dragon before going back to hers.

"...I should have smothered you the second you were born," he seethed. "I should have slit your throat before you learned how to use that damn mouth. I should have disposed of you the same way I got rid of your useless mother. I should have known that damn witch would bring me nothing but trouble."

Alezya froze. A sharp, suffocating weight settled in her chest.

"Why?" she asked, her voice tight with emotion. "Why did you even marry my mother? You didn't love her."

"That witch turned out to be useless," he sneered. "Given her wretched clan, I thought she would at least be of some use to me. Show me how they avoided the dragon, teach me their secrets. But she never trusted me with anything. She was a disobedient, worthless, arrogant bitch who didn't know her fucking place. She dared to talk back to me in front of my men! She tried to take my place, insult me! She thought she was so special because she came from that crazy clan of witches. She thought she was smarter than me. I tried to teach her her place quickly, but no, that insufferable bitch wouldn't take it. I would have thrown her back to the pack of rabid mutts she belonged to if she hadn't been pregnant with you! I had to suffer her cocky, know-it-all bitch mouth for months! I tried to endure her yapping, but she was an insufferable, pathetic excuse of a woman. I was merciful to even let her carry you! More than once, I thought that even a son wasn't worth enduring her disobedience!"

"...So you killed her," Alezya muttered. "Instead of letting my mom leave, you just killed her."

"Of course I killed her!" he scoffed. "What else was I supposed to do with that useless wench? Her clan was hounding me about sending her back! There were rumors about me being violent, unfair, or such nonsense coming from those harpies! As if it wasn't my right to discipline my disobedient bitch of a wife! Even other clans were pestering me, putting their noses in my clan as if she were some precious princess! All she was was a venomous snake, going around seducing men and poisoning minds! She would have taken my whole clan from me! She strutted around like some high-born empress when she was just a mouthy little slut who forgot her place!"

"You killed her because she spoke up," Alezya hissed. "She wasn't just fighting back, she was telling everyone about your abuse."

A victorious, cruel smirk twisted his lips.

"She left me no choice," he snarled. "She kept challenging me, and if she was so smart, she should have known better. It was almost too easy. She was so desperate to leave me, to go back to her clan, that in the end, she even agreed to leave without you. She died in one of those crevices, forgotten, with no one to listen to her stupid yapping anymore. When her clan came for her, I pretended she had gone and disappeared into the mountains. Everyone but her wretched fucking clan bought it. They ran their mouths incessantly instead of shutting up and moving on. They harassed me relentlessly, looking for their precious princess and dragging my name through the mud. What good was a clan of women, anyway? Always acting like they were so smart too. All I could see was a bunch of snakes spreading their poison and acting like they were men."

"...So you killed the Lumiata," Alezya choked out, her voice barely a whisper. "They didn't just disappear. It was all you. You... You did this."

The truth slammed into her like a blade to the gut.

So many times she had wondered why no one ever spoke of her mother's people, why she couldn't finally meet her mother's relatives. She had dreamt of meeting them, often. Dreamt of a place where she belonged, where she could be accepted. That fateful day, when she had run with Lumie, she had prayed that, of all people, her daughter could find her way to her mother's kin.

But there was no one to get to. They were gone, all of them. Not scattered, not missing, but dead. Slaughtered. Erased because her father couldn't stand a woman defying him.

Her heart ached, thinking about all those women. They had tried to speak up for her mother, and her father had done exactly what he always did to those who dared to raise their voices: he silenced them.

He hadn't just stolen her mother. He had stolen her history. Her people. Her *freedom*. Alezya's eyes burned with tears as, for the first time, she was hit with the reality of why her mom had named her so.

It had been her last wish, or a prayer.

"They had to disappear," he shrugged. "They had all this witchcraft nonsense going on. They knew how to survive the dragon attacks and wouldn't share their secrets. Those witches were all damned wenches, most likely plotting to bring clans to their downfall. They seduced men but wouldn't bow to them, what kind of a woman is that? They're better off dead. All the foolish rumors died after those witches were gone."

"...Gods, you're a coward."

His gaze fixated on Alezya, staring at her like he couldn't believe she'd said that after all he'd just revealed. But Alezya acted far from scared. Instead, she didn't even try to hide her snarl of contempt.

"The truth is, you weren't strong enough to handle her. You were terrified of my mother," she hissed. "You couldn't take a woman being smarter than you. You might have murdered my mom, but you're the one who was afraid of her, because she saw you for the weak, pathetic excuse of a man you are. All I hear is that she was brilliant, kind, and loved, and you couldn't stomach how weak she made you feel. You chose to kill her rather than face the fact that she was a better leader than you. My mother was everything you'll never be."

"She was a witch!" he barked. "She was a weak woman! She could never be a leader! She died the pathetic death she deserved–"

"You know nothing about being a leader," Alezya snarled. "You're the worst of them all. You rule through tyranny and ignorance. ...For so long, I thought that was your right. That it was the only way, the one all clans had to be. But in the past few weeks, all I've seen is how wrong I was, and how inadequate, awful, and despicable you are."

Her father's hand twitched at the side, his lips curled, but Alezya didn't leave him time to shout again.

"There's a man out there who is as strong as a dragon, and he fights on the frontlines of a war he didn't start," she said, her voice choking with emotion. "That's the same man who can kill another man with his bare hands, and grows scales instead of bleeding. Do you know what that man did, when he first found me, Father? He protected me. He didn't know my name, nor why I'd been cast out and nearly killed, and he didn't care. He gave me medicine, food, clothes, and he asked for nothing in return. He slept on the floor for days so I could have his bed. His dragon killed men who insulted me. He killed a man who touched me. And never, once, did he expect a single damn thing from me. He never yelled at me, hit me, forced himself on me. And right now, he is down there, fighting in front of hundreds of men who respect him. For me. For a woman who launched a war he doesn't understand, just because he believes in me. While you're up here, hiding with your so-called warriors, still barking and shouting at a woman who is smarter than you. Because you think leadership is power, and power is violence. Because that's your only way to stay relevant. Silencing everyone who shows you you're wrong, who can call you out on your weakness. You couldn't take my mother being a better leader than you. You couldn't take her family calling you out on your crime, so you murdered an entire clan out of sheer, stupid, vain pride. You are so scared to die in a war you started that you're hiding up here while our people die. You're no leader. You're not even a man. You're just worthless."

The silence that followed was deafening, every word slowly sinking in. Then, gradually, his face turned so red it looked like it might explode.

"I AM A CLAN CHIEF!" he roared, his face contorted with pure rage. "I DECIDE WHO LIVES AND DIES! I AM THE MOST RESPECTED LEADER IN ALL–"

"You're going to die," Alezya cut him off with an eerie calm. "You're going to die, and I'm going to tell them all what a coward you are, Father. I'll let them know that Darak of the Deklaan Clan was a coward who hid in the mountains during the war. How you cowered behind your men, too afraid to even set foot on the battlefield with your own clan. I'll let them know how you murdered my mother and her entire clan. I'll tell them the Lumiata was murdered by a coward!"

"SHUT UP!" he barked. "If anyone will die, it's you and the bastard you whored yourself to!"

Just then, Niiru let out an angry growl and suddenly turned around.

Two of her father's men had tried to creep up on her from behind, and she realized that's where they had gone. Somehow, they had found a way to go around and corner her into the end of the tunnel.

Her father stood at the entrance, suddenly far too confident, while two of his men and their weapons were blocking any chance of escape.

While Niiru kept growling at them, Alezya turned her eyes back to her father; an insufferable smug expression now gradually replaced his previous glower.

"Clan chiefs make strategic decisions, Daughter," he sneered, "and out of compassion and mercy, I am willing to make a deal with you."

"...A deal?" Alezya repeated, doubtful.

"I will let you live," he stated with an arrogant tone. "I am willing to offer you mercy and let you and your bastard live. You go out there with us and tell the Dragon Clan the war is over. Tell their dragon to go away. We could put an end to this war, Alezya."

Alezya was utterly confused. His offer didn't make sense at all. He had provoked this war, not her. She'd offered peace with the Dragon Clan to the other clans before.

"...You want me to ask the Dragon Clan to back down?"

"You understand those tyrants," he nodded. "You are essential to negotiations, are you not? If you die unfortunately here, this war will end with many of our people dead, all because of you."

"I didn't start this."

"Oh, but you did," he hissed. "You brought the damn Dragon Clan all the way here, to our mountains. You're the one who started this war, Alezya, not me."

"I offered peace," she retorted. "You lied to the other clans that they had a chance to win a war against the Dragon Clan!

"They have a dragon," he snarled. "That's the only reason those barbarians could win. If you tell them to stand the fuck down, they will submit to us. The dragon listens to you, and so does their tyrant leader. Whatever witchcraft you did to achieve that should serve us, the clans. We are your people."

"Oh, no," she scoffed. "Don't you dare give me the family speech now, Father. I'm not that stupid. What do you want? What are you actually after? If the Dragon Clan stops fighting, they'll all see you lied."

"Of course not," he retorted. "They will see I brought them the peace I promised. I'll convince the Dragon Clan to never attack us again. I will show them that we, the Deklaan Clan, are the ones who can achieve peace. I'm even willing to start trading with the Dragon Clan. I can unify all the clans as one and start a new era. We can–"

"There it is," Alezya muttered. "Your grand scheme, as always. You want to use the Dragon Clan to threaten the other clans into submission."

"It is my right as the war's winner. I will achieve the peace I promised, and the clans will follow my lead. You'll get to live, and I'll never touch you or your bastard again. Think about it, Alezya. You get to remain the Dragon Clan's whore. You'll see the war is over for yourself. Isn't this what you wanted? You and your bastard spawn will be safe with those savages. I'll decide whatever happens to the clans."

It hit Alezya hard to think that not so long ago, that was exactly what she would have wanted. Lumie's safety and hers guaranteed.

Even if she doubted her father's word, so long as he got her back to Kassein, chances were she'd be safe forever. She could wash her hands of what happened up here and live the rest of her days with the most powerful clan of all. Kassein didn't have anything to win in this war; he and Kein would stand down if she asked. It would be pretty much what she had always wanted.

Except that she would be signing over every other clan's submission to her father.

The Deklaan Clan would emerge as the victor who got the Dragon Clan to stand down, her father claiming all the glory he'd gotten just from using her as a hostage. He was undeniably good at twisting facts to serve his agenda. The

Dragon Clan would go back to being a threat only the Deklaan Clan could control, and all the clans would be forced to endure his tyranny.

The saddest part was, if it had been anyone but her father asking her to stop the war this way, it would have been good. But Darak wasn't a good man, and Alezya knew it all too well. She knew exactly what she would be subjecting every clan to if he won this war.

She thought about Lumie, her precious baby girl, who was waiting for her at *Kalat Unshreik*. Lumie, who'd been able to roam around for the first time, who had giggled so happily in Kassein's arms. Lumie, who'd gotten her own dragon, and as much food as she wanted. Clean clothes, a warm bed, and a nice room.

Tears sprang to her eyes. Sometimes, Alezya had wondered why her mom had left her. Even now, she wondered if her mom had been this torn between remaining subjected to her father and keeping Alezya, or going back to the safety of her clan.

This was a choice about the future. About the clans' futures, and Lumie's. The choice of being a mother, or a fighter.

Alezya knew her father's plan wasn't a deal, it was an ultimatum.

She knew exactly what would happen if she refused. Either they would kill her here and let the war go on, or worse, they would use her as a hostage. Her father had already clearly understood Kein wouldn't risk harming her. He would use her as leverage, forcing Kein to surrender, manipulating both Kassein and the dragon into submission, perhaps even convincing the entire Dragon Clan to bow. It wasn't a choice when she had to pick between submission, coercion, or death.

He was staring at her with his smug expression, so certain he had her cornered. And she was.

But right at this instant, Alezya's mind was drifting between memories of Lumie and thoughts of her mother. And suddenly, she understood.

She finally knew why her mother had tried to go, leaving her behind.

Because against her father, fighting back was impossible.

Because he always found a way to twist the world to his advantage.

Because against him, there was no victory, only sacrifices.

Only the cold, familiar wind that seemed to be whispering her name like an old friend.

"...Do you think she would have won?" she suddenly asked, a single tear tracing its way down her cheek as she spoke, her voice ragged with sorrow and fury.

"What?"

"My mom." Alezya's breath hitched, broken with a raw edge. "If she had been given a chance to face you... do you think she would have won?"

Alezya lunged, seizing him with every ounce of strength she had left.

His startled gasp was lost in the wind as they tumbled together over the edge and into the abyss below.

Chapter 20

Kassein glanced up, checking the skies again as they finally reached the edge of the Wailing Rift.

His dragon was still up there, carrying Alezya on its back. He let out a long, quiet exhale and stared as Kein was just a bright orange dot among the dark clouds and battering rain, lost between the high mountains surrounding them. Everything looked darker and more sinister in this area, as if the landscape and the skies were bracing for the battle too.

If it weren't for Kein's vivid bronze color, it would have vanished quickly into the growing darkness. Kiki, who was flying nearby, already blended in with its dark gray scales.

"Sir," Captain Dajan's voice came from a few steps behind him. "The troops are all set and ready to go. The first lines of men are ready for battle, and General Sazaran is taking the lead in bringing them down this gorge. We've secured a large enough path. They've sent me to let you know the infirmary is set up and ready in the secure location they'd picked too."

Kassein remained quiet for a few seconds; he lowered his gaze from the thunderstorm coming their way to what was supposed to become their battlefield in just a few moments.

He had to admit, whoever the leaders were on the other side, they knew how to pick their landscape. It had been obvious the minute they'd arrived that their only reason for choosing this place was to hinder his dragon and nothing else. Sure, having Kein able to join the battle would have guaranteed them victory, but with this new configuration, he wasn't sure things looked much better for their opponents. The generals, Tievin, Kiera, and their scouts had discussed at length the difficulties of the battleground, which parts to avoid, and how to proceed to limit accidental deaths.

The only good part was that their enemies were likely to try and surround them, but they would have to go down steep cliffs for that, and there were high chances of accidents happening. Or they could make them happen, as Kiera had noted with a sinister grin. Kiki would have had trouble getting down there, but his sister's dragon would be sure to cause a lot of damage elsewhere, and his sister was likely gearing herself up to do the same on the battlefield; neither half of that duo had ever been one to shy away from a fight.

"...I hope Lady Alezya will be alright," Dajan suddenly muttered.

Kassein turned to him, and as soon as he did, he found the man blushing and waving his hands with a panicked expression.

"I-I-I am merely concerned for the lady's safety!" he hurriedly said. "She's b-been really nice to us, and, uh... I-I admire her as a leader. F-from what I gathered, Lady Alezya went through a lot..."

He went quiet and looked down, probably thinking he had said too much, but Kassein kept his gaze on the young Captain. At eighteen, Kassein was younger than most of the men he gave orders to. But Dajan was among the younger men too, and he didn't look more than five years older at most.

"...Why are you here?"

Dajan blinked at his question, looking confused for a second.

"I-I won't shy away from a battle, Commander," he said, his voice growing firmer. "It's my duty, and I'm proud to fight for our army–"

"The north," Kassein cut him off. "Why were you sent?"

Dajan's chest deflated right away, and he was back to staring at his feet. After a second, he inhaled and lifted his eyes again.

"...I killed a man, sir," he said with a hoarse voice. "I was sentenced for murder."

"Why?"

There was no judgment in Kassein's tone, but this time, a flash of anger passed over Dajan's face.

"He killed my mother, sir," he said, holding Kassein's gaze. "So I killed him. I was condemned for patricide."

He kept staring back at Kassein with his fists clenched for several long seconds, and for once, he was visibly making an effort not to look away. He didn't give any more information, but the clench in his jaw and his tense shoulders said it all.

"...I would kill anyone who harmed my mother too," Kassein finally said.

Dajan said nothing, pressing his lips together, but his shoulders relaxed slightly.

Kassein's gaze went behind him to his men, who were all ready for battle, leaving or about to, in tight ranks, wearing the same uniform and armor. Some looked tense and silent, others chatted hurriedly. He caught some men bumping fists, exchanging determined nods, and even sharing a couple of hugs with their brothers in arms.

He wondered how many of those men had been sent here because their crimes were too bad to stay in the Empire but not bad enough to die.

The Dragon Empire still had the death penalty. It wasn't applied often because the law required that the crime had to be the worst, and there had to be no doubt about the culprit.

He knew some real criminals would have been dead already if there hadn't been reasonable doubt or a lack of witnesses. Rapists whose word had been against their victims', for example. Those who had killed without witnesses and those who had claimed self-defense. Those who had no history before their crime. And those, like Dajan, whose crime was motivated by another crime and whose circumstances were somewhat understandable but not to be forgiven.

The North Army had become an open-air penitentiary, the one where no more mistakes were allowed. It was like a final trial, where those who never committed a crime again could survive, and those who did died. Kein had killed men trying to run away from the camp more than once, and enough that they'd stopped trying. The threat of an angry dragon was enough to keep most men behind invisible walls, and the threat of its owner was just as efficient in keeping them in line most days.

Kassein was well-aware that there was second-hand justice served in the ranks; if a man had been sent here for rape, he usually only survived as long as it wasn't known. The violent ones didn't make it long either if they didn't save their urges for battles and training.

He had never spent time thinking about why all those men were sent to the north; he just knew they were here for a second chance some of them didn't deserve. He and Kein were the judge and jury for a years-long trial.

This was the first time he realized some of them did deserve that second chance and thought sincerely about those men. Dajan was a murderer, but right here, in the north, he could stand among other men guilty of similar crimes and fight for his second chance.

And unbeknownst to most, Kassein wasn't any different.

"Will you go back to the Empire once this is over?" Kassein asked, his eyes back on the rift.

"I don't think so, sir," Dajan said after a short hesitation. "No one is waiting for me there... I don't think I'd want to go back."

"What about a new life here? Once this war is over, if you get your freedom?"

"...That would be nice, Commander."

Kassein remained silent for a few seconds, and Dajan waited for him, his eyes hopeful. After a few seconds, Kassein cracked his neck and suddenly moved, patting Dajan's shoulder once as he walked past him.

"Make sure you survive. She likes you."

"Yes, Commander!"

Dajan ran after him as Kassein walked back to his army, determined.

The Captain took a different route to find his place amongst the brigades without a word, but his head was now held high. Kassein had been truthful in his words: he hoped Dajan and more men like him made it out of this alive. Meanwhile, he crossed the ranks of men, hundreds of them lined up in tight formation, in their armor and carrying their weapons, greeting him with determined nods and shy cheers.

It only took him a handful of minutes to hurry past those who were already marching forward and make his way to the front, where General Sazaran stood at the helm, all geared up in his heavy armor.

"Ready for a good brawl, Commander?" The General grinned, looking excited.

"Try to stay alive, old man," Kassein smirked.

The General blinked a couple of times, shocked, before he erupted in a loud, thunderous laugh that made the men behind them jump and Kassein wince.

"Ha! Haven't heard you be this brash in a while, Commander!"

"Are you trying to warn the enemy we're here?" Kiera grimaced as she joined them. "What did I miss?"

"Only the excitement of the upcoming battle, Princess Kiera!"

"Call me princess again and you won't make it to the battle, old man," she hissed.

That only made Sazaran laugh more and louder while she rolled her eyes. Kassein knew there was no point in hiding their arrival, anyway.

Their opponent had spotted them, and on the opposite side of the rift, they could see the black sea of fighters heading toward them, their two armies descending into what was to be their arena.

Kassein glanced up at the skies as thunder erupted in the distance, definitely looming to overtake the battle. It was hard to say if the sun had already set or not; it was eerily dark already. This would make things harder for everyone, but mostly, he was worried about Alezya riding his dragon in a thunderstorm. As much as he knew his dragon wouldn't take any risks because of its rider, he regretted letting her join this battle at all.

Alezya was too fierce and determined, and he wasn't sure she would put her safety first if things got worse.

"She'll be fine," Kiera sighed next to him.

When he directed an annoyed glance at his sister, she rolled her eyes.

"Your woman is a lot of things, and if I've seen anything, it's that she is a survivor, Kassein," Kiera insisted. "Not everyone grows up being taught how to fight as we were, but she's a damn fighter in her own right. She's come out of her shell so much since you showed me that shivery little thing cornered in your tent. Look around. She launched a war, for dragon's sake. She didn't convince just you, but other people to fight against the tribes who wronged her. The reason I agreed to this is because if so many people are willing to fight with us, it means the battle's worth it."

"I thought you were just here to brawl."

"That too," she grinned, "but I respect the hell out of your woman, Kassein. She's as sharp as my blade, and she's got the heart of a dragon. I can't say I don't understand why you and Kein tripped over yourselves for her."

Kassein smiled. That moment he had set his eyes on her, battered and bruised in the snow, felt like ages ago already. The woman who was now riding his dragon because she had refused to stay away from this battlefield felt like a completely different person. And he loved her even more for that.

"Ugh, stop making that face," his sister groaned. "You'll get to see her after the fight, but I need your head here first, Brother. ...They're coming."

He schooled his expression immediately.

Indeed, both armies were getting closer to each other, and just like the thunder rumbling above, the tension was rising quickly as the armies filled each end of the rift, their numbers making their way down the tortuous pathways.

Kassein felt the pair of sibling tribe leaders step up to their side, and he exchanged a quiet, understanding nod with them.

Those two were clearly fighters, ready to lead their people into battle. He could tell by their build, lean and muscular, shaped by movement and endurance, and by the weapons they carried. Both wielded long, double-headed spears, and their people carried similar ones. Their warriors were few, at least compared to his army, but they didn't hesitate. Their stance showed discipline, and the way they moved suggested they had received some level of training.

None of them had tried to avoid the fight. If anything, they had insisted on standing at the front. They had explained their plan at length, including his army for sure, but this was still very much their battle; they weren't cowering behind Kassein or expecting his men to do all the work, regardless of the numbers. Instead, the two leaders were standing on the same line as Kassein, Kiera, and Sazaran as soon as there was enough space for it, and he knew that the other tribe leader had led some of his warriors on a different route to bring them support from the side.

When both armies got closer, Kassein surveyed their ranks, evaluating them to be in the hundreds too.

For now, the size of their armies looked somewhat equal, but he had kept some of his men at the back with Herken as reinforcements. If the tribe leaders were right, their opponents also had more tribes that would probably attack from the flanks of the rift as well, using the dangerous descents to try and trap them down here. Kassein's eyes scoured the heights, spotting several men indeed lurking there.

"The little rats are hiding," his sister hissed with vicious glee.

Their eyesight as bearers of Dragon Blood was better than humans', and without it, Kassein doubted they would have been able to spot this many men stalking them from all corners of the surrounding heights. He glared at those he sighted before redirecting his gaze to their main forces, still yards away, squeezing themselves into the rift, progressing slowly but surely toward the inevitable.

The main difference between their armies was how disparate the enemy's was.

He couldn't even begin to guess how many different tribes they were facing, but as they got closer, it became evident that unlike the Munsa, who had made a point to blend in with his men, their tribes weren't even trying to be homogenous, making them look as uncoordinated as possible.

Each group among the gathered men had distinct features, such as tribal paintings, piercings, color-coded accessories or clothing, specific hairstyles, or face tattoos. There were even what looked like dogs in a corner, held on a leash by one of the tribes and growling in warning; one glare from Kassein had some of them stop and whimper instead.

"Wait," Kassein said aloud as he saw the Munsa Tribe's male leader step forward.

He raised his hand, and his army stopped as one.

Both sides now stood at a distance, facing each other with a stretch of muddy ground between them. It was a gap that a running man could cross in under a minute, yet it felt wider than ever.

Tension rose again as thunder cracked above their heads, followed by a flash of lightning that lit up the field for a heartbeat.

It felt like the calm before the storm, but the storm was already raging angrily above their heads in anticipation of the fierce battle.

And yet, there was this eerie pause, during which men on both sides considered one another, staring, gauging, tensing up as the inevitable loomed closer and closer.

Eventually, the Munsa Tribe leader next to him cleared his throat.

Kassein turned to watch as the man stepped forward, just enough to make his voice carry across the field. He shouted toward the enemy line, loud enough for the front ranks to hear. His words echoed against the stone walls that bordered the ravine, cutting through the wind and rain.

He could guess it was a last ditch attempt at peace, although it felt far too late for that. Not now. Not when both sides stood ankle-deep in mud, armed and ready for blood.

Still, Kassein waited patiently, using that brief pause to gauge their enemy tribe leaders with his eyes, wondering which of them had hurt Alezya, which were the ones he had to kill first, and those he could let die a slow, painful death. He had no personal vendetta against any of those men but the ones who had injured Alezya and made her cry. He would ask for no unnecessary deaths so long as her abusers paid. Although most eyes were on him, their gazes ranging from fearful to excited, they were all listening to Ekut. Some of the men had their fear written all over them, Kassein thought. Some of those men might run before the battle began if there was anywhere to run.

As a man on the opposite side also stepped up, the shouting between both sides went back and forth for a while, but their demeanors showed little promise of stopping this war. Many of those men looked determined, while the Munsa Tribe's male leader's tone sounded pleading. Kassein didn't need to understand a word he said to know he was pleading with them to give up and surrender before they launched into this war. While he could see many fearful faces, more men looked determined, especially those who appeared to be the leaders.

Kassein let out a faint sigh; only foolish leaders would lead their people to a certain death.

"They're not going to give up, are they?" Kiera muttered lightly as if she were commenting on the weather.

"Doesn't look like it," Sazaran nodded. "Well. We came all the way for this, didn't we? Might as well show them how we–"

"Don't kill them all," Kassein cut him off, their gazes snapping to him. "Lots of them are scared. Some will flee. Some will try to survive. Only kill when they don't give up."

"Are you sure?" Kiera raised an eyebrow. "They surrounded us down here; I doubt it was to extend the same courtesy."

"Alezya was forced to flee by her tribe," he said. "Look at those men. They're terrified. Their leaders forced them into a fight they already have little chance of winning in a place like this."

"Since when do we care?" Kiera groaned.

"Since Alezya does."

His sister rolled her eyes. She didn't say anything for a while, and Kassein could feel she was also scouring the ranks, glancing up at the men standing in the deadly heights or hiding between crevices. He had often cared very little about their opponents' survival, but things were different since he had seen things from Alezya's perspective. She had done everything she could to prevent this fight. She had been the first one horrified by the battleground and what it would imply too. He had mastered very little of their language, but if he had understood one thing from all their exchanges and what he'd observed, it was that this battle had not been her and her allies' doing; they had sought peace as much as they'd been able to until this very moment.

"...Fine," Kiera finally sighed. "There's no fun in fighting cowards anyway."

"Target the leaders," Kassein hissed, his tone getting angrier as the negotiations seemed to reach a dead-end. "From what we've seen of the tribes, they'll be in disarray once we get rid of their heads."

"That I can do," Kiera grinned. "...Any idea which of those dragon dungs is that Darak bastard?"

"Not yet," he groaned.

Alezya's and Lumie's fathers were his priority targets, but for now, he had no idea where they were in the sea of men. He would have expected the man who had initiated this war to be at the forefront, but none of those men seemed to look anything like Alezya, and he couldn't pinpoint anyone who looked like they belonged to her tribe.

He leaned toward the Munsa Tribe's female leader, Ekata, to ask.

"Deklaan *Kulani*?" he did his best to pronounce it right. "Darak?"

She glanced at him, visibly slightly surprised he was addressing her, but after a glance at the army they faced, she shook her head, confirming what he had already guessed: neither Alezya's father nor her tribe was on the frontlines.

"Well," Kiera sighed, swinging her favorite sword, "guess we'll have to do a bit of cleaning first."

Just then, silence reigned, the negotiations having obviously failed.

The Munsa Tribe's male leader, Ekut, glanced at Kassein and shook his head in a defeated expression. Kassein took a deep breath and stepped forward, effectively standing a couple of steps ahead of his army and fellow leaders.

Then, he slowly drew his large, giant sword from its sheath, causing some gasps among the ranks. It had been almost inconspicuous while hidden in the leather, but his sword was too heavy for most normal men to even carry, and its size was as impressive as the shine of its blade. This was a weapon that had heavy damage and mass casualty written all over it, and the men on the frontlines paled at the sight of it in Kassein's hand.

Slowly and deliberately, he pointed it at the man who had been shouting back at Ekut.

"...You chose to die," he hissed.

In the distance, Kein let out a deafening growl, and Kassein took the first step. At first, he walked, almost casually, rain dripping down his hair and face, his dark green eyes riveted on the man who, for a split second, seemed to deeply regret his decision.

Then, Kassein accelerated, and he heard steps behind him. One pair of feet splashing the mud following him, then another, then another, then a dozen, then twice as many. After what looked like a second of hesitation, the first enemy line marched forward too.

Thunder suddenly boomed over their heads, and it was like chaos erupted all at once. Kassein ran, men shouted, and a head flew off. The war had begun.

Kassein had fought in a lot of battles before, but for the first time, he was experiencing the difference between being in battle and leading a war. When he had stood in battle, he had always been able to see the end. See the men fall, one after another, gauge the chaos around him, and know when the end was near. But standing down here, in this hellish rift, there was no way to tell the end, no way to tell how many more men he'd have to slay before it was over.

It felt endless.

The rain was battering the troops, the mud was climbing up their ankles and licking their shins, and the thunder was raging along with the chorus of clashing blades and human cries. It was sheer chaos all around him, and for a while, all he could do was slay, stab, and swing his sword as the men kept coming at him. There was no room for him to check on his troops, let alone establish any kind of strategy. He had a faint sense that they were trying to gang up on him, like they were trying to take down a giant. Still, Kassein kept going, ignoring everything else, kicking bodies out of his way, focusing on his movements, staying aware of his blind spots, and spotting any enemies that dared to approach.

He had been trained to fight from the minute he had been able to hold a sword, and he'd had the strength of a dragon since his birth, but there was nothing that could test a man like hundreds of men coming at him and hoping to be the one to sever his head from his body. Some men came howling, roaring, shouting like their battle cry was going to grant them some invisible power, only to be rendered mute or choking on their own blood seconds later. It was all the warriors seeking glory in taking down the strongest of them all, and for a while, Kassein didn't have the time to bother with mercy. He acted like a mindless instrument of death, killing, slashing, and breaking anything that came his way with ill intent. He didn't bother with any war cry, only releasing grunts when his muscles began to ache, hot breaths when his skin burned, and spitting when something foreign entered his mouth. There were no superficial movements, no speeches like some of those men did, for whatever reasons their customs or pride led them to. Kassein didn't care; he had a war to win and an opponent to defeat.

It took a long while before he was finally able to slow down just enough to check on everyone else, somewhere behind him.

He was standing at the very helm of his army, with Kiera, Ekata, Ekut, and Sazaran scattered a few paces behind and on the sides with their men, like he was leading an arrow's head piercing through and behind enemy lines. All of them seemed to be holding their ground with various amounts of fatigue showing; Sazaran's arm was bleeding, and Ekata had changed weapons for some reason, but they were still going strong, flanked by allies and, instead of shouting orders few would hear, they led by example. Kassein had to slay some more men who'd rushed at him before he could take another short break to check farther back.

Their army held the ranks tight with the Munsa Tribe, but as anticipated, more enemies had descended from the sides, and now, all the brigades were forced to battle, even those at the very back.

The enemy was trying to trap them, but that would be impossible so long as Kassein's army didn't let them win any ground. For now, their exit route still looked solid, and no brigade was conceding. Some tight pockets were forming around the injured to evacuate them, and Kassein could guess that although he was too far to be seen, Kauser had to be leading the troops at the rear and, if it was still possible, coordinating evacuations for whoever had a chance to make it. They had established a post about a mile before the battlefield with an infirmary, with Tievin supervising it and a brigade to defend it, and Kassein hoped they'd manage to stay unharmed long enough.

He refocused on his end, but gradually, it became clear the enemies had stopped trying to charge him and were making efforts to avoid him instead; the path of defeated enemies behind him served as a clear warning to anyone who took the main route and tried to rush past Kassein.

Sadly for both armies, this rift offered absolutely no such thing as a safe route anywhere. The terrain was just as dangerous as the blades they carried, and in the very first minutes of the battle alone, dozens of men had been injured or killed by unforeseen crevices, rocks suddenly falling, and underestimated cliff heights.

Even Kassein had felt sharp rocks stab his boots, soles, or skin several times as he'd been forced to step on them without looking. This place was a nightmare to walk around in, let alone try to fight in; the ground was uneven, and unpredictable sharp-edged rocks were hidden in the growing amount of bloody mud pooling around them. He'd learned enough medicinal basics from his mother to know many who survived this fight might die from infections, and it made him even more furious.

Whoever had picked this battleground had no regard for the lives of their soldiers. The thunderstorm was making the already treacherous terrain twice as bad, and he was starting to understand the absolute horror the Munsa and Alezya had shown when their battlefield had been announced; their enemies were madmen.

When Ekata let out a frustrated cry, he glanced back and saw that she'd stuck her ankle in a crevice, tripped, and injured herself.

He was too far to help, but in a matter of seconds, Sazaran was over to shield her from enemies while she recovered and stood back up. They had to admit that the tribes weren't shying away from the fight, at least the ones on their side. The same couldn't be said for their opponents.

The trained warriors had obviously stood at the front, but the more Kassein pierced through enemy lines, the more he came across scared expressions, shivering hands, and tearful eyes. Maybe some were just cold from the rain. Still, either way, he slightly changed his attacks from then on, trying to focus his fatal blows on the most determined fighters and sparing the lives of anyone who showed weakness, satisfying himself by just harming them until they fell or gave up.

More than once, he saw a man fall, injured, and cower in the mud; Kassein moved on without looking back. He also stopped trying to make more progress through the battleground; there was no point in burying themselves deeper into this hellhole. Instead, Kassein determined that if their opponents were that eager to fight, they could cross the hellhole they'd picked to get to him; he would rather stand his ground and let them come than pull his men any deeper into this treacherous area.

"This. Fucking. Mud!" his sister barked from somewhere behind.

When he glanced back, Kiera was absolutely covered in mud, like she'd been hit by a wave of it, and the downpour wasn't washing it off of her fast enough; he grimaced, unsure of what his sister had done to end up like this. Maybe she had tripped at some point too because she looked positively pissed. It took Kassein a second to realize that the only reason she had time to rant was that, like him, Kiera had reached a point where the enemy had deemed it better to try and avoid facing her at all.

She spat out something dark and kicked a man who was trying to get back up before she glanced up and smirked.

"Looks like our girl's doing great."

Kassein whipped his head around toward the skies. It took him less than a second to spot his dragon, right before it dove with a furious growl onto the flank of one of the mountains surrounding the rift. With all the chaos down there and the thunder above, Kassein had completely tuned out his own dragon's furious growls, but now, it was clear that they echoed just as loudly as the skies all around them.

He watched as Kein furiously clawed at the mountain, effectively breaking through rocks and triggering an avalanche over the neighboring cliffs. His dragon attacking the ridge high in the heights sent a crushing tide of rocks, snow, and dust, and Kassein watched as it hit the enemy's flank without warning and without anywhere for them to run.

"Darsan would be a big fan," his sister scoffed with a hint of amusement in her voice.

Indeed, their older brother had an uncanny reputation for willingly or unwillingly breaking mountains and causing avalanches when they were younger, but never had it been used in combat like this.

Even Kassein was filled with silent admiration as he realized that Alezya and Kein's attack on the mountains had probably been helping them in more than one way. He had wondered why none of their enemies had tried attacking them from above with arrows or the like, and now he knew: with Alezya and Kein roaming the skies, there wasn't a single man who would dare to peek out.

Kassein grinned, proud of his woman, and swiftly spun the blade in his hand, suddenly eager to do his fair share of the work down here too; Kein and Alezya were taking down a lot of men at once, and he couldn't wait for them to be reunited once this would all be over.

For now, however, there was still a lot of work to be done.

This war was an ongoing nightmare.

As the downpour got worse, the thunderstorm arrived with a loud boom to throw a dark shadow over the battlefield. Kassein heard the voices of men fighting coming from everywhere, as both armies were now a confused mix, stepping over mud, rocks, and bodies, many whipping their blades in disorganized chaos at whoever came their way. He realized his bronze armor had become a shining beacon, with a lot of his men following in his wake, while the enemy tried to run away from whichever area he approached. Whenever he could check on the others, he did.

He was aware he would lose men no matter what, and they had already likely lost dozens, but he had to keep an eye on his sister, the Munsa Tribe leaders, and Sazaran. Kiera seemed to be doing fine; the rain had become heavy enough to wash the mud off her body, and instead, he could see the dark gray scales that covered her skin, testaments to the scratches and cuts she'd suffered, but it wasn't much compared to the volume of men trying to take her down. If he had to guess, Kassein thought those men were hoping they'd have a better chance at taking down his sister than him, and they were fatally wrong. Kiera loved fighting, and she didn't often have the chance to use her full strength.

Not only that, but even if she didn't look like it, his sister was about eight years older; that meant she'd had eight more years of training than him, and their father had never been one to train his daughters any less than his sons unless they chose not to. Their oldest sister, Cessilia, was an excellent fighter, but she didn't particularly enjoy it, and Sadara, the youngest sister, didn't like fighting at all; Kiera was the only one of his sisters who had been eager to train as much as she could before she left the nest, and right now, it was showing. She was absolutely slaughtering everyone around her, her dual swords swinging around her with impressive speed. She had even picked up a couple of new blades along the way as he noticed a spear and two knives attached to her belt or armor.

It was like watching a small tornado whirling around on the battlefield; her armor was dark gray, like her dragon's scales they were made of, and a flash of silver was all he could see while she spun, moved, and fought like a lightning bolt. Kiera had never bothered looking graceful; instead, she was focused on being fast and lethal. Her fighting style was closer to that of an assassin than his brute style, but here, it served her well; she was jumping from one prey to another like a snowcat on a rampage, looking like she flew in her determined fighting space. She might complain about the mud, but it didn't look like it slowed her one bit.

Her dragon, Kiki, looked like her reptilian double. The dark gray dragon was hard to spot against the landscape, but whenever it made an appearance, it was to dislodge rocks from the cliffs and send them crashing down, dart into an area where it had just enough space to drill through enemy lines, or fly back up to terrorize those in the nearest cliffs.

Kiera's dragon wasn't loud, but it was easy to follow its path, for it caused waves of mayhem and panic wherever it appeared. Its best work was in the heights, though. Kiki wasn't flying as high as Kein was, but it was making full use of its snake-like figure and rock-like color for sneak attacks. Instead of being as loud and furious as its sibling, his sister's dragon seemed to be leaping around just above their heads, a flash of ashen scales dancing around the mid-height cliffs its bigger sibling couldn't reach, pouncing on any archer that thought it had a chance with Kein busy elsewhere.

Kiki was just as fast and efficient as Kiera, making appearances everywhere they needed before they even knew and disappearing into the storm again before the enemy could retaliate. They would have been in a much more compromising situation if it hadn't been for the pair of dragons terrifying everyone who wasn't down there.

Kassein was forced to focus on the men who had approached in front of him for a few minutes before he was finally able to steal glances at their other allies.

He'd lost sight of the Munsa Tribe's male leader, Ekut, but his sister was doing alright on her own; unlike them, she couldn't grow scales to heal her injuries, so her cuts and bruises were in plain sight, but he had to admit, she was still looking as fierce and determined as when the battle had begun, aside from that permanent grimace. She had a slight limp from her earlier injury, but she was doing fine otherwise, standing her ground thanks to Sazaran protecting her blind spot and her sharp, long spear that allowed her a wide range of motion without moving too much. Kassein had only noticed she'd changed weapons again because the spear before was shorter, and he guessed the Munsa Tribe stuck close and had prepared many replacement weapons. Ekata also kept one of their army's smaller blades at her waist, probably in case she had to defend herself in close quarters. She looked tired, but she was still leading her people by example, and it was Kassein's first time realizing she was the only other female fighter on the battlefield.

It should have made her an easier target, perhaps, but the Munsa Tribe seemed determined to protect their leader. Thus, she was well surrounded by some of their people, all of them easily distinguishable by their unique spears and the small fishnets some of them used to trap their enemies' legs or block their attacks.

Sazaran was also looking tired but putting up a good front; Kassein was surprised the older man still found the strength to bark orders and motivate their troops at regular intervals. Kassein let the General direct their forces as he saw fit. While Kassein led the front of the army with few words and mostly action, Sazaran was in a better position to assess the troops' morale and strength from the middle ranks.

He focused on the fighting ahead of him again, but by all accounts, the troops didn't seem to diminish, only slow down.

As they'd anticipated, the nightmare they had for a battlefield was doing a lot of damage. Since Kassein had decided to stop making deliberate efforts to move forward, keeping his men from advancing any farther even when they had a chance, the opposite army was struggling to get to him. It wouldn't have been a good move to stay rooted where they were on many battlefields, but here, it was proving to be a good decision; by the time the new waves of opponents reached Kassein, they had gathered all sorts of little injuries and fatigue. They weren't letting themselves get to an area where they could be enclosed and isolated, either. By keeping his army from stretching, Kassein ensured they didn't lose the connection at the back or weaken their flanks.

Moreover, Alezya and Kein kept damaging the rival army farther down the rift, burying their flanks under snow and rocks, forcing them to stay in tight, uneven, and slow ranks and advance arduous routes before they could make their way to Kassein's army. Their initial plan to trap them by attacking the flanks continued to backfire. Between the dragons and the terrain, they were losing ground before some of their men even reached the fight.

After a few glances upward, Kassein noticed what had to be their allied tribes finally appearing in the heights and engaging in the fight where they could.

It was oddly satisfying to see that many tribes, aside from the Munsa, had answered the call to battle, even if they seemed late. Perhaps they had hesitated, waiting to see which way the fight would turn, or maybe they had been frightened by the dragons. But now, they were fully committed to the war. They were small groups, appearing throughout the cliffs on this or that mountain, but they were fiercely defending themselves against the enemy tribes. Unlike their foes, their allies did not fear his dragon as much, allowing them to fight openly in the heights, exposed to the relentless rain and wind, while many of their opponents tried to hide whenever they heard a growl or a flap of wings. Kassein wasn't sure how Alezya had managed to distinguish friend from foe in the chaos, but one thing was clear: she had done most of the work in the heights already.

"Kassein!"

He turned to his sister, but she was looking up, and for the first time, she looked worried. He turned his head back to the skies, looking for whatever had alarmed Kiera, and it took him a while to realize what was wrong; Kein was still attacking mountains, letting out furious growls and looking more enraged than ever before, but the dragon was alone.

Alezya was gone from its back.

Kein had already spun, and he couldn't see the dragon's back, but Kassein kept staring, horror creeping up his spine.

He had to be wrong.

Things were so chaotic, he'd only gotten a glimpse of his dragon for a fraction of a second.

He waited, his throat tight. His heartbeat pounded so loud in his ears that he barely heard the chaos around him; the chaos in his head was much louder. His fingers curled, tightening around his sword's hilt so hard his knuckles went white.

She has to be there, a panic-rising voice in his head kept repeating, begging, chanting internally like a prayer. His green eyes remained fixed on his dragon's back, willing his vision to sharpen through the thick rain, mist, and snow. His heart was drumming furiously in his chest; he had to be wrong.

No one should have been that still on a battlefield, but he was frozen, his entire body resisting the horrible realization that was about to break over him like a crashing wave. He could vaguely hear his men calling him, warning him, but he didn't move. He couldn't. He was paralyzed by fear like he'd never experienced before, and hundreds of men lunging at him with sharp blades had nothing to do with it.

Something sharp suddenly pinched somewhere against his ribs.

Kassein barely noticed at first, and he cared even less. But he felt that nagging pinch, a bothersome tug he couldn't shake off. For a second, he willed his eyes back down, and found the bewildered face of a man in front of him, oddly close.

His eyes dropped more. A dagger was buried in his side, hilt-deep, and a trembling hand was holding it. As soon as he saw it, the man's hand let go as if his weapon had burned him, as if he second-guessed landing that stab. Kassein stared, feeling strangely removed from it all.

Then, his hand moved, almost by itself, slowly, grabbed the weapon, and pulled it out. He barely flinched as another wave of pain hit him sharply, and his body flexed for the split second his blood flew. The man gasped, paled some more, and stumbled back, slipping in the mud.

Kassein reversed the blade and slit his throat in a single motion without thinking much about it. He didn't even watch the body fall, nor the shocked gazes around him; his head had already snapped back up.

His dragon was going mad against a mountain, and its back showed no rider.

A block of ice sank in Kassein's stomach. Where was Alezya? Why had she left the safety of his dragon's back?

Something red distorted his vision, and something deafening blocked his hearing. Alezya was gone. Alezya wasn't safe on Kein's back anymore, and a tidal wave of rage quietly, dangerously, rose as that realization sunk in. She was missing. She was somewhere, and he couldn't protect her.

He didn't know what had happened to her. What was happening to her. He had failed to protect someone. *Again.*

Something snapped inside him. It was a crack in the wall at first, and then, a dam burst. Alezya was gone, and with her, something that had been holding back the chaos all along.

Kassein's green eyes turned back to a movement in front of him, and suddenly, something that wasn't human took over. Sheer instinct, guided by fury.

The first wave of men that reached him didn't have time to realize their mistake. They got too close, reacted too late, and Kassein's blade flashed like the lightning bolt above. Two men were cut down in one movement, dead before their bodies hit the ground. And then another one followed, and another one.

The large sword swung, slashing so fast and vicious that it looked more like a whip than a heavy blade, and no one could escape it. Kassein let out a loud, frustrated roar of rage, his anger taking over. He swung his sword, not worrying about allowing survivors anymore; he was far too anxious, irate, and agitated to care. He didn't hold back, his large blade ripping through flesh, shedding blood, and breaking bones. It was like he had snapped, turning into a raging beast on the battlefield.

There was no more standing his ground, no more holding back. For the first time in months, he was the Wild Prince again, blinded by his wrath, a god of war and destruction, leaving nothing in his wake. Kassein roared against the opponents and shouted back at the thunderstorm, at his growling dragon. He vaguely heard Kiera barking at their men to stay back and away from him while he tore deeper into enemy lines.

Kassein was ready to fight an entire army alone so long as he could find

Alezya. The last bit of reason he held onto was telling him to find her. No matter how many he'd have to cut down in his path, he had to find her. Alezya was lost, somewhere in this sea of rocks, snow, mud, and men, and absolutely nothing else mattered. He let out another animalistic shout, one aimed at his dragon, letting Kein know how furious its owner was. The dragon growled back, a ferocious warning. There was a dangerous tension in the air, and a brewing sense of doom as a feeling of anticipation settled between them, as if they hadn't both been busy fighting an entire army at the same time.

Suddenly, Kein's growl thundered above them, and chaos unleashed on the battlefield; Kein was diving down as if there hadn't been sharp peaks and jagged cliffs in its path.

The orange dragon had gone wild again, and all it cared about was fighting its owner; Kassein was aching for that fight too. It was like their sanity had snapped the moment Alezya had disappeared. Kassein didn't hear his sister's shouts nor the panicked screams around him. All he did was glare at the incoming building of orange scales, the sharp claws aimed right at him, and readied himself for a fight.

"EKUT!"

The female shout got his attention.

Kassein whipped his head just as Kein flew above their heads with a loud growl, the force throwing him and everyone around to the ground.

The dragon didn't touch the ground, but it hit some walls of rock around, and dozens of boulders rained on the battlefield. Thankfully, most of it hammered the enemy lines, forcing their troops to scatter in screaming, panicked chaos and disarray.

Kassein scrambled to his knees and ran back to his troops, his thoughts somewhat clear again; in his rage, he'd mistaken Ekata's scream for Alezya's, but it had been enough to snap him out of his rampage. He ran toward where he'd last seen her, realizing how far ahead of his troops his frenzy had taken him.

Finally, he found Ekata and, sadly, her brother.

It was far too late by the time Kassein reached them, and Sazaran also stood nearby, looking sorry. There was no hope; it was painfully obvious Ekut was already dead, his eyes left wide open. He was covered in so much blood and mud it was hard to tell which injury had caused it, but if Kassein had to guess, it was the one that horribly dented his head.

Her brother's passing had utterly defeated Ekata; she had let go of her spear and was down on her knees, cradling his body, her frame hunched over his as uncontrollable sobs shook her. Her wails were the saddest Kassein had ever heard, barely sounding human. She wasn't going to fight anymore, and Sazaran and her people had taken over defending the mourning tribe leader.

Kassein found his sister's gaze across the battlefield, all traces of joy gone; Kiera was as shocked by their ally's death as he was, and with Kein having scared half of both armies away, the battle had subdued considerably. Kassein resented himself for his outburst of rage, but right then, his mind was clearer than ever before; this war had to end.

He turned back toward the opposing army, and strangely, things had considerably calmed on their side of the battlefield too.

Kein's sudden attack had terrified them all enough that they'd stopped fighting to take into account the state of their army, take in all the bodies surrounding them, and realize that they were all headed toward the inevitable unless they did something now. Kassein could see many of them weren't willing to resume the battle, their eyes distraught or contemplating, horrified, the accumulated bodies around them.

It had taken a woman's scream and a dragon's attack, but suddenly, an eerie suspense settled over the rift as both armies regarded one another, hesitant.

Many of their leaders were dead, and the men didn't seem eager to run headfirst into the same fate.

Then, a deafening crack echoed through the rift, breaking the tension.

Men on both sides looked around and up, trying to find the source of the sound. Then another crack was heard, louder, and all eyes shifted to one of the largest mountains overlooking the area. A block of snow had detached itself from somewhere under the tip of it.

At first, and with the distance, it only seemed like an inconsequential event, but the sound it had made upon detaching itself indicated it was going to be anything but. Every single fighter in the area was frozen in nervous anticipation, watching with growing horror as it slowly rolled down and more and more snow toppled, blowing thick clouds of white smoke in its wake. It was picking up speed, and more chunks of snow were detaching, adding to the white tidal wave.

"...That can't be good," Kiera swallowed.

Kassein was the first to snap his focus back to the battlefield. That avalanche was going to hit the rift. There was no way around it.

With the way that mountain was positioned, it was going to tumble straight toward them. It was coming down fast, growing larger by the second, and they probably had less than a minute before it struck.

The trajectory itself was hard to predict, but if he had to guess, Kassein estimated it was going to hit somewhere between where their armies met, and farther down, where he'd forced their opponent to come to them. The enemy would be the most impacted, but the men who'd followed him to the frontline were also at the forefront of the impending catastrophe, and there was no time to evacuate them. Kein wouldn't be able to carry dozens of men to safety, and he couldn't even predict how far that avalanche was going to reach.

Kassein began to frantically look for a solution, glancing at the mud-covered cliffs, the dozens of men standing there in petrified shock, and the jagged stone pillars scattered along the floor of the rift. His heart accelerated. They were massive. Sharp, towering like the fangs of some buried monster pointed toward the sky, and they were all standing in its open maw. He glanced up again at the avalanche, the looming wave of snow gathering speed and heading straight for them.

"...Kiera," he called his sister with a hoarse voice.

"We don't have time to evacuate," she retorted with a tight jaw.

"No, we don't."

He turned to her as she approached, her eyes riveted on the impending catastrophe.

"Then what do we–"

"You have to use your water thing."

His sister's eyes snapped back to him, and after a second of taking in what he'd said, her jaw dropped. She let out a nervous laugh.

"You can't be serious," she muttered.

"You have to," he insisted.

"Kassein, I haven't-... I haven't done it in years, and I've only succeeded twice!"

"It doesn't matter," he retorted. "It's all ice and snow. Do it."

"But–!"

He didn't stay to listen to her protests. He vaguely heard his sister complain and maybe let out a couple of bad words, but he was already running, his eyes riveted on the incoming disaster.

"Sir, what do you want us to–"

"Run! Find cover!" he barked behind him.

He left his men, charging ahead. No one stopped him when he pushed past the enemy lines; most were frozen with fear, and those who weren't had already begun to run. But the rift was too deep, and there was nowhere they could escape to before the avalanche reached them.

If they couldn't stop it, they had to block it.

That was Kassein's plan as he darted toward the largest spiked boulder he could find. It was half-buried in ice, the tallest of the jagged rock formations scattered through the rift, at least five or six times his height, but that didn't stop him. He threw his sword to the ground and lunged at it, ignoring the shouted warnings from behind. His body slammed into the rock, shaking loose a shower of ice and, against all odds, triggering a sharp crack. His shoulder flared with pain, but he didn't stop. He slammed it again, this time angling himself toward the weak spot he'd felt at chest height. He planted his boots in the mud and shoved with everything he had. Another crack. Another wave of pain.

Yells and chaos echoed around him, but all he registered was Kiki's shriek above, Kiera urging her dragon into the air. Somewhere down the rift, a rock spire collapsed with a thunderous crash; Kein was doing the same. But Kassein was alone with this one. He gritted his teeth and slammed his shoulder once more. Blood hit his tongue, but he ignored it. The crack was growing. He dug in again, using his hands now. His palms bled against the stone, bronze scales beginning to creep along his fingers. He pushed harder. His boots slipped an inch, sweat running down his back, and the roar of the avalanche grew louder by the second.

He let out a breath, gathered his strength, and slammed forward.

This time, the crack split wide. One final push, and the column gave way, crashing heavily into the snow.

"*HIDE!*" he roared, one of the few words he'd learned in their language.

It took a second, but then, dozens of men from the opposite side glanced at the collapsed trunk of rocks and threw themselves behind the barrier he'd just created. Seconds later, the rumble of the avalanche grew louder and louder, until there was a split second of haunting silence.

And then, all hell broke loose above their heads.

The avalanche didn't come down as solid snow to bury them.

It slammed into them like a freezing wall of sleet and water. The force alone pinned them to the ground, the weight of it knocking the breath from their lungs. The jagged rock column shook, but it held, and the men braced themselves against the slick, frozen stone, gritting their teeth as the relentless downpour battered them.

The flood didn't stop. It pounded over them in crashing waves, drenching them from head to toe, soaking through armor and cloth until the cold felt like it had seeped into their bones. Men coughed and sputtered, spitting out water, their hands gripping anything solid as the muddy, freezing current surged up to their waists, their chests, threatening to swallow them before, finally, it began to recede. The flood drained as fast as it had come, leaving behind knee-deep pools of slush and icy mud.

Kassein spat out water and pushed himself back, his boots sinking into the flooded ground. He glanced up, catching sight of his sister.

Kiera was standing, her arms raised, but her entire frame seemed arched with immeasurable effort, her body shaking violently as she held the massive, white, and terrifying frozen storm at bay. The avalanche hadn't disappeared. It was right there, hovering dangerously just above Kiera, frozen mid-collapse, a massive wall of ice and snow ready to crash down at any second. It churned like a storm caught in place, twisting and writhing, fighting against the force that held it back, the invisible barrier Kiera's hands held. Instead, it was falling slowly, controlled, inch by inch, turning into thick, steady streams of water that rushed past her ankles and knees, the same water that ran like a heavy downpour into the battlefield and drenched the men below.

Kiki had to be somewhere ahead of her, likely taking the brunt of it, shielding Kiera from the worst of the force, but it was clear this was Kiera's doing. She stood at the center of the chaos, the avalanche roaring around her like a beast on the verge of collapse. But she wouldn't let it.

A proud smirk appeared on Kassein's lips as he witnessed his sister's power.

All around him, the men clung to the barricade of jagged stone, shivering and coughing, still in tight bundles, but the worst of it was over. Farther down the rift, the soldiers in the collapsed tunnels were in the same condition, half-drowned but alive.

Kassein looked up. The avalanche had broken apart, crashing at Kiera's feet in heavy waves. It was a waterfall now, its crushing force spent. It wasn't a perfect save, but it had been enough.

Kein swooped low overhead, skimming just above the battlefield now that the jagged stone barriers no longer threatened it. As the dragon passed, Kassein didn't hesitate. He leapt, catching onto Kein's extended paw and letting the dragon launch him toward the ridge, toward where Kiera had just stood, locked in the fight of her life.

He found her on her knees beside Kiki, both of them drenched and breathing hard.

"...You did it," he said.

"Shut up," Kiera hissed angrily. "I didn't think I'd be able to do it again. You are mad! That was a crazy idea!"

"But you did it."

His sister rolled her eyes.

"Yeah, well... I'm not Cessilia, but Kiki's still a *Water* Dragon, so... I figured it was easier to turn it all into water... Well, most of it. We did what we could."

He walked over and offered a hand to help her up. She sighed but took it, getting up with visible exhaustion.

"How are things down there?"

"Hopefully over," Kassein hissed.

Kiera nodded, and the two of them jumped back down into the rift, landing from a height that would have shattered a normal human's knees.

The fighters on both sides were slowly recovering. Many were shivering, coughing up water, or helping by patting backs, while others were staying down on their knees, looking exhausted. Some were staring at Kassein with confusion written all over their faces. They all knew he didn't have to save a single one of them, but he had nearly broken a shoulder to protect hundreds of them.

He and Kiera slowly walked back together to their army, checking on their men as everyone was getting back up and stepping away from the other collapsed columns or emerging from whichever hideouts they'd found. Those who weren't moving were already being dragged or carried to the back. Someone brought Kiera's blades to her, and two of the few men who'd followed Kassein handed him his weapon; it was nearly impossible for one of them to carry it alone.

Overall, it was clear their end of the rift had been mostly spared, as expected. The damages were mostly on the other side, and it would have been far worse if they hadn't intervened.

Kassein realized the thunder had stopped. His dragon was no longer furiously growling and attacking mountains, either, causing an eerie calm in the rift. Everyone had stopped fighting, as the thwarted catastrophe had broken the armies apart, leaving them in a suspended interlude, an impossible pause in the chaos.

Heavy rain was quietly washing over the battleground in a strange, somber atmosphere, only broken by Ekata's heartbreaking wails.

"Is it over?" Sazaran grunted.

"...We're about to find out," Kiera muttered.

Without exchanging a word, she and her brother turned around and marched ahead calmly rather than menacingly. They stopped to stand side by side ahead of their troops, quietly daring anyone to resume the fight.

Kassein's green eyes scoured the enemy lines, looking each man in the eye, reading their fear, their confusion, their panic. Now that the water had washed a lot of the mud and blood away, they could see the bodies of their fallen brothers all around them; they could see the fate that awaited them if this fight went on any longer. Whatever their leaders had promised, it was lying dead in the mud along with their heads.

Several long seconds passed, but before hope could take root, furious voices came from the rear of the enemy lines. Kassein tilted his head angrily, and a handful of men stepped forward, looking belligerent and, more annoyingly, pretty unharmed. They carried cuts and bruises, but it was easy to see that those were most likely caused from being hit by fallen rocks and treacherous ground than any actual fight.

"Here come the cowards," Kiera hissed.

Indeed, the only way those men were this fine so late in the battle meant they'd been standing at the rear all along. Kassein had cut pretty deep behind enemy lines before the avalanche, and there were very few men who hadn't been pulled into the fight; the two armies had been forced to meet where they hadn't been pressured by the snowfalls and landslides his dragon had triggered. Things were quiet on all sides now, and the avalanche had cooled most fighting spirits, but those men were walking ahead, looking determined, angry, and infuriatingly fine.

One of them stepped forward.

His equipment was slightly better than the others', with thick fur draped over his shoulders, his sword looking sharp and unused. He was tall, though not as tall as Kassein, his long hair held back by a circlet, fully exposing the disfigurement along the side of his face. A web of dark, unnatural veins sprawled across his jaw and neck, twisting beneath his skin like something diseased, poisoned. The scarring was uneven, creeping in jagged patterns, the sickly color standing out in stark contrast to the rest of his flesh. When he clenched his jaw, the veins pulsed slightly, as if whatever had damaged him still lingered.

Kassein had seen many wounds, but none quite like this. The man's fingers twitched briefly at his throat before curling into a fist, as if resisting the urge to claw at the scars, but his eyes burned with hatred, locked entirely on Kassein. There was something about this man that unnerved Kassein, although he couldn't exactly pinpoint why. An instinct, perhaps, his stomach curling to let him know this was a natural enemy.

"Why does that ugly bastard feel slightly familiar?" His sister similarly tilted her head with a frown.

The man stepped in front of the others, visibly putting on some sort of show. He raised his blade, pointing the tip at Kassein, and spoke loudly in that tongue of theirs. Kassein, who hadn't spent nearly enough time trying to learn Alezya's tongue, still managed to recognize the words "dragon" and "woman" in his long speech. It was obviously meant for the tribes to hear, but his eyes were glaring at Kassein the whole time.

But then, the man said one word even his sister understood, who immediately straightened herself with anger.

"*Miski ti loptaa latka, sinun kayarun! Vikaya labga hamrun! Deklaan Kulani loyka tyo kutiya Alezya ra tyo ho dryagaan bastarko ilkat agadi taneka hanra!*"

He finished his spiel by spitting in the mud at their feet. Kiera clicked her tongue, a sound their family used when they were getting annoyed.

"...Fine," she muttered. "This one's yours."

Kassein didn't reply because this wasn't up for debate.

His dark green eyes were locked on his prey, watching as the man tried and failed to rouse their troops. Except for the handful of men around him, he was standing alone to face the two of them, and clearly, he was trying hard to convince their army to resume the fight.

"We need to find Alezya," he said to his sister, glancing up as Kein was making nervous loops above them.

"Kiki's looking for her too."

As grateful as he was for his sister's dragon helping out, Kassein needed to find Alezya himself. He needed this fight to be over so he could find her, hold her, make sure she was safe and sound. He wouldn't stop until then. He didn't like not knowing where she was or how she was, and he hated even more that his dragon seemed as concerned and clueless as he was. Kein's frustrated growls were now like a heavy thunder above their heads as his dragon was getting just as restless as he was.

"Let's end this," he hissed, stepping forward.

His opponent let out a loud shout that could have been a convincing war cry if his army hadn't remained rooted in place, refusing to resume the fight before them, turning their heads away. Undeterred, he lunged at Kassein with his blade leading the charge, his determined gaze suggesting he truly believed he had a chance.

In other circumstances, Kassein might have taken his time. He would have let the man get a few swings at him, making him believe they were on the same level. He would have made this duel last longer, inflicting small but painful wounds on his opponent, making him suffer, and using him as an example. Kassein wasn't much of a merciful man, and he had never claimed to be one. But right then, he didn't have the patience to indulge in this madman; he had to end this and find Alezya.

He had led this war for her, and it would all mean nothing without her. He certainly didn't care to entertain a man who had spat in the mud in the same breath he'd dared to utter her name. Everything happened in a short moment; the man jumped at Kassein, his sword held high to slice him from above—a bold move, but too slow. Kassein stepped aside, spun around, and slashed the man's heels.

A horrible scream echoed as his opponent fell on his face into the mud and coughed, his tears adding to the wet ground.

"Seriously?" his sister panted between two strikes.

Kassein didn't answer; instead, he helped her finish the handful of madmen who had seriously thought they could take the two of them on. It would have taken at least three times as many for them to even have a chance at defeating one of them. When they were done, Kiera wiped the sweat off her forehead with a groan.

"You think they're done now?" she hissed, glaring at the rest of the tribes, challenging them with her eyes.

Kassein looked around, but this time, no one pushed through or stepped forward; they had just seen a handful of men fall in seconds.

The outcome was clear if they decided to foolishly risk their lives attempting to do the same. Someone moved, and Kassein glared fiercely, Kein echoing his annoyance with a growl from above, but against all odds, the man suddenly got down to his knees. With a fearful glance at Kassein, who looked pissed enough already, he threw his weapon in the mud and put his hands on his knees, his head low in an obvious sign of submission. The man looked slightly older than most, in his fifties or older, and as soon as they saw this, some of the younger men behind him exchanged looks, and after glancing nervously at the siblings, they did the same.

It was only one tribe at first, but Kiera and Kassein didn't move. A lot of the other tribes hesitated and waited, apprehensive, almost waiting to see if either of them would use their weak position to finish them off.

But Kassein and Kiera remained still; instead, their eyes scrutinized all the men still standing. They didn't need to speak the same language to make their intentions known. All the tribes present quickly understood, and, one by one, men's knees and weapons hit the ground.

Kiera and Kassein waited until not a single head was raised, all eyes cast on the ground.

"...That will do, I guess," Kiera finally said.

But Kassein had already moved on. As soon as the last man's knees had hit the ground, he began running toward them.

"Kassein!"

His sister's call was lost behind him.

Frightening the kneeling men nearby, Kassein ran past, ignoring them all as he ran deeper into the rift, his eyes scouring the area.

He glanced up at his dragon, who landed on a mountain, letting out a loud, long, and frustrated growl, and began scratching it furiously. Kassein immediately understood and ran even faster to reach the point under the mountain where his dragon had last seen Alezya. He glanced up, and a wall of snow and mud-covered dark rock stared back. It was humongous and ominous, but he didn't care.

If he had to search an entire mountain for Alezya, he would.

"Alezya!" he called, his voice echoing in the mountain.

He had a dreadful feeling, and he couldn't shake it off. The fact that she'd disappeared during a battle, vanished from the safe position of his dragon's back, was gnawing at his insides.

Something had gone wrong, and he had to find her, quickly.

"Commander!"

He barely glanced back to find Dajan and the handful of his men who had followed him. There were still kneeling tribesmen surrounding them, and Kassein wasn't sure if his men had followed him out of curiosity, to offer support, or ensure the enemy was subdued, but he didn't care.

He swallowed.

"Alezya," he muttered. "I need to find her. ...Help me find her."

He heard a quiet gasp. Kassein had never asked anything of his men. And he had certainly never asked for *help*. But right then, he didn't care.

He would ask and beg anyone he needed to so he could find Alezya even a second faster. Kassein knew precisely why he was more terrified than ever before: Alezya could be anywhere, and in those mountains, it wasn't a good thing. The burning memory of her limp body, bruised and battered in the snow, came to mind. He couldn't see her like that again. He shouldn't have let her go at all. This was like the night Cessilia had gone off. He had let her go, and he shouldn't have. If anything had happened to Alezya and their child...

"We will find her, sir," Dajan replied with a determined voice, pulling him out of his dark thoughts. "We will find Lady Alezya."

Then, he turned around, speaking to his unit.

"Come on! I need a unit in the heights to look for the nearby cliffs and two units down here!" he spoke with sudden urgency. "Somebody go and warn General Sazaran we're looking for Lady Alezya, and I want someone to report to Grand Intendant Tievin too! Dispatch medical units over here immediately! Also, offer medical assistance to the tribespeople who will take it! Kill anyone who tries to start a fight again! And bring some torches! Come on, the Commander in Chief needs us! Let's move!"

Kassein was already arms-deep into the snow, searching for Alezya, when the first men moved. He didn't care about what they were doing. He was focused on one thing only, and nothing else mattered.

He searched and searched, using every ounce of strength he had left and then some, drilling furiously, shoveling through the wall of snow and mud facing him. Kassein would have rather faced twice as many armies alone than this feeling, than not knowing where Alezya was.

Why had she left his dragon? Why wasn't she back already? Was she hiding away safely? She had to have heard the war had stopped, so why wasn't she coming out? The feeling of dread was numbing his mind, making him fear in a way he hadn't experienced in years. All of a sudden, Kassein was that four-year-old boy again, shivering in the Onyx Castle's garden while waiting for his siblings to find his missing older sister.

Except this time, he was the one searching and the one who would have to face whatever they found.

"Kassein!"

His sister's voice pulled him from the grip of panic.

Looking up, he saw Kiera waving from above. He had barely looked around when Kiki came in to scoop him up and flew up there. Now several dozen feet higher, Kiera stood on a cliff with a somber expression, her back turned to the opening as she stared into the mountain.

Kassein found the body she was staring at just as he stepped inside.

A man was lying in a pool of blood, his throat ripped wide open. He immediately knew a blade hadn't caused the wound; it was too large, like it had been ripped open, not sliced.

"Looks like a baby dragon's work," Kiera commented.

"Niiru," Kassein muttered.

It was the only dragon they knew who would have been the right size for this injury and had all the reasons to be there. Kassein swallowed and moved deeper into the cave, his heart anxiously thumping faster and faster as they found one body after another.

While a young dragon's sharp fangs had obviously ripped apart the first one, this one had been violently stabbed by a proper blade.

"Alezya," he muttered.

After the second body, Kassein's eyes stopped on what, at first, looked like just a lump of bloodied fur. He almost threw himself on his knees, his hands frantically grabbing the ripped coat while his heart pounded in his chest. He'd put that very coat on Alezya just hours ago.

Now, it was ripped in multiple places, and worse, it was stained with blood. A lot of blood. Kassein's mouth was horribly dry.

"Looks like our girl fought and took this off," Kiera noted.

His sister's voice barely reached him. He scrambled to his feet and continued down the tunnel, finding two more dead men, but no Alezya.

He reached the end of the tunnel, and that was it.

Four dead men, a ripped coat, signs that she and Niiru had been there, but Alezya was nowhere to be found.

"She had to have come out either way–"

He didn't listen to the end of his sister's sentence; Kassein ran back to the cliff, and looked down at the impossible height. Kiera let out a faint, ragged breath behind him.

"Kassein, if she fell–"

"Don't say it," he cut her off angrily.

Kein growled in the distance too. He was staring down from that height, and there was nothing his sister could say that he didn't already know. Kassein forced himself to breathe; even his throat was impossibly tight and painful. He had to find her.

He took out his blade, ignoring the protests of his sore, aching muscles as he began to climb down. Maybe she'd managed to fall on a cliff somewhere below. Maybe she'd landed in a shallow crevice, and the snow had stopped her fall. Maybe she was just stuck somewhere. Maybe she just couldn't hear him calling her name. Maybe she couldn't hear all his men calling her name.

Kassein climbed down, and his sister flew on Kiki, making another loop around the mountain, looking for an impossible scenario, something they might have missed. It was about a fifty-foot drop from the cliff to where Dajan and his men were searching the hill of snow and rocks.

The rain had stopped, and it was night now, dark, infinite, and cold. The temperatures were dropping scarily low, the ice-cold air biting. Kein growled in the distance, his dragon touring the entire rift as if Alezya could appear anywhere.

Kassein climbed down, looking for any crevice, any small hill, anything he could have missed between the cliff and the ground. The minutes stretched into hours. He was vaguely aware that the gorge had emptied, the men had been taken to the infirmary, and his generals and Tievin were leading the other rescues and assessing the aftermath.

Kassein couldn't have cared less. All he cared about was this small area and finding Alezya, wherever she was.

"Commander!"

He heard Dajan's voice and jumped down as fast as he could, not caring how painfully he landed. The Captain's voice made it seem like they had found something, and Kassein couldn't tell if his tone had sounded good, bad, or just shocked. He ran to them, and his heart sank as they were slowly extracting a body. They had gotten rid of most of the snow, but it took Kassein seconds to focus, and recognize that the broken mound of blood-covered limbs wasn't Alezya. It was an older man, whose body had visibly been broken in several places in the fall; he had probably died on impact, given the state of his skull.

"Darak," one of the nearby tribesmen gasped.

Kassein's eyes whipped to them. That man was the Deklaan Tribe leader? The man who had spoken paled under his stare, but pointed a shivering finger.

"*Tyo Darak!*" he exclaimed. "*Te Deklaan Kulani bastarko!*"

And then, the man spat at Darak's body.

Many other tribesmen reacted angrily too, sending obscene gestures at the dead man's body, some of them glancing up at the mountain before they got even angrier for some reason.

"I guess they won't fight anymore now," Dajan commented.

"...Keep searching," Kassein muttered in a broken voice.

Now he knew why Alezya had been up there. She'd dug out the man responsible for this war. She had killed her father, the one responsible for all this, the one who'd caused her so much hurt. But at what cost?

Kassein glanced up, his heart turning to stone as he contemplated the height. The horrible, gaping height from which her father's body had fallen.

Suddenly, a sound reached his ear, immediately followed by Kein's louder growl above. Kassein blinked, staring at the snow, wondering if he had hallucinated when he heard it again.

A high-pitched, weak sound.

"...Niiru," he muttered.

Kassein threw himself into the snow, scooping and pushing through armfuls of ice and rocks. His fingers were turning purple from the cold and painfully numb. His arms were gradually covered in bronze scales, but he ignored all of it and kept digging, his heart in his throat.

Niiru's weak whines were scarily faint. Kassein realized he was shaking violently, but he wasn't sure if it was the cold or fear; it felt like a block of ice had settled in his stomach while a dangerous blend of despair and hope kept him moving. Tears were pricking his eyes too, but he ignored it all, the pain and the fear, and he kept going.

It felt like miles of snow between him and the baby dragon's wails despite all the men who were also digging around him.

The snow was turning into slush at their feet, slowly licking their ankles, but they didn't stop.

Finally, Kassein's fingers grazed something more solid, and he froze. He kept digging more cautiously, and a little bundle of black scales appeared, trapped between two cold, white limbs. His heart stopped.

He forced himself to take one breath in and dug even further, cautiously sweeping the snow off her arms and shoulders. Finally, her face appeared. Kassein let out a strangled sound. Her eyes were closed, her expression incredibly serene, like she was sleeping. He pulled more of the snow that was trapping her, and eventually, her limp body slowly fell into his arms; Alezya didn't react.

She had never been so pale nor so cold. His hand that was holding her head returned covered in blood, and only then did he notice the gash on her head, the blood soaking her dark hair.

"Call a medic!" Dajan shouted. "C-Commander, is she alive?"

Was she? She looked so pale and so cold, but it took Kassein a second to realize that Alezya had turned white not because of snow or cold but because her entire body was covered in thin white scales. Every bit of her limbs had turned reptilian, cold and rigid. He had never seen this amount of scales on someone before. He forced himself to check her body, his trembling fingers moving very cautiously. She'd fallen from the same height as her father, but because of the scales, it was hard to assess the damage. The wound on her head was horrifying, but it was the only obvious one, and the sight of her blood made

Kassein sick.

"We should take her to–"

"Don't touch her," Kassein growled, his instincts taking over.

He could barely think; the sight of that wound on her head and the stillness of her body was dragging him down into a pit of darkness. He felt numb and terrified, and nothing but his instincts could make him move at that very moment. Kassein couldn't think, he couldn't formulate a single thought, but he knew he didn't want anyone touching her. She was his. It didn't matter what was left; she was his. And like a dragon, he guarded his treasure, threatening anyone who came near to take her away from him.

Very slowly and cautiously, moving his arms as little as possible, he gently put her down and lay next to her, his warm and large body shielding hers. He ignored the voices around them, his confused men, and those who looked with pity in their eyes. He heard, but he didn't care what it looked like. What Alezya looked like. And he didn't want to think about that. He didn't want to think about anything.

All he wanted to do was lie there, next to her, and wait. He would wait, no matter how long. He would wait.

"Kassein, what–"

His sister's voice trailed off as she came to an audible halt somewhere nearby, and gasped.

"Fuck," she hissed. "Is... Is she...?"

"We don't know. He-... The Commander wouldn't let us come near..."

Kiera let out a long exhale.

"...Leave them alone."

"But–"

"With that wound on her head, it's either too late, or there's nothing we can do. We shouldn't move her at all. Just... leave them there. Focus on the tribes and ensuring their surrender. We've got plenty to do already. Report everything to me and the generals. I need to hear how many men we lost and the state of the medical unit. Did you round up the surviving tribe leaders? Make sure Darak's body is somewhere they can see."

"Yes, Your Highness!"

He heard movement, voices, steps, and people busy evacuating the injured, gathering bodies, and looking for whoever was missing, but Kassein didn't react.

Not even when he heard Tievin nearby assessing the damage and trying to communicate with the tribe leaders. Not when Kein finally was able to land nearby, after Dajan and his men had spent more time digging and shoveling, until there was enough space for his dragon to land, crawl to Alezya's other side, and extend a wing to shield them.

All he could hear was Niiru's faint whining.

The baby dragon kept letting out little wails and sniffing Alezya's face. It was curled up in her arms, its eyes wide open, glancing at her and Kassein, waiting. Kassein didn't speak. He was staring at her face too.

He couldn't tell if she was breathing. He couldn't know if she was warmer since Kein had landed behind her. He couldn't tell if the white scales were fading or still. He couldn't know if she was asleep or already gone. She was too still. They were eerily still compared to everything that was going on around them. Under Kein's wing, in the darkness, lying as if they were in a cocoon, shielded from the rest of the world.

"...I need you," Kassein rasped after a long time had passed, and things had gone quiet around them. "...I feel like a man with you. A man I want to be. You make me feel strong, yet weak at the same time. You make me want to love and protect. Before you came, there was nothing but chaos in my head."

He forced himself to breathe as his throat hurt, and his eyes prickled.

"I wanted to die before you came," he muttered. "I never... I couldn't forgive what I'd done. I felt like I was living for nothing. For no one. But then, you..."

He swallowed a sob.

"You fought so hard to live, Alezya. You wanted to live. I'd never seen someone as brave as you. You were hurt, but you were... so, so courageous and so beautiful. I grew up surrounded by strong people, but I never knew what brave meant until I met you. I fought to die, and you fought to live. I'd never met someone as radiant as you, my moonlight. You shine in the dark, my moonlight. So bright, so blinding."

He dared to move, and with trembling fingers, he caressed her pale cheek.

"...I love you," he whispered. "I love you so much that I can't go on hating myself. I forget it all when you're near. You make me want to live and be alive. You make me want to have the world with you."

He closed his eyes, and very carefully, he moved even closer to lean his forehead against hers.

"You terrify me," he whispered. "You make me fear a world where you don't... you don't..."

He swallowed again, and forced himself to take a shallow, shivering breath in.

"Where you're not here," he mumbled, "and I know I'd have to go on without you. Because I'd have to be there for them. For Lumie. For all those who need me. You're the one who made me care, and now, you can't leave me to... to face it all alone. Please. Please, please, please, my moonlight. Please wake up. Please come back to me again. I'll never let you go ever again. I've learned my lesson this time. I miss your eyes... I miss you. Please. Please. Please, please, please..."

He kept repeating it over and over again, like a quiet, whispered prayer that got lost in the wind. Niiru stopped whining, leaning against Alezya's chest and closing its tiny eyes.

The hours passed.

The night grew colder as the aftermath of the battle disappeared.

The mud turned solid, and a gentle rain flushed the blood down the rift, washing it all away.

The voices gradually disappeared. The crowd grew distant, except for steps approaching now and then, stopping somewhere nearby, and then leaving again. Then, none was left.

The rift turned quiet as it emptied of all human life. Nothing else moved. It all went away, replaced by the quiet drumming of the rain against rocks, the faint stream of water.

Then, just before dawn, steps were heard again.

The rain had stopped, and the sounds of heavy boots, coming closer, could be heard in faint splashes.

Kassein let out a heavy breath as a large, warm hand landed on his shoulder.

"You did good, son," a familiar male voice whispered. "Now let me help."

Only then did Kassein let a sob shake him.

Chapter 21

Her body had never felt so heavy. Nor so cold. It didn't feel like her body, but a mountain: cold, hard, still, and impossible to move. Everything felt off, like she was floating in a shell of herself. The first sensation was pain. Her head ached in a dull, slow throb. It was numbing and overtaking all of her senses. She couldn't remember anything; the pain was tainting and blurring everything. She had the vague sensation that she should have remembered something. Anything really. But right now, it felt too hard, too much of a task. So, she let herself drift away softly, away from the pain, away from everything.

Faint voices reached her through the fog of her mind. Whispers she couldn't understand, lingering at the borders of her consciousness, titillating her senses. She couldn't remember who those voices belonged to, but they felt familiar, even pleasant. She tried listening, but even that felt like an overwhelming effort. So, she let them be, like a lingering sound she didn't need to hold on to. They felt nice, she thought, so nice that it made her happy for a reason she couldn't quite pinpoint. Thinking felt like too much work, but listening was passive; it was easy.

"Ma!"

The cute little voice nearby got her attention. She couldn't figure out how to wake up fully, but she didn't need to. Even through the fog, she felt something small touch her cheek, and a cute giggle followed. It brought her a mysterious joy.

"*Natim, Lumie. Natim.*"

Another voice, familiar too. That one was soft and soothing. Then, another sound followed, one she couldn't decipher this time. It was cute too, and made her feel warm inside, like the child's soft chuckles. A second gentle tap on her face followed.

"*Ma...*"

The other voice replied, something Alezya couldn't quite understand. She tried to focus, but each attempt felt too strenuous and tiresome. Listening was the only thing she could seem to do without feeling overwhelmed. Something painful pulsated in her head, making her efforts feel worthless. Her heart sank a bit as the only thing she could do was listen, and not think. Yet, the little sounds that came felt like enough of a comfort. Yes, those gentle, peaceful sounds were nice. It was enough for now.

Another set of voices brought her back to consciousness sometime later. This time, Alezya remembered herself, and she remembered enough to recognize the low rumble of Kassein's voice. It felt like a warm blanket enveloping her senses, gentle and familiar. The other voice was even lower than his but so similar that it felt familiar too. They spoke in that frustrating, nonsensical language of theirs. She could have understood better if she didn't feel so... tired. The pain in her head was still there, bothersome but not as bad. It felt like an irritating knock, a sore throb she could ignore.

She heard her name among the flowing grunts and odd words a couple of times, and it made her happy. Something warm was holding her too. Her hand, she realized after focusing for a couple of seconds. They were holding her hand in a soft, warm grip. She tried to focus on the sensations of her body, as heavy and bothersome as it was... She couldn't move, but she could get a vague sense of her limbs, lying like useless growths that weighed her down. She was resting on something soft that made her body feel like it was sinking in. It was nice, but she felt restless, and while her body was unresponsive, her mind was bored. She wanted to know what they were saying. She wanted to talk, to ask, to let them know she was there, but nothing worked, nothing responded. She was just there, helpless. Trapped in an unresponsive body, too tired for anything, her senses were her only tool. So, she focused on those like they were her rope to hold onto this glimpse of reality. The voices were easy to listen to; they remained nearby and floated to her ears, a solemn, continuous melody she could rely on. A faint, lovely sound of rain too. It had taken her a while to realize it was there, but now, she could hear it in the background, soft, steady, and familiar. Rain, hitting the ground, the walls, from close and far away. And something light and flowery. No, that was a smell, she realized. The smell of rain and the smell of some flowers. Or wet grass. Or wet flowers. Either way, she focused on the smells, and there was something even better, smelling good and familiar, nearby. She couldn't remember what it was, but she knew she loved that smell very much. It made her happy.

"Ma!"

The little voice was growing impatient. Alezya listened, fighting to find her way to the surface.

"Ma... Ma..."

She felt tiny hands tapping lightly on her shoulder. Alezya focused on that until she finally followed her urge to open her eyes. It took her a second, and the first thing she saw was Lumie's blinding smile, right next to her face. The little girl squealed in delight.

"Ma!" she exclaimed fiercely, looking pleased.

Her little eyes were bright, her cheeks a subtle pink, and someone had put her white curls into two tiny pigtails that bounced with her. It was adorable. She sat back, wiggling and clapping her hands in delight.

"Ma! Ma! Ma!" she kept chanting.

"Hey..." Alezya's hoarse voice managed.

Her throat felt tight and dry, and she swallowed with difficulty. Her body was still heavy, and the pain in her head was a dull throb, but she managed to glance around the room. After a second, she noticed a large figure sitting nearby.

It took her a second to realize the man sitting there wasn't Kassein, but the resemblance was striking. This man had a longer, thicker mane of darker hair, with streaks of white, although some of it was braided back. He had darker skin, too, and his eyes were a warm, dark brown instead of the gentle forest green she was used to. He was just as large, though, and his facial features were nearly identical to Kassein's. He also had a beard covering his chin, with little patches of white in it.

"You're awake," he noted with an incredibly low voice.

"Where...?"

But upon recognizing the dark walls, she realized where she was. *Kalat Unshreik*. Kassein's home. She was resting in a large bed in one of those rooms. It was dark outside, but the sky was a soft purple, indicating dawn or sunset; she wasn't sure.

Alezya looked back at the man, and suddenly, she realized what had been nagging at the back of her mind.

"You speak our language," she muttered, stunned. "You speak... our clans' tongue."

"Not well," he shook his head, "but yes, I learned."

"How...?"

"Another clan taught us," he explained. "From the mountains."

His pronunciation was indeed off, and she had to focus to understand some of the words he used, but he was far more fluent in her language than she was in theirs.

"I see... Kassein," she rasped. "How is he?"

The man let out a shadow of a smile, and she relaxed; Kassein had to be fine.

Alezya nodded, before regretting the movement as a dull ache in her head made her wince. She could feel something pressing around her head and the pungent smell of medicine. Someone had braided her hair to one side, but something ached more strongly on the other side. She couldn't remember hitting her head, but she vaguely remembered the fall. It was blurry, but it somewhat made sense. She let out a faint breath and ignored the pain, focusing on the man instead.

"...My son loves you," the man suddenly spoke again.

Alezya blushed, but she didn't shy away from his gaze.

"I love him too," she whispered.

He gave her a slow nod.

"...Thank you," he finally said.

"For what?"

"For loving him," he replied.

Alezya was slightly confused, but Lumie stole her attention with another tap on her arm. She smiled at her baby, cupping her cheek and caressing it with her thumb. That's when she noticed that, in the darkness, Niiru was also curled up against her. The baby dragon was right behind Lumie, with her bum resting against it like a tiny seat of dark scales. Niiru's head was on Alezya's leg, its little eyes on her. Its tail was swishing left and right, tapping Lumie's leg until she grabbed it and tugged it with a frown; Niiru didn't complain.

"...You look a lot like him," Alezya commented, glancing back at the man.

The man nodded with another of his faint smiles.

"I'm Kairen," he said. "Kassein's father."

"I heard you," she said just as she realized it, "while I was unconscious. Talking with Kassein."

He nodded again.

"He refused to leave your side. Or Lumie's."

Recognizing her name, Lumie snapped her head back to him and immediately granted the man a bright, beaming smile that showed she was familiar with him already. Ignoring her mom, she crawled across the covers to him, extending her arms with a demanding gesture, and let herself be scooped up into his arms. The man immediately placed the baby girl on his knee, bouncing her into a tiny fit of excited giggles. He was obviously used to young children, and Lumie seemed entirely at ease with him. This was an unexpected sight that made Alezya incredibly happy. Lumie had never had the chance to enjoy having a loving grandparent before, but there she was, all smiles and giggles on this imposing man's knee. Meanwhile, Niiru took this opportunity to crawl closer, putting its head on Alezya's belly. That movement awakened a whole bunch of memories in her mind.

"Oh gods," she gasped. "The war, how did it end? And the clans? And... my father. I fell with him. How am I-...? And is the baby...?"

"You're fine," Kairen said with that low, deep but gentle voice. "My wife examined you."

He put one of his large hands on her leg, in a gesture to calm her down. Her head ached again. Everything seemed jumbled, and it was painfully hard to actually think, with her head throbbing non-stop. Alezya glanced down at her body and, for the first time, she noticed her arm, the other one, lying on top of the covers. It was partially bandaged, but... there were patches of white scales peeking through from underneath. She tried moving her hand, and while the effort was strenuous, everything moved almost as usual. Still, she stared at the patches of white scales, confused.

"Dragon skin," Kairen said. "It will fade."

"My baby?" she dared to ask.

"Your baby is fine too."

Alezya let out a breath of relief. That was all she needed to know. With difficulty, she shifted her hand to her stomach and took a deep breath; Niiru put its head on her hand and let out a soft growl. Her memories were still a blur, but she knew her baby had saved her life. Those white scales all over her body were proof of it. She frowned, remembering why she'd fallen... No, why she had jumped in the first place.

"What about the clans?" she couldn't help but ask. "...Darak?"

Those man's dark eyes were intimidating, and yet, seeing him bounce her baby on his knee, knowing he'd spent time with Kassein watching her, had Alezya trust him instantly. Perhaps, for the first time in her life, she trusted a man she'd barely met because he looked so much like Kassein.

"That man is dead," he said in a neutral tone. "The war is over."

"...Kassein won the war," Alezya muttered as realization sank in.

He had won the war for her, and then, he had let his father and sister deal with the aftermath while he watched over her. She smiled, and the man mimicked her grin.

"He's my son," he said, as if that explained it all.

They exchanged a complicit look, full of love for Kassein.

"...I'm Alezya," she said, because it felt right to introduce herself, even out of order.

The man nodded and slowly stood.

She smiled. She wouldn't have thought it felt so nice to meet someone from the Dragon Clan who spoke their tongue, and certainly not well enough to know what her name meant. When he was standing, Kassein's father was even more imposing. Perhaps it was worse because she was lying down, but he looked like a dark mountain, not unlike their home. He gently put Lumie back on the bed, and she clumsily crawled back to her mom until her head landed heavily on Alezya's chest.

Just then, they heard steps coming up. The door opened, and Kassein appeared in the doorway. He briefly glanced at her, but then, his gaze did a double-take, and once his eyes landed on Alezya again, and he realized she was awake, they opened even wider in surprise, his shock written all over his face.

She wasn't prepared to see him, and he gave her no time to figure out what to do or say. One second he was at the door, and the next, he'd ran across the room to be by her side, his weight pressing the mattress next to her. His wide hand cupped her cheek, his gaze still wide and breath suddenly close while he studied her.

"Alezya," he let out in a shaky breath.

She smiled because any head movement was painful, but that was enough. He replied with the first sincere smile she had seen on him in a while, one of relief. Then, his smile broke a little, and he sunk forward, hiding his face in her hair, hugging her into the bed. It took her a second to realize his shoulders were shaking, and her heart sunk.

"*Kassein… Are you crying?*" Her throat tightened as she asked.

He didn't move, but she could feel that man's large body trembling in her arms. He let out a strangled, muted sob, and she felt her own tears escape. She could feel all of his emotions crashing all over him, the heavy relief of seeing her awake. Gently, she forced herself to move to press kiss after kiss on his raspy cheek, lifting her hand to caress his nape, her thumb rubbing his cheek softly.

"I'm sorry, baby," she cried, the nickname in her language coming naturally. "I'm sorry… I'm fine. *I'm fine.*"

It took a few seconds for Kassein to calm down, and slowly pull back, his eyes red and his jaw still trembling. Never had she thought she would ever see this man cry, but the misty sheen on those green eyes she adored wrecked her heart. She cupped his wet cheeks, wiping them with her thumbs, and brought him in for a long, tender and overdue kiss. Then, he pulled back, still looking at her like he couldn't believe his eyes, relief written all over his face.

"I love you."

Him suddenly using her language to say those three words shook Alezya.

She didn't even know how to react, but before she did, he smiled, and pressed another long kiss against her forehead. Next to them, Lumie suddenly let out a delighted giggle, reminding them they weren't alone.

"*Mama is awake,*" he whispered to the baby girl, who squealed at him.

"*Are you alright?*" Alezya asked, fighting the heaviness in her limbs again to touch his warm arm.

He gave her a strong nod, immediately followed by a frown.

"*You? Pain?*"

Alezya went for a shrug, but that made her wince too. She sighed and nodded.

"*Yes,*" she confessed, "*and I'm tired.*"

He nodded and pressed another long kiss to her forehead before he glanced back, saying something to his father, who nodded and left the room.

"*Your dad,*" she said, still amazed.

He nodded.

"*He helped,*" he said, "*with* kulani. *He speaks like you.*"

"*Not you? You didn't speak to the* kulani?"

Kassein hesitated, before he shook his head, and leaned in even more, his cheek against her cheek, breathing in deeply under her ear.

"*With you,*" he whispered. "*I stayed with you. Kiera and Father spoke to the* kulani."

Alezya let out a sigh and lifted her hand further to run her fingers through his hair. He felt warm, with that faint smell of sweat she didn't hate and the fresh scent of the forest. Stuck under his arm as he hugged them both, Lumie decided to lean against her mom too, wrapping her tiny chubby arms around Alezya's neck. She exhaled slowly, sinking into his warmth and reality. She had survived. They had survived.

"...Kiera?" she asked. "Lorey? Ekata? Ekut? Tievin?"

She had missed him, but now that her memories were coming back, so was her sense of duty. She had more or less triggered that war; she needed to know the outcome. Kassein let out a sigh and slowly pulled back a few inches. He lay on the edge of the bed, next to Niiru, and leaned his upper body next to her on the bed, propped on his elbow, while Lumie had decided to stay on her mom, playing with her hair in her fist. He was careful to keep at a distance this time, visibly worried about touching her anywhere that could hurt, his hand only caressing hers softly.

"...*Ekut is dead,*" Kassein admitted.

That sobered the happiness out of Alezya immediately. She felt her worries soar, but before she could panic, Kassein gently pressed her hand.

"*Others are fine,*" he said. "*Kiera and Tievin are in the mountains. With the* kulanis. *Lorey here. I stayed here to watch you.*"

"*I slept... long?*"

Kassein nodded.

"*Three days, three nights,*" he said, glancing at what was now the sunrise.

It would be too bright for Lumie soon, and Kassein seemed to come to the same realization because he pulled a blanket over the little girl, who didn't protest. Alezya noticed that Lumie's breathing had slowed down, and she was now snoozing against her chest. She turned her eyes back to Kassein, and for a while, they exchanged a long look, not saying anything. Then, something prickled behind her eyes, and she let a tear fall.

"*It's over,*" she whispered.

Kassein leaned over, placing another long kiss on her forehead. Then, he gently kissed one wet cheek, and then the other, before he pressed his forehead against hers once again, and his thumb came to wipe her tears.

"*You're here,*" he said. "*With me. And Lumie.*"

The truth was slowly sinking in, but it was hard to realize.

Her father was dead. The clans who had wanted her dead were either dead or had submitted to Kassein's clan. For the first time, it slowly hit Alezya that they had won this war and with it, her freedom. There would be no one to use her anymore. No more battles to come, no more need to run. She was free to stay or go wherever she pleased with Lumie. She was free to be happy and be loved by Kassein. So many invisible chains she hadn't realized had been weighing her down suddenly disappeared. For the first time in years, or maybe ever, she felt safe and free. The future felt so bright now, and it was almost... scary. Blinding with possibilities. Was that it? There was nothing more to worry about, nothing else to fear? She could just... live?

"*Food?*" Kassein asked.

It snapped her back to reality, and made her smile.

"*Meat?*" she asked.

But he shook his head.

"*Mother said no meat for you. Not yet.*"

Alezya immediately pouted, a bit annoyed, but Kassein smiled and pressed a gentle kiss to her lips. He was about to back away, probably to go and get her food, but she grabbed his wrist. He immediately turned back to her, worry all over his features, but she smiled.

"Wait," she whispered, gently pulling him back to her.

She pulled him close for a longer, more delicate kiss. Not a mere peck, but one full of softness and longing. One to tell this man how much she had missed him. One to tell him how sorry she was. The glimpses of the war she remembered were scary, but more than anything, she remembered how she'd feared for his life. She was the one to have caused all this, and if anything had happened to Kassein, Alezya knew she might not have survived.

She *knew* she shouldn't have survived. She hadn't been sure they'd meet again when she had flown away on Kein, and it had been the worst of their separations. Even now, she didn't want him to leave the room, even for a moment. Their time together felt too precious. She had chosen to jump, knowing she wasn't supposed to make it. She had survived, and she would spend the rest of her life being grateful for that miracle.

Kassein seemed to read her mind because he leaned over, careful about her injuries and yet getting as close as he could, to caress her cheek, fully take her lips with his, fill her space with his smell, and fulfill her need for his presence. They didn't need to speak; every apology, every "I missed you," every breath of relief was passed into their sweet kiss and tender gestures.

After a few more kisses, Kassein slowly pulled back, giving her one more loving gaze before he eventually left the room. Alezya didn't have to wait long as he quickly returned with a bowl of warm soup that smelled heavenly. It had a faint taste of meat but no actual chunks in it, and truthfully, she wasn't sure she would have had the strength to chew. Kassein helped her eat, bringing each spoonful to her lips, as any head movement made her wince, and Lumie was holding her down. She was more hungry than she'd realized, and before she knew it, Alezya had finished a second bowl. It made sense, given how long she had been asleep. Kassein seemed pleased with her eating, and she wondered how tired and frail she must look for him to seem constantly worried, unwilling to look away from her any second longer than necessary.

"*You hurt?*" she asked Kassein, still concerned.

But he shook his head and showed her the last of the bronze scales on his hands, then lifted his shirt to reveal a large patch of them on his flank. She frowned, but he shrugged, clearly over it already.

"*Kiera hurt?*"

He grinned.

"*Kiera's fine. She's angry at me.*"

"*Angry? Why?*"

"*Because she does Aqayir work, and I am here.*"

Alezya smiled.

"*Kiera is a good Aqayir.*"

"Yes," he nodded. *"She can be Aqayir. I stay."*

As if to show her, he leaned more into the bed next to her like he was about to take a nap. It was the first time he was acting a bit childish like this, and Alezya had a feeling that was his way of comforting her, of showing her things were fine.

"Kassein," she whispered. *"...You hurt?"*

She had already asked, but this time, she wasn't asking about physical pain, and her gaze conveyed that. He frowned for a second before she saw him swallow. He sighed, staring at her with a deep, sorrowful look. The mist in his eyes came back for a second.

"I was scared," he muttered. *"Scared I lost you. You were... cold."*

Alezya let out a faint, pained breath.

"I'm sorry," she said. "I'm so sorry."

She brought his hand to her lips and kissed it as tears pearled in her eyes, staring into his hurt, dark green gaze. She was sorry he'd had to go through that. She had made her decision on that mountain, but she knew she would carry that guilt for the rest of her life. It hadn't felt like a right or a good choice, and she didn't believe there was such a thing, but it was the one she'd made for the sake of many.

Kassein swallowed again, and he leaned until his face rested in the crook of her neck, opposite to Lumie's. Only Alezya was close enough that she heard the broken breath he let out. She held his hand tighter, but he moved it over her stomach, splaying it there, and she realized he had been worried about losing their baby too. She put her hand over his, caressing his skin with her thumb.

"I'm sorry," she whispered.

"Don't go," he muttered. *"Don't go ever again."*

"No," she said. "I swear. *With you. I'll stay with you."*

The two of them remained like that for a while, in silence, until Kassein calmed down, breathing peacefully against her neck, and Alezya fell back asleep again, listening to the soothing rhythm of his breath against her neck.

When she woke up again a while later, the sun was high. Alezya had to blink a few times before her eyes got used to the influx of light, though the sunshine felt nice on her skin. Kassein was gone from her side, and so were Niiru and Lumie. Instead, the chair next to the bed was now occupied by a beautiful woman who was busy sewing something. Alezya was slightly confused. She had never seen someone with such pale skin aside from her daughter. It wasn't as snow-white as Lumie's, more like a pale, warm beige color. It made a beautiful contrast to the woman's thick, long, wavy chestnut-brown hair held in a half-up hairdo, and the beautiful dusty pink gown she was wearing. Alezya had never seen such amazing fabric, and it was half covered by the thick cloak of fur wrapped around the woman's shoulders.

When she glanced up and their eyes met, she smiled, her eyes a beautiful green color like the fresh grass in spring.

"Hello," the woman said.

"...Hello," Alezya muttered, feeling slightly intimidated for some reason.

The woman put aside her work, which looked like a small dragon plushie, and leaned over to check something on Alezya's head.

"Does your head hurt?"

"It's... fine."

It was. There was still a lingering pain, but now, it was so faint it was almost forgettable. It certainly wasn't as bothersome as how heavy Alezya felt. Her entire body felt unwilling to move, even as she was dying to stretch a bit. The woman gave her a gentle smile.

"It looks fine," she said, putting something back on the injury. "Do you hurt elsewhere?"

"No," Alezya said, which was true. "...Where is Kassein?"

"He went to the mountain for a bit," the woman replied with a sorry smile. "Tievin insisted he come and help. He will be back soon. He didn't want to leave you."

Alezya blushed, pleased but feeling a bit shy.

"You're... his older sister?"

The woman raised her eyebrows.

"I'm his mom," she said.

Alezya's jaw dropped. Kassein's mother? There was no way. That woman didn't look forty! And didn't Kassein have many older siblings? She was scared to ask that woman's age. Reading her surprise, the woman chuckled.

"You've met my husband already," she said, "but you were asleep every time I came."

"You're a healer," Alezya remembered. "They... told me."

The woman nodded.

"I am Cassandra."

"You're not... like the others of the Dragon Clan."

Alezya wasn't sure how to say it without sounding offensive, but that woman looked different from her husband and the two of her children Alezya knew. She looked different from the men at the camp too, and as different as Alezya was from all of them. Cassandra smiled.

"I am from a different clan," she explained. "The Rain Clan."

"...The Rain Clan? From the mountains too?"

"No," Kassein's mother gently shook her head. "I came from somewhere more south. East of the Dragon Clan's territory."

"Is that why you speak our tongue?"

"No. My language is different too. But we met another clan from the north, the Lumiata Clan. They taught us-"

"The Lumiata?" Alezya exclaimed, nearly sitting up. "You met the Lumiata? When?"

Cassandra rose, gently pushing her to lean back before she answered.

"Yes," she said as she tucked the blanket around her. "They descended from the mountains, one bad winter, many years ago. They knew a bit of our language, and taught us theirs, and once we understood, they said they were in danger and wanted to find another land to live on. We gave them a safe route to the west, but I do not know where they went next. ...Do you know them?"

"...My mother was a Lumiata," Alezya said. "She is dead, and... I thought her clan was dead too."

"I think some of them stayed behind in the mountains," Cassandra nodded, "but others left... after they spent the winter here."

Alezya felt tears spring to her eyes. For some reason, knowing that some of her mother's clan had survived brought her a wave of relief she didn't know she needed; her father hadn't killed them all, after all... Had they sensed the danger coming? Had they fled after knowing what had happened to her mom?

"Kiera likes to explore the west," Cassandra smiled. "Would you like to find them?"

Alezya took a few seconds to actually think about it, but eventually, she slowly shook her head.

"No," she said. "Well... Maybe one day, but not now. For now, I want to stay... To stay here for a bit. With Kassein. I want... I want to be happy here."

She felt a bit shy announcing this to Kassein's mother, but to her relief, Cassandra smiled gently.

"That sounds like a wonderful plan," she said. "You can teach Kassein your language. From what I heard, he needs it."

Alezya laughed, amused.

"...I will. Are you staying here?"

"Not long," Cassandra shook her head. "Just to be sure you'll recover. We were on our way to visit our daughter in the east, but Darsan said his little brother might need us here, so we flew back north first."

"He told me this was your home."

"It used to be," she nodded, looking around the walls. "This is where we raised our children... But now that we're older, it should belong to them. We live a bit farther south-east, with Kassein's grandmother. We visit our children east, south, or north when we get bored."

Alezya suddenly remembered that the woman had birthed eight children. Was it even possible to look so beautiful and young after eight children? Alezya hoped she would get to ask her a few questions before she left...

"Do you know what happened?" Alezya asked. "In the mountains?"

"I do. It sounds like you're a very brave young woman."

Alezya blushed.

"Kassein and Kiera... I put them in a lot of danger," she muttered. "They didn't have to fight this war."

"A lot of men do terrible things for much worse reasons," Cassandra said, a mysterious expression in her eyes. "My son fought this war because he trusts you, Alezya. Because he loves you, and because he saw what you were capable of, and what you needed. Kassein spent a lot of years fighting against himself most of all. But you came, and for the first time, you gave him a reason to fight for someone else."

"Still," she mumbled, feeling choked up. "He didn't have to... I used him. I used his love for me, and I-"

"No," Cassandra interrupted her with a chuckle. "Alezya, dear, if there is one thing I have learned over all these years, it is that, eventually, a dragon will always do what a dragon wants, and none of my children are any different. Kassein..."

She took a deep breath, her eyes getting misty for a second.

"Kassein has been unhappy for a long time," she said, "and there was nothing we could do or say to help. You're a mother too, and I am sure you know that there is nothing more painful than to be helpless to help your child. Kassein didn't fit anywhere, and he and Kein were always, always fighting. Trying to... harm each other. And then, all of a sudden, I hear that my son and his dragon are fighting, not against one another, but together, for a woman and her baby."

Alezya blushed. How odd must the situation have sounded for Kassein's parents...? But his mother smiled.

"I hadn't seen Kassein in a long while, and the first thing he says when he sees me, is to help you. It's the first thing he asks of me in *years,* and it's to save someone. So, of course, I do. And as soon as he knows you'll be alright, he tells me everything about you, how brave, kind, courageous you are, and all I see is my son finally *happy*. Happy here, and most importantly, happy with you. And then I saw him holding your baby girl, and by the Water God, I cried happy tears."

She looked on the verge of tears now, and one escaped as she gently pressed Alezya's hand.

"My children can destroy buildings, bridges, mountains," she chuckled, "and they have. They can fly to the end of the world, lead armies, disappear for weeks without notice. They can love and marry whomever they please, and they can certainly give me dozens of grandbabies. The one and only thing that I ask is for each and every one of them to be happy. And you gave me that for Kassein. So, no, darling, I do not care that my son fought a war for you. So long as he is happy, you can ask of him whatever you want, Alezya."

Now Alezya was the one choking back tears, and the two women exchanged a long, compassionate, and understanding gaze.

"I want to be happy too," she finally muttered. "With him."

"That's all I wish for you two," Cassandra smiled. "You both deserve it."

Alezya forced herself to take a deep breath and smiled back. Then, after another silence, she frowned.

"Is... Is everything alright?" she asked shyly. "With the clans?"

"Yes," Cassandra nodded. "Don't worry. Kassein will take you up there soon enough for you to see. Right now, all that matters is that you recover first. Lots of rest, soups, and, once you can, some meat. Kassein told me you're quite fond of it."

Alezya wanted to melt under the covers, but she only gave her a nod while she turned a terrible shade of red.

"Alezya!"

She turned toward the door and blinked. Lorey stood there, beaming, a vase of flowers in her arms. She barely had time to react before the young woman crossed the room, dropped the vase on the bedside table, and pulled her into a hug without warning. The hug was so unexpected and blunt it caught her off guard, and yet, Alezya found herself returning it without hesitation. She wasn't sure when it had happened, but she knew Lorey was the first friend she'd had in a long while, maybe ever, and she was so grateful for the kindness and patience she'd shown her.

"Lorey," she smiled in her shoulder.

Her friend pulled back, her eyes sparkling with happiness, and she cupped Alezya's cheek.

"*You hurt?*" she asked. "*You alright?*"

Alezya wasn't sure which to answer, so she just smiled back, feeling her throat tight with emotion. Then, Kassein's mom spoke, and Lorey relaxed, visibly pleased with whatever she'd said about Alezya's condition. She turned back to smile at her, and the two young women exchanged a long, complicit look.

"Kiera?" Alezya asked.

"*Kiera is fine,*" Lorey smiled. "*She is hunting some people.*"

"*Hunting again?*" Alezya worried.

"Kiera's gone to track down those who refused the peace treaty Kassein offered," Cassandra explained. "Most of the Northern clans were happy to end the war, but a few individuals have acted dishonorably. She's making sure they will not be a problem in the future."

Alezya nodded. She knew better than most that there would be some unwilling to let go of the old ways. They had profited off the weakness of others for too many years, and the Dragon Clan coming to establish a society where fear of dragons would no longer be a tool for control was bound to carve a very different future for the Northern clans...

She turned back to Lorey, who shrugged, like her partner going to hunt down some men was just some regular errand. But Alezya took her friend's hand, giving her a serious expression that had Lorey raise her eyebrow questioningly.

"*...Thank you,*" Alezya said. "*Thank you, Lorey.*"

Lorey seemed slightly confused, but she smiled back softly.

It didn't matter if Alezya couldn't translate all her words of gratitude into the Dragon Clan's language yet; she just needed to say them. After everything she had gone through, after she'd had such a close encounter with death, Alezya felt like she could finally look back on her journey and see who had helped her survive it.

Right after Kassein, Lorey was at the very top of that list. She wasn't a fighter like Kassein or Kiera, but she had shown Alezya so much kindness it felt like she had been fighting alongside her from the beginning. Lorey had helped her navigate a foreign world, teaching her their language without hesitation, being a constant, reassuring presence when anyone but Kassein had been too frightening. And when the battle had come, Lorey had stayed behind to keep Lumie safe. Having someone she could fully trust with her baby meant more to Alezya than she could ever put into words.

So, she just smiled at her friend, and tried to show her gratitude with her eyes. Lorey must have felt something, because her eyes got misty for a bit, and she leaned in again for another long hug.

"You're home," she whispered to Alezya.

After that, Lorey and Kassein's mother, Cassandra, stayed by her side whenever he wasn't, never leaving her alone for a moment. His father made a few quiet appearances, but by all accounts, he seemed to be Lumie's new favorite as the little girl seemed stuck to his side and beamed whenever she spotted him. She was going as far as learning to walk at a scary pace to be able to follow Kassein's father around in the rare instances he wasn't carrying her. While Alezya remained stuck in bed, her headaches easing and injuries slowly healing, the hours passed quickly with Kassein's mother at her side. Cassandra was incredibly lovely and easy to talk to, and eager to learn all she could about Alezya and Lumie, asking lots of questions about the north, and how different their cultures were.

Whenever Kassein returned and crossed paths with his mom in her room, she witnessed him acting a bit shyer than usual, something she loved. It was clear, no matter what had happened, that his parents cherished him dearly.

Alezya had a million questions about what was happening in the mountains, but Kassein refused to answer any of them. She tried to plead many times, but it soon became clear that not only Kassein but his parents and Lorey were all in agreement to insist she rest and recover first, promising everything was fine.

It was only a couple of days later that she was finally allowed to leave her room, just in time to say goodbye to Kassein's parents. That morning, just before sunrise, Alezya stepped outside for the first time since waking. Cassandra and Kairen were preparing to resume their journey to the east, and Kiera had returned from the mountains to bid them farewell.

That's when she found out that, for the past couple of days, another dragon had been around. It took her a moment to realize that the massive black dragon, the one whose shadow had once sent whole clans running for cover, was now gently nudging Niiru with its snout like an overgrown kitten. Now that she could see it from up close, she realized the large black dragon was nearly as big as Kein, but not quite, which was probably why she was disappointed not to find the bronze dragon in the gardens; there was no way both dragons could have fit.

She stood off to the side with Lorey, watching as Kassein and Kiera spoke with their parents. Kiera was laughing, her eyes bright as she talked excitedly with their father. Kairen didn't talk much, but he did ruffle her hair affectionately while Cassandra eventually pulled her son into a long, tight hug despite the height advantage he had on her. Even Lorey had gotten a hug from both of them, and something ached quietly in Alezya's chest, something that felt like quiet envy.

But then, to her surprise, Kassein's mom turned to her with a soft smile, and walked over to grant her a tight hug, before she pulled back, her cold, soft hand gently caressing Alezya's cheek.

"Take good care of yourself, and take good care of him, darling," she whispered. "We will be back before your baby is born to help you out."

Alezya could only nod, her throat choked with a thick swirl of emotions. She was already grateful for how kindly they treated her; knowing that they planned to come back to help with her child meant the world to her. To distract herself and blink back the tears, she smiled, and looked at the others.

Kairen, who had used that moment to also hug Lorey and give another quick tickle to Lumie, who was standing and holding on to his pants, turned to his son. Quietly, he wrapped his arm around Kassein's shoulders, and pulled his son over, pressing their foreheads together. He said something in a low voice, and Alezya watched as Kassein held his dad's gaze before he gave him what she could only describe as a confident nod. Something silent passed between them, and then, Kairen pulled back with one of his rare, barely-there smiles.

Next, he turned to Alezya. She wasn't sure what to say, but he opened his arms in a quiet, unmistakable gesture, and she gladly closed the distance between them to hug him. He was a massive man, solid and strong, but she didn't feel afraid when he wrapped his arms around her. She felt safe.

When he pulled back, he gave her another small smile before turning to his wife and helping her onto his dragon's back. Alezya felt Kassein's hand rest on her shoulder, and she smiled up at him before they both turned to watch the large black dragon take off and vanish into the sky, heading east.

Down in the grass, Lumie watched the clouds with wide eyes. As the dragon disappeared, she pointed up with a confused sound and tugged on Kassein's pant leg, her expression wobbling between tears and questions. Alezya bent down to scoop her up, holding her close.

"Don't worry, my snowflake," she whispered. "They'll be back."

She was already looking forward to seeing Kassein's parents again, she realized, and with that thought, a fresh wave of gratitude filled her. This man had given her a family. A big, strong, and warm family she couldn't wait to know better.

Sadly, Lumie didn't see things the same way. She burst into tears in her mother's arms, inconsolable. It took a while to coax her back inside and settle her back to her usual morning sleep, even with Lorey's help.

Once they did, Alezya took the chance to insist she was healthy enough to go out. And this time, Kassein finally gave in. He bundled her in new, heavy fur cloaks and waited for the skies to be cloudless and the sun to be higher up before agreeing to take her to the mountains.

When Alezya stepped back into the gardens, she found the orange dragon curled around the remaining small but growing egg. Kein lifted its head upon sniffing her and slowly walked to her. It was the first time she was seeing Kein since the war that day, and it made Alezya sad to see how cautiously the dragon approached her, like it was... nervous. But she smiled, and as soon as it was close enough, she hugged its large head, pressing her forehead between the dragon's eyes.

"I'm sorry, friend," she whispered. "Thank you for protecting me."

Kein replied with a long, low, and soft growl. Then, the dragon huffed a breath of hot air onto her face, making her laugh, and everything seemed a whole lot better all of a sudden. Niiru ran between Kein's legs, and when they took off, the little black dragon followed, flying under the large bronze wings.

Once they were up in the skies, Alezya leaned back into Kassein's embrace, letting the sunshine hit her face, and closed her eyes. She didn't want to ever get tired of flying. This was what freedom felt like, she thought. Kassein's warmth behind her, a dragon's wings carrying her, and the whole, wide world ahead. She took a deep breath, and when Kassein pressed his lips to her head, she smiled. As always, he was holding her, but this time, he kept his hand splayed on her belly.

To her surprise, they made a large, pleasant loop, but they eventually landed in a nice clearing, close to her home mountain, where she recognized some of the Dragon Clan's habitations they had built up there, with a little crowd gathered around. Almost immediately after they had landed and Kassein had helped her down, Ekata ran to them, hugging Alezya without warning. She was still somewhat tired, but she had been recovering more so from days without food or water than her injuries, and the sudden gesture didn't make her more than slightly dizzy. Her headaches had passed, and the dragon scales were still there, but nothing hurt anymore. Hugging her friend back felt good.

"How are you?" Alezya immediately asked. "I'm so sorry about Ekut..."

Ekata pulled back from their embrace first and gave her a sad smile, nodding. Her eyes were a bit red, and she looked tired.

"Thank you," she muttered. "We... We buried him two days ago. It was... It was a beautiful ceremony."

"I'm sorry I missed it."

Ekata shook her head, taking Alezya's hands in hers.

"Don't. Ekut... My brother died for the sake of future generations, and he died on the battlefield, a hero of our clan. I'll make sure he is remembered for many years to come as he deserves."

"He deserves it," Alezya nodded. "...How about you? How are you?"

"Well, aside from the funeral, it's been... quite intense, actually," Ekata sighed. "How much do you know?"

"Almost nothing," Alezya said, pouting in Kassein's direction. "He's kept me away from it all while I recovered. I know his father came and helped with the negotiations...?"

"Oh, that," Ekata nodded. "I wish you had seen it! Once they saw that the Dragon Clan Chief could speak our language, the clan chiefs tripped over themselves to finalize agreements. It has been insane. Well, many clan chiefs who were against us died in the war, but their successors were surprisingly eager to make peace with everyone, especially the Dragon Clan."

"Lesson learned?"

"More than that, I think many were... doubtful about Darak from the start. Once everyone realized he was dead, that he'd even hidden from his clan, and that most of his so-called warriors hadn't even taken part in the battle, people just... got furious. A lot of them are using him as a scapegoat to reduce their share of the blame, for sure, but at least they were quick to agree to our terms. The others who were most against peace with the Dragon Clan are dead anyway, so... they didn't have a choice but to agree."

"What are the terms, then? Just peace?"

"Oh, it's so much better than that!" Ekata beamed. "That skinny guy, Tievin, he showed us a map of the mountains. Like a real, very large map, with all the mountains on it! It was fascinating. He showed us routes we could use, where we should create more, and spoke about trading things, not only between our clans but with the Dragon Clan as well. He drew routes to their clan too, and now, there are people from several clans going there, down the mountains, for the first time in their lives."

"Did you see it's just... a bit of their clan?"

Ekata sighed.

"Yeah, I realized that when I saw his map. I'm not the only one. I think a lot of clan leaders were shocked when he explained that what we thought was their territory was just a little bit of it. He even explained how far the place you were resting was, and everyone was stunned. I suppose the journey is faster if you have a dragon, but for us, it just means the world beyond our mountains is... so, so much bigger than we thought!"

She was almost beaming, and Alezya smiled. She had felt the same way when she had stared at the mountains for hours and at the horizon toward the south. Now, many children of the clans would grow up with the same vision, of a world much, much bigger that was waiting for them. Sure, the Dragon Clan was still too grand and too intimidating, a world of mysteries, but still, at the very least, no one would have to grow up confined in a cave anymore. With the threat of dragon attacks gone, they would be free to live outside, run down the hills, or stand at the tops of a cliffs.

"Lady Alezya."

Alezya turned to find Tievin, looking tired but strangely surrounded by young children who were playing and tugging on his robes, trying to get a reaction out of him while he clung onto one of his usual paper pads.

"Tievin," she smiled. "Lady?"

"*I learned the word from* Lady Cassandra," he nodded. "*I will learn.*"

"*Thank you.* Thank you for helping the clans," Alezya said.

He let out a long sigh, glancing around at the kids who were laughing at his reactions.

"*Yes,*" he shrugged.

"*You look tired,*" Kassein told his second without an ounce of apology in his tone.

Alezya laughed while Tievin gave his *Aqayir* a pissed-off look.

"*Yes, I am, Aqayir,*" he groaned. "*I am very, very much tired while you rested at Kalat Unshreik with Lady Alezya. Very, very tired.*"

With a pout, he went to make a theatrical exit, but he spun so fast while the children held onto his cloak that he nearly fell on his face, making all the children bark in laughter. Alezya bit her lip too and turned to Kassein with an admonishing look.

"*Be nice to Tievin,*" she said.

Kassein shrugged.

"*Mom said he needs a wife.*"

"...Oh," Alezya blinked, before smiling. "We can definitely find him a wife."

She did not doubt that there would be plenty of young ladies willing to marry a scholar from the Dragon Clan. Maybe plenty of widows too. If many women, like her, had been forced into marriage without a clue about their partner, some might be happy to enjoy their freedom, but some might enjoy even more having a man they picked... She looked around, seeing men of the Dragon Clan helping build new habitations, and a bunch of women nearby from other clans who were glancing in the foreign men's directions. They weren't even trying to hide their curiosity and kept peering the other way while they were busy helping with chores or rounding up the children. There were people from many different clans coming and going, and few supplies, but some tables were set up outside, and some men seemed to be coming back from a hunt.

"...What is this place?" she asked Ekata.

"This is the spot we chose for negotiations," Ekata explained. "We needed some place central and large enough for, uh, the dragons to land. People representing their clans can come and go easily, and those who need help can stay and request help from other clans. Some cannot go back to their homes, so we are scouting for options. We're not far from the Wailing Rift, either. Many were still recovering and burying bodies until recently, and a handful of people are still missing."

"Do you know where my clan is?"

Ekata frowned.

"Some of them are here," she said, "but things have been... complicated. Many don't want anything to do with Darak's clan."

"They're here?" Alezya blinked in surprise.

Ekata nodded, and she led her through the clearing. On the way there, and as they passed by many people, all from different clans, Alezya noted that some of the children were playing around chasing Niiru. When she glanced back, she saw a handful of others were having some kind of dare game about who would be brave enough to approach Kein, and that made her smile.

Eventually, they approached a little spot on the edge of the clearing, where a handful of people were gathered. Alezya froze as she recognized the faces before they even saw her. Then, slowly, she witnessed her cousin's gaze reaching her, her eyes opening wide, and she ran to her.

"Alezya!"

"Zenia?"

She had barely spoken her name when her cousin closed the distance and wrapped her in a hug. It was so out of the blue, so unexpected, that Alezya couldn't decide whether to return her hug or not before Zenia stepped back, her cheeks red.

"Sorry, I'm just... I'm so, so sorry," Zenia said, tears appearing in her eyes already. "I... It's been so eventful, and... and we heard everything that you did, and... then, the war..."

"Are you alright?" Alezya asked after her mind cleared, taking her cousin's hand gently.

Zenia blinked at where their hands were joined, like she couldn't understand the movement. Then, her hand tightened back, and she swallowed a sob.

"I should be the one asking you that," she mumbled. "We heard bits and pieces, but..."

She glanced nervously behind Alezya.

"No one is very fond of us at the moment," she chuckled nervously.

"Did anyone harm you?"

"No," Zenia quickly shook her head, but her voice broke with the next words, "but the other clans... They wanted to kill the men we had left. Including Suolk."

"Is Suolk fine?" Alezya immediately asked, remembering how well he'd treated Lumie.

"He is," Zenia nodded. "I thought... I thought we were all going to die. But when they found us, the Dragon Clan... They told the other clans not to touch us. That you didn't want them to."

Her cousin finally broke into a sob, and Alezya let out a sigh of relief. She knew it couldn't have been easy for them. They were too closely tied to Darak; of course, many had blamed them for this... for what their clan leader had done. Too many had died because of him. Alezya hugged her cousin, this time, and glanced over Zenia's shoulder. The few men and women gathered were all familiar faces, tired-looking faces she had known most of her life. The same faces that had shown her nothing but contempt and disdain for the past couple of years. And yet, the very faces that had once looked down on her were now staring at her with something else entirely, something that almost resembled hope.

Just beyond them, three Dragon Clan warriors stood guard, silent and alert. Among them was Dajan, a fresh cut marking his temple and one shoulder was still bandaged, but he held himself with quiet confidence. When their eyes met, he gave her a firm, confident nod, and Alezya smiled back, her chest tightening with something like pride.

"Thank you," she whispered for him to see, and he replied with another nod, a slight blush appearing on his cheeks.

Then, she caressed her cousin's hair while she cried.

"Many died," Zenia mumbled. "Many men... Your father took the best fighters with him, and they were all killed too. And the men he sent down... Suolk survived, but so many died..."

"Did you get to bury them?" Alezya asked.

"Yeah... Yeah, we did," her cousin nodded, pulling back a bit to look her in the eyes, "but we don't know what to do next... We don't have a clan chief, Alezya. No one wants to do it. We have dozens of widows and children, and we can't provide for everyone... The Dragon Clan helped us for the past few days, but then what? I don't... I know you don't owe us anything, but... Please. I know we don't deserve anything from you, but please, can you help us?"

Alezya took in her cousin's forlorn expression, her pleading eyes, and then, all the gazes she felt on her. She glanced at what remained of her clan again. She spotted Suolk, stepping out of the line of trees, and their eyes met for a brief second, before she noticed what he had in his hand. A hare. He'd gone to hunt to feed them, she realized. And that was all he'd come back with... It brought back some sour memories for her.

When she had been the one outcasted, the one in need of help, none of them had lent a hand. No one had given her food or even kindness. They'd treated her like a pariah and Lumie like a disease.

Now they were the ones desperate for help. A clan with only a handful of men and with no one willing to help out wouldn't recover. The other clans would be able to trade, lean on each other, and maybe even flourish once those routes were opened between their homes. But the Deklaan Clan was unwelcome. What remained of her father's people would forever be outcasts in the mountains, the ones held responsible for the war and all the losses. The women hadn't been taught to hunt or even pick herbs. There were too few men left to feed them all. She doubted the widows would even find anyone willing to take them in, not when there were dozens of women from other clans in the same situation.

Alezya glanced back at Kassein. He was standing still, a hand on her lower back, waiting for her, as always. Patient, kind, and willing to support whatever she decided. She could let go, she thought. She could let her cousin and her clan fend for themselves. She would have had every right to, after what had happened. They had rejected her first. She could have died in a crevice or bled out in the snow, if it had been up to them. She wasn't sure a single one of them would have shed a tear.

But then, she looked again beyond Zenia's shoulders. At the children. There was a handful of them, being bounced in their mother's arms, or for the oldest ones, peeking with envy at the dragons through the trees. She could see in their eyes they were dying to chase after Niiru with the others or eager to approach Kein. Alezya took in a deep breath and returned her gaze to Zenia.

"...I want you to leave the mountains," she calmly said.

"W-what?" Zenia blinked, just as her husband walked up to them.

"There's nothing left for you here," Alezya calmly explained to the two of them. "The Deklaan Clan needs to disappear. No other clan will be willing to trade with you, and no mountain will be welcoming. Take the men, women, and children that are left and come down the mountains."

"How could we?" Zenia cried. "We've never lived anywhere but here. We wouldn't know how to start over—"

But Suolk put a hand on her shoulder, interrupting her, and, with a resolute look, turned his eyes to Alezya.

"...Where do you think we should go?" he asked calmly.

It was the first time ever that a man from her clan was asking Alezya a question, and genuinely asking her for guidance. She swallowed, and held her cousin's husband's gaze.

"Come to the Dragon Clan. They won't care about what you did as the other clans do."

"But..." her cousin frowned, glancing at the Dragon Clan's men. "...Are you sure? They're... you know."

"If I survived down there, you will," Alezya said. "They could use some women down there, to be honest. They can't even make proper tea, and they could use some hands to help with chores. You could earn your keep doing what you know, like sewing, making food, or laundry, and the men could hunt. There's more to their territory, where you could relocate."

"...They can't make tea?" Zenia frowned, confused.

"They keep drinking hot water for some reason; it's disgusting."

Her cousin chuckled but glanced at the men off to the side. Dajan and his two companions blushed and looked at their feet. Dajan's bandages on his shoulder were messy, their hair was poorly cut, and they had dirt behind their ears.

"It looks like they could use some women indeed," Zenia smiled.

Alezya nodded before looking back at the two of them.

"That's my offer," she said. "The Deklaan Clan doesn't need a new leader; it needs a new life."

After a hesitation, Suolk nodded.

"Thank you, Alezya," he said. "I know we... None of us deserve your kindness."

"It's not kindness," Alezya replied, "but... the ones I resented the most are already dead, and being cast out set me free. And now I'm free to choose the future I want. And the future I want isn't to let women and children suffer like I did out of resentment. I'm choosing to move forward. I got a second chance at life. I think everyone deserves one."

She took a step back, leaning into Kassein's embrace as she smiled at him. He smiled back and leaned over to press a kiss to the top of her head, unbothered by all the eyes on them. She felt his arm move from her lower back to curl around her waist until he splayed his hand on her belly again. She let out a peaceful sigh and glanced up at the blue sky beyond the mountains.

"...I used to fear the future. Now I think I'm looking forward to it," she whispered.

6 months later

Kassein was on his way out of the castle's kitchens, a crate in his arms, when he was stopped by the sound of a giggle, followed by a suspicious shushing. He frowned, set the crate down, and leaned over to peer under the nearest table.

"Hi, Daddy," Lumie beamed up at him.

"Hello, snowflake," he smiled. "What are you and Auntie doing?"

"Candies!" she announced proudly.

"Hush, you snitch!" Kiera hissed. "You can't give us away like that!"

Lumie giggled and crawled out from their hiding spot, visibly unbothered.

"Hiding from what?" Kassein asked.

"From your woman," Kiera muttered. "I don't know if it's the pregnancy or the fact she finally speaks our language fluently, but your wife terrifies me. She's been working us to death all day."

"There's a lot to prepare," he shrugged. "And what were you hiding for, snowflake?"

"Candies!" Lumie repeated, gleefully.

"No! I said I'd give you candies if you *didn't* tell anyone where I was—"

But Lumie was already holding her arms out expectantly, grinning. Kassein lifted her into his arms with a chuckle.

"You have a good nap, baby?"

"Grandpa?" Lumie asked hopefully.

"Not yet," he said with a smile. "One more sleep. He'll be here for the party tomorrow."

She pouted but leaned her head against his shoulder. Her vocabulary was growing fast, picking up from both languages, but her favorite word, without contest, was "Grandpa."

Kiera groaned as she crawled out from under the table.

"We shouldn't have come back early," she muttered, stretching. "Lorey was worried about Alezya's pregnancy, so we came to help, but your wife is like

Tievin on a bad day, plus a dragon sidekick."

"He's gotten softer since he got married," Kassein offered.

"Right. I forgot he has his own dragon sidekick now," Kiera snorted. "I think his wife's even scarier than yours…"

"Grab the crate," Kassein simply said with a smile.

He carried Lumie outside. The Onyx Castle's gardens were nearly unrecognizable. Every patch of earth had been trimmed, rearranged, uprooted, or replanted under Alezya's watchful eye. His mother's once-abandoned greenhouse had been claimed and brought back to life, but today, the greenhouse faded into the background behind the chaos of the celebration setup. Lanterns had been strung from newly installed poles, tables and benches were scattered across the garden like fallen chess pieces, and one long banquet table was commanding the center like a throne. At the moment, Alezya and his sister-in-law Naptunie were pointing at a corner of the lawn, instructing his brother where to drag yet another table. Lorey stood beside them, nodding along and holding a notepad.

Due to being the mother of nine children, Naptunie was followed by a small herd of young dragons at nearly all times, and presently, three of them were now brawling around her in the grass with Niiru in their midst.

"A bit more to the left," Alezya called. "Not too close to the wall."

"Right there, honey!" Naptunie nodded. "Perfect!"

"Oh, speaking of—do we have enough honey for the beignet sauce?" Lorey asked, frowning. "Tievin put a note that your mom adores that one."

"As do my Darsan, the kids, and Tessa," Naptunie added. "We'll need a lot."

"I only got four pots," Alezya said, looking worried. "Do you think that's enough?"

"I'll send the kids to get some more! Dada?"

The largest of the young dragons perked up immediately.

"Go find the kids. We have a new errand!"

With a low growl, the dragon took off into the sunset.

"Mama!"

Lumie squirmed in Kassein's arms, and as soon as she was down, ran toward her mother. She hugged Alezya's legs and promptly left loud kisses on her baby bump.

"Hi, baby!" she cooed at the bump.

"Hello, baby," Alezya smiled, brushing her daughter's snow-white curls aside. "You found Auntie Kiera, I see."

"What? I was checking the wine," Kiera said defensively.

"For half an hour?" Lorey asked, eyebrows raised.

"It was a lot of wine."

"Mama! Kein?" Lumie chirped.

"Kein's outside the garden, my love. Go find him with Niiru."

"Daddy Dragon!" she shrieked and took off, Niiru right behind her.

The adults laughed. Now that she knew how to walk, Lumie had only one speed: full sprint. If she wasn't running around the grounds, she was trying to scale Kein like he was a playground. Whenever he saw the young girl running happily like that, Kassein always thought of that tiny, cramped space she'd grown in during the first months of her life. And every time, it made his chest swell with quiet relief.

Kiera dropped the crate at Alezya's feet.

"Where do you want this, *Commander*?"

"Oh, are those the candles for the tables? Leave them by the greenhouse, we'll set them up tomorrow."

"Do we *need* candles?" Kiera asked, glancing up at all the lanterns strung around the garden.

"They're sage-scented," Alezya replied firmly, "and green, your mom's favorite color. I ordered them especially from the new trading hub!"

Alezya was extremely passionate about the new, budding trading hub that had been recently established up north. It was a fresh enterprise between Kassein's army and the clans descended from the mountains, and any excuse was good to go check on the growing trades or order products there. When Kassein had floated the idea of offering to host his mother's birthday party after his parents had mentioned that Kairen's mother might not be able to make the trip to the east where they'd originally planned it, she had been all for it, and had immediately tried to place as many orders as she could.

Kiera exchanged a look with her brother, but he shrugged, amused.

Then, he walked around to hug Alezya from behind, cupping her belly with his large hands.

"How are you feeling?" he asked, pressing a kiss on her cheek.

"Nervous," she sighed. "We still have so much to prepare tomorrow, and once we have so many people and dragons around..."

"It will be fine," Lorey smiled. "Everyone's just happy to gather and they will all be willing to help."

"And with my Dran and Krai around," Naptunie added, beaming, "the kids will stay in line!"

"Damn right," Darsan grinned, slinging an arm over his wife's shoulder.

"But it's your mother's birthday, and this is your childhood home," Alezya sighed. "I really want it to be–"

"It *will* be perfect, my moonlight," he whispered in her ear. "All Mom wants is for all of us to be together. The whole family, together."

"There will definitely be mayhem," Kiera scoffed. "It wouldn't be a family gathering if half of us don't end up drunk, lost, or passed out!"

"Oh, no," Naptunie pouted. "The children better stay where I expect them this time!"

Alezya smiled. Ever since they had discovered that, by dragon flight, the Onyx Castle was close to their parents' house, Kassein's nieces and nephews had taken to sneaking off to visit. Lumie now enjoyed a rotating door of cousins coming to play in the gardens, and Naptunie and Alezya had inevitably become close. She was getting to know Kassein's family while settling her own there, and while it came with some challenges, Alezya loved it.

"You should get some rest," Lorey smiled at her gently. "You've been on your feet all day, Alezya. Don't worry about the party, everyone will be happy to help tomorrow."

"All that's left is the final decorations and food," Naptunie chimed in cheerfully. "That'll be fun to finish together!"

"And it'll keep the kids busy," Darsan added with a grin.

"Yeah, the four of us and Tievin's legendary notes can handle the rest," Kiera said, half-sighing, half-smirking. "Go rest, sister. We've got this."

Alezya smiled at Kiera; now that they could communicate, she and Kiera had gotten closer, and she found that they both loved to banter any chance they got. Though she and Lorey had left shortly after their parents had, the two of them came back so often that they now had a bedroom permanently waiting for them at the Onyx Castle.

"Come on," Kassein said gently, nudging her toward the castle. "Let's get some rest."

Alezya nodded, smiling shyly as everyone around them bid her goodnight.

Kassein escorted her inside, and helped her lie in their bed; it was a brand new bed Darsan had gifted them after their wedding ceremony. It was ridiculously large, but she loved it, and she loved the idea that someday they'd sleep there together with more of their children.

"How's baby?" he asked, softly caressing her bump.

"He's been moving a lot," Alezya chuckled. "I think he's excited to see the family too."

"Good," Kassein kissed her belly. "We can't wait to meet him."

Tears welled in her eyes. That had become ridiculously common lately, and she wasn't sure if she had always been emotional, if she should blame the pregnancy, or just how happy she had been in the past six months. Kassein was used to it by now. He didn't panic like he used to, especially back when he was still learning how to understand her.

Now, he simply held her. He leaned over, pulling her gently into his arms, and kissed her deeply, his hand never leaving her stomach. When he pulled back, his green eyes stayed locked on hers.

"Get some rest, my moonlight," he whispered.

Alezya nodded sleepily, eyes fluttering shut as she curled into him. The baby gave one last soft kick beneath his palm, and Kassein smiled.

From the windows, she could hear the faint laughter of their family, the evening breeze, and the faraway growls of dragons small and large. Tomorrow would bring even more noise and dragons and laughter and chaos, and she would love that. But tonight, there was only the two of them, and love, and that wonderful bliss of that future that was waiting for them.

Epilogue

"Lumie?" Alezya called, glancing around. "Lumie!"

A flash of white darted behind her, and she sighed, turning around.

"I know it's you, Oshu," she said. "If you try to scare me again, you're going to be in trou–"

A high-pitched growl cut off her sentence, and a mass of black and white scales rolled in a scuffle around her feet. Then, Niiru got the upper hand, pinning the smaller white dragon to the dark stone floor. Alezya sighed.

"Niiru," she said. "Where's Lumie?"

But Niiru ignored her, busy chewing its dragon sibling's tail. Oshu was smaller, half Niiru's size, and as white as Niiru was black. The two dragons were perfect opposites, except that they shared the same bright amber-colored eyes.

"Niiru," she called again. "Let your baby brother go."

Niiru growled but eventually moved aside, letting Oshu run behind Alezya's leg with a sulky grunt. She sighed but kept walking down the corridor with both dragons at her feet, glancing around. Eventually, she reached the gardens of the Onyx Castle and let out another sigh. Oshu and Niiru ran ahead to Kein, who was napping in the high grass. The dragon was curled around a new egg, its snout against it. Alezya walked up to the tall dragon, who barely opened an eye as she caressed its head.

Then, on the other side of the mountain of bronze scales, she found the three of them. Lying on the grass with his back resting against his dragon, Kassein had their son sleeping on his bare torso. His hand was under the baby's bum, and Shuryo's tiny fist was clutched under his chin. Lumie was cradled between his legs. The two of them were busy with their favorite activity together: watching the stars.

"There you are," Alezya said.

"Good evening, Mama!" Lumie beamed as Alezya came to sit next to them, her back immediately warmed up by Kein's scales.

Kassein smiled, pressing a kiss to her lips as his free hand gently caressed the small curve of her belly. His mother had warned them, but it had not taken long for Alezya to get pregnant again after Shuryo was born. Their son was barely six months old, and she was already carrying their next child. Not that she minded. Cassandra had given her a contraceptive medicine in case she needed it, but the truth was that this second pregnancy had only made her love Kassein even more. She had never realized how much of a difference it made to have a partner who truly cared, one who was more nervous about the pregnancy than she was.

Even when she had been much sicker while carrying Shuryo, it had felt easier with Kassein at her side. He had been there for every step, waiting on her hand and foot at all hours, never letting her feel alone in it. He had stayed with her during the birth, and afterward, he had been even more helpful, making sure she could focus on both children without feeling overwhelmed. He was patient, reliable, and endlessly caring. Knowing he would always be there gave her so much confidence in growing their family. Maybe not eight children like his mother or nine like his older brother, but she definitely wanted at least one or two more.

Any lingering doubt that Kassein would be a good father had disappeared the moment Shuryo was born.

What had moved her most wasn't how naturally he had taken to caring for a newborn, but how nothing had changed with Lumie. Alezya had been worried, even if she hadn't dared to voice it aloud. Worried that a new baby might shift something, even just a little. That Lumie might feel left out, or that Kassein's love for her might somehow dim. She had known plenty of men who wouldn't have spared a second glance at an adoptive daughter after a son of their blood was born. Kassein wasn't one of those men. He had loved Lumie from the second he'd met her, and that love had never wavered. If anything, he'd made sure to cater to the little girl even more while Alezya had been busy nursing her baby brother. He could have let his family take care of Lumie, as they'd come to help, but no. Kassein had been the one to make sure Lumie was cared for while everyone was focused on their newborn. If anything, Lumie had probably felt more loved than ever during her baby brother's first months, with everyone coming to see them.

And once they had been gone, they'd enjoyed simply being a family of four. Kassein had made sure to keep Lumie involved in everything regarding her younger brother, and yet still saved time just for her. Kassein had become a better father for both children, and he had made it seem effortless. Sometimes, Alezya almost forgot that Lumie wasn't biologically his, because Kassein never acted like she wasn't, not once. If anything, she suspected that as the children grew older, he might end up taking Lumie's side more often than not. He had a special fondness for her, and she loved him all the more for it.

"You guys snuck away again," she sighed, leaning against his shoulder.

"Lumie wanted to see the stars."

"It is a nice night," she smiled, looking up.

Since they'd worked out a schedule to spend more time outside with Lumie, sleeping late into the day and staying up past midnight, Kassein and the children had fallen into the habit of going out into the garden whenever the weather allowed to watch the stars. It had become their favorite thing to do together. It had started one night when Shuryo wouldn't settle, and he'd taken both children outside to look at the stars so Alezya could get some rest. After that, it had just become their thing, something the three of them did when Alezya needed sleep, and sometimes, she would come out and join them. Even though his work often took him away from the Onyx Castle during the day, Kassein always made sure to be home before it got too late, just so he wouldn't miss putting the kids to bed.

The North Camp was now shaping up to become a proper village, built by his army and those who had come from the town to mix with them. If Alezya hadn't flown there often, she wouldn't have recognized the place, which was now full of little houses, growing families, and a popular stop for trade between the mountains and the rest of the continent.

When Kassein had taken her to see how large his clan's land was, Alezya had needed a few hours to recover. Their first trip had been to his grandmother's house, which was one of the most beautiful places she'd ever seen, but knowing that the journey to the tip of his country took three or four times as long had made her dizzy. Once she had been alright with traveling again, they had gone farther, to the east to meet his older sister's family, and to the south, in their country's capital, to meet his oldest brother, whom she had learned was the current, actual leader of their Empire and some of his other siblings. By now, Alezya had seen more land than she would have ever imagined and met all of Kassein's family.

Yet, it had actually made her realize the north was her home. Lumie had been born in the mountains and Shuryo in the Onyx Castle. The nights were long enough here for her daughter to enjoy them, and Alezya could spend time with all the clans, shaping the future of the north alongside Kassein.

Now, together, they ruled the Northern Kingdom. Kassein hated the title of King, and aside from residing in the Onyx Castle, they lived like most families up here. However, the country's border had been set, the Empire no longer disposed of convicts here, and they were making new decisions weekly that would shape many people's futures. Tievin was still Kassein's advisor and was still doing a lot of his beloved paperwork, although now, and thanks to Alezya's suggestion, he had taken on a handful of assistants to have time with his wife, who had just given him a son. Dajan had also found love, with a young woman from a northern clan. It was new, as he had met her after the war while he had helped establish a route between the mountains and the camp, but now, he spent more time in the heights than not, and was learning the northern language at remarkable speed.

Much to Alezya's sadness, Lorey and Kiera still spent a lot of time travelling and exploring the west. The pair always came back whenever they felt like it, but at least, it still looked like they made a point to come back fairly regularly. The Onyx Castle had become the place they called "home" whenever they returned, in need of a break from their travels and dying to spend time with their nieces and nephews.

The pair had found traces of the Lumiata Clan during their journeys, but they weren't sure what had happened to them. Kiera suspected many clans like their mother's before had been attacked by slave traders. More optimistic, Lorey thought they might have sailed away to explore the sea west of the continent. Alezya sometimes wondered if she would ever meet them. But even if she didn't, a part of her was satisfied enough knowing they lived. She had her own family here, and she didn't feel the need to seek out more.

"How are you feeling?" Kassein gently asked.

She let out a faint sigh.

"A bit better. I can't wait for this one to be born, though. I keep falling asleep in every room of the castle I sit in..."

"It's fine," he smiled. "That's why we have pillows everywhere."

"You promised you didn't mind the new pillows," she pouted.

"I don't."

The Onyx Castle had never felt more like a home than it did today. When Kassein was a child, his mother had been more interested in the gardens and too busy raising eight children to make many changes inside. Alezya, however, was different. After spending years confined in a tight cave with Lumie, she had been determined to turn the castle into a proper home. Every room had been renovated with the blessing of his siblings and parents, including some he had nearly forgotten existed. Alezya had a knack for trade and made every trip to the villages worthwhile. She loved learning about new techniques, fabrics, and materials, always eager to explore the expanding trade hubs in the mountains.

Kassein had fallen into a habit of going on long hunts in the days leading up to their trips, knowing how much she loved returning home with new goods in exchange for the pelts and meat he procured. She had a map from Tievin, carefully marked with every trading hub, ensuring she always knew where their next stop would be. When she had been too pregnant to travel, she had been just as involved, making detailed lists of what she wanted and sending Dajan to gather everything for Kassein to collect later.

"...I heard something interesting today," he smiled.

"What? At the Dragon's Haven?" she asked, using the new name for the North Camp, which honored Kein for some reason.

"In the mountains," Kassein shook his head. "They were talking about the Onyx Princess."

"Who?"

But Alezya's jaw dropped when he smiled.

"*Me?*" she exclaimed. "They're calling me the Onyx Princess?"

"I think the Onyx Queen would be more accurate," he frowned.

"You're one to talk! You won't even let anyone call you King."

"That's different," Kassein rolled his eyes.

"How? You're more of a king than I am a queen. Or a princess."

"You work with the clan chiefs to expand trade, you manage an entire castle, you had a school built for the clans' children, and you're an incredible mother to ours. Meanwhile, I go out to hunt, settle a few disputes, and come home to nap with our kids."

Alezya blushed but shook her head.

"That's nonsense," she said. "You hunt for *hours* to feed people who can't feed themselves. You teach men twice your age how to coexist. And when you're gone, you make sure they're too scared to misbehave. Then you come home to *our* castle and take care of me and our babies. That's more than enough. People who once feared you now rely on you to survive the winter, my love. The north is harsh, but no one went hungry last season because of you."

"Because of your trade routes too," he reminded her, before shrugging. "... It's a wild land. It doesn't need much managing, not compared to my brother's Empire."

"I'm happy with that," Alezya sighed, leaning against his shoulder. "Let's keep the north wild and free. I think that's exactly what it's meant to be."

"Agreed."

She smiled. She loved that they were fluent enough in each other's language to have long discussions or even arguments like this. In the beginning, whenever she got upset, she would speak so fast in her own language that Kassein couldn't keep up. In the end, he would just apologize, even if it had nothing to do with him. Now, she knew that when they did fight, he let her win. He was fluent enough to argue back if he wanted to, but the only fights he actually cared to have the last word over were the ones about her safety. If it involved riding Kein on bad days or staying put when she was too pregnant and exhausted, Kassein refused to back down.

She turned to check on Shuryo, who was frowning and wiping his face against his father's torso. Their son was a miniature copy of Kassein, with his dad's facial features and his skin the same dark shade. The only difference was his onyx-black eyes and messy mop of dark hair, which were like hers. He definitely had her temper too, and she was glad for Kassein's patience because at six months old, the baby boy was already able to throw dragon-sized temper tantrums. At the moment, though, he was sleeping adorably, and as usual, he would sleep through the night, unshakeable like his father when they were napping. She smiled and pressed a kiss against his chubby cheek. She had named him after the sun in her language, and she found it incredibly fitting.

"I'm excited to see the family," she smiled. "Lumie is going to have fun with all her cousins. And your grandpa, Lumie?"

"*Ababi* will come?" Lumie whipped her head around.

"Yes, my snowflake, *Ababi* is coming tomorrow."

"Yeah!" she punched her fists to the skies happily.

Alezya felt her heart so warm and full, a tear reached her eye. Just over a year ago, she would have never dreamed of Lumie having such a big family who adored her. A couple of months after the war, Lumie had started calling Kassein "Dad" in his language. Alezya had cried when she had finally realized the word he'd taught her patiently for weeks. Then, when Kassein's parents visited right before Shuryo's birth, Lumie had learned a lot more words, including grandpa and grandma. It wasn't just Lumie; Kassein's siblings and parents treated Alezya like she was one of their own too. She was close to his mom, and whenever she bickered with his siblings and the in-laws, Kassein's much-feared and respected paternal grandmother often favored her.

She felt at home. With Kassein, their children, their garden full of dragons, and the black walls of the Onyx Castle surrounding them, she felt more at home than she had ever felt before in any cave. She was free to go wherever she wanted, but this was the one place she always wanted to return to. She looked up at the stars, the same stars she had once been too afraid to admire in the open. Once, she had feared the skies. Now, she lay beneath them, unafraid. With her family, her future, and her freedom.

"Thank you," she said, the tear escaping her eye, "for finding me."

Kassein smiled, leaning his forehead against hers.

"Thank you for loving me."

The End.

The Dragon Empire Saga will continue in

The Emperor's Favorite

(Coming Soon)

Aknowledgements

First, I have to thank my editors, who believed in my stories from the beginning. I wouldn't be here if it weren't for April and Wendy telling me readers loved what I wrote—and that I had to write more. Thank you both, deeply.

Next, a massive thank-you to the amazing team of proofreaders who painstakingly read this story over and over again, doubted every comma, checked every spelling, and tirelessly hammered me on my (many) inconsistencies to bring you what may be my most polished story yet. There were laughs, some tears, plenty of frustration—and even a full-blown campaign to keep Kassein shirtless. So you can thank them for *that*, too. Huge thanks as well to my beta readers, who gave me raw, honest, thoughtful feedback. You shed tears, laughed, and reassured me through every moment of doubt—and it meant the world.

I wouldn't have made it here without my incredible friends. I can't count the number of hours they've listened to me panic, rave, complain, and get wildly excited over this book. To my best friend, Amelie, who spent hours listening to my ideas, nodding patiently through my headless musings, and helping me unpack every thought to see if it was worth chasing—thank you. To Michaela and Alex, who generously offered me my favorite writing retreat: their house in the Scottish countryside. Nothing like the peaceful wilds of Scotland and absolute silence to help me knock down thousands of words at once. And to my friends in London—thank you for letting me unwind when I needed it, and offering help whenever I asked (and even when I didn't).

Of course, I have to thank my family for always encouraging my love of books. To my mom, who tirelessly took me to the library, bought me books, and now displays my published works on her shelf like hunting trophies. To my dad, who'll follow me for hours in bookstores, recommends my books to everyone around him, and listens to me ramble about whatever I'm working on—even when he has no idea what I'm on about. And to my brother, who always updates me on which manga I need to catch up on, and is my favorite person to geek out with about shows we love.

Finally, thank you, dear reader. Whether you're a long-term Foxie or this is your first time picking up one of my books, thank you for helping me live my dream—and letting me turn my passion into something real.

Bio

Jenny Fox is a French fantasy author who lives off caffeine, emotions, and just enough chaos to keep things interesting. She started reading young and so obsessively that her mom once used "no books" as a legit (and effective) time-out. She wrote her first story at nine, which her teacher read aloud to the whole class. After receiving her friends' praise, she never stopped.

In 2019, snowed in during a Boston winter, Jenny began posting fantasy stories online to pass the time. By 2020, writing had become her escape during lockdown—and, unknowingly, it became that for thousands of readers too.

That unexpected connection launched her full-time author career.

Her stories feature strong heroines, found families, emotional gut-punches, and morally grey heroes that readers love to hate (or just love). Her growing international fanbase affectionately calls themselves the "Foxies," and they remain her greatest motivation.

Now living in London, Jenny writes full-time and balances her storytelling habit with regular runs, meditation, music-fueled brainstorming, and cozy gaming nights with The Sims, Pokémon, or Animal Crossing—depending on the day and how much she needs to unwind.

She's currently obsessed with Ali Hazelwood, Elsie Silver, Stephanie Archer, cowboy romances, and the occasional dark mafia bad boy.

You can find her on Instagram or Facebook at **@AuthorJennyFox**, most likely plotting her next fictional heartbreak with a very full cup of tea.

Novels by Jenny Fox

THE SILVER CITY SERIES
His Blue Moon Princess
His Sunshine Baby
His Blazing Witch

*

THE DRAGON EMPIRE SAGA
The War God's Favorite
The White King's Favorite
The Wild Prince's Favorite

*

STAND-ALONE STORIES
Lady Dhampir
The Songbird's Love
A Love Cookie
Hera, Love & Revenge
The HellFlower
Dhampir Knight

*

THE FLOWER ROMANCE SERIES